PENGUIN CLASSICS

THE IDIOT

FYODOR MIKHAILOVICH DOSTOYEVSKY was born in Moscow in 1821, the second of a physician's seven children. When he left his private boarding school in Moscow he studied from 1838 to 1843 at the Academy of Military Engineers in St Petersburg, graduating with officer's rank. His first novel to be published, *Poor Folk* (1846), was a great success. In 1849 he was arrested and sentenced to death for participating in the 'Petrashevsky circle'; he was reprieved at the last moment but sentenced to penal servitude, and until 1854 he lived in a convict prison at Omsk, Siberia. Out of this experience he wrote *The House of the Dead* (1860). In 1860 he began the review *Vremya (Time)* with his brother; in 1862 and 1863 he went abroad, where he strengthened his anti-European outlook, met Apollinaria Suslova, who was the model for many of his heroines, and gave way to his passion for gambling. In the following years he fell deeply in debt, but in 1867 he married Anna Grigoryevna Snitkina (his second wife), who helped to rescue him from his financial morass. They lived abroad for four years, then in 1873 he was invited to edit *Grazhdanin (The Citizen)*, to which he contributed his *Diary of a Writer*. From 1876 the latter was issued separately and had a large circulation. In 1880 he delivered his famous address at the unveiling of Pushkin's memorial in Moscow; he died six months later in 1881. Most of his important works were written after 1864: *Notes from Underground* (1864), *Crime and Punishment* (1865–6), *The Gambler* (1866), *The Idiot* (1868), *The Devils* (1871–2) and *The Brothers Karamazov* (1880).

DAVID MCDUFF was born in 1945 and was educated at the University of Edinburgh. His publications comprise a large number of translations of foreign verse and prose, including poems by Joseph Brodsky and Tomas Venclova, as well as contemporary Scandinavian work; *Selected Poems* of Osip Mandelstam; *Complete Poems* of Edith Södergran; and *No I'm Not Afraid* by Irina Ratushinskaya. His first book of verse, *Words in Nature*, appeared in 1972. He has translated a number of nineteenth-century Russian prose works for the Penguin Classics series. These include Dostoyevsky's *The Brothers Karamazov*, *The House of the Dead*, *Poor Folk and Other Stories* and *The Idiot* (2004), Tolstoy's *The Kreutzer Sonata and Other Stories* and *The Sebastopol Sketches*, and Nikolai Leskov's *Lady Macbeth of Mtsensk*. He has also translated Babel's *Collected Stories* and Bely's *Petersburg* for Penguin.

WILLIAM MILLS TODD III was educated at Dartmouth College, Oxford University and Columbia University and is Harry Tuchman Levin Professor of Literature at Harvard University. He has published *The Familiar Letter as a Literary Genre in the Age of Pushkin* (1976), *Fiction and Society in the Age of Pushkin* (1986), and many articles on theory of narrative, sociology of literature and nineteenth-century fiction.

FYODOR DOSTOYEVSKY

The Idiot

Translated with Notes by DAVID McDUFF
With an Introduction by WILLIAM MILLS TODD III

PENGUIN BOOKS

PENGUIN BOOKS

Published by the Penguin Group
Penguin Books Ltd, 80 Strand, London WC2R ORL, England
Penguin Group (USA) Inc., 375 Hudson Street, New York, New York 10014, USA
Penguin Books Australia Ltd, 250 Camberwell Road, Camberwell, Victoria 3124, Australia
Penguin Books Canada Ltd, 10 Alcorn Avenue, Toronto, Ontario, Canada M4V 3B2
Penguin Books India (P) Ltd, 11, Community Centre, Panchsheel Park, New Delhi – 110 017, India
Penguin Books (NZ) Ltd, Cnr Rosedale and Airborne Roads, Albany, Auckland, New Zealand
Penguin Books (South Africa) (Pty) Ltd, 24 Sturdee Avenue, Rosebank 2196, South Africa

Penguin Books Ltd, Registered Offices: 80 Strand, London WC2R ORL, England

www.penguin.com

First published 1868
This translation first published 2004

041

Translation and editorial material copyright © David McDuff, 2004
Introduction copyright © William Mills Todd III, 2004
All rights reserved

The moral rights of the translator and introducer have been asserted

Set in 10.25/12.25 pt PostScript Adobe Sabon
Typeset by Rowland Phototypesetting Ltd, Bury St Edmunds, Suffolk
Printed and bound in Great Britain by Clays Ltd, Elcograf S.p.A.

ISBN-13: 978-0-140-44792-7

www.greenpenguin.co.uk

Penguin Books is committed to a sustainable
future for our business, our readers and our planet.
This book is made from Forest Stewardship
Council™ certified paper.

Contents

Chronology

1821 Born Fyodor Mikhailovich Dostoyevsky, in Moscow, the son of Mikhail Andreyevich, head physician at Marlinsky Hospital for the Poor, and Marya Fyodorovna, daughter of a merchant family.

1823 Pushkin begins *Eugene Onegin*.

1825 Decembrist uprising.

1830 Revolt in the Polish provinces.

1831–6 Attends boarding schools in Moscow together with his brother Mikhail (b. 1820).

1837 Pushkin is killed in a duel.
   Their mother dies and the brothers are sent to a preparatory school in St Petersburg.

1838 Enters the St Petersburg Academy of Military Engineers as an army cadet (Mikhail is not admitted to the Academy).

1839 Father dies, apparently murdered by his serfs on his estate.

1840 Lermontov's *A Hero of Our Time*.

1841 Obtains a commission. Early works, now lost, include two historical plays, 'Mary Stuart' and 'Boris Godunov'.

1842 Gogol's *Dead Souls*.
   Promoted to second lieutenant.

1843 Graduates from the Academy. Attached to St Petersburg Army Engineering Corps. Translates Balzac's *Eugénie Grandet*.

1844 Resigns his commission. Translates George Sand's *La Dernière Aldini*. Works on *Poor Folk*, his first novel.

1845 Establishes a friendship with Russia's most prominent and influential literary critic, the liberal Vissarion Belinsky, who praises *Poor Folk* and acclaims its author as Gogol's successor.

1846 *Poor Folk* and *The Double* published. While *Poor Folk* is widely praised, *The Double* is much less successful. 'Mr Prokharchin' also published. Utopian socialist M. V. Butashevich-Petrashevsky becomes an acquaintance.

1847 Nervous ailments and the onset of epilepsy. *A Novel in Nine Letters* published, with a number of short stories including 'The Landlady', 'Polzunkov', 'White Nights' and 'A Weak Heart'.

1848 Several short stories published, including 'A Jealous Husband' and 'A Christmas Tree Party and a Wedding'.

1849 *Netochka Nezvanova* published. Arrested and convicted of political offences against the Russian state. Sentenced to death, and taken out to Semyonovsky Square to be shot by firing squad, but reprieved moments before execution. Instead, sentenced to an indefinite period of exile in Siberia, to begin with eight years of penal servitude, later reduced to four years by Tsar Nicholas I.

1850 Prison and hard labour in Omsk, western Siberia.

1853 Outbreak of Crimean War.
        Beginning of periodic epileptic seizures.

1854 Released from prison, but immediately sent to do compulsory military service as a private in the Seventh Line infantry battalion at Semipalatinsk, south-western Siberia. Friendship with Baron Wrangel, as a result of which he meets his future wife, Marya Dmitriyevna Isayeva.

1855 Alexander II succeeds Nicholas I as Tsar: some relaxation of state censorship.
        Promoted to non-commissioned officer.

1856 Promoted to lieutenant. Still forbidden to leave Siberia.

1857 Marries the widowed Marya Dmitriyevna.

1858 Works on *The Village of Stepanchikovo and its Inhabitants* and 'Uncle's Dream'.

1859 Allowed to return to live in European Russia; in December, the Dostoyevskys return to St Petersburg. First chapters of *The Village of Stepanchikovo and its Inhabitants* (the serialized novella is released between 1859 and 1861) and 'Uncle's Dream' published.

1860 Vladivostok is founded.

Mikhail starts a new literary journal, *Vremya (Time)*. Dostoyevsky is not officially an editor, because of his convict status. First two chapters of *The House of the Dead* published.

1861 Emancipation of serfs. Turgenev's *Fathers and Sons*.

Vremya begins publication. *The Insulted and the Injured* and *A Silly Story* published in *Vremya*. First part of *The House of the Dead* published.

1862 Second part of *The House of the Dead* and *A Nasty Tale* published in *Vremya*. Makes first trip abroad, to Europe, including England, France and Switzerland. Meets Alexander Herzen in London.

1863 *Winter Notes on Summer Impressions* published in *Vremya*. After Marya Dmitriyevna is taken seriously ill, travels abroad again. Begins liaison with Apollinaria Suslova.

1864 First part of Tolstoy's *War and Peace*.

In March with Mikhail founds the journal *Epokha (Epoch)* as successor to *Vremya*, now banned by the Russian authorities. *Notes from Underground* published in *Epokha*. In April death of Marya Dmitriyevna. In July death of Mikhail.

1865 *Epokha* ceases publication because of lack of funds. *An Unusual Happening* published. Suslova rejects his proposal of marriage. Gambles in Wiesbaden. Works on *Crime and Punishment*.

1866 Dmitry Karakozov attempts to assassinate Tsar Alexander II. *The Gambler* and *Crime and Punishment* published.

1867 Alaska is sold by Russia to the United States for $7,200,000.

Marries his twenty-year-old stenographer, Anna Grigoryevna Snitkina, and they settle in Dresden.

1868 Birth of daughter, Sofia, who dies only three months old. *The Idiot* published in serial form.

1869 Birth of daughter, Lyubov.

1870 V. I. Lenin is born in the town of Simbirsk, on the banks of the Volga.

The Eternal Husband published.

1871 Moves back to St Petersburg with his wife and family. Birth of son, Fyodor.

1871–2 Serial publication of *The Devils*.

1873 First *khozdenie v narod* ('To the People' movement).
Becomes contributing editor of conservative weekly journal
Grazhdanin (*The Citizen*), where his *Diary of a Writer* is
published as a regular column. 'Bobok' published.

1874 Arrested and imprisoned again, for offences against the
political censorship regulations.

1875 *A Raw Youth* published. Birth of son, Aleksey.

1877 'The Gentle Creature' and 'The Dream of a Ridiculous
Man' published in *Grazhdanin*.

1878 Death of Aleksey. Works on *The Brothers Karamazov*.

1879 Iosif Vissarionovich Dzhugashvili (later known as Stalin)
born in Gori, Georgia.
First part of *The Brothers Karamazov* published.

1880 *The Brothers Karamazov* published (in complete form).
Anna starts a book service, where her husband's works may
be ordered by mail. Speech in Moscow at the unveiling of a
monument to Pushkin is greeted with wild enthusiasm.

1881 Assassination of Tsar Alexander II (1 March).
Dostoyevsky dies in St Petersburg (28 January). Buried in
the cemetery of the Alexander Nevsky Monastery.

Introduction

This Introduction reveals elements of the plot.

One of Dostoyevsky's favourite words, often used ironically, was 'fact' (*fakt*, a harsh-sounding foreign loan word in the Russian language), and it figures prominently in the characters' rumour-mongering, through which readers must attempt to make sense of *The Idiot*. The novelist's own life has entered public mythology with a dazzling series of such 'facts': the brutal father murdered by his serfs (perhaps not so brutal, perhaps not murdered), the molestation of a young girl (a vicious rumour utterly without proof), temporal lobe epilepsy, extraordinary poverty, flight from creditors, arrest and near-execution for 'seditious conspiracy', penal servitude and Siberian exile, a six-year intoxication with gambling. These events and situations have been the stuff of many biographies and psychoanalytic accounts, of which Freud's is the most notorious and Joseph Frank's the most judicious and comprehensive.

These facts, most of them registered in this volume's Chronology, blend in the popular imagination with material from Dostoyevsky's fiction (the murder of Fyodor Karamazov, numerous scenes of violated innocence, Prince Myshkin's seizures in *The Idiot*, Makar Devyushkin's hand-to-mouth existence in *Poor Folk*, hellish scenes from *The House of the Dead* and from *The Gambler*). Dostoyevsky's Russian critics processed his fiction in these terms, and 'scientific criticism' of foreign scholars was quick to build upon this shaky foundation. The most reckless diagnosis no doubt belongs to Emile Hennequin:

Dostoyevsky's ultimate originality, the feature which distinguishes and characterizes him, is his enormous imbalance between

feeling and reason. This man sees things and beings with the
vividness and surprise of someone half insane. And since anticipa-
tion neither prepares him for their movement nor the need for
reasoning impels him to sort out causes and effects, he looks
wildly upon a spectacle which assaults his senses in disconnected
shocks. Likewise, an intellect little developed, to which the senses
ceaselessly bear disconnected impressions, would be at a loss to
imagine the idea of development, be it in a narrative or in a
characterization, and would conceive instead uncertainty in a
story and instability in a soul ... Hence, once these aptitudes
are amplified to the level of genius, the marvellous design of
Dostoyevsky's characters; hence, above all, their carnal, wild,
violent, brutal, unintelligent nature, which Dostoyevsky must
have discovered latent in his own unpolished character, more
animal than spiritual.[1]

As a description of Dostoyevsky's characters in their most desperate moments, this has some plausibility; and the narrator of
The Idiot – by no means equal in intelligence and understanding
to its author – seems often at a loss when dealing with the
development of plot and character. And to be sure Dostoyevsky
himself could be irascible, unreasonable and, in polite society,
notoriously 'unpolished'. Recent novels by John Coetzee (*The
Master of St Petersburg*) and Leonid Tsypkin (*Summer in Baden-
Baden*)[2] have imagined these aspects of the author's personality
more successfully than the scholars and psychologists. Dostoyevsky's was, indeed, a life lived on the edge of physical break-
down, financial ruin and mental depression. By his own estimate
he endured, beginning at the age of twenty-six, an epileptic
seizure every three weeks.[3]

All of these sensational details of his life and work are, however, subject to qualification. James Rice, in a thorough and
insightful study of Dostoyevsky's illness, notes that unlike the
hero of *The Idiot*, Dostoyevsky could generally anticipate his
seizures and rarely suffered them in public.[4] He was able, ultimately, to control and terminate his obsession with gambling,
and to write his way out of debt. The madness, violence and
irrationality of his characters – denigrated by his contemporary

Russian critics and celebrated by his first foreign ones – were more often than not creative transformations of his childhood reading of early nineteenth-century European literature. In ways unrecognized by his first European readers, he was returning them the themes, plots and characters of their own Romantic fiction, drama and poetry.

By studying Dostoyevsky's letters, notebooks and revisions – most fully collected in the thirty-volume Soviet collection of his works (1972–90) – later twentieth-century scholars began to show the extent to which his choices were the products of a deep understanding of literary art. Unlike Henry James, who famously undervalued Russian craftsmanship (except Turgenev's), Dostoyevsky did not publish prefaces to his works, nor did he author an essay on the art of the novel. But the notebooks show that he had a nuanced understanding of the rhetorical and aesthetic consequences of his choices of narrative viewpoint, archetype, plot sequence and mode (comic, tragic, satiric, ironic). Robin Miller's magisterial reading of the notebooks for *The Idiot*, in particular, opened new perspectives on Dostoyevsky's art.

By countering the initial response to Dostoyevsky as an untutored savage, such detailed studies of his texts and writing process enable us to understand him as a gambler in a new and different sense. While he is famous for his compulsive gambling sprees at a game of chance, roulette, his greatest gamble was one that he indulged not for six years, but for nearly four decades: that he could support himself exclusively by his writing, by becoming one of Russia's first truly professional writers.

To appreciate this risk one must understand the circumstances in which Dostoyevsky worked. Secular Russian literature was scarcely a century older than Dostoyevsky himself. And the first tentative steps toward a viable, prestigious literature that was not a matter of salon play or court patronage had been taken by writers but a generation or two older than Dostoyevsky: Nikolai Novikov (1744–1818), Nikolai Karamzin (1766–1826), Aleksandr Pushkin (1799–1837), Nikolai Gogol (1809–52) and Mikhail Lermontov (1814–41) among them. These writers contended with conditions far from conducive to the

development of a literary marketplace. For a start, the autocracy
was inconsistent in dealing with what the Emperor Alexander
II would call 'the ungovernability and excesses of the printed
word'.[5] During the period 1750–1854 private presses were
permitted, banned and re-established; ambiguous passages in a
text were held against the author, then discarded, and – *de
facto* – held against him; the importation of foreign books was
banned, permitted, then severely curtailed. And agencies with
censorship powers proliferated, often contradicting one
another. The imperial government had so little respect for the
laws it promulgated that one of the censors would justly complain that 'there is no legality in Russia'.[6] With Russia's defeat
in the Crimean War and the accession of a new emperor in 1855,
the situation became better, but still far from ideal. Dostoyevsky
would feel the lash on his own back in 1863, when *Vremya*
(*Time*), the very successful journal that he and his brother
Mikhail had founded, was shut down over an innocuous article
on the Polish Uprising of that year. That Dostoyevsky, an ardent
Russian nationalist who sprinkled unsympathetic Polish characters across his novels, should have suffered this disaster indicates
the continuing capriciousness of the government, which, even
as it was banning *Vremya*, was allowing the publication of
Nikolai Chernyshevsky's utopian novel, *What Is to Be Done?*,
which would become gospel for radical youth, including, later,
Vladimir Ilyich Lenin.

So high were the barriers to successful professional authorship
that few of Dostoyevsky's fellow writers risked hurdling them;
a contemporary survey by S. S. Shashkov argued that few writers
earned the 2,000 roubles a year necessary to support a family
and that the situation in the 1870s was little better than it had
been four decades earlier.[7] Even prominent writers relied on
independent means or hedged their bets with official positions.
Leo Tolstoy inherited a large estate (approximately 800 taxable
serfs), Ivan Turgenev divided an estate of 4,000 with his brother.
These grand holdings considerably dwarfed the small debt-
ridden property of Dostoyevsky's father. Both Ivan Goncharov
and Mikhail Saltykov-Shchedrin came from families that
enjoyed noble status and merchant wealth, and both made

significant careers in state service, from which Dostoyevsky had quickly resigned upon graduating from the Academy of Military Engineers. Dostoyevsky's family background was decidedly modest – his mother came from the merchant estate and his father had worked his way into the lower nobility from the even less prosperous parish clergy. Once Dostoyevsky had surrendered his ensign's pay and exchanged his share of his father's insignificant estate for 1,000 roubles, he had no other sources of support than small loans from friends and relations and income from his writing.

To count on finding a readership was no less a gamble than was braving the Russian legal system. Five years before beginning *The Idiot* Dostoyevsky estimated that only one Russian in 500 was sufficiently educated to read the literature that he and his fellow writers were publishing in a handful of journals, in an increasing number of newspapers and in small editions of individual volumes.[8] Eight years of penal servitude and Siberian exile, most of them spent in the company of non-intellectuals, had made him acutely conscious of the cultural schism between the empire's minuscule Westernized elite and the illiterate masses which preserved Russia's traditional Orthodox culture. He had come to deplore this schism; he sought enduring value in the people's way of life, and he dedicated his post-exile career to reconciling intellectuals who looked to the modern West ('Westernizers') and to the Russian past ('Slavophiles') through a policy of *pochvennichestvo* (a term derived from the Russian word for soil) in his short-lived journal *Vremya*. But Dostoyevsky attempted to do this as a professional author, not as a gentleman-pamphleteer or salon debater, and, as a professional, he knew that he not only had to argue with the cultured elite, but also entertain it and seize its imagination.

Dostoyevsky may not have had financial resources, but the cultural capital he could stake was not insignificant by the standards of his time. He had acquired a love of literature in his family surroundings and at school. At the Imperial Academy of Military Engineers he received instruction in Russian and French literature, German and history. In these early years at home, at school and in St Petersburg he pored over and passionately discussed the books of the Bible; Job, Revelation and the Gospels, especially John, shaped his view of the world. The Dostoyevsky family, far socially from the Francophone elite, taught him to revere the best of Russian literature, and his texts – including *The Idiot* – reverberate with quotations from the works of Pushkin, Gogol and Karamzin. Gogol's impact is particularly noticeable throughout Dostoyevsky's career in the uncanny relationships between his characters, in his often fantastic treatment of St Petersburg, and in his use of multiple narrative positions within a single fiction. Pushkin and Gogol had helped foster a vision of St Petersburg as a city of extremes, of inhumane destructiveness, of sudden transformations. Dostoyevsky's very notion of reality, 'fantastic' as he called it shortly after completing *The Idiot*,[9] derived in large part from the experience of these two predecessors in thematizing the capital of the Russian bureaucracy, 'the most abstract and intentional city on the entire globe', as one of his characters, the Underground Man, would put it. But Dostoyevsky would tether his predecessors' balloon of fantasy to social, economic and cultural situations they had not envisioned, as is immediately apparent from the opening chapters of *The Idiot*, set in a railway car and in the home of a newly enriched capitalist.

Nabokov, mocking Dostoyevsky's Russian nationalism, could not resist the temptation to call him 'the most European of the Russian writers',[10] and Dostoyevsky's early letters and late journalistic essays, to say nothing of his fiction, show an intense, enduring fascination with several interrelated genres imported into Russia by translators and literary journals. The German writer Friedrich Schiller gave him a sense of life as festival, an ecstatic sense that humanity could be perfected and that people could become brothers through achieving a harmonious balance between mental, emotional and sensual activities. Such visions extend from Dostoyevsky's early teens through Prince Myshkin's visions in *The Idiot* to Dmitri Karamazov's confessions in verse and Alyosha Karamazov's final speech. Gothic fiction, another youthful fascination, transects all of Dostoyevsky's fiction with mysterious settings, characters beset by mental dysfunction and plots set in motion by violations of the divine order. If we could use the term 'Gothic' in its historical sense and not in its present, pejorative one, we would find much of it in Dostoyevsky, whose mature fiction centres around daring challenges to moral and divine authority. French social Romanticism (Georges Sand, Victor Hugo, Honoré de Balzac, the Utopian Socialists) figures no less prominently in his early reading, and it gave him lessons in criticizing contemporary society and dreaming of a potentially harmonious social order. Dostoyevsky would begin his literary career with a translation of Balzac's *Eugénie Grandet* (1833). Canonical works sanctified by Romanticism, such as Shakespeare's, would lend Dostoyevsky citations and plot structures for the rest of his career. So, from the other end of the literary hierarchy, would his immersion in the columns and serialized novels of the popular newspapers. A glance at the annotations to the present volume will show how well all of this youthful reading stayed with Dostoyevsky, to be supplemented with references to later writing, such as Gustave Flaubert's *Madame Bovary* (1857) and Alexandre Dumas' *La Dame aux camélias* (1848), to the heroines of which he will sharply contrast *The Idiot*'s tormented Nastasya Filippovna.

This varied material staked Dostoyevsky well, and his gamble on professional authorship paid off, at least initially. His first novel, *Poor Folk* (1846), earned him critical attention and steady honoraria for his ensuing pre-exile fictions. The happy few who comprised the reading public welcomed him back from political imprisonment and exile in 1859. He published a two-volume collection of his pre-exile fiction in 1860, a relatively rare event at a time when most successful literary commerce was conducted through a handful of so-called 'thick journals' – the reading public and distribution networks were not sufficiently capacious to make individual volumes profitable. His work for *Vremya* and the pseudo-memoir of his prison experience, *The House of the Dead*, earned him a handsome income of 8,000–10,000 roubles a year.

The closing of *Vremya*, however, became but the first in a series of catastrophes that preceded the writing of *The Idiot*. The deaths of Dostoyevsky's niece (February 1864), wife (April

1864) and brother Mikhail (July 1864) were profound personal misfortunes, and they had a major impact on Dostoyevsky's ability to conduct his professional life. A new journal which his brother had received permission to publish, *Epokha* (*Epoch*), got off to a slow start, each issue appearing two months late throughout the first year. It produced little income because subscribers to *Vremya* had to be compensated for the issues they had not received when the journal was banned. To make matters worse, the new journal's fiction did not meet the standards that *Vremya* had set. The one exception was Dostoyevsky's own *Notes from Underground*, which would become one of his best-known and most respected fictions only in the twentieth century. But in 1864 the circumstances of serialization worked against this challenging novella: over two months elapsed between the appearance of the first and second parts, giving the journal's readers little chance to see the intricate connections between the two parts. The critics dismissed it with silence.

Meanwhile, Mikhail's family, a widow and young children, had inherited an immense debt of 33,000 roubles, and Dostoyevsky took responsibility for their well-being. In an effort to support himself, his stepson and his brother's family, Dostoyevsky made two exceedingly risky business decisions. The first was to continue *Epokha* instead of abandoning it to his brother's creditors as a liquefiable asset. It soon folded from want of subscribers. This drove Dostoyevsky to take a second major risk, agreeing to finish two novels in 1866, a Trollope-like rate of production which he never before or afterwards met. For the first novel, the future *Crime and Punishment*, he secured a place in Mikhail Katkov's 'thick journal' *The Russian Herald*, at a rate – 150 roubles a signature (a printed sheet equivalent to twelve pages) – that he would continue to receive for his next two major novels, *The Idiot* and *The Devils*. This journal was one of a handful that supported major Russian novelists during the 1860s–1880s, and Katkov would regularly send Dostoyevsky advances during the late 1860s, thereby providing a sort of salary, but at a cost. The rate Katkov paid took Dostoyevsky out of the very first rank of Russian writers. Rates were well known in the literary world, and this drop in income would have brought with it a concomitant drop in prestige, a handicap in negotiating future honoraria.

Publishing with *The Russian Herald* entailed artistic and ideological hazards. Dostoyevsky suspected that Katkov was knocking down his rate to compel him to produce a longer work. 'A novel is a poetic matter,' he wrote to A. E. Vrangel, 'it demands spiritual calm and imagination' (28:ii.150–51). In the years to come Dostoyevsky would discover that Katkov's journal impinged not only on the 'poetry' of his novels, but on their concrete realization, their 'art', as he called it. Katkov, a political and cultural conservative, would insist that Dostoyevsky change the scene of the prostitute Sonia reading the Gospels in *Crime and Punishment* and that he drop Stavrogin's confession to Tikhon from *The Devils*. The publishing pressures on *The Idiot* were less a matter of censorship than ones of pace and deadline, but they would constantly challenge Dostoyevsky to solve problems of plot and characterization on the fly, giving him no chance to return and revise previous parts as he moved forward with the process of serialization.

The contract for Dostoyevsky's other novel of 1866, *The Gambler*, was even more threatening to his art and livelihood than the contract with Katkov. Tempted by the possibility of publishing another collected edition of his works, Dostoyevsky agreed to a contract with F. T. Stellovsky that is legendary for its penalty clause: if he did not deliver a novel of twelve or more signatures by 1 November 1866, Stellovsky would acquire the right to publish Dostoyevsky's works for nine years – with no compensation for the author. This proved as melodramatic a predicament as any Victorian novelist, including Dostoyevsky, ever invented. Fortunately for Dostoyevsky, the melodrama's opening acts of tragedy were followed by the obligatory comic ending, a rescue-in-the-nick-of-time. The hero of the piece turned out to be one of Russia's first stenographers, Anna Grigoryevna Snitkina. He would work late into the night over his notebooks, jotting down ideas. Then, by day, he would dictate passages to her, and she would transcribe them and promptly return them neatly copied for editing. With her help he not only met Stellovsky's deadline, he also found a work rhythm that he

would continue for the remaining fifteen years of his career.
Jacques Catteau argues that the insistent peculiarities of Dostoyevsky's mature style owe much to this mode of creativity:

> While Dostoyevsky was dictating, he never stopped pacing around
> the room and even, at difficult moments, pulled his hair . . . The
> style with its triple repetitions, its sentences punctuated as in
> speech, its accumulation of nouns and adjectives with similar
> meanings, its constant reticence, reflects this uninterrupted pacing
> within a confined space. From this time on, the rhythm of the
> Dostoevskian sentence may be defined as a walking movement,
> where the breath of the spoken word is marked in the written
> style.[11]

The final text would be an amalgam of feverishly jotted, dis-
jointed notebook entries, oral dictation and careful polishing of
the day's efforts. It required immense powers of concentration
and nearly unimaginable intensity to keep in mind hundreds of
pages created in this way, because Dostoyevsky did not draft
his major novels in their entirety before serialization, and, once
serialization was complete, he would not revise the instalments
(except for a few corrections of typographical mistakes) before
publishing them as separate volumes. *The Idiot* itself would
appear in book form only in 1874, five years after serialization
had been completed.

Born the year Dostoyevsky published his first novel, Anna
Grigoryevna was half his age. Broadly educated and fluent in
German, she was, like other literate young Russians of her time,
devoted to literature. She became Dostoyevsky's wife in early
1867, shortly before the newlyweds were forced abroad by
debts. No account of Dostoyevsky's work can neglect the extraordinary contributions she made to his career and reputation.
Not only did he dictate all his remaining fiction to her, she
managed his publishing affairs and a book-setting business after
they returned from four years of wandering in Europe. Dissemi-
nating his works is only a part of what she did to secure his
legacy. She kept a stenographic diary of their time abroad, she
wrote valuable memoirs, and she prepared Dostoyevsky's letters

to her for publication. The diary – more than the worshipful memoirs – chronicles his gambling sprees, his bursts of temper, friction with relatives and other daily trials that he would make, much reworked, the stuff of his fiction. The letters show the agony Dostoyevsky experienced in dealing with journals, editors and publishers.

It is to Anna Grigoryevna that we owe our best record of the process of writing *The Idiot*, the notes that Dostoyevsky jotted down in three notebooks as he planned and drafted the novel. Fearing a lengthy customs inspection, he had planned to destroy them, as he destroyed the novel's drafts, before crossing the border back into Russia, but she managed to save them, and their crying child distracted the officials, who did not detain the family.

In the best of times writing for serial publication without a completed novel was a nerve-racking process, a gamble by the author that he would be able to pull the work together within the course of the journal's subscription year. But for the Dostoyevsky family these were not the best of times. As he worked fitfully on the novel between September 1867 and January 1869, Dostoyevsky and Anna Grigoryevna moved between four different cities (Geneva, Vevey, Milan, Florence), enduring a number of seizures, gambling episodes, grinding poverty and, most disheartening of all, the death of their baby daughter Sofia (May 1868). The writing in the notebooks reflects this desperate situation. Earlier editions neatly lay them out into eight plans for the novel, followed by notes for Parts Two–Four, but the most recent edition reproduces them precisely, not as discrete plans, but as a chaotic set of brief comments on plot and character, a few long paragraphs and many feverish '*Nota bene*' asides. A sequence of headings that Dostoyevsky gave some of his notes captures his attempts to give himself confidence in the novel's direction and, then, his failure to do so: 'new and *final* plan', 'new plan', 'new plan', 'final plan', 'final plan', 'plan based on Iago', 'again a new plan'. None of these 'plans' is more than two printed pages in length; most of the material they contain is not to be found in the final version of the novel. The notes are at times remarkable, as I have noted, for their awareness of problems of characterization, plotting and rhetoric. They make subtle distinctions which help our understanding of the novel, as when the author differentiates three different kinds of love that his principal male characters exhibit – '1) passionately direct love, Rogozhin; 2) love from vanity, Ganya; 3) Christian love, the prince' (9:220) – or when he differentiates his approach to depicting a virtuous character ('innocent') from those of Cervantes and Dickens (Don Quixote and Pickwick are 'comical', 9:239).

More remarkable still, however, is the extent to which the notes and plans show novelistic dead ends, character traits and events rejected from the final version, as Dostoyevsky discards possibilities both extremely sensational and novelistically conventional. The future Prince Myshkin in early versions rapes his adopted sister (the future Nastasya Filippovna), sets fire to their house, is a figure of proud self-mastery, a figure based on Shakespeare's Iago and a wife-murderer. Nastasya Filippovna herself and her rival for the affections of Prince Myshkin, Aglaya Yepanchin, show similar instability, the former – as rape victim (in one version by the Idiot, in another by his handsome brother, cut from the final text) who marries the prince and runs off to a brothel, the latter in vacillating relationships with the prince, with Nastasya Filippovna and with Ganya Ivolgin.

Dostoyevsky struggled with these possibilities throughout the autumn of 1867, eventually rejecting the biographical development of his future hero's oppressive past, the most brutal events and a number of the hero's family entanglements. The novel became, thereby, much less a Gothic thriller or a work of social Romanticism, in which the characters are crushed by the circumstances of their milieu. He discarded one false start to the novel before starting anew in early December. By 18 December a new novel had taken shape from these confused beginnings, and by 5 January 1868 be was able to send off the first five chapters of Part One to *The Russian Herald*; two more chapters followed on 11 January, and the first journal instalment was complete; he had written nearly a hundred pages in less than a month.[12] The remainder of Part One constituted the second, February, instalment. As was often the case in his years as a serial novelist,

Dostoyevsky met his deadline, but allowed himself no time to correct the proofs of the instalment. Living abroad further limited his opportunity to make last-minute changes.

Discarding the bric-à-brac of conventionally sensational fiction opened the way for Dostoyevsky to undertake the radical novelistic gamble that lies at the centre of the finished novel. In a letter to his friend Apollon Maikov, Dostoyevsky spelled out the direction that his writing had taken him:

> I have long been tormented by one idea, but I have been afraid to make a novel out of it, because this idea is too difficult and I am not prepared for it, although it is a fully tempting one and I love it. This idea is to *depict a completely beautiful human being*. Nothing can be more difficult than this, in my opinion, and especially in our time . . . This idea flashed before me previously in a certain artistic idea, but only to a *certain extent*, and it has to be complete. Only my desperate situation forced me to seize upon this premature idea. (28.ii.240–41, 12 January 1868).

With the privilege of hindsight we can look back over the notebooks and see this solution taking shape, as the hero becomes a prince and a holy fool (a type of Eastern Orthodox saint, particularly prevalent in Russia, who imitates Christ in extreme humility and who speaks truth to the powerful of the world) and, finally, in a cryptic notebook entry from 10 April: 'Prince Christ' (9:253).

Dostoyevsky well understood the problem of depicting positive characters, as he had witnessed Gogol's failure with the sequel to *Dead Souls* (usually published as Part Two of the novel in English translation), the exemplary landowners of which he had himself mocked. Chernyshevsky's no less exemplary and no less wooden 'new people' in *What Is to Be Done?* had won acceptance, but on ideological, not aesthetic grounds, and Dostoyevsky knew that a Christ-like hero would win him little praise from the radical intelligentsia. To place such a character at the centre of his novel was, indeed, a gamble, probably the greatest of Dostoyevsky's career, more even than the theodicy that is part and parcel of *The Brothers Karamazov*, which also ran counter to the prevailing scepticism of the intelligentsia, but was undertaken at a time when he held a much more secure place in public opinion.

Dostoyevsky was gambling, moreover, not only with his finances and with his literary future, but with his most sacred beliefs. Well before he immersed himself in Orthodox theology and the history of Orthodoxy, before he became friendly with Orthodox thinkers and clerics in the 1870s, he had developed an image of Christ that was inextricably joined in his mind with beauty, truth, brotherhood and Russia. He did not stake this image and these beliefs lightly. Nor did he turn to personal experience – epilepsy, near-execution – for plot material in any simple or straightforward fashion. Like his faith and his image of Christ these experiences are worked into intricate, non-obvious and non-didactic elements of plot and characterization. Cherished ideas – such as the fear that the modern world lacks a positive guiding idea – appear in the mouths of buffoons, such as the corrupt schemer Lebedev. Truth becomes something a character tells by accident, as another buffoon, General Ivolgin, does with Aglaya. A consumptive fourteen-year-old, Ippolit, will make a mockery of the beauty and harmony of God's world, and, as the other characters mock him, the prince will be rendered silent.

Dostoyevsky's inclination to make Prince Myshkin an 'innocent', not primarily a figure of comic excess, might have entailed a particular treatment, one which goes back to the philosophical tales of the Enlightenment, such as Voltaire's *Candide* (1759), in which the innocent character becomes a satiric instrument for revealing the corruption of society, the inadequacy of its value systems or the stultifying nature of its institutions. Certainly the novel uses him to this end, as he is confronted with calculating capitalists, scheming members of high society, corrupt bureaucrats and other denizens of the nineteenth-century novel's St Petersburg. But he far exceeds this satiric role, as soon becomes apparent in the novel's quickly paced, dazzlingly comprehensive first part.

Readers familiar with nineteenth-century Russian novels will be struck by the intensity of the novel's opening: not in a carriage, but in a railway car, not on a warm summer day, but in cold, foggy November. Thrown together in a third-class compartment, a dissolute merchant's son (Rogozhin), a know-it-all bureaucrat (Lebedev) and an ethereal young man (Prince Myshkin) immediately begin telling the most intimate details of their lives. There is no escape from the crowded, uncomfortable situation, and the prince can recall the beauty of Switzerland only as an ecstatic act, for there is no relieving view of the countryside through the opaque windows. This scene uses the techniques for which Dostoyevsky has become justly famous: dramatic confrontations, developed in fragments of conversation, with relatively little background biographical development of the characters. The time spanned by the first part will only be fifteen hours; there are only ten days' worth of narrated action over the whole course of the novel. Compressing the action of the novel into such a brief time span allows the author to rub their psyches raw. Rogozhin by the end of the first part will not have slept for forty-eight hours; the third part will keep the prince and many of the other characters awake through the night, which culminates in Ippolit's failed attempt at suicide.

Part One takes familiar novelistic structures and sets them spinning. The wealth which differentiates characters is no longer hereditary and based in agriculture. It is measured by money, unprecedentedly large sums gained and lost with hyperbolic speed. The narrator and many of the characters are obsessed with it. Ptitsyn and the Terentyev widow are loan sharks; General Ivolgin and Ferdyshchenko are spongers; General Yepanchin rents almost all of his house and is caught up in his enterprises; Ganya believes that money will buy him talent and lend him the 'originality' he sadly lacks. Family groupings are introduced only to show their fragility; as an institution the family is nowhere in Dostoyevsky's fiction so vulnerable. The family as a traditional centre of patriarchal life becomes, instead, the locus of greed, falsehood and contention. The Rogozhins cheat each other, and one brother cuts the gold tassels from their father's coffin. The Myshkins are dying out. Ganya Ivolgin is ashamed of his father and makes him use the back staircase; his younger brother, Kolya, wants to disown his family. Totsky raises his ward, Nastasya Filippovna, only to make her his adolescent concubine. The Yepanchins are the most conventionally stable of the families, yet even here the three headstrong girls control their parents, and, as the novel opens, General Yepanchin is hoping to purchase Nastasya Filippovna's favours with a very expensive necklace. The individual characters dream of, and achieve, extremes of mobility. The two generals cross paths as they ascend and descend the social hierarchy: General Yepanchin, a private's son, has become a wealthy investor, while General Ivolgin has become a drunkard and buffoon who maintains his status only in his hyperbolic lies.

Already in this opening part Dostoyevsky develops the extreme egocentricity of his characters, both major and minor, and contrasts it with that of the prince. These other characters, in seeking to define themselves and realize their ambitions, resist patterns and definitions imposed on them by others, lashing out verbally and physically. Dostoyevsky introduces the theme of illness in this part – epilepsy (the Prince), consumption (the Swiss girl, Marie and Ippolit) and self-destructiveness ('hara-kiri', Nastasya Filippovna). These three illnesses will come to dominate Parts Two, Three and Four of the novel, respectively, as physical, psychological and philosophical problems.

Among these unusual characters the prince stands out as the most unusual, precisely because he eludes the understanding of the others. Unashamedly ignorant of social conventions, he turns immediately to large, ultimate issues, indecorously talking of a seduced girl and executions in the Yepanchin drawing room. Ungoverned by a sense of shame, he is the only character in the novel who can laugh at himself. He is, without trying to be, unsystematic, and this frustrates his interlocutors, who see him as someone to distrust (as a sponger, a fraud), an ideologue, an object of mockery, a cause of irritation and an easy dupe. His approach to art captures his artlessness when he tells Adelaida: 'I think one simply looks and paints' (Part One, chapter 5). The Prince calls forth a 'dialectical' pattern, as the narrator calls it (Part Two, chapter 5), or 'double thoughts', as the Prince calls them (Part Two, chapter 11) in the adult characters throughout the novel, bringing out the worst in them, the best, and again the worst. Thus Rogozhin will call him a 'holy fool', offer him clothes, exchange crosses with him, only to try to slit his throat; General Yepanchin will suspect him, welcome him with money, then plan to trap him. Ganya will become irritated with him, slap him, beg forgiveness, and then try to exploit him. The Yepanchin girls will mock him, accept him and confide in him, but ultimately turn away.

It becomes clear early on that the prince has a special part to play among the characters of the novel. Because he will not be offended, does not compete with people and does not judge them, he has the ability to defuse tense situations and quarrels, if only the other characters will respond to this in a positive fashion, appreciating his gentleness and sharing his ecstatic sense of joy, as in the passage on the donkey or in his story about the mother taking delight in her child. It is his tragedy that very few characters, such as the Swiss children, can accept him in these terms. The others fit him into their own patterns of distrust, self-hatred, lying and fraud. They project their corruption and tortuous psychology on to him. Totsky, the most corrupt, will suspect that the Prince is also on the make.

All of the failed interpretations and poisoned relationships come together in the final four chapters of Part One, at Nastasya Filippovna's party, which, together with the epileptic seizure in Part Two, Ippolit's rebellion in Part Three and Aglaya's meeting with with Nastasya Filippovna in Part Four, provides some of Dostoyevsky's most intense writing. Here at Nastasya Filippovna's not only do we have the relationships and themes gathered around the fireplace, we have almost all of the characters, except the Yepanchin women, together with the hatreds and resentments that have been brewing for nine years and 200 pages. The 'scandalous scene' (*skandal* in Russian) is a favourite compositional device in Dostoyevsky's mature fiction. This one, like others, has four moments: (1) the characters come together in a fever pitch of excitement, already resenting and fearing each other; (2) some explosion occurs on various psychological, social, political or religious levels; (3) the characters challenge and expose each other, uttering extreme statements and wounding each other psychologically and even physically; (4) the characters then fly off in different directions and configurations, to prepare for the next 'scandalous scene'. The Dostoyevskian scandalous scene joins the subjective, selfish motivations of the individual characters to the broader philosophical issues. Thus the principal one in Part Two with Burdovsky and the 'post-nihilists' involves economics and politics; the one in Part Three with Ippolit involves philosophy and religion. But this first great scandalous scene keeps to the social, economic and moral issues of the first part of the novel, including the themes of illness and love.

At the centre of this confrontation is the breathtakingly beautiful Nastasya Filippovna, whose anger burns white hot from the narratives told for Ferdyshchenko's game. Totsky and General Yepanchin have each promised to tell the truth for the novelty of it, and each has come up with a highly 'literary' and ultimately self-flattering piece of trivia. Meanwhile, Totsky has refused to admit that his violation of the teenaged Nastasya Filippovna was an unbelievably shameful act. The narrator shows her listening to his account with flashing eyes, and we know she will make him pay. Surrounded by the three men who love her in terms of the three kinds of love that Dostoyevsky outlined in his notebooks, vain (Ganya), passionate (Rogozhin) and Christ-like (the prince), each offering more money than the one before, Nastasya Filippovna snaps. Why can she not accept the prince's love? The answer shows once again the working of Dostoyevskian psychology, as she vacillates between her role as victim (which implicates Totsky) and her role as moral agent (which implicates herself). By rejecting the offers she makes it impossible for Totsky to be free to make an advantageous marriage with the oldest Yepanchin girl, thereby taking vengeance on her molester. By rejecting the prince's title and fortune, she can rise above all of society's values, showing that she is not for sale. The prince has compassionately negated her declaration of independence, that she is 'in charge' (Part One, chapter 14) by declaring her ill, 'in a fever' (Part One, chapter 16), and not responsible for her situation. She retaliates by calling him ill in return, and she rejects the opportunity to break out of her five-year cycle of humiliating herself and others.

A bystander aptly compares her act to the Japanese ritual of hara-kiri.

Part One of *The Idiot* represents Dostoyevsky's writing at its best. But he concluded it not really knowing where to proceed from the concluding scandalous scene, and the flurry of 'plans' in his notebooks did not immediately help him. He did not have an instalment for the March issue of *The Russian Herald*, and the plotting of the novel moves fitfully forward through the next two parts. Two of the novel's most intriguing and powerful characters, Rogozhin and Nastasya Filippovna, the characters who best understand the prince, are absent from most of these central sections, and remain in the reader's mind largely through rumour and letters.

In his desperation to continue, Dostoyevsky hit upon a mode of narration that he would develop further in *The Devils* and in *The Brothers Karamazov*. Although the narrator occasionally has the power of omniscience, the power to enter the minds of the characters, for the most part the story is told by a chronicler-narrator who follows closely upon the events, reporting them in terms of the characters' own understanding of them. He sometimes learns of events long after they happen, and he registers material that he does not analyse: rumours, visits, letters. This technique forces the reader to try to see beyond the narrator, who, as becomes clear from his rather wordy and inappropriate digression on the 'practical man' at the opening of Part Three, becomes progressively inadequate to the complexity of the situation. The narrator opts out of explaining the really difficult matters, pontificating instead on things he can comprehend, such as the social types of his time. He would be adequate to a standard Victorian novel of manners, perhaps, or to a newspaper column on contemporary life, but his limited understanding is not adequate to these characters and situations. In his confusion the narrator often gives us the illusion of plottedness – he refers to meetings of characters we never see, such as the meetings between Ippolit and Rogozhin. But we often do not learn what happens and are left with a vague sense of suspense. Of the six months that elapse between Part One and Part Two, we learn of only a few events, and these from rumours or from brief reminiscences of the characters in their conversations. Readers are compelled to speculate, infer and, increasingly, explain and piece together the novel for themselves. This mode of narration constitutes a daring risk on the author's part, but it is a brilliant solution to his problems with the plot, a way of getting his readers to share the burden of putting all of these characters and incidents together. He asks his readers to reach back hundreds of pages to recall details, scenes and important dialogue, a difficult enough task for the modern reader of this one-volume edition. Imagine the burden that it placed upon the original readers of the serialized version, who had to read the novel over the course of a year!

Dostoyevsky picked up the threads of his novel not so much through conventional plotting as through the introduction of a few new characters and new themes, as he underscores the sickness of the novel's world with reference to two different diseases: epilepsy (Part Two) and consumption (Part Three). Confrontations between the prince and Rogozhin (Part Two) and between the prince and Ippolit (Part Three) bring themes and illness into sharp focus. Both serve to take *The Idiot* outside the bounds of the family novel that it becomes when it centres on the prince's growing intimacy with the Yepanchins, with Aglaya in particular. Ippolit and Rogozhin are similar to each other in several ways that make them ideal figures for the discussion of ultimate issues. Both live outside polite society and lack Radomsky's polished irony and Mrs Yepanchin's common sense. Each lives on the brink of death, madness and destruction, like the prince himself. Rogozhin's negation of life by violent passion and murder parallels Ippolit's negation of life by blasphemy and attempted suicide. They give us two visions of ugliness set against the prince's ecstatic sense of beauty and life: Rogozhin's dark house, haunted by the sect of Castrates, Ippolit's excruciatingly terrifying monster. Each character is developed in connection with a reproduction of Holbein's 1522 painting 'Christ in the Tomb'.

To Rogozhin the prince speaks, Christ-like, in parables, which he does not interpret. It becomes clear that his is a religion of ecstasy or rejoicing, not of rituals, institutions or formalized precepts. As the prince's epileptic seizure is about to begin, he faces the possibility that his sense of joy, hope and higher understanding might be nothing more than a fleeting product of his illness, like the mental darkness and idiocy that threatened him in its wake (Part Two, chapter 5). Here and elsewhere, he does not succumb to the possibility.

More intellectual than Rogozhin, Ippolit represents the spirit of negation on a conscious, premeditated, rational level. It is Ippolit, whose consumption dooms him to a life of endless contemplation, who draws the most negative meaning from Holbein's portrait. Rogozhin owns the reproduction and is aware that it is special, but cannot analyse its effect. Ippolit, the former student, understands the full horror of the portrait's message, that even the most perfect and beautiful of men is subject to the impersonal, monstrous laws of nature. The painting would seem even more terrifying to Ippolit because its Christ looks so consumptive, so pained and wasted.

Dostoyevsky arranges Ippolit's confrontation with the prince with an elegance and symmetry that are rare in this novel. The two of them are each on the brink of death. Each has an illness which can eventuate in madness, each has had doubts about the justice of God's world, and each has felt alienated from nature's 'feast' (Part Three, chapter 7). Yet they respond very differently. The prince embraces nature in a leap of faith, while Ippolit perceives himself apart from nature and hates the prince for his love of life. The prince sees compassion as the only law of existence; the pronoun 'I' appears infrequently in his discourse, while Ippolit sees suicide as the only meaningful act he can complete, and his discourse is replete with the first-person pronoun. The prince suffers from the sacred illness; his is the psychology of epilepsy. Ippolit's consumption – a slow, painful wasting disease – drives him to irritability, and, by the end of the novel, he has become insufferable.

Ippolit's reading of his 'Necessary Explanation' is a savage scene. Everyone is drunk, including the prince and Ippolit, who have each had three glasses of champagne in quick succession. Everyone is exhausted and has been awake for many hours. The raucous and generally uninvited guests are waiting to see Ippolit die and mock him. He is abandoned by his family. The narrative stresses his bad luck, and the prince can only ask his forgiveness, not provide a counter-argument. Meanwhile, Part Three's argument in favour of a 'binding idea' is delivered by Lebedev. His critique of modern secular civilization is presented as a parody of a modern legal defence, that is, Dostoyevsky shows us one institution (the church) through the rhetoric of another (the legal system), in the words and intonations of a drunkard. Life and joy are a matter of forgiving absurdity. Christ's promise of redemption is as yet unfulfilled, and the Holbein portrait remains the very image of this unfulfilment.

Problems of understanding, truth and falsehood dominate Part Four, and the reader must face them with even less help from the chronicler-narrator than in Parts Two and Three. The sequence of events becomes more difficult to follow, their significance even harder to comprehend. The narrator gives up, devoting his attention to secondary characters and allowing that 'sometimes it is best for the narrator to confine himself to a simple exposition of events' (Part Four, chapter 1). By chapter 9 he has abdicated the authority to explain the prince's failure with Aglaya to Radomsky, whose understanding is, by this time, more limited than the reader's and grounded in a series of inadequate determinist propositions (nerves, epilepsy, the St Petersburg weather, etc.). Aglaya, too, has failed to understand him, grounding her sense of his extraordinary nature in a series of conventionally heroic poses: knight, duelist, judge.

Aglaya's treatment of the prince in Part Four is one of the most salient of a series of misunderstandings and rejections, rejections which call to mind Nastasya Filippovna's insightful comment in a letter to Aglaya that Christ should be painted alone, with a child. The plot has not made it easy for these other characters, as the prince is generally presented in terms of negatives or symbols. He is not moralistic or judgemental and does not make conscious choices, acting, instead, compassionately and intuitively. Nor is he formal or ritualistic. He is not conscious of institutions but is vaguely communitarian in his desire to reconcile the characters, uniting them in brotherhood. This makes him particularly vulnerable to the rituals of politeness at the Yepanchin's party; he can read the faces of children and of characters, such as Rogozhin and Nastasya Filippovna, who are marginal to society, but he cannot read the faces of those who are trained to dissemble. The prince's values, if we may use so formal a term, centre on beauty, broadly understood to comprise physical and spiritual beauty, natural beauty, the innocence of children and brotherly (not egotistical) love. These are values that the others will not try to grasp and that he cannot express in a logically coherent fashion, only through parable-like narratives. Aglaya specifically forbids him to speak of beauty at her family's party.

The ending brings together Nastasya Filippovna, Rogozhin and the prince in tragic symmetry. Lying near her, they represent the two aspects of her potential that the prince recognized at first glance, destructively passionate and compassionately gentle. The ending, in turn, leaves the reader with two vexing questions. What has been the prince's effect on the world of the novel? What has been the world's effect on the prince? The novel gives many answers to these questions. Ultimately the prince is seen to have 'fallen' (the Russian term for epilepsy is the 'falling sickness') into a world which expects no Messiah, which cannot understand him and which mistrusts the gifts he brings it, gifts which may themselves become tarnished in this corrosive atmosphere. His passionately ideological speech at the Yepanchins' party may be just such a tarnished gift.

Whatever Dostoyevsky's intentions to create a 'completely beautiful human being', he did not make the world of *The Idiot* the world of the Gospels. The corrupt, fearful officials and lawyers of the Gospels seem rather tame beside the characters of this novel. And Christ never had to deal simultaneously with the likes of Aglaya and Nastasya Filippovna. The Christ of the Gospels performed miracles, but always in connection with the faith of those around Him. The world of this novel is very different: a world of cynicism, greed and rampant egocentricity. Its sense of beauty is superficial, not spiritual, and, in the final analysis, it extends the prince no understanding. And he can bring it no miracles.

NOTES

1. Emile Hennequin, *Etudes de critique scientifique: Ecrivains francisés: Dickens, Heine, Tourguenef, Poe, Dostoiewski, Tolstoi* (Paris: Perrin et Cie., 1889), pp. 181–2.

2. John Coetzee, *The Master of St Petersburg* (London: Secker and Warburg, 1994); Leonid Tsypkin, *Summer in Baden-Baden*, translated by Roger and Angela Keys (New York: New Directions, 2001).

3. James L. Rice, *Dostoevsky and the Healing Art: An Essay in Literary and Medical History* (Ann Arbor: Ardis, 1985), pp. xiii–xiv.

4. Rice, *Dostoevsky and the Healing Art*, p. 77.

5. Quoted in Charles A. Ruud, *Fighting Words: Imperial Censorship and the Russian Press, 1804–1906* (Toronto: Toronto University Press, 1982), p. 186.

6. Aleksandr Nikitenko, *The Diary of a Russian Censor*, abridged, edited and translated by H. S. Jacobson (Amherst: University of Massachusetts Press, 1975), p. 30.

7. S. S. Shashkov, 'Literaturnyi trud v Rossii', *Delo* 8 (1876), p. 43.

8. Fyodor Dostoevsky, *Winter Notes on Summer Impressions*, trans. David Patterson (Evanston: Northwestern University Press, 1988), p. 8.

9. F. M. Dostoevsky, *Polnoe sobranie sochinenii v tridtsati tomakh* (Leningrad: Nauka, 1972–90) 29:i.19, letter of 28 February 1869 to N. N. Strakhov. Subsequent references to this edition will appear in parentheses in the text.

10. Vladimir Nabokov, *Lectures on Russian Literature* (New York: Harcourt Brace Jovanovich, 1981), p. 103.

11. Jacques Catteau, *Dostoyevsky and the Process of Literary Creation* (Cambridge: Cambridge University Press, 1989), p. 178.

12. Dates are given according to the Gregorian Calendar, in use in Western Europe. The Russian Empire used the Julian Calendar, which was twelve days behind the Gregorian one. Thus the January issue of *The Russian Herald* came out on 31 January according to the Russian calendar, but on 12 February according to the calendar in use in Western Europe.

Further Reading

Bakhtin, Mikhail, *Problems of Dostoevsky's Poetics*, ed. and trans. Caryl Emerson (University of Minnesota Press, 1984).

Berdyaev, Nicholas, *Dostoevsky* (Sheed & Ward, 1934). Not a biography in the strict sense, but rather a philosophical study of Dostoyevsky's world view and aesthetics by a major Christian existentialist thinker.

Catteau, Jacques, *Dostoyevsky and the Process of Literary Creation* (Cambridge University Press, 1989).

Coetzee, J. M., *The Master of Petersburg* (Secker and Warburg, 1994).

Dalton, Elizabeth, *Unconscious Structure in* The Idiot: *A Study in Literature and Psychoanalysis* (Princeton University Press, 1979).

Dostoevskaya, Anna Grigoryevna Snitkina, *Dostoevsky: Reminiscences* (Liveright, 1975).

Fanger, Donald, *Dostoevsky and Romantic Realism: A Study of Dostoevsky in Relation to Balzac, Dickens, and Gogol* (Harvard University Press 1965).

Frank, Joseph, *Dostoevsky: The Seeds of Revolt, 1821–1849* (Princeton University Press, 1979).

—, *Dostoevsky: The Years of Ordeal, 1850–1859* (Princeton University Press, 1983).

—, *Dostoevsky: The Stir of Liberation, 1860–1865* (Princeton University Press, 1986).

—, *Dostoevsky: The Miraculous Years, 1865–1871* (Princeton University Press, 1995).

—, *Dostoevsky: The Mantle of the Prophet, 1871–1881* (Princeton University Press, 2002).

Freud, Sigmund, 'Dostoevsky and Parricide', in René Wellek (ed.), *Dostoevsky: A Collection of Critical Essays* (Prentice-Hall, 1962), pp. 98–111.

Gide, André, *Dostoevsky* (Secker & Warburg, 1949).

Holquist, Michael, *Dostoevsky and the Novel* (Princeton University Press, 1977).

Jackson, Robert Louis, *Dostoevsky's Quest for Form: A Study of his Philosophy of Art*, 2nd edn (Physsardt Publishers, 1978).

Jones, Malcolm V., *Dostoyevsky: The Novel of Discord* (Barnes and Noble Books, 1976).

Kjetsaa, Geir, *Fyodor Dostoyevsky: A Writer's Life* (Viking, 1987). A good general and comprehensive overview of Dostoyevsky's life and work for the non-specialist reader.

Knapp, Liza, *The Annihilation of Inertia: Dostoevsky and Metaphysics* (Northwestern University Press, 1966).

— (ed.), *Dostoevsky's* The Idiot: *A Critical Companion* (Northwestern University Press, 1998).

Lary, N. M., *Dostoevsky and Dickens: A Study of Literary Influence* (Routledge and Kegan Paul, 1973).

Martinsen, Deborah A., *Surprised by Shame: Dostoevsky's Liars and Narrative Exposure* (Ohio State University Press, 2003).

Miller, Robin Feuer, *Dostoevsky and* The Idiot: *Author, Narrator, and Reader* (Harvard University Press, 1981).

Mochulsky, K., *Dostoevsky: His Life and Work*, trans. Michael A. Minihan (Princeton University Press, 1967).

Muchnic, Helen, *Dostoevsky's English Reputation, 1881–1936* (Octagon Books, 1969). Dostoyevsky seen through the eyes of English writers and novelists, and a study of his effect on the development of English literature.

Murav, Harriet, *Holy Foolishness: Dostoevsky's Novels and the Poetics of Cultural Critique* (Stanford University Press, 1992).

Peace, Richard Arthur, *Dostoyevsky: An Examination of the Major Novels* (Cambridge University Press, 1971).

Rice, James L., *Dostoevsky and the Healing Art: An Essay in Literary and Medical History* (Ardis, 1985).

Terras, Victor, The Idiot: *An Interpretation* (Twayne Publishers, 1990).

Tsypkin, Leonid, *Summer in Baden-Baden: A Novel*, trans. Roger and Angela Keys (New Directions, 2001).

Wasiolek, Edward, *Dostoevsky: The Major Fiction* (MIT Press, 1964).

A Note on the Translation

Dostoyevsky is often characterized as a writer of Russian nationalist tendencies, his world view seen as an assertion of Russian Orthodox and Russian national ideas. Yet his books are thoroughly steeped in the writing of other nations and cultures, especially Western ones. Like that of Pushkin, of Turgenev and Tolstoy, his Russian-ness is defined against the background of his wide and varied reading of West European literature. The works of Dante, Shakespeare, Cervantes, Goethe and Schiller are the starting-points of his aesthetic – these sources meet and coincide with the work of his Russian antecedents, particularly Gogol, to produce an œuvre that is at once a universal human tragicomedy and a cultural-historical debate between East and West. In translating Dostoyevsky's works into English, one is constantly aware of this tension and interaction between literary cultures. In *Crime and Punishment* it is echoes of the Anglo-Saxon tradition that predominate: Dickens, but above all Hawthorne, with his themes of sin, punishment and atonement, and Poe, with his invention of the detective story and his researches into the human psyche (in 1861 Dostoyevsky published his own critical comparison of the stories of Poe and E. T. A. Hoffmann). Victor Hugo is present, but more as a topical reference than a literary model. In *The Brothers Karamazov* there are echoes of all of these, but with the addition of Shakespeare and the Germanic influence of Schiller.

The Idiot differs from many of Dostoyevsky's other works in showing influences and a psychological ambience that are predominantly French: the writing of Jean-Jacques Rousseau, Georges Sand, Alexandre Dumas, Victor Hugo, Ernest Renan and Gustave Flaubert is vital to a deeper understanding of the novel's characterization and intention. References to works by some of these authors actually figure directly in the plot: Dumas's *The Lady with Camellias* (in the *petit jeu*, or game of 'forfeits' at Nastasya Filippovna's birthday soirée), Flaubert's *Madame Bovary* (in the scene where Myshkin and Rogozhin sit beside the corpse of Nastasya Filippovna), and Hugo's *The Last Day of a Man Condemned to Death* (in Myshkin's description of the execution he watched in France). In addition, the structure of the novel, and its setting in an environment that is very different from that of its predecessor, *Crime and Punishment* – the high society salons and houses of St Petersburg – show affinities with the structure and setting of novels by Georges Sand, whose work Dostoyevsky had read and admired.

It may, therefore, be plain that the challenges posed to the English translator by a novel like *The Idiot* are of a different nature from those present in other works of Dostoyevsky, in particular the novel *Crime and Punishment*, with its, to some extent, 'Anglo-Saxon' literary background and precedents. For one thing, the 'Frenchness' of *The Idiot* is difficult to render in English. In the dialogue, Dostoyevsky often has a habit of inserting Russified French words into the text: *petizhyo* (*petit jeu*), *prues* (*prouesse*), *afishevanye* (from Fr. *afficher*), *frappirovan* (from Fr. *frapper*), *konsekventnyi* (from Fr. *conséquent*) and so on, and this effect is heightened by a peppering of phrases that either mimic French constructions or are directly written in French. For another, the characters speak in formal styles, which are sometimes, as in the case of the Yepanchin family, those of the French-educated upper middle class, but are also – as in the case of Lebedev and Rogozhin – urban idioms that have ceased to exist in contemporary Russian and cannot be easily transposed into another language. Lebedev speaks a Russian that lies somewhere between the lingo of nineteenth-century petty civil servants and the rhetoric of religious sects such as the Old Believers. Rogozhin's speech is derived from, among other things, that of nineteenth-century Russian merchants. To attempt to put it into English as 'Cockney' or Dickensian substandard English is to miss its essence, for it, too, is a formal style of speech, with its own special – and sometimes even 'specialist' – vocabulary, grammar and syntax.

A further challenge to the task of translation is represented by the presence in the novel of a fictional narrator, a device that is also a feature of other novels of Dostoyevsky, in particular *The Brothers Karamazov*. In *The Idiot*, the narrator, when present, writes in a style which the author deliberately intends to be clumsy, and even comical at times – laborious, pedantic and unconsciously self-contradictory, the chronicles of an untalented local newspaper journalist in charge of society columns of his publication. This fictional narrator moves in and out of the novel – it is not always absolutely clear where his contributions begin and end, or exactly where Dostoyevsky takes over. This tongue-in-cheek element of burlesque in the writing is hard to catch in translation, but I have attempted it, and the reader must judge the degree of my success.

Amidst the polyphonic richness of the text, I have mostly opted for maximum comprehensibility, while remaining as close to the original Russian as possible. The reader should not forget, however, that to Russians Dostoyevsky's prose can seem strange and even perverse at times, while none the less possessing an almost magical quality. It is, I believe, the translator's task to preserve the nervous, electric flow of the writing, while still preserving the idiosyncrasies of the author's style – from the repetition of words like 'even' and 'again', which crop up with disconcerting frequency in many of the sentences, to the more extended repetitions which are also Dostoyevsky's hallmarks. Also, the sheer oddity of some of the dialogue cannot really be disguised without betraying the author's aesthetic purpose, which is to create a world that superficially resembles the 'real' world, but is much more akin to the landscape of a dream.

Where Russian names are concerned, I have kept the forms that appear in the original Russian text, in most cases giving name and patronymic where Dostoyevsky does this: Lev Nikolayevich, Ivan Fyodorovich, Nina Alexandrovna, Afanasy Ivanovich, Darya Alexeyevna, etc. I have also preserved the contractions of the patronymic – Pavlych for Pavlovich, Ivanych for Ivanovich, etc. – which are commonly used by Russians in colloquial speech. The diminutive forms of names have also been kept where they are used in the original – Ganka (Ganya), Varya (Varvara), Kolya (Nikolai), etc., as these denote affection, and are important psychological elements in the narrative.

The text used for this translation is that contained in F. M. Dostoevskii, *Polnoe sobranie sochinenii v tridsati tomakh* (Complete collection of works in thirty volumes), Leningrad, Nauka, 1972–90, vol. 8.

David McDuff

The Idiot

PART ONE

At about nine o'clock one morning, at the end of November, during a thaw, a train of the St Petersburg–Warsaw line was approaching St Petersburg at full steam. Such were the damp and the fog that it was a while before daylight broke; at ten yards to the right and the left of the track it was hard to make out anything at all from the windows of the carriage. The passengers included some returning from abroad; but the third-class compartments were the most crowded, with ordinary folk and those on business, who had not travelled far. Everyone, as is usually the case, was tired, with eyes heavy after the night, everyone was cold, every face was pale yellow, the colour of the fog.

In one of the third-class carriages, since dawn, two passengers had found themselves opposite each other close by the window – both young men, both with almost no luggage to speak of, both unostentatiously dressed, both with rather remarkable facial features, and both wishing to enter into conversation with the other. If each had known what was especially remarkable about each other at that moment, they would certainly have marvelled that chance had so strangely put them opposite each other in a third-class carriage of the Warsaw–St Petersburg train. One of them was rather short, about twenty-seven, with almost black curly hair, and small, grey, but fiery eyes. His nose was broad and flat, and he had high cheek-bones; his thin lips were constantly creased in a kind of brazen, mocking and even cruel smile; but his brow was high and well formed and did much to compensate for the ignobly developed lower part of his face. Especially striking in that face was its deathly pallor, which gave the whole of the young man's physiognomy an emaciated look, in spite of his rather sturdy build, at the same time imparting to it something passionate, to the point of suffering, that was out of harmony with his coarse and insolent smile and his harsh, self-satisfied gaze. He was warmly dressed, in a wide, black wool-lined sheepskin overcoat, and had not felt the cold overnight, whereas his neighbour had been compelled to endure on his shivering back all the delights of a damp November Russian night, for which he was obviously not prepared. He wore a rather capacious, thick sleeveless cloak with an enormous hood, of the kind often used in winter, in such far-off places such as Switzerland or northern Italy, by travellers who do not, of course, have to reckon with the distance between points so far removed as Eidkuhnen[1] and St Petersburg. But what had been suitable and thoroughly satisfactory in Italy turned out to be not wholly so in Russia. The wearer of the cloak with the hood was a young man, also about twenty-six or twenty-seven, of slightly above-average height, with very thick, fair hair, sunken cheeks and a light, pointed, almost completely white little beard. His eyes were large, blue and fixed; in their gaze there was something quiet but heavy, and they were filled with that strange expression by which some can detect epilepsy on first glance at a person. The young man's face was, however, pleasant, delicate and lean, though colourless, and now so cold that it was positively blue. In his hands dangled a thin bundle made of old, faded silk, apparently containing all his travelling possessions. He wore thick-soled shoes with buttoned gaiters – all quite un-Russian. The dark-haired neighbour in the wool-lined sheepskin coat observed all this, partly because he had nothing else to do, and, at last, with that insensitive smile in which people so unceremoniously and carelessly express their satisfaction at the misfortunes of a neighbour, inquired:

'Chilly?'

And hunched his shoulders.

'Yes, indeed,' the neighbour replied with extreme readiness, 'and, mind you, there's still a thaw. What would it be like in a frost? I really didn't think it could be as cold as this in our country. I'm not used to it.'

'Come from abroad, have you?'

'Yes, from Switzerland.'

'Whew! You don't say! . . .'

The dark-haired man whistled and began to laugh.

A conversation ensued. The willingness of the fair-haired young man in the Swiss cloak to answer every question from his swarthy neighbour was remarkable, and he appeared to have no inkling of the utterly casual, inappropriate and idle nature of some of the questions. In replying he declared, among other things, that he had not been in Russia for a long time, four years or more, and that he had been sent abroad because of an illness, some strange nervous illness, akin to epilepsy or St Vitus's dance, with tremors and convulsions. As he listened to him, the swarthy man grinned several times; he laughed especially when to the question: 'Well, and did they cure you?' the fair-haired man replied: 'No, they didn't.'

'Heh! You probably paid them a lot of money for nothing, and here we still go on believing in them,' the swarthy man observed caustically.

'Very true!' said a shabbily dressed gentleman who was sitting near by, some sort of minor official hardened in the work of the civil service, aged about forty, strongly built, with a red nose and a face covered in blackheads, as he joined the conversation: 'Very true, sir, all they do is use up all Russia's strength for their own benefit and give nothing in return!'

'Oh, but in my own case you're very mistaken,' the Swiss patient rejoined in a quiet and conciliatory voice. 'Of course, I can't argue, for there are many things I don't know, but my doctor gave me the money for my fare here out of the last he had, having supported me at his own expense for almost two years.'

'Why? Was there no one to pay for you?' asked the swarthy man.

'Well, you see, Mr Pavlishchev, who was supporting me, died two years ago; then I wrote to Mrs Yepanchin, the general's wife, a distant relation of mine in St Petersburg, but received no reply. And so that's why I've returned.'

'Returned where, exactly?'

'You mean, where will I stay? . . . Well, I don't really know yet . . . that is . . .'

'You haven't decided yet?'

And both listeners again burst into laughter.

'And I suppose all your worldly possessions are in that bundle?' asked the swarthy man.

'I'm willing to bet on that,' the red-nosed official said with a look of extreme satisfaction, 'and that he has nothing in the luggage van, though poverty's no sin, we mustn't omit to point that out.'

This also turned out to be true: the fair-haired young man admitted it at once, and with unexpected haste.

'Your bundle does have a certain significance, however,' the official continued, once they had finished laughing (remarkably enough, the owner of the bundle himself eventually began to laugh as he surveyed them, which increased their merriment), 'and though I'm willing to bet there are no gold coins in it, no foreign bags of Napoléons d'or and Friedrichs d'or, let alone Dutch *arapchiki*,[2] all of which may be deduced if only by the gaiters that are wrapped round your foreign shoes, still . . . if one were to add to your bundle a relative such as the general's lady, Mrs Yepanchin, then it would take on a rather different meaning, in the event, of course, that Mrs Yepanchin really is a relation of yours, and you're not mistaken, because of absent-mindedness . . . something that's very, very common in people, well, because of . . . an over-abundance of imagination.'

'Oh, you've guessed right again,' the fair-haired young man rejoined, 'though I really am almost mistaken, because she's scarcely a relation at all; and indeed I really wasn't at all surprised when I received no reply from her. That was what I expected.'

'You wasted your money on the postage stamp. Hmm . . . well, at least you're honest and sincere about it, and that's to be commended! Hmm . . . As for General Yepanchin, sir, we know him for the simple reason that he's well known;[3] and also the late Mr Pavlishchev, who supported you in Switzerland, he was also well known, sir, if he was Nikolai Andreyevich Pavlishchev, because there were two cousins. The other one still lives in the

Crimea, but Nikolai Andreyevich, the deceased, was a much respected man and had connections, owned four thousand souls in his day, sir . . .'

'That's right, his name was Nikolai Andreyevich Pavlishchev.' And, having offered his reply, the young man gave this Mr Know-all a fixed and searching look.

These Mr Know-alls are sometimes encountered, even rather frequently, at a certain level of society. They know everything; all the restless curiosity of their mind and faculties is irrepressibly aimed in one direction, because of the absence of any more important opinions or interests in life, as a contemporary thinker would say. However, this 'knowing everything' refers to a rather narrow area: where such-and-such a person works, who his friends are, how much he is worth, where he was governor, who he is married to, how much his wife's dowry was, who his cousin is, and his second cousin, etcetera, etcetera, and all that kind of thing. For the most part these know-alls have worn elbows and earn a salary of seventeen roubles a month. The people of whom they know all the details could never, of course, imagine the interests that guide them, and yet many of these know-alls derive positive consolation from this knowledge, which is equivalent to a whole science, finding self-respect and even the loftiest spiritual fulfilment in it. And it is a seductive science, too. I have seen scholars, men of letters, poets, political activists, seeking and achieving their highest ambitions and goals in this science, even making it the sole foundation of their careers.

Throughout this entire conversation the swarthy young man yawned, looked aimlessly out of the window and awaited the end of the journey with impatience. He seemed distracted, really very distracted, well nigh agitated, and his behaviour was even becoming rather strange: from time to time he would listen and then not listen, look and then look the other way, laugh and then seem unaware of what he was laughing at.

'But permit me to ask with whom I have the honour . . .' the gentleman with the blackheads said, suddenly addressing the fair-haired young man with the bundle.

'Prince Lev Nikolayevich Myshkin,' the other replied with complete and instant readiness.

'Prince Myshkin? Lev Nikolayevich? I don't know that one, sir. In fact I've never heard of him, sir,' the official answered, reflectively. 'I don't mean the name, of course, the name is a historic one, you'll find it in Karamzin's *History*, it must be there, no, I mean the person, sir, and somehow one doesn't encounter any Prince Myshkins anywhere, not even stories about them at second hand, sir.'

'Oh, of course not!' the prince replied at once. 'There aren't any Prince Myshkins now at all, except for me; I think I'm the last. And as for our forefathers, some of them were only smallholders. My father was a sub-lieutenant in the army, by the way, a military cadet. And so I really don't know how Mrs Yepanchin managed to become a Princess Myshkin, the last of her kind, too . . .'

'Heh-heh-heh! The last of her kind! Heh-heh! That was well put,' the official giggled.

The swarthy man also smiled. The fair-haired man was slightly surprised that he had succeeded in making a witty remark, even though it was really rather a bad one.

'But imagine, I said it quite without thinking,' he explained, at last, in surprise.

'Of course, of course, sir,' the official cheerfully confirmed.

'And so, Prince, did you study the sciences with that professor?' the swarthy man asked suddenly.

'Yes . . . I did . . .'

'You know, I've never studied anything.'

'Oh, I just dabbled in a couple of things,' the prince added, almost in apology. 'They couldn't teach me systematically because of my illness.'

'Do you know the Rogozhins?' the swarthy man asked quickly.

'No, I don't, not at all. But then, I know very few people in Russia. Are you a Rogozhin?'

'Yes, I'm a Rogozhin, Parfyon.'

'Parfyon? Not the Rogozhins who . . .' the official began, with increasing solemnity.

'Yes, them,' the swarthy man interrupted rudely and impatiently, without ever once having actually addressed the official with the blackheads, his remarks addressed only to the prince.

'But . . . How can this be?' the official was astonished to the point of stupor, his eyes very nearly starting out of his head; the whole of his face at once began to collapse into a kind of servile reverence, something even resembling fear – 'Your father is the same Semyon Parfyonovich Rogozhin, the hereditary distinguished burgher,[4] who passed away a month ago, leaving capital of two and a half million?'

'And how do you know that he left net capital of two and a half million?' the swarthy man interrupted, this time not even deigning to glance at the official. 'Will you look at him (he winked at the prince, to draw his attention), what do they think they'll gain by crawling like vermin? But it's true that my father died, and I came home from Pskov a month later, almost without a pair of boots to my name. Neither my scoundrel of a brother nor my mother sent money or word – nothing! As if I were a dog! In Pskov I was in bed for a whole month with a fever! . . .'

'And now you'll receive a nice little million and a bit, at the very least. Good heavens!' the official threw up his hands.

'Well, what does it have to do with him, I ask you, if you please!' Rogozhin said, nodding towards him again in irritation and hostility. 'Why, I wouldn't give you a copeck, not even if you walked on your hands in front of me.'

'And I will, I will.'

'Would you believe it! And I won't give you anything, not a thing, not even if you dance for a week!'

'Then don't give me anything! That's what I deserve; don't give me anything! But I'll dance. I'll leave my wife and my little children, and I'll dance in front of you. And crawl, crawl!'

'Confound you!' the swarthy man spat. 'Five weeks ago I was like you,' he said, turning to the prince, 'ran away from my father to my aunt in Pskov with nothing but a bundle; and I caught a fever there and had to lie in bed, and he died while I was away. He had a stroke. May his soul find peace in eternity, but before that he'd nearly beaten me to death! Would you believe it, Prince, I swear to God! If I hadn't run away when I did, he'd have killed me on the spot.'

'Did you do something to make him angry?' the prince responded, studying the millionaire in the sheepskin with particular curiosity. But although the million roubles and the receipt of an inheritance might have been remarkable in themselves, it was something else that had struck the prince and aroused his interest; and indeed, Rogozhin himself was for some reason particularly eager to converse with the prince, though his need for such conversation was, it seemed, more automatic than intentional; stemming more from distraction than from genuine feeling; from alarm, from agitation, just so as to have someone to look at, and something to exercise his tongue about. He still seemed to be in an ague, or at least a fever. As for the official, he hovered very close to Rogozhin, not daring to breathe, catching and weighing each word as though in search of a diamond.

'He just got angry, and perhaps he had good reason for that,' Rogozhin answered, 'but it was my brother who really annoyed me. One can't blame Mother, she's getting on in years, reads the Lives of the Saints, sits with the old women, and whatever brother Senka decides is right as far as she's concerned. But why didn't he tell me in time? We know why, sir! It's true that I was unconscious at the time. Also, they say that a telegram was sent. But the telegram was delivered to my aunt. And she's been a widow for thirty years, and sits around with the holy fools from morning to night. Like a nun, like a nun, but worse. The telegram frightened her and, without opening it, she took it to the police station and that's where it remains to this day. In the event, Konyov, Vasily Vasilyich, lent a helping hand, wrote to me with all the details. At night my brother cut the gold tassels off the brocade covering of my father's coffin: "They cost a vast amount of money," he said. I mean, he could go to Siberia if I wanted him sent there, because that's sacrilege. Hey you, scarecrow buffoon!' he turned to the official. 'What does the law say: is it sacrilege?'

'Oh yes, it's sacrilege! Sacrilege!' the official at once agreed.

'One could be sent to Siberia for it?'

'Yes indeed, to Siberia, Siberia! Straight to Siberia!'

'They still think I'm ill,' Rogozhin continued to the prince, 'but without a word to anyone I boarded the train in secret, and

off I went: "Open the gates, dear brother Semyon Semyonych!"
He said bad things about me to our dear dead father, I know
that. Well, I really did annoy father over Nastasya Filippovna,
that's true. It was all my fault. Sin led me astray.'

'Because of Nastasya Filippovna?' the official babbled obsequiously, as if he were putting two and two together.

'Oh come, you don't know her too!' Rogozhin shouted at
him in exasperation.

'I do!' the official replied triumphantly.

'Get away with you! There are lots of Nastasya Filippovnas!
And you're an insolent creature, too, I'll tell you that! You
know, I had a feeling some creature like this would start latching
on to me!' he continued to the prince.

'But perhaps I do know her, sir!' the official was agitated.
'Lebedev knows! Your Grace, you saw fit to reproach me, but
what if I can prove it? The same Nastasya Filippovna because of
whom your father chastised you with a hazel rod, and Nastasya
Filippovna is a Barashkov, even a high-born lady, in a sense,
and also a princess of a kind, and consorts exclusively with a
certain Totsky, Afanasy Ivanovich, a landowner and important
capitalist, a board member of companies and societies, and great
friends on that account with General Yepanchin . . .'

'Aha, so that's it!' Rogozhin said at last in genuine surprise.
'Confound it and damn it, he really does know.'

'He knows everything! Lebedev knows everything! Your
Grace, I travelled around with Alexashka Likhachov for two
months, and also after the death of his father, and so I know it
all, all the nooks and crannies, and it got to the point where he
couldn't take a step without Lebedev. Now he's in prison, in
the debtors' wing, but back then I had occasion to make the
acquaintance of Armance and Coralie, and Princess Patskaya
and Nastasya Filippovna, too, and I had occasion to learn a
great many things.'

'Nastasya Filippovna? Did she and Likhachov . . .' Rogozhin
looked at him with animosity, and his lips even grew pale and
began to tremble.

'N-nothing! N-n-nothing! Nothing, I swear it!' the official
recollected himself and hurried on. 'That's to say, no money

could ever buy Likhachov what he wanted! Not like Armance. No, Totsky was the only one. In the evenings she would sit in her own box at the Bolshoi or the French Theatre.[5] The officers talked a lot among themselves, but they couldn't prove anything: "There," they'd say, "that's the famous Nastasya Filippovna," but that was all, and as for the rest of it – nothing! Because there wasn't anything.'

'That's all true,' Rogozhin confirmed gloomily, knitting his brow, 'Zalyozhev told me the same thing at the time. That day, Prince, I was running across Nevsky Prospect wearing my father's three-year-old fur jacket, and there she was coming out of a shop and getting into a carriage. It burned me right through. I met Zalyozhev, he's not like me, he goes about like a barber's assistant, even has a monocle in one eye, while we had a high old time at my father's with blacked boots and cabbage soup without meat. She's not for the likes of you, she's a princess, he says, she's called Nastasya Filippovna, Barashkova's her last name, she lives with Totsky, but Totsky doesn't know how to get rid of her, for he's reached a regular age, he says, fifty-five, and wants to marry the most beautiful woman in St Petersburg. Then he also suggested to me that I could see Nastasya Filippovna at the Bolshoi Theatre that very day, at the ballet, she'd be sitting in her box, in the *baignoire*. Just try getting out of my father's house to go to the ballet – he'd have no mercy – he'd kill me! However, I did manage to sneak out for an hour and saw Nastasya Filippovna again; I didn't get any sleep that night. In the morning my deceased father gave me two five per cent credit notes, each worth five thousand, go and sell them, he said, and take seven thousand five hundred to Andreyev at his office, pay it to him, and bring the rest of the change of the ten thousand back to me, and don't drop in anywhere on your way; I'll be waiting for you. I sold the notes, took the money, but didn't go to Andreyev's office, no, instead, without giving it a further thought, I went to the English shop and spent it all, chose a pair of earrings with a nice little diamond in each of them, about the size of a nut they were, I still owed four hundred, told them my name, they gave me credit. I took the earrings to Zalyozhev: told him this and that and said, brother, let's go and see Nastasya

Filippovna. We set off. What was under my feet, what in front of me, what to the sides – none of that do I know or remember. We walked straight into her entrance hall, and she came out to us herself. You see, I didn't let on who I was; and Zalyozhev just said: "From Parfyon Rogozhin, as a memento of his meeting with you yesterday; please be so good as to accept it." She opened it, glanced inside, and smiled thinly: "Thank your friend Mr Rogozhin for his kind attention," she said – took her leave and went away. Well, why didn't I just die right there and then? I mean, I'd only gone there because I'd thought: "Say what you like, I won't return alive!" The most offensive thing was that rogue Zalyozhev taking all the limelight. I'm quite short, and I was dressed like a lackey, and I stood there, saying nothing, staring at her, because I was embarrassed, while he was dressed in the latest fashion, his hair all pomaded and waved, ruddy-cheeked, with a check cravat – ingratiating himself, bowing and scraping, and she probably thought he was me! "Well," I said as we went out, "don't go getting any ideas in your head, you understand?" He laughed: "And how are you going to smooth things over with Semyon Parfyonych?" To tell the truth, I was just about ready to throw myself in the water right there on the spot, without going home, but I thought: "Well it's all the same, anyway," and went off home like a man who's been damned.'

'Ooh! Aah!' the official grimaced, and was even seized by a shudder. 'You know, the deceased used to hound men to the next life for ten roubles, let alone ten thousand,' he nodded to the prince. The prince was studying Rogozhin with curiosity; the latter seemed even paler at that moment.

'Used to hound them?' Rogozhin said, interrupting him. 'What do you know about it? He immediately found out everything,' he continued, turning to the prince, 'and of course Zalyozhev went off to tell everyone he met. My father grabbed me, locked me in upstairs, and thrashed me for an hour. "That was just to prepare you," he said. "I'll be back to say goodnight to you as well." And what do you think? The grey-headed fellow went off to see Nastasya Filippovna, bowed to the ground, implored her and wept; at last she brought out the box to him, and snapped: "Here you are," she said, "here are your earrings, old greybeard, and they're ten times more precious to me now that I know the danger Parfyon faced in going to get them. Give him my greetings," she said, "and thank Parfyon Semyonych." Well, meanwhile I got twenty roubles from Seryozhka Protushin, with Mother's blessing, and set off by train for Pskov, arriving there in a fever; the old women began to recite the saints' days over me, and I sat there drunk, and then went crawling round the taverns on the last of my money, and lay all night sprawled in the street, and by morning my fever had got worse, and meanwhile during the night the dogs had worried at me. I only just managed to come to.'

'Well, sir, well, sir, now Nastasya Filippovna will sing a different tune for us!' the official giggled, rubbing his hands. 'What are those earrings now, sir? Now we shall reward her with such earrings that . . .'

'And if you say one more word about Nastasya Filippovna, as God is my witness I'll thrash you, and I don't care if you did travel about with Likhachov!' shouted Rogozhin, seizing him violently by the arm.

'If you thrash me it means you don't reject me! Thrash me! If you thrash me, it means you'll have placed your seal on me . . . But look, we've arrived!'

Indeed, they were entering the station. Although Rogozhin had said he had left in secret, several people were waiting for him. They were shouting and waving their caps at him.

'Look, Zalyozhev's here, too!' Rogozhin muttered, gazing at them with a smile that was triumphant and even somehow malicious, and suddenly turned to the prince. 'Prince, I don't know why, but I've developed a liking for you. Maybe it's because I met you at a moment like this, and after all I met him, too (he pointed to Lebedev), and I didn't develop a liking for him. Come to my house, Prince. We'll take off those silly gaiters, and I'll dress you in a first-class marten fur coat; I'll have a first-class frock coat made for you, too, a white waistcoat, or whatever you want, I'll stuff your pockets full of money, and . . . we'll go and see Nastasya Filippovna! Will you come, or not?'

'Pay heed to what he says, Lev Nikolayevich!' Lebedev chimed in with imposing solemnity. 'Oh, don't let the chance slip! Oh, don't let it slip! . . .'

Prince Myshkin half rose to his feet, politely extended his hand to Rogozhin and said to him graciously:

'I'll come with the greatest of pleasure, and I thank you very much for liking me. I may even come today, if I can manage to. Because, I'll tell you candidly, I also like you very much, especially after what you told me about the diamond earrings. I liked you even before the earrings, though you have a gloomy face. Thank you also for the promised clothes and for the fur coat, because I will indeed soon need clothes and a fur coat. As for money, at the present moment I've hardly a copeck.'

'There'll be money, there'll be money by this evening, come to my house!'

'There'll be money, there'll be money,' the official chimed in. 'From this evening until break of day there'll be money!'

'And how about the female sex, Prince, are you a great admirer? Let me know in advance.'

'I, n-n-no! You see, I . . . Perhaps you don't know, but you see, because of my congenital illness I don't have any experience of women at all.'

'Well, if that's how it is,' Rogozhin exclaimed, 'you really are a holy fool, and such men as you God loveth!'

'And such as these the Lord God loveth,' the official chimed in.

'As for you, quill-driver, you can follow me,' Rogozhin said to Lebedev as they all got out of the carriage.

Lebedev had ended up by achieving his goal. Soon the noisy throng moved away in the direction of Voznesensky Prospect.[6] The prince's way led towards Liteinaya. It was damp and wet; the prince asked passers-by for directions – there were still more than two miles to the end of the journey that awaited him, and he decided to take a cab.

2

General Yepanchin lived in his own house, just off Liteinaya, towards the Church of the Transfiguration.[1] Besides this (magnificent) dwelling, five-sixths of which was rented out, General Yepanchin owned another enormous house on Sadovaya, which also brought in an exceedingly large income. In addition to these two houses, he had an extremely profitable estate of considerable size, just outside St Petersburg; there was also a factory of some kind in the St Petersburg province. In the old days General Yepanchin, as everyone knew, had shared in the farming of revenues.[2] Now he held shares in several solid joint-stock companies, where his voice carried very considerable weight. He passed for a man with big money, big projects and big connections. In some places he was able to make himself quite indispensable, and these places included his own government office. And yet it was also well known that Ivan Fyodorovich Yepanchin was a man who lacked education and was descended from the offspring of a soldier; without doubt, this latter circumstance could only redound to his honour, but the general, though an intelligent man, was also not without some small, highly pardonable weaknesses, and did not take certain hints kindly. But an intelligent and shrewd man he unquestionably was. It was, for example, a rule of his never to push himself forward in situations where it was better to retire into the background, and many valued him precisely for his simplicity, precisely for the fact that he always knew his place. And yet, if those judges had only known the things that sometimes took place in the soul of Ivan Fyodorovich, who knew his place so well! Though he did indeed have both practical sense and experience of worldly matters, and certain very remarkable abilities, he liked to present himself more as the executor of other people's ideas rather than as a man of wisdom, a man 'devoted without flattery',[3] and – where will our age not lead? – even Russian and stout of heart. In the latter connection he had even been involved in a number of amusing incidents; but the general never lost heart, even in the most amusing incidents; he was, moreover, lucky, even at cards, and he played for exceedingly high stakes, and was not only intentionally reluctant to conceal this small apparent weakness for cards, a weakness that had been of such material advantage to him on many occasions, but actually displayed it for all to see. The society he kept was mixed, though it was, of course, composed of the 'top brass'. But everything lay ahead, there was plenty of time, there was really plenty of time, and everything could not fail to come to him eventually, in its turn. And indeed, where years were concerned, General Yepanchin was, as they say, in the very prime of life, fifty-six and not a day more, which is of course a flourishing age, an age when *real* life truly begins. His good health, his facial complexion, his strong though blackened teeth, his stocky, thick-set build, the preoccupied expression of his physiognomy in the morning at his work in the office, the cheerful one in the evening at cards or at the count's – it all made possible his present and future success, and strewed his excellency's path with roses.

The general possessed a flourishing family. To be sure, not all was roses there, but there were on the other hand many things on which, both seriously and stout-heartedly, his excellency had long begun to concentrate his principal hopes and aims. And indeed, what aim in life is more important and sacred than a father's? To what should one adhere, if not to one's family? The general's family consisted of his spouse and three grown-up daughters. Very long ago, while still a lieutenant, the general had married a girl of almost his own age, possessing neither beauty nor education, and for whom he had received a dowry of only fifty serfs – which had, it was true, served as the basis of his subsequent fortune. But the general never grumbled later about his early marriage, never spoke of it slightingly as an infatuation of extravagant youth, and his respect for his spouse and occasional fear of her were so great that it could even be said that he loved her. The general's wife was from the line of the Princes Myshkin, a family which, though it did not shine, was very ancient, and her descent was a great source of pride to her. A certain influential person of those days, one of those patrons whose patronage does not really cost them anything, agreed to take an interest in the marriage of the young princess.

He opened the door for the young officer and pushed him through; though the officer did not even need a push, for a mere look would have been enough – it would not have been wasted! With a few exceptions, the married couple spent the entire period of their long jubilee in harmony. At a very young age, as a born princess and the last in her family, and also, perhaps, because of her personal qualities, the general's wife had been able to find herself several very highly placed patronesses. Later, because of her spouse's wealth and official standing, she even began to feel somewhat at ease in this higher circle.

During these recent years all three of the general's daughters – Alexandra, Adelaida and Aglaya – had grown up and matured. To be sure, all three were only Yepanchins, but descended from princes on their mother's side, with sizeable dowries, with a father who might later lay claim to a very high social position, and, what was also rather important, all three were remarkably pretty, including the eldest, Alexandra, who was already over twenty-five. The middle daughter was twenty-three, while the youngest, Aglaya, had just had her twentieth birthday. This youngest was even quite a beauty, and beginning to attract much attention in society. But this, too, was not all: all three were distinguished by their education, intelligence and talents. It was well known that they were wonderfully fond of one another and that they each supported one another. There was even talk of some kind of sacrifices that were said to have been made by the two elder daughters for the sake of the family idol – the youngest. They were not only reluctant to push themselves forward in company, but were even too modest. No one could reproach them for being haughty or overbearing, and yet everyone knew that they were proud, and aware of their own worth. The eldest was a musician, and the middle one was an excellent painter; but almost no one knew anything about this for many years, and it had only been discovered in the very recent past, and even then by accident.[4] In a word, exceeding praise was lavished on them. But there were also those who did not wish them well. People spoke in horror of how many books they had read. They were in no hurry to get married; though they cherished a certain circle of society, they did not make too much of it. This was all the more remarkable since everyone knew the turn of mind, the character, aims and wishes of their father.

It was already nearly eleven o'clock when the prince rang the bell of the general's apartment. The general lived on the first floor and occupied quarters that were as modest as possible, though in keeping with his social station. A liveried servant opened the door to the prince, who was obliged to explain himself for a long time to this man: right from the outset the servant looked suspiciously at him and his bundle. At last, after repeated and precise declarations that he really was Prince Myshkin and needed to see the general on urgent business, the perplexed servant took him into a small vestibule, right outside the reception room, next to the study, handing him into the charge of another servant who was usually on duty in this vestibule in the mornings and who announced visitors to the general. This second servant, over forty, in a frock coat, with a preoccupied mien, was his excellency's special study-attendant and announcer, and consequently aware of his own worth.

'Wait in the reception room and leave your bundle here,' he said, seating himself unhurriedly in his armchair and looking with stern astonishment at the prince, who had instantly disposed himself on a chair beside him, his little bundle in his arms.

'If you please,' said the prince, 'I'd rather wait here with you, for what would I do alone in there?'

'You can't wait in the vestibule as you're a visitor, a guest, in other words. You wish to see the general himself?'

It was plain that the lackey could not reconcile himself to the idea of admitting a visitor such as this, and he decided to put the question to him yet again.

'Yes, I have business . . .' the prince began.

'I do not inquire as to the precise nature of your business – my task is merely to announce you. And I have said that I will not do so until the secretary arrives.'

This servant's mistrust seemed to be increasing more and more; the prince was too unlike the usual run of daily visitors, and although at a certain hour the general quite often, very nearly every day, had to receive, especially on 'business', guests who were sometimes even very multifarious, in spite of custom and rather broad instructions the valet was doubtful in the extreme: for an announcement to be made the secretary's permission was indispensable.

'Have you really . . . come from abroad?' he asked, almost in spite of himself, at last – and grew embarrassed; perhaps he had wanted to ask: 'Are you really Prince Myshkin?'

'Yes, straight off the train. I think you wanted to ask if I'm really Prince Myshkin, but didn't, out of politeness.'

'Hmm . . .' the astonished lackey grunted.

'I assure you that I haven't lied to you, and you will not be held responsible for me. And as for my looking like this and carrying a bundle, there's no need for it to surprise you: my circumstances aren't much to boast about at present.'

'Hmm. That is not what disturbs me. You see, I'm obliged to announce you, and the secretary will come out to you, unless you . . . And that's the sticking point – unless . . . You haven't come to ask the general for money, if I may make so bold as to ask?'

'Oh, no, you may be quite assured of that. I'm here on a different matter.'

'You must forgive me, I merely asked because of your appearance. Wait for the secretary; the general is busy with the colonel at present, and then the secretary will be here . . . the company secretary.'

'Well, if I shall have to wait a long time, I have a request: is there anywhere here where I could smoke? I've a pipe and tobacco with me.'

'Sm-o-ke?' the valet hurled him a glance of bewildered contempt, as though he still could not believe his ears. 'Smoke? No, here you may not smoke, and what is more you ought to be ashamed to even think of such a thing. Heh . . . extraordinary, sir!'

'Oh, I wasn't asking to smoke in this room; I mean, I know what's right and proper; but I could go outside somewhere, if you'd show me where, because I have the habit, and I haven't smoked my pipe for about three hours. However, as you please, and there's a proverb, you know: "When in Rome . . ."'

'Well, how am I to announce someone like you?' the valet

muttered almost in spite of himself. 'For one thing, you oughtn't to be here, you should be sitting in the reception room, because you're in the way of being a visitor, or a guest, in other words, and I shall have to answer for it . . . You're not planning to stay with us, are you?' he added, once again taking a sidelong look at the prince's bundle, which was obviously giving him no rest.

'No, I don't think so. Even were I to be invited, I shouldn't stay. I've simply come to introduce myself, no more than that.'

'What? To introduce yourself?' the valet asked, surprised and doubly suspicious. 'Then why did you say at first that you were here on business?'

'Oh, hardly on business at all! That's to say, if you will, I do have a certain item of business, but it's simply about asking for advice, and the main reason I'm here is to present myself, because I'm Prince Myshkin, and Mrs Yepanchin is the last of the Princess Myshkins, and, apart from her and myself there aren't any Myshkins left.'

'So you're a relation, too?' the lackey, by now almost thoroughly alarmed, asked with a start.

'Hardly that, either. As a matter of fact, if one stretches a point, we are, of course, relations, but so distant that it doesn't really count. I once wrote a letter to Mrs Yepanchin from abroad, but she didn't reply to me. I nonetheless considered it necessary to initiate contact on my return. I'm explaining all this to you now so that you shouldn't be in any doubt, for I see that you're still uneasy: if you'll just announce that Prince Myshkin is here, the very announcement itself will explain the reason for my visit. If they receive me – well and good, if they don't – also, perhaps, well and good. But I think they will receive me: the general's wife will of course want to see the eldest and only representative of her family, for I've heard it said of her, and reliably so, that she attaches great value to her descent.'

The prince's conversation was, to all appearances, very simple; but the simpler it was, the more absurd did it become in the present situation, and the experienced valet could not but feel that what was completely appropriate between one man and another was completely inappropriate between a guest and a manservant. And as servants are generally much more intelligent

than their masters suppose them to be, it occurred to the valet
that there were two possibilities here: either the prince was some
kind of vagrant who had come to ask for money, or he was
simply an imbecile with no ambition, because a clever prince
with ambition would not sit in a vestibule telling a lackey about
his business – and so, in either case, would he not be held
responsible for him?

'All the same, you really would do better to wait in the
reception room,' he observed as pressingly as he could.

'But if I'd sat in there I wouldn't have explained it all to you,'
the prince laughed cheerfully, 'and so you'd still be worried by
the sight of my cloak and bundle. Anyway, perhaps there's no
need for you to wait for the secretary now – you can just go and
announce me yourself.'

'I can't announce a visitor such as yourself without the secretary's permission, especially as the general himself gave orders
a short time ago that they were not to be disturbed for any
reason while the colonel is there, and only Gavrila Ardalionych
may go in unannounced.'

'An official?'

'Gavrila Ardalionych? No. He works for the company in a
private capacity. At least put your bundle over there.'

'I'd already thought of doing so, if you'll let me. And I tell
you what, may I take off my cloak as well?'

'Of course, why, you can hardly go in there wearing a cloak.'

The prince got up, hurriedly removed his cloak and proved
to be wearing a fairly respectable and smartly cut, though now
somewhat threadbare, jacket. His waistcoat bore a steel chain.
The chain turned out to have a silver Geneva watch on the end
of it.

Though the prince was an imbecile – the lackey had already
decided this – to a general's valet it none the less seemed
improper to prolong any further a conversation between himself
and a visitor, even though for some reason he liked the prince,
in his own way, of course. From another point of view, however,
the prince aroused in him a pronounced and gross indignation.

'And when does Mrs Yepanchin receive guests, sir?' the prince
asked, sitting down again in his previous place.

'That's not my business, sir. She receives at different times, depending on who it is. The milliner is admitted at eleven. Gavrila Ardalionych is admitted earlier than anyone else, even for breakfast.'

'It's warmer here in your rooms than it would be in winter abroad,' the prince observed, 'and although over there it's warmer out in the streets than it is in our country, a Russian finds it hard to live in their houses in winter because he isn't used to it.'

'They don't heat them?'

'No, and their houses are arranged differently, the stoves and windows, that is.'

'Hmm! And were you away for a long time, sir?'

'Four years. As a matter of fact, I stayed in one place, in the country.'

'Our way of life grew foreign to you?'

'That's also true. You know, I marvel at myself for not having forgotten how to speak Russian. Here I am talking to you now, and all the time I'm thinking: "I say, I speak the language quite well after all." Perhaps that's why I'm talking such a lot. It's true that since yesterday I've wanted to speak Russian all the time.'

'Hmm! Heh! Did you live in St Petersburg before, then?' (Try as he might, the lackey found it impossible not to sustain such a courteous and polite conversation.)

'In St Petersburg? Hardly at all, I only stayed here when passing through. Even before, I didn't know anything of the place, and now I hear so much is new that they say those who did know are learning it all over again. There's a lot of talk here just now about the courts.'

'Hmm! . . . The courts. Courts, yes, there certainly are courts. Well, and how is it over there, are their courts fairer than ours?'

'I don't know. I've heard a lot that is good about ours. And then again, we don't have capital punishment.'[5]

'Do they have it over there?'

'Yes. I saw it in France, at Lyons. Schneider took me with him to see it.'

'Do they hang them?'

'No, in France they cut off their heads.'

'Does the fellow yell, then?'

'Oh no! It takes only a single instant. The man is put in place, and a sort of broad knife falls on him, it's part of a machine called a guillotine, it's a heavy thing, powerful . . . The head flies off so quickly you don't have time to blink. The preparations are hideous. It's when they read out the sentence, set up the machine, bind the man, lead him out to the scaffold, that's the dreadful part! People gather round, even women, though they don't like women to watch.'

'Not the sort of thing for them.'

'No, of course not! Of course not! Such torment! . . . The criminal was an intelligent man, fearless, strong, getting on in years, Legros by name. Well, I'll tell you, believe it or not, when he mounted the scaffold he wept, with a face as white as a sheet. Is it possible? Isn't it horrible? Whoever weeps from fear? I'd never imagined that a man could weep from fear – not a child, after all, but a man who'd never wept in his life, a man of forty-five. What must be happening in his soul at that moment, for a man to be brought to such convulsions? An outrage on the soul, nothing less! It is said: "Thou shalt not kill" – so does that mean because he has killed he, too, must be killed? No, it's wrong. I saw it a month ago, and I can still see it even now. I've dreamed about it repeatedly.'

The prince grew more animated as he spoke, and a faint flush emerged on his pale face, though his voice was quiet as before. The valet followed his words with sympathetic interest, reluctant, it appeared, to tear himself away; he was also, perhaps, a man with imagination who made some attempt to think for himself.

'It's a good thing at least that the suffering is short,' he observed, 'when the head flies off.'

'Do you know what?' the prince broke in heatedly. 'You've made that observation, it's exactly the same observation that everyone makes, and that's why this machine, the guillotine, was invented. But then a thought came into my head: what if it's even worse? You may find this ridiculous, it may seem outrageous to you, but if you've any imagination, an idea like this will leap into your head. Just think: if there was torture, for example, it would involve suffering and injuries, physical torment and all that would probably distract you from the mental suffering, so that your injuries would be all that you'd suffer, right up to the time you died. For after all, perhaps the worst, most violent pain lies not in injuries, but in the fact that you know for certain that within the space of an hour, then ten minutes, then half a minute, then now, right at this moment – your soul will fly out of your body, and you'll no longer be a human being, and that this is certain; the main thing is that it's *certain*. When you put your head right under the guillotine and hear it sliding above your head, it's that quarter of a second that's most terrible of all. This isn't my imagination, you know, many people have said the same thing.[6] I believe this so strongly that I'll tell you my opinion straight out. To kill for murder is an immeasurably greater evil than the crime itself. Murder by judicial sentence is immeasurably more horrible than murder committed by a bandit. The person who's murdered by a bandit has his throat cut at night, in a forest, or somewhere like that, and he certainly hopes to be rescued, right up to the very last moment. There have been examples of people whose throats have been cut still hoping, or running away, or begging for their lives. But here, all this final hope, with which it's ten times easier to die, is taken away *for certain*; the terrible torment remains, and there's nothing in the world more powerful than that torment. Take a soldier and put him right in front of a cannon in a battle and fire it at him, and he'll go on hoping, but read out a *certain* death sentence to that same soldier, and he'll go mad, or start to weep. Who can say that human nature is able to endure such a thing without going mad? Why such mockery – ugly, superfluous, futile? Perhaps the man exists to whom his sentence has been read out, has been allowed to suffer, and then been told: "Off you go, you've been pardoned." A man like that could tell us, perhaps. Such suffering and terror were what Christ spoke of.[7] No, a human being should not be treated like that!'

Although he could not have put all this into words as the prince had done, the valet understood, if not all of it, then the main point, and this was even visible in his features, which showed that he was moved.

'If you really need to smoke,' he said quietly, 'you may, but you'll have to be quick about it. Because they may suddenly ask for you, and you wouldn't be there. Look, through there, under the stairs there's a door. Go through the door, and on your right there's a little room; you can smoke in there, but be sure to open the ventilation window, because it's not allowed . . .'

But the prince did not have time to go and smoke. A young man with papers in his hands suddenly came into the vestibule. The valet began to help him off with his fur coat. The young man gave the prince a sidelong look.

'Gavrila Ardalionych,' the valet began confidentially and almost with familiarity, 'this gentleman says he is Prince Myshkin and a relation of the mistress, he's arrived by train from abroad with nothing but a bundle in his hand, but . . .'

The prince did not catch any more, for the valet had begun to whisper. Gavrila Ardalionovich listened attentively, and kept looking at the prince with great curiosity. At length he stopped listening and eagerly approached him.

'You're Prince Myshkin?' he asked, with extreme good nature and politeness. He was a very handsome young man, also about twenty-eight, slender and fair-haired, with a small Napoleonic beard,[8] and a clever and very attractive face. Only his smile, for all its good nature, was slightly too refined; his teeth were somehow too pearly and evenly spaced; his gaze, in spite of all its cheerfulness and apparent sincerity, was a little too fixed and probing.

'I expect that when he's alone he doesn't look anything like that, and perhaps never laughs at all,' the prince found himself sensing.

The prince explained all that he could in a hurry, in almost the same words he had used to the valet, and before that to Rogozhin. Meanwhile, Gavrila Ardalionovich seemed to remember something.

'Wasn't it you,' he asked, 'who about a year ago, or even more recently, sent a letter from Switzerland to Yelizaveta Pro- kofyevna?'

'Yes, it was.'

'Then you're known here and will surely be remembered. You want to see his excellency? I'll announce you in a moment . . . He'll be free presently. Only you should . . . you ought to be waiting in the reception room . . . Why is the gentleman here?' he asked sternly, turning to the valet.

'I told him, but he didn't want to . . .'

At this point the door to the study suddenly opened, and some kind of military gentleman holding a briefcase emerged, talking loudly and taking his leave.

'Is that you, Ganya?' a voice shouted from the study. 'Come in!'

Gavrila Ardalionovich nodded to the prince, and quickly entered the study.

About two minutes later the door opened again, and Gavrila Ardalionovich's resonant and affable voice was heard:

'Prince, do come in!'

3

The general, Ivan Fyodorovich Yepanchin, stood in the middle of his study and looked at the prince with extreme curiosity as he entered, even taking two paces towards him. The prince went up to him and introduced himself.

'Well, sir,' the general replied, 'how can I be of service?'

'I have no pressing business; my aim was simply to make your acquaintance. I should not like to inconvenience you, as I know neither the order of your day nor your arrangements . . . But I'm just off the train myself . . . I've come from Switzerland.'

The general was on the verge of smiling, but reflected and checked himself; then he reflected again, narrowed his eyes, surveyed his guest once more from head to toe, then quickly showed him to a chair, sat down himself, somewhat at an angle from him, and turned to him in impatient expectation. Ganya stood in a corner of the study, by the writing desk, sorting some papers.

'On the whole I don't have much time for making acquaintances,' said the general, 'but since you, of course, have some
purpose of your own, then . . .'

'I had a feeling,' the prince interrupted, 'that you would be
bound to see some special purpose in my visit. But to be quite
honest, apart from the pleasure of making your acquaintance,
I have no private purpose.'

'It's also, of course, a great pleasure for me, too, but life is not
all enjoyment, after all – sometimes business must be attended to
. . . What is more, I still cannot perceive between us any common
. . . pretext, as it were.'

'No pretext, indisputably, and little in common, of course.
For, if I am Prince Myshkin and your spouse is of our family,
that is of course not a pretext. I understand that very well. Yet,
none the less, all of my reason for coming to see you lies in the
fact that I haven't been in Russia for more than four years; and
when I left, I wasn't really in my right mind! Back then I knew
nothing, and now I know even less. I'm in need of good people;
I even have a certain item of business to attend to and don't
know where to start. Back in Berlin I thought: "They're almost
relatives, I'll start with them; perhaps we shall be of use to one
another, they to me and I to them – if they're good people."
And I'd heard that you are good people.'

'I'm very grateful to you, sir,' the general said in surprise.
'May one ask where you are staying?'

'I'm not staying anywhere yet.'

'You mean, straight off the train, and to me? And . . . with
luggage?'

'My luggage is only one small bundle of linen, and that's all;
I usually carry it in my hand. I shall manage to rent a room this
evening.'

'So you still intend to rent a room?'

'Oh yes, of course.'

'To judge from what you said, I almost thought you had come
straight to me.'

'That might have been possible, but not unless you'd invited
me. I admit that I wouldn't have stayed even if you'd invited me,
not for any special reason, but . . . because that's what I'm like.'

'Well, in that case it's just as well I didn't invite you and do not invite you now. Allow me also, Prince, to clear the matter up once and for all: as we have just agreed that there can be no more talk of family kinship between us – though it would, of course, have been most flattering for me – it follows that . . .'

'It follows that I should get up and go away?' the prince said, half rising, and even with a cheerful laugh, in spite of all the evident difficulty of his circumstances. 'And to be quite honest, General, though I know practically nothing of either the local customs or of how people live here, things have worked out between us exactly as I thought they would. Who knows, perhaps it's best that way . . . And I received no reply to the letter I wrote then, either . . . Well, goodbye, and forgive me for troubling you.'

So affectionate was the prince's gaze at that moment, his smile so devoid of even the slightest nuance of concealed hostility, that the general suddenly paused and saw his guest, as it were, in a different light; the entire change in his expression took place in a single instant.

'Listen, Prince,' he said in an almost entirely different voice, 'the fact remains that I don't know you, and it may be that Yelizaveta Prokofyevna would like to take a look at someone who shares her family's name . . . Wait awhile, if you like, and if you have time.'

'Oh, I've plenty of that; my time is completely my own (and the prince at once placed his soft, round hat on the table). I will admit that I was counting on the possibility that Yelizaveta Prokofyevna might perhaps remember I wrote to her. Just now, while I was waiting for you out there, your servant thought I'd come to beg money from you; I noticed it, and I expect you've given strict instructions in that regard; but truly, I haven't come for that, I really have come only in order to make people's acquaintance. Only I have a slight feeling that I've disturbed you, and that troubles me.'

'I tell you what, Prince,' the general said with a jovial smile, 'if you are indeed the man you seem to be, I think it will be nice to make your acquaintance; only you see, I'm a busy man, and very soon I must sit down and look through some papers and sign them, and then I must go and see his excellency the count, and then to my office at the department, and so as a result I'm glad to see people . . . good people, that is . . . but . . . As a matter of fact, I'm so convinced that you're someone of very good breeding that . . . How old are you, Prince?'

'Twenty-six.'

'Oh! And I thought much less.'

'Yes, they say I have a young-looking face. But I shall soon learn not to be a nuisance to you, as I really don't like to be a nuisance . . . And also, I think, we are very different . . . in many ways, and cannot perhaps have many points in common, but you know, I don't place much faith in that last idea, for it very often merely *seems* that there are no points in common, while in reality there are lots . . . it's because people are lazy that they sort themselves into categories, and therefore can't find anything . . . But perhaps I've begun to bore you? You seem . . .'

'I'll be quite brief, sir: do you have private means of any kind? Or do you intend to take up some kind of occupation? Forgive me for . . .'

'Oh good heavens, I greatly appreciate your question and understand it perfectly. At present I have no private means, and no occupation, also at present, but I need one, sir. The money I've had so far has been someone else's, Schneider, my professor, who treated me and taught me in Switzerland, gave me it for the journey, and it was only just enough, so that now, you see, I've only a few copecks left. It's true that I do have some business, and I'm in need of advice, but . . .'

'Tell me, what do you intend to live on at present, and what are your plans?' the general interrupted.

'I should like to do some kind of work.'

'Oh, and you're a philosopher, too; however . . . have you any talents, abilities, of a sort by which one may earn one's daily bread? Forgive me again . . .'

'Oh, don't apologize. No, sir, I'm afraid I have neither talents nor special abilities; the contrary, even, for I'm an invalid and did not receive a proper education. As for bread, I think that . . .'

Again the general interrupted, and again he began to ask

questions. Once more the prince told him what has already
been told. It transpired that the general had heard of the late
Pavlishchev, and had even known him personally. Why Pavlishchev had taken an interest in his education the prince himself
could not explain – but perhaps it was simply because of his old
friendship with the prince's late father. The prince's parents had
died when he was still a young child; he had spent all his life in
villages of one kind or another and had grown up there, as his
health required country air. Pavlishchev had entrusted him to
some elderly female landowners, kinsfolk of his; first a governess
had been hired for him, then a tutor; he declared, however, that
although he remembered it all, there was not much he could
satisfactorily explain, as there were many things he had not been
aware of. The frequent attacks of his illness had made of him
almost a complete idiot (the prince actually used the word
'idiot'). He said, at last, that in Berlin one day Pavlishchev had
met Professor Schneider, who specialized in precisely this form
of illness and had a clinic in the Swiss canton of Valais, where
he gave treatment that combined a cold-water method with
gymnastics, for the cure of idiotism and insanity, while at the
same time providing education and seeing to his patients' spiritual development; that Pavlishchev had sent him to Schneider
in Switzerland some five years earlier and had died two years
ago, suddenly, without having made any arrangements: that
Schneider had supported him and continued his treatment for
about another two years; that he had not cured him, but had
helped him greatly; and that finally, at the prince's own request
and because of a certain circumstance that had arisen, he had
now sent him back to Russia.

The general was very astonished.

'And you have no one in Russia, absolutely no one?' he asked.

'At present I have no one, but I have hopes . . . what's more,
I've had a letter . . .'

'At least,' the general interrupted, not hearing the part about
the letter, 'you have obtained some kind of education, and your
illness would not prevent you occupying some, shall we say,
undemanding post, in some office?'

'Oh, it certainly wouldn't prevent me from doing that. And

as regards a post, I should even be rather eager, for I should like to see what I am capable of. For I studied constantly all those four years, though not quite properly, but according to a special system. And I also managed to read a very large number of Russian books.'

'Russian books? So you can read and write – write without mistakes?'

'Oh, very much so.'

'Splendid, sir; and your handwriting?'

'My handwriting is first-rate. You see, I have a sort of talent for it; I'm a real calligrapher. With your permission I'll write something for you now, as a sample,' the prince said with eagerness.

'I'd be much obliged. In fact, it's even required . . . And I like this enthusiasm of yours, Prince, truly you are most kind.'

'You have such wonderful writing things, so many pencils, so many pens, what wonderful thick paper . . . And what a wonderful study you have! That landscape there, I know it, it's a Swiss view. I'm sure the artist painted it from nature, and I'm sure I have seen that place: it's in the canton of Uri . . .'

'That may very well be so, though it was bought here. Ganya, give the prince some paper; here are some pens and paper, we'll put them on this table, if you like. What's this?' the general asked turning to Ganya, who had meanwhile taken from his briefcase a large photographic portrait and handed it to him. 'Bah! Nastasya Filippovna! Did she send you this, she, herself?' he asked Ganya with animation and intense curiosity.

'Just now, when I went to see her with my congratulations, she gave it to me. I've been asking her for one for ages. I'm not sure it wasn't a hint on her part, for having come to her empty-handed, without a present, on such a day,' Ganya added, smiling unpleasantly.

'Oh, no,' the general interrupted with conviction, 'and really, what a cast of mind you have! She would never hint . . . she's not self-seeking at all. And in any case, what are you going to give her as a present: I mean, one would need thousands! Not your portrait, anyway! By the way, has she asked you for your portrait yet?'

'No, she hasn't; and perhaps she never will. Ivan Fyodorovich, you do remember about the soirée this evening? After all, you are one of the specially invited guests.'

'Yes, yes, of course I remember, and I shall be there. Especially as it's her birthday, and she's twenty-five! Hmm . . . And listen, Ganya, I may as well tell you, I'm going to reveal something, so prepare yourself. She has promised Afanasy Ivanovich and me that at this evening's soirée she will deliver her final word: to be or not to be! So let me tell you: watch out.'

Ganya suddenly became embarrassed, so much so that he even turned slightly pale.

'Did she really say that?' he asked, and his voice seemed to tremble.

'She promised it the day before yesterday. We were both so insistent that she had no option. Only she asked us not to tell you in advance.'

The general was studying Ganya fixedly; Ganya's embarrassment was evidently not to his liking.

'Remember, Ivan Fyodorovich,' Ganya said, uneasily and hesitantly, 'that she gave me complete freedom of decision until such time as she herself would resolve the matter, and even then would I still have the last word . . .'

'I say, you haven't . . . you haven't . . .' the general suddenly exclaimed in alarm.

'I haven't said anything.'

'But for pity's sake, what are you trying to do to us?'

'I'm not refusing her. Perhaps I didn't express myself properly . . .'

'I should think you're not refusing her!' the general said with annoyance, not even trying to restrain himself. 'What matters here, brother, is not your refusal, what matters is your eagerness, your pleasure, the joy with which you will receive her words . . . How are things with you at home?'

'What is there to say about home? At home my will prevails in everything, except that Father is playing the fool as usual – he's become a complete ruffian; I don't talk to him any more, but I keep tight control of him, and really, were it not for Mother, I would have shown him the door. Mother cries all the time, of course; my sister is in a violent temper, but I finally told them straight out that I am the master of my fate, and that in the house I wish to be . . . obeyed. I spelt it out for my sister, at least, in my mother's presence.'

'Well, brother, I still fail to perceive,' the general observed reflectively, with a slight shrug of his shoulders, spreading his arms a little. 'Nina Alexandrovna, your mother, when she came here the other day – you remember? – also kept moaning and groaning all the time. "What's the matter with you?" I asked. It turned out that to them it's some kind of *dishonour*. What kind of dishonour is there in it, permit me to ask? Who can reproach Nastasya Filippovna with anything, or raise anything against her? Surely not that she'd been with Totsky? But that's plain rubbish, especially in view of certain circumstances! "You won't let her near your daughters, will you?" she said. Well! I never! Dear me, Nina Alexandrovna! I mean, how can you not understand, how can you not understand . . .'

'Your position?' Ganya said to the flabbergasted general. 'She does understand; don't be angry with her. Actually, at the time I gave her a good talking to, and told her not to meddle in other people's business. So far, however, the house still stands only because the last word has not yet been spoken; but the storm is gathering. If the last word is spoken this evening, then everything else will come out, too.'

The prince heard the whole of this conversation as he sat in the corner at his calligraphic sample. He finished it, walked round to the table and handed over his sheet of paper.

'So that's Nastasya Filippovna?' he said quietly, looking at the portrait attentively and inquisitively for a moment. 'Astonishingly good looking!' he added at once, with ardour.

The portrait really did depict a woman of unusual beauty. She had been photographed in a black silk dress of exceedingly simple and elegant cut; her hair, apparently dark russet, was done up simply, in domestic fashion; her eyes were dark and deep, her forehead pensive; the expression of her face was passionate and slightly haughty. She was somewhat thin in the face, perhaps, and pale . . . Ganya and the general looked at the prince in bewilderment . . .

'What, Nastasya Filippovna? Do you know Nastasya Filip-povna, too?' asked the general.

'Yes; only twenty-four hours in Russia and I know a great beauty like her,' replied the prince, and at once told them about his meeting with Rogozhin, retelling his entire story.

'This is news, indeed!' the general began to worry again, having listened to the story with extreme attention, and giving Ganya a searching look.

'Probably just some disreputable caper,' muttered Ganya, whose composure was also somewhat ruffled. 'A merchant's son on the spree. I've already heard something about him.'

'And so have I, brother,' the general broke in. 'That day, after the earrings, Nastasya Filippovna told me the whole incident. But you know, it's a different matter now. We really are talking of perhaps a million here, and . . . passion, grotesque passion, admittedly, but there is a whiff of passion all the same, and, after all, we know what these gentlemen are capable of when they're in a state of complete intoxication! . . . Hmm! . . . I hope there won't be an "incident"!' the general concluded reflectively.

'Are you worried about the million?' Ganya grinned.

'You're not, of course?'

'How did he seem to you, Prince?' Ganya said, suddenly addressing him. 'What is he, a serious man or just a ruffian? Your personal opinion?'

Something strange took place in Ganya as he asked this question. It was as though some new and strange idea began to burn in his brain, glittering impatiently in his eyes. As for the general, who was seriously and genuinely troubled, he also gave the prince a sidelong glance, but as though he did not expect much from his reply.

'I don't know how to put it,' the prince replied, 'but it seemed to me that there was a lot of passion in him, and even a kind of morbid passion. And he also seems to be quite ill. It may very well be that he'll take to his bed again in his first few days in St Petersburg, especially if he starts drinking.'

'Really? Was that what you thought?'

'Yes, I did.'

'And in any case, that kind of scandal could take place

this very evening, never mind in a few days' time. Perhaps something will happen tonight,' Ganya said, smiling crookedly at the general.

'Hmm! . . . Of course . . . In a way it all depends on what passes through her head,' said the general.

'And after all, you know what she can be like sometimes, don't you?'

'What on earth are you trying to say?' the general blurted out again, having now reached an extreme point of agitation. 'Listen, Ganya, please don't contradict her too much today and try, you know, to be . . . in short, to get along with her . . . Hmm! . . . Why are you twisting your mouth like that? Listen, Gavrila Ardalionovich, this may be a good opportunity, a very good opportunity, to say to you now: why are we going to all this trouble? You understand that as far as my personal advantage, which is involved here, goes, it has long ago been secured; one way or another, I shall resolve this matter in my favour. Totsky has taken his decision and will stand by it, of that I am quite certain. And so if I desire anything now, it is only your own good interests. Judge for yourself; what's the matter, don't you trust me? Besides, you're a man . . . a man . . . in a word, an intelligent man and I have placed my trust in you . . . and in the present situation that's . . . that's . . .'

'That's the main thing,' Ganya said, completing the sentence, once again helping the flabbergasted general, and twisting his lips into the most poisonous smile, which he no longer tried to conceal. With his inflamed gaze he stared the general straight in the face, as if in his eyes he wanted him to read everything he was thinking. The general turned crimson with anger, and blazed up.

'Well yes, intelligence is the main thing!' he assented, looking sharply at Ganya. 'And you're a ridiculous fellow, Gavrila Ardalionych! I mean, I can't help noticing that you're simply glad of this merchant chap as a way out for yourself. Well, this is where intelligence should have been used right from the start; this is where you should have understood and . . . and dealt honestly and plainly with both sides, or else . . . given advance warning so as not to compromise others, particularly as there was enough time to do so, and there remains enough time even now (the general raised his eyebrows meaningfully), even though it's only a few hours . . . Do you understand? Do you? Are you willing to go through with it or not? If not, say so, and – that will be all right! No one is holding you back, Gavrila Ardalionych, no one is luring you into a trap, if a trap is what you see here.'

'I'm willing to go through with it,' Ganya said in a low but firm voice, dropping his gaze and lapsing into gloomy silence.

The general was satisfied. The general had lost his temper, but evidently felt remorse at having gone too far. He suddenly turned to the prince and his face seemed traversed by the uneasy thought that the prince was there and had heard everything. He was, however, instantly reassured: one look at the prince was enough to entirely reassure him.

'Oho!' the general exclaimed, looking at the specimen of calligraphy the prince was presenting. 'Now there's a sample for you! And a rare one, too! Come and take a look, Ganya, what talent!'

On a thick sheet of vellum the prince had written in medieval Russian script: 'The humble Abbot Pafnuty hath signed this with his hand.'

'Now this,' the prince explained with great delight and enthusiasm, 'this is the personal signature of the Abbot Pafnuty, from a fourteenth-century copy. They had magnificent signatures, all those old abbots and metropolitans of ours, and sometimes wrote them with such taste, such diligence! You must have Pogodin's edition, at least, general? Then here I've written in a different script: this is a large round French script of the last century, some letters were even written differently, a script of the market place, a script of the public scribes, adapted from their samples (I used to own one) – you'll agree that it's not without its merits. Look at those round d's and a's. I've transferred the French style to the Russian letters, which is very difficult, but it's worked out well. Here is another fine, original script, in this sentence: "Hard work conquers all."[1] This is a Russian script, used by clerks, or possibly military clerks. It was used to write official memos to persons of importance, and it's also a round script, a wonderful *black* script, written in black but with remarkable taste. A calligraphist would not allow those flourishes or, rather, those attempts at flourishes, those unfinished half-tails – you will observe – but taken as a whole, look, it makes their character, and truly, the very soul of the military clerk peeps out: it would like to break loose, and the talent is there; but the military collar is tightly buttoned, the discipline has come out in the script, too, delightful! I was struck by a sample of this kind not long ago, found it by chance, and where do you suppose? In Switzerland! Well, and this is a plain, ordinary English script: elegance can go no further, here all is charm, beads, pearls; it's quite perfect; but here's a variation, and again a French one, I copied it from a travelling French *commis*:[2] the same English script, but the black line a touch blacker and thicker than in the English one – and the proportion of light has been destroyed; and observe also: the oval has been changed, a touch rounder, and in addition a flourish has been permitted, but flourishes are a most dangerous thing! Flourishes demand unusual taste; but if they succeed, if the proportion is found, then a script like that is not to be compared with any other, so much so that one may even fall in love with it.'

'Oho! What subtleties you're entering into,' laughed the general, 'but you, sir, are not merely a calligrapher, you're an artist, eh, Ganya?'

'Astonishing,' said Ganya, 'And even with an awareness of his calling,' he added, laughing sarcastically.

'Laugh, laugh, but I'll tell you, there's a career in this,' said the general. 'Do you know how important the person is, the one we shall give you memos to write to? Why, you can count on earning thirty-five roubles a month, from your very first step. But it's already half-past twelve,' he concluded, glancing at his watch. 'To business, Prince, for I must hurry, and you and I may not meet again today! Sit down for a moment; I have already explained to you that I am not in a position to meet you very often; but I sincerely wish to help you a little, a little, of course, that's to say in the form of the most necessary things, and after that you shall do as you please. I'll give you a little job in the office, not a very demanding one, but it will require accuracy. Now, sir, as regards the rest; at the house, in the household of Gavrila Ardalionych Ivolgin, that is, this same young friend of mine to whom I should like to introduce you, his mother and sister have prepared two or three furnished rooms in their apartments, which they rent out to highly recommended tenants, with meals and a maid. I am sure that Nina Alexandrovna will accept my recommendation. And for you, Prince, this will be more than precious, above all because you won't be alone, but, so to speak, in the bosom of a family, for in my view it is out of the question for you to find yourself alone on your first steps in a capital city such as St Petersburg. Nina Alexandrovna, the mother, and Varvara Ardalionovna, Gavrila Ardalionych's sister, are ladies for whom I have the greatest respect. Nina Alexandrovna is the wife of Ardalion Alexandrovich, a retired general, a former comrade of mine from my early army days, but with whom, because of certain circumstances, I have severed relations: which does not, however, prevent me from respecting him in my own way. I am explaining all this to you, Prince, so that you realize that I am, so to speak, recommending you personally, and consequently, as it were, taking responsibility for you. The rent is extremely modest, and I hope that your salary will soon be quite sufficient for it. To be sure, a man also needs pocket money, even if just a little, but please don't be angry, Prince, if I observe to you that you would do better to avoid pocket money, and indeed any kind of money, in your pocket. I say this after having taken a look at you. But since at present your purse is absolutely empty, then, as a beginning, permit me to offer you these twenty-five roubles. We'll settle up later on, of course, and if you're the sincere and straightforward man you seem to be from the way you talk, there can be no problems between us there. As for my taking such an interest in you, I actually have a certain purpose in your regard; you will learn about it subsequently. You see, I'm being perfectly open with you; Ganya, I hope you have nothing against the prince being lodged in your apartment?'

'Oh, on the contrary! And mother will be very pleased too . . .' Ganya confirmed politely and courteously.

'After all, I think you only have one other room occupied. It's that, what's his name, Ferd . . . Fer . . .'

'Ferdyshchenko.'

'Ah yes; I don't like him, that Ferdyshchenko of yours; he's some sort of lewd buffoon. And I don't understand why Nastasya Filippovna encourages him, either. Is he really a relative of hers?'

'Oh no, that's all a joke! He doesn't even come close to being a relative.'

'Well, the devil take him! So, then, how do you like it, Prince, are you pleased or not?'

'Thank you, General, you've treated me in the most kindly fashion, all the more so as I did not even ask; I say it not from pride, but I really didn't know where I was going to lay my head. It's true that Rogozhin invited me a while back.'

'Rogozhin? Ah, no; I would give you my fatherly, or, if you prefer, friendly advice to forget about Mr Rogozhin. And on the whole I'd counsel you to stick to the family you are about to enter.'

'As you're being so kind,' the prince began, 'I do have one item of business. I've received notification . . .'

'Now, excuse me,' the general interrupted, 'I can spare not a moment more. I'll tell Lizaveta Prokofyevna about you directly: if she is willing to receive you right now (I shall try to introduce you on that pretext), I advise you to take the opportunity to see that she takes a liking to you, for Lizaveta Prokofyevna could be very useful to you; after all, you share her family name. If she is not willing, then please forgive me, some other time. And you, Ganya, take a look at these accounts, Fedoseyev and I were struggling with them just now. We mustn't forget to include them . . .'

The general went out, and thus the prince had still not succeeded in telling him his business, the matter of which he had tried to raise three or four times now. Ganya lit a cigarette and offered another to the prince; the prince accepted it, but remained silent, not wishing to be in the way, and began to examine the study; but Ganya barely glanced at the sheet of paper covered in figures, which the general had pointed out to him. His mind was elsewhere; Ganya's smile, gaze and pensiveness were even more painful, it seemed to the prince, than when they had both been left alone. Suddenly he approached the prince; at that moment, the latter was again standing over the portrait of Nastasya Filippovna and examining it.

'So you like that sort of woman, do you, Prince?' he asked him suddenly, giving him a penetrating look. And as though he had some extraordinary purpose.

'An astonishing face!' the prince replied. 'And I'm certain that her fate is not of an ordinary kind. Her face is cheerful, but she has suffered dreadfully, don't you think? Her eyes betray it, those two little bones here, two points under her eyes where her cheeks begin. It's a proud face, a dreadfully proud one, and I simply can't tell if she is good or not. Oh, if only she were good! It would redeem everything!'

'And would *you* marry that sort of woman?' Ganya continued, keeping his inflamed gaze trained on him.

'I can't marry anyone, I'm an invalid,' said the prince.

'And would Rogozhin marry her? What do you think?'

'Well, he might marry her tomorrow; might marry her, and a week later, perhaps, cut her throat.'

No sooner had the prince said this than Ganya gave such a start that the prince nearly cried out.

'What's wrong?' he said, clutching his arm.

'Your grace! His excellency requests you to attend upon her excellency,' a lackey announced, appearing in the doorway. The prince set off after the lackey.

4

All three of the Yepanchin girls were healthy young ladies, blossoming, tall, with striking shoulders, powerful bosoms, strong arms, almost like men's arms, and, of course, because of their strength and health, liked to eat well now and then, something they did not even try to conceal. Their mother, the general's wife, Lizaveta Prokofyevna, sometimes looked askance at the frankness of their appetites, but as some of her opinions, in spite of all the outward respect with which they were received by her daughters, had in essence long ago lost

their original and unquestionable authority over them, and to
such a degree that the harmonious conclave established by the
three girls more often than not began to be predominant, the
general's wife, in the interests of her own dignity, found it
more convenient not to argue, but to yield. To be sure, her
temperament very often would not obey, and would not submit
to the decisions of common sense; with each year Lizaveta
Prokofyevna became more and more capricious and impatient,
was even becoming a sort of eccentric, but as a most obedient
and well-trained husband remained to hand, the excessive and
accumulated emotions were usually poured on to his head,
whereupon harmony was once again restored to the household,
and everything went as well as it possibly could.

As a matter of fact, the general's wife had not lost her appetite
either, and usually, at half-past twelve, partook of an abundant
breakfast, almost resembling a dinner, together with her daughters. The young ladies each had a cup of coffee even earlier, at
exactly ten o'clock, in bed, as soon as they woke up. They
liked this routine and it had become firmly established. And at
half-past twelve the table would be laid in the small dining room,
near the mother's rooms, and this intimate family breakfast was
sometimes attended by the general himself, if time permitted. In
addition to tea, coffee, cheese, honey, butter, the special thick
pancakes that were the favourite of the general's wife, rissoles
and so on, a strong, hot bouillon was even sometimes served.
On the morning our narrative begins, the entire household had
gathered in the dining room in expectation of the general, who
had promised to appear at half-past twelve. If he had been only
a minute late, they would have sent for him at once; but he
appeared punctually. As he approached his spouse to greet her
and kiss her hand, on this occasion he noticed something rather
strange in the look on her face. And although the night before
he had had a presentiment that this would indeed be so today
because of a certain 'incident' (as he was in the habit of putting
it), and had been worried about it as he dropped off to sleep,
yet none the less his nerve failed him now. His daughters came
up to him to give him a kiss; here, though they were not angry
with him, and here too there was something strange. To be

sure, the general, because of certain circumstances, had become excessively suspicious; but as he was an experienced and skilful husband, he at once took measures of his own.

Perhaps we shall do no great harm to the vividness of our narrative if we pause here and have recourse to a few explanations, in order to establish, in the most straightforward and precise manner, the relations and circumstances that we find in General Yepanchin's household at the beginning of our tale. We said just now that the general, though not a man of great education, but, on the contrary, as he said of himself, 'a man self-taught', was, however, an experienced husband and a skilful father. Among other things, he had adopted the system of not hurrying his daughters into marriage, in other words not 'worrying the life out of them' and not troubling them with an excessive paternal love of their happiness, as happens more often than not, involuntarily and naturally, even in the most intelligent families where there is an accumulation of grown-up daughters. He even managed to win Lizaveta Prokofyevna over to his system, though it was on the whole a difficult task – difficult because unnatural; but the general's arguments were extremely cogent, and were grounded on tangible facts. What was more, left entirely their own will and resolve, the future brides would naturally be constrained to make up their own minds, and then things would start to happen fast, because they would set to work with a will, putting aside their caprices and excessive discrimination; their parents would merely need to keep a more watchful and unobtrusive eye on them, lest any strange choice or unnatural aberration occur, and then, seizing the proper moment, do all that they could to help them and direct the matter with all their influence. Finally, the very fact that with each year that passed their wealth and social standing grew in geometrical progression meant that, the more time went by, the more the daughters gained, even as future brides. But among all these incontrovertible facts yet one more fact emerged: suddenly, and almost quite unexpectedly (as is always the case) the eldest daughter, Alexandra, turned twenty-five. At almost the same time, Afanasy Ivanovich Totsky, a man of the highest society, with the highest connections and extraordinary wealth, again

disclosed his long-felt desire to marry. He was a man of about
fifty-five, of exquisite character, and with uncommon refinement
of taste. He wanted to marry well; he was a great connoisseur
of beauty. As for some time he had been on unusually close
terms of friendship with General Yepanchin, a friendship
strengthened by their mutual participation in certain financial
undertakings, he now, as it were, told him about it, requesting
friendly advice and guidance: would it or would it not be possible for him to enter into a marriage with one of his daughters?
In the quiet and splendid flow of General Yepanchin's family
life an evident upheaval was in the offing.

The undoubted beauty of the family was, as we have already
said, the youngest, Aglaya. But even Totsky himself, a man of
exceeding egoism, realized that there was no point in looking
there, and that Aglaya was not intended for him. It is possible
that the sisters' somewhat blind love and overly warm friendship
exaggerated the matter, but they had, in the most sincere
fashion, earmarked Aglaya's destiny to be not merely a destiny
but the reachable ideal of an earthly paradise. Aglaya's future
husband was to be the holder of every perfection and success, not
to mention wealth. The sisters had even agreed among themselves, and without much in the way of superfluous words, on
the possibility that, if necessary, they would make sacrifices for
Aglaya's sake; her dowry was to be colossal, and out of the ordinary. The parents knew of this agreement between the two elder
sisters and so, when Totsky asked for advice, they had little doubt
that one of the elder sisters would certainly agree to crown their
desires, all the more so as Afanasy Ivanovich could not make
difficulties concerning the dowry. As for Totsky's proposal, the
general himself, with the knowledge of life that was characteristic
of him, at once placed an exceedingly high value on it. Since Totsky, because of certain special circumstances, was at present
observing extreme caution in the steps he took, and as yet doing
no more than sounding out the matter, the parents presented it
all to their daughters as only the most remote hypothesis. In
response to this they issued a declaration, likewise not entirely
definite, but at least reassuring, that the elder sister, Alexandra,
might not refuse. She was a girl of firm character, but kind, sen-

sible and of an exceedingly lenient disposition; might even be keen to marry Totsky and, if she gave her word, would keep it honourably. She was not fond of surface brilliance, and not only did she eschew all threats of trouble and sudden upheaval: she was even able to sweeten life and soothe it. She was very pretty, though not ostentatiously so. What could be better for Totsky?

And yet, the matter was still proceeding by tentative fits and starts. Totsky and the general had come to a mutual and friendly agreement to avoid taking any formal and irrevocable step before it was time. The parents had not yet even begun to talk quite frankly with their daughters; a kind of discord had begun to develop: for some reason Mrs Yepanchina, the mother of the family, was becoming displeased, and this was very serious. Here a circumstance was involved that interfered with everything, a tricky and bothersome incident that might cause the entire arrangement to collapse irrevocably.

This tricky and bothersome 'incident' (as Totsky himself expressed it) had begun a very long time ago, some eighteen years earlier. Adjoining one of Afanasy Ivanovich's wealthiest estates, in one of the central provinces, a certain small and utterly destitute landowner lived a life of poverty. This was a man remarkable for his constant and 'anecdotal' failures – a retired officer, from a good family of gentlefolk, even superior to Totsky in this respect, a certain Filipp Alexandrovich Barashkov. Entirely submerged in debt and mortgages, he finally managed, after back-breaking, almost muzhik-like labours, in more or less putting his small farm in satisfactory order. The slightest success cheered him inordinately. Cheered, and glowing with hope, he absented himself for a few days on a visit to the chief town of his district in order to meet and, if possible, come to a final agreement with one of his principal creditors. On the third day of his visit to the town the elder of his village came to see him, on horseback, his cheek and beard scorched, and announced to him that his 'patrimony' had 'burned to nought', the previous day, at the stroke of noon, in addition to which 'herself, your wife' had been burned to death, though 'the little ones' were safe. Not even Barashkov, schooled to the 'blows of fortune' as he was, was able to withstand this; he went mad and within a month died of a fever. The burned-down farm, with its muzhiks, who now wandered homeless, was sold to pay off the debts; as for the two little girls, six and seven years old, Barashkov's children, they were taken as dependants to be fostered under the generous tutelage of Afanasy Ivanovich Totsky. They were brought up together with the children of Afanasy Ivanovich's estate manager, a retired official with a large family, who was, moreover, a German. Soon only one of the little girls, Nastya, remained, the younger having died of whooping-cough; as for Totsky, he soon completely forgot about them both, spending the time in Europe. One day about five years later, Afanasy Ivanovich, passing through, thought he would drop in on his estate and his German, and suddenly noticed in his house, in his German's family, a delightful child, a girl some twelve years old, playful, intelligent and promising unusual beauty; in this respect, Afanasy Ivanovich was an unerring connoisseur. This time he only stayed on the estate for a few days, but managed to make the necessary arrangements; and a considerable change occurred in the little girl's upbringing: a respectable elderly governess, experienced in the higher education of young ladies, a Swiss woman, progressively educated, who in addition to French taught various sciences, was engaged. She took up residence in the house, and the education of little Nastasya acquired extraordinary dimensions. At the end of exactly four years this education was terminated; the governess departed, and a lady, who was also some sort of landowner, and one of Mr Totsky's neighbours, but in another, far-off province, came to fetch Nastya and took her with her in accordance with Afanasy Ivanovich's instructions and authority. On this little estate there was also a wooden house, though a small one, which had just been built; it was furnished with particular elegance, and the little village, as if on purpose, was called the hamlet of Otradnoye.[1] The lady landowner brought Nastya straight to this quiet little house, and as she herself, a childless widow, lived only a verst[2] away, she decided to live there with Nastya. An old female housekeeper and a young, experienced chambermaid also made their appearance around Nastya. The house contained musical instruments, an exquisite young ladies' library, pictures, prints, pencils, brushes, paints and a wonderful little greyhound, and at the end of two weeks Afanasy Ivanovich himself arrived on a visit . . . Since then he had seemed to acquire a particular fondness for this far-flung little village in the steppes, and stayed there for two, even three months, and thus a rather long period of time went by, some four years, peacefully and happily, amid taste and elegance.

It chanced one day at the onset of winter, some four months after one of Afanasy Ivanovich's summer visits to Otradnoye, on this occasion of but two weeks' duration, that a rumour went round, or rather, a rumour somehow reached Nastasya Filippovna, that Afanasy Ivanovich was getting married in St Petersburg to a beautiful woman, who was rich, of high society – in a word, he was making a sound and brilliant match. This rumour later turned out to be not quite true in every detail: even then the wedding was merely at the stage of planning, and all of it was still very vague, but at this time an extraordinary upheaval none the less took place in Nastasya Filippovna's fortunes. She suddenly showed unusual determination, displaying a most unexpected character. Without thinking long about it, she left her little house in the country and suddenly appeared in St Petersburg, going straight to see Totsky, all on her very own. He was amazed and began to talk; but it suddenly turned out, almost from the first word, that he would have to completely change his style, the diapason of his voice, the former subjects of pleasant and elegant conversation he had hitherto employed with such success, his logic – everything, everything, everything! Before him sat a completely different woman, not at all resembling the one he had hitherto known and had left in the hamlet of Otradnoye only that July.

For one thing, this new woman, it turned out, knew and understood an extraordinary amount – so much that one could only wonder where she had acquired such knowledge, cultivated such precise ideas within herself. (Not in her young ladies' library, surely?) What was more, she even understood a great deal about juridical matters and had a positive knowledge, if not of the world, then at least of how certain matters proceed in the world; for another thing, she had not at all the same character as previously, and was no longer timid and vague in the manner of a schoolgirl, sometimes enchanting in her unaffected playfulness and naivety, sometimes sad and pensive, surprised, mistrustful, tearful and restless.

No: here, laughing in his face and stabbing him with the most venomous sarcasms was an extraordinary and unexpected creature who told him directly that she had never had anything for him in her heart but the most profound contempt, contempt that rose to the point of nausea, and had begun immediately after her initial astonishment. This new woman declared that in the full sense of the word it was a matter of indifference to her how soon he married, or whom, but that she had come here in order to prevent this marriage, and to prevent it out of spite, solely because she felt like it, and because, consequently, that was how it must be – 'if only so I can laugh at you as much I want to, because now I, too, want to laugh at last'.

That, at least, was how she expressed it; she did not, perhaps, tell all that was in her mind. But while the new Nastasya Filippovna laughed and set forth all this, Afanasy Ivanovich considered the matter and, as far as possible, put his somewhat bruised thoughts in order. His consideration lasted quite a long time; he spent nearly two weeks pondering and trying to make up his mind: but at the end of two weeks his decision was made. The fact was that Afanasy Ivanovich was then almost fifty, and he was a man in the highest degree respected and settled. His position in the world and in society had long ago been established on the firmest of foundations. More than anything else in the world he loved and valued himself, his peace and comfort, as befitted a man upright in the highest degree. Not the slightest infraction, not the slightest hesitation could be permitted in what, throughout all his life, had been in the making and had now assumed such a pleasant form. On the other hand, his experience and penetrating view of things very quickly and with unusual certainty made him realize that he now had to deal with a creature entirely out of the ordinary, that this really was a creature that would not merely make threats, but also carry them out and, above all, would decidedly stop at nothing, all the more so as she decidedly attached no value to anything in

the world, so that it was even impossible to offer her inducements. Here, evidently, there was something else, some kind of
mental and emotional mish-mash was at work – something akin
to a romantic anger, goodness only knew at whom and at
what, some kind of insatiable contempt that had leaped entirely
beyond all measure – in a word, something in the highest degree
ridiculous and impermissible in decent society and to encounter
which, for any decent person, was simply divine retribution. Of
course, with his wealth and connections Totsky could easily
commit some minor and completely innocent act of villainy in
order to rid himself of the unpleasantness. On the other hand,
it was obvious that Nastasya Filippovna herself was not really
in a position to cause any harm, even, for example, in a juridical
sense; she would not even be able to make a significant scandal,
for it would always be so easy to keep her within bounds. But
all this was true only in the event that Nastasya Filippovna
decided to act as most people act in such cases, without leaping
too eccentrically beyond all measure. Here it was, however, that
Totsky's sureness of vision came into play: he was able to
guess that Nastasya Filippovna herself knew perfectly well how
harmless she was in a juridical sense, but that she had something
entirely different in her mind and . . . in her flashing eyes. Valuing
nothing, and least of all herself (a great deal of intelligence and
insight was needed in order to realize at that moment that she
had long ago ceased to value herself, and for him, a sceptic and
worldly cynic, to believe in the seriousness of this emotion),
Nastasya Filippovna was capable of ruining herself, irrevocably
and hideously, with Siberia and penal labour, as long as she
could treat outrageously the man for whom she felt such
inhuman revulsion. Afanasy Ivanovich never concealed that he
was somewhat cowardly or, more precisely, in the highest degree
conservative. Had he known, for example, that he was going to
be murdered at the altar, or that something of that kind was
about to happen to him, something exceedingly improper, ridiculous and unpleasant in the company of others, then, naturally, he would have been alarmed, but not so much about being
murdered and bloodied and injured, or spat in the face in public
in front of everyone, etcetera, etcetera, as about the fact that

this would happen to him in such an unnatural and unpleasant manner. And yet this was exactly what Nastasya Filippovna was predicting, though she was still keeping quiet about it; he knew that, to the highest degree, she had understood him and studied him, and consequently knew where to strike at him. And as the wedding was really still only a plan, Afanasy Ivanovich resigned himself and let Nastasya Filippovna have her way.

He was helped in this decision by one other circumstance: it was hard to imagine the degree to which this new Nastasya Filippovna differed from the former one in facial appearance. Before, she had been merely a very pretty girl, but now ... For a long time Totsky could not forgive himself for having looked for four years without seeing. To be sure, it meant a great deal when on both sides, inwardly and outwardly, a great change took place. He recalled, however, that, even before, there had been moments when, for example, strange thoughts had sometimes come to him from outside at the sight of those eyes: in them one somehow felt the imminence of some deep and mysterious darkness. This gaze looked as though it were asking him a riddle. In the past two years he had often been surprised by the alteration in Nastasya Filippovna's complexion; she was becoming dreadfully pallid and – strangely – was even more beautiful for it. Totsky, who, like all gentlemen who have sown their wild oats in their day, had initially watched with contempt how cheaply this inexperienced soul fell into his hands, had of late begun to have doubts about his opinion. At any rate, he had decided as long ago as last spring to marry Nastasya Filippovna off in the near future, well and with a reasonable dowry, to some sensible and decent gentleman who served in another province. (Oh, how horribly and how cruelly Nastasya Filippovna now laughed at this!) But now Afanasy Ivanovich, fascinated by the novel situation, even thought that he might once again exploit this woman. He decided to settle Nastasya Filippovna in St Petersburg and to surround her with luxurious comfort. If not the one, then the other: Nastasya Filippovna could be shown off and even boasted about, within a certain little circle. For Afanasy Ivanovich was very proud of his reputation in that department, after all.

Five years of life in St Petersburg had passed, and, of course, in that time many things had become clear. Afanasy Ivanovich's position was not a favourable one; worst of all was the fact that, having once lost his nerve, he was subsequently quite unable to put his mind at rest. He was afraid – and did not even himself know why – he was simply afraid of Nastasya Filippovna. For some time, during the first two years, he began to suspect that Nastasya Filippovna wanted to marry him herself, but that she kept silent because of extraordinary vanity, tenaciously waiting for him to propose to her. It would have been a strange claim; Afanasy Ivanovich frowned. To his great and (such is the human heart!) somewhat unpleasant astonishment, he was suddenly, in the aftermath of a certain incident, convinced that even had he made a proposal, it would not have been accepted. For a long time he was unable to understand this. The only explanation that seemed possible to him was that the pride of the 'humiliated and fantastical' woman had now attained such frenzy that she found it more agreeable to display her contempt in a refusal than to finally normalize her position and attain an inaccessible grandeur. Worst of all was that Nastasya Filippovna had, to such a disastrous degree, got the upper hand. Nor would she submit to financial inducements, even very large ones, and though she accepted the comfort that was offered to her, she lived very modestly, and saved almost nothing during those five years. Afanasy Ivanovich began to risk a very cunning method in order to break his fetters: unobtrusively and cleverly, employing the assistance of skilful accomplices, he began to seduce her with sundry ideal temptations; but the personified ideals – princes, hussars, secretaries of embassies, poets, novelists, socialists even – made not the slightest impression on Nastasya Filippovna, as though in place of a heart she had a stone, and her feelings had withered and died once and for all. She lived mostly alone, read, even studied, was fond of music. She had few acquaintances; she mostly associated with some poor and ridiculous officials' wives, knew two actresses of some sort, old women of some sort, was very fond of the large family of a respectable schoolteacher, and in this family she was much liked, and received with pleasure. Quite often in the evenings five or six acquaintances would call on her, no more. Totsky announced himself very frequently and punctually. Of late General Yepanchin had, not without difficulty, made her acquaintance. At the same time, easily and without any difficulty, a certain young official, Ferdyshchenko by name, a very disreputable and salacious-minded buffoon who drank a great deal and had pretensions to gaiety, also made her acquaintance. Another of her acquaintances was a strange young man by the name of Ptitsyn, a modest, punctual and dandified fellow who had risen from poverty and become a moneylender. Lastly, Gavrila Ivolgin made her acquaintance . . . The end of it was that Nastasya Filippovna established a strange reputation: everyone knew of her beauty, but that was all; no one could boast of anything, no one could tell any stories. A reputation like this, her education, her elegant manner, her wit – all this finally confirmed Afanasy Ivanovich in a certain plan. It was at this moment that General Yepanchin began to take such an active and extraordinary part in the story.

When Totsky so courteously turned to him for friendly advice with regard to one of his daughters, he at once, in a most noble fashion, made the fullest and frankest of confessions. He disclosed that he was resolved to stop at *nothing* to obtain his freedom; that he would not rest easy even were Nastasya Filippovna herself to tell him that in future she would leave him in perfect peace; that words were not enough for him, that he required the fullest guarantees. They came to an agreement and determined to act jointly. It was initially decided to try the most gentle methods and to touch, as it were, only 'the heart's noble strings'. They both arrived at Nastasya Filippovna's house, and Totsky began quite bluntly by telling her of the unendurable horror of his position; he blamed himself for everything; said frankly that he could not repent of his original action with her, as he was a hardened voluptuary and not his own master, but that now he wished to be married and that the entire fate of this extremely proper and society marriage was in her hands; in a word, that he expected everything of her noble heart. Then General Yepanchin began to speak, in his capacity of father, and spoke reasonably, avoiding pathos, and merely mentioning

that he fully acknowledged her right to decide Afanasy Ivanovich's fate, cleverly showing off his own resigned attitude by
pointing out that the fate of his daughter, and possibly that of
his two other daughters, now depended on her decision. To
Nastasya Filippovna's question: 'Just what is it that you want
of me?' Totsky confessed to her, with the same open bluntness,
that he had been so intimidated by her five years earlier that
even now he could not quite rest easy until Nastasya Filippovna
herself had married someone. He at once added that this request
would, of course, have been a preposterous one on his part had
he not had certain reasons for making it. He had taken very
good note and positively knew for a fact that a young man of
very good family, living in the most worthy of households,
namely Gavrila Ardalionovich Ivolgin, whom she knew and
received in her house, had for a long time loved her with all the
strength of passion and would, of course, have given half his
life for the hope of acquiring her favour. Gavrila Ardalionovich
had made these confessions to him, Afanasy Ivanovich, a long
time ago, in a friendly way and out of a pure young heart, and
Ivan Fyodorovich, the young man's benefactor, had also long
known about it. Lastly, if he was not mistaken, the young man's
love had also long been known to Nastasya Filippovna herself,
and he even fancied that she looked upon this love with indul-
gence. Of course, it was harder for him to talk about this than
anyone else. But if Nastasya Filippovna was willing to allow
that he, Totsky, in addition to egoism and a desire to arrange
his own destiny, had at least some good feeling towards her, she
would have realized that he had long found it strange and even
painful to look upon her loneliness: that here was nothing but
an uncertain darkness, a complete lack of faith in a renewal of
life, which could have been resurrected so beautifully in love
and a family and thus acquired a new goal; that here was
a waste of talents, which were perhaps brilliant, a voluntary
brooding on her own anguish, in a word, even a certain romanticism, worthy neither of Nastasya Filippovna's sensible mind
nor of her noble heart. Repeating again that it was harder for
him to speak than others, he concluded by saying that he could
not reject the hope that Nastasya Filippovna would not respond

with contempt if he expressed his sincere desire to make her future secure and offered her the sum of seventy-five thousand roubles. He added, in explanation, that this sum was in any case already allotted to her in his will; in a word, that here there was no question of a reward of some kind . . . and that, finally, why not allow and excuse him the human desire to at least relieve his conscience in some way, etcetera, etcetera – all the things that are said on this subject in such cases. Afanasy Ivanovich spoke long and eloquently, adding, as it were, in passing, the very curious information that this was the first time he had alluded to this seventy-five thousand, and that not even Ivan Fyodorovich himself, who was sitting right there, knew about it; in a word, no one did.

Nastasya Filippovna's reply dumbfounded the two friends.

Not only was there not the slightest trace in her of her former mockery, her former hostility and hatred, her former laughter, the mere recollection of which had hitherto sent shivers down Totsky's spine, but, on the contrary, she seemed to rejoice that she was at last able to talk to someone in an open and friendly manner. She confessed that she herself had long wanted to ask for friendly advice, that only pride had stood in her way, but that now that the ice was broken, there could be nothing better. At first with a sad smile, but then laughing cheerfully and playfully, she admitted that at any rate there could be no question of her earlier storms; that she had long ago partly altered her view of things, and that although she had not altered in her heart, she was still compelled to accept many things as facts that had been accomplished; what was done was done, what was past was past, so that she even found it strange that Afanasy Ivanovich still continued to be so alarmed. Here she turned to Ivan Fyodorovich and, with a look of the most profound respect, declared that she had long heard a very great deal about his daughters and had long grown accustomed to respecting them deeply and sincerely. The very thought that she might be in any way at all useful to them, would, it seemed, have made her happy and proud. It was true that she felt wretched and low just now, very low; Afanasy Ivanovich had guessed her dreams; she would have liked to resurrect herself, if not in love then in a family, conscious of a new goal; but of Gavrila Ardalionovich she could say almost nothing. It seemed to be true that he loved her; she felt that she herself could fall in love with him, if she could believe in the firmness of his affection; but he was very young, even if he was sincere; it was hard to make a decision. What appealed to her most, however, was the fact that he was in work, that he toiled and supported his family alone. She had heard that he was a man of energy and pride, wanted a career, wanted to make his mark. She had also heard that Nina Alexandrovna Ivolgina, Gavrila Ardalionovich's mother, was a magnificent and in the highest degree estimable woman; that his sister, Varvara Ardalionovna, was a very remarkable and energetic girl; she had heard much about her from Ptitsyn. She had heard that they were cheerfully enduring their misfortunes; she would very much have liked to make their acquaintance, but there was a question as to whether they would welcome her into their family. On the whole, she would not say anything against the possibility of this marriage, but she really needed to think about it carefully; she would prefer it if they did not hurry her. As for the seventy-five thousand – there was no need for Afanasy Ivanovich to be so embarrassed about speaking of it. She knew the value of money and would, of course, take it. She was grateful to Afanasy Ivanovich for his tact, for not speaking of it even to the general, let alone to Gavrila Ardalionovich, but then why should he not know of it in advance? She had no reason to be ashamed on account of this money, on entering their family. At any rate, she had no intention of asking anyone for forgiveness for anything, and wanted them to know that. She would not marry Gavrila Ardalionovich until she was quite certain that neither he nor his family had any hidden thoughts in her regard. At all events, she did not consider that she was to blame for anything, and it would be better if Gavrila Ardalionovich knew on what basis she had been living in St Petersburg these last five years, in what relation to Afanasy Ivanovich, and how much of a fortune she had put together. Finally, if she were to accept this capital now, it was in no way as payment for her maidenly disgrace, for which she was not to blame, but simply as recompense for a corrupted destiny.

Towards the end, so excited and irritable did she become as she set forth all this (which was, however, so natural), that General Yepanchin was quite satisfied and considered the matter finished; but even now the alarmed Totsky did not quite believe in it, and for a long time feared that a serpent might lurk beneath the flowers. But the negotiations began; the point on which the entire manoeuvre of the two friends was based, namely the possibility that Nastasya Filippovna was in love with Ganya, gradually started to become clear and to find its justification, so that even Totsky sometimes began to believe in the possibility of success. Meanwhile, Nastasya Filippovna had a confrontation with Ganya: very few words were spoken, as though her modesty experienced pain during the course of it. But she acknowledged and allowed his love, insistently declaring, however, that she was not willing to restrict herself in any way; that until the day of the wedding (if there was to be a wedding) she reserved to herself the right to say 'no', even at the very last moment; she offered Ganya that entire same right. Soon Ganya learned for a fact, through a stroke of chance, that the whole extent of his family's ill-will towards this marriage and towards Nastasya Filippovna personally, something that had been revealed in domestic scenes, was already known to Nastasya Filippovna; she herself had not broached the subject with him, though he expected it daily. As a matter of fact, one might tell much of all the stories and circumstances that came to light apropos of this matchmaking and the negotiations; but as it is, we have run on ahead, especially as some of the circumstances appeared in the form of extremely vague rumours. For example, Totsky was supposed to have learned from somewhere that Nastasya Filippovna had entered into some kind of vague and secret relations with the Yepanchin girls – a quite unlikely rumour. On the other hand, there was another rumour which he believed in spite of himself, and which he feared to the point of nightmare: he had heard for a fact that Nastasya Filippovna was perfectly aware that Ganya was marrying only for money, that Ganya's soul was dark, grasping, impatient, envious and immensely, out of all proportion, self-proud; that although Ganya had indeed passionately tried to achieve victory over Nastasya Filippovna earlier, when the two friends decided to exploit this passion, which had begun on both sides, to their advantage and buy Ganya by selling him Nastasya Filippovna as his lawful wife, he began to hate her like the nightmare he had had. In his soul there seemed to be a strange fusion of passion and hatred, and although at last, after agonizing hesitations, he agreed to marry the 'vile woman', he swore in his soul to take a bitter revenge on her for it and to 'harry her to death' later on, as he apparently expressed it. Nastasya Filippovna apparently knew all this and was preparing something in secret. By this time Totsky was in such a state of funk that he even stopped telling Yepanchin about his worries; but there were moments when, like the weak man he was, he decidedly took heart again and swiftly regained his spirits: he took heart exceedingly, for example, when Nastasya Filippovna at last promised the two friends that on the evening of her birthday she would deliver her final word. On the other hand, a most strange and most unlikely rumour concerning the respected Ivan Fyodorovich turned out – alas! – to be more and more correct.

At first glance the whole thing seemed the purest rubbish. It was hard to believe that Ivan Fyodorovich, at his venerable age, with his splendid intellect and positive knowledge of life, etcetera, etcetera, could ever be seduced by Nastasya Filippovna – but such, apparently, was the case and, it was said, to such a degree that this caprice almost resembled passion. What his hopes were in this instance it was hard to imagine; perhaps he was even relying on Ganya's assistance. Totsky at least suspected something of this kind, suspected the existence of some almost tacit concordat, founded upon mutual discernment, between the general and Ganya. As a matter of fact, it is well known that a man excessively carried away by passion, especially if he is getting on in years, becomes completely blind and is ready to suspect hope where there is none at all; not only that, but he loses his reason and acts like a silly child, though he may be a Solomon of wisdom. It was known that the general was preparing to give Nastasya Filippovna a present of some wonderful pearls, costing a vast sum, for her birthday, and that he had a considerable interest in this present, though he knew that

Nastasya Filippovna was a disinterested woman. On the eve of
Nastasya Filippovna's birthday he was almost in a fever, though
he skilfully concealed it. It was of these pearls that the general's
wife, Mrs Yepanchina, had heard. True, Yelizaveta Prokofyevna
had long experienced her spouse's fickleness, and was even to
some extent accustomed to it; but after all, a case like this could
not possibly be overlooked: the rumour of the pearls interested
her exceedingly. The general sniffed this out in good time; the
previous day certain words had passed between them; he had
forebodings of a major confrontation, and was afraid of it. This
was why, on the morning where we begin our story, he so
dreadfully did not want to go to have breakfast in the bosom of
his family. Even before the prince appeared he had decided to
plead pressure of business, and thus to avoid it. For the general,
avoidance sometimes simply meant running away. He merely
wished to get through that day and, especially, that evening,
without unpleasantness. And suddenly, so opportunely, the
prince had arrived. 'As though God had sent him!' the general
thought to himself as he went in to his wife.

5

The general's wife guarded her lineage jealously. So it may
be imagined what she felt upon hearing, directly and without
preparation, that this Prince Myshkin, the last in the family, a
man of whom she had already heard something, was no more
than a pathetic idiot and almost a beggar, and accepting alms
because of poverty. For the general had striven for effect, so as
to engage her interest at once and somehow deflect it from
himself.

In extreme situations the general's wife's eyes usually bulged
exceedingly as, with a slight backwards tilt of her body, she
looked vaguely ahead of her, not saying a word. She was a tall
woman, the same age as her husband, with dark hair that
contained much grey, but was still luxuriant, a slightly aquiline
nose, and a rather thin look, with hollow, sallow cheeks and

sunken lips. Her forehead was high, but narrow; her grey, rather large eyes sometimes had a most startling expression. At one time she had the foible of believing that her gaze was uncommonly effective; this conviction had remained with her, and nothing could efface it.

'Receive him? You say we must receive him, now, this instant?' And the general's wife made her eyes bulge with all her might at Ivan Fyodorovich, as he stood fidgeting before her.

'Oh, where that's concerned you need not stand on any ceremony, if only you will see him, my dear,' the general hurried to explain. 'He's a perfect child, and even a rather pathetic one; he has some kind of morbid fits; he is newly arrived from Switzerland, just off the train, dressed strangely, in a sort of German style, and in addition without a copeck, literally; he is almost in tears. I gave him twenty-five roubles and am going to find him some little clerking job in our office. And you, *mesdames*, I should like you to give him something to eat and drink, because I think he is hungry, too . . .'

'You astonish me,' the general's wife continued as before. 'Hungry and fits! What kind of fits?'

"Oh, they don't occur so often, and moreover he's almost like a child, though an educated one. I was going to ask you, *mesdames*,' he addressed his daughters again, 'to give him an examination, for it really would be good to know what he is able to do.'

'An ex-am-in-ation?' the general's wife said slowly, and in the most profound bewilderment began once more to roll her eyes from her daughters to her husband and back again.

'Oh, my dear, don't give it such a meaning . . . Anyway, it's as you please; I thought we might be kind to him and bring him into our home, as it's almost a charitable act.'

'Bring him into our home? From Switzerland?'

'In this case Switzerland may come in useful; but anyway, I repeat, it's as you like. You see I want to do it because, firstly, he shares our family name, and may even be a relative of ours, and secondly, he has nowhere to lay his head. I actually thought it might be rather interesting for you, as whatever else he is, he's from our family.'

'Of course, *Maman*, if we don't need to stand on ceremony with him; what's more, he is hungry after his journey, why not feed him, if he has nowhere else to go?' the eldest, Alexandra, said.

'And also a perfect child, we can play blind man's buff with him.'

'Blind man's buff? What on earth?'

'Oh, *Maman*, do stop play-acting, please,' Aglaya interrupted in vexation.

The middle daughter, Adelaida, much given to mirth, could not restrain herself and burst out laughing.

'Call him in, Papa,' Aglaya decided. The general rang the bell and had the prince called in.

'But only on condition he has a napkin tied round his neck when he sits down at table,' the general's wife decided. 'Call Fyodor, or let it be Mavra ... to stand behind him and look after him while he's eating. Is he quiet during his fits, at least? He doesn't make gestures?'

'On the contrary, he is even very nicely brought up and has beautiful manners. He's sometimes a bit simple-minded ... But here he is! So now, madam, let me introduce you, the last Prince Myshkin of his line, who shares your family name and may also be a relative of yours, receive him and be kind to him. Breakfast will be served in a moment, Prince, please do us the honour ... But you must forgive me, I'm late, I must hurry ...'

'We know where you're hurrying to,' the general's wife said with a consequential air.

'I'm in a hurry, a hurry, my dear, I'm late! And give him your albums, *mesdames*, let him write something in them, he's such a calligrapher, you have never seen the like! A talent; the way he wrote out for me in my study: "The Abbot Pafnuty hath signed this with his hand" ... Well, goodbye.'

'Pafnuty? An abbot? But wait, wait, where are you going, and who is this Pafnuty?' in stubborn vexation, very nearly bordering on anxiety, the general's wife cried to her spouse as he ran away.

'Yes, yes, my dear, he was an abbot in olden times, but I'm

off to the count's, he's been waiting for ages, and the fact is that he set our appointment himself . . . Prince, goodbye!'

The general set off, with swift steps.

'I know what sort of count *he's* off to see!' Yelizaveta Proko-fyevna said sharply, transferring her gaze irritably to the prince. 'What was I saying?' she began, trying to remember, with dis-taste and annoyance. 'Oh, what was it? Ah yes: now, who was this abbot?'

'*Maman*,' Alexandra began, while Aglaya even stamped her foot.

'Don't interrupt me, Alexandra Ivanovna,' the general's wife rapped out. 'I also want to know. Sit down here, Prince, in this armchair here, opposite, no, here, where there's some sun, move into the light so I can see you. Well now, who was this abbot?'

'The Abbot Pafnuty,' the prince replied, with serious attention.

'Pafnuty? That's interesting; well, what of him, then?'

The general's wife asked her questions impatiently, swiftly and sharply, never taking her eyes off the prince, and whenever the prince replied she nodded her head after each word he spoke.

'The Abbot Pafnuty, of the fourteenth century,' the prince began. 'He governed a monastery on the Volga, in what today is the province of Kostroma. He was well known for his holy life, travelled to the Horde,[1] helped to organize the business of those times, and signed a certain deed, and I have seen a copy of that signature. I liked the handwriting, and I learned the knack of it. When the general wanted to see my writing just now, so that he could assign me a job, I wrote a few sentences in different scripts, including "The Abbot Pafnuty hath signed this with his hand" in the Abbot Pafnuty's own handwriting. The general liked it very much, and so he remembered it just now.'

'Aglaya,' said the general's wife, 'remember: Pafnuty, or better, write it down, for I always forget things. Actually, I thought it would be more interesting. Where is this signature, then?'

'I think it's still on the table in the general's study.'

'Have it brought here at once.'

'Oh, I think it would be better if I wrote it for you another time, if you would like that.'

'Of course, *Maman*,' said Alexandra, 'but now it would be better to have breakfast; we're hungry.'

'There's that, too,' the general's wife decided. 'Come along, Prince; are you very hungry?'

'Yes, I've begun to feel very hungry, and I am very grateful to you.'

'It's very good that you're so polite, and I can see that you are not at all the . . . eccentric you were introduced as. Come along. Sit down here, opposite me,' she fussed, seating the prince when they arrived in the dining room, 'I want to look at you. Alexandra, Adelaida, help to serve the prince. He's not such an . . . invalid after all, is he? Perhaps the napkin isn't necessary . . . Prince, are you used to having a napkin tied round your neck at meal-times?'

'I think that formerly, when I was about seven years old, I used to have that done, but now I usually put the napkin on my knees when I'm eating.'

'Quite right. And your fits?'

'Fits?' The prince was slightly astonished. 'My fits are rather infrequent now. However, I don't know, they say that the climate here will be bad for me.'

'He speaks well,' the general's wife remarked, turning to her daughters and continuing to nod her head after the prince's every word, 'I really didn't expect it. It must all be nonsense and fabrication – as usual. Eat, Prince, and tell me: where were you born, where were you raised? I want to know it all; I find you extremely interesting.'

The prince thanked her and, while eating with hearty appetite, again began to tell everything he had already had to say several times that morning. The general's wife grew more and more content. The girls also listened quite closely. They considered their degree of kinship; it turned out that the prince knew his family tree rather well; but no matter how hard they tried, there proved to be no almost no relation between him and the general's wife. There might have been a distant kinship among the grandfathers and grandmothers. This arid subject particularly appealed to the general's wife, who hardly ever had the opportunity of talking about her family tree as much as she wanted to, and she rose from the table in an excited state of mind.

'Let's all go to our salon,' she said, 'and they'll bring the coffee there. We have a room we share,' she addressed the prince, leading him out, 'really my own little drawing room where, when we are on our own, we sit together and each of us gets on with her own work: Alexandra here, my eldest daughter, plays the piano, or reads, or sews; Adelaida paints landscapes and portraits (and is incapable of finishing anything) and Aglaya just sits and does nothing. I'm no good with my hands, either: nothing works out right. Well, here we are; you sit down here, Prince, by the fire, and tell us something. I want to know how you tell a story. I want to be quite convinced, and when I see old Princess Belokonskaya I shall tell her all about you. I want them all to take an interest in you, too. Well, then, speak.'

'*Maman*, but that's a very strange way to ask someone to tell a story,' observed Adelaida, who had meanwhile straightened her easel, taken her brushes and palette and begun to copy a landscape she had begun long ago, from a print. Alexandra and Aglaya sat down together on the small sofa and, folding their arms, prepared to listen to the conversation. The prince noticed that special attention was being directed towards him from all sides.

'If I were ordered like that, I shouldn't say anything,' Aglaya observed.

'Why not? What's strange about it? Why shouldn't he tell us something? He has a tongue. I want to find out how well he talks. About anything, really. Tell us your view of Switzerland, your first impression. Now you'll see, he'll begin at once, and begin splendidly . . .'

'The impression it made on me was a powerful one . . .' the prince began.

'There you are,' the impatient Lizaveta Prokofyevna chipped in, turning to her daughters, 'he's begun.'

'Then at least let him speak, *Maman*,' Alexandra stopped her.

'This prince may be a great fraud, and not an idiot at all,' she whispered to Aglaya.

'Probably, I saw it long ago,' Aglaya replied. 'And it's vile of him to play a role like this. What does he expect to gain from it?'

'My first impression was a very powerful one,' the prince repeated. 'When I was taken out of Russia, through various German towns, I merely looked in silence and, I remember, did not even ask any questions. This was after a series of violent and agonizing attacks of my illness, and always, if the illness got worse and the fits were repeated several times in a row, I used to fall into a complete torpor, wholly lost consciousness, and although my mind continued to function, it was as if the logical flow of my thoughts was broken off. I couldn't connect more than two or three ideas in consecutive order. So it seems to me. But when the fits died down, I again became healthy and strong, as I am now. I remember: there was an unendurable sadness in me; I even wanted to cry; I was constantly astonished and anxious: it had a dreadful effect on me that all this was *foreign*; that I understood. The foreign-ness crushed me. I completely awoke from this darkness, I remember, in the evening, at Basle, on entering Switzerland, and what woke me up was the hee-hawing of a donkey in the town market. The donkey gave me a dreadful shock and for some reason greatly appealed to me, and at the same time it was as if everything in my head suddenly cleared.'

'A donkey? That's strange,' the general's wife observed. 'Though actually, there's nothing strange about it, one of us might easily fall in love with a donkey,' she observed, with an angry glance at the laughing girls. 'It happened in mythology. Continue, prince.'

'Since then I've had a dreadful soft spot for donkeys. There's even a kind of sympathy between us. I began to make inquiries about them, as I'd never seen them before, and was at once convinced that they're a most useful animal, hard-working, strong, patient, inexpensive and long-suffering; and through that donkey I suddenly began to like the whole of Switzerland, so that my earlier sadness passed completely.'

'This is all very strange, but you may omit the donkey; let us go on to another subject. Why do you keep laughing, Aglaya? And you, Adelaida? The prince gave us a splendid description of the donkey. He saw it himself, and what have you seen? Have you been abroad?'

'I've seen a donkey, *Maman*,' said Alexandra.

'And I've heard one, too,' Aglaya chimed in. All three again began to laugh. The prince laughed along with them.

'That's very naughty of you,' the general's wife observed. 'You must excuse them, Prince, they're good-hearted, really. I'm forever quarrelling with them, but I love them. They're giddy and frivolous, crazy.'

'But why?' the prince laughed. 'If I'd been in their place I wouldn't have let the opportunity slip either. I'm still on the donkey's side though: the donkey is a good-hearted and useful fellow.'

'And are you good-hearted, Prince? I ask out of curiosity,' the general's wife inquired.

They all began to laugh again.

'It's that confounded donkey, back again; I wasn't thinking of it!' cried the general's wife. 'Please believe me, Prince, I had no thought of . . .'

'Hinting? Oh, I believe you, beyond all doubt!'

And the prince laughed and laughed.

'It's good that you can laugh. I see that you're a most good-hearted young man,' said the general's wife.

'Sometimes I'm not good-hearted,' the prince replied.

'Well, I *am* good-hearted,' the general's wife inserted unexpectedly. 'And if you really want to know, I'm always good-hearted, and that is my only failing, for one shouldn't always be good-hearted. I very frequently lose my temper, with them, and with Ivan Fyodorovich especially, but the dreadful thing is that when I'm angry I'm at my most good-hearted. Just before your arrival I lost my temper and indulged in play-acting as though I didn't understand anything and couldn't understand anything. I do that sometimes; like a child. Aglaya took me to task for it; thank you, Aglaya. As a matter of fact, it's all nonsense. I'm not as stupid as I seem, and as my daughters would like to make out. I have character, and make no bones about showing it. But I should make clear that I say this without malice. Come here, Aglaya, give me a kiss, that's right . . . and that will do with expressions of affection,' she observed, when Aglaya had kissed her on the lips and on the hand with emotion. 'Continue, Prince. Perhaps you will remember something more interesting than a donkey.'

'I really don't understand how one can tell a story so directly,' Adelaida observed again. 'I would be quite at a loss.'

'But the prince won't be at a loss, because the prince is extremely clever and at least ten times, possibly a dozen times more clever than you. I hope you will be aware of that after this. Prove it to them, Prince; continue. We really can move on from the donkey at last. Well, what did you see abroad apart from a donkey?'

'The bit about the donkey was clever, too,' observed Alexandra. 'The prince was very interesting when he described his bout of illness, and also how after that one external shock he began to like everything. I've always been interested in how people go mad and then recover again. Especially if it happens suddenly.'

'Is that so? Is that so?' the general's wife hurled back at her. 'I see that you can sometimes be clever, too; well, that's enough laughter! You had reached the subject of Switzerland's natural environment, I believe, Prince. Well?'

'We arrived in Lucerne, and I was taken out on the lake. I was aware of how marvellous it was, but at the same time I felt dreadfully miserable,' said the prince.

'Why?' asked Alexandra.

'I don't know. Seeing nature like that for the first time always makes me unhappy and anxious; but this all happened when my illness was still with me.'

'Oh no, but I'd like to see it very much,' said Adelaida. 'And I don't know when we'll be going abroad. I haven't been able to find a subject for a painting for two years: "The East and South were long ago depicted. . ."[2] Prince, find me a subject for a painting.'

'I don't know anything about it. I think one simply looks and paints.'

'I don't know how to look.'

'Why are you talking in riddles? I don't understand any of it,' the general's wife interrupted. 'What do you mean: "I don't know how to look"? You have eyes, so look. If you don't know how to look here, you won't learn abroad either. You had better tell us how you yourself looked, Prince.'

'Yes, that would be better,' Adelaida added. 'After all, the prince learned to look abroad.'

'I don't know; I merely got my health back there; I don't know if I learned to look. Though I was very happy nearly all of the time.'

'Happy? Do you know how to be happy?' exclaimed Aglaya. 'Then how can you say that you didn't learn to look? I expect you could teach us.'

'Yes, do teach us, please,' Adelaida laughed.

'I can't teach anything,' the prince laughed, too. 'I spent nearly all my time abroad in that Swiss village; very rarely I made a short trip somewhere close at hand; so what can I teach you? At first it was merely diverting; I quickly began to recover; then each day became precious to me, and the longer I was there the more precious they became, so I that began to notice it. I would go to bed very contented, and get up even happier. But why it was so it's rather hard to say.'

'So you never felt like going anywhere, you never felt an urge to go anywhere?' asked Adelaida.

'At first, right at the outset, yes, I did feel an urge, and I lapsed into great anxiety. I kept thinking all the time of how I was going to live; I wanted to test my fate, felt anxious particularly at certain moments. You know, there are such moments, particularly when one is in seclusion. We had a waterfall there, a small one, it fell high from the mountain, almost like a fine thread, perpendicular – white, noisy, foaming; it fell from high up but seemed quite low, was more than half a mile distant, but seemed only about fifty yards away. I liked to listen to its noise at night; it was at those moments that I sometimes reached great anxiety. Also sometimes at noon, when I'd go up into the mountains somewhere, stand alone amidst the mountains, around me pine trees, old, large and resinous; on the top of a rock an old

medieval castle, ruins; our little village far below, scarcely visible; a bright sun, a blue sky, a terrible silence. It was there that
something kept calling me somewhere, and I kept thinking that
if I were to walk straight, walk for a very long time and go beyond
that line, the line where earth meets sky, there the whole riddle
around me would be solved and instantly I would see a new life,
a thousand times more powerful and noisy than our own; I kept
dreaming of a big city like Naples, with palaces, noise, thunder,
life . . . Oh, what didn't I dream! And then it seemed to me that
even in prison one might discover an immense life.'

'That last edifying thought is one that I read in my "Reader"
when I was twelve years old,' said Aglaya.

'It's all philosophy,' observed Adelaida. 'You're a philosopher
and have come to teach us.'

'You may be right,' smiled the prince. 'I may be a philosopher,
and, who knows, I may indeed have the aim of teaching people
. . . That may be so; truly, it may.'

'And your philosophy is just the same as Yevlampia Niko-
layevna's,' Aglaya again chimed in. 'She's an official's widow
and comes to see us, a sort of dependant. All she cares about in
life is cheapness; all that matters is how cheaply one can live, all
she talks about is copecks, and, yet, mind you, she has money,
she's an impostor. It's just the same with your immense life in
prison, and perhaps your four years of happiness in the country,
for which you sold your city of Naples, and at a profit, too,
though only a few copecks.'

'On the subject of life in prison one might disagree,' said the
prince. 'I heard the story of a man who spent about twelve years
in prison; he was one of the patients receiving treatment from
my professor. He had fits, was anxious sometimes, wept and
even once tried to kill himself. His life in prison was very sad, I
assure you, but it was not, of course, a matter of copecks. And
all the friends he had were a spider and a little tree that grew
under his window . . . But I'd do better to tell you about another
encounter I had last year with another man. Here there was one
very strange circumstance – strange, really, because incidents of
this kind happen very rarely. This man was once taken up with
others to the scaffold, and the death sentence by firing squad

was read out to him, for a political offence. Some twenty minutes later a reprieve was read out to him, and a different degree of punishment was fixed, but in the interval between the two sentences, twenty minutes, or at least quarter of an hour, he lived in the unquestionable conviction that in a few minutes' time he would face sudden death. I was dreadfully keen to listen when he sometimes recalled his impressions of that time, and I asked him questions about it again on several occasions. He remembered it all with uncommon clarity and said he would never forget anything of those minutes. Some twenty paces from the scaffold, around which stood the people and the soldiers, three posts had been dug into the ground, as there were several criminals. The first three were led up to the posts, bound, dressed in the death apparel (long white loose overalls), and white caps were pulled down over their eyes so that they could not see the rifles; then a company of several soldiers was lined up opposite each post. My acquaintance was eighth on the list, and so he would have to go out to the posts in the third group. A priest went round them all with a cross. It turned out that the man had about five minutes left to live, no more. He said that those five minutes seemed to him an infinite length of time, an immense richness; it seemed to him that during those five minutes he would live so many lives that there was no point in thinking about the last moment yet, so he made various allocations: he calculated the time he needed to say goodbye to his companions, and allotted some two minutes to it, then he allotted another two minutes to think about himself for the last time, and then look around him for the last time. He remembered very well making precisely these three allocations, and that he calculated in precisely this way. He was dying at the age of twenty-seven, healthy and strong; he recalled that as he said farewell to his companions he asked one of them a rather irrelevant question and was even very interested in the reply. Then, after he had taken leave of his companions, came the two minutes he had set aside for *thinking about himself*; he knew in advance what he was going to think about: he kept wanting to imagine as quickly and vividly as he could how it could be like this: now he existed and was alive, but in three minutes' time he would be *something*, someone or something – but who? And where? He thought he would be able to determine all this in those two minutes! Not far away there was a church, and the top of it, with its gilded roof, was sparkling in the bright sunlight. He remembered looking at that roof with awful persistence, and at the beams of light that sparkled from it; he could not tear himself away from them; it seemed to him that they were his new nature, those beams, that in three minutes' time he would somehow fuse with them ... The unknown quality of this new phenomenon and the revulsion which it inspired in him, now that it was coming and would soon be upon him, were dreadful; but he says that nothing was so hard for him at the time as the incessant thought: "What if I didn't have to die? What if I could get my life back – what an infinity it would be! And it would all be mine! Then I would make each minute into a whole lifetime, I would lose nothing, would account for each minute, waste nothing in vain!" He said that this idea finally turned into such fury that he wanted them to shoot him as quickly as possible.'

The prince suddenly fell silent; they all waited for him to continue and draw a conclusion.

'Have you finished?' asked Aglaya.

'What? Yes, I have,' said the prince, emerging from his momentary reflection.

'But why did you tell us about this?'

'I just ... remembered it ... I was making conversation ...'

'You're very abrupt,' observed Alexandra. 'I expect, Prince, you intended to show that not a single moment may be valued in mere copecks, and that sometimes five minutes are more precious than treasure. All that is commendable, but permit me to ask, this friend of yours who told you of such sufferings ... I mean, his sentence was commuted, so he was given that "eternal life". Well, what did he do with that wealth later on? Did he live each minute "accounting" for it?'

'Oh no, he told me himself – I'd already asked him about it – he didn't live like that at all, and wasted far too many minutes.'

'Well then, there's your proof, that means it's impossible to live "counting each minute". For some reason, it's impossible.'

'Yes, for some reason it's impossible,' the prince repeated.

'That's what I thought, too . . . And yet somehow I don't believe it . . .'

'You mean you think you'll live more wisely than anyone else?' said Aglaya.

'Yes, that has sometimes occurred to me.'

'And does it still?'

'Yes . . . it does,' replied the prince, looking at Aglaya as before with a quiet and even timid smile; but at once burst out laughing again and gave her a cheerful look.

'Such modesty!' said Aglaya, almost irritated.

'But how brave you are, here you are laughing, and I was so shocked by all the things in his story that I kept having dreams about it afterwards, kept dreaming about those five minutes . . .'

Once more he cast a searching and earnest gaze over his female listeners.

'You're not angry with me about something, are you?' he asked suddenly, as if embarrassed, but looking them all straight in the eye.

'What for?' all three girls exclaimed in surprise.

'Well, because it's as if I were lecturing you all the time . . .'

They all began to laugh.

'If you're angry, then don't be,' he said. 'I mean, I myself know that I have lived less than others and have less understanding of life. It's possible that I sometimes talk very strangely . . .'

And he decidedly lost his composure.

'If you say you were happy you must have lived more and not less; so why are you wriggling and making excuses?' Aglaya began, sternly and captiously. 'And please do not worry about lecturing us, there is no superiority there on your part. With quiet-ism like yours one could fill a hundred years with happiness. Whether one showed you an execution or a little finger, you would extract an equally edifying thought from both of them, and would still be content. That's the way to get on in life.'

'What you are so angry about, I don't understand,' the gen-eral's wife chimed in, having long been observing their faces as they talked, 'and what you are talking about I don't understand, either. What little finger, and what nonsense is this? The prince speaks beautifully, just a little sadly, that's all. Why are you discouraging him? When he began he was laughing, but now he has gone all dazed and dreamy.'

'Never mind, *Maman*. But Prince, it's a pity you've never seen an execution, there was one thing I wanted to ask you about.'

'I *have* seen a execution,' replied the prince.

'You have?' Aglaya exclaimed. 'I ought to have guessed it! That crowns everything. If you've seen one, how can you say that you lived happily all the time? Well, I'm right am I not?'

'But do they execute people in your village?'

'I saw it at Lyons, I went there with Schneider, he took me. It was the first thing I saw when I arrived.'

'Well, did it appeal to you greatly? Was it very educational? Useful?' asked Aglaya.

'It did not appeal to me at all, and I was rather ill after it, but I will confess that the spectacle riveted me, I couldn't tear my eyes from it.'

'I wouldn't have been able to either,' said Aglaya.

'Over there they don't like women to go and look, there are even articles about those women in the newspapers afterwards.'

'That means that if they don't consider it a matter for women, by the same right they mean to say (and, I suppose, claim in justification) that it's a matter for men. I congratulate them on their logic. And you think the same way, of course?'

'Tell us about the execution,' Adelaida broke in.

'I'd much rather not at the moment . . .' the prince said, becoming embarrassed, and apparently frowning.

'It's as if you grudged telling us,' Aglaya inserted sharply.

'No, it's because I have just been telling someone about that execution.'

'Telling whom?'

'Your valet, while I was waiting . . .'

'What valet?' resounded from all sides.

'The one who sits in the vestibule, he has greying hair and a reddish face; I was sitting in the vestibule waiting to go into Ivan Fyodorovich's study.'

'That's strange,' the general's wife observed.

'The prince is a democrat,' Aglaya snapped. 'Well, if you told Alexey, you really can't refuse to tell us.'

'I certainly want to hear it,' Adelaida repeated.

'Actually, just now,' the prince said turning to her, rather animated again (he seemed to grow animated very quickly and trustingly), 'I actually had the idea, when you asked me for a subject for a painting, of giving you a subject: to paint the face of a condemned man a minute before the guillotine falls, while he's still standing on the scaffold and before he lies down on that plank.'

'You mean the face? Only the face?' asked Adelaida. 'That would be a strange subject, and what sort of painting would it be?'

'I don't know, but why not?' the prince insisted with heat. 'I saw a painting like that at Basle once.[3] I would very much like to tell you . . . I will tell you some time . . . It made a great impression on me.'

'You shall certainly tell us about the Basle painting later,' said Adelaida, 'but now I want you to explain to me the painting of this execution. Can you tell it to me as you imagine it to yourself? How is this face to be painted? Just the face, yes? What is this face like?'

'It's exactly a minute before death,' the prince began with perfect willingness, carried along by memory and, it seemed, at once forgetting about everything else, 'at the very moment he has climbed the short stepladder and has just mounted the scaffold. At that point he glanced in my direction; I looked at his face and understood everything . . . But I mean, how is one to describe it? I should like it terribly, terribly much if you or someone else would paint it! Best if it were you! I thought at the time that a painting would be useful. You know, in this case everything must be portrayed as it was beforehand, everything, everything. He'd been living in prison, expecting his sentence to be at least a week hence; he had somehow been relying on the usual formalities, on the likelihood that the document would have to go somewhere and would take a week to come back. But then suddenly for some reason the procedure was curtailed. At five o'clock in the morning he was asleep. It was the end of October; at five o'clock in the morning it's still cold and dark. The head gaoler came in, quietly, with a guard and cautiously touched him on the shoulder, the man raised himself on one elbow and saw the light: "What is it?" "The execution is at ten." Half awake, he did not believe it, began to argue that the document would not come back for a week yet, but when he had completely woken he stopped arguing and fell silent – so it is told – then said: "All the same, it's hard, coming all of a sudden . . .", again fell silent, and did not want to say any more. At this point three or four hours go by on the usual things: a priest, a breakfast at which he is served wine, coffee and beef (well, is that not mockery? I mean, think how cruel it is, yet on the other hand, as God is their witness, those innocent people are acting from purity of heart and are convinced that it is philanthropy), then the dressing (do you know what dressing is like for a condemned man?), and at last he is taken through the town to the scaffold . . . It seems to me he probably thought on the way: "There's a long time, three streets to live yet; when I've gone along this one, there will still be another, and then yet another, where there's a bakery on the right . . . it will be a long time before we get to the bakery!" All around the crowd, shouting, noise, ten thousand faces, ten thousand eyes – all that has to be borne, and above all, the thought: "Look, there are ten thousand of them, and none of them is being executed, but I'm being executed!" Well, this is all as a preliminary. A short stepladder leads up to the scaffold; at this point, in front of the steps, he suddenly burst into tears, yet this is a strong and courageous man whom they say was a great villain. The priest has been with him constantly, riding with him in the cart, and talking all the time – though the man has scarcely been listening to him: and if he begins to listen, understands no more than a couple of words. That is how it is bound to be. At last he begins to climb the steps; now his legs are tied and so he moves with short steps. The priest, who is doubtless an intelligent man, has stopped talking, and keeps giving him the cross to kiss. At the foot of the steps he was very pale, but when he had climbed them and stood on the scaffold he suddenly turned as white as paper, just like white writing paper. His legs had probably gone weak and numb, and then he felt nausea – as though his throat were being constricted, making it tickle – have you ever felt that, when you were frightened or at moments of great terror, when all of your reason remains but has no power any more? I think that if, for example, doom is inevitable, and the house is collapsing on top of one, one will have a sudden urge to sit down and close one's eyes and wait for what may come next! ... It was at this very point, when this weakness was beginning, that the priest rather more quickly, with a swift gesture, suddenly began to put the cross right to the man's lips without a word, a small cross, silver, four-pointed – doing so frequently, every minute. And as soon as the cross touched his lips, he would open his eyes, and again for a few seconds come to life again, as it were, and his legs moved forward. He kissed the cross avidly, hurried to kiss it, as though he were hurrying lest he forget to take something with him in reserve, just in case, but he would hardly have been aware of anything religious at that moment. And so it continued right up to the plank itself ... It's strange that men seldom faint at these very last seconds! On the contrary, the brain is horribly alive and must work fiercely, fiercely, fiercely, like an engine in motion; I imagine various thoughts chattering, all unfinished, and perhaps ridiculous ones, too, irrelevant ones: "Look at that man staring – he has a wart on his forehead, look at the executioner, one of his lower buttons is rusty" ... and all the while you keep remembering; there is one point like that, which you cannot forget, and you must not faint, and everything moves and whirls around it, around that point. And to think that this goes on until the very last quarter of a second, when your head lies on the block, waits, and *knows*, and suddenly it hears above it the sliding of the iron! That you would certainly hear! If I were lying there I would make a special point of listening for it and hearing it! At that point there would perhaps only be one-tenth of a moment left, but you would certainly hear it! And imagine, to this day there are those who argue that when the head flies off it may possibly for a second know that it has flown off – what a conception! And what if it were five seconds? ... Paint the scaffold so that only the last stair can be seen clearly and closely; the condemned man has stepped on to it: his head, white as paper, the priest holding out the cross, the man extending his blue lips and staring – and *knowing everything.* The cross and the head – that is the paint-ing, the face of the priest, of the executioner, of his two assistants and a few heads and eyes from below – all that may be painted on a tertiary level, as it were, in a mist, as a background . . . That's what the painting should be like.'

The prince fell silent and looked round at them all.

'That is rather different from quietism, of course,' Alexandra said to herself.

'Well, now tell us about when you were in love,' said Adelaida.

The prince looked at her with surprise.

'Listen,' Adelaida went on, as if in a hurry, 'you have still to tell us the story about the Basle painting, but now I want to hear about when you were in love; don't deny it, you've been in love. What's more, as soon as you begin to tell a story you stop being a philosopher.'

'As soon as you finish telling something you at once begin to be ashamed of what you have told,' Aglaya suddenly observed. 'Why is that?'

'Really, how stupid this is,' snapped the general's wife, look-ing at Aglaya in indignation.

'It's not clever,' Alexandra confirmed.

'Don't listen to her, Prince,' the general's wife said, turning to him. 'She's doing it on purpose, out of some kind of spite; she really hasn't been brought up as stupidly as that; don't go away with the idea that they're out to tease you. They've prob-ably got something up their sleeve, but they already like you. I know by their faces.'

'I know by their faces, too,' said the prince, giving his words particular emphasis.

'How can that be?' Adelaida asked with curiosity.

'What do you know about our faces?' the two others also asked curiously.

But the prince said nothing, and looked earnest; they all awaited his reply.

'I'll tell you later,' he said quietly and earnestly.

'You really are trying to arouse our interest,' exclaimed Aglaya, 'and what solemnity!'

'Oh, very well,' Adelaida hurried on again, 'but if you are

such an expert on faces, you must have been in love; so I guessed correctly. Now tell us.'

'I've never been in love,' the prince replied, quietly and gravely as before. 'I . . . was happy in a different way.'

'How, in what way?'

'Very well, I shall tell you,' the prince said softly, as if in deep reflection.

6

'At the moment,' the prince began, 'you're all looking at me with such curiosity that if I don't satisfy it you may perhaps get angry with me. No, I'm joking,' he added quickly with a smile. 'There . . . there it was children all the time, and I spent all my time there with children, only with children. They were the children of that village, a whole band of children who attended the school there. Not that I taught them; oh no, for that there was a schoolteacher, Jules Thibaud; I may have also taught them in a way, but I was mostly just with them, and that was how all my four years passed. I needed nothing more. I told them everything, hid nothing from them. Their fathers and relatives got angry with me because in the end their children couldn't do without me and kept crowding around me, and the school-teacher even became my principal enemy. I made a lot of enemies there, and all because of the children. Even Schneider tried to make me feel ashamed. And what were they so afraid of? One can tell a child everything – everything; I have always been struck by how little adults understand children, even the fathers and mothers of their own children. Nothing should be hidden from children on the pretext that they're too young and it's too soon for them to know. What a sad and unhappy idea! And how well children themselves notice that their fathers consider them too young and devoid of comprehension, while in fact they comprehend everything. Adults don't realize that even in the most difficult matter a child can give extremely useful advice. Oh Lord! When that pretty little bird looks at you, trustingly and happily, why, you feel ashamed to deceive it! I call them little birds because there is nothing finer than a bird in all the world. However, everyone in the village got angry with me most of all because of a certain incident . . . and Thibaud was just envious of me; at first he simply shook his head and wondered how it was that the children understood everything I taught them and almost nothing he did, and then began to laugh at me when I told him that neither of us would teach them anything, but that they would teach us instead. And how could he envy me and spread false rumours about me when he himself lived among the children? Through children the soul is healed . . . There was a certain patient in Schneider's establishment, a very unfortunate man. It was such a dreadful misfortune that there can hardly be anything like it. He had been sent to be treated for insanity; in my opinion, he wasn't insane, he was just suffering horribly – that was all his illness was. And if you knew what our children finally became to him . . . But I had better tell you about that patient later on; for the moment I'll just tell you how it all began. At first the children didn't like me. I was so big, I'm always so awkward; I also know that I'm not good-looking . . . and lastly, I was a foreigner. At first the children laughed at me, and they even began throwing stones at me, when they saw me kissing Marie. And I only kissed her once . . . No, don't laugh,' the prince hurried to check the smiles of his female listeners, 'it had nothing to do with love at all. If you knew what an unhappy creature she was, you would be very sorry for her, as I was. She was from our village. Her mother was an old woman, and in her house, in that small, quite ramshackle cottage, which had two windows, one window was partitioned off, by permission of the village authorities; from that window she was allowed to sell laces, thread, tobacco and soap, all for the most meagre coppers, on which she lived. She was an invalid, and her legs kept swelling up, so that she had to sit still where she was. Marie was her daughter, about twenty, weak and thin; she had long ago begun to suffer from consumption, but she still went from house to house to do heavy work by the day – scrubbed floors, washed linen, swept yards, tended the cattle. A passing French *commis* seduced her and abducted her, but a week later left her alone on the road and quietly rode off. She arrived home, having begged her way, bespattered with mud, in rags, her shoes ripped and torn; she had travelled a whole week on foot, sleeping in fields, and had caught a very bad chill; her feet were covered in lacerations, and her hands were swollen and chapped. Even before that she had not been very pretty, it must be said; though her eyes were quiet, good-natured and innocent. She was terribly quiet. On one occasion, before all this, while at work, she had suddenly started to sing, and I remember that everyone was surprised and began to laugh: "Marie's singing! How do you like that? Marie's singing!" – and she was dreadfully embarrassed and was silent for ever after that. At that time people were still kind to her, but when she returned, ill and tormented, no one had any compassion for her at all! How cruel they are about this! What harsh ideas they have about it! Her mother was the first to receive her with spite and contempt: "You have dishonoured me now." She was also the first to expose her to disgrace: when the people of the village heard that Marie had returned, they all came running to look at her, and almost the whole village crammed itself into the old woman's cottage: old men, children, women, girls, all in such a hurrying, eager crowd. Marie lay on the floor, at the old woman's feet, hungry, ragged, and crying. When they all came running, she hid her bedraggled hair and just pressed herself face down on the floor. Everyone around looked on her as a loathsome creature; the old men condemned her and shouted abuse at her, the young even laughed, the women scolded her, condemned her, regarded her with contempt as if she were some sort of spider. Her mother allowed all this to continue, just sat there, nodding her head and approving. Her mother was very ill at that time, and almost dying; two months later she did indeed die; she knew she was dying, and yet had no thought of being reconciled with her daughter right up to the time of her death, said not a word to her, chased her out to sleep in the passage, almost did not even feed her. She frequently had to put her infirm legs in warm water; each day Marie washed her legs and looked after her; she accepted all her services in silence and never said a kind word to her. Marie endured it all, and later, when I got to know her,

I noticed that she herself approved of all this, and considered herself the very lowest of creatures. When the old woman took to her bed for good, the old women of the village came to look after her, in turn, as is the way there. Then they stopped feeding Marie altogether; and in the village everyone chased her away and no one would even give her any work, as they had done formerly. It was as if everyone spat on her, and the men even stopped thinking of her as a woman, kept saying such vile things to her. Sometimes, very rarely, on a Sunday, when the drunks were in their cups, they would throw her coppers, right there, straight on the ground; Marie would pick them up without saying anything. By then she had begun to cough blood. At last her tattered clothes became real rags, so that she was ashamed to show herself in the village; since the time of her return she had gone barefoot. It was at this point that children in particular, a whole crowd – there were over forty of them, schoolboys – began to tease her and even threw mud at her. She asked the herdsman to let her tend the cows, but the herdsman chased her away. Then she began to take the herd out herself, without permission, spending the whole day away from the house. As she was of great use to the herdsman, and he noticed this, he stopped chasing her away and would sometimes even give her the remains of his own dinner, cheese and bread. He considered this a great kindness on his part. But when her mother died, the pastor at the church had no qualms about holding Marie up to universal disgrace. Marie stood behind the coffin, as she was, in her rags, and cried. Many people had gathered to watch her cry and walk behind the coffin; then the pastor – he was still a young man, and his whole ambition was to became a great preacher – turned to them all and pointed at Marie. "There is the one who caused the death of this respected woman" (which wasn't true, as she had already been ill for two years), "there she is standing before you, not daring to look up, because she has been marked by the finger of God; there she is, barefoot and in rags – an example to those who lose their virtue! And who is she? She is this woman's daughter!", and so on in that vein. And imagine, this base talk found favour with nearly all of them, but . . . at this point something unusual happened; at this point the children

intervened, because by now the children were all on my side and
had begun to love Marie. It happened like this. I wanted to do
something for Marie; she was very much in need of money, but
I never had so much as a copeck while I was there. I had a small
diamond pin, and I sold it to a second-hand dealer; he travelled
about the villages and dealt in old clothes. He gave me eight
francs, though it was probably worth forty. For a long time I
tried to meet Marie alone; at last we met outside the village, by
the fence, on a side path that led up the mountain, behind a tree.
There I gave her the eight francs and told her to look after the
money, as I would not have any more, and then kissed her and
told her she should not think that I had any bad intention, and
that I kissed her not because I was in love with her, but because
I felt very sorry for her and because right from the outset I had
not considered her guilty in any way, but only as someone who
was unfortunate. I very much wanted to comfort her right there
and then and to assure her that she should not consider herself
so inferior to everyone else, but I don't think she understood. I
noticed that immediately, though she hardly said anything all
the time and stood before me with her eyes lowered, and terribly
ashamed. When I had finished, she kissed my hand, and I at
once took hers and was about to kiss it, but she quickly pulled
it away. Then suddenly the children saw us, the whole crowd of
them; I learned afterwards that they had been spying on me for
a long time. They began to whistle, clap their hands and laugh,
but Marie ran away as fast as she could. I wanted to talk to
them, but they started to throw stones at me. That same day
everyone found out about it, and the whole village again
pounced on Marie; their dislike of her grew even worse. I even
heard that they wanted to have her punished by the court, but
nothing was done about this, thank God; on the other hand, the
children would not give her a chance, and teased her worse than
before, throwing mud at her; they chased her, she, with her
weak chest, ran away from them, panting for breath, they followed her, shouting abuse at her. On one occasion I even rushed
at them and fought them. Then I began to talk to them, talked
every day, whenever I could. They would sometimes stop and
listen, though they still shouted at her. I told them how unhappy

Marie was; soon they stopped shouting at her and went away in silence. Little by little, we began to talk, and I hid nothing from them; I told them everything. They listened to me with great interest and soon began to feel sorry for Marie. Some of them, when they met her, began to greet her with affection; people there have a custom, when meeting one another – friends or not – of bowing and saying: "How do you do?" I can imagine how astonished Marie must have been. One day two little girls obtained some food and took it to her, delivered it, then came and told me. They said that Marie burst into tears and that now they loved her very much. Soon they all began to love her, and at the same time they suddenly began to love me, too. They took to coming to see me often and kept asking me to tell them things; I think I must have been good at this, because they were very fond of listening to me. And after that I studied and read things just in order to tell them about them later, and I did this for a whole three years. When later everyone – including Schneider – accused me of talking to them like grown-ups, of concealing nothing from them, I replied to them that lying to them was shameful, that they knew it all in any case, no matter how much one tried to hide it from them, and would probably find things out in the wrong sort of way, which they did not with me. All anyone had to do was remember what it was like when they were children. They did not agree . . . I kissed Marie two weeks before her mother died; but by the time the pastor preached his sermon, all the children were on my side. I told them at once of what the pastor had done and helped them to understand what it meant; they all got angry with him, and some went so far as to break his windows with stones. I stopped them because this was bad behaviour, but everyone found out about it at once, and then they began to accuse me of corrupting the children. Then they all discovered that the children loved Marie, and were terribly alarmed; but Marie was happy now. The children were even forbidden to meet her, but they ran to see her and the herd in secret, quite far away, almost half a verst from the village; they brought her sweets, and some simply ran there in order to hug her, give her a kiss, and say: "*Je vous aime, Marie!*" – and then run back at top speed. Marie almost went out of her mind with such sudden happiness; she had never even dreamed of this; she was embarrassed and overjoyed, but above all, the children, especially the little girls, wanted to run to her to tell her that I loved her and talked to them about her an awful lot. They said to her that I had told them all about it, and that now they loved her and felt sorry for her, and always would. Then they ran to me and told me with such joyful, bustling little faces that they had just seen Marie and that Marie sent me her greetings. In the evenings I walked to the waterfall; there was a spot there that was completely closed off from the village side, and around it poplars grew; there in the evenings they came running to me, some of them even secretly. I think that my love for Marie was frightfully pleasing to them, and in this one thing, in all the time I lived there, I deceived them. I did not try to open their eyes to the fact that I did not love Marie at all, or rather, that I was not in love with her, that I was only very sorry for her; I could see by all the signs that they would much prefer it to be as they imagined and had decided between themselves, so I said nothing and maintained the pretence that they had guessed correctly. And to what a degree were those little hearts tactful and affectionate: it seemed to them, among other things, impossible that their good *Léon* should love Marie so, when Marie was so poorly dressed and had no shoes. Imagine, they got her shoes, and stockings, and linen, and even some sort of dress; how they contrived this I do not know; the whole crowd of them worked at it. When I asked them about it they just laughed merrily, while the little girls clapped their hands and gave me a kiss. I sometimes also went in secret to see Marie myself. By now she was very ill, and could only just walk; at last she stopped working for the herdsman, but every morning she went off with the herd none the less. She would sit down apart, on her own; there, beneath an almost straight, sheer rock, there was a ledge; she sat right in the corner, concealed from everyone, on a stone, and sat there all day almost without moving, from early morning until the hour when the herd went back. She was already so weak from consumption that most of the time she sat with her eyes closed, leaning her head against the rock, dozing and breathing heavily; her face had grown as thin as a skeleton's,

and sweat stood out on her forehead and temples. That was
how I always found her. I only came to see her for a minute,
and I also did not want anyone to see me. As soon as I appeared,
Marie at once quivered, opened her eyes and rushed to kiss my
hands. I did not take them away any more, because it made her
happy; all the time I sat there she trembled and cried; several
times, it was true, she started to speak, but it was hard to
understand her. She was like a mad girl, in dreadful agitation
and ecstasy. Sometimes the children came with me. When they
did, they usually stood close by, guarding us from something or
someone, and from this they derived extraordinary pleasure.
When we went away, Marie again remained alone, unmoving
as before, her eyes closed, and leaning her head against the rock;
she was, perhaps, dreaming of something. One morning she
could no longer go out to the herd and remained at home in her
empty house. The children at once found out, and nearly all of
them went to visit her that day; she lay all alone, in her bed. For
two days the children alone looked after her, taking it in turns
to call, but later, when people in the village heard that Marie
was actually dying, old women began to come from the village,
to sit and watch by the bedside. It seemed that the village had
begun to take pity on Marie, for at any rate the children were
not stopped or scolded as they had been formerly. Marie was in
a state of drowsiness all the time, her sleep was uneasy: she kept
coughing dreadfully. The old women would shoo the children
away, but they came running up to the window, sometimes only
for a minute, just to say: "*Bonjour, notre bonne Marie.*" And
as soon as she saw or heard them, she would spring to life, and
at once, not heeding the old women, make efforts to raise herself
on one elbow, nod her head to them, thank them. They brought
her sweets as before, but she hardly ate anything. Because of
them, I assure you, she died almost happy. Because of them she
forgot her black misfortune, as if she had accepted forgiveness
from them, for to the very end she considered herself a great
sinner. Like little birds they beat their wings at her windows
and called to her each morning: "*Nous t'aimons, Marie.*" She
died very soon after that. I had thought she would live much
longer. On the day that preceded her death, before sunset, I

went to see her; I think she recognized me, and I pressed her hand for the last time; how it had withered away! And then suddenly in the morning they came and told me that Marie had died. Now there was no holding the children back: they decked her coffin with flowers and put a garland on her head. Now that she was dead, the pastor at the church did not pour shame on her, and indeed there were very few people at the funeral, only a few who looked in out of curiosity; but when the coffin had to be carried, the children all rushed together to carry it themselves. As they could not manage it alone, they helped, running after the coffin, and crying. Ever since then, the children have constantly honoured Marie's little grave; they deck it with flowers every year, have planted it round with roses. But that funeral marked the beginning of the worst of my persecution by the whole village because of the children. Its main instigators were the pastor and the schoolteacher. The children were firmly forbidden even to meet me, and Schneider even pledged to see to this. But we saw one another none the less, and communicated by means of signs. They would send me little notes they had written. Later on it all settled down, but even at the time it was all right: because of this persecution, I came even closer to the children. In my last year I even almost made it up with Thibaud and the pastor. But Schneider talked to me a lot and argued with me about my harmful "system" with the children. What kind of system did I have? At last, Schneider expressed to me a certain strange thought he had had – this was right before my departure – he told me he was quite convinced that I myself was a complete child, a child, that is, in every sense, that only in my face and stature did I resemble an adult, but that in development, soul, character and, perhaps, even intelligence I was not an adult, and thus I would remain, even were I to live to the age of sixty. I laughed a great deal: he's not right, of course, because what sort of little boy am I? Only one thing is true, however, and that is that I am indeed not fond of being with adults, with people, with grown-ups – and have long noticed this – I'm not fond of it, because I don't know how to be with them. No matter what they say to me, no matter how kind they are to me, for some reason I always find it awkward to be with them, and I'm dreadfully glad when I can get away to my companions, and my companions have always been children, but not because I myself was a child, but because I was simply drawn to children. When, right at the beginning of my life in the village – that was when I used to go off to be melancholy on my own in the mountains – when, wandering alone, I sometimes began to meet them, especially at noon, when that whole noisy crowd was let out of school, running with their little satchels and their slates, with shouting, laughter and games – my entire soul would suddenly begin to strive towards them. I don't know, but I began to feel something exceedingly powerful in every encounter I had with them. I used to stop and laugh with happiness, as I looked at their little darting legs eternally running, at the boys and girls running together, at the laughter and tears (because many of them managed to fight, burst into tears, make it up again, and start another game while they were running home from school), and then I would forget all my melancholy. And later, through-out the whole of those three years, I could never understand how people could be melancholy, or why they felt that way. The whole of my fortunes settled on them. I never even dreamed that I would leave the village, and it never entered my mind that I would ever come here, to Russia. I thought I would be there for ever, but in the end I saw that Schneider could not go on paying for my keep, but then something turned up, something apparently so important that Schneider himself began to press me to go and wrote a letter of reply on my behalf. I shall look into it, and talk it over with someone. It may be that my fortunes will alter entirely, but that is not the point and not the main thing. The main thing is that my entire life has already altered. I left many things there, too many. They have all vanished. I sat in the train and thought: "Now I'm going out among people; it may be that I don't know anything, but a new life has begun."[1] I decided that I would discharge my task honestly and firmly. I might find it boring and awkward to be among people. I made it my top priority to be polite and candid with everyone; after all, no one can demand more of me than that. Perhaps here too I would be considered a child – then let it be so! Everyone regards me as an idiot for some reason. At one time I really was so ill that I did resemble an idiot; but what kind of idiot am I now, when I myself am aware of the fact that people consider me an idiot? I go in and think: 'Very well, they regard me as an idiot, but I'm intelligent, and they don't realize it . . .' I often have that thought. It was only when, in Berlin, I received some little letters from them they had managed to write to me that I realized how much I loved them. It was very painful to get that first letter! How sad they were when they saw me off! They had started saying goodbye to me a month earlier: *"Léon s'en va, Léon s'en va pour toujours!"* Every evening we gathered by the waterfall, and talked all the time about our parting. Sometimes we had just as much fun as we had before; except that, as we went our separate ways for the night, they began to give me tight and ardent hugs, which they had not done before. Some of them used to run to see me in secret, one at a time, simply in order to hug and kiss me in private, not in front of everyone. When I was already setting out on my journey they all, the whole flock of them, accompanied me to the railway station. The station was about a verst away from our village. They tried not to cry, but many of them could not help themselves and sobbed out loud, especially the girls. We were hurrying not to miss the train, but first one and then another would suddenly rush towards me in the middle of the road, embrace me with his little arms and kiss me, holding up the whole crowd only for that; but although we were in a hurry, they would all stop and wait for him to say his farewell. When I got into the carriage and the train moved off, they all shouted "hurrah!" to me and stood there for a long time, until it had completely gone. And I looked, too . . . You know, when I came in here just now and beheld your nice faces – I study faces closely now – and heard your first words, I felt a weight lift from my soul for the first time since then. I was already thinking just now that perhaps I really was one of the fortunate ones: I mean, I know that it isn't easy to find people whom one likes straight away, but I met you as soon as I got off the train. I'm well aware that everyone finds it embarrassing to talk about their feelings, and yet here I am talking to you about them, and with you I don't feel embarrassed. I'm an unsociable person, and it may be that it will be a

long time before I come and visit you. But don't take that as an
unkind thought: I didn't say it because I don't value you; and
please don't think that I've taken offence at anything, either.
You asked me about your faces, and what I could see in them. I
will tell you that with great pleasure. You, Adelaida Ivanovna,
have a happy face, the most sympathetic face of the three. In
addition to the fact that you are very pretty, when one looks at
you, one says: "She has a face like that of a kind sister." Your
approach is simple and cheerful, but you are quickly able to
understand someone's heart. That's my impression of your face.
Your face, Alexandra Ivanovna, is also beautiful and very nice,
but perhaps you have some secret sadness; your soul is without
doubt most kind, but you are not cheerful. You have a certain
nuance in your face; it resembles that of the Holbein Madonna
in Dresden.[2] Well, that's what I think of your face; am I a good
diviner? After all, you yourselves consider me a diviner. But of
your face, Lizaveta Prokofyevna,' he said, turning to the general's wife suddenly, 'of your face I don't merely think, I am quite
certain that you are a perfect child, in everything, everything, in
all that is good and all that is bad, in spite of the fact that you
are the age you are. You're not angry with me for putting it like
that? After all, you know the respect I have for children! And
don't go thinking that I've said all these candid things about
your faces out of naivety; oh no, not at all! Perhaps I have a
motive of my own, too.'

7

When the prince fell silent they all looked at him cheerfully,
even Aglaya, but especially Lizaveta Prokofyevna.

'There, they've given you an examination!' she exclaimed.
'Well, dear ladies, you thought you would make him a protégé,
like some poor little thing, but he scarcely deigned to choose
you, even adding the proviso that he'll only come and see you
now and then. Now it's our turn to look foolish, and I'm glad;
and Ivan Fyodorovich looks most foolish of all. Bravo, Prince,

we were told to subject you to an examination just now. And what you said about my face was all quite true: I am a child, I know that. I was aware of it even before you told me; you really did express my own thoughts in a single word. I consider your character entirely like my own, and am very glad; like two drops of water. Only you're a man and I'm a woman and have never been in Switzerland; that's the only difference.'

'Don't be too hasty, *Maman*,' exclaimed Aglaya. 'The prince says that in all his confessions he had a special motive and was speaking with some hidden design.'

'Yes, yes,' the others laughed.

'Do not mock him, my dears, he may be more cunning than all three of you put together. You'll see. The only thing, Prince, is why didn't you say anything about Aglaya? Aglaya is waiting, and I am waiting.'

'I can't say anything just now; I'll say it later.'

'Why? She is striking, is she not?'

'Oh yes, indeed; you are extremely beautiful, Aglaya Ivanovna. You are so pretty that one is afraid to look at you.'

'Is that all? What about her qualities?' the general's wife insisted.

'Beauty is difficult to judge; I'm not ready yet. Beauty is a riddle.'

'That means you've set Aglaya a riddle,' said Adelaida. 'Solve it, Aglaya. But she's pretty, Prince, she's pretty, isn't she?'

'Extremely!' the prince replied warmly, glancing at Aglaya with animation. 'Almost like Nastasya Filippovna, though her face is quite different! . . .'

They all exchanged looks in surprise.

'Like who-o-o?' the general's wife said slowly. 'Like Nastasya Filippovna? Where did you see Nastasya Filippovna? Which Nastasya Filippovna?'

'Gavrila Ardalionovich was showing Ivan Fyodorovich a portrait of her just now.'

'What, he brought Ivan Fyodorovich a portrait?'

'To show it. Nastasya Filippovna made a present of her portrait to Gavrila Ardalionovich today, and he brought it to show.'

'I want to see it!' the general's wife leaped to her feet. 'Where is this portrait? If she gave it to him, it must be in his study, and, of course, he's still in there. On Wednesdays he always comes in to work and he never leaves before four. Summon Gavrila Ardalionovich at once! No, I'm not exactly dying with eagerness to see him. Do me a favour, Prince, dear, go into his study, get the portrait from him and bring it here. Tell him it's so we can have a look at it. Please.'

'He's nice, but a bit simple-minded,' said Adelaida, when the prince had gone out.

'Yes, rather too much so,' Alexandra confirmed. 'So much that it's even slightly ridiculous.'

Neither the one nor the other seemed to be expressing all that was in their thoughts.

'Though he got out of that part about our faces very well,' said Aglaya. 'He flattered everyone, even *Maman*.'

'No witticisms, please!' exclaimed the general's wife. 'It wasn't he who did the flattering, but I who was flattered.'

'You think he was trying to get out of it?' asked Adelaida.

'I don't think he's so simple-minded.'

'Oh, get along with you!' the general's wife said, losing her temper. 'And if you ask me, you're more ridiculous than he is. He's simple-minded, but he has all his wits about him, in the most noble sense of the word, of course. Just as I do.'

'It was bad of me to let it slip about the portrait, of course,' the prince mused to himself, going through to the study and feeling a certain pang of conscience. 'But . . . perhaps I did well to let it slip . . .' A strange idea, though it was not yet quite clear, was beginning to flit through his head.

Gavrila Ardalionovich was still sitting in the study, immersed in his papers. It must have been true that he did not draw his salary from the joint-stock company for nothing. He was dreadfully embarrassed when the prince asked for the portrait and told him how they had found out about it.

'E-e-ch! And why did you have to blab about it,' he exclaimed in angry vexation. 'You don't know anything . . . Idiot!' he muttered to himself.

'I'm sorry, I did it quite without thinking; it seemed apropos.

I said that Aglaya was almost as pretty as Nastasya Filippovna.'

Ganya asked him to recount the matter in more detail; the prince did so. Ganya looked at him mockingly again.

'You've got Nastasya Filippovna on the brain . . .' he muttered, but did not finish his sentence, and fell to brooding.

He was visibly anxious. The prince reminded him about the portrait.

'Listen, Prince,' Ganya said suddenly, as though an unexpected thought had struck him. 'I have an enormous favour to ask of you . . . But I really don't know . . .'

He became confused, and did not finish what he was saying; he was trying to make his mind up about something, and seemed to be struggling with himself. The prince waited in silence. Once more, Ganya surveyed him with a fixed, searching stare.

'Prince,' he began again, 'in there just now . . . because of a certain very strange circumstance . . . and also a ridiculous one . . . for which I am not to blame . . . well, actually, this is superfluous . . . I think they're a little angry with me, so I don't want to go in for a while unless I'm asked. I really do terribly need to talk to Aglaya Ivanovna now. I've written a few words just in case (he was holding a small, folded piece of paper) – but I don't know how to get it to her. Prince, would you undertake to give it to Aglaya Ivanovna, right now, but only to Aglaya Ivanovna, that's to say, so that no one else sees it, you understand? Lord knows, it isn't any kind of a secret, there's nothing of that sort . . . but . . . will you do it?'

'I don't feel very comfortable about it,' the prince replied.

'Oh, Prince, it's really urgent!' Ganya began to implore. 'She may reply . . . Believe me, I would only have turned to you in an extreme, in the most extreme situation . . . Who can I get to deliver it? . . . It's very important . . . Terribly important to me . . .'

Ganya was horribly afraid that the prince would not agree, and began to look him in the eye, with a gaze of timid pleading.

'Very well, I'll give it to her.'

'Only it must be done so no one notices,' Ganya beseeched, overjoyed, 'and I say, Prince – I mean, I rely on your word of honour, eh?'

'I won't show it to anyone,' said the prince.

'The note isn't sealed, but . . .' Ganya let slip in his turmoil, and stopped in embarrassment.

'Oh, I shan't read it,' the prince replied quite simply, took the portrait and walked out of the study.

Ganya, left alone, clutched his head.

'A single word from her, and . . . and truly, I may break it off with her! . . .'

He could no longer sit down at his papers again, so excited and expectant was he, and began to wander about the study from one corner to another.

The prince went off, in reflection; the errand had struck him unpleasantly, as had the thought of Ganya's note to Aglaya. But while he was still two rooms away from the drawing room, he suddenly stopped, as though remembering something, looked round, went over to the window, closer to the light, and began to look at the portrait of Nastasya Filippovna.

It was as if he were trying to decipher something that was hidden in this face and had struck him earlier. His earlier impression had remained with him almost intact, and now he seemed to be hurrying to check something again. This face, unusual in its beauty and also for some other quality, struck him even more powerfully now. There was in this face something that resembled an immense pride and contempt, hatred, almost, and at the same time something trusting, something extremely artless; as one beheld these features, the two contrasts even seemed to arouse a kind of compassion. This dazzling beauty was positively unendurable, the beauty of the pale face, the almost hollow cheeks and the burning eyes; a strange beauty! The prince looked for about a minute, then suddenly recollected himself, glanced about him, and hurriedly brought the portrait to his lips, and kissed it. When, a minute later, he entered the drawing room, his face was completely calm.

But no sooner had he stepped into the dining room (one room away from the drawing room) than he almost collided in the doorway with Aglaya, who was coming out. She was alone.

'Gavrila Ardalionovich asked me to bring this to you,' said the prince, giving her the note.

Aglaya stopped, took the note, and gave the prince a rather strange look. There was not the slightest embarrassment in her gaze, except perhaps for a certain glint of surprise, and even that seemed to relate only to the prince. It was as if, with her gaze, Aglaya were demanding that he account for himself – how had he got involved in this business with Ganya? – and demanding calmly, and from a position of superiority. For a moment or two they stood facing each other; at last, a kind of mocking expression was barely delineated in her features; she smiled faintly and walked past.

The general's wife examined the portrait of Nastasya Filippovna for some time, silently and with a nuance of disdain, holding it in front of her with her arm outstretched, keeping it at a distance from her gaze, and with much effect.

'Yes, pretty,' she said quietly, at last, 'even very pretty. I've seen her twice, but only from afar. So that's the sort of beauty you like?' she said, turning to the prince suddenly.

'Yes . . . that sort . . .' the prince replied with a certain effort.

'You mean precisely that sort?'

'Precisely that sort.'

'Why?'

'In that face . . . there is much suffering . . .' the prince said quietly, almost involuntarily, as though he were talking to himself, and not answering a question.

'Well, I really think you may be talking nonsense,' the general's wife decided, and with a haughty gesture threw the portrait away from her on to the table.

Alexandra took the portrait, Adelaida went over to her, and they both began to examine it. At that moment Aglaya returned to the drawing room.

'What power!' Adelaida suddenly exclaimed, eagerly scrutinizing the portrait over her sister's shoulder.

'Where? What power?' Lizaveta Prokofyevna asked sharply.

'Beauty like that is power,' Adelaida said hotly. 'With beauty like that one may turn the world upside down!'

Reflectively, she walked over to her easel. Aglaya gave the portrait only a fleeting glance, narrowed her eyes, stuck out her lower lip, and went to sit down at one side, with her arms folded.

The general's wife rang the bell.

'Tell Gavrila Ardalionovich to come here, he's in the study,' she ordered the servant who entered.

'*Maman!*' Alexandra exclaimed meaningfully.

'I just want to say a couple of words to him!' the general's wife snapped quickly, stopping the objection. She was apparently irritated. 'As you can see, Prince, we have nothing but secrets here just now. Nothing but secrets! It's *de rigueur*, a kind of etiquette, a stupid one. And this in a matter that demands the greatest possible frankness, clarity and honesty. There's marriage in the air, and not the kind of marriage for which I particularly care . . .'

'*Maman*, what *are* you talking about?' Alexandra hurried to stop her again.

'What is it to you, dear daughter? Do *you* care for it? Let the prince hear, for we are friends. He and I are, at least. God looks for people, good ones, of course, but he has no use for the bad and capricious; especially the capricious, who today decide one thing, and tomorrow say another. Do you understand, Alexandra Ivanovna? They say I'm an eccentric, Prince, but I have discernment. For the heart is the main thing, and the rest is rubbish. Intelligence plays a role, too, of course . . . perhaps intelligence is the main thing. Don't smile like that, Aglaya, I'm not contradicting myself: a silly woman with a heart and no intelligence is just as unhappy as one with intelligence and no heart. That's an old truth. I'm a silly woman with a heart and no intelligence, and you're a silly woman with intelligence and no heart; we're both unhappy, and we both suffer.'

'What makes you so unhappy, *Maman*?' Adelaida could not help asking, apparently alone among the whole company in not having lost her cheerful disposition.

'For one thing, educated daughters do,' snapped the general's wife, 'and as that in itself is enough, there's no point in going into the rest. There's been enough verbosity. We shall see how the two of you (I don't count Aglaya) get out of it with your intelligence and verbosity, and whether you, my much esteemed Alexandra Ivanovna, will be happy with your honourable gentleman ... Ah! ...' she exclaimed, seeing Ganya enter. 'Here's another matrimonial union. How do you do?' she replied to Ganya's bow, without asking him to sit down. 'Are you entering upon marriage?'

'Marriage? ... What ...? What marriage?' Gavrila Ardalionovich muttered, astounded. He was dreadfully taken aback.

'I'm asking you, are you about to be wedded, if you prefer that expression?'

'N-no ... I ... n-no ...' Gavrila Ardalionvich lied, and a blush of shame suffused his face. He cast a fleeting glance at Aglaya, where she sat to one side, and quickly took his eyes away again. Aglaya stared at him coldly, fixedly and calmly, not averting her gaze, and observing his confusion.

'No? Did you say no?' the inexorable Lizaveta Prokofyevna continued to question him. 'That will do, I shall remember that today, Wednesday morning, you answered "no" to my question. It's Wednesday today, isn't it?'

'I think so, *Maman.*'

'They never know what day it is. What's the date?'

'The twenty-seventh,' replied Ganya.

'The twenty-seventh? That's good, for a certain reason. Goodbye. I am sure you have a lot to do, and I must dress and go out; take your portrait with you. Give my greetings to poor Nina Alexandrovna. *Au revoir*, dear Prince! Come and see us often, and I shall drop in on old Belokonskaya with the express purpose of telling her about you. And listen, my dear: I believe that God has brought you to St Petersburg from Switzerland especially for me. It may be that you will have other things to do as well, but it is mainly for me. God has arranged it specially this way. *Au revoir*, my dears. Alexandra, come through and see me for a moment, dear.'

The general's wife went out. Ganya, frustrated, embarrassed, and full of anger, took the portrait from the table and, with a twisted smile, addressed the prince:

'Prince, I'm going home now. If you haven't changed your mind about staying with us, I'll take you there, for you don't even know the address.'

'Wait, Prince,' said Aglaya, suddenly rising from her armchair.

'I want you to write something in my album. Papa said you're a calligraphist. I'll bring it to you in a moment . . .'

And she went out.

'*Au revoir*, Prince, I'm leaving, too,' said Adelaida.

She squeezed the prince's hand tightly, smiled at him affably and kindly, and went out.

'It was you,' Ganya began to grind out, suddenly hurling himself on the prince as soon as they had all left, 'it was you who blabbed that I'm getting married!' he muttered in a quick semi-whisper, his face livid and his eyes flashing with spite. 'You shameless blabbermouth!'

'I assure you that you are mistaken,' the prince replied calmly and politely. 'I didn't even know that you are getting married.'

'You heard Ivan Fyodorovich say earlier on that everything will be decided at Nastasya Filippovna's this evening, and that's what you told them! You're lying! Where else could they have heard it from? The devil take it, who could have told them apart from you? The old woman hinted as much to me, didn't she?'

'You're the one who should know who told them if you think you were given a hint, I said not a word about it.'

'Did you deliver the note? Was there a reply?' Ganya interrupted him with feverish impatience. But at that very moment Aglaya returned, and the prince had no time to answer.

'Here, Prince,' said Aglaya, putting her album on the table. 'Choose a page and write something for me. Here is a pen, and a new one, too. Is it all right that it's a steel one? I've heard that calligraphists don't use steel ones.'

As she talked to the prince, she did not seem to notice Ganya's presence. But while the prince adjusted the pen, found the right page and got himself ready, Ganya went over to the fireplace, where Aglaya was standing, immediately on the prince's right, and in a trembling, faltering voice said, almost straight into her ear:

'One word, only one word from you – and I am saved.'

The prince turned quickly and looked at them both. In Ganya's face there was real despair; he seemed to utter these words almost without thinking, at lightning speed. Aglaya

looked at him for a few seconds with exactly the same calm
surprise as she had earlier looked at the prince, and this calm
surprise of hers, this bewilderment, as if stemming from a complete failure to understand what was being said to her, was at
that moment more dreadful to Ganya than the most withering
contempt.

'What shall I write, then?' asked the prince.

'I'll dictate it to you in a moment,' said Aglaya, turning to
him. 'Ready? Write: "I do not bargain." Now write the date
and the month underneath. Show me.'

The prince handed her the album.

'Magnificent! You've done it splendidly: you have wonderful
handwriting. Thank you. *Au revoir*, Prince . . . Wait,' she added,
as if remembering something. 'Come along, I want to give you
something as a keepsake.'

The prince followed her; but, as they entered the dining room,
Aglaya paused.

'Read this,' she said, giving him Ganya's note.

The prince took the note and looked at Aglaya in bewilderment.

'After all, I know you haven't read it and cannot possibly be
that man's confidant. Read it, I want you to read it through.'

The note had obviously been written in a hurry:

Today my fate will be decided, you know in what way. Today I
will have to give my word irrevocably. I have no right to your
sympathy, I do not dare to have any hopes; but once you uttered
one word, one single word, and that word illumined the whole of
my life's dark night and became for me a beacon. Say one more
such word to me now – and you will save me from perdition! Say
to me only: *break it all off*, and I will break it off today. Oh, what
will it cost you to say it? In that word I beg only a sign of your
sympathy and pity for me – and that is all, *all*! And nothing more,
nothing! I do not dare to contemplate any hope, because I am not
worthy of it. But after your word I will again accept my poverty
and with joy will start to endure my desperate position. I will face
the struggle, I will be glad of it, I will rise up again in it with new
strength!

Send me this word of compassion (of compassion *alone*, I swear
to you!). Do not be angry at the insolence of a desperate, a
drowning man, for having dared to make a last attempt to save
himself from perdition.

G. I.

'This man assures me,' Aglaya said sharply, when the prince
had finished reading, 'that the words: *break it all off* will not
compromise me and will not bind me to anything, and himself
gives me a written guarantee of this, as you can see from this
note. Observe how naively he has hurried to underline certain
words, and how crudely his secret motive shows through. He
knows, however, that if he broke it all off himself, alone, without
waiting for my word and not even telling me about it, without
any hopes of me, then I would change my feelings for him and
perhaps become his friend. He knows it for certain! But he has
a sordid soul: he knows and cannot make up his mind; he knows
and yet asks for a guarantee. He is not able to act on faith. He
wants me to give him hope of obtaining me in exchange for a
hundred thousand. With regard to my earlier word, which he
mentions in the note and which is supposed to have illumined
his life, he is brazenly lying. I once merely felt sorry for him. But
he is insolent and shameless: the thought then at once flashed
across his mind that there was the chance of hope; I realized
that instantly. Ever since then he has begun to try to ensnare
me; he is doing so still. But enough; take the note and give it
back to him, in a moment, when you have left our house, of
course, not before.'

'And what shall I say to him in reply?'

'Nothing, of course. That is the best reply. So you want to
stay at his house, do you?'

'Ivan Fyodorovich himself earlier recommended me to do so,'
said the prince.

'Then beware of him, I warn you; he will not forgive you now
for returning his note to him.'

Aglaya gave the prince's hand a light squeeze and went out.
Her face was serious and frowning, and she did not even smile
as she nodded to him in farewell.

'I'll be with you in a moment, I'll just get my bundle,' said the prince to Ganya, 'and then we can go.'

Ganya stamped his foot with impatience. His face even darkened with fury. At last they both came out on to the street, the prince holding his bundle.

'The reply? The reply?' Ganya pounced on him. 'What did she say to you? Did you give her the letter?'

The prince silently handed him the note. Ganya was speechless.

'What? My note!' he exclaimed. 'He didn't even deliver it! Oh, I should have guessed! Oh, damn-ation . . . Now I see why she didn't understand anything just now! But why, why did you not deliver it, oh, damn-ation . . .'

'Forgive me, on the contrary, I succeeded in giving her your note at once, straight after you gave it to me, and exactly as you asked. I had it again because Aglaya Ivanovna gave it back to me just now.'

'When? When?'

'As soon as I'd finished writing in her album, and when she asked me to accompany her. (Did you hear?) We went into the dining room and she gave me your note, asked me to read it, and told me to give it back to you.'

'Re-e-ad it?' Ganya shouted, almost at the top of his voice. 'Read it? You read it?'

And again he stood rigid in the middle of the pavement, but so amazed that his mouth even fell open.

'Yes, I did, just now.'

'And she herself, she herself let you read it? She herself?'

'Yes, and you must believe me, I wouldn't have read it had she not asked me to.'

Ganya said nothing for a minute, working something out with agonizing effort, and then suddenly exclaimed:

'It can't be true! She couldn't possibly have asked to read it. You're lying! You read it yourself!'

'I'm telling the truth,' the prince replied in his earlier, completely imperturbable tone, 'and you must believe me: I'm very sorry that it makes you feel so bad.'

'But wretched man, did she not at least say something to you at the time? Did she not make some reply?'

'Yes, of course.'

'Then tell me, tell me, oh, the devil! . . .'

And Ganya stamped his right foot, in its galosh, twice upon the pavement.

'As soon as I'd read it, she told me that you were angling for her; that you wanted to compromise her in order to receive hope from her, and, while gaining support from that hope, to give up the other hope of a hundred thousand. That if you had done so without bargaining with her, if you had broken it all off yourself, without asking her for a guarantee in advance, she might perhaps have become your friend. I think that's all. Yes, also: when, having taken the note, I asked if there was any reply, she said that the best reply would be no reply – I think that's what she said; I'm sorry if I've forgotten her exact words, I'm telling it as I understood it.'

A boundless spite took possession of Ganya, and his rabid fury broke through without any restraint.

'Hah! So that's it!' he ground out. 'She throws my notes out of the window! Hah! *She* doesn't bargain – then I will! And we shall see! I've a trick or two left yet . . . we shall see! . . . I'll make her toe the line! . . .'

He grimaced, turned pale, foamed at the mouth; he shook his fist. They walked several yards like this. He stood not on the slightest ceremony with the prince, as though he were in his own room, because he really did consider the prince a total nonentity. But suddenly he thought of something, and pulled himself together.

'But how was it,' he suddenly addressed the prince, 'how was it that you' (an idiot, he added to himself) 'were suddenly taken into such confidence only two hours after your first acquaintance? How was that?'

Of all his torments, only envy was missing. It suddenly bit him to the heart.

'I'm really not able to explain that to you,' replied the prince.

Ganya looked at him with spite.

'It wasn't in order to take you into her confidence that she asked you to go into the dining room, was it? I mean, she was going to give you something, wasn't she?'

'I can't account for it otherwise.'

'But why, the devil take it? What did you do there? Why did they like you? Listen,' he said, agitated in every fibre of his being (at that moment everything in him was somehow scattered and seething with disorder, so that he could not gather his thoughts), 'listen, can't you remember at least something and work out in order what you actually talked about, all your words, right from the beginning? Didn't you notice anything, don't you recall?'

'Oh, I can easily do that,' the prince replied. 'Right at the start, when I came in and was introduced, we began to talk about Switzerland.'

'Oh, to the devil with Switzerland!'

'Then about the death penalty . . .'

'The death penalty?'

Yes; it was apropos of something . . . then I told them about the three years I lived there, and a story about a poor village girl . . .'

'Oh, to the devil with the poor village girl! Go on!' Ganya burst out in impatience.

'Then how Schneider told me his opinion of my character and compelled me to . . .'

'May the deuce swallow Schneider and spit on his opinions! Go on!'

'Then, apropos of something, I began to talk about faces, that is, the expression of faces, and said that Aglaya Ivanovna was almost as pretty as Nastasya Filippovna. It was then that I let it slip about the portrait . . .'

'But you did not retell, I mean to say, you did not retell what you had earlier heard in the study? Did you? Did you?'

'I repeat to you, I did not.'

'Then how the devil . . . Bah! Aglaya didn't show the note to the old woman, did she?'

'On that account I can most fully guarantee that she did not. I was there throughout; and in any case, she had no time.'

'Well, perhaps there was something you didn't notice . . . Oh, damn-able idiot!' he exclaimed, now completely beside himself, 'he can't even tell anything properly!'

Ganya, once he had begun to hurl abuse and encountered no

resistance, little by little lost all restraint, as is always the case with some people. A little longer, and he would perhaps have begun to spit, so rabidly furious was he. But it was precisely this fury that made him blind; otherwise he would long ago have paid attention to the fact that this 'idiot' whom he was slighting in this way was sometimes able only too swiftly and subtly to understand everything and tell it all in an exceedingly satisfactory manner. But suddenly something unexpected happened.

'I must observe to you, Gavrila Ardalionovich,' the prince said suddenly, 'that earlier I really was so unwell that I was indeed almost an idiot; but now I have long since recovered, and so I find it somewhat unpleasant when I am called an idiot to my face. Although you may be forgiven, taking into account the setbacks you have met with, in your vexation you have even abused me a couple of times. I really do not wish it, especially like this, suddenly, right from the outset; and as we are now standing at a crossroads, would it not be better for us to go our separate ways? You can turn to the right, and go home, and I will turn left. I have twenty-five roubles and I'm sure I can find some *hôtel garni*.'

Ganya was horribly embarrassed, and even blushed with shame.

'Forgive me, Prince,' he exclaimed hotly, suddenly changing his abusive tone to one of exceeding politeness, 'for God's sake, forgive me! You see what trouble I'm in. You know almost nothing, but if you knew everything you would probably forgive me at least a little; although, of course, I am beyond forgiveness . . .'

'Oh, I don't need such profuse apologies,' the prince hurried to reply. 'I mean, I understand how unpleasant it is for you, and that is why you are being so rude. Well, let us go to your house. I shall come with pleasure . . .'

'No, I can't let him off the hook that easily,' Ganya thought to himself, looking spitefully at the prince as they walked, 'that rogue wheedled everything out of me and then suddenly took off his mask . . . That means something. Well, we shall see! Everything will be decided, everything, everything! This very day!'

They were already standing outside the house.

8

Ganya's apartment was on the third floor, on a very clean, light and spacious staircase, and consisted of six or seven rooms and roomlets, in themselves unremarkable, but at any rate not quite affordable by a functionary with a family, even if he were in receipt of a two-thousand-rouble salary. It was, however, intended for the keeping of lodgers with meals and service, and had been occupied by Ganya and his household no more than two months earlier, to the very great displeasure of Ganya himself, on the pleas and insistence of Nina Alexandrovna and Varvara Ardalionovna, who wished in their turn to be useful and at least increase the family income somewhat. Ganya would frown and call the keeping of lodgers a disgrace; after this he seemed to become ashamed in society, where he was accustomed to appearing as a brilliant young man with a fine future ahead of him. All these concessions to fate and all this annoying crowdedness – these were deep spiritual wounds for him. For some time now he had begun to be irritated beyond measure and proportion by all kinds of trivial things, and if temporarily he agreed to concede and endure, it was only because he had decided to change and modify all this in a very short space of time. And yet this very change, this way out he had determined on, constituted no small task – a task whose imminent solution threatened to be more troublesome and tormenting than all that had gone before.

The apartment was divided by a corridor, which began right in the entrance hall. On one side of the corridor were the three rooms that were intended to be rented out to 'specially recommended' lodgers; in addition, on the same side of the corridor, right at its far end, next to the kitchen, there was a fourth small room, more cramped than all the others, in which retired General Ivolgin himself, the father of the household, had his quarters, sleeping on a broad sofa and obliged to leave or enter the apartment through the kitchen, and by the back stairs. Gavrila Ardalionovich's thirteen-year-old brother, the schoolboy Kolya, was also accommodated in this room; he was also destined to be squeezed in here, to study, sleep on another, very old, narrow and short little sofa, with a sheet full of holes, and, above all, to tend to and look after his father, who was becoming less and less able to manage without this. The prince was allocated the middle of the three rooms; in the first, to the right, lived Ferdyshchenko, while the third, to the left, was still empty. But first Ganya took the prince to the family quarters. These family quarters consisted of a reception room, which was turned, when necessary, into a dining room; a drawing room, which was actually only a drawing room in the morning, and in the evening became Ganya's study and his bedroom; and, finally, a third room, narrow and always closed: this was the bedroom of Nina Alexandrovna and Varvara Ardalionovna. In a word, everything in this apartment was crowded and cramped; Ganya just gritted his teeth and kept going; although he was, and wanted to be, deferential to his mother, it was obvious from one's first moment in their home that he was the household's great despot.

Nina Alexandrovna was not alone in the drawing room, Varvara Ardalionovna was sitting with her; they were both occupied with some sort of knitting and were talking to a visitor, Ivan Petrovich Ptitsyn. Nina Alexandrovna appeared to be about fifty, with a thin, drawn face and pronounced dark circles under her eyes. She had an ill and somewhat mournful look, but her face and gaze were rather pleasant; from her first words, a serious character full of genuine dignity announced itself. In spite of her sorrowful look, one sensed in her firmness, and even determination. She was dressed with exceeding modesty, in something black and quite old-lady-like, but her ways, conversation and entire manner revealed a woman who had seen the best society. Varvara Ardalionovna was a girl of about twenty-three, of medium stature and rather thin, with a face which, although it was not markedly pretty, had the secret of appealing without beauty, and being inordinately attractive. She looked very like her mother, was even dressed in the same way as her mother, out of a complete reluctance to array herself in fine clothes. The gaze of her grey eyes might sometimes have been very cheerful and affectionate, if it was not most frequently serious and reflective, sometimes even too much so, especially of late. Firmness and determination were also visible in her face, but one had a sense that this firmness could be even more energetic and enterprising than her mother's. Varvara Ardalionovna was rather quick-tempered, and her brother was sometimes even rather afraid of this quick temper. The visitor who sat with them now, Ivan Petrovich Ptitsyn, was also rather afraid of it. He was still quite a young man, aged around thirty, modestly but elegantly dressed, with pleasant but somehow excessively sedate manners. A small dark brown beard designated him as someone who was not employed in the civil service.[1] He was able to converse intelligently and interestingly, but more frequently said nothing. In general he even made a pleasant impression. He was apparently not indifferent to Varvara Ardalionovna and did not hide his feelings. Varvara Ardalionovna treated him in a friendly way, but to some of his questions she still delayed in making a reply, did not like them, even; Ptitsyn was, however, far from being discouraged. Nina Alexandrovna was affectionate towards him, and had recently begun to confide many things to him. It was, however, known that his speciality was the lending of money at high interest on more or less guaranteed security. With Ganya he was on exceedingly close terms.

After a detailed but jerky introduction from Ganya (who greeted his mother very coldly, did not greet his sister at all and at once led Ptitsyn out of the room somewhere) Nina Alexandrovna said a few words of welcome to the prince and told Kolya, who emerged through the door, to take him to the middle room. Kolya was a boy with a cheerful and rather sweet face, and a trusting and straightforward manner.

'But where's your luggage?' he asked, leading the prince into the room.

'I have a bundle; I left it in the vestibule.'

'I'll bring it to you at once. Our only servants are the cook and Matryona, so I help as well. Varya inspects everything and gets cross. Ganya says you came from Switzerland today?'

'Yes.'

'And is it nice in Switzerland?'

'Very.'

'Mountains?'

'Yes.'

'I'll go and get your bundles at once.'

Varvara Ardalionovna came in.

'Matryona will make your bed in a moment. Have you a trunk?'

'No, a bundle. Your brother has gone to get it; it's in the vestibule.'

'There are no bundles there apart from this little one; where did you put them?' asked Kolya, returning to the room again.

'That's the only one there is,' the prince announced, taking his bundle.

'Aha! And I thought Ferdyshchenko might have walked off with them.'

'Don't talk nonsense,' Varya said in a stern tone of voice – even to the prince she spoke very coldly, in a tone that was only just polite.

'*Chère Babette*, you could treat me a little more kindly, I'm not Ptitsyn, after all.'

'Why, Kolya, you need a thrashing, you're so stupid. You may ask Matryona for anything you require; dinner is at half-past four. You may dine with us, or in your room, as you please. Come along, Kolya, don't get in his way.'

'Let us go, O woman of determined character!'

On their way out they collided with Ganya.

'Is father at home?' Ganya asked Kolya, and in answer to Kolya's affirmative reply whispered something in his ear.

Kolya nodded, and followed Varvara Ardalionovna out.

'Prince, there is something I forgot to say to you about all this . . . business. One request: please do me the favour – if it won't be too much of a strain for you – of not blabbing here either about what passed between Aglaya and myself just now, or *there* about what you find here; because there are also enough disgraceful things happening here. To the devil with it, though . . . At least restrain yourself for today.'

'But I assure you that I've blabbed far less than you think,' said the prince with a certain irritation, in answer to Ganya's reproaches. Relations between them were clearly deteriorating.

'Well, I've endured enough on your account today. In short, I request this of you.'

'Please note, Gavrila Ardalionovich, that I was in no way bound not to mention the portrait earlier today. I mean, you didn't ask me.'

'Ugh, what a foul room,' Ganya observed, looking round contemptuously, 'dark, and windows facing the courtyard. In all respects you've come to our place at the wrong time . . . Well, that's not my business; I'm not the one who lets the apartments.'

Ptitsyn looked in and called Ganya; the latter hastily abandoned the prince and went out even though there was still something he wanted to say, but was apparently hesitant, and seemingly afraid to broach the matter; and he had cursed the room in a way that suggested embarrassment.

No sooner had the prince washed, and managed to smarten himself up a little, than the door opened again, and a new figure emerged.

He was a gentleman of about thirty, of considerable stature, broad-shouldered, with an enormous head of reddish, curly hair. His face was fleshy and rubicund, his lips thick, his nose broad and flat, his eyes small, with swollen lids, and mocking, as though he were constantly winking. The general impression he made was one of insolence. His clothes were slightly dirty.

At first, he opened the door just wide enough to thrust his head through. For about five seconds, the inserted head looked round the room, and then the door slowly began to open, and the whole of his figure appeared in the doorway, yet still the visitor did not enter, but continued to study the prince from the doorway, narrowing his eyes as he did so. At last he closed the door behind him, approached, sat down on a chair, took the prince firmly by the arm and made him sit down on the sofa, at an angle to him.

'Ferdyshchenko,' he said, looking the prince in the face intently and questioningly.

'Very well – and?' the prince replied, almost bursting into laughter.

'Lodger,' Ferdyshchenko said softly again, lost in contemplation of the prince as before.

'Do you want to make my acquaintance?'

'E-ech!' the visitor said, rumpling his hair and sighing, and began to look at the opposite corner. 'Have you any money?' he asked suddenly, turning to the prince.

'A little.'

'How much?'

'Twenty-five roubles.'

'Show me.'

The prince fished the twenty-five-rouble note out of his waistcoat pocket and gave it to Ferdyshchenko. The latter unfolded it, looked at it, then turned it over, and held it up to the light.

'It's strange,' he said as if in reflection. 'Why do they go brown? These twenty-five-rouble notes sometimes go awfully brown, while others lose their colour altogether. Here.'

The prince took his note back. Ferdyshchenko got up from the chair.

'I've come to warn you: above all, don't lend me money, because I'll certainly ask you to.'

'Very well.'

'Do you intend to pay while you're here?'

'Yes.'

'Well, I don't; thank you. I'm the first door on your right here, did you see? Try not to come and see me very often; I'll come and see you, don't worry. Have you seen the general?'

'No.'

'And you haven't heard him?'

'Of course not.'

'Well, you'll see him and hear him; what's more, he even tries to borrow money from me! *Avis au lecteur*.² Goodbye. Do you think a man can live with a name like Ferdyshchenko? Eh?'

'But why not?'

'Goodbye.'

And he walked to the door. The prince later discovered that this gentleman had taken upon himself, as if it were an obligation, the task of astonishing everyone with his eccentricity and joviality, though it somehow never worked properly. On some people he even made a rather unpleasant impression, something that sincerely grieved him, though it did not lead him to abandon his task. In the doorway he almost succeeded in regaining his composure, colliding with a gentleman who was on his way in; having admitted to the room this new visitor, whom the prince did not know, he gave the prince several warning winks from behind his back and thus made a tolerable exit, not without aplomb.

The new gentleman was tall of stature, about fifty-five or even a little more, rather corpulent, with a purplish-red, fleshy and flaccid face, framed in thick grey side-whiskers, moustached, with large, rather protuberant eyes. His figure would have been rather dignified, had there not been something seedy, shabby, even soiled about it. He was dressed in a little old frock coat, with elbows that were nearly worn through; his linen was also stained with grease – in a homely sort of way. If one got near him there was a slight smell of vodka; but his manner was calculated for effect, slightly studied and with an obvious fervent desire to impress by his dignity. The gentleman approached the prince slowly, with a cordial smile, silently took his hand and, keeping it in his own, looked into his face for some time, as if discerning familiar features.

'It's him! It's him!' he said quietly, but solemnly. 'To the life! I hear the familiar, beloved name repeated, and I remember the irretrievable past . . . Prince Myshkin?'

'That's correct, sir.'

'General Ivolgin, retired and unfortunate. Your name and patronymic, if I may make so bold to ask?'

'Lev Nikolayevich.'

'That's it, that's it! The son of my friend, my childhood companion, Nikolai Petrovich?'

'My father's name was Nikolai Lvovich.'

'Lvovich,' the general corrected himself, but without haste, and with complete confidence, as though he had not forgotten at all, but had merely made an inadvertent slip of the tongue. He sat down and, taking the prince by the hand, seated him beside him. 'I carried you in my arms, sir.'

'Really?' asked the prince. 'My father died a good twenty years ago.'

'Yes; twenty years; twenty years and three months. We were at school together; I went straight into the army . . .'

'My father was in the army, too, as a second lieutenant in the Vasilkovsky regiment.'

'The Belomirsky. He was transferred to the Belomirsky almost the day before he died. I stood there and blessed him into eternity. Your dear mother . . .'

The general paused, as if struck by a sad memory.

'She also died, six months later, from a chill,' said the prince.

'It wasn't a chill. Not a chill, believe what an old man tells you. I was there, and I helped to see her into the ground. It was grief for her prince, and not from a chill. Yes, sir, I remember the princess too! Youth! Because of her, the prince and I, friends from childhood, very nearly became each other's murderer.'

The prince was beginning to listen with some distrust.

'I was passionately in love with your mother when she was engaged to be married – married to my friend. The prince noticed it and was *frappé*. He came to me in the morning, between six and seven, woke me up. I got dressed in amazement; silence on both sides; I understood everything. From his pocket he took two pistols. Across a handkerchief. Without witnesses. What did we need witnesses for, when in five minutes' time we would send each other into eternity? We loaded, spread the handkerchief, stood, put the pistols to each other's heart and looked into each other's faces. Suddenly a flood of tears came to the eyes of us both, our hands shook. Both of us, both of us at once! Well, of course, there were embraces, and we tried to outdo each other in generosity. The prince cried: "She's yours!" I cried: "She's yours!" So . . . so . . . you've come to . . . stay with us?'

'Yes, for a time, perhaps,' the prince said with a slight stammer.

'Prince, Mama wants you to go and see her,' Kolya shouted, looking in at the doorway. The prince half rose to go, but the general put his right palm on his shoulder and pressed him down to the sofa again in friendly fashion.

'As a true friend of your father I want to warn you,' said the general. 'You can see for yourself that I have suffered a tragic misfortune; but there was no trouble with the law! No trial, or anything like that! Nina Aleksandrovna is a rare woman. Varvara Alexandrovna, my daughter, is a rare daughter! Because of our circumstances, we rent out lodgings – a disgraceful fall! For me, who might have been a governor-general! . . . But you, you we are always glad to see. Yet there is tragedy in my house! . . .'

The prince looked at him questioningly and with great curiosity.

'A matrimonial union is being prepared, and it's a rare union. The union of a woman of easy virtue and a young man who might have become a gentleman of the royal bedchamber. This woman will be brought into the house where my daughter and my wife are living! But while yet I breathe, she shall not enter! I'll lie down on the threshold, and she'll have to step over my body! . . . I hardly speak to Ganya now, I even avoid meeting him. I warn you in advance: if you're going to stay with us, you will be a witness to it all in any case. But you are the son of my friend, and I have a right to rely . . .'

'Prince, please be so good as to come and see me in the drawing room,' called Nina Alexandrovna, appearing in the doorway.

'Imagine, my dear,' the general exclaimed. 'It turns out that I dandled the prince in my arms!'

Nina Alexandrovna gave the general a reproachful look and the prince a searching one, but did not say a word. The prince set off after her; but no sooner had they arrived in the drawing room and sat down, and Nina Alexandrovna had begun to tell the prince something in a great hurry, and in an undertone, than the general himself suddenly appeared in the room. Nina Alexandrovna at once fell silent and bent over her knitting in evident vexation. It was possible that the general noticed this vexation, but he continued to be in a most excellent mood.

'The son of my friend!' he exclaimed, turning to Nina Alexandrovna. 'And so unexpected, too! I had long ago ceased even to imagine such a thing. But, my dear, don't you remember the late Nikolai Lvovich? You met him in . . . Tver, didn't you?'

'I don't remember any Nikolai Lvovich. Was he your father?' she asked the prince.

'Yes, he was; but I think he died in Yelisavetgrad, not in Tver,' the prince observed to the general, timidly. 'I heard it from Pavlishchev . . .'

'Yes, it was Tver,' the general confirmed, 'his transfer to Tver came through just before his death, and even before he developed his illness. You were too young then to remember either the transfer or the journey; but Pavlishchev could sometimes be mistaken, though he was a most excellent man.'

'You knew Pavlishchev, too?'

'He was a rare fellow, but I was a personal witness. I blessed your father on his deathbed . . .'

'You see, my father died awaiting trial,' the prince observed again, 'though I was never able to find out precisely what for; he died in the military hospital.'

'Oh, it concerned the case of Private Kolpakov, and the prince would have been acquitted, without a doubt.'

'Is that so? Do you know for sure?' the prince asked with particular curiosity.

'Most certainly I do!' the general exclaimed. 'The trial broke up without resolving anything. An impossible case! A case that was even, one may say, mysterious: Staff-captain Larionov, the company commander, dies; the prince is temporarily appointed in his place; very well. Private Kolpakov commits a theft – some boots from a comrade – and sells them for drink; very well. The prince – and observe, this was in the presence of a sergeant major and a corporal – hauls Kolpakov over the coals and threatens him with a flogging. Very well, indeed. Kolpakov goes to the barracks, lies down on his bunk, and a quarter of an hour later dies. Splendid, but it's an unexpected incident, impossible, almost. One way or another, Kolpakov is given a funeral; the prince files a report, and then Kolpakov is removed from the lists. What could be better, you might think? But just six months later, at a brigade inspection, Private Kolpakov turns up, as though nothing were the matter, in the third company of the second battalion of the Novaya Zemlya infantry regiment,[3] in the same brigade and the same division!'

'What?' the prince exclaimed, beside himself with astonishment.

'That's not true, it's a mistake!' Nina Alexandrovna said, turning to him suddenly, looking at him almost with anguish. '*Mon mari se trompe.*'[4]

'But my dear, *se trompe*, that's easy to say, but try to solve an incident like that yourself! Everyone was at a loss. I would be the first to say *qu'on se trompe*. But unfortunately, I was a witness and sat on the commission myself. All the witnesses testified that this was definitely the same Private Kolpakov who some six months earlier had been buried with the usual parade and tattoo of drums. Truly a rare incident, almost an impossible one, I agree, but . . .'

'Papa, your dinner is on the table,' Varvara Ardalionovna announced, entering the room.

'Ah, that's splendid, magnificent! I'm so hungry . . . But as for that case, it is even, one may say, a psychological one . . .'

'The soup will get cold again,' Varya said with impatience.

'I'm coming, I'm coming,' muttered the general as he went out of the room. 'And in spite of all the inquiries,' could still be heard from the corridor.

'You will have to excuse Ardalion Alexandrovich many things if you stay with us,' Nina Alexandrovna said to the prince. 'However, he won't be much trouble to you; he even eats his dinner alone. I think you'll agree that everyone has their short-comings and their . . . peculiar features, some, perhaps, even more than those at whom we are accustomed to point our fingers. There is one thing I particularly want to ask you: if my husband should ever address you on the subject of payment for your lodging, please tell him that you have given it to me. That's to say, anything you gave Ardalion Alexandrovich would be deducted from your bill, but I ask you solely for the sake of accuracy . . . What's that, Varya?'

Varya had returned to the room and silently handed her mother the portrait of Nastasya Filippovna. Nina Alexandrovna started, and at first with a kind of alarm, and then with a sense of overwhelming bitterness, examined it for a while. At last she looked questioningly at Varya.

'It's a present she gave him today,' said Varya, 'and this evening it's all to be decided between them.'

'This evening!' Nina Alexandrovna echoed in a low voice, as if in despair. 'What can one say? At any rate, there's no more doubt, and there's no hope left, either; the portrait says it all . . . Did he show it to you himself?' she added in surprise.

'You know, we've hardly exchanged a word all month. Ptitsyn told me about it, and the portrait was just lying on the floor in there; I picked it up.'

'Prince,' Nina Alexandrovna suddenly addressed him, 'I wanted to ask you (that's really why I asked you to come here) how long you have known my son. I think he said you have only just arrived from somewhere?'

The prince explained briefly about himself, omitting the greater part. Nina Alexandrovna and Varya listened to it all.

'I'm not trying to find out something about Gavrila Arda-lionovich by asking you questions,' observed Nina Alex-androvna, 'you mustn't get the wrong idea. If there's something he can't admit to me himself, I don't intend to try to make inquiries behind his back. I'm doing it really because earlier Ganya, when you were there, and later, when you had gone, in reply to my question about you, replied: "He knows everything, there's no need to stand on ceremony!" What does that mean? That's to say, I would like to know how far . . .'

Suddenly Ganya and Ptitsyn came in; Nina Alexandrovna at once fell silent. The prince remained in the chair beside her, but Varya withdrew to the side: the portrait of Nastasya Filippovna lay in a most conspicuous place, on Nina Alexandrovna's work table, right in front of her. Ganya, catching sight of it, frowned, picked it up from the table in vexation and threw it on to his writing desk, which stood at the other end of the room.

'Today, Ganya?' Nina Alexandrovna suddenly asked.

'What do you mean, today?' Ganya said, starting, and sud-denly hurled himself on the prince. 'Ah, I might have known you were here! . . . Really, what's wrong with you, some kind of illness, or what? You can't restrain yourself, can you? Well let me tell you this, your excellency . . .'

'I'm the one who's to blame here, Ganya, no one else,' Ptitsyn broke in.

Ganya looked at him questioningly.

'I mean, it's better like this, Ganya, all the more so as, from one point of view, the matter is settled,' muttered Ptitsyn and, going off to the side, sat down by the table, took some sort of pencil-scribbled sheet of paper out of his pocket and began to study it intently. Ganya stood in gloom, uneasily awaiting a family row. He had no thought of apologizing to the prince.

'If everything is settled, then Ivan Petrovich is right, of course,' said Nina Alexandrovna. 'Don't frown, please, and don't get irritated. Ganya, I shall not ask you anything you do not want to tell me yourself, and I assure you that I'm completely resigned, so do me a favour and don't be worried.'

She said this without interrupting her work and, it seemed, calmly. Ganya was surprised, but cautiously refrained from saying anything and looked at his mother, waiting for her to express herself more clearly. Domestic rows had already cost him too dear. Nina Alexandrovna noticed this caution and, with a bitter smile, added:

'You still have doubts and don't believe me; don't worry, there will be neither tears nor entreaties, like before, on my part at least. All I desire is that you should be happy, and you know that; I've resigned myself to fate, but my heart will always be with you, whether we stay together or whether we go our separate ways. Of course, I answer only for myself; you can't demand the same of your sister . . .'

'Ah, her again!' exclaimed Ganya, looking at his sister with mocking hatred. 'Dear Mother! I swear again to you what I have already given you my word on: no one shall ever treat you with disrespect while I am here, while I am alive. No matter who it may be, I shall insist on the most complete respect for you, no matter who crosses our threshold . . .'

Ganya was so relieved that he looked at his mother in a way that was almost conciliatory, almost tender.

'I have never been afraid on my own account, Ganya, you know that; it's not about myself that I have experienced such anxiety and torment all this time. They say that everything is to be settled between you today! What is to be settled?'

'This evening, at her house, she promised to announce whether she consents or not,' replied Ganya.

'We've been avoiding that subject for nearly three weeks now, and that was for the best. Now that everything is settled, I will only permit myself to ask one thing: how could she give you her consent and even give you her portrait, when you don't love her? Do you really think that with a woman like her, so . . . so . . .'

'Er, experienced, you mean?'

'That's not how I was going to put it. Do you really think you could deceive her to that extent?'

There was suddenly an extraordinary irritation in this question. Ganya stood still, thought for a moment and, not concealing his derision, said quietly:

'You've got carried away, Mother dear, couldn't hold out again, that's the way these scenes have always begun and flared up between us. You said there would be no questions or reproaches, but they've already started! We'd better stop; really, let's stop; at least we tried . . . I'll never leave you, not for any reason; another man would have run away from a sister like that – look at her staring at me now! Let's end it here! I was beginning to feel so pleased . . . And how do you know that I'm deceiving Nastasya Filippovna? And as for Varya – she can do as she likes and – that's enough. Yes, now we've really had enough!'

Ganya was becoming more and more excited with each word, pacing aimlessly about the room. Conversations like this at once became a painful experience for all the members of the family.

'I said that if she comes in here I'll leave, and I will also keep my word,' said Varya.

'It's stubbornness!' exclaimed Ganya. 'It's stubbornness that makes you refuse to get married! What are you snorting at me for? I don't give a damn, Varvara Ardalionovna; you may carry out your intention at once, if you like. I'm really sick of you now. You're finally deciding to leave us, Prince!' he shouted to the prince, seeing him get from his chair.

In Ganya's voice could be heard that degree of irritation in which a man is almost glad of that irritation, abandons himself to it without any restraint and almost with growing enjoyment, whatever it may lead to. The prince had started to turn round in the doorway in order make some reply but, seeing by the unhealthy expression on his assailant's face that now all was needed was the drop that would make the cup run over, he turned back and went out in silence. A few minutes later he heard by the noise from the drawing room that in his absence the conversation was even louder and more outspoken.

He walked through the reception room into the hallway, in order to reach the corridor, and from it his room. As he passed close by the door that gave on to the staircase, he heard and observed that on the other side of it someone was furiously trying to ring the bell; but there must have been something wrong with the bell: it merely shook a little, but there was no sound. The prince slid the bolt, opened the door and – stepped back in amazement, even shuddered all over: before him stood Nastasya Filippovna. He instantly recognized her from the portrait. Her eyes flashed with a burst of annoyance when she saw him; she quickly walked into the hallway, pushing him out of the way with her shoulder, and said angrily, as she threw off her fur coat:

'If you're too lazy to mend the bell, you might at least be sitting in the hallway when people knock. Look, now you've dropped my coat, fool!'

The coat was indeed lying on the floor; Nastasya Filippovna, not waiting for the prince to help her off with it, had thrown it into his hands without looking, from behind, but the prince had missed it.

'They ought to get rid of you. In you go, announce me.'

The prince was about to say something, but was so embarrassed that he could get nothing out, and holding the coat which he had picked up from the floor, entered the drawing room.

'Look, now he's going in with the coat! Why are you carrying the coat? Ha-ha-ha! Are you insane, or what?'

The prince came back, and looked at her like a dummy; when she began to laugh, he also smiled, but still could not find his tongue. At the initial moment when he opened the door to her he had been pale, but now the colour suddenly flooded his face.

'But what kind of idiot is this?' Nastasya Filippovna exclaimed in indignation, stamping her foot at him. 'Well, where are you going? Who are you going to announce?'

'Nastasya Filippovna,' muttered the prince.

'How do you know who I am?' she asked him quickly. 'I've never seen you before! In you go, announce me . . . What's all that shouting?'

'They're quarrelling,' the prince replied, and went into the drawing room.

He entered it at a rather decisive moment: Nina Alexandrovna was by now on the point of entirely forgetting that she had 'resigned herself to it all'; she was, however, defending Varya. Ptitsyn was also standing beside Varya, having abandoned his pencil-scribbled sheet of paper. Varya herself was not afraid, and was indeed a girl not easily frightened; but with every word her brother's crassness was becoming more and more blatant and intolerable. In such cases she usually stopped talking and merely stared at her brother mockingly and in silence, fixing her eyes on him. This manoeuvre, as she well knew, was capable of driving him beyond the limit. At this very moment the prince stepped into the room and proclaimed:

'Nastasya Filippovna!'

9

A universal silence ensued; they all looked at the prince as though they did not understand, and did not want to understand. Ganya went stiff with fright.

Nastasya Filippovna's arrival, especially at the present moment, was a most strange and troubling surprise for them all. There was the very fact that Nastasya Filippovna was visiting for the first time: hitherto she had held herself so aloof that in conversations with Ganya she had not even expressed a desire to be introduced to his relatives, and most recently had not even mentioned them at all, as though they did not exist. Though Ganya was in some respects pleased to be rid of a subject of conversation that was so troubling to him, in his heart he had set this aloofness against her. At any rate, he expected mocking and caustic remarks about his family from her rather than a visit to him; he knew for certain that she was privy to all that was taking place in his house in connection with his preparations for marriage and how these were viewed by his relatives. Her visit, *now*, after the gift of the portrait and on her birthday, the day on which she had promised to decide his fate, almost signi-fied that decision itself . . .

The bewilderment with which they all looked at the prince did not continue for long: Nastasya Filippovna appeared in the doorway of the drawing room, and again, as she entered, pushed the prince slightly aside.

'At last I've managed to get in . . . why do you tie up the doorbell?' she said cheerfully, giving her hand to Ganya, who had rushed towards her as fast as his legs would carry him. 'Why the long face? Introduce me, please . . .'

Ganya, completely embarrassed, introduced her first to Varya, and the two women exchanged odd looks before extending their hands to each other. Nastasya Filippovna, how-ever, laughed and put on a mask of cheerfulness; but Varya did not want to put on a mask, and her gaze was fixed and gloomy; not even the shadow of a smile demanded by simple politeness was visible in her face. Ganya was horrified; there was no point in pleading with her, and not time to do so, and he cast such a threatening look at Varya that by it alone she understood what this moment meant for her brother. It seemed that then she decided to yield to him, and smiled faintly to Nastasya Filippovna. (They were all still, as a family, very fond of one another.) The situation was rescued to some extent by Nina Alexandrovna, whom Ganya, utterly flustered by now, intro-duced after his sister, and even led up to Nastasya Filippovna first. But no sooner did Nina Alexandrovna begin to speak of her 'great pleasure', than Nastasya Filippovna, without waiting to hear her through, quickly turned to Ganya and, sitting down (without so much as an invitation to do so) on the little sofa, in the corner by the window, exclaimed:

'But where is your study? And . . . and where are the lodgers? I mean, you have lodgers, don't you?'

Ganya blushed terribly, and began to stammer something in reply, but Nastasya Filippovna at once added:

'But where is there to keep lodgers here? You haven't even got a study. And does it pay?' she suddenly addressed Nina Alexandrovna.

'It's quite a lot of trouble,' the latter replied. 'Of course, it ought to pay. Actually, we've only just . . .'

But Nastasya Filippovna was not listening again: she was staring at Ganya, laughing and shouting to him:

'What sort of look is that on your face? Oh my God, what a face you've got on at this moment!'

Several seconds of this laughter went by, and indeed, Ganya's face really was very distorted; his rigid stupor, his comical, timorous embarrassment, suddenly left him; but he turned dreadfully pale; his lips began to twist convulsively; silently, fixedly and with an evil gaze, not moving away, he looked into the face of his visitor, who continued to laugh.

There was also another observer here, who had likewise not yet recovered from his numbed shock at the sight of Nastasya Filippovna; but although he stood 'as stiff as a post', in his former position, in the doorway of the drawing room, he had time to notice the pallor and ominous change in Ganya's features. This observer was the prince. Almost in fear, he suddenly, mechanically, stepped forward.

'Take a drink of water,' he whispered to Ganya. 'And don't look like that . . .'

It was clear that he had said this with no calculation, no particular intention, no thought, at the first prompting; but his words produced an extraordinary effect. All Ganya's anger was suddenly unloaded on the prince: Ganya seized him by the shoulder and looked at him in silent, vengeful hatred, almost unable to get a word out. There was a general commotion: Nina Alexandrovna even uttered a little scream, Ptitsyn stepped forward in concern, Kolya and Ferdyshchenko, appearing in the doorway, stood in amazement, and Varya alone glowered as before, though attentively observing. She did not sit down, but stood to the side, next to her mother, her arms folded on her bosom.

But Ganya at once pulled himself together, almost in the first moment of his gesture, and began to laugh nervously. He recovered himself completely.

'I say, Prince, are you a doctor, then?' he exclaimed, as cheerfully and naturally as he could. 'You really gave me a fright; Nastasya Filippovna, allow me to introduce him to you, he's a most valuable fellow, though I've only known him since this morning.'

Nastasya Filippovna looked at the prince in bewilderment.

'A prince? He's a prince? Imagine, just now, in the hallway, I thought he was a lackey and sent him in here to announce me! Ha-ha-ha!'

'No harm done, no harm done,' Ferdyshchenko chimed in, quickly going up to them and relieved that they had begun to laugh. 'No harm done: *se non è vero . . .*'[1]

'And I very nearly gave you a scolding, Prince. Please forgive me. Ferdyshchenko, what are you doing here, at this hour? I didn't think I would find you here, at least. Who? What prince? Myshkin?' she again asked Ganya, who had meanwhile succeeded in introducing him, his hand around the prince's shoulder.

'Our lodger,' repeated Ganya.

Evidently, the prince was being presented as something rare (and useful to them all, as a way out of their false position), and was almost being thrust on Nastasya Filippovna; the prince even distinctly heard the word 'idiot', whispered from behind him, apparently by Ferdyshchenko, as an explanation for Nastasya Filippovna.

'Tell me, why didn't you set me right just now, when I made such a dreadful . . . mistake about you?' Nastasya Filippovna continued, surveying the prince from head to foot in the most unceremonious fashion; she awaited his reply impatiently, as if wholly convinced the reply would be so stupid that it would be impossible to avoid laughing.

'I was surprised at seeing you so suddenly . . .' the prince began to mutter.

'But how did you know it was me? Where had you seen me before? What is this? It's as if I had really seen him somewhere before . . . And permit me to ask you, why were you dumbfounded just now? What is so dumbfounding about me?'

'For heaven's sake, man!' Ferdyshchenko continued to

grimace, 'for heaven's sake! Oh Lord, the things I should say were I to be asked such a question! For heaven's sake . . . Prince, after this you're a bumpkin!'

'And I would have said a lot in your place, too,' the prince began to laugh to Ferdyshchenko. 'Your portrait made a great impression on me earlier,' he continued to Nastasya Filippovna. 'Then I talked about you with the Yepanchins . . . and early this morning, before I had even got to St Petersburg, on the train, Parfyon Rogozhin told me a great deal about you . . . And at the very minute I opened the door to you I was also thinking about you, and suddenly here you are.'

'But how did you know it was me?'

'By your portrait and . . .'

'And what else?'

'And because you were exactly as I imagined you . . . I also thought I had seen you somewhere.'

'Where? Where?'

'I've seen your eyes somewhere before . . . but it isn't possible! I'm just making it up . . . I've never been here. Perhaps in a dream . . .'

'Well done, Prince!' cried Ferdyshchenko. 'No, I take back my *se non è vero*. Unfortunately, though, unfortunately, it's all because of his innocence!' he added with regret.

The prince had delivered his few sentences in an anxious voice, faltering, and frequently pausing for breath. Everything about him indicated extreme agitation. Nastasya Filippovna looked at him with curiosity, but was not laughing now. At this same moment a new, loud voice, which could be heard from the other side of the crowd that densely surrounded the prince and Nastasya Filippovna, parted the crowd and, as it were, split it in two. Before Nastasya Filippovna stood the *paterfamilias* himself, General Ivolgin. He was wearing a tailcoat and a clean dickey; his moustache was dyed . . .

This was more than Ganya could endure.

Proud and conceited to the point of morbid suspicion, of hypochondria; having sought all these past two months at least some point on which he could support himself more decently and present himself more nobly; feeling that he was as yet a

PART ONE, CHAPTER 9

novice on his chosen path, and that he might not last the course; having resolved at last in despair to settle in his own home, where he was a despot, upon complete brazenry, but not daring to settle on it in front of Nastasya Filippovna, who to the very last had confounded his stratagems and mercilessly kept the upper hand over him; 'an impatient beggar', to use Nastasya Filippovna's own expression, which had already been reported to him; swearing by all the oaths to recompense her painfully for all this later and at the same time childishly dreaming now and then of making both ends meet and reconciling all the opposites – he must now also drain this horrible cup, and, what was more, at such a moment! One more unforeseen, but most terrible torment for a conceited man – the agony of blushing for his own relatives, in his own home, had fallen to his lot. 'But is the reward worth it?' flashed through Ganya's head at that instant.

What was occurring at that very moment was what he had dreamed of these last two months only at nights, in the form of a nightmare that froze him with horror and burned him with shame: the meeting of his father with Nastasya Filippovna. Sometimes, to tease and torment himself, he had tried to picture the general during the wedding ceremony, but had never been able to finish the tormenting scene and had soon abandoned it. Perhaps he boundlessly exaggerated the calamity; but such is always the way with conceited men. During those two months he had had time to make up his mind and muster his resolve, and had promised himself that whatever else happened, he would somehow get rid of his father, at least for a time, and keep him in the background, even out of St Petersburg altogether, if possible, whether his mother agreed to it or not. Ten minutes earlier, when Nastasya Filippovna walked in, he had been so shocked, so stunned that he had completely forgotten the possibility of Ardalion Alexandrovich's appearance on the scene and had done nothing about it. And now here was the general, in front of them all, and, what was more, in evening dress and a tailcoat, and this at the very moment when Nastasya Filippovna 'was only looking for a chance to shower him and his family with mocking gibes'. (Of this he was convinced.) And indeed,

what was the meaning of her visit now, if not this? Had she
come in order to make friends with his mother and sister or in
order to insult them in his own home? But from the way in
which the two sides were disposed, there could be no further
doubt: his mother and sister sat to one side as though they had
been reviled, while Nastasya Filippovna even seemed to have
forgotten that they were in the same room as her . . . And if she
was behaving like that, then, of course, she must have her
purpose!

Ferdyshchenko took hold of the general and led him over.

'Ardalion Alexandrovich Ivolgin,' the bowing and smiling
general enunciated with dignity, 'an unfortunate old soldier and
father of a family that is happy in the expectation of including
within it such a charming . . .'

He did not get to the end; Ferdyshchenko quickly moved up
a chair for him from behind, and the general, somewhat weak
in the legs at this post-prandial hour, fairly flopped, or rather
fell, into it; this did not disconcert him, however. He settled
down directly facing Nastasya Filippovna and, with a pleasant
grimace, slowly and ostentatiously, brought her fingers to his
lips. It was, on the whole, rather hard to disconcert the general.
His appearance, apart from a certain unkemptness, was still
quite respectable, something of which he was very well aware.
He had formerly had occasion to move in very good society,
from which he had been excluded only two or three years before.
Since then, he had abandoned himself with rather too little
restraint to some of his weaknesses; but a nimble and pleasant
manner remained with him to this day. Nastasya Filippovna
seemed extremely pleased at the appearance of Ardalion Alexandrovich, of whom she had, of course, heard at second hand.

'I have heard that my son . . .' Ardalion Ardalionovich began.

'Oh, your son! You're handsome, too, Papa, are you not?
Why do you never show your face at my house? What is it, are
you hiding yourself away or is your son hiding you? You of all
people can come and see me without compromising anyone.'

'Nineteenth-century children and their parents . . .' the general began again.

'Nastasya Filippovna! Let Ardalion Alexandrovich go for a

moment, please, someone is asking for him,' Nina Alexandrovna said loudly.

'Let him go? For heaven's sake, I've heard so much about
him, have wanted to see him for so long! And what sort of
business can he have? I mean, he's retired, isn't he? You won't
leave me, General, you won't go away, will you?'

'I give you my word that he'll come and see you in person,
but now he is in need of rest.'

'Ardalion Alexandrovich, they say you're in need of rest!'
Nastasya Filippovna exclaimed with a resentful and peevish
face, like a thoughtless little girl who has had a toy taken away
from her. The general at once tried to make himself look even
more foolish.

'My dear! My dear!' he said reproachfully, solemnly turning
to his wife and putting his hand on his heart.

'Will you not come away, Mama?' Varya asked loudly.

'No, Varya, I shall stay here to the end.'

Nastasya Filippovna could not have failed to hear the question
and the answer, but this only seemed to make her cheerfulness
all the greater. She at once began to shower the general with
questions again, and within five minutes the general was in the
most festive mood, launching into oratory, to the loud laughter
of those present.

Kolya tugged the prince by his coat tail.

'Get him out of here somehow! Can't you? Please!' And
tears of indignation even burned in the poor boy's eyes. 'Oh,
confound Ganka!' he added to himself.

'I did indeed have a great friendship with Ivan Fyodorovich
Yepanchin,' the general gushed, in response to Nastasya Filippovna's questions. 'He, I and the late Prince Lev Nikolayevich
Myshkin, whose son I have today embraced after a twenty years'
separation, were three inseparables, so to speak, a cavalcade:
Athos, Porthos and Aramis.[2] But alas, one is in the grave,
struck down by slander and a bullet, another is before you, still
struggling with slander and bullets . . .'

'Bullets?' Nastasya Filippovna exclaimed.

'They are here, in my chest, I received them at Kars,[3] and
in bad weather I feel them. In all other respects I live like a

philosopher, I go out, take walks, play draughts at my café, like a *bourgeois* who has retired from practical affairs, and read the *Indépendance*.[4] But with our Porthos, Yepanchin, after the business with the lap-dog on the train three years ago, I have had absolutely nothing further to do.'

'A lap-dog? But what was that about?' Nastasya Filippovna asked with particular curiosity. 'A lap-dog? You don't say, and on a train! . . .' she said, as if remembering something.

'Oh, a stupid story, it's not worth repeating: it involved Princess Belokonskaya's governess, Mistress Schmidt, but . . . it's not worth repeating.'

'But you absolutely must tell me!' Nastasya Filippovna exclaimed merrily.

'I haven't heard it yet, either!' observed Ferdyshchenko. '*C'est du nouveau.*'[5]

'Ardalion Alexandrovich!' Nina Alexandrovna's imploring voice again rang out.

'Papa, someone's asking for you!' cried Kolya.

'A stupid story, and one that can be told in a few words,' the general began complacently. 'Two years ago, yes, more or less, just after the opening of the new — Railway, when attending to some business that was extremely important to me, about retiring from my position in the service (by that time I was back in civilian clothes), I took a ticket, first class: I got in, sat down, had a smoke. That's to say, I continued to smoke, I had lit my cigar earlier. I was alone in the compartment. Smoking is not prohibited, but it's not permitted either; it's just semi-permitted, as a matter of custom; well, and depending on the person. The window had been lowered. Suddenly, just before the whistle for departure, two ladies with a lap-dog got in and occupied the seats directly opposite me; they were late for the train; one of them was dressed in the most eye-catching manner, in light blue; the other more modestly, in black silk and a pelerine. They were quite good-looking, gazed at me haughtily, were talking English. I, of course, paid no attention; I smoked. That's to say, I thought about it, but I continued to smoke, because the window was open, and I smoked out of the window. The lap-dog was resting on the light-blue lady's knees, it was small, no bigger than my fist, black, with little white paws, a curiosity, even. It had a silver collar with a motto. I paid no attention. Though I did notice that the ladies seemed to be angry, about my cigar, of course. One of them trained her lorgnette on me, a tortoiseshell one. Again I paid no attention: because, after all, they didn't say anything! If they'd said something, warned me, asked me, I mean, after all, there is such a thing as the human tongue! But they said nothing . . . then suddenly – and it came, I tell you, with not the slightest forewarning, I mean not the very slightest, every bit as though she had gone quite out of her mind – the light-blue lady snatched my cigar from me and threw it out of the window. The train hurtled along, I stared at her like a halfwit. The woman was wild; a wild woman, quite as if she were from some savage society; but a stout woman, plump, tall, fair-haired, red-cheeked (even too much so), her eyes flashing at me. Without saying a word, but with uncommon politeness, with the most complete politeness, with the most refined, so to speak, politeness, I approached the lap-dog with two fingers, delicately picked it up by the collar and flung it out of the window after the cigar! You should have heard the squeals! The train continued to speed along . . .'

'You're a monster!' exclaimed Nastasya Filippovna, roaring with laughter and clapping her hands like a little girl.

'Bravo, bravo!' cried Ferdyshchenko. Ptitsyn also smiled ironically, though he had found the general's arrival much to his distaste; even Kolya laughed, and also cried, 'Bravo!'

'And I was right, I was right, right three times over!' the triumphant general continued, with heat. 'Because if cigars are prohibited on trains, dogs are even more so!'

'Bravo, Papa!' Kolya exclaimed in rapture. 'That's magnificent! I would certainly, certainly have done the same!'

'But what about the lady?' Nastasya Filippovna questioned impatiently.

'The lady? Well, that is where the unpleasant part comes in,' the general continued, frowning. 'Without so much as a word, and again without the slightest warning, she slapped me on the cheek! A wild woman; quite as if she were from some savage society!'

'And your response?'

The general lowered his eyes, raised his eyebrows, raised his shoulders, pursed his lips, spread his arms, was silent for a moment, and then suddenly said quietly:

'I got carried away!'

'And did you strike her hard? Hard?'

'I swear to God, not hard! There was a scandal, but I didn't strike her hard. I only brushed her aside once, solely in order to brush her aside. But then Satan himself took a hand: the light-blue one turned out to be an Englishwoman, a governess or even some sort of friend of Princess Belokonskaya's family, and the one in the black dress was the eldest of the Belokonskaya daughters, an old maid of about thirty-five. And you know how close the wife of General Yepanchin is to the Belokonskaya household. All the princesses in a swoon, tears, mourning for their beloved lap-dog, the shrieking of six princesses, the shrieking of the Englishwoman – Armageddon! Well, of course, I went to tender my remorse, asked for forgiveness, wrote a letter, but they wouldn't accept it, neither me nor the letter, and I quarrelled with the Yepanchins, was excluded, banished!'

'But excuse me, how can this be?' Nastasya Filippovna asked suddenly. 'Five or six days ago I read in the *Indépendance* – I subscribe to the *Indépendance* – exactly the same story! I mean really exactly the same! It happened on one of the railways in the Rhineland, on board a train, between a Frenchman and an Englishwoman: the cigar was snatched in exactly the same way, the lap-dog was thrown out of the window in exactly the same way, and it ended exactly as you described. The dress was even light-blue!'

The general blushed horribly. Kolya also blushed, and clutched his head with his hands; Ptitsyn quickly turned away. Only Ferdyshchenko roared with laughter as before. Of Ganya there was nothing to be said: he had stood throughout, enduring a speechless and intolerable agony.

'I assure you,' the general muttered, 'that exactly the same thing happened to me.'

'Papa really did have an unpleasant encounter with Mistress Schmidt, the Belokonskayas' governess,' exclaimed Kolya, 'I remember.'

'What? Exactly the same? The same story at both ends of Europe and exactly the same in every detail, right down to the light-blue dress?' Nastasya Filippovna insisted mercilessly. 'I'll send you the *Indépendance Belge*!'

'But please observe,' the general continued to insist, 'that it happened to me two years earlier . . .'

'Ah, there is that, perhaps!'

Nastasya Filippovna roared with laughter, almost in hysterics.

'Papa, I want you to come outside for a word or two,' Ganya said in a trembling, exhausted voice, mechanically seizing his father by the shoulder. An infinite hatred boiled in his gaze.

At that same moment there was an exceptionally loud ring of the bell in the entrance hall. It was the kind of ring that might easily have pulled the bell off. It presaged an extraordinary visit. Kolya ran to open the door.

10

The hallway suddenly became extremely noisy and crowded; from the drawing room it seemed that several people had entered from outside and that more were still continuing to enter. Several voices were talking and shouting at once; there was also talking and shouting on the staircase, where the door from the hallway, as could be heard, had not been closed. The visit was turning out to be an exceedingly strange one. They all looked at one another; Ganya rushed into the reception room, but several people had gone in there, too.

'Ah, there he is, the Judas!' exclaimed a voice that was familiar to the prince. 'Hello, Ganka, you villain!'

'That's him, that's the man!' another voice confirmed.

It was impossible for the prince to be in any doubt: one voice was that of Rogozhin, and the other that of Lebedev.

Ganya stood, almost in stupefaction, in the doorway of the drawing room and stared in silence, taking no steps to prevent the entry to the reception room of some ten or twelve people who came in one after the other, following Parfyon Rogozhin. The company was extremely diverse, and was characterized not only by diversity, but also by its disgraceful behaviour. Some came in just as they had been on the street, in topcoats and furs. None was completely drunk, however; on the other hand, they all seemed to have had a good few too many. None of them seemed able to enter without the others; not one of them would have had the boldness to enter alone, but all appeared to be pushing one another. Even Rogozhin stepped cautiously at the head of the crowd, but he had some kind of plan, and he looked gloomily and irritably preoccupied. As for the rest, they merely formed a chorus, or rather a gang, to provide support. In addition to Lebedev there was the wavy-haired Zalyozhev, who had thrown off his fur coat in the hallway and entered with the casual air of a dandy, and two or three other gentlemen like him, who were obviously merchants. There was a man in a semi-military greatcoat; there was a small and exceedingly fat man, who laughed constantly; there was an enormous gentle-man, over six feet tall, who was also extraordinarily fat, extremely surly and silent, and obviously powerfully reliant on his fists. There was a medical student; there was a little Polish hanger-on. From the staircase two ladies of some kind looked into the hallway, but did not venture inside; Kolya slammed the door in their noses, and fastened the hook.

'Hello, Ganka, you villain! Well, did you not expect Parfyon Rogozhin?' Rogozhin repeated, reaching the drawing room and stopping in the doorway facing Ganya. But at that moment he suddenly espied in the drawing room, directly facing him, Nastasya Filippovna. He had obviously had no idea that he would encounter her here, because the sight of her had an extraordinary effect on him; he went so pale that his lips even turned slightly blue. 'So it's true!' he said quietly and as if to himself, looking completely lost – 'the end! Well . . . You'll answer to me now!' he ground out suddenly, looking at Ganya with violent hostility. 'Well . . . ach! . . .'

He was even panting, even finding it hard to get his words out. Mechanically he advanced into the drawing room, but on crossing the threshold suddenly caught sight of Nina Alexandrovna and Varya and stopped, somewhat embarrassed, in spite of all his excitement. Behind him came Lebedev, cleaving to him like a shadow and already very drunk, then the student, the gentleman with the fists and Zalyozhev, bowing to right and left; and lastly, the short little fat man squeezed himself in. The presence of the ladies held them all back slightly, and was, of course, obviously only a severe restraint on them until the *beginning*, until the first pretext for shouting and *beginning* . . . After that, no ladies in the world could have got in their way.

'What? Are you here, too, Prince?' Rogozhin said absent-mindedly, in partial surprise at encountering the prince. 'Still in your gaiters, e-ech!' he sighed, now forgetting the prince and transferring his gaze back to Nastasya Filippovna, still advancing towards her as if drawn to a magnet.

Nastasya Filippovna was also staring at the visitors with uneasy curiosity.

Ganya, at last, pulled himself together.

'But really, what's the meaning of this?' he began in a loud voice, sternly surveying those who had come in, and addressing himself primarily to Rogozhin. 'This is not a horse stable, you know, gentlemen, my mother and sister are here . . .'

'We can see it's your mother and sister,' Rogozhin muttered through his teeth.

'One can indeed see it's your mother and sister,' Lebedev confirmed, to keep himself in countenance.

The gentleman with the fists, probably supposing that his moment had come, began to growl something.

'But I mean to say!' Ganya's voice rose suddenly, and somehow excessively, like an explosion. 'In the first place, I want you all to go through to the reception room, and then I wish to know . . .'

'I like that, he doesn't recognize me,' Rogozhin grinned with hostility, not budging. 'Don't you recognize Rogozhin?'

'I expect I have met you somewhere, but . . .'

'I like that, met you somewhere! Why, only three months ago I lost two hundred roubles of my father's money to you, and then the old man died, before he'd had time to find out; you dragged me into it, and Knif cheated. You don't recognize me?

Ptitsyn was a witness! If I were to show you three roubles, if I took them out of my pocket right now, you'd crawl on all fours all the way to Vasilevsky Island for them – that's what you're like! That's what your soul is like! And now I've come here to buy you off for money, you don't need to stare at the boots I'm wearing, I have money, brother, lots of it, I'll buy you, buy you up and all your living too . . . if I want to, I'll buy the lot of you! I'll buy the lot of you!' Rogozhin was working himself up more and more, and seemed to be getting more and more drunk. 'E-ech!' he cried. 'Nastasya Filippovna! Don't show me the door, just say one little word: are you going to marry him or not?'

Rogozhin asked the question like a man who was done for, as though addressing it to some deity, but with the boldness of one sentenced to execution, who no longer had anything to lose. In deathly anguish he awaited her reply.

Nastasya Filippovna measured him with a mocking and haughty gaze, but glanced at Varya and at Nina Alexandrovna, looked at Ganya and suddenly changed her tone.

'Of course not, what has got into you? And what makes you ask such a question?' she replied quietly and earnestly and as if with a certain surprise.

'No? No?' Rogozhin shouted, almost in an ecstasy of joy. 'So you're not going to? And they told me . . . Oh! Well! Nastasya Filippovna! They say that you're engaged to Ganka! To him? I mean, is it possible? (That's what I say to them all!) And I'll buy him out, if I gave him a thousand, no, three, to withdraw, he'd run away on the eve of his wedding, and leave his fiancée to me! It's true, Ganya, you villain, isn't it? I mean, you'd take the three thousand, wouldn't you? Here it is, here! That's why I came, to take your signature; I said: I'll buy you – and I will!'

'Get out of here, you're drunk!' cried Ganya, flushing and turning pale.

After his shout there was a sudden explosion of several voices; the whole of Rogozhin's brigade had long been awaiting the first challenge. Lebedev was whispering something in Rogozhin's ear with extreme alacrity.

'True, civil servant!' Rogozhin replied, 'true, drunken soul! Ech, to hell with it, Nastasya Filippovna!' he exclaimed, staring at her like a halfwit, losing his nerve and then suddenly recovering it to the point of insolence, 'here's eighteen thousand!' And he slapped on to the table in front of her a white paper package tied across with string. 'Here! And . . . and there'll be more!'

He did not dare to say what it was he wanted.

'No, no, no!' Lebedev began to whisper to him again, with a look of terrible alarm; one could guess that he was alarmed by the huge size of the sum and was suggesting that a much smaller one be tried.

'No, brother, in this matter you're a fool, and don't know what you're getting yourself into . . . and, clearly, I'm a fool, too!' Rogozhin said, recovering himself with a start, under the flashing gaze of Nastasya Filippovna. 'E-ech! I should never have listened to you,' he added with deep remorse.

Nastasya Filippovna, who had been looking narrowly at Rogozhin's downcast features, suddenly began to laugh.

'Eighteen thousand, for me? That's the muzhik in you talking,' she added suddenly, with brazen familiarity, getting up from the sofa as though she were preparing to leave. Ganya watched the whole scene with a sinking heart.

'Then forty thousand, forty, not eighteen!' cried Rogozhin. 'Vanka Ptitsyn and Biskup have promised to get forty thousand here by seven o'clock. Forty thousand! All on the table.'

The scene was becoming extremely disgraceful, but Nastasya Filippovna continued to laugh and did not leave, as though she were indeed prolonging it intentionally. Nina Alexandrovna and Varya also rose from their places and fearfully, silently waited to see what this might come to; Varya's eyes flashed, but it all had a morbid effect on Nina Alexandrovna; she was trembling and seemed to be on the point of fainting.

'Well, if that's how it is – a hundred! I'll get you a hundred thousand this very day! Ptitsyn, help me, you'll do well out of this!'

'You've taken leave of your senses!' Ptitsyn whispered suddenly, going over to him quickly, and seizing him by the arm. 'You're drunk, they'll send for the police. Where do you think you are?'

'He's drunk, and talking nonsense,' said Nastasya Filippovna, as if teasing him.

'It isn't nonsense, the money will be here! It will be here by this evening! Ptitsyn, help me, you interest-grasping soul, take what you want, but get me a hundred thousand by this evening; I'll prove that I stick by what I promise!' Rogozhin suddenly grew animated to the point of ecstasy.

'But really, what is all this?' a wrathful Ardalion Alexandrovich exclaimed suddenly and menacingly, drawing close to Rogozhin. The suddenness of the old man's behaviour, following upon the silence he had kept until now, made it seem very comical. Laughter was heard.

'What is all what?' Rogozhin began to laugh. 'Come and join us, old man, you're going to get drunk!'

'That's just vile!' cried Kolya, in tears now, from shame and vexation.

'Is there really not one among you who will take this shameless creature out of here!' Varya exclaimed suddenly, trembling all over with anger.

'They call me shameless!' Nastasya Filippovna parried with cheerful disdain. 'And I, like a fool, came to invite them to my soirée! Look how your sister treats me, Gavrila Ardalionovich!'

Ganya stood for a while in the wake of his sister's behaviour as if struck by lightning; but observing that this time Nastasya Filippovna really was leaving, he threw himself upon Varya like a frenetic, seizing her arm in rabid fury.

'What have you done?' he cried, staring at her as though he wanted to reduce her to ashes on the spot. He had decidedly reached the end of his tether, and was scarcely conscious of what was happening.

'What have you done? What are you getting me into? You want me to apologize to her for having insulted your mother and having come here to cover your house in shame, you base man?' Varya shouted again, exultant, and staring at her brother in defiance.

For a few moments they stood like this, one against the other, face to face. Ganya was still holding her arm. Varya tugged once, twice, with all her strength, but could not control herself, and suddenly, beside herself, spat at her brother in the face.

'That's the way, girl!' shouted Nastasya Filippovna. 'Bravo, Ptitsyn, I congratulate you!'

Ganya's head spun, and, in complete oblivion, he lashed out at his sister with all his might. The blow would certainly have struck her in the face. But suddenly, another arm stopped Ganya's arm in flight.

Between Ganya and his sister stood the prince.

'That will do, enough!' he said insistently, but also trembling all over, as from an extremely violent shock.

'Are you forever going to block my path?' roared Ganya, letting go of Varya's arm, and with his free hand, in the last degree of rabid fury, dealt the prince a slap in the face with all his might.

'Oh!' Kolya lifted his hands. 'Oh, my God!'

There were exclamations on all sides. The prince turned pale. With a strange and reproachful gaze he looked Ganya straight in the eye; his lips were trembling and trying to say something; they were twisted into a strange and completely inappropriate smile.

'Well, you may do it to me . . . but I won't let you do it to her! . . .' he said quietly, at last; but suddenly lost his nerve, abandoned Ganya, covered his face with his hands, went off into a corner, stood with his face to the wall, and said in a faltering voice:

'Oh, how ashamed you will be for what you have done!'

Indeed, Ganya stood like a man who had been annihilated. Kolya rushed to embrace and kiss the prince; behind him jostled Rogozhin, Varya, Ptitsyn, Nina Alexandrovna, all of them, even the old man Ardalion Alexandrovich.

'I'm all right, I'm all right!' the prince muttered in all directions, with the same inappropriate smile.

'And he'll be sorry!' shouted Rogozhin. 'You'll be ashamed, Ganya, for having insulted such a . . . sheep! (He could not find another word.) Prince, my dear fellow, leave them be; spit on them, let's go! You'll find out what Rogozhin's love is like!'

Nastasya Filippovna was also very shocked, both by Ganya's

action and by the prince's response. Her usually pale and reflective face, which had all the time been out of harmony with her earlier apparently affected laughter, was now evidently agitated by a new emotion; and yet she none the less seemed unwilling to display it, and it was as if the mocking smile were struggling to remain on her features.

'It's true, I have seen his face somewhere before!' she said suddenly in an earnest voice, abruptly recalling her earlier question.

'And aren't you ashamed of yourself? You're not like that, not like the person you pretended to be just now, are you? Is it really possible?' the prince suddenly exclaimed with a deep, heartfelt reproach.

Nastasya Filippovna was surprised; she smiled, but, as though she were hiding something under the smile, somewhat embarrassed, gave Ganya a look, and went out of the drawing room. Before she reached the hallway, however, she suddenly turned back, quickly went over to Nina Alexandrovna, took her hand, and brought it to her lips.

'Indeed I am not like that, he has guessed,' she whispered quickly, hotly, suddenly flaring and blushing all over, and, turning away, this time went out so quickly that no one had time to work out why she had come back again. All they saw was her whispering something to Nina Alexandrovna and apparently kissing her hand. But Varya saw and heard it all and followed her with a surprised gaze.

Ganya pulled himself together, and rushed to say goodbye to Nastasya Filippovna, but she had already left. He caught up with her on the staircase.

'You don't need to see me to the door!' she shouted to him. '*Au revoir*, till this evening! Without fail, do you hear!'

He returned confused, reflective; a heavy enigma had descended on his soul, even heavier than before. The prince was in it, too ... So wrapped in oblivion was he that he hardly noticed Rogozhin's entire crowd flocking past him and even jostling him in the doorway, as they hurriedly made their way out of the apartment in Rogozhin's footsteps. They were all loudly, at the top of their voices, discussing something. Rogozhin himself walked with Ptitsyn, insistently repeating some important and apparently urgent remark.

'You lost, Ganka!' he shouted, as they walked past.

Anxiously, Ganya watched them go.

11

The prince left the drawing room and shut himself up in his own room. Kolya at once ran in to console him. The poor boy, it seemed, was now unable to leave him alone.

'You did well to leave,' he said. 'There'll be an even worse row than before, it's like that every day with us, and the trouble all started because of that Nastasya Filippovna.'

'Many different kinds of unhappiness have accumulated here in your home, Kolya,' observed the prince.

'Yes, that's true. But it's our own fault. We ourselves are to blame for it all. But I have a great friend, and he's even more unfortunate. Would you like me to introduce him to you?'

'I'd like that very much. Is he a friend of yours?'

'Yes, almost like a friend. I'll explain it all to you later . . . I say, Nastasya Filippovna is pretty, don't you think? I had never seen her before now, though I'd tried terribly to. Simply dazzling. I would forgive Ganka everything if he were doing it out of love; but why is he taking the money, that's the bad thing!'

'Yes, I don't like your brother very much.'

'Well, of course you don't! Especially after . . . You know, it's all these different opinions I can't stand. Some madman, or fool, or evildoer in a state of madness gives a man a slap in the face and then the man is dishonoured for the rest of his life, and can't wash the dishonour away except with blood, or has to beg for forgiveness on his knees. In my view it's absurd, despotism. Lermontov's drama *Masquerade* is based on it, and it's stupid, in my view. What I mean is, it's unnatural. But after all, he wrote it when he was little more than a child.'[1]

'I liked your sister very much.'

'How she spat in Ganka's mug! Bold Varka! But you didn't

do that, and I'm sure it was not from lack of boldness. Why, here she is now, talk of the devil. I knew she would come: she is noble, though she has her faults.'

'And you have no business here,' Varya pounced on Kolya first of all. 'Go and see your father. Is he being a nuisance, prince?'

'Not at all, on the contrary.'

'Oh, big sister, there she goes again! Now that's the really nasty thing about her. Actually, I thought father would be sure to leave with Rogozhin. I expect he regrets not going now. I'd better go and see how he is,' Kolya added, as he went out.

'Thank goodness, I got mother away and put her to bed, and there's been no more trouble. Ganya is embarrassed, and very pensive. And he has reason to be. Quite a lesson for him! . . . I came to thank you again and to ask you, Prince: you didn't know Nastasya Filippovna before you came here, did you?'

'No, I didn't.'

'Then what made you tell her straight to her face that she was "not like that"? And, it seems, guessed correctly? It turned out that perhaps she really isn't like that. Though as a matter of fact, I can't make her out! Of course her aim was to insult, that's clear. I've also heard many strange things about her before. But if she came to invite us, how could she treat mother like that? Ptitsyn knows her well, he says he could not fathom her just now. And with Rogozhin? One may not talk like that, if one has any self-respect, in the house of one's . . . Mother's also very worried about you.'

'I'm all right!' said the prince, with a wave of his hand.

'And the way she obeyed you . . .'

'How do you mean, obeyed?'

'You told her she ought to be ashamed, and she suddenly changed completely. You have an influence on her, Prince,' Varya added, with the merest of smiles.

The door opened, and quite unexpectedly Ganya walked in.

He did not even hesitate when he saw Varya; he stood in the doorway for a moment and then suddenly, with determination, approached the prince.

'Prince, I behaved basely, forgive me, my dear man,' he said suddenly with intense emotion. The features of his face expressed intense pain. The prince looked in wonder, and did not reply immediately. 'Well, forgive me, please forgive me!' Ganya impatiently insisted. 'If you like, I will kiss your hand!'

The prince was extremely moved, and silently, with both arms, embraced Ganya. They kissed each other sincerely.

'I never, never thought you were like that,' the prince said at last, taking breath with difficulty. 'I didn't think you . . . were capable.'

'Of admitting my guilt? . . . And where I did get the notion earlier that you're an idiot? You notice things that others would never notice. One could talk to you, but . . . better not to talk!'

'Here's someone else to whom you should admit your guilt,' said the prince, pointing to Varya.

'No, these are all my enemies. You may be assured, Prince, many attempts have been made; there is no sincere forgiveness here!' Ganya exclaimed heatedly, and he turned away from Varya to the side.

'No, I forgive you!' Varya said suddenly.

'And will you go to Nastasya Filippovna's this evening?'

'I will go if you tell me to, but you had better judge for yourself: is there even the slightest possibility for me to go now?'

'Look, she's not like that. You see the sort of riddles she poses! Caprices!' and Ganya began to laugh spitefully.

'I know that she's not like that, and has caprices, but what kind of caprices are they? And moreover, watch out, Ganya: what do you think she takes you for? Very well, so she kissed mother's hand. Very well, so these were some kind of caprices, but all the same, I mean to say, she was laughing at you! That's not worth seventy-five thousand, brother, I swear to God it isn't! You're still capable of noble feelings, that's why I'm talking to you. Oh, don't you go there, either! Beware! It will all end badly, you mark my words!'

Having said this, the utterly agitated Varya quickly went out of the room . . .

'That's what they all say!' said Ganya, with an ironic smile. 'And do they really think I don't know it myself? Why, I know far more than they do.'

Having said this, Ganya seated himself on the sofa, evidently wishing to prolong the visit.

'If you already know it,' asked the prince, rather timidly, 'why have you chosen such torment, when you know that it's not really worth seventy-five thousand?'

'I'm not talking about that,' muttered Ganya, 'and by the way, tell me, what do you think, I particularly want to hear your opinion: is this "torment" worth seventy-five thousand or isn't it?'

'In my view, it isn't.'

'Well, now I know. And is it shameful to marry like this?'

'Very shameful.'

'Well, then let me tell you that I'm going to marry her, and it's certain now. Even earlier today I hesitated, but now I don't! Don't say anything! I know what you are going to say . . .'

'I wasn't going to say what you think I was, but I am very astonished at your extreme certainty . . .'

'About what? What certainty?'

'That Nastasya Filippovna will be bound to marry you and that it's all settled now, and secondly, that even if she does marry you, the seventy-five thousand will go straight into your pocket. Of course, there are many aspects of the matter that I don't know . . .'

Ganya moved violently towards the prince.

'That's right, you don't know everything,' he said, 'and why would I take on a burden like that?'

'I think it happens quite a lot: people marry for money, and the wife keeps the money.'

'N-no, that's not how it will be with us . . . there are . . . there are circumstances . . .' Ganya muttered, anxiously brooding. 'And as for her answer, there's no doubt about it now,' he added quickly. 'What makes you think she'll refuse me?'

'I know nothing except what I've seen; and Varvara Arda-lionovna was saying just now . . .'

'Eh! That's just what they're like, they don't really know what to say . . . But as for Rogozhin, she was laughing at him, rest assured. I saw it. It was obvious. I was a little afraid earlier, but now I've seen it. Or perhaps it's because of the way she behaved with mother, father and Varya?'

'And you.'

'Maybe; but it's just the age-old female revenge, and nothing more. She's a fearfully petulant, suspicious and touchy woman. Like a civil servant passed over for promotion! She felt like showing herself off, and all her disdain for him ... well, and also for me; that's true, I don't deny it ... And yet she'll marry me. You have no inkling of the caprices human vanity is capable of: you see, she thinks I'm a scoundrel because I'm taking her, another man's mistress, so openly for her money, and doesn't realize that another man would swindle her even more basely: he'd attach himself to her and start showering her with liberal-progressive ideas and wheeling out various aspects of the woman question, so she'd be like putty in his hands. He would assure the silly vain woman (and so easily!) that he was taking her solely for "the nobility of her heart, and for her misfortune", but he'd be marrying for money all the same. I'm found wanting here because I don't want to prevaricate; but I ought to. But what does she do? Isn't it the same thing? So why then does she despise me and invent these games? Because I don't give in, and show some pride. Well, we shall see!'

'Did you really love her before this?'

'I loved her to begin with. Well, enough said ... There are women who are fit only to be mistresses and nothing else. I'm not saying she was my mistress. If she wants to live quietly, I'll live quietly; but if she rebels, I'll leave her at once, and take the money with me. I don't want to look ridiculous; above all I don't want to look ridiculous.'

'I can't help thinking,' the prince observed cautiously, 'that Nastasya Filippovna is clever. Why, sensing such torment in advance, would she walk into the trap? I mean, she could marry someone else. That's what I find astonishing.'

'But that's where the calculation comes in! You don't know it all, Prince ... it's ... and what's more, she's convinced that I love her to the point of insanity, I swear to you, and you know, I strongly suspect that she loves me, in her own way, that is, you know the saying: "You always hurt the one you love." All her life she will regard me as a *valet de carreau*[2] (and perhaps that's what she needs), and yet love me in her own way; she's preparing to do that, it's in her character. She's an extremely Russian woman, I tell you; well, and I'm also preparing a surprise of my own for her. That scene with Varya just now was an accident, but it was to my advantage: now she has seen and been convinced of my devotion and that I'll break off all ties for her. Which means that we're no fools, either. By the way, I hope you don't think I'm always such a chatterbox? My dear Prince, I may indeed be acting badly by taking you into my confidence. But it's precisely because you're the first decent person to come my way that I've pounced on you, and please don't take that in the wrong way. You're not angry about what happened just now, are you? It's the first time I've spoken from the heart in possibly all of two years. There's an awful lack of honest people here; Ptitsyn is about as honest as they get. Well, are you laughing or aren't you? Scoundrels like honest people – didn't you know that? Though as a matter of fact, in what way am I a scoundrel, tell me, in all conscience? Why do they all follow her in calling me a scoundrel? And you know, I follow her and them in calling myself a scoundrel! That's scoundrelly indeed!'

'I shall never consider you a scoundrel now,' said the prince. 'Earlier today I thought you were an out-and-out evildoer, and you suddenly made me so glad – there is a lesson: not to judge without experience. Now I see that one can consider you neither an evildoer nor even a very corrupt man. In my opinion, you are just the most ordinary man there could be, except that you're very weak and not original at all.'

Ganya smiled caustically to himself, but said nothing. The prince saw that his challenge had not met with approval, grew embarrassed and also fell silent.

'Has father asked you for money?' Ganya asked suddenly.

'No.'

'He will, but don't give him any. And yet you know he was even a respectable man, I remember. He was admitted to polite society. And how quickly they all meet their end, all those respectable old men! The moment their circumstances change there's nothing left, as though their powder had gone up in smoke. He didn't use to lie like that, I assure you; he used simply to be a man with too much enthusiasm, and – look at what it's

resolved itself into! Of course, drink is to blame. Do you know
that he keeps a mistress? He's not just an innocent little old liar
now. I can't understand how mother puts up with it. Has
he told you about the siege of Kars? Or about how his grey
trace-horse began talking? I mean, it even goes as far as that.'

And Ganya fairly shook with sudden laughter.

'Why are you looking at me like that?' he asked the prince.

'It's just that I was surprised you laughed so sincerely. You
really do still have the laugh of a child. Just now you came in
to make amends and said: "If you like, I'll kiss your hand" –
that's exactly how a child would make amends. So you're
still capable of such words and gestures. And suddenly you
start giving an entire lecture about this murky affair and the
seventy-five thousand. Really, it's all rather absurd and hard to
countenance.'

'So what are you trying to conclude from this?'

'That perhaps you're acting too thoughtlessly, and shouldn't
you take your bearings first? Perhaps Varvara Ardalionovna is
right.'

'Ah, morality! I myself am well aware that I'm still a little
boy,' Ganya interrupted hotly. 'Prince, I'm not going into this
murky affair out of calculation,' he continued, letting out his
secret like a young man whose vanity has been wounded. 'If
that were the case, I would have certainly have been in error,
because I am not yet strong in mind and character. I am going
into it because of passion, because of inclination, because I have
a supreme purpose. I expect you think that as soon as I get the
seventy-five thousand I'll buy myself a carriage. No, sir, when
it happens, I shall wear out my three-year-old frock coat and give
up all my club acquaintances. We have few men of perseverance,
though we have plenty of moneylenders, and I want to persevere.
The main thing is to carry it through to the end – that's the
whole task! Ptitsyn was sleeping in the street at seventeen, sold
penknives and began with copecks; now he has sixty thousand,
but only after goodness knows what gymnastics! Now I am
going to jump over the gymnastics, and begin with capital; in
fifteen years' time I shall say: "Behold Ivolgin, King of the Jews."
You say I'm a man with no originality. Bear in mind, dear

Prince, that there is nothing more hurtful to a man of our time and race than to tell him he has no originality, has a weak character, lacks any particular talent and is an ordinary fellow. You didn't even consider me worthy of being called a decent scoundrel, you know, I wanted to eat your bones for that just now! You insulted me worse than Yepanchin, who considers me (without words or wiles, in the simplicity of my soul, bear that in mind) capable of selling him my wife! That has been driving me insane for a long time, and I want money. Once I've made money, you know, I'll be a man of the greatest originality. The most vile and hateful thing about money is that it even imparts talent. And will go on doing so until the end of the world. You may say that this is all childish talk, or poetry, perhaps – what of it, I'll be all the merrier, but the business will be done all the same. I'll go through with it, and persevere. *Rira bien qui rira le dernier!*[3] Why does Yepanchin insult me like that? Out of spite? Never, sir. Simply because I'm too insignificant. Well, sir, but then . . . However, enough, and it's time to go. Kolya has already peeked round the door twice; he's calling you to dinner. But I must be off. I shall drop by and visit you now and then. You'll have quite a nice time with us; now you'll be part of the family. But see that you don't give me away. I think you and I will either be friends, or enemies. What do you suppose, Prince, if I had kissed your hand (as I sincerely offered to do), would I have been your enemy thereafter, as a result?'

'Of course you would, only not for ever, later you wouldn't have been able to keep it up, and you'd have forgiven me,' the prince decided, after some thought and beginning to laugh.

'E-heh! One must be more cautious with you. The devil, you've put some poison into that, too. And who knows, perhaps you're my enemy too? By the way, ha-ha-ha! I forgot to ask: was I correct in thinking that you're rather taken with Nastasya Filippovna? Eh?'

'Yes . . . I am.'

'You're in love?'

'N-no.'

'But he's blushing all over, and suffering. Well, it's all right, it's all right, I'm not going to laugh; *au revoir*. But you know, I mean, she's a woman of virtue, can you believe that? You think she lives with the other one, with Totsky? Not a bit of it! And hasn't for a long time. And did you notice that she's terribly awkward, and was embarrassed at certain moments just now? It's true. Those are the ones who like to wield power. Well, goodbye!'

Ganya went out far more at ease than he had been when he came in, and was now in a good mood. The prince remained motionless for some ten minutes, thinking.

Kolya again stuck his head round the door.

'I don't want dinner, Kolya; I had a good lunch at the Yepanchins' earlier.'

Kolya came all the way round the door and handed the prince a note. It was from the general, folded and sealed. It was clear from Kolya's face that he found it a painful task. The prince read the note, got up and took his hat.

'It's only a couple of blocks away,' Kolya said, starting to grow embarrassed. 'He's sitting there now, with a bottle. Though how he gets credit there, I really don't know. Prince, dear fellow, please don't say anything to the family about my bringing you the note! I've sworn a thousand times not take these notes, but I feel sorry for him; but look, please don't stand on ceremony with him; give him some change, and let that be an end of it.'

'Actually, Kolya, I had the same thought myself; I need to see your papa . . . about a certain matter . . . Come on, let's go.'

I 2

Kolya took the prince a short way, to Liteinaya and a café and billiards room, on the ground floor, the entrance from the street. Here on the right, in a corner of a small, separate room, like an old regular, Ardalion Alexandrovich sat with a bottle in front of him on the table and, indeed, with a copy of the *Indépendance Belge* in his hands. He was expecting the prince; as soon as he caught sight of him he at once put down his newspaper and began a heated and verbose explanation, of which, however, the prince understood nothing, as the general was by now more or less 'primed'.

'I haven't got ten roubles,' the prince interrupted, 'but here's twenty-five, change it, and give me fifteen, for otherwise I myself won't have anything left.'

'Oh, naturally; and you may rest assured that it will be this very moment . . .'

'In addition, I have a request to make of you, General. You've never been at Nastasya Filippovna's, have you?'

'I? Never been? You say this to me? Several times, my dear fellow, several times!' the general exclaimed, in a fit of complacent and triumphant irony. 'But in the end I broke it off myself because I didn't want to encourage an improper union. You have seen for yourself, you were a witness this morning: I have done all that a father could do, but a meek and lenient father; well, now a different sort of father is going to enter the stage, and then – we shall see, we shall see if an honourable old soldier can defeat the intrigue, or if a shameless "camellia" will enter a most noble family.'

'What I particularly wanted to ask you is, could you not, as an acquaintance, take me to Nastasya Filippovna's this evening? I absolutely need to do this today; I have business; but I really don't know how to get in. I was introduced earlier today, but not invited: the soirée is a formal one. However, I'm prepared to overlook certain proprieties, and I don't even mind being laughed at, as long as I can get in somehow.'

'And you have quite, quite coincided with my plan, my young friend,' the general exclaimed in rapture. 'I didn't ask you to come here for this trivial matter!' he continued, taking the money all the same, and putting it in his pocket. 'I really asked you to come here in order to invite you as a companion on a visit to Nastasya Filippovna, or rather on a campaign against Nastasya Filippovna! General Ivolgin and Prince Myshkin! That will surely make her sit up and take notice! And I, on the pretext of an act of kindness on her birthday, will at last make known my will – obliquely, not directly, but it will be the same as if it were directly. Then Ganya himself will see his position: whether it's to be his father, an honourable man and . . . so to speak . . .

etcetera, or . . . But what will be will be! Your plan is a most
fertile one. We shall set off at nine, we still have plenty of time.'

'Where does she live?'

'A long way from here: near the Bolshoi Theatre,
Mytovtsova's house, almost right on the square, on the first
floor . . . It won't be a large gathering, even though it's her
birthday, and they'll break up early . . .'

It had now long been evening; the prince still sat waiting,
listening to the general, who had begun a countless multitude
of anecdotes and had not finished one of them. On the prince's
arrival he had asked for a new bottle and took an hour to finish
it, then asked for another, and finished that one, too. It was a
fair guess that during this time the general succeeded in telling
very nearly the whole of his story. At last, the prince got up and
said he could not wait any longer. The general drained the last
dregs of the bottle, got up and went out of the room, walking
very unsteadily. The prince was in despair. He could not understand how he could have so stupid as to let himself be taken in.
In reality, he never had been; he had placed his reliance on the
general in order to somehow find a way to get into Nastasya
Filippovna's, even if it caused a scandal, but had not reckoned
on a major scandal: the general proved to be decidedly drunk,
in a state of the most violent eloquence, and spoke incessantly,
with emotion, with tears in his soul. The constant gist of it was
that because of the bad behaviour of all the members of his
family everything had gone to pot, and that it was now time for
him to draw the line. At last they came out on to Liteinaya. The
thaw still continued; a dismal, warm, damp wind whistled about
the streets, carriages splashed through the mud, the hooves
of trotting-horse and cart-horse resonantly struck the cobbles.
Pedestrians wandered along the pavements in a wet and dismal
throng. There were drunks here and there among them.

'Do you see those lit-up windows on the first floor?' the
general was saying. 'That's where my comrades live, while I,
who've served longer and suffered more than any of them, have
gone on foot to the Bolshoi Theatre, to the apartment of a
woman of doubtful reputation! A man with thirteen bullets in
his chest . . . you don't believe me? And yet it was exclusively

for me that Pirogov telegraphed Paris and left besieged Sebastopol for a while, and Nélaton, the Paris court physician, got
a safe conduct in the name of science and came to besieged
Sebastopol in order to examine me.[1] The very highest command
knows about it: "Oh, that's the Ivolgin who got thirteen
bullets! . . ." That's how they talk, sir! Do you see that house,
Prince? On the first floor there lives my old comrade General
Sokolovich, with a most noble and numerous family. Well,
that house and another three houses on Nevsky and two on
Morskaya – that's the entire present circle of my acquaintances,
my purely personal acquaintances, that is. Nina Alexandrovna
long ago resigned herself to circumstances. But I still remember
. . . and, as it were, relax in the educated circle of the company
of my former comrades and subordinates, who adore me to this
day. This General Sokolovich (as a matter of fact, I haven't
been to see him for a very long time, nor have I seen Anna
Fyodorovna) . . . you know, dear Prince, when you don't receive
guests yourself, you somehow find yourself giving up visiting
other people. But . . . ahem . . . you don't look as though you
believe me . . . However, why should I not introduce the son of
my best friend and childhood companion into this charming
family home? General Ivolgin and Prince Myshkin! You will
see an astounding girl, and not just one: two, even three, the
ornament of the capital and of society: beauty, progressive
education, progressive orientation . . . the woman question,
poetry – all this has been combined into a happy, diversified
mixture, not to mention a dowry of eighty thousand roubles, in
cash, for each of them, which never does any harm, no matter
what woman questions and social questions there may be . . . in
other words, I have an absolute, total duty and obligation to
introduce you. General Ivolgin and Prince Myshkin!'

'This minute? Now? But you've forgotten,' the prince began.

'I've forgotten nothing, nothing, come along! This way, up
this magnificent staircase. I'm surprised there is no hall porter,
but . . . it's a holiday, and the porter has taken the day off. They
haven't sacked the drunkard yet. This Sokolovich owes all the
happiness of his life and position to me, to me alone, and no
one else, but . . . here we are.'

By now, the prince had stopped objecting to the visit, and obediently followed the general, in order not to irritate him, in the sanguine hope that General Sokolovich and all his household would gradually evaporate like a mirage and prove to be non-existent, so that they could, very calmly, come back down the staircase again. But, to his horror, this hope began to recede; the general led him up the staircase like a man who really did have acquaintances here, and kept constantly inserting bio-graphical and topographical details that were full of a math-ematical precision. At last, when they reached the first floor and stopped on the right, facing the door of a wealthy apartment, and the general took hold of the doorbell handle, the prince decided to run away; but at that moment a strange circumstance stopped him.

'You're mistaken, general,' he said. 'The name on the door is Kulakov, but it's Sokolovich you want.'

'Kulakov . . . Kulakov proves nothing. This is Sokolovich's apartment, and I'm ringing for Sokolovich; I don't give a damn about Kulakov . . . There, now they're coming to open.'

The door really had opened. A lackey peered out and announced: 'The master and mistress are not at home, sir.'

'What a pity, what a pity, and what bad luck,' Ardalion Alexandrovich repeated several times with the most profound regret. 'Then please tell them, my dear fellow, that General Ivolgin and Prince Myshkin wished to pay their respects and were extremely, extremely sorry . . .'

At this moment another face peeped through the door from the interior of the apartment, apparently that of a housekeeper, or possibly even a governess, a lady of about forty, wearing a dark dress. On hearing the names of General Ivolgin and Prince Myshkin she approached with curiosity and mistrust.

'Marya Alexandrovna is not at home,' she said, giving the general a particularly close look. 'She's gone away with the young lady, Alexandra Mikhailovna, to the young lady's grand-mother.'

'And Alexandra Mikhailovna with her, good Lord, what misfortune! And imagine, madam, I always have such mis-fortune! I most humbly ask you to convey my greeting, and remember me to Alexandra Mikhailovna ... in a word, give them my heartfelt wishes for what they themselves wished for on Thursday, in the evening, to the strains of one of Chopin's Ballades; they will remember ... My heartfelt wishes! General Ivolgin and Prince Myshkin!'

'I won't forget, sir,' the lady said with a bow of farewell, more trusting now.

As they went down the staircase, the general, still with ardour uncooled, continued to express regret that they had not found them at home and that the prince had been deprived of such a charming acquaintance.

'You know, my dear fellow, I'm something of a poet at heart, have you noticed that? However ... however, I think we didn't quite go to the right place,' he concluded, apropos of nothing at all. 'The Sokoloviches, I remember now, live in another house and even, I think, in Moscow now. Yes, I was slightly mistaken, but it ... doesn't matter.'

'There's only one thing I should like to know,' the prince observed dismally. 'Ought I to stop relying on you altogether and go on my own?'

'Stop? Relying? On your own? But for what reason, when for me this is a most capital enterprise, on which so much of the fate of my household depends? But, my young friend, you don't know Ivolgin very well. Whoever says "Ivolgin" says "a wall"; you can rely on Ivolgin like a wall, that's what they used to say in the squadron where I began my service. All I want to do is to call in for a moment at a certain house where my soul finds repose, and has done for some years now, after many trials and tribulations ...'

'You want to call in at your home?'

'No! I want ... to go and see the widow of Captain Terentyev, my former subordinate ... There, at the captain's widow's house, I am reborn in spirit, and bring her the unhappiness of my everyday and family life ... And as today there is a great weight upon my mind, I ...'

'I think I've already done something very stupid,' the prince muttered, 'by having troubled you this evening. What's more, now you're ... Goodbye!'

'But I cannot, I cannot let you go, my young friend!' the general flung back at him. 'A widow, the mother of a family, and she pulls from her heart the strings that respond in all my being. A visit to her would take five minutes, in that house I don't stand on ceremony, I almost live there; I shall have a wash, attend to the most essential items of dress, and then we shall take a cab to the Bolshoi Theatre. I assure you that I have need of you for the whole evening ... It's this house here, we've arrived ... Ah, Kolya, are you here already? Well, is Marfa Borisovna at home, or have you only just got here yourself?'

'Oh no,' replied Kolya, who had just collided with them in the gateway of the house, 'I've been here for ages, with Ippolit, he's worse, he was in bed this morning. I've come down now to get some cards at the shop. Marfa Borisovna is waiting for you. But, Papa, oh, look at you! . . .' Kolya concluded, staring fixedly at the general's walk and stance. 'Well then, come on!'

The encounter with Kolya induced the prince to accompany the general to Marfa Borisovna's, too, but only for a minute. The prince needed Kolya; as for the general, however, he had made up his mind to abandon him, and was kicking himself for having earlier thought he could rely on him. The ascent was a long one, to the fourth floor, and by the back stairs.

'Are you going to introduce the prince?' asked Kolya, on the way.

'Yes, *mon ami*, I am: General Ivolgin and Prince Myshkin, but tell me . . . how is . . . Marfa Borisovna . . .'

'You know, Papa, you'd better not go in there! She'll eat you alive! You haven't shown your face for three days, and she's waiting for the money. Why did you promise her that money? You're always like that! Now you'll have to settle with her.'

On the fourth floor they stopped in front of a low door. The general was visibly afraid, and pushed the prince ahead of him.

'I'll stay here,' he muttered. 'I want to make it a surprise . . .'

Kolya went in first. Some lady or other kind, aged about forty, heavily powdered and rouged, in slippers and a dressing-jacket, her hair plaited in pigtails, peeped from the doorway, and the general's surprise suddenly vanished. As soon as the lady caught sight of him she immediately began to shout:

'There he is, the vile, insidious man, I knew it in my heart!'

'Let's go in, it's all right,' the general muttered to the prince, still trying to laugh it off innocently.

But it was not all right. No sooner had they entered, through a dark, low-ceilinged hallway, into a narrow sitting room lined with half a dozen wicker chairs and two card tables, than the mistress of the chambers continued in a studied, plaintive voice, the voice of habit:

'And are you not ashamed, ashamed, you barbarian and tyrant of my household, barbarian and monster! You've robbed me of everything, sucked all the vital juices out of me and are still not satisfied! How much longer must I put up with you, you shameless and dishonourable man?'

'Marfa Borisovna, Marfa Borisovna! This is ... Prince Myshkin. General Ivolgin and Prince Myshkin,' muttered the trembling and flustered general.

'Would you believe,' the captain's widow suddenly addressed the prince, 'would you believe that this shameless man has had no mercy on my orphaned children! He has robbed me of everything, stolen everything, sold everything and pawned it, has left me with nothing. What am I to do with your IOUs, you sly and unscrupulous man? Answer me, sly-boots, answer me, insatiable heart: how, how am I going to feed my orphaned children? Now he turns up drunk, hardly able to stand upright ... What have I done to incur the wrath of the Lord, infamous and disgraceful man, answer me that?'

But the general's mind was elsewhere.

'Marfa Borisovna, twenty-five roubles ... all I can manage, with the help of my most noble friend. Prince! I am cruelly mistaken! Such ... is life ... But now ... forgive me, I'm tired,' the general continued, standing in the middle of the room and bowing in all directions, 'I'm tired, forgive me! Lenochka! A pillow ... my dear!'

Lenochka, an eight-year-old girl, at once ran for a pillow and put it on the hard and tattered oilcloth-covered sofa. The general sat down on it, intending to say more, but as soon as he touched the sofa he at once slumped on his side, turned to the wall and fell into the sleep of the just. Marfa Borisovna ceremoniously

and sorrowfully showed the prince to a chair at a card table, sat
down opposite him, propped her right cheek in her hand, and
silently began to sigh as she looked at the prince. Three small
children, two girls and a boy, of whom Lenochka was the eldest,
approached the table, all three put their hands on the table, and
all three also began to watch the prince closely. Kolya appeared
from the other room.

'I'm very glad that I met you here, Kolya,' the prince addressed
him, 'I wonder if you can help me? I absolutely must be at
Nastasya Filippovna's this evening. I asked Ardalion Ardalionovich earlier today, but now he's fallen asleep. Please come with
me, for I know neither the streets nor the way. I do, however
have the address: near the Bolshoi Theatre, Mytovtsova's house.

'Nastasya Filippovna? But she's never lived near the Bolshoi
Theatre, and father has never been to Nastasya Filippovna's, if
you want to know; it's strange that you expected anything of
him. She lives near Vladimirskaya, by the Five Corners, that's
much closer to here. Do you want to go right now? It's half past
nine. If you like, I'll take you there.'

The prince and Kolya went out at once. Alas! The prince had
no money for a cab, and they had to go on foot.

'I was going to introduce you to Ippolit,' said Kolya. 'He's
the eldest son of that captain's widow in the dressing-jacket,
and he was in the other room; he's ill, and has been in bed all
day today. But he's a strange fellow; he's terribly touchy, and I
thought he might be ashamed in front of you, because you'd
come at such a moment . . . All the same, I'm not as ashamed as
he is, because I have a father, and he has a mother, it makes all
the difference, because the male sex is not disgraced by such
a situation. Though actually, it may perhaps be a prejudice
regarding the predomination of one sex in this case. Ippolit is a
splendid fellow, but he's a slave to certain prejudices.'

'You say he has consumption?'

'Yes, apparently, he'd do better to die as soon as possible. If
I were in his place I'd certainly want to die. He feels sorry for
his brothers and sisters, those little ones, you know. If it were
possible, if only we had the money, he and I would have rented
separate lodgings and renounced our families. That is our

dream. And you know, when I told him earlier about your
incident, he even got angry, and said that anyone who allows
his face to be slapped and doesn't challenge the man who did it
to a duel is a scoundrel. However, he's dreadfully excitable, and
I've given up arguing with him. So let's see, Nastasya Filippovna
invited you to her house straight away, did she?'

'Well, no, not exactly – she didn't.'

'Then why are you going?' exclaimed Kolya, even stopping
in the middle of the pavement. 'And . . . in such clothes, and it's
a formal soirée.'

'I honestly really don't know how I shall get in. If I'm received
– good, if not – it means the business falls through. And as far
as clothes are concerned – what can I do?'

'So you have business? Or are you just going *pour passer le
temps*[2] in "good society"?'

'No, I actually . . . that is, I'm going on business . . . it's hard
for me to explain, but . . .'

'Well, as to its precise nature, let that be as you wish, but
for me the important thing is that you shouldn't simply go
gate-crashing a soirée to join the charming company of
"camellias", generals and moneylenders. If that were the case,
forgive me, Prince, but I should laugh at you and begin to despise
you. There are awfully few decent people here, there's even no
one to respect at all. One finds oneself looking down on them,
but they all demand respect; Varya's the first among them.
And have you noticed, Prince, that in our age everyone is an
adventurer! Especially here in Russia, in our dear fatherland.
And how it all came to be like this, I don't understand. Everything seemed to be so solid, but what do we see now? Everyone
talks about it and writes about it everywhere. They accuse. In
our country everyone accuses. The parents are the first to go
back on their word, and are ashamed of their former moral
probity. Down there in Moscow a father tried to persuade his
son not to stop *at anything* in order to get money; it was in the
press.[3] Take my general. Well, what has become of him? Though
actually, you know: I think my general is an honourable man; I
honestly do! It's all just confusion and drink. It honestly is so! I
even feel sorry for him; I'm just afraid to say it, because everyone

laughs; but quite honestly, I feel sorry for him. And what about them, the clever ones? They're all moneylenders, every last one of them! Ippolit says that money-lending is justified, he says it has to be that way, the economic crisis, some kind of ebb and flow, the devil take it. I find it awfully annoying when he says that, but he's embittered. Imagine, his mother, the captain's widow there, gets money from the general and then lends it back to him at high interest; horribly shameful! And you know, Mother, my mother that is, Nina Alexandrovna, the general's wife, helps Ippolit with money, clothes, linen and everything, and she even helps the children, too, through Ippolit, because they're neglected by their own mother. And Varya helps, too.'

'There you are, you see, you say there are no decent, strong people, and they're all just moneylenders; but there are strong people, your mother and Varya. Isn't helping here and in such circumstances a sign of moral strength?'

'Varka does it out of vanity, out of vainglory, in order not to be outdone by mother; well, and mother really does . . . I respect her. Yes, I respect it, and I think it is justified. Even Ippolit feels that, and he is almost completely embittered. At first he used to laugh and call it baseness on my mother's part; but now he sometimes starts to feel there's something in it. Hmm! So you call that strength, do you? I'll make a note of that. Ganya doesn't know about it, if he did he'd call it "pandering".'

'And Ganya doesn't know? It seems to me there are many things that Ganya doesn't know,' the reflective prince uttered involuntarily.

'But listen, Prince, I like you very much. I keep thinking about that incident of yours earlier today.'

'And I like you very much, Kolya.'

'I say, how long do you plan to live here? I shall soon be getting myself a job and earning something, let's you, I, and Ippolit, all three of us together, rent some lodgings; and we'll invite the general to come and see us.'

'With the greatest of pleasure. However, we shall see. I'm very . . . very unsettled just now. What? Are we here already? This house has . . . such a magnificent doorway! And a hall porter. Well, Kolya, I don't know what's going to come of this.'

The prince stood like one who was lost.

'Tell me about it tomorrow! Don't be too timid. May God grant you success, because I share your convictions about everything! Goodbye. I'll go back there now and tell Ippolit. And as for them letting you in, there's no doubt of that, have no fear! She's terribly eccentric. Up this staircase to the first floor, the hall porter will show you the way!'

13

As he climbed the stairs the prince was very anxious, and tried with all his might to keep his spirits up. 'The worst thing that can happen,' he thought, 'is that they won't let me in and will think badly of me, or, perhaps let me in and then laugh in my face ... Oh, it doesn't matter!' And indeed, this did not yet alarm him very much, but the question: 'what am I going to do there and why am I going?' – to this question he decidedly could not find a reassuring answer. Even if somehow, catching an opportunity, he were able to say to Nastasya Filippovna: 'Don't marry this man and don't ruin yourself, he loves not you but your money, he told me that himself, and so did Aglaya Yepanchina, and I've come to tell you,' it would hardly sound right in every respect. There was yet another unresolved question, and such an important one that the prince was even afraid to think about it, could not and did not dare even admit it, nor know how to formulate it, blushed and trembled at the very thought of it. The upshot of it was, however, that in spite of all these anxieties and doubts he none the less went in and asked for Nastasya Filippovna.

Nastasya Filippovna occupied an apartment that was not very large, but magnificently appointed. In these past five years of her life in St Petersburg there had been a time, at the beginning, when Afanasy Ivanovich was particularly lavish with the money he spent on her; at that time he still had hopes of winning her love, and thought he could seduce her mainly by comfort and luxury, knowing how easily the habits of luxury are acquired and how difficult it is later to give them up, when luxury gradually turns into necessity. From this point of view, Totsky remained faithful to the good old traditions, not changing them in any way, and with a boundless respect for all the invincible power of sensual influences. Nastasya Filippovna did not turn her nose up at luxury, was even fond of it, but – and this seemed exceedingly strange – in no way surrendered to it, as though she could always manage without it; she even tried to put this into words on this occasion, something that struck Totsky unpleasantly. There were, however, many things about Nastasya Filippovna that struck Afanasy Ivanovich unpleasantly (and subsequently even to the point of contempt). Not to speak of the lack of refinement of the class of people she sometimes brought close to herself, and must therefore have been inclined to bring close, there were signs in her of other, quite strange inclinations: there asserted itself a kind of barbarous mixture of two tastes, a capacity for making do and being content with such things and resources the very existence of which one might have thought no decent and educated person could allow. Indeed, if, to take an example, Nastasya Filippovna had suddenly displayed a charming and refined ignorance of, say, the fact that peasant women could not afford to wear the cambric underwear she wore, Afanasy Ivanovich would, it seems, have been exceedingly content. It was at such results that the whole of Nastasya Filippovna's upbringing had been originally aimed, in accordance with the programme devised by Totsky, who in this respect was a man of great understanding; but alas, the results turned out to be bizarre. In spite of this, however, there was and remained something in Nastasya Filippovna that occasionally even struck Afanasy Ivanovich himself by its extraordinary and fascinating originality, a kind of power, and it sometimes enticed him even now, when all his former plans for her had come to nought.

The prince was met by a maid (Nastasya Filippovna's servants were always female) and, to his surprise, she listened to his request to be announced without any perplexity at all. Neither his muddy boots, nor his wide-brimmed hat, nor his sleeveless cloak, nor his flustered look caused her the slightest hesitation.

She helped him off with his cloak, asked him to wait in the hallway, and at once set off to announce him.

The company that had assembled at Nastasya Filippovna's consisted of her most ordinary and usual friends and acquaintances. It was even rather sparse, compared to previous annual gatherings on this day. Those present included, first and foremost, and as the main guests, Afanasy Ivanovich Totsky and Ivan Fyodorovich Yepanchin; both were polite, but both were in a state of some hidden anxiety, which stemmed from their poorly concealed expectation of the promised announcement concerning Ganya. In addition to them, of course, there was Ganya – also very gloomy, very pensive and even almost 'impolite', for the most part standing to the side, at a distance, and not saying anything. He had not dared to bring Varya, but Nastasya Filippovna never even mentioned her; on the other hand, no sooner had she greeted him than she reminded him of his earlier scene with the prince. The general, who had not yet heard about it, began to grow interested. Then Ganya coolly, with reserve, but also with complete candour, related all that had happened earlier, and how he had already gone to see the prince in order to apologize. As he did so, he warmly expressed his opinion that it was very strange, and Lord knew why the prince should be called an 'idiot', that he thought 'quite the opposite' of him, and that 'of course the man was in his right mind'. Nastasya Filippovna listened to this testimonial with close attention, watching Ganya inquisitively, but the talk at once passed to Rogozhin, who had played such an important part in the morning's events, and who also began to arouse the interest and extreme curiosity of Afanasy Ivanovich and Ivan Fyodorovich. It turned out that some special information about Rogozhin was available from Ptitsyn, who had been helping him with business matters until nearly nine o'clock in the evening. Rogozhin had insisted with all his might that a hundred thousand roubles be obtained that very day. 'He was drunk, of course,' Ptitsyn commented, 'but it seems that, however difficult it may be, he'll get a hundred thousand, only I don't know if it will all be here today; but many people are working on it, Kinder, Trepalov, Biskup; he's willing to pay any rate of interest at all, though of course it's just drunken talk and the first flush of joy . . .' Ptitsyn concluded. All this news was received with interest, partly of a gloomy sort; Nastasya Filippovna kept silent, evidently not wishing to express an opinion; Ganya, too. General Yepanchin was secretly almost more anxious than anyone else; the pearl necklace he had presented that morning had been accepted with too cold a politeness, and even with a kind of peculiar smile. Ferdyshchenko, alone of all the guests, was in a merry, festive mood, laughing loudly from time to time at no one knew what, and only because he had taken upon himself the role of jester. As for Afanasy Ivanovich, who had the reputation of being a subtle and elegant raconteur, and who on previous occasions had led the conversation at these soirées, he was evidently not in a good mood and even in a kind of perplexity that was uncharacteristic of him. The remaining guests, of whom there were, as a matter of fact, not many (one wretched old schoolmaster, invited heaven knows why, a very young man whom no one knew, dreadfully shy, who never opened his mouth, a pert lady of about forty who was an actress, and an exceedingly beautiful, exceedingly well and richly dressed and extraordinarily silent young lady), were not only unable to enliven the conversation much, but were even at a loss to know what to talk about.

Thus, the appearance of the prince even came at the right time. The announcement of his arrival caused bewilderment and several strange smiles, especially when, from Nastasya Filippovna's surprised look, it was learned that she had not thought of inviting him at all. But after her initial surprise, Nastasya Filippovna suddenly displayed so much delight that most of those present at once prepared to greet the uninvited guest with both laughter and cheerfulness.

'I expect this has happened because of his innocence,' concluded Ivan Fyodorovich Yepanchin, 'and as a general rule it's rather dangerous to encourage such tendencies, but it's true that at the present moment it's not a bad thing that he's decided to come visiting, even though in such an original manner: perhaps he will cheer us up a bit, at least if I'm any judge.'

'All the more so since he's invited himself!' Ferdyshchenko at once inserted.

'And what follows from that?' the general, who loathed Ferdyshchenko, asked sourly.

'That he'll have to pay for admittance.'

'Well, sir, but Prince Myshkin is not Ferdyshchenko,' the general could not restrain himself from saying; he had still not been able to reconcile himself with the thought of being in the same company with Ferdyshchenko, and on an equal footing with him.

'Oh, General, don't be too hard on Ferdyshchenko,' the latter replied, smirking. 'I have special rights, you know.'

'And what sort of special rights would those be?'

'Last time I had the honour of explaining it in detail to the company; for your excellency I'll repeat it once more. Be so good as to observe, your excellency: everyone has wit, but I have none. As a reward, I have obtained permission to tell the truth, as everyone knows that the truth is only told by those who have no wit. In addition, I am a very vindictive man, and that is also because I have no wit. I will meekly endure all kind of insults, but only until my insulter suffers a setback; at his first setback I immediately remember it all and at once take my revenge in some way, I kick, as has been said of me by Ivan Petrovich Ptitsyn, who himself, of course, never kicks anyone. Your excellency, do you know Krylov's fable *The Lion and the Donkey*? Well, that's the two of us, it was written about us.'

'I think you're talking rot again, Ferdyshchenko,' the general flared up again.

'But what's wrong, your excellency?' retorted Ferdyshchenko, who had been relying on the possibility of making some retort and of spreading himself still wider. 'Don't worry, your excellency, I know my place: if I said that you and I are the Lion and the Donkey from Krylov's fable, then of course I take the role of Donkey on myself, while your excellency is the Lion, as it goes in Krylov's fable:

> The mighty Lion, tempest of the woods,
> With age his strength had yielded.[1]

While I, your excellency, am the Donkey.'

'With the last part I agree,' the general blurted rashly.

All of this was crude, of course, and deliberately manufactured, but it was indeed now accepted that Ferdyshchenko should be allowed to play the role of jester.

'And I am only admitted here on sufferance,' Ferdyshchenko had once exclaimed, 'in order to talk in precisely this vein. Well, is it really possible to receive someone like me? I mean, I understand that. Can I, a Ferdyshchenko such as I, be seated beside a refined gentleman like Afanasy Ivanovich? There remains, willy-nilly, but one explanation: I am seated beside him because such a thing is impossible to imagine.'

But although it was crude, it was also caustic, sometimes even very much so, and it seemed it was this that appealed to Nastasya Filippovna. Those who were desirous of her company had to put up with Ferdyshchenko. He had perhaps guessed the whole truth in supposing that he was received because from the very first Totsky found his presence unendurable. Ganya, for his part, had endured from him a whole infinity of torments, and in this respect Ferdyshchenko had succeeded in being very useful to Nastasya Filippovna.

'Well, the prince can make a start by singing us a popular romance,' concluded Ferdyshchenko, looking to see what Nastasya Filippovna would say.

'I don't think so, Ferdyshchenko, and please don't get so excited,' she observed coldly.

'Aha! If he's under special protection then I, too, relent . . .'

But Nastasya Filippovna got up without listening, and went to greet the prince herself.

'I'm sorry', she said, suddenly presenting herself to the prince, 'that earlier, in my haste, I forgot to invite you to my home, and I'm very glad that you yourself now afford me the chance of thanking and praising you for your resolve.'

As she said this she stared fixedly at the prince, endeavouring to interpret his action to herself in some way.

The prince would, perhaps, have made some reply to her kind words, but was so dazzled and struck that he could not even utter a word. Nastasya Filippovna observed this with satisfaction. This evening she was in full dress attire, and produced an extraordinary impression. She took him by the arm and led him towards the guests. Right at the entrance to the drawing room the prince suddenly halted and, in extraordinary agitation, hurriedly whispered to her:

'Everything about you is perfection . . . even that you're thin and pale . . . one would not wish to imagine you differently . . . I so much wanted to come and see you . . . I . . . forgive me . . .'

'Don't apologize,' Nastasya Filippovna began to laugh, 'it will spoil all the strangeness and originality. So it's true what they say about you, that you're a strange man. So you think I am perfection, do you?'

'Yes.'

'Though you may be a master of guesswork, you are mistaken. I shall remind you of that later this evening . . .'

She introduced the prince to the guests, to more than half of whom he was already known. Totsky at once made some kind of complimentary remark. Everyone seemed to liven up a little, they all began to talk and laugh together. Nastasya Filippovna made the prince sit down beside her.

'But what's so surprising about the prince showing up?' Ferdyshchenko shouted louder than any of them. 'The matter is clear, the matter speaks for itself!'

'The matter is all too clear and speaks for itself all too well,' Ganya, who had been silent, chipped in. 'I have been observing the prince almost constantly today, right from the moment he looked at Nastasya Filippovna's portrait earlier, on Ivan Fyodorovich's desk. I very well remember at the time thinking something of which I now quite convinced and which, by the way, the prince himself confessed to me.'

Ganya spoke this entire sentence extremely earnestly, without the slightest jocularity, even gloomily, which seemed slightly strange.

'I didn't make any confessions to you,' replied the prince, blushing, 'I merely replied to your question.'

'Bravo, bravo!' cried Ferdyshchenko. 'Honest, at least, both cunning and honest!'

They all laughed loudly.

'Oh, stop shouting, Ferdyshchenko,' Ptitsyn observed to him in a low voice, with revulsion.

'I didn't expect such prowess from you, Prince,' Ivan Fydorov-ich said softly. 'It's not the kind of thing I'd expect you to say. And there was I thinking you were a philosopher! Oh, the quiet ones!'

'And judging from the way the prince blushes at an innocent joke like an innocent young girl, I conclude that, as a well-bred young man, he nourishes the most praiseworthy intentions within his heart,' the toothless and until now completely silent septuagenarian schoolmaster, whom no one could have expected even to utter a word that evening, said, or rather mumbled, quite suddenly and unexpectedly. This made them all laugh even more. The old man, probably thinking that they were laughing at his wit, began, as he looked at them all, to laugh even more, which caused him to have a severe fit of coughing, so that Nastasya Filippovna, who was for some reason inordinately fond of all such eccentric old men and old women, and even of holy fools, at once began to lavish affection on him, kissing him and ordering more tea for him. Of the maid who entered she also asked for a mantilla to be brought for her, in which she wrapped herself, and gave instructions for more wood be put on the fire. In response to the question of what time it was, the maid replied that it was already half-past ten.

'Would you like some champagne, gentlemen?' Nastasya Filippovna asked them suddenly. 'I have some ready. Perhaps it will cheer your mood. Please help yourselves, without ceremony.'

The invitation to drink, especially phrased in such naive terms, seemed very strange coming from Nastasya Filippovna. Every-one knew the extraordinary decorum that had characterized her previous soirées. On the whole, the soirée did become more cheerful, but not in the usual way. The wine was, however, accepted, first by the general himself, second by the pert lady, the old man, Ferdyshchenko, and after that, by everyone else. Totsky also took a glass, hoping to harmonize the new tone that was beginning to emerge by giving it as far as possible the character of a charming joke. Ganya alone took none. Of the

strange, sometimes very abrupt and swift caprices of Nastasya
Filippovna, who also took wine and announced that this evening
she would have three glasses, of her hysterical and aimless
laughter, which alternated suddenly with silent and even,
gloomy pensiveness, it was hard to make much sense. Some
suspected she was suffering from a fever; they began, at last, to
notice that she seemed to be waiting for something, frequently
looking at the clock, becoming impatient and listless.

'Do you have a slight fever, perhaps?' the pert lady asked.

'Quite a bad one, not a slight one, that's why I've put on
this mantilla,' replied Nastasya Filippovna, who had indeed
become paler, and seemed at times to be suppressing a violent
shiver.

They all began to be concerned, and there was a general stir.

'Shouldn't we give our hostess some rest?' ventured Totsky,
looking at Ivan Fyodorovich.

'On no account, gentlemen! I particularly request you to
stay. I especially need your presence this evening,' Nastasya
Filippovna declared with meaningful insistence. And since
nearly all the guests had learned that on this evening a very
important decision was to be made, these words carried
exceeding weight. The general and Totsky again exchanged
glances, and Ganya made a convulsive twitch.

'It would be nice to play a *petit jeu*,'[2] said the pert lady.

'I know a new and most marvellous *petit jeu*,' Ferdyshchenko
chimed in, 'or at least one that has only been played once, and
then not successfully.'

'What was it?' asked the pert lady.

'One day a company of us got together, well, we'd been
drinking a bit, it's true, and suddenly someone proposed that
each of us, without getting up from the table, should tell the
others something about himself, but something that he himself,
in sincere conscience, viewed as the worst of all the bad things
he'd done during the whole of his life; but he should be sincere,
that was the main thing, sincere, and he must not lie!'

'A strange idea,' said the general.

'Indeed, what could be stranger, your excellency, and that is
what makes it so good.'

'A ridiculous idea,' said Totsky, 'though in fact it's easy to understand: it's a special kind of boasting.'

'Perhaps that was the whole purpose of it, Afanasy Ivanovich.'

'I think one would end up crying, not laughing, in such a game,' the pert lady observed.

'It's quite impossible and absurd,' was Ptitsyn's opinion.

'And did it succeed?' asked Nastasya Filippovna.

'That's just the point, it didn't, it all went wrong, each person did tell something, many told the truth, and imagine, some even enjoyed the telling, but then they all felt ashamed, couldn't keep it up! On the whole, though, it was great fun, in its own way.'

'Yes, it would indeed be fun!' observed Nastasya Filippovna, growing suddenly animated in the whole of her being. 'Indeed, let us try, gentlemen! We really could do with cheering up. If each of us would agree to tell something . . . of that kind . . . by consent, of course, everyone is completely free, all right? Perhaps we might be able to keep it up? At any rate it's terribly original . . .'

'A brilliant idea!' Ferdyshchenko chimed in. 'However, the ladies are excused, the men shall begin; the matter will be settled by drawing lots, like last time! Yes, we must certainly do it that way! If anyone really doesn't want to, he need not tell anything, but that will be churlish of him! Cast your lots here, gentlemen, over here to me, into my hat, the prince will make the draw. A very simple task, to describe the worst thing you ever did in your life – it's terribly easy, gentlemen! You'll see! If anyone has forgotten, I shall at once undertake to remind him!'

No one liked the idea. Some frowned, others slyly smiled. Some protested, but not greatly – Ivan Fyodorovich, for example, who did not want to go against Nastasya Filippovna's wishes, and had noticed how attracted she was by this strange notion. Nastasya Filippovna was always unyieldingly relentless in her desires once she had determined to express them, no matter how capricious, and even, from her point of view, how completely useless, those desires might be. And now she was almost in a state of hysteria, agitated, in fits of convulsive laughter, especially at the objections of the alarmed Totsky. Her dark eyes began to glitter, two red spots appeared on her pale cheeks. Perhaps the despondent and squeamish look on the physiognomies of some of the guests inflamed her mocking desire even more; perhaps it was precisely the cynicism and cruelty of the idea that appealed to her. Some were even sure that she had some special calculation in it. However, they began to give their consent: at all events it was intriguing, and for many of them quite tempting. Ferdyshchenko was more agitated than anyone else.

'But what if it's something that can't be told . . . in the presence of ladies,' the silent youth observed timidly.

'Then don't tell it; you must have done enough bad things without it,' replied Ferdyshchenko. 'Oh, you young people!'

'But I really don't know which things I've done that I consider the worst,' the pert lady inserted.

'Ladies are exempt from the obligation of telling,' Ferdyshchenko repeated, 'but are only exempt; the inspiration of the moment is gratefully permitted. As for the men, if they really don't want to take part, they're exempt, too'

'But how am I to prove that I'm not lying?' Ganya asked. 'And if I lie, the whole object of the game is defeated. And who will not lie? I'm sure everyone will.'

'Well, that in itself is rather alluring, to see the way in which people will lie. But you, Ganechka, have no particular need to be afraid of lying, as everyone already knows the worst thing you've done. And just think, gentlemen,' Ferdyshchenko suddenly exclaimed in a kind of inspiration, 'just think with what eyes we'll look at one another afterwards, tomorrow, for example, after the stories we've heard!'

'But is this possible? Are you really in earnest, Nastasya Filippovna?' Totsky inquired with dignity.

'If you're frightened of wolves, don't go into the forest!' Nastasya Filippovna observed with an ironic smile.

'But forgive me, Mr Ferdyshchenko, is it really possible to make a parlour game out of this?' Totsky continued, growing more and more anxious. 'I assure you that such things are never a success; you say yourself that it didn't succeed last time.'

'How do you mean, didn't succeed? Last time I told the story of how I stole three roubles, I just went ahead and told it!'

'Very well. But after all, there was no possibility of you telling it in such a way that so as to make it resemble the truth and be believed, was there? And as Gavrila Ardalionovich quite correctly observed, as soon as the slightest note of insincerity is heard, the whole object of the game is defeated. The truth is possible here only accidentally, in a special kind of boastful mood that is in bad taste, unthinkable here and totally indecent.'

'But what a subtle man you are, Afanasy Ivanovich, why, you even astonish me!' exclaimed Ferdyshchenko. 'Imagine, gentlemen: by his observing that I couldn't possibly tell the story of my theft in such a way that it would resemble the truth, Afanasy Ivanovich is hinting in the most subtle way that I couldn't possibly commit a theft in real life (because to say so out loud would be indecent), even though he may privately be quite certain that there is every likelihood Ferdyshchenko is capable of theft! But to the matter at hand, gentlemen, to the matter at hand, the lots are gathered and you, Afanasy Ivanovich, have put yours in, too, and therefore no one has refused! Prince, make the draw!'

The prince silently lowered his hand into the hat and took out the first lot – Ferdyshchenko, the second – Ptitsyn, the third – the general, the fourth – Afanasy Ivanovich, the fifth – himself, the sixth – Ganya, and so on. The ladies had not cast any lots.

'Oh Lord, what misfortune!' exclaimed Ferdyshchenko. 'And there was I thinking that the prince would be first, and the general would be second. But thank goodness, at least I'm before Ivan Petrovich, and that will be some recompense. Well, gentlemen, of course, I'm obliged to set a noble example, but my principal regret at this moment is that I'm so contemptible and lack distinction in any way; even my rank is the very, very lowest; well, what is there of any interest in the fact that Ferdyshchenko has done something bad? And indeed, what is my most reprehensible deed? I have an *embarras de richesse*. Must I really tell that same story about my theft, in order to convince Afanasy Ivanovich that it's possible to steal without being a thief?'

'You're convincing me, Mr Ferdyshchenko, that one may indeed feel satisfaction to the point of rapture in telling of one's rotten actions, even though one has never been asked about them . . . Though, actually . . . Forgive me, Mr Ferdyschchenko.'

'Do get on with it, Ferdyshchenko, you ramble far too long and never arrive at the end,' Nastasya Filippovna commanded with irritable impatience.

They all noticed that after her recent convulsive laughter she had suddenly become gloomy, peevish and irritable; none the less, with despotic obstinacy she insisted on her impossible caprice. Afanasy Ivanovich was suffering horribly. Ivan Fyodorovich was also driving him mad: he sat there drinking his champagne as though nothing were the matter and was even, perhaps, planning to tell something of his own when his turn came.

14

'I have no wit, Nastasya Filippovna, and that's why I talk too much!' exclaimed Ferdyshchenko, as he began his story. 'Had I the wit of Afanasy Ivanovich or Ivan Petrovich, then I would have sat and kept quiet all evening, like Afanasy Ivanovich and Ivan Petrovich. Prince, allow me to ask you, what do you think, it seems to me that there are many more thieves in the world than there are non-thieves, and that there is not even the most honest man who has not at least once in his life stolen something. That's my opinion, from which, however, I do not at all conclude that all people are thieves, although, quite honestly, I'm sometimes terribly inclined to suppose that they are. But what do you think?'

'Fie, what a silly way you have of telling a story,' replied Darya Alexeyevna, 'and what nonsense, it cannot possibly be true that everyone has stolen something; I've never stolen anything.'

'You may never have stolen anything, Darya Alexeyevna; but what will the prince say, who has suddenly blushed all over?'

'I think what you say is true, but you exaggerate too much,' said the prince, who really had begun to blush for some reason.

'Well, Prince, have you never stolen anything?'

'Fie! How ridiculous this is! Remember where you are, Mr Ferdyshchenko,' the general intervened.

'It's plain to see that when it comes down to it, you're ashamed to tell your story, so you try to drag the prince with you, because he's so meek and mild,' Darya Alexeyevna rapped out.

'Ferdyshchenko, either tell your story or be quiet and mind your own business. You're exhausting our patience,' Nastasya Filippovna said sharply and with annoyance.

'At once, Nastasya Filippovna; but if the prince has confessed, for I insist all the same that the prince has confessed, then what, for example, would someone else (I mention no names) say, if he wanted to tell the truth? With regard to myself, gentlemen, there's really nothing more to tell: it's all very simple, stupid, and bad. But I assure you that I'm not a thief; I just stole something, I don't know why. It was the year before last, at the dacha of Semyon Ivanovich Ishchenko, on a Sunday. He had some guests to dinner. After dinner the gentlemen sat on over their wine. I had the idea of asking Marya Semyonovna, his daughter, a young lady, to play something on the piano. I passed through the corner room, and there was a green three-rouble note lying on Marya Ivanovna's work box: she had got it out to pay some household expense. There was no one in the room. I picked up the note and put it in my pocket. I don't know what got into me. But I quickly went back and sat down at the table. I continued to sit and wait, in a state of rather violent agitation, talking without cease, telling anecdotes, laughing; then I went in and sat with the ladies. Approximately half an hour later, the absence of the money was noticed, and they began to question the maids. The maid Darya was suspected of having taken it. I displayed extraordinary curiosity and sympathy, and I remember that when Darya completely broke down, I even began to try to persuade her that she should confess her guilt, staking everything on Marya Ivanovna's kindness, and this out loud, in everyone's presence. They all stared at me, and I felt extraordinary satisfaction because I was preaching while the note was in my pocket. That evening I spent the three roubles in a restaurant, on drink. Went in and asked for a bottle of Lafite; never before had I asked for a bottle of wine on its own like that, without anything else; I wanted to spend the money quickly. Neither then nor later did I feel any particular qualms of conscience. I probably wouldn't have done it a second time; you may believe it or not, as you will, but it doesn't interest me. Well, gentlemen, that is all.'

'Except, of course, that it's not the worst thing you've ever done,' said Darya Alexeyevna, with disgust.

'It's a psychological case, not something you did,' observed Afanasy Ivanovich.

'And the maid?' asked Nastasya Filippovna, not trying to conceal a most fastidious distaste.

'The maid was dismissed the very next day, of course. It's a strict household.'

'And you allowed it to happen?'

'I like that! You really think I should have gone and owned up?' giggled Ferdyshchenko, struck, however, by the very unpleasant impression his story had left.

'What a filthy thing to do!' exclaimed Nastasya Filippovna.

'Bah! You want to hear about the worst thing a man has done, and demand brilliance at the same time! The worst actions are always filthy, we shall hear it from Ivan Petrovich in a moment; and there are not a few people who show a brilliant exterior and think they look virtuous because they own their own carriage. There are not a few people who own their own carriage . . . Though by what means . . .'

In a word, Ferdyshchenko was quite unable to control himself, and suddenly lapsed into a frantic rage, even to the point of forgetting himself and going beyond all limits; his whole face was positively contorted. However strange it might seem, it was very possible that he had expected quite a different response to his story. These 'blunders' of taste and this 'special kind of boasting', as Totsky had expressed it, happened very often with Ferdyshchenko and were an integral part of his character.

Nastasya Filippovna even shuddered with anger, and stared intently at Ferdyshchenko; in an instant he lost his nerve and fell silent, almost turning cold with fright; for he had gone too far.

'Don't you think we ought to give this up?' Afanasy Ivanovich asked, slyly.

'It's my turn now, but I'm going to claim my privilege, and shall not tell a story,' Ptitsyn said resolutely.

'You don't want to?'

'I can't, Nastasya Filippovna; and in any case, I consider a *petit jeu* of this kind impossible and out of the question.'

'General, it seems that you are next in our line,' Nastasya Filippovna said, turning to him. 'If you refuse, the whole thing will fall apart in our hands, and I shall be sorry, as I'd been planning to round things off by telling something "from my own life", but wanted to do so after you and Afanasy Ivanovich, because I need you to give me courage,' she concluded, bursting into laughter.

'Oh well, if that's what you're promising,' the general exclaimed warmly, 'I'm willing to tell you my entire life story, but I must confess that while waiting for my turn I've already prepared my own anecdote . . .'

'And by his excellency's look alone one may conclude with what literary satisfaction he has worked out his little anecdote,' the still somewhat flustered Ferdyshchenko summoned up the boldness to observe, smiling poisonously.

Nastasya Filippovna glanced briefly at the general, and also smiled to herself. But it was evident that *ennui* and irritation were intensifying in her more and more. Afanasy Ivanovich was doubly alarmed at her promise to tell a story of her own.

'It has happened, gentlemen, to me as to everyone else, that in the course of my life I have done some things that were not very pretty,' began the general, 'but the strangest aspect of it is that I myself consider the short little anecdote I shall tell you in a moment the ugliest one of my entire existence. Moreover, almost thirty-five years have passed since it took place; but when I remember it I can never free myself from a certain, as it were, clawing sensation in my heart. It was, however, an exceedingly stupid affair: I was then only an ensign, drudging my way through the army. Well, you know what an ensign is like: blood at boiling point and housekeeping run on copecks; in those days I had a batman, Nikifor, who took a keen concern for my housekeeping, saving, sewing, scrubbing and cleaning, and even stealing anything he could get his hands on just in order to add a few items to the house; he was the most loyal and honest of men. I, of course, was strict but fair. For a while, we happened to be stationed in a small town. I was billeted in a suburb with a second lieutenant's wife, who was in fact a widow. The old woman must have been about eighty, or at least something approaching it. Her little house was tumbledown, wretched, made of timber, and she even had no maid, because she was so poor. She was mainly distinguished, however, by once having had a numerous family and relatives; but during the course of her life some had died, others had gone their separate ways, others still had forgotten about the old woman, and she had buried her husband some forty-five years earlier. A few years before this a niece had lived with her, hunchbacked and as nasty as a witch, who had even once bitten the old woman's finger, but she too had died, and the old woman had now been struggling along all on her own for some three years. It was pretty boring at her place, and the old woman was so senile that one couldn't get anything out of her. At last she stole a cockerel from me. It was an obscure business, but it could only have been her. We quarrelled about the cockerel, and considerably so, and then it so happened that right on my first application I was transferred to another billet, in a suburb on the other side of the town, in the numerous family of a merchant with a very large beard, as I remember him now. Nikifor and I were glad to move, but we left the old woman in a state of indignation. Some three days went by, I came back from drill, and Nikifor announced that "we shouldn't have left our tureen at the old landlady's, sir, there's nothing to serve the soup in now". I was taken aback, of course: "How can it be, how did our tureen get left behind at the landlady's?" The astonished Nikifor continued to report that while we were moving out the landlady had refused to give him our tureen, on the grounds that, as I had broken a pot of hers, she was going to keep our tureen, and that I had offered it to her. Such meanness on her part, of course, drove me beyond the limit; my blood began to boil, I leaped to my feet, went rushing off. I arrived at the old woman's place practically beside myself; I saw her sitting in the passage all on her own, in the corner, as though she were hiding from the sun, propping her cheek in her hand. Well, I at once brought a thunderbolt down on her, telling her she was "this" and "that", you know, in the Russian way. But then I looked, and saw something strange: she sat staring with her face towards me, her eyes bulged, and she said not a word in reply, looking so strangely, strangely, and as if she were rocking to and fro. At last I calmed down, took a closer look, asked her some questions: not a word in reply. I stood for a while, undecided; flies were buzzing, the sun was setting, silence; at last, completely baffled, I went away. I hadn't yet reached home when I was summoned to the major, then I had to look in at company headquarters, so I didn't get home until far into the evening. The first thing Nikifor said was: "You know, sir, our landlady has died." "When?" "This evening, about an hour and a half ago." This meant that at the very time I had been shouting at her, she had been departing this world. This gave me such a shock, I tell you, I could barely pull myself together. You know, I even began to brood about it, even dreamed about it at night. Of course, I'm not superstitious, but on the third day I went to church for the funeral. In short, the more time passes, the more I think about it. Not that it really worries me, but sometimes I imagine it, and it doesn't feel good. I've worked out what the main point of it is. In the first place, she was a woman, so to speak, a human being, as it's called in our time, *être humain*, she had lived, lived a long time, and had finally come to the end of her life. Once she had had children, a husband, a family, relatives, all that had effervesced around her, so to speak, all those smiles, and suddenly – a total void, everything flown up the chimney, she was left alone, like ... some kind of housefly, bearing a curse from time immemorial. And now, at last, God had led her to the end. With the setting of the sun, on a quiet summer evening, my old woman also flew away – of course, there's a certain moral to be drawn here; and then at that very moment, instead of tears of farewell, so to speak, there's a desperate young ensign, with his hands on his hips and a self-satisfied look, seeing her off from the crust of the earth with a stream of Russian curses about a missing tureen! There's no doubt, I was guilty, and although, because of the remoteness of the years and the change in my nature, I have long viewed my action as that of another man, I none the less continue to be sorry. So that, I repeat, it even seems strange to me, and all the more so since, if I was to blame, I was not so entirely: I mean, why did she decide to die at that particular moment? There is, of course, an excuse: that my action was in some sense a psychological one, but all the same I could find no rest until, about fifteen years ago, at my own expense I settled two chronically ill old women in the almshouse, with the object of softening the last days of their earthly life by having them decently looked after. I plan to turn it into a permanent one, and have left capital in my will. Well, gentlemen, that is all, gentlemen. I repeat that although I may have been guilty of very many things in my life, I consider that incident to be the worst action of my whole life.'

'And instead of the worst action of your life, your excellency has told us one of your good deeds; you've cheated Ferdyshchenko!' said Ferdyshchenko.

'Indeed, general, I never imagined that you had a kind heart in spite of it all; I'm almost sorry,' Nastasya Filippovna said carelessly.

'Sorry? But why?' the general asked with a polite laugh, and took a sip of his champagne, not without self-satisfaction.

But now it was the turn of Afanasy Ivanovich, who had also prepared himself. Everyone had guessed that, unlike Ivan Petrovich, he would not refuse, and for several reasons, they awaited his story with particular curiosity, looking at Nastasya Filippovna now and then. With extraordinary dignity, quite in harmony with his portly appearance, and in a courteous voice, Afanasy Ivanovich began one of his 'charming stories'. (Incidentally, he was a man imposing in his presence, portly, tall of stature, slightly balding, slightly greying, and rather stout, with soft, rubicund, slightly flabby cheeks, and false teeth. He dressed in loose, elegant clothes, and wore magnificent linen. His plump white hands made one want to stare in wonderment. On the index finger of his right hand there was an expensive diamond ring.) Throughout the whole of his story, Nastasya Filippovna fixedly studied the lace of the frill on her sleeve, pinching it with two fingers of her left hand, so that never once did she so much as glance at the story's teller.

'What makes my task easier, above all,' Afanasy Ivanovich began, 'is the absolute obligation to describe the very worst thing I have ever done in my whole life. In such a case, there can, of course, be no hesitation: one's conscience and the memory of the heart at once tell one exactly what to say. I confess with sorrow that among all the countless possibly frivolous and . . . fickle actions of my life there is one that has imprinted itself all too painfully on my memory. It was about twenty years ago; at the time I was staying on Platon Ordyntsev's country estate. He had just been elected marshal of nobility and had arrived with his young wife to spend the winter holidays. Anfisa Alexeyevna's birthday happened to fall at the same time, and two balls were arranged. In those days the height of fashion was represented by the delightful novel of Dumas *fils*, *La Dame aux camélias*, a poem which had taken society by storm and which, in my opinion, is destined neither to die nor to grow old. In the provinces all the ladies, or at least, those ladies who had read it, were in raptures of ecstasy over it. The delightful quality of the narrative, the originality of the main character's presentation, that alluring world, analysed to the point of subtlety, and, of course, all those enchanting details that are scattered through the book (concerning, for example, the circumstances in which bouquets of white and pink camellias are to be used in turn),[1] in short, all those delightful details, and the whole thing together, caused a virtual earthquake. The flowers of the camellia enjoyed an extraordinary vogue. Everyone wanted camellias, everyone was looking for them. I ask you, how many camellias could one hope to obtain in the district of a province when everyone wanted them for balls, even though there weren't many balls? At the time, Petya Vorkhovskoy, poor fellow, was pining away for Anfisa Alexeyevna. To be sure, I don't know whether there was anything between them, that is, I mean, whether he could have entertained any serious hope. The poor man was going out of his mind in an effort to get hold of some camellias in time for the night of Anfisa Alexeyevna's ball. Countess Sotskaya from St Petersburg, a guest of the governor's wife, and Sofya Bespalova, it became known, would certainly be bringing bouquets, white ones. Anfisa Alexeyevna, for the sake of special effect,

wanted red ones. Poor Platon was nearly driven frantic; naturally – he was her husband; he undertook to get a bouquet for
her, and – what do you suppose? On the eve of the ball he was
beaten to it by Mytyshcheva, Katerina Alexandrovna, a fierce
rival of Anfisa Alexeyevna in everything; they were at daggers
drawn. Of course there were hysterics, fainting fits. Platon was
done for. It wasn't hard to see that if Petya were able to produce
a bouquet from somewhere at that interesting moment, his
chances would be greatly improved; in such situations, a
woman's gratitude knows no bounds. He rushed about like a
madman; but, needless to say, it was an impossible task. I
suddenly bumped into him at eleven o'clock the night before
the birthday and the ball, at the house of Marya Petrovna
Zubkova, a neighbour of Ordyntsev's. He was beaming with
smiles. "What's up?" "I've found them! *Eureka!*" "Well,
brother, that's a surprise! Where? How?" "In Yekshaisk (there
is a little town of that name there, about twenty versts away, in
another district), there's a merchant called Trepalov, with a big
beard and bags of money, lives with his old woman, and canaries
instead of children. They're both crazy about flowers, and he
has camellias." "For heaven's sake, but it's not certain, I mean,
what if he won't give you them?" "I'll get down on my knees
and grovel at his feet until he does, or I won't go away." "When
are you going, then?" "At first light tomorrow, at five." "Well,
good luck!" And I really was so glad for him, you know; I
returned to Ordyntsev's house; by now it was already two in
the morning, but you know, my mind kept racing. Just as I was
about to go to bed, I suddenly had a most original idea! I
immediately made my way to the kitchen, roused Savely the
coachman and gave him fifteen roubles: "Have the horses ready
in half an hour!" Half an hour later, of course, the sleigh was at
the gates; Anfisa Alexeyevna, I was told, had a migraine, fever
and delirium – I got in and drove. Before five I was in Yekshaisk,
at the coaching inn; I waited until dawn, and only until dawn;
by seven I was at Trepalov's, "Have you any camellias? Little
Father, dear Father of mine, help me, save me, I'll get down at
your feet!" I saw him, an old man, tall, grey-haired, stern – a
terrifying old chap. "No, no, on no account! I won't consent!"

Down I went, bang, at his feet! Fairly stretched myself out! "What's up, little Father, what's up, Father of mine?" – he was frightened, even. "Why, there's a man's life at stake!" I shouted to him. "If that's so, then take them, may God go with you." Then I cut red camellias, as many as I wanted! Wonderful, lovely ones, he had a whole little greenhouse full of them. The old man sighed. I took out a hundred roubles. "No, little Father, please don't insult me like this." "Well, if that's how it is, dear sir," I said, "donate the hundred roubles to the local hospital to improve the upkeep and food." "Now that, little Father," he said, "is a different cause, and a good one, a noble one and one that is pleasing to God; I'll donate it in the name of your health and welfare." And I liked him, you know, that old Russian fellow, so to speak, a real "Russky", *de la vraie souche*.[2] Delighted by my success, I at once went back; returning by a circuitous route so as not to encounter Petya. When I got there, I sent the bouquet so it would be there for Anfisa Alexeyevna when she woke up. You can imagine the delight, the gratitude, the tears of gratitude! Platon, yesterday's crushed and annihilated Platon – sobbing on my chest. Alas! All husbands have been like that since the creation . . . of lawful wedlock! I don't dare to add any more, except that with this episode poor Petya's chances were finally destroyed. At first I thought he would kill me when he found out, I even got ready for an encounter with him, but then something happened, something which I would not have believed was possible: he fell down in a swoon, by evening he was in delirium, and by morning had a fever of the blood; he was sobbing like a child, in convulsions. A month later, when he had only just recovered, he asked to be posted to the Crimea; it became a real romantic novel! In the end he was killed in the Crimea. At the time his brother, Stepan Vorkhovskoy, was in command of a regiment, and distinguished himself in action. I will confess that I was tormented by pangs of conscience for many years afterwards: why, for what purpose had I struck him such a blow? There might have been some excuse had I been in love myself at the time. I mean, it was just plain mischief, nothing more. And had I not outbid him for that bouquet, who knows, the man might still be alive, happy and successful, and it would never have crossed his mind to go and fight the Turks.'

Afanasy Ivanovich fell silent with the same solid dignity with which he had begun the story. They noticed that Nastasya Filippovna's eyes had begun to glitter peculiarly, and her lips even trembled when Afanasy Ivanovich had finished. Everyone looked at them both with curiosity.

'Ferdyshchenko's been cheated! He's been cheated! Yes, that's what it is, cheated!' Ferdyshchenko exclaimed in a plaintive voice, realizing that he could, and must, insert a word or two here, for the sake of effect.

'And whose fault is it you didn't catch on? Learn from clever people!' the almost triumphant Darya Alexeyevna (an old and loyal friend and accomplice of Totsky's) snapped at him.

'You're right, Afanasy Ivanovich, it's a very boring parlour game, and we must quickly end it,' Nastasya Filippovna said carelessly. 'I shall tell the story I promised to tell, and then let's play cards.'

'But first the promised anecdote!' the general approved warmly.

'Prince,' Nastasya Filippovna said, suddenly addressing him sharply and unexpectedly, 'look: here are my old friends, the general and Afanasy Ivanovich, they keep wanting to give me away in marriage. Tell me, what do you think: should I get married or not? Whatever you say, I shall do it.'

Afanasy Ivanovich turned pale, the general went as stiff as a post; everyone stared, craning their necks. Ganya froze on the spot.

'Married to ... to whom?' the prince asked with a sinking heart.

'To Gavrila Ardalionovich Ivolgin,' Nastasya Filippovna continued, sharply, firmly and clearly as before.

Several seconds of silence went by; the prince seemed to be making an effort to get the words out, as though a dreadful weight were crushing his chest.

'N-no ... don't!' he whispered, at last, drawing breath with an effort.

'Then that is how it shall be! Gavrila Ardalionovich!' she

addressed him imperiously, and almost with triumph. 'You heard the prince's decision? Well, it also contains my reply; and let this be an end of the matter for once and for all!'

'Nastasya Filippovna!' Afanasy Ivanovich said in a trembling voice.

'Nastasya Filippovna!' the general enunciated, in a voice of persuasion, but also of anxiety.

Everyone began to stir and grow uneasy.

'What's wrong, gentlemen?' she continued, looking intently at her guests as though in surprise. 'Why are you so alarmed? And what looks you all have on your faces!'

'But . . . remember, Nastasya Filippovna,' Totsky muttered, hesitantly, 'you gave a promise . . . a completely voluntary one, and could to some extent have spared us this . . . I find it difficult and . . . am of course, embarrassed, but . . . In short, now, at a moment like this, and in front of . . . of people, and to . . . to settle a serious matter by a parlour game like this, a matter of honour and of the heart . . . on which depends . . .'

'I don't understand you, Afanasy Ivanovich; you really are quite confused. For one thing, what you mean "in front of people"? Are we not in splendid, intimate company? And why "a parlour game"? I really did want to tell my anecdote, well, now I have told it; it's a good one, isn't it? And why do you say that it's not serious? It is serious, isn't it? You heard me say to the prince: "Whatever you say, it shall be so"; if he had said *yes*, I would at once have given my consent, but he said *no*, and I refused. At that moment my whole life hung by a thread; what could be more serious?'

'But the prince, why is the prince involved in it? And who is the prince, after all?' muttered the general, almost unable to control his indignation that the prince should have such a positively offensive authority.

'Well, for me the prince means this: he is the first man I have ever met in my whole life in whom I can believe as one who is truly devoted. He believed in me at first sight, and I trust him.'

'It only remains for me to thank Nastasya Filippovna for the exceeding delicacy with which she . . . has treated me,' a pale Ganya said at last in a trembling voice, and with twisted lips.

'Of course, it was what I deserved . . . But . . . the prince . . . The prince's role in this matter . . .'

'Is to get hold of the seventy-five thousand?' Nastasya Filippovna suddenly interrupted. 'Is that what you meant? Don't deny it, that's just what you meant! Afanasy Ivanovich, I forgot to add: you can take that seventy-five thousand in the knowledge that I am setting you free for nothing. Enough! You too need to draw breath! Nine years and three months! Tomorrow everything shall be different, but today is my birthday and I am in charge for the first time in my whole life! General, you can take your pearl necklace, too, give it to your wife, here it is; and as from tomorrow I am moving out of this apartment for good. And there will be no more soirées, gentlemen!'

Having said this, she suddenly got up, as if wishing to leave.

'Nastasya Filippovna! Nastasya Filippovna!' was heard from every side. They all began to grow agitated, they all rose from their seats; they all surrounded her, they all listened to these jerky, feverish, frenzied words with anxiety; they all sensed some kind of disorder, no one could make head or tail of it, no one could understand anything of it. At that moment there was suddenly a loud, resonant ringing of the bell, just as there had been earlier at Ganechka's apartment.

'Aha-a! This is the dénouement! At last! It's half-past eleven!' exclaimed Nastasya Filippovna. 'Please sit down, ladies and gentlemen, this is the dénouement!'

Saying this, she herself sat down. A strange laughter quivered on her lips. She sat silently, in feverish expectation, looking at the door.

'Rogozhin and the hundred thousand, there can be no doubt,' Ptitsyn muttered to himself.

15

Katya the room maid came in, much alarmed.

'Lord only knows what's going on out there, Nastasya Filippovna, about ten men have barged in, and they're all drunk, ma'am, asking to be let in here, they say it's Rogozhin, and that you know about it.'

'That's true, Katya, let them in at once, then.'

'Surely . . . not all of them, Nastasya Filippovna, ma'am? I mean, they're in a shocking state! Awful!'

'Let them all in, all of them, Katya, don't be afraid, every single one, otherwise they'll ignore you and come in anyway. What a noise they're making, just like this morning. Gentlemen, I suppose you may be offended,' she addressed the guests, 'that I'm receiving such company in your presence? I'm very sorry and I apologize, but I should very, very much like you to be my witnesses to this dénouement, although, of course, it's as you please . . .'

The guests continued to show bewilderment, whisper and exchange glances, but it became perfectly clear that all this had been calculated and arranged beforehand and that Nastasya Filippovna – although she had, of course, taken leave of her senses – would not be deflected from her course. They were all racked with curiosity. Moreover, no one there was likely to be too intimidated. There were only two ladies: Darya Alexeyevna, the pert lady, who had seen all manner of things and would be hard to disconcert, and the beautiful, but silent stranger. But the silent stranger would hardly understand anything: she was a visiting German, and knew nothing of the Russian language; in addition, she seemed to be as stupid as she was beautiful. She was new here, and it was already the accepted thing to invite her to certain soirées, in the most extravagant attire, with her hair done up as for a fashion show, and have her sit like a charming picture in order to adorn the soirée in just the same way as some people obtain from friends, for a single evening, a picture, a vase, a statue or a screen in order to adorn their soirées. As for the men, Ptitsyn, for example, was a friend of Rogozhin's; Ferdyshchenko was like a fish in water; Ganechka was still unable to pull himself together, but had a dim though irresistible sense of the need for him to stand at his pillory to the end; the old schoolmaster, who had little idea of what it was all about, was very nearly in tears and literally trembled with fear as he noticed the extraordinary state of anxiety in those around him and in Nastasya Filippovna, whom he worshipped like his grandchild; but he would rather have died than abandon her at such a moment. As for Afanasy Ivanovich, he could not, of course, compromise himself with such adventures; but he had too much at stake in the matter, even though it had taken such a crazy turn; and in any case, Nastasya Filippovna had dropped a few remarks in his regard which had been such that it would be impossible for him to leave without having finally cleared up the matter. He resolved to stay to the end and keep silent altogether, remaining solely as an observer, something that was, of course, demanded by his dignity. Only General Yepanchin, who had just before this been deeply insulted by the unceremonious and ridiculous return of his present to him, might possibly be even more insulted by all these extraordinary eccentricities or, for example, by Rogozhin's arrival; and indeed a man like him had already sunk low enough by bringing himself to sit beside Ptitsyn and Ferdyshchenko; but what the power of passion was able to do was, at last, overcome by a feeling of obligation, a sense of duty, rank and self-respect, so that Rogozhin and his company, in his excellency's presence, at any rate, were out of the question.

'Oh, General,' Nastasya Filippovna at once interrupted him, no sooner had he addressed her with his statement, 'I forgot! But rest assured that I had foreseen your position. If you feel so insulted, I won't insist and won't detain you, though I very much wanted to see you here with me now. At any rate, I thank you very much for your acquaintance and flattering attention, but if you're afraid . . .'

'Forgive me, Nastasya Filippovna,' the general exclaimed in a fit of chivalrous magnanimity, 'but think who you are addressing! I shall remain beside you now out of devotion, and if, for example, there is any danger . . . What's more, I confess that I'm extremely curious. All I meant was that they will spoil the carpets and may possibly break something . . . And they shouldn't be here at all, in my opinion, Nastasya Filippovna!'

'Here's Rogozhin!' proclaimed Ferdyshchenko.

'What do you think, Afanasy Ivanovich,' the general managed to whisper quickly. 'Has she taken leave of her senses? I mean, not metaphorically, but in the real medical sense, eh?'

'I always told you she was inclined that way,' Afanasy Ivanovich whispered slyly.

'And a fever as well . . .'

Rogozhin's company was made up of almost the same
members as in the morning; the only additions were a disreputable old man who had once been the editor of some sort of
indecent newspaper that published exposés, and of whom the
anecdote circulated that he had pawned his gold teeth, and a
retired second lieutenant, a determined rival and competitor, in
trade and calling, with that morning's gentleman with the fists,
and completely unknown to any of the Rogozhinites, but picked
up in the street on the sunny side of Nevsky Prospect, where he
was stopping passers-by and, in the style of Marlinsky,[1] begging
for assistance on the insidious pretext that he himself 'used to
give beggars fifteen roubles each in his day'. The two rivals at
once took a hostile attitude to each other. The earlier gentleman
with the fists even considered himself insulted after the reception
into the company of the 'beggar' and, being taciturn by nature,
merely growled from time to time like a bear, looking with profound contempt on the sycophancy and advances of the 'beggar',
who turned out to be a worldly, political fellow. From the look of
it, the second lieutenant was likely to gain more 'in the business'
by means of skill and resourcefulness rather than by strength, and
was indeed shorter of stature than the fisted gentleman. Tactfully,
without entering into open argument, but boasting horribly, he
had already several times alluded to the superiority of English
boxing and, in a word, turned out to be a Westernizer of the purest
sort. At the word 'boxing' the fisted gentleman merely smiled
with bristling contempt and, for his part, not deeming his rival
worthy of an open debate, now and then quietly displayed, as if
by accident, or, rather, allowed to be displayed now and then, a
wholly national object – an enormous fist, sinewy, knotted,
covered in a kind of reddish down – and it became clear to
everyone that if this profoundly national object were to land on
its target without error, it would reduce it to a jelly.

Besides, none of them was well and truly 'primed', as earlier,
this as a result of efforts on the part of Rogozhin himself, who
had had his visit to Nastasya Filippovna in view all day. He

himself had managed to sober up almost completely, but was on the other hand almost stupefied by all the impressions he had endured on this outrageous day of his life, a day that was unlike any other. One thing only remained constantly in view for him, in his memory and heart, at every minute, at every moment. For the sake of this *one thing* he had spent the whole time, from five o'clock in the afternoon to eleven at night, in a state of boundless anguish and anxiety, dealing with various Kinders and Biskups, who had also nearly gone mad, rushing about like scalded cats on his behalf. And yet, even so, they had managed to raise the hundred thousand roubles in cash to which Nastasya Filippovna had fleetingly, mockingly and very vaguely referred, at rates of interest which even Biskup himself, from shame, talked about with Kinder not aloud, but only in a whisper.

As earlier, Rogozhin strode out at the front, with the rest of them following after him, though still somewhat fearfully. Principally, they were afraid of Nastasya Filippovna. Some of them even thought, for some reason, that they would all be promptly 'kicked downstairs'. Among those who thought this way was Zalyozhev, the dandy and vanquisher of hearts. But the others, and especially the gentleman with the fists, viewed Nastasya Filippovna with the most profound contempt and even with hatred, and had gone to her abode as to a siege. However, the magnificent appointment of the first two rooms, the objects they had never heard of or seen before, the rare furniture, the pictures, the enormous statue of Venus – all this made on them an irresistible impression of reverence and even almost of fear. This did not, however, prevent them all from, gradually, and with impudent curiosity, in spite of their fear, crowding after Rogozhin into the drawing room; but when the gentleman with the fists, the 'beggar', and several others noticed General Yepanchin among the guests, they were at first so discouraged that they even began to gradually retreat into the other room. Only Lebedev was sufficiently courageous and convinced, and strode along beside Rogozhin, realizing the significance of a million four hundred thousand in cash and a hundred thousand now, this very moment, in hand. It should, however, be noted that all of them, even the expert Lebedev, were somewhat unsure about the limits and bounds of their powers and whether everything was now permitted to them, or not. At some moments Lebedev was ready to swear that it was, but at others felt an uneasy need to call to mind, just in case, some encouraging and reassuring articles of civil law.

On Rogozhin himself, Nastasya Filippovna's drawing room made an impression that was the reverse of that produced on all his companions. No sooner had the door curtain been raised, and he caught sight of Nastasya Filippovna, than everything else ceased to exist for him, as it had done earlier, in the morning, and even more powerfully than in the morning. He went pale, and stopped for a moment; one could guess that his heart was beating horribly. In timid perplexity he stared at Nastasya Filippovna for several seconds. Suddenly, as if he had lost all his reason, and almost staggering, he approached the table; on the way he knocked into Ptitsyn's chair and trod with his great, dirty boots on the lace trimmings of the silent German beauty's magnificent blue dress; did not apologize and did not notice. Approaching the table, he placed upon it the strange object with which he had stepped into the drawing room, holding it before him in both hands. It was a large paper parcel, some three vershoks[2] thick and some four vershoks long, wrapped firmly and compactly in *The Stock Exchange Gazette*, and tied very tightly on all sides and twice across the middle with string of the kind that is used for binding sugar loaves. Then he stood without saying a word, his arms at his sides, as though awaiting sentence. His clothes were just the same as they had been earlier, except for a brand new silk scarf, bright green and red, with an enormous diamond pin in the form of a beetle, and a massive diamond ring on a grimy finger of his right hand. Lebedev came to a halt about three paces from the table; the others, as mentioned, were gradually making their way into the drawing room. Katya and Pasha, Nastasya Filippovna's room maids, also came running to stare from behind the raised door curtain, in deep bewilderment and fear.

'What's that?' asked Nastasya Filippovna, surveying Rogozhin intently and curiously, and indicating the 'object' with her eyes.

'A hundred thousand!' the latter replied, almost in a whisper.

'Ah, so you kept your word, well, well. Sit down, please, here, here on this chair; I shall tell you something later. Who is with you? The whole company who were with you earlier? Well, let them come in and sit down; they can sit on the sofa, there's another sofa over there. There are two armchairs . . . but what's wrong, don't they want to?'

Indeed, some were positively confounded, beat a retreat and settled down to wait in the other room, but some remained and took their seats when invited to, but as far from the table as possible, mostly in the corners, while some still wanted to merge into the background, and others seemed to regain their courage with unnatural swiftness the farther away they sat. Rogozhin also sat down where he was shown to, but did not remain there for long; he soon got up, and did not sit down again. Little by little he began to survey the guests, identifying them. On seeing Ganya, he smiled poisonously and whispered to himself: 'Just look at him!' At the general and Afanasy Ivanovich he glanced without embarrassment and even without particular curiosity. But when he noticed the prince beside Nastasya Filippovna, for a long time he was unable to tear himself away from him, in extreme surprise and as if he were unable to admit the reality of this encounter. One could suspect that at moments he was in a genuine state of delirium. In addition to all the upheavals of this day, he had spent the whole of the night before on the train and had not slept for almost forty-eight hours.

'This, gentlemen, is a hundred thousand,' said Nastasya Filippovna, addressing them all with a kind of feverish, impatient challenge, 'here, in this dirty parcel. Earlier today he shouted like a madman that he would bring me a hundred thousand in the evening, and I've been waiting for him. He bargained for me: began with eighteen thousand, then suddenly bumped it up to forty, and then to this hundred. He certainly kept his word! Ugh, how pale he is! . . . It all happened at Ganechka's earlier on: I arrived to see his mother on a visit, to my future family, and his sister shouted in my face: "Why don't they throw this shameless woman out of here?", and spat in her own brother Ganechka's face! A girl of character!'

'Nastasya Filippovna!' the general said reproachfully.

He was beginning to understand the matter a little, in his own way.

'What's wrong, General? Indecent, is it? But enough of this showing off! The fact that I sat in a box of the French Theatre like a personification of inaccessible dress-circle virtue, avoiding like a savage all those who had been chasing me for five years, and gazing down like proud innocence itself, well, it was stupidity that made me do it! Now, right in front of your eyes, he has come and put a hundred thousand on the table, after those five years of innocence, and I bet they have a troika outside waiting for me. He has valued me at a hundred thousand! Ganechka, I see that you are still angry with me? Did you really want to take me into your family? I, who belong to Rogozhin? What did the prince say earlier?'

'I didn't say that you belong to Rogozhin!' the prince got out in a trembling voice.

'Nastasya Filippovna, enough, little mother, enough, little dove,' Darya Alexeyevna suddenly lost patience. 'If you've suffered so much because of them, why bother paying any attention to them? And do you really want to go off with a man like that, even for a hundred thousand! True, a hundred thousand is not to be sneezed at! So take the hundred thousand and chase him away, that's how to deal with them; oh, in your place I would tell them all where to go . . . so I would!'

Darya Alexeyevna had really worked herself into a state of anger. She was a good-hearted woman, and highly impressionable.

'Don't get angry, Darya Alexeyevna,' Nastasya Filippovna smiled to her, thinly. 'After all, I didn't speak to him in anger. I mean, did I rebuke him? I really can't understand how I could ever have been so stupid as to want to enter a decent family. I've seen his mother, and kissed her hand. And as for my mocking you earlier, Ganechka, I did it on purpose in order to see for the last time how far you would go. Well, and you surprised me, truly you did. I had expected many things, but not that! I mean, could you really have married me, knowing that he would give me a pearl necklace like that practically on the eve of your wedding, and that I would accept it? And Rogozhin? After all he bargained for me in your house, in the presence of your mother and sister, and yet you came to seek my hand in marriage after that, and nearly brought your sister with you? Is what Rogozhin said of you really true, that you would crawl on your hands and knees to Vasilyevsky Island for three roubles?'

'He would,' Rogozhin suddenly said quietly, but with a look of the utmost conviction.

'And it would be all very well if you were dying of hunger, but after all, they say you get a good salary! And as if that weren't enough, in addition to the disgrace, to bring a hated wife into your home! (Because you do hate me, I know that!) No, now I believe that such a man could kill for money! I mean, now they are all in the grip of such a craving, they're so torn apart for money, that it's as if they'd lost their minds. Just a child, but he aspires to become a moneylender! I can imagine him wrapping the silk round the razor, tightening it, and quietly cutting his friend's throat from behind, as though he were a sheep, as I read recently. Oh, you shameless man! I'm shameless, but you're worse. To say nothing of that bouquet-collector . . .'

'Is it you, is it you, Nastasya Filippovna?' the general said, clasping his hands in genuine grief. 'You, so delicate, with such refined ideas, and now! What language! What a manner of speech!'

'I'm intoxicated now, General,' Nastasya Filippovna laughed suddenly, 'and I want to enjoy myself! Today is my day, my appointed day, my high holiday, I have waited for it a long time. Darya Alexeyevna, you see that bouquet-collector, that *monsieur aux camélias*? He's sitting there laughing at us . . .'

'I'm not laughing, Nastasya Filippovna, I am merely listening with the greatest attention,' Totsky parried with dignity.

'Well then, so why have I tormented him for a whole five years and not let him go? Was he worth it? He's simply the way he's supposed to be . . . He also thinks I'm guilty in his regard: after all he gave me my upbringing, kept me like a countess, and the money, the money he spent, found me a decent husband back there, and here Ganechka; and what do you suppose: I haven't lived with him these past five years, but I've taken money

from him and thought I was in the right! I mean, I've completely
confused myself! You say, take the hundred thousand and chase
him away, if you find it disgusting. Yes, it's true, it's disgusting
. . . I could have got married long ago, and not to Ganechka
either, but that would also have been too disgusting . . . And
why have I wasted five years of my life in this spite and anger?
Believe it or not, but about four years ago there were times when
I thought: why don't I just marry my Afanasy Ivanovich? I
thought it out of malice at the time; there were a lot of things
going through my head in those days; yet, it's true, I could have
made him do it! He suggested it himself, would you believe it?
He wasn't being sincere, of course, but then he's easy prey, has
no self-control. And after that, thank God, I thought: is he
worth such malice? And then I got so disgusted by him that even
if he'd come and offered me his hand himself I wouldn't have
married him. And for five whole years I pranced about like
this! No, better out on the street, where I ought to be! Have a
fling with Rogozhin, or become a washerwoman tomorrow!
Because, after all, I have nothing of my own; if I go, I'll leave
everything to him, down to my last rag, and who will take me
without anything. Ask Ganya if he'll take me. Why, not even
Ferdyshchenko will take me! . . .'

'Ferdyshchenko might not take you, Nastasya Filippovna,
I'm a candid fellow,' Ferdyshchenko broke in, 'but the prince
will take you! There you sit lamenting, but just look at the
prince! I've been watching him for a long time . . .'

Nastasya Filippovna turned to the prince with curiosity.

'Really?' she asked.

'Really,' whispered the prince.

'You'll take me as I am, without anything?'

'I will, Nastasya Filippovna . . .'

'Here's another anecdote!' muttered the general. 'It was to be
expected.'

The prince looked with a sorrowful, stern and penetrating
gaze into the features of Nastasya Filippovna, who continued
to survey him.

'He always knows how to say the right thing!' she said suddenly, addressing Darya Alexeyevna again. 'And I mean, it really

is from a kind heart, I know him. I've found a benefactor! Though, as a matter of fact, they do say that he's . . . *you know* . . . What are you going to live on if you're so in love that you'll take Rogozhin's woman for yourself, a prince?'

'I'll take you as an honest woman, Nastasya Filippovna, and not as Rogozhin's,' said the prince.

'I'm an honest woman?'

'Yes.'

'Oh, that's . . . stuff out of novels! That's a lot of old claptrap, Prince, dear, the world's grown a bit wiser now, and all that is nonsense. And what would you be doing getting married when you still need a nanny to look after you?'

The prince rose, and in a trembling, timid voice, but at the same time with the look of one deeply convinced, said:

'I don't know anything, Nastasya Filippovna, I haven't seen anything, you're right, but I . . . I consider that you'll be doing me an honour, and not vice versa. I'm nothing, while you have suffered and have emerged pure from a hell like that, and that is a lot. So why are you ashamed, and planning to go with Rogozhin? It's your fever . . . You've given Mr Totsky his seventy thousand and say you are going to turn your back on everything, everything, and there is no one here who could do that. I . . . Nastasya Filippovna . . . I love you. I'll die for you, Nastasya Filippovna. I won't let anyone say a word against you, Nastasya Filippovna . . . If we're poor, I shall work, Nastasya Filippovna . . .'

At the last words the sniggering of Ferdyshchenko and Lebedev could be heard, and even the general seemed to grunt to himself in great displeasure. Ptitsyn and Totsky could not help smiling, but restrained themselves. The rest simply opened their mouths wide with astonishment.

'. . . But perhaps we shall not be poor, but very rich, Nastasya Filippovna,' the prince continued in the same timid voice. 'However, I don't know for certain, and I'm sorry I haven't been able to find out anything about it all day, but in Switzerland I got a letter from a Mr Salazkin, and he informs me that I may apparently receive a very large inheritance. This is the letter, here . . .'

And the prince actually took a letter out of his pocket.

'He's raving, isn't he?' muttered the general. 'This is a real madhouse!'

For a moment, silence ensued.

'Did you say that you have a letter from Salazkin, Prince?' asked Ptitsyn. 'He's a man very well known in his circle; he's a very well-known solicitor, and if the letter really is from him, you may believe him completely. Fortunately, I know his handwriting, as I recently had business with him . . . If you would let me have a look, perhaps I could tell you something.'

The prince silently held out the letter to him in a trembling hand.

'What on earth, what on earth?' the general said, recovering himself, staring at them all like a halfwit. 'Is it really an inheritance?'

They all fixed their eyes on Ptitsyn as he read the letter. The universal curiosity had received a new and extreme impetus. Ferdyshchenko could not sit still; Rogozhin stared in bewilderment and kept transferring his gaze now to the prince, now to Ptitsyn, with dreadful anxiety. Darya Alexeyevna looked on, in expectancy, as though she were sitting on needles. Even Lebedev was unable to hold out, emerged from his corner and, craning his neck for all he was worth, began to peer at the letter over Ptitsyn's shoulder with the look of a man who feared he might at any moment receive a clout for doing so.

16

'It's genuine,' Ptitsyn announced, at last, folding the letter and handing it back to the prince. 'You will receive, under the terms of your aunt's incontestable will, without any need for petition, an extremely large sum of capital.'

'Impossible!' exclaimed the general, as though firing a shot.

Their mouths all fell open again.

Ptitsyn explained, addressing himself primarily to Ivan Fyodorovich, that five months earlier the death had occurred of the prince's aunt, whom he had never known personally, his mother's eldest sister, the daughter of a Moscow merchant of the Third Guild, Papushin by name, who had died in poverty and bankruptcy. But this Papushin's elder brother, who had also died recently, was a well-known and rich merchant. About a year earlier his only two sons had died, almost within a month of each other. This had been such a shock to the old man that, not long after, he himself fell ill and died. He was a widower, there were no heirs at all apart from the prince's aunt, his niece, a very poor woman who lived with relatives. At the time she received the inheritance this aunt was almost dying of dropsy, but she had at once begun to seek out the prince, entrusting this to Salazkin, and managed to make a will. It appeared that neither the prince nor the doctor, in whose home he lived in Switzerland, had been willing to wait for official notification or to make inquiries, and the prince, with Salazkin's letter in his pocket, decided to set off on his own . . .

'There is one thing I can tell you,' concluded Ptitsyn, turning to the prince, 'and that is that all this cannot be anything but correct and beyond dispute, and everything that Salazkin writes to you about the indisputability and legality of your case you may take as ready money in your pocket. I congratulate you, Prince! Perhaps you will also get a million and a half, and possibly more. Papushin was a very rich merchant.'

'Hurrah for the last Prince Myshkin of his line!' whooped Ferdyshchenko.

'Hurrah!' Lebedev wheezed in a drunken little voice.

'And I lent him twenty-five roubles earlier, the poor fellow, ha-ha-ha! A phantasmagoria, it truly is!' almost stunned with amazement, the general said. 'Well, congratulations, congratulations!' And, rising from his seat, he went over to the prince to embrace him. Others also began to get up, following his example, and also sidled over to the prince. Even those who had retreated behind the door curtain began to appear in the drawing room. There was a vague ripple of talk, there were exclamations, there were even demands for champagne; everyone began to jostle and bustle. For a moment they seemed to have forgotten Nastasya Filippovna, and that she was still the hostess of her own soirée. But little by little, almost at the same time, it dawned on them that the prince had just proposed to her. This made it all seem three times as mad and extraordinary as before. The profoundly amazed Totsky shrugged his shoulders; he was almost the only one still seated, all the rest of the crowd were thronging round the table in disorder. They all maintained afterwards that it was from that moment that Nastasya Filippovna went mad. She continued to sit in her chair and for some time surveyed them all with a strange, astonished look, as though she did not understand and were trying to work something out. Then, suddenly, she turned to the prince and, with a menacing frown, scrutinized him intently; but this was only for a moment; perhaps it suddenly seemed to her that it was all a joke, a piece of mockery; but the prince's look at once broke the illusion. She began to reflect, then smiled again, as though not clearly aware that she was doing so . . .

'This means I really am a princess!' she whispered, as if mocking herself, and, as she happened to glance at Darya Alexeyvna, began to laugh. 'An unexpected dénouement . . . I . . . didn't expect this . . . But gentlemen, why are you standing, please sit down and congratulate me and the prince! I think someone asked for champagne? Ferdyshchenko, go and tell them to bring some. Katya, Pasha,' – she suddenly caught sight of her maids in the doorway – 'come here, I'm going to be married, do you hear? To the prince, he has a million and a half, he's Prince Myshkin, and he's marrying me!'

'And may God bless you, my dear, it's not before time! Don't let the opportunity slip!' cried Darya Alexeyevna, deeply moved by what had taken place.

'Now, you sit beside me, Prince,' Nastasya Filippovna went on. 'That's right, and here comes the wine. Congratulate us, gentlemen!'

'Hurrah!' cried a large number of voices. Many people began to crowd round the wine, including nearly all the Rogozhinites. But although they were shouting and eager to shout, many, in spite of all the strangeness of the circumstances and the surroundings, sensed that the scene was changing. Others were disconcerted, and waiting with mistrust. But many whispered to one another that after all it was a perfectly ordinary occurrence, that princes married all sorts of women, even gypsy girls from encampments. As for Rogozhin, he stood and stared, contorting his features into a rigid smile of bewilderment.

'Prince, old fellow, think what you're doing!' the general whispered in horror, approaching from the side and tugging the prince by the sleeve.

Nastasya Filippovna observed this, and began to laugh out loud.

'No, General! I'm a princess now, do you hear – the prince won't allow me to be insulted! Afanasy Ivanovich, you congratulate me, too; now I shall sit next to your wife everywhere; what do you think, does it pay to have a husband like that? A million and a half, and a prince, too, and, they say, an idiot into the bargain, what more could one want? Real life is only beginning! You're too late, Rogozhin! Take your parcel of money away, I'm marrying the prince and am richer than you!'

But Rogozhin had grasped what was happening. Inexpressible suffering left its imprint on his face. He clasped his hands, as a groan burst from his chest.

'Give her up!' he shouted to the prince.

There was laughter all around.

'Is it you he's to give her up for?' Darya Alexeyevna chimed in, triumphantly. 'We all saw the way you dumped your money on the table, muzhik! The prince is going to take her in marriage, but you've just come to make a nuisance of yourself!'

'I'll marry her, too! I'll marry her now, this very minute! I'll give anything.'

'Look at you, a drunkard from a tavern, you ought to be shown the door!' Darya Alexeyevna repeated in indignation.

The laughter grew louder.

'Listen, Prince,' Nastasya Filippovna addressed him, 'there's the muzhik bargaining for your bride.'

'He's drunk,' said the prince. 'He loves you very much.'

'But won't you feel ashamed later on that your bride nearly went away with Rogozhin?'

'You were in a fever, and you're still in a fever, you are almost delirious.'

'And you won't feel ashamed when they tell you later on that your wife was kept by Totsky?'

'No, I won't . . . You were with Totsky against your will.'

'And you'll never reproach me?'

'I won't reproach you.'

'Well, be careful you don't swear your whole life on it!'

'Nastasya Filippovna,' the prince said quietly, and as if with compassion, 'I told you earlier that I would take your consent as an honour and that it is you who are doing me an honour, and not I you. You smiled at those words, and I also heard laughter around us. Perhaps I expressed myself too absurdly and was myself absurd, but it still seemed to me that I . . . understood what the honour was, and am certain that I told the truth. You were on the point of ruining yourself just now, irrevocably, because you would never have forgiven yourself for it later: but you're not guilty of anything. It cannot be that your life should be completely ruined. What does it matter that Rogozhin came to see you, and Gavrila Ardalionovich tried to deceive you? Why do you constantly mention that? What you have done, few people are capable of doing, I repeat that to you again, and your wanting to go away with Rogozhin was something you decided in a morbid fit. You are in a fit even now, and would do better to go to bed. Tomorrow you'd have gone and become a washerwoman, and you wouldn't have stayed with Rogozhin. You are proud, Nastasya Filippovna, but perhaps you're now so happy that you really do consider yourself guilty. You need much looking after, Nastasya Filippovna. I will look after you. I saw your portrait earlier, and it was as if I recognized a familiar face. It seemed to me at once that you were already somehow calling me . . . I . . . will respect you all my life, Nastasya Filippovna,' the prince concluded suddenly, as though suddenly remembering where he was, blushing and realizing the kind of people in front of whom he was saying this.

Ptitsyn even went so far as to chastely incline his head and look at the floor. Totsky thought to himself: 'An idiot, but he knows that flattery is the best policy; it's second nature to him!' The prince also began to notice Ganya's flashing gaze from the corner, a gaze with which the latter seemed to be trying to reduce him to ashes.

'What a kind man!' Darya Alexeyevna proclaimed, touched.

'An educated man, but a ruined one!' the general whispered in an undertone.

Totsky picked up his hat and prepared to get to his feet in order to quietly make himself scarce. He and the general exchanged glances, as a sign they were going to leave together.

'Thank you, Prince, no one has spoken to me like that before,' said Nastasya Filippovna. 'They're always bargaining for me, but no decent man has ever sought my hand in marriage. Did you hear, Afanasy Ivanovich? What do you think of all the things the prince was saying? I mean, it's almost indecent . . . Rogozhin! Wait a while, don't go yet. And you're not going anyway, I can see. Perhaps I may come with you after all. Where were you going to take me?'

'To Yekaterinhof,' Lebedev said from the corner, while Rogozhin merely started, and stared with all his might, as though he could not believe his ears. He was completely stupefied, as from a terrible blow to the head.

'But what are you thinking of, my dear! You really are in a fit: have you gone mad?' cried the frightened Darya Alexeyevna.

'Did you think I meant it?' Nastasya Filippovna jumped up from the sofa in loud laughter. 'Do you think I would ruin a baby like him? That's more in Afanasy Ivanovich's line: he's the one who's fond of children! Let's be off, Rogozhin! Get your parcel ready! It doesn't matter if you don't want to get married, but let's have the money all the same. I may not marry you anyway, perhaps. Did you think that if you decided to get married you could keep the parcel? You were wrong! I have no shame! I was Totsky's concubine . . . Prince! You need Aglaya Yepanchina now, not Nastasya Filippovna, or else – Ferdyshchenko will be pointing his finger! You're not afraid, but I'll be afraid that I've ruined you and that you'll reproach me for it later! And as for your declaring that I'm doing you an honour, Totsky knows about that. But Ganechka, you've missed Aglaya Yepanchina; did you know that? If you hadn't bargained with her she would have married you instantly! That applies to all of

you: either go around with women who are honourable or
with those who are dishonourable – there's only one choice.
Otherwise you will certainly get confused . . . Look at the general
staring, his mouth is open . . .'

'This is a Sodom, a Sodom!' the general repeated, shrugging
his shoulders. He had also got up from the sofa; they were all
on their feet again. Nastasya Filippovna was almost in a frenzy.

'Is it possible?' the prince groaned, wringing his hands.

'Did you think it wasn't? Perhaps I am proud in my own way,
whether I'm a shameless hussy or not! You called me perfection
earlier; well, it's a nice kind of perfection to go slumming just
in order to be able to boast of having spurned a million and a
princess's title! Well, what sort of a wife am I for you after
that? Afanasy Ivanovich, I really have thrown a million out
of the window, you know! What did you think, that I'd consider myself lucky to marry Ganechka on your seventy-five
thousand? You may keep your seventy-five thousand, Afanasy
Ivanovich (you didn't even go up to a hundred, Rogozhin
outdid you!); as for Ganechka, I'll console him, I've had an idea.
But now I want to enjoy myself, I'm a woman of the streets,
after all! I've spent ten years in prison, now my happiness
has arrived! What's wrong with you, Rogozhin? Get ready, let's
be off!'

'Let's be off!' roared Rogozhin, almost in a frenzy of joy.
'Hey, you there . . . wine! . . . lots of it . . . Hah! . . .'

'Let's have lots of wine, I want to drink. And will there be
music?'

'There will, there will! Keep away!' Rogozhin howled in a
frenzy, seeing Darya Alexeyevna going up to Nastasya Filippovna. 'She's mine! It's all mine! The queen! That's the end
of it!'

He was panting with joy; he walked round Nastasya Filippovna, shouting at them all: 'Keep away!' The whole company
was now jammed into the drawing room. Some were drinking,
others shouting and laughing loudly, they were all in a most
excited and unrestrained frame of mind. Ferdyshchenko was
making efforts to join them. The general and Totsky again
moved to get out as quickly as possible. Ganya also had his hat

in his hand, but he stood silently, as if still unable to tear himself away from the scene that was unfolding before him.

'Keep away!' Rogozhin kept shouting.

'What are you bawling like that for?' Nastasya Filippovna laughed at him: 'I'm still the hostess here; if I want, I can throw you out. I haven't taken your money yet, look, it's over there; give it to me, the whole parcel! This is the parcel that contains a hundred thousand? Ugh, how loathsome! What's wrong, Darya Alexeyevna? But should I really have ruined him?' (She pointed at the prince.) 'What's the point of him marrying, he still needs a nanny; the general there can be his nanny – look how he hangs around him! Look, Prince, your bride-to-be has taken the money because she's a loose woman, and you wanted to take her in marriage! But why are you crying? Does it leave a bitter taste? But in my opinion you ought to be laughing,' continued Nastasya Filippovna, on whose cheeks two large tears had begun to glisten. 'Trust in time – all things will pass! Better safe than sorry ... But why are you all crying? There's Katya crying! I'm leaving a lot to you and Pasha, I've already made the arrangements, but now farewell! I've forced you, a decent girl, to look after me, a loose woman ... It's better like this, Prince, truly it's better, later you would have begun to despise me, and there'd have been no happiness for us! Don't swear it's not true, I don't believe you! And how stupid it would have been! ... No, it's better that we say farewell on friendly terms, I mean, I myself am a dreamer, and no good would have come of it. Haven't I dreamed about you? You're right, I did, a long time ago, in the house on his estate, for five years I lived there all on my own; one thinks and thinks, I used to dream and dream – and always imagining someone like you, kind, honest, good and a bit stupid, that you would suddenly arrive and say: "You bear no guilt, Nastasya Filippovna, and I adore you!" And I used to get so lost in daydreams that I nearly went mad ... And then that man over there would arrive: he would stay for a couple of months of the year, to disgrace, outrage, infuriate, deprave, and leave – so that a thousand times I wanted to hurl myself into the pond, but I was base, I didn't have the courage; well, and now ... Rogozhin, are you ready?'

'It's all ready! Keep away!'

'Everything's ready!' several voices rang out.

'Troikas are waiting, with bells!'

Nastasya Filippovna snatched up the parcel.

'Ganka, I've had an idea: I want to reward you, because why should you lose everything? Rogozhin, would he crawl to Vasilyevsky Island for three roubles?'

'He would!'

'Well then, listen, Ganya, I want to look at your soul for the last time; you've tormented me for a whole three months; now it's my turn. Do you see this parcel, it contains a hundred thousand! In a moment I'm going to throw it into the fireplace, into the flames, in front of everyone, they're all witnesses! As soon as the flames catch hold of it – crawl into the fireplace, but without gloves, mind, with your bare hands, your sleeves rolled up, and pull the parcel out of the fire! If you pull it out it's yours, the whole hundred thousand is yours! You'll burn your fingers a tiny bit – but I mean, it's a hundred thousand, think of it! It won't take long to pull it out! And I'll feast my eyes on your soul as you crawl into the fire for my money. All are witnesses that the parcel will be yours! And if you don't crawl, it will burn away: I won't let anyone else have it. Keep away! Keep away, all of you! It's my money! I took it for a night with Rogozhin. It's my money, isn't it, Rogozhin?'

'It's yours, my joy! It's yours, my queen!'

'Well, then keep away, all of you, I shall do as I want! Don't interfere! Ferdyshchenko, rake up the fire!'

'Nastasya Filippovna, my hands won't rise to the task!' replied the stunned Ferdyshchenko.

'E-ech!' cried Nastasya Filippovna. She seized the tongs, raked two smouldering logs and, as soon as the flames leapt up, threw the parcel on them.

A shout went up all round; many even crossed themselves.

'She's gone mad, she's gone mad!' came the cry from all round.

'Shouldn't we . . . shouldn't we . . . tie her up?' whispered the general to Ptitsyn, 'or send for the . . . I mean, she's gone mad, hasn't she? Hasn't she?'

'N-no, this may not quite be madness,' whispered Ptitsyn, trembling and pale as a handkerchief, unable to take his eyes off the smouldering parcel.

'She's mad, isn't she? I mean, she's mad?' the general insisted to Totsky.

'I told you she was a *colourful* woman,' muttered the also rather pale Afanasy Ivanovich.

'But I mean to say, dash it, a hundred thousand! . . .'

'Good Lord, good Lord!' came the cry from all round. They all began to crowd around the fireplace, they all clambered to look, they all exclaimed . . . Some even jumped on to chairs in order to look over the heads of the others. Darya Alexeyevna darted through to the other room and whispered something in terror to Katya and Pasha. The beautiful German lady ran away.

'Dear lady! Queen! All powerful one!' howled Lebedev, crawling on his hands and knees before Nastasya Filippovna and stretching out his arms towards the fireplace. 'A hundred thousand! A hundred thousand! I saw it myself, they wrapped it up in front of me! Dear lady! Your highness! Order me into the fireplace: I'll crawl right in, I'll put my grey-haired head right into the flames! . . . A sick wife who's lost the use of her legs, thirteen children – all orphans, I buried my father last week, he was starving, Nastasya Filippovna!' – and having howled this out, he began to crawl towards the fireplace.

'Keep away!' Nastasya Filippovna began to shout, pushing him back. 'Make room, all of you! Ganya, but why are you standing there? Don't be ashamed! Crawl! You're in luck!'

But Ganya had already endured too much that day and that evening and was not prepared for this last unexpected ordeal. The crowd parted before them into two halves, and he remained eye to eye with Nastasya Filippovna, at a distance of three paces from her. She stood right by the fireplace, waiting, not lowering her burning, fixed gaze from him. Ganya, in evening dress, his hat in his hand, and his gloves, stood before her silently and meekly, his arms folded, looking at the fire. An insane smile wandered across his face, which was as pale as a handkerchief. To be sure, he was unable to take his eyes off the flames, off the smouldering parcel; but something new seemed to have ascended into his soul; as though he had sworn to endure the torture; he did not move from where he stood; after a few moments it became clear to them all that he would not go to retrieve the parcel, that he did not want to.

'I say, it will burn, and make a fool of you,' Nastasya Filippovna shouted to him. 'I mean, you'll want to hang yourself afterwards, I'm not joking!'

The fire that had initially leaped up between the two smouldering logs nearly went out when the parcel fell on it, weighing it down. But a small blue flame still clung to one corner of the lower log, from underneath. At last a long, thin tongue of flame licked the parcel, too, the fire took hold and ran up the corners of the paper, and suddenly the whole parcel flared up in the fireplace and a bright flame shot upwards. Everyone gasped.

'Dear lady!' Lebedev went on howling, again trying to move forwards, but Rogozhin pulled him aside and repulsed him again.

Rogozhin himself had turned into a single, motionless stare. He was unable to tear himself away from Nastasya Filippovna, he was intoxicated, he was in seventh heaven.

'That's how a queen behaves!' he repeated every moment, addressing whoever happened to be around. 'That's how our kind behaves!' he shrieked, beside himself. 'Well, which of you swindlers would do a thing like that, eh?'

The prince watched in silent sadness.

'I'll snatch it out with my teeth for only a thousand!' Ferdyshchenko began to offer.

'If I had any teeth I'd do it, too!' the gentleman with the fists ground out from behind them all in a fit of positive despair. 'The d-devil take it! It's burning, it will all burn away!' he exclaimed, seeing the flame.

'It's burning, it's burning!' they all cried with one voice, almost all of them trying to get to the fireplace as well.

'Ganya, don't be a fool, I tell you for the last time!'

'Crawl for it!' roared Ferdyshchenko, hurling himself at Ganya in a genuine frenzy and tugging his sleeve, 'crawl for it, you wretched braggart! It'll burn away! Oh, accur-r-r-sed man!'

Ganya pushed Ferdyshchenko away by force, turned and walked towards the door; but, without even having gone two paces, he began to stagger and crashed to the floor.

'He's passed out!' people began to cry all round.

'Dear lady, it'll burn away!' howled Lebedev.

'It'll burn away for nothing!' came a roar from every side.

'Katya, Pasha, bring him water, spirits!' cried Nastasya Filippovna, seizing the tongs and snatching out the parcel.

Almost all the outer paper was scorched and smouldering, but it was at once evident that the inside was not touched. The parcel was wrapped in a sheet of newspaper folded round three times, and the money was intact. Everyone breathed a sigh of relief.

'Perhaps just a wretched little thousand has been damaged, but the rest is all safe,' Lebedev said with tender emotion.

'It's all his! The whole parcel is his! You hear, gentlemen!' Nastasya Filippovna proclaimed, putting the parcel beside Ganya. 'And he didn't crawl, he endured! That means his vanity is even greater than his craving for money. Never mind, he'll come to! He'd have cut my throat, otherwise . . . There, he's coming round. General, Ivan Petrovich, Darya Alexeyevna, Katya, Pasha, Rogozhin, did you hear? The parcel is his, Ganya's. I'm giving it to him as his own property, as a reward . . . well, for whatever it may be! Tell him. Let it lie beside him here . . . Rogozhin, quick march! Farewell, Prince, it's the first time I've ever seen a human being! Farewell, Afanasy Ivanovich, *merci!*'

Rogozhin's entire gang swept through the rooms with noise, with thunder, with shouts towards the exit, following Rogozhin and Nastasya Filippovna. In the reception room the maids handed her fur coat to her; Marfa the cook came running from the kitchen. Nastasya Filippovna kissed them all several times.

'But are you really leaving us altogether, little mother? But where are you going? And on your birthday, too, on such a day!' asked the tearful maids, kissing her hands.

'I'm going on the streets, Katya, you heard, that is my place, and if not there, then I'll be a washerwoman! Enough of Afanasy

Ivanovich! Give him my farewell greetings, and don't think ill of me . . .'

The prince rushed headlong to the entrance, where everyone was getting into four troikas with bells. The general managed to catch up with him on the staircase.

'For pity's sake, Prince, bethink yourself!' he said, seizing him by the arm. 'Give her up! You see what she's like! I say it as a father . . .'

The prince looked at him, but not saying a word tore himself free and ran downstairs.

By the entrance from which the troikas had just moved away the general could discern the prince hailing the first cab that came along and telling the driver to follow the troikas to Yekaterinhof. Then the general's little grey trotter arrived and took the general home, with new hopes and plans, and with the pearl necklace, which the general had not forgotten to take with him. Amidst the plans he fleetingly glimpsed the seductive figure of Nastasya Filippovna once or twice; the general sighed:

'A pity! A real pity! A lost woman! A mad woman! . . . Well, sirs, but it's not Nastasya Filippovna the prince needs now.'

A few edifying and parting words in this same vein were uttered by two other partners in conversation, guests of Nastasya Filippovna who had decided to go some of the way on foot.

'You know, Afanasy Ivanovich, they say that something of this kind happens among the Japanese,' said Ivan Petrovich Ptitsyn. 'The man who has been insulted apparently goes up to his insulter and says to him: "You've insulted me, so I've come to slit open my belly in front of you," and with these words he really does slit open his belly in front of his insulter's eyes and, it would seem, experiences a sense of extreme satisfaction, as though he had really obtained his revenge. There are strange characters in the world, Afanasy Ivanovich!'

'And you think there was something of that kind here?' Afanasy Ivanovich replied with a smile. 'Hm! That's clever . . . and your comparison is an excellent one. But dash it, you saw yourself, dearest Ivan Petrovich, that I did everything I could; I mean, I couldn't have done any more, could I? But you'll also agree that there were some capital qualities present in that woman . . . brilliant features. I even wanted to shout to her just now, if I could have brought myself to do so in that Sodom, that she herself is my best defence against her accusations. Well, who wouldn't sometimes be captivated by that woman to the point of forgetting his reason and . . . everything? Look at that muzhik Rogozhin, chucking a hundred thousand at her! Granted, everything that happened in there just now was ephemeral, romantic, indecent, but also colourful and original, you will agree. Lord, what might have come of such a character, and with such beauty! But in spite of all my efforts, and an education, even – it's all gone to waste! An uncut diamond – I've said that more than once . . .'

And Afanasy Ivanovich heaved a deep sigh.

PART TWO

I

About two days after the strange incidents at Nastasya Filippovna's soirée, with which we concluded the first part of our story, Prince Myshkin hurried to leave for Moscow to see about receiving his unexpected inheritance. It was said at the time that there might be other reasons for the haste of his departure; but about this, as about the prince's adventures in Moscow and in general during his absence from St Petersburg, we can offer very little information. The prince was absent for exactly six months, and even those who had certain reasons for being interested in his fate were unable to find out very much about him during this time. Rumours of a sort did, it is true, reach some of them, though very infrequently, but these were for the most part strange, and almost always contradicted one another. The greatest amount of interest in the prince was shown, of course, in the house of the Yepanchins, to whom he had not even had time to say goodbye before leaving. The general had, however, seen him at the time, and even on two or three occasions; they had had a serious discussion about something. But if Yepanchin saw him, he did not announce it to his family. And on the whole, initially, that is to say for a whole month after the prince's departure, it was not done to speak of him in the Yepanchins' house. Only the general's wife, Lizaveta Prokofyevna, delivered herself right at the outset of the opinion that she had been 'cruelly mistaken about the prince'. Then, some two or three days later she added, without mentioning the prince this time, but in general terms, that the principal feature of her life was 'being constantly

mistaken about people'. And, at last, some ten days later, irritated at her daughters for some reason, she concluded in the
form of a maxim: 'Enough of mistakes! There shall be no more
of them.' In this connection it cannot be left unnoticed that a
rather unpleasant atmosphere had existed in the house for quite
some time. There was something in the air that was painful,
strained, unspoken, quarrelsome; everyone frowned. Night and
day the general was occupied, attending to business; rarely had
he been seen so busy and active – especially on official duties.
The family were scarcely able to catch a glimpse of him. As for
the Yepanchin girls, they expressed no opinions, of course.
Quite possibly very little was said even when they were alone.
They were proud girls, haughty and sometimes diffident even
among themselves, though they understood one another not
only from the first verbal hint, but even from the first glance, so
that quite often there was no point in any of them saying much.

Only one conclusion could have been drawn by an outside
observer, had one happened to be there: that, judging by all the
evidence given above, scanty though it may be, the prince had
succeeded in leaving a certain impression in the house of
the Yepanchins, though he had appeared in it but once, and
then only fleetingly. It was, perhaps, an impression of simple
curiosity, explained by some of the prince's eccentric conduct.
Whatever it was, the impression remained.

Little by little, the darkness of ignorance managed to obscure
even the rumours that had begun to spread around the town.
There was talk, it was true, of some little prince and fool (no
one could put a definite name to him) who had suddenly received
an enormous inheritance and married a visiting Frenchwoman,
a well-known cancan artiste from the Château de Fleurs in Paris.
But others said that the inheritance had been received by some
general, and that the visiting Frenchwoman had been married to
a young Russian merchant and unimaginably wealthy Croesus
who, drunk at his own wedding, out of sheer bravado, had
burned on a candle no fewer than seven hundred thousand
roubles' worth of the latest issue of lottery tickets. But all
these rumours very soon died down, something that was greatly
assisted by circumstances. For example, Rogozhin's entire com-

pany, many of whom might have been able to tell something, had all set off for Moscow *en masse*, led by Rogozhin himself, almost exactly a week after the dreadful orgy in the Yekaterinhof pleasure gardens,[1] at which Nastasya Filippovna had also been present. One or two people, the very few who were interested, learned from passing rumours that on the very next day after the incident at Yekaterinhof Nastasya Filippovna had fled, vanished, and that it was finally discovered she had set off for Moscow; the result of this was that Rogozhin's own departure for Moscow began to be viewed as more than a coincidence.

Rumours also began to circulate about Gavrila Ardalionovich Ivolgin, who was also rather well known in his circle. But with him too something occurred, the gossip about which quickly grew cold, but which subsequently quite put to rest all the unkind stories in his regard: he became very ill and was not only unable to present himself anywhere in society, but even at work. Having been ill for a month, he recovered, but for some reason refused point blank to continue in his job at the joint-stock company, and his post was filled by someone else. He did not appear at the house of General Yepanchin even once, so that another civil servant began to visit the general instead. Gavrila Ardalionovich's enemies might have supposed that he was so embarrassed by all that had happened to him that he was even too ashamed to leave the house; but he really did appear to be indisposed: he even fell into a state of morbid preoccupation with his health, brooded, grew irritable. That winter Varvara Ardalionovna married Ptitsyn; everyone who knew them directly ascribed this marriage to the circumstance that Ganya did not want to go back to his job and had not only ceased to support the household but had even begun to stand in need of assistance himself and almost of being looked after.

We shall note in parenthesis that Gavrila Ardalionovich was likewise never even mentioned in the house of the Yepanchins – as if there were no such person in the world, let alone in their house. And yet all the same everyone learned (and even very quickly) of a certain remarkable circumstance concerning him, namely, that on that same night that had been so fateful for him, after the unpleasant incident at Nastasya Filippovna's,

Ganya, returning home, did not go to bed but began to await the prince's return with feverish impatience. The prince, who had travelled to Yekaterinhof, returned from there between five and six in the morning. Then Ganya entered his room and placed before him on the table the scorched parcel of money that had been given him by Nastasya Filippovna as he lay unconscious. He insistently begged the prince to return this gift to Nastasya Filippovna at the first opportunity. On entering the prince's room, Ganya was in a hostile and almost desperate state of mind; but some words apparently passed between him and the prince, whereupon Ganya stayed with the prince for two hours, sobbing most bitterly all the while. They parted on friendly terms.

As subsequently confirmed, this news, which reached all the Yepanchins, was entirely correct. It was, of course, strange that news of such a kind should have reached them and become known to them all so quickly; for example, everything that had taken place at Nastasya Filippovna's became known in the house of the Yepanchins almost on the very next day, and even in rather precise detail. As for the news about Gavrila Ardalionovich, it was not too much to suppose that it had been brought by Varvara Ardalionovna, who suddenly began to pay visits to the Yepanchin girls and was even within a very short time on the closest of terms with them, which astonished Lizaveta Prokofyevna exceedingly. But Varvara Ardalionovna, though for some reason she had found it necessary to associate so closely with the Yepanchins, would certainly not have talked to them about her brother. She was also a rather proud woman in her own way, even though she had made friends with people in a house in which her brother had almost been shown the door. Before this, though she had been acquainted with the Yepanchin girls, they had not seen one another very often. Even now, she hardly ever showed herself in the drawing room, and visited by dropping in, as it were, by way of the back staircase. Lizaveta Prokofyevna had never regarded her with favour, either before or now, though she had great respect for Nina Alexandrovna, Varvara Ardalionovna's mother. She was surprised and angry, ascribing her daughters' friendship with Varya to their caprice and love of power, and their tendency 'to think of nothing but going against her wishes'; nevertheless, Varvara Ardalionovna continued to visit them before and after her marriage.

But when about a month had passed since the prince's departure, Mrs Yepanchina received a letter from old Princess Belokonskaya, who had left some two weeks earlier for Moscow to stay with her eldest married daughter, and this letter had a visible effect on her. Though she disclosed its contents neither to her daughters nor to Ivan Fyodorovich, the family began to notice by a number of signs that she was somehow oddly excited, even agitated. She began to talk to her daughters in a very strange way, and always about most the unusual things; she clearly wished to express her opinion, but was for some reason holding back. On the day she received the letter she was very affectionate to them all, even kissed Aglaya and Alexandra, was apologetic about something in their regard, though precisely what it was they could not ascertain. Even towards Ivan Fyodorovich, whom she had kept in disgrace for a whole month, she suddenly began to be indulgent. Of course, on the very next day she was dreadfully angry about her sentimentality of the day before, and even managed to quarrel with them all before dinner, but towards evening the horizon cleared once again. Indeed, for a whole week she continued to be in a rather serene frame of mind, something that had not been the case for a long time.

After another week, however, another letter arrived from Belokonskaya, and this time the general's wife decided to make her opinion known. She solemnly declared that 'old Belokonskaya' (she never called the princess anything else when talking about her in her absence) had imparted to her some very comforting information about that . . . 'eccentric, oh, you know, the prince!' The old woman had sought him out in Moscow, made inquiries about him, and learned some very good things about him; the prince, at last, had come to see her himself and had made an almost extraordinarily fine impression on her. 'That's clear from the fact that she's invited him to visit her each morning from one to two, and he goes trailing over there every day and hasn't got tired of it so far' – the general's wife concluded, adding that through the 'old woman' the prince had begun to be received in two or three good houses. 'It's good that he's not just staying at home being shy like a fool.' The girls, who were informed of all this, at once observed that their mother had concealed from them a good portion of her letter. It is possible that they discovered it through Varvara Ardalionovna, who might have known and who of course did know everything that Ptitsyn knew about the prince and his stay in Moscow. And Ptitsyn may have known even more than anyone else. However, where business was concerned he was a man of extreme reticence, though he did, of course, tell things to Varya. Because of this the general's wife instantly took an even greater dislike to Varya.

But whatever the truth of the matter, the ice was now broken, and it suddenly began to be possible to speak of the prince out loud. In addition, it was once again clearly revealed what an extraordinary impression and exceedingly great interest the prince had awoken and left in the house of the Yepanchins. The general's wife was positively astonished at the impression the news from Moscow made on her daughters. And the daughters were also astonished at their mother for so solemnly declaring to them that the principal feature of her life was 'being constantly mistaken in people', while at the same time entrusting the prince to the attention of the 'powerful' old Belokonskaya in Moscow, attention which she must of course have had to beg on bended knee, as the 'old woman' was hard to rouse in such cases.

But as soon as the ice had been broken and the wind was blowing in a new direction, the general, too, hurried to express an opinion. It turned out that he too was particularly interested. He talked, however, only about 'the business side of the subject'. It turned out that in the prince's interests he had appointed two very reliable gentlemen, who were in their own way influential in Moscow, to keep an eye on him, and particularly on the prince's business attorney, Salazkin. Everything that had been said about the inheritance, 'the fact of the inheritance, as it were', turned out to be true, but the inheritance itself had proved

PART TWO, CHAPTER I

to be not at all as considerable as rumour had had it at first. The estate was in something of a muddle; there proved to be debts, and claimants of various sorts, and the prince, in spite of all the guidance he had received, had behaved in the most unbusiness-like fashion. 'God bless him, of course'; now that the 'ice of silence' was broken, the general was glad to announce this 'with all the sincerity of his soul', for 'although the fellow's a little *you know*', he deserved the inheritance none the less. Yet all the same, he had done some foolish things: for example, the credi-tors of the deceased merchant had appeared, with documents that were questionable and worthless, and other creditors, hav-ing scented a prince, with no documents at all – and what had happened? The prince had met nearly all the claims, in spite of all the insistence of his friends that these wretched little people, these creditors, had no claim at all; and met them for the sole reason that, it transpired, some of them really had suffered.

The general's wife responded to this by saying that Belokon-skaya had also written to her in this vein, and that it was 'stupid, very stupid; once a fool, always a fool', she added sharply, though from her face it was clear that she was pleased by the actions of the 'fool'. To conclude it all, the general observed that his wife cared for the prince as though he were her own son, and that she had begun to be very affectionate towards Aglaya; seeing this, Ivan Fyodorovich assumed a very business-like air for some time.

This pleasant atmosphere did not, however, last for long. After only two weeks had passed, something suddenly changed again; the general's wife frowned, and the general, shrugging his shoulders a few times, again submitted to 'the ice of silence'. The fact was that only two weeks earlier he had received a report which, though short and therefore not quite unambiguous, was none the less reliable, to the effect that Nastasya Filippovna, who had first disappeared in Moscow, and then been tracked down there by Rogozhin, then disappeared somewhere again, and again tracked down by him, had at last given him her almost certain promise to marry him. And now, only two weeks later, his excellency had suddenly received intelligence that Nastasya Filippovna had run away a third time, almost from the altar, and had this time disappeared somewhere in the surrounding province, while in the meantime Prince Myshkin had also vanished from Moscow, leaving all his business matters in the hands of Salazkin. 'We don't know whether he accompanied her or just went rushing off after her, but something is going on here,' the general concluded. Lizaveta Prokofyevna, for her part, had also received some unpleasant news. In the end, two months after the prince's departure almost all the rumours about him had finally died away in St Petersburg, and once again the 'ice of silence' in the house of the Yepanchins remained unbroken. On the other hand, Varvara Ardalionovna still came to visit the girls.

In order to put an end to all these rumours and reports, we should also add that by the time spring arrived there were a great many upheavals in the Yepanchin household, so that it was hard not to forget the prince, who sent no news of himself and perhaps did not want to send any. Gradually, in the course of the winter, they decided to go abroad for the summer, Lizaveta Prokofyevna and the daughters, that is; it was, of course, out of the question for the general to waste time on 'empty amusement'. The decision was taken at the extreme and obstinate insistence of the girls, who had become quite convinced that their parents did not want to take them abroad because of their ceaseless concern with marrying them off and finding them husbands. It is possible that the parents, too, had at last been persuaded that prospective husbands might be met abroad, and that one summer trip might not only not be harmless but might even possibly 'facilitate matters'. Here it is relevant to note that the plans for the marriage of Afanasy Ivanovich Totsky and the eldest Yepanchin daughter had completely foundered, and no formal proposal had materialized at all. This had happened almost of its own accord, without lengthy discussions and without any family strife. Since the prince's departure, it had all suddenly petered out on both sides. This circumstance, too, was among the reasons for the painful atmosphere in the Yepanchin household, even though the general's wife had said at the time she was now so glad she could 'cross herself with both hands'. Although the general was in disgrace and felt that he was to blame, for a long time he sulked; he felt sorry for Afanasy Ivanovich: 'such a fortune and such a smart fellow!' Not long afterwards the general learned that Afanasy Ivanovich had been captivated by a visiting Frenchwoman of high society, a marquise and legitimist, that they were going to be married and that Afanasy Ivanovich would be taken off to Paris, and then to somewhere in Brittany. 'Well, the Frenchwoman will be his downfall,' the general decided.

So the Yepanchins prepared to go abroad for the summer. Then suddenly something happened that altered everything again, and again the trip was postponed, to the great delight of the general and his wife. There arrived in St Petersburg from Moscow a certain prince, Prince Shch., a man who was well known, and well known in a very, very good sense. He was one of those men, or even, one might say, men of action of our modern age, decent, modest, who sincerely and consciously desire the useful, are always working and are distinguished by the rare and happy quality of always finding work to do. Not parading himself, avoiding the bitterness and empty talk of the political parties, not considering himself among the leaders, the prince was none the less very thoroughly acquainted with much that had taken place in recent times. He had earlier been in government service, then began to take part in the running of the *zemstva*.[2] In addition, he was a useful corresponding member of several Russian learned societies. Together with an engineer of his acquaintance he had made possible, by the information they collected and the surveys they had made, an improved route for one of the most important railways then being planned. He was about thirty-five years of age. He was a man of the 'very highest society' and, moreover, with a 'good, serious, indisputable' fortune, as the general, who in connection with a rather serious matter had had occasion to meet him and make his acquaintance at the house of the count, his superior, put it. The prince, out of a certain special curiosity, never avoided the acquaintance of Russian 'men of business'. It happened that the prince also became acquainted with the general's family. Adelaida Ivanovna, the middle of the three sisters, made a rather strong impression on him. Towards the spring, the prince proposed to her. He liked Adelaida very much, and also liked Lizaveta Prokofyevna. The general was very pleased. Naturally, the trip abroad was postponed. The wedding was set for the spring.

As a matter of fact, the trip might still have taken place either towards the middle or the end of the summer, though only in the form of an excursion lasting a month or two by Lizaveta Prokofyevna and the two daughters remaining to her, in order to dispel the sadness caused by Adelaida leaving them. But again something happened: in late spring (Adelaida's wedding was slightly delayed and was postponed until the middle of the summer) Prince Shch. introduced to the house of the Yepanchins one of his distant relatives, who was, however, rather well known to him. This was a certain Yevgeny Pavlovich R., a man still young, about twenty-eight, an aide-de-camp to the Tsar, a picture of handsomeness, 'of noble birth', a man who was witty, brilliant, 'new', 'extremely well-educated', and possessed of some truly unheard-of wealth. Concerning this last point, the general was invariably cautious. He made inquiries: 'There does indeed turn out to be something of the kind – however, one must check further.' This young aide-de-camp 'with a future' was much elevated by a recommendation from old Princess Belokonskaya from Moscow. Only one aspect of his glory was slightly ticklish: there had been several liaisons and, it was asserted, 'conquests' of unfortunate hearts. Having set eyes on Aglaya, he became uncommonly assiduous in his visits to the house of the Yepanchins. While it was true that nothing had yet been said, no hints had even yet been made, to the parents it none the less seemed that a trip abroad that summer was out of the question. Aglaya herself was possibly of a different opinion.

This happened just before the second appearance of our hero on the scene of our narrative. By this time, to judge by appearances, people in St Petersburg had managed to completely forget about poor Prince Myshkin. If now he appeared among those who knew him, it was as if he had fallen from the sky. But meanwhile we shall report one more fact and with it conclude our introduction.

After the prince's departure, Kolya Ivolgin at first continued to lead the life he had led previously, that is, he attended school, visited his friend Ippolit, looked after the general and helped Varya with the running of the household, going out on errands for her. But the lodgers quickly disappeared: Ferdyshchenko went off somewhere three days after the adventure at Nastasya Filippovna's and rather soon vanished from sight, so that every rumour about him died away; he was said to be drinking somewhere, but this could not be verified. The prince went away to Moscow; that was the end of the lodgers. Later, after Varya had got married, Nina Alexandrovna and Ganya moved together with her to Ptitsyn's quarters in Izmailovsky Regiment;³ as for General Ivolgin, almost at the same time an entirely unforeseen circumstance befell him: he was put in the debtors' prison. He was dispatched there by his friend the captain's widow because of documents he had issued to her at various times, to the value of some two thousand roubles. All this came as a complete surprise to him, and the poor general was 'decidedly a victim of his own immoderate faith in the nobleness of the human heart, broadly speaking'. Having acquired the reassuring habit of signing IOUs and promissory notes, he had never even dreamed of the possibility that this might have any effect, even in the distant future, and went on thinking that it was *all right*. It turned out not to be. 'How can one trust people after this, how can one show them a noble trust?' he explained in sorrow, as he sat with his new friends in Tarasov House (the debtors' prison), over a bottle of wine, telling them anecdotes about the siege of Kars and the soldier who came back from the dead. He began a new life, and for him it was, moreover, an excellent one. Ptitsyn and Varya said it was the best place for him; Ganya was in thorough agreement on this. Only poor Nina Alexandrovna wept bitterly to herself (which rather astonished the rest of the family) and, eternally ailing, dragged herself to see her husband as often as she could.

But ever since 'the incident with the general', as Kolya expressed it, and indeed ever since his sister's marriage, Kolya had got almost completely out of hand, and it had even got to the point that he seldom appeared in the household and spent the night there. According to rumours, he had made a great many new friends; in addition, he had become all too familiar a face at the debtors' prison. Nina Alexandrovna was unable to manage there without him; while at home he was no longer even troubled by the curiosity of the others. Varya, who had treated him so strictly before, now did not subject him to the slightest interrogation about his wanderings; while Ganya, to the family's great astonishment, spoke to him and sometimes treated him in quite a friendly manner, in spite of all his hypochondria, something that had never happened earlier, as the twenty-seven-year-old Ganya had naturally never paid his fifteen-year-old brother the slightest friendly attention, dealing roughly with him, demanding that all the members of the household be strict with him, and constantly threatening to 'take him by the ears', which drove Kolya 'beyond the final limits of human endurance'. One could almost suppose that now Kolya was sometimes even indispensable to Ganya. He had been greatly struck when Ganya returned the money that day; for that, he was prepared to forgive him many things.

Some three months had passed since the prince's departure, and news reached the Ivolgins' household that Kolya had suddenly got to know the Yepanchins and was very well received by the girls. Varya soon found out about this; however, Kolya had made their acquaintance not through Varya, but 'on his own account'. Little by little, the Yepanchins grew fond of him. At first the general's wife was very displeased with him, but soon she began to show him affection 'for his openness, and because he doesn't flatter anyone'. That Kolya did not flatter anyone was perfectly true; he was able to be on a completely equal and independent footing with them, though he sometimes read books and newspapers to the general's wife – but then, he was always helpful and obliging. On a couple of occasions he had, however, fiercely quarrelled with Lizaveta Prokofyevna, told her that she was a despot and that he would not set foot in her house again. On the first occasion the argument had stemmed from the 'woman question', and on the second from the question of the best time of year for catching siskins. However improbable it might seem, on the third day after the quarrel she sent a lackey with a note asking him to visit her without fail; Kolya did not make difficulties, and at once presented himself. Only Aglaya was for some reason forever ill-disposed towards him, and treated him condescendingly. She it was, however, who was destined to receive something of a surprise from him. One day – it was in Holy Week – having snatched a moment when they were alone, Kolya handed Aglaya a letter, saying merely that he had been told to deliver it to her in person. Aglaya looked the 'conceited urchin' sternly up and down, but Kolya did not wait, and left the room. She unfolded the note and read:

> At one time you honoured me with your trust. It may be that you have now forgotten me entirely. How has it come to pass that I am writing to you? I do not know; but there has appeared in me an irrepressible longing to remind you of me, and you in particular. How many times I have needed all three of you, but of all three I saw only you. I need you, very much. I have nothing to write to you about myself, nothing to tell you. I did not want that, either; I should terribly like you to be happy. Are you happy? That is all I wanted to say to you.
>
> Your brother Pr. L. Myshkin.

As she read this short and rather incoherent note, Aglaya suddenly flushed all over and began to reflect. It would be hard for us to describe the current of her thoughts. Among other things, she asked herself: 'Should I show this to anyone?' She somehow felt ashamed. In the end, however, with a strange, mocking smile she threw the letter into her writing desk. The next day, she took it out and put it into a thick book with a strong binding (she always did this with her papers, in order to locate them more quickly when she needed them). And only a week later she happened to notice what book it was. It was *Don Quixote*. Aglaya burst into peels of laughter – for no reason that is known.

Nor is it known if she showed her acquisition to either of her sisters.

But when she read the letter again, the thought suddenly entered her mind: had that conceited urchin and wretched little braggart really been chosen by the prince as his correspondent – and, for all she knew, his only correspondent here? Though she did so with an air of great disdain, she none the less subjected Kolya to questioning. On this occasion, however, the ever touchy 'urchin' paid not the slightest attention to the disdain; in very brief and rather dry terms, he explained to Aglaya that although he had told the prince his permanent address just in case, before the prince's departure from St Petersburg, and had at the same time offered him his services, this was the first commission and the first note he had been given by him, while as a proof of his words he presented the letter he had himself received. Aglaya had no scruples about reading it. The letter to Kolya said:

Dear Kolya,
Please give the enclosed sealed note to Aglaya Ivanovna. Stay well.

Your loving L. Myshkin.

'But it's absurd to confide in a little brat like you,' Aglaya said huffily, handing the note back to Kolya, and walking contemptuously past him.

This was more than Kolya could endure: for this occasion, without explaining the reason, he had especially asked Ganya to let him wear Ganya's brand new green scarf. He was deeply offended.

2

It was early June, and the weather in St Petersburg had been unusually fine for a whole week. The Yepanchins owned a splendid dacha in Pavlovsk, and Lizaveta Prokofyevna suddenly got excited and burst into action; before two days of bustle had passed, they had moved.

On the second or third day after the Yepanchins' move, Lev Nikolayevich Myshkin arrived from Moscow by the morning train. No one met him at the station, but while disembarking from the carriage the prince suddenly fancied that he saw the strange, hot gaze of someone's eyes,[1] in the crowd, importuning the arrivals from the train. Taking a closer look, he could make out nothing more. Of course, he had only fancied it; but it left an unpleasant impression. Moreover, the prince was in any case sad and reflective, and seemed to be preoccupied about something.

A cab took him to a hotel not far from Liteinaya. The hotel was an inferior one. The prince took two small rooms, dark and poorly furnished, washed, dressed, asked for nothing, and hurriedly left, as though afraid of wasting time, or of not finding someone at home.

If any of those who had known him six months earlier in St Petersburg, on his first arrival, had glanced at him now they might have concluded that his appearance had altered considerably for the better. But this was not really true. In his dress alone was there a complete change: all his clothes were different, cut in Moscow by a good tailor; but even in his clothes there was something not quite right: they were cut too fashionably (as conscientious but not very talented tailors always cut them) and in addition they were worn by a man who had no interest in such things at all, so that on a close look at the prince, someone rather too fond of a chuckle might perhaps have found something to smile about. But many things are a source of amusement, are they not?

The prince took a cab and set off for Peski.[2] In one of the Rozhdestvensky streets he soon located a small wooden house. To his astonishment, this house turned out to be attractive to the eye, well kept, in good order, with a front garden in which grew flowers. The windows facing the street were open, and from them came a strident, unbroken stream of talk, of shouting, almost, as though someone were reading aloud or even giving a speech; the voice was interrupted from time to time by the laughter of several resonant voices. The prince entered the courtyard, climbed the front steps, and asked for Mr Lebedev.

'He's in there,' replied the cook who opened the door, her

sleeves rolled up to the elbows, poking her finger towards the 'drawing room'.

In the middle of this drawing room, which was papered with dark blue wallpaper and furnished neatly and somewhat pretentiously, that is to say, with a round table and a sofa, a bronze clock under a glass cover, a narrow mirror in the space between the two windows and a small, extremely ancient chandelier with crystal pendants, hanging on a bronze chain from the ceiling, stood Mr Lebedev himself, who, with his back to the prince as he entered, in his waistcoat, but without his jacket, summer style, was striking his chest and bitterly orating on some subject or other. His listeners were: a boy of about fifteen, with a rather cheerful and intelligent face and a book in his hands, a young girl of about twenty, in mourning attire with a babe in arms, a girl of thirteen, also in mourning, who laughed a great deal, her mouth gaping dreadfully as she did so, and, lastly, a very strange listener indeed, a fellow of about twenty who lay on the sofa, rather handsome, darkish, with long, thick hair, large black eyes, and feeble efforts at sideburns and a beard. This listener seemed frequently to interrupt and argue with the orating Lebedev; this was probably what the rest of the audience were laughing at.

'Lukyan Timofeich, Lukyan Timofeich! For heaven's sake! Look this way! . . . Well, to the devil with you, then!'

And the cook went away with a wave of her arms, and so angry that she even blushed all over.

Lebedev turned round and, catching sight of the prince, stood for some time as if struck by lightning, then rushed over to him with an obsequious smile, but on the way seemed to freeze again, saying:

'M-m-most illustrious Prince!'

But then suddenly, still as though he were unable to regain his self-control, he turned and, for no apparent reason, first rounded on the girl in mourning with the babe in her arms, so that she staggered backwards a little in surprise; then, however, at once abandoning her, he turned on the thirteen-year-old girl who was standing in the doorway of the next room and was still smiling, the remnants of her recent laughter still on her lips. She could not endure his shouting and at once made a bolt for the kitchen; Lebedev even stamped his feet after her, as an added warning, but meeting the gaze of the prince, who was staring in bewilderment, said by way of explanation:

'To make her . . . show some respect, heh-heh-heh!'

'There's really no need for you to . . .' the prince began.

'One moment, one moment, one moment . . . in two shakes of a lamb's tail!'

And Lebedev quickly vanished from the room. The prince looked in astonishment at the girl, the boy and the fellow lying on the sofa; they were all laughing. The prince also began to laugh.

'He's gone to put on his frock coat,' said the boy.

'How vexing this all is,' the prince began, 'and I thought . . . tell me, is he . . .'

'Drunk, you mean?' cried a voice from the sofa. 'Not on your life! Maybe three or four glasses, well, or five, but for him that's – discipline.'

The prince was about to address the voice from the sofa, but the girl began to speak, and with a look of the utmost candour on her pretty face said:

'He never drinks much in the morning; if you've come to see him on some business matter, do it now. Now's the time to catch him. It's only when he comes back in the evening that he's drunk; and even then he's more likely to cry all night and read aloud to us from Holy Scripture, because our mother died five weeks ago.'

'He probably ran away because he found it hard to answer you,' the young man from the sofa began to laugh. 'I bet he's already working out how to swindle you right now.'

'Only five weeks! Only five weeks!' Lebedev chimed in, returning now in his frock coat, blinking and pulling from his pocket a handkerchief to wipe away the tears. 'Orphans!'

'But why have you come out dressed in those old rags?' said the girl. 'I mean, you've a brand new frock coat hanging behind the door, didn't you see it, or what?'

'Be quiet, vixen!' Lebedev shouted at her. 'Oh, you bad girl!' He began to stamp his feet at her. But this time she merely burst out laughing.

'What are you trying to frighten me for? I'm not Tanya, you know, I won't run away. But you'll wake up Lyubochka, and give her convulsions, too . . . why are you shouting?'

'Sh-sh-sh! Curse that tongue of yours . . .' Lebedev said suddenly in fearful alarm, rushing up to the child that slept in his daughter's arms and making the sign of the cross over it several times with a frightened look. 'Lord preserve her, Lord protect her! This is my own baby, my daughter Lyubov,' he said, turning to the prince, 'and she was born in the most lawful wedlock to my lately deceased wife Yelena, who died in childbirth. And this little sprout is my daughter Vera, dressed in mourning . . . And this, this, oh, this . . .'

'What have you stopped for?' cried the young man. 'Go on, don't be embarassed.'

'Your excellency!' Lebedev suddenly exclaimed with a kind of rush. 'Have you had occasion to follow the murder of the Zhemarin family in the newspaper?'[3]

'I have,' said the prince with some surprise.

'Well, this is the real murderer of the Zhemarin family, he's the man himself!'

'What do you mean?' asked the prince.

'Figuratively speaking, of course, the future second murderer of the second Zhemarin family, if there turns out to be one. He's preparing himself for it . . .'

They all laughed. It occurred to the prince that Lebedev might very well be prevaricating and cringing because, anticipating the prince's questions, he did not know how to reply to them, and was stalling for time.

'He's a man in revolt! He's brewing conspiracies!' shouted Lebedev, as though no longer able to contain himself. 'Well, can I, well, have I the right to consider such a slanderer, such a monster and whore of cruelty, one might even say, as my own nephew, as the only son of my sister Anisa, now deceased?'

'Oh stop it, you drunken man! Would you believe it, Prince, now he's taken it into his head to take up the profession of lawyer, and is attending trials at the courts; he's studying eloquence, and talks to his children at home in high-flown language all the time. He spoke before the magistrates five days ago. And who had he undertaken to defend: not the old woman who begged and beseeched him and whom a scoundrel of a moneylender had robbed, five hundred roubles he'd taken from her, all that she owned, but the moneylender, some Yid called Zaydler, all because he'd promised him him fifty roubles . . .'

'Fifty roubles if I won, and only five if I lost,' Lebedev suddenly exclaimed in a voice that was completely different from the one in which he had spoken hitherto, and as though he had never been shouting at all.

'Well, and he put his foot in it, of course, things are not how they used to be, after all, they just laughed at him. But my, how pleased with himself he was; remember, he said, impartial gentlemen judges, that a melancholy senior citizen, without the use of his legs, living by honest toil, is deprived of his last piece of bread; remember the wise words of the legislator: 'Let mercy reign in the courts.'[4] And would you believe: every morning he repeats the same speech to us, exactly as he gave it there; it's the fifth time today; he was even reciting it just before you arrived, that's how pleased he is with it. He's preening himself in delight. And he's going to defend someone else as well. I believe you're Prince Myshkin? Kolya told me about you, he said he'd never met anyone cleverer in all the world . . .'

'And there isn't! There isn't! There isn't anyone cleverer in all the world!' Lebedev at once chimed in.

'Well, this one, I think, is lying. One loves you, but the other is trying to curry favour with you; and I don't intend to flatter you, let me tell you that now. But you're not without sense: so judge between him and me. I say, would you like the prince to judge between us?' he said turning to his uncle. 'I'm rather glad that you've turned up, Prince!'

'Yes, I would!' Lebedev cried determinedly, casting an involuntary glance at his audience, which was beginning to draw closer again.

'But what's going on here?' said the prince, frowning.

He really did have a headache and, moreover, he was growing more and more convinced that Lebedev was trying to pull the wool over his eyes, glad that the essential business was being postponed.

'Exposition of the matter. I'm his nephew, about that he did not lie, though he lies all the time. I haven't graduated yet, but I want to graduate and shall insist on doing so, for I have character. And meanwhile, in order to exist, I'm going to take a job on the railway at twenty-five roubles. I will admit, moreover, that he has helped me on two or three occasions. I had twenty roubles, and I lost them. Well, would you believe it, Prince, I was so vile, so base, that I lost them, too!'

'To a villain, a villain who ought not to have been paid!' cried Lebedev.

'Yes, a villain, but one who had to be paid,' the young man went on. 'And that he's a villain, I will bear testimony to that, and not only because he gave you a drubbing, Prince; he's an officer who was dismissed from the service, a retired lieutenant from the old Rogozhin gang who teaches boxing now. Now that Rogozhin's dispersed them, they're roaming about all over the place. But what's worst of all is that I knew he was a villain, a rogue and a wretched little thief, and yet I sat down to play cards with him, and, playing my last rouble (we were playing *palki*),[5] I thought to myself: if I lose, I'll go to Uncle Lukyan, I'll bow to him – he won't refuse. Now that is baseness, that really is baseness! That is conscious vileness!'

'Now that is conscious vileness!' Lebedev repeated.

'Now don't crow, wait a moment,' cried the nephew, touchily. 'He's actually rather pleased. I came to see him here, Prince, and confessed to everything; I acted decently, I didn't spare myself; I cursed myself before him, for all I was worth, everyone here was a witness. In order to take up this job on the railway I shall have to kit myself out somehow, for I'm all in rags. Here, look at my boots! I can't turn up at the job like this, and if I don't turn up when I'm supposed to, someone else will get the job, and then I'll be back at square one again, and when will I ever find another job? I'm only asking him for fifteen roubles now, and I promise I'll never ask him again and, on top of that, during the first three months I'll pay back the whole debt to him, right down to the last copeck. I'll keep my word. I'm able to live on bread and kvass for whole months on end, for I have character. For three months I'll get seventy-five roubles. With the old money, I'll only owe him thirty-five roubles, so I'll have enough to pay him. Well, let him fix any interest he likes, the devil take it! He knows me, doesn't he? Ask him, Prince: before, when he helped me, did I pay him or didn't I? So why doesn't he want to lend to me now? He's angry with me because I paid that lieutenant; there's no other reason! That's what this man is like – he'll give neither to himself, nor to others!'

'And he won't go away!' exclaimed Lebedev. 'He lies on the sofa here and won't go away.'

'That's what I told you. I won't go away until you give it to me. Are you smiling, Prince? I believe you think I am in the wrong?'

'I'm not smiling, but in my view you are indeed somewhat in the wrong,' the prince volunteered reluctantly.

'Then say it straight, that I'm totally in the wrong, don't beat about the bush; what do you mean, "somewhat"?'

'If you like, then you're totally in the wrong.'

'If I like! That's comical! Do you really think I don't know that to act like that is questionable, that the money is his, that he has the freedom to do what he likes with it, while I for my part am merely exercising force? But you don't know much about life, Prince . . . If you don't teach them a lesson, you won't get anywhere. You have to teach them. I mean, my conscience is clear; in all good conscience, I won't involve him in any loss, I'll return the money with interest. He's also obtained moral satisfaction: he's seen me humiliated. So what more does he want? What good is he if he's no use to anyone? For pity's sake, what does he do himself? Ask him what he gets up to with other people, and how he swindles them. How did he get this house? And I'll put my head on the block if he hasn't already swindled you and hasn't already thought about how he could swindle you some more! You smile, you don't believe it?'

'I don't think all this is quite relevant to your case,' observed the prince.

'I've been lying here for three days now, and I've seen enough!' the young man shouted, not listening. 'Imagine, this angel here, this girl, who is now orphaned, my cousin, his daughter, he's suspicious of her, goes looking for lovers in her room every night! He comes in here on the sly, looks under the sofa I'm lying on, too. He's gone mad with suspicion; sees thieves in every corner. Keeps leaping up at all hours of the night, examining the windows to see if they're properly closed, trying the doors, looking inside the stove, and on and on like that more than half a dozen times a night. Pleads the defence of swindlers in court, but gets up about three times every night, right here in this room, on his knees, knocking his forehead on the floor for half an hour at a time, and who does he not pray for, who do you think he mourns when he's drunk? He was praying for the repose of the soul of the Countess Du Barry,[6] I heard it with my own ears; Kolya also heard it: he's gone completely mad!'

'You see, you hear how he heaps infamy on me, Prince?' Lebedev exclaimed, flushing and really beside himself now. 'But what he doesn't know is while I may be a drunkard and a vagrant, a robber and an evildoer, there is one thing I can be proud of, and that is that that scoffer there, when he was still an infant, I wrapped him in swaddling clothes, and washed him in the tub, and sat up at nights never sleeping a wink, with my sister Anisya who was widowed and destitute, and I was destitute as well, looked after them both when they were ill, stole firewood from the yardkeeper downstairs, sang songs to him and snapped my fingers for him, with hunger in my belly, and look at what I nursed him into, there he is now, laughing at me! And what business is it of yours, if I did once cross my forehead for the repose of the Countess Du Barry? Prince, three days ago I read her biography in an encyclopedia. Well, do you know what she was like, *la Du Barry*? Tell me, do you know or don't you?'

'I suppose you think you're the only one who knows?' the young man muttered derisively, but with reluctance.

'She was a countess who, risen from disgrace, reigned in place of the queen and to whom a great empress, in a letter in her own hand, wrote *"ma cousine"*. A cardinal, a papal nuncio, offered to put silk stockings on her bare legs at a *levée du roi* (do you know what a *levée du roi* is?) considering it an honour – an exalted and most holy personage like him! Do you know that? By your face I can see that you don't! Well, how did she die? Answer, if you know?'

'Clear off! You're annoying me.'

'She died in such a manner that after all that honour, this former ruler of the land was dragged to the guillotine by the executioner Samson, innocent as she was, for the entertainment of the Parisian *poissardes*, and she, from terror, didn't know what was happening to her. When she saw that he was bending her down by the neck under the blade, pushing her under it, kicking her – the others were laughing – she began to shout: "*Encore un moment, monsieur le bourreau, encore un moment!*" Which means: "Wait just one little moment, Mr Executioner, just one!" And for that moment, perhaps, the Lord will forgive her, because a *misère* worse than that is impossible to imagine for a human soul. Do you know what the word *misère* means? Well, that is the very personification of *misère*. That cry of the countess's, for one little moment, when I read about it, seized my heart with pincers. And what is it to you, you worm, that I, on going to bed for the night, had the notion of mentioning her, great sinner that she was, in a prayer? Perhaps I mentioned her because probably never since the world came into being has anyone ever made the sign of the cross over his forehead for her sake, or thought of her. I think she'll find it pleasant in the next world to feel that there was a sinner like her who prayed for her at least once on this earth. What are you laughing for? Atheist, you have no faith. Anyway, how do you know? And you were wrong, if you did overhear me: I didn't just pray for the Countess Du Barry; my prayer went like this: "Grant repose, O Lord, to the soul of the great sinner the Countess Du Barry, and of all those like her," and that's quite different; for there are many such great female sinners and examples of the changes of fortune, who have suffered much, who are without rest there now, groaning, and waiting; and at the same time I prayed for you, and for those like you, impudent, offensive boors, if you'd really taken it upon yourself to overhear my prayers . . .'

'Well, that will do, enough, pray to anyone you like, the devil take you, you've done enough shouting!' the nephew interrupted in vexation. 'Why, he's very well read, this man of ours, didn't you know, Prince?' he added with an awkward, ironic smile. 'He's forever reading books and memoirs of that kind nowadays.'

'All the same, your uncle is . . . not a man without a heart,' the prince observed reluctantly. This young man was becoming quite repugnant to him.

'Now that's the way to praise him! You see, he's already put his hand on his heart, and his mouth's curled into a smile, he's got a taste for it at once! He may not lack a heart, perhaps, but he's a swindler, that's the trouble; and what's more, he's drunk, he's come completely unhinged, like any man who's been a drunkard for several years, that's why everything about him creaks. He loves his children, let's grant him that, he respected my deceased aunt . . . He even loves me, and has left me something in his will, I swear to God . . .'

'N-nothing will I leave you!' Lebedev exclaimed with frantic energy.

'Look, Lebedev,' the prince said firmly, turning away from the young man. 'I mean, I know from experience that you're a man of business when you want to be . . . I don't have much time now, and if you . . . Forgive me, what are your name and patronymic? I've forgotten.'

'Ti-Ti-Timofei.'

'And?'

'Lukyanovich.'

All who were in the room again burst into laughter.

'He's lying!' cried the nephew. 'He's even lying about that! Prince, his name isn't Timofei Lukyanovich at all, but Lukyan Timofeyevich! Well, tell me, why did you lie? Isn't it all the same to you if it's Lukyan or Timofei, and what does the prince care about it? I mean, he lies out of sheer habit, I assure you!'

'Is it so?' the prince asked in impatience.

'My name's really Lukyan Timofeyevich,' Lebedev agreed, starting to grow embarrassed, lowering his eyes submissively, and putting his hand on his heart again.

'But why do you do this, for heaven's sake?'

'Out of self-depreciation,' whispered Lebedev, hanging his head more and more submissively.

'Oh, what self-depreciation is there in that? If only I knew where to find Kolya now!' said the prince, turning to go.

'I can tell you where Kolya is,' the young man volunteered again.

'No, no, no!' Lebedev jumped up and began to bustle about.

'Kolya spent the night here, but this morning he went to look for his general, whom you, Prince, bailed out of prison, Lord knows why. Yesterday the general promised to come and spend the night here, but he never turned up. He most likely spent the night at the "Scales" Hotel, very near here. Kolya must either be there or in Pavlovsk, at the Yepanchins'. He had money, he wanted to go there yesterday. So he must either be at the "Scales" or in Pavlovsk.'

'Pavlovsk, Pavlovsk! . . . But let's go outside, out to the garden and . . . have coffee . . .'

And Lebedev pulled the prince by the arm. They emerged from the room, walked across the small courtyard and went in at the wicker gate. Here there really was a very small and very charming little garden, in which thanks to the good weather all the trees had already opened their leaves. Lebedev showed the prince to a green wooden bench, at a green table set into the ground, and himself sat opposite him. A moment later the coffee really did appear. The prince did not refuse. Lebedev continued to gaze obsequiously and avidly into his eyes.

'I didn't know you had a place like this,' said the prince with the look of a man who was thinking about something else entirely.

'O-orphans,' Lebedev began, wriggling into life, but stopped: the prince was gazing distractedly in front of him and had, of course, forgotten his own question. Another minute or so passed; Lebedev watched and waited.

'Well, where was I?' said the prince, as though waking up. 'Ah yes! Why, you yourself know what our business is, Lebedev: I've come in response to your letter. So tell me all about it.'

Lebedev grew embarrassed, was about to say something, but merely stammered: no words came out. The prince waited and sadly smiled.

'I think I understand you very well, Lukyan Timofeyevich: you probably weren't expecting me. You thought I wouldn't emerge from my backwoods the first time you notified me, and wrote to me in order to clear your conscience. But here I am.

Well, enough, don't try to deceive me. Enough of serving two masters. Rogozhin's already been here for three weeks, I know it all. Have you managed to sell her to him, as you did last time, or not? Tell the truth, now.'

'The monster found out by himself, all by himself.'

'Don't call him names; he behaved badly to you, of course . . .'

'He thrashed me, thrashed me!' Lebedev retorted with the most frightful intensity. 'And set his dog on me in Moscow, all the way down the street, his borzoi bitch. A horrible bitch.'

'You take me for a child, Lebedev. Tell me, has she seriously left him now, in Moscow, that is?'

'Seriously, seriously, right at the altar again. He was already counting the minutes, but she came here to St Petersburg and straight to me: "Save me, preserve me, Lukyan, and don't tell the prince . . ." Prince, she's more afraid of you than of him, and therein lies an enigma!'

And Lebedev slyly put a finger to his forehead.

'And now you've brought them together again?'

'Most illustrious Prince, how could . . . how could I have not allowed it?'

'Well, enough, I'll find it all out for myself. Just tell me, where is she now? At his house?'

'Oh no! No, no! Still by herself. I'm free, she says, and you know, Prince, she insists on it, I'm still completely free, she says! She is still living on the St Petersburg Side, in the house of my wife's sister, as I wrote to you.'

'And she's there now?'

'Yes, if she's not in Pavlovsk, on account of the good weather, staying with Darya Alexeyevna at her dacha. I'm completely free, she says; just yesterday she was boasting a lot to Nikolai Ardalionovich about her freedom. A bad sign, sir!'

And Lebedev showed his teeth in a grin.

'Is Kolya often at her house?'

'He's flippant and unfathomable, but not secretive.'

'Have you been there recently?'

'Every day, every day.'

'Yesterday, then?'

'N-no; three days ago, sir.'

'What a pity you've been drinking, Lebedev! Otherwise there is something I would have asked you.'

'No, no, no, not a drop!'

Lebedev fairly stared at him.

'Tell me, how was she when you left her?'

'S-seeking . . .'

'Seeking?'

'As though she were in search of something, something she'd lost. Even the thought of the forthcoming marriage revolts her, she sees it as an insult. She thinks no more of *him* than of an orange peel, or rather more, with fear and terror, even forbids anyone to talk about it, and they only see each other if it's absolutely necessary . . . and he feels it all too keenly! But there's no way round it, sir! . . . She's restless, mocking, double-tongued and snipey . . .'

'Double-tongued and snipey?'

'Snipey: for last time she nearly grabbed me by the hair because of something I said. I'd begun to lecture her from Revelation.'

'How's that again?' the prince asked, thinking he had misheard.

'I was reading Revelation. A lady with a restless imagination, heh-heh! And what's more, I've deduced the observation that she's excessively inclined to serious topics, even though they're strange ones. She likes them, she likes them and even takes them as a mark of particular respect for her. Yes, sir. I'm good at interpreting Revelation, and I've been doing it for fifteen years. She agreed with me that we're at the third horse, the black one, and the horseman who has the pair of balances in his hand, as in the present age everything is by measure and agreement, and all men seek nothing but their own right: "A measure of wheat for a penny, and three measures of barley for a penny"[7] . . . and also a free spirit and a pure heart, and at the same time they want to preserve all God's gifts. But they can't preserve these things by right alone, and after this will follow the pale horse and the one whose name is Death, and after him Hell . . . Whenever we meet we discuss this, and – it's had a powerful effect on her.'

'Do you believe it yourself?' asked the prince, surveying Lebedev with an odd look.

'I believe it and interpret it. For I am destitute and naked, and an atom in the cycle of mankind. And who will respect Lebedev? Everyone falls over backwards to mock him, and everyone more or less sees him off with a kick. Here, on the other hand, in this interpretation, I'm equal to a high official. For I have intellect! And a high official trembled before me . . . in his armchair, as his intellect grasped it. Two years ago, before Holy Week, his exalted excellency, Nil Alexeyevich, heard about me – while I was still working in his department – and specially asked me, through Pyotr Zakharych, to come from the orderly office to see him in his study and when we were alone asked me: "Is it true that you're a professor of the Antichrist?" And I didn't hide it: "I am," I said, and expounded, and presented, and didn't tone down the horror, but even deliberately heightened it, unfolding the allegorical scroll, and adducing the figures. And he laughed, but at the figures and analogies he began to tremble, and asked me to close the book and leave, and saw to it that by Holy Week I received promotion, and then at the Feast of St Thomas he gave up his soul to God.'

'Surely not, Lebedev?'

'It's true. He fell out of his carriage after a dinner . . . hit his temple on a post and, like a little child, like a little child, instantly departed this world. Seventy-three years old according to his record of service; somewhat red in complexion, somewhat grey-haired, sprinkled all over with scent, and always smiling, smiling, like a little child. Pyotr Zakharych recalled at the time: "It was you who foretold it," he said.'

The prince began to get up. Lebedev was surprised, and even puzzled, that the prince was already getting up.

'You've become very indifferent, sir, heh-heh!' he ventured to comment, obsequiously.

'It's true, I don't feel very well, I have a headache from the journey, I suppose,' the prince replied, frowning.

'You should go to a country dacha, sir,' Lebedev timidly suggested.

The prince stood lost in reflection.

'In another three days I'm going to a dacha myself, with all my family, in order to look after the health of the newborn chick and at the same time have the house put in order. And I'm also going to Pavlovsk.'[8]

'You, too?' asked the prince, suddenly. 'But what is all this, is everyone here going to Pavlovsk? And you say you have your own dacha there?'

'Not everyone's going to Pavlovsk, sir. But Ivan Petrovich Ptitsyn let me have cheaply one of the dachas he's acquired. It's pleasant, and high up, and leafy, and cheap, and *bon ton*, and musical, and that's why everyone goes to Pavlovsk. Actually, I'm in a small wing, and the dacha itself . . .'

'You've rented it out?'

'N-n-no. Not . . . not quite, sir.'

'Rent it to me,' the prince suggested suddenly.

This was apparently what Lebedev had been leading up to. This idea had flashed through his mind three minutes earlier. And yet he was in no need of a tenant now; he already had a prospective tenant for the dacha who had told him he might perhaps take it. Lebedev knew for a fact, however, that it was not merely 'perhaps', and that the man would take it. But suddenly a very promising idea, as he saw it, occurred to him: he could rent the dacha to the prince, taking advantage of the fact that the previous applicant had expressed himself only in vague terms. 'A real collision and a whole new turn of events,' suddenly presented itself to his imagination. He accepted the prince's offer almost with delight, so that in response to his direct question about the terms he simply waved his arms.

'Well, as you like; I'll manage; you won't lose out.'

They were both now leaving the garden.

'I could . . . I could . . . if you like, I could tell you something very interesting, esteemed Prince, relating to the same subject,' Lebedev muttered, trailing along by the prince's side.

The prince came to a halt.

'Darya Alexeyevna also has a dacha in Pavlovsk, sir.'

'Well?'

'And a certain lady person is a friend of hers, and, it seems, plans to visit her often in Pavlovsk.'

'Well?'

'Aglaya Ivanovna . . .'

'Oh, enough, Lebedev!' the prince interrupted, experiencing an unpleasant sensation, as though he had been touched on a sore spot. 'All that is . . . not what you think. Tell me rather, when are you moving? For me, the sooner the better, as I'm in a hotel . . .'

As they talked, they came out of the garden and, without going into the house, crossed the courtyard and reached the wicket gate.

'Well, what could be better?' Lebedev thought at last. 'Move straight into my house from the hotel, this very day, and the day after tomorrow we'll go to Pavlovsk together.'

'I'll see,' said the prince, reflectively, and went out of the gate.

Lebedev watched him go. He was struck by the prince's sudden air of distraction. As the prince went out, he even forgot to say goodbye, did not even nod, something that was out of character with what Lebedev knew of the prince's courtesy and consideration.

3

By now it was getting on for twelve o'clock. The prince knew that at the Yepanchins' house in town he might find only the general now, attending to his business, and even that was not very likely. It crossed his mind that the general might possibly whisk him off to Pavlovsk at once, and there was a visit that he very much wanted to make before that. At the risk of missing Yepanchin and delaying his trip to Pavlovsk until the following day, the prince made up his mind to go and find the house he so much wanted to visit.

This visit was, however, in a certain sense risky for him. He found himself in a quandary, and hesitated. Of the house he knew that it was situated on Gorokhovaya Street, not far from Sadovaya, and decided to walk there, in the hope that when he arrived at the place he would at last be able to finally make up his mind.

As he approached the intersection of Gorokhovaya and Sadovaya, he was surprised at his own extraordinary agitation; he
had not expected that his heart would beat so painfully. One
house, probably because of its odd physiognomy, began to
attract his attention while he was still some way off, and the
prince remembered later that he said to himself: 'That must be
the house.' With intense curiosity, he went closer to verify his
guess; he felt that for some reason he would find it very
unpleasant if his guess proved to be correct. This house was
large, gloomy, three storeys high, without any architectural
merit, a dirty green colour. Some houses in this genre, though
very few in number, built at the end of the last century, have
survived in precisely these streets of St Petersburg (in which
everything alters so quickly) nearly unaltered. They are built
solidly, with thick walls and exceedingly few windows; on the
ground floor the windows sometimes have bars. Usually the
ground floor is taken up by a moneychanger's shop. The *skopets*[1]
who sits in the shop rents the floor above. Both outside and
inside the place feels somehow inhospitable and arid, everything
appears to be screening and concealing itself, but why it seems
this way purely from the house's physiognomy would be hard
to explain. Architectural combinations of lines have their secret,
of course. These houses are almost exclusively inhabited by
tradesfolk. As he approached the gates and glanced at the
inscription, the prince read: 'The House of Hereditary Distinguished Burgher Rogozhin'.[2]

Ceasing to hesitate, he opened the glass door that slammed
noisily behind him, and began to climb the main staircase to the
second storey. The staircase was dark, made of stone, crudely
constructed, and the walls were coloured with red paint. He
knew that the whole second storey of this dreary house was
occupied by Rogozhin, with his mother and brother. The servant
who opened the door to the prince let him in without announcing him and led him a long way; they walked through a large
hall with walls of 'imitation marble', a slatted oak floor, and
furniture of the 1820s, crude and heavy; they also walked
through some tiny rooms, making sudden detours and zigzags,
ascending two or three steps and descending the same number

again, and, at last, knocked on a door. The door was opened by
Parfyon Semyonych himself; seeing the prince, he turned so pale
and went so rigid that for a time he looked like a stone statue,
staring with an immobile and frightened gaze, and twisting his
mouth into a smile of extreme bewilderment – as though in
the prince's visit he found something impossible and almost
miraculous. The prince, although he had expected something of
this kind, was positively astonished.

'Parfyon, perhaps I've come at a bad moment, look, I'll go
away,' he said at last in embarrassment.

'Not at all! Not at all!' Parfyon said, recovering himself at
last. 'Welcome, enter!'

They spoke to each other on 'thou' terms. In Moscow they
had chanced to meet often and spent a lot of time together, there
were even some moments in their meetings that had imprinted
themselves all too memorably on their hearts. Now, however,
it was more than three months since they had seen each other.

The pallor, and a kind of minor, fleeting convulsion, had still
not left Rogozhin's face. Though he had invited his guest in, his
extraordinary embarrassment continued. As he was showing
the prince to the armchairs and seating him at the table, the
prince happened to turn round to face him and stopped under
the effect of his exceedingly strange and turbid gaze. Something
seemed to transfix the prince, and at the same time he seemed
to remember – something recent, painful, and sombre. Without
sitting down, for some time he looked Rogozhin straight in the
eyes; they seemed to glitter even more powerfully in that initial
moment. At last, Rogozhin smiled, but in some discomfiture,
and as if at a loss.

'Why are you staring like that?' he muttered. 'Sit down!'

The prince sat down.

'Parfyon,' he said, 'tell me straight, did you know I was
coming to St Petersburg today?'

'That you'd come, I thought as much, and, you see, I wasn't
mistaken,' the latter added, with a caustic smile, 'but how could
I have known that you'd come today?'

A certain harsh abruptness and the strange irritability of the
question contained in the reply struck the prince even more.

'Well, even if you'd known it was *today*, why get so irritated?' the prince said, quietly perplexed.

'But why do you ask?'

'Earlier today, when I got off the train, I saw a pair of eyes looking at me in exactly the way you looked at me just now behind me.'

'Oho! And whose eyes were they, then?' Rogozhin muttered suspiciously. It seemed to the prince that he gave a start.

'I don't know; I think I might even have imagined them in the crowd; I'm beginning to imagine things all the time. I feel, brother Parfyon, almost as I did about five years ago, when I was still having fits.'

'Well, perhaps you did imagine them; I don't know . . .' muttered Parfyon.

The affectionate smile on his face did not seem right at that moment, as though something in that smile had broken, and as though he were utterly unable to glue it back together, no matter how he tried.

'What, off abroad again, are you?' he asked, suddenly adding: 'Do you remember our train journey from Pskov last autumn, when I was on my way to this house and you were . . . in that cloak, do you remember, those wretched gaiters?'

And Rogozhin suddenly began to laugh, this time with a kind of open malice, and as if he were glad to have succeeded in expressing it in some way.

'Are you quite settled here?' asked the prince, surveying the study.

'Yes, this is my home. Where else would I be?'

'It's a long time since we saw one another. I've heard things about you that don't sound like you at all.'

'People say all kinds of things behind one's back,' Rogozhin observed dryly.

'But you've broken up that gang of yours; here you are, not playing pranks any more, but sitting in your father's house. Well, that's good. Is the house your own, or do you share it?'

'It's mother's house. She's through there, along the corridor.'

'And where does your brother live?'

'Semyon Semyonych lives in the wing.'

'Does he have a family?'

'He's a widower. Why do you want to know?'

The prince looked, and did not answer; he suddenly fell into reflection and did not seem to hear the question. Rogozhin did not press him, and waited. They were silent for a while.

'I guessed that this was your house when I was still a hundred yards away,' said the prince.

'How was that?'

'I really don't know. Your house bears the physiognomy of your whole family and the whole of your Rogozhin way of life, but ask why I came to that conclusion, and I can't explain it. It's delirium, of course. I'm even frightened that it troubles me so much. Before it would never have crossed my mind that you would live in a house like this, but as soon as I caught sight of it I at once thought: "Why, but that's exactly the sort of house he'd be bound to have!"'

'Nonsense!' Rogozhin smiled vaguely, not quite comprehending the prince's obscure thought. 'My grandfather built this house,' he observed. '*Skoptsy* have always lived here, the Khludyakovs, and even now they rent from us.'

'Such gloom! It's a gloomy place you live in,' said the prince, surveying the study.

It was a large room, high-ceilinged, rather dark, crammed with all sorts of furniture – mostly large office desks, bureaux, cupboards, in which ledgers and some kind of documents were kept. A wide, red morocco leather sofa obviously served Rogozhin as a bed. The prince observed on the table beside which Rogozhin had seated him two or three books; one of them, Solovyov's *History*,[3] was open, and there was a bookmark in it. Along the walls, in tarnished gilt frames, hung several oil paintings, dark and soot-begrimed, in which it was hard to discern anything. One full-length portrait drew the prince's attention: it depicted a man of about fifty, in a frock coat of German cut, but long-skirted, with two state decorations, a very sparse and short greyish beard, a yellow, wrinkled face, and a suspicious, reserved and sorrowful gaze.

'That's not your father, is it?'

'That is indeed who it is,' Rogozhin answered with an

unpleasant smile, as though he were preparing for some instant unceremonious joke about his deceased father.

'He wasn't an Old Believer, was he?'

'No, he went to church, but it's true that he used to say the old faith was more correct. He also greatly respected the *skoptsy*. This used to be his study. Why did you ask if he was an Old Believer?'

'Will you be having your wedding here?'

'Y-yes,' Rogozhin answered, almost startled by the unexpected question.

'Will it be soon?'

'You know yourself that it doesn't depend on me.'

'Parfyon, I'm not your enemy and I don't plan to interfere in anything you do. I repeat this now as I said it earlier, once, on a similar occasion. When your wedding was being prepared in Moscow, I didn't interfere, you know that. The first time *she* herself came rushing to me, nearly from the altar, beseeching me to "save" her from you. I'm repeating her words to you. Then she ran away from me, too, you tracked her down again and took her to the altar and now, they say, she's run away from you again here. Is it true? Lebedev informed me of it, and so I came. That there's harmony between you again I only learned for the first time yesterday on the train from one of your former friends, Zalyozhev, if you want to know. I came here with a purpose: I wanted to finally persuade *her* to go abroad, to restore her health; she is very disturbed both in body and in soul, in her mind especially, and in my opinion requires much looking after. I did not want to accompany her abroad myself, but thought I might arrange all this in my absence. I'm telling you the honest truth. If it really is true that this matter has been resolved between you again, then I won't show my face to her again and I won't come and see you any more, either. You know yourself that I'm not deceiving you, because I've always been open with you. I've never concealed from you my thoughts about this and have always said that to marry you would be *her* certain ruin. Ruin for you, too . . . perhaps even more than for her. If you were to part again, I would be very pleased; but I don't plan to upset you or come between you. So be assured, and don't suspect me. And in any case, you yourself know: was I ever your *real* rival, even when she ran away to me? You laughed just now; I know what you were laughing at. Yes, we lived separately there and in different cities, and you know all that *for a fact*. I mean, I explained to you before that I don't love *her* with love, but with pity. I think I'm defining that precisely. You said at the time that you understood those words of mine; is it true? Did you understand? My, what a look of hatred you're giving me! I've come to reassure you because you are dear to me. I like you very much, Parfyon. But now I shall go and will never return again. Farewell.'

The prince stood up.

'Sit with me for a while,' Parfyon said quietly, not getting up from his seat and leaning his head on his right palm. 'It's a long time since I've seen you.'

The prince sat down. They both fell silent again.

'When you're not there in front of me, I at once feel malice towards you, Lev Nikolayevich. These last three months, when I haven't seen you, I've felt bitter towards you every moment, by God, I have. I could have gone and poisoned you! It was like that. Now you've scarcely been sitting with me for quarter of an hour, yet all my malice is passing, and you're as dear to me as you used to be. Sit with me for a while . . .'

'When I'm with you, you trust me, but when I'm not there, you at once cease to trust me and suspect me again. You take after your father!' the prince answered, smiling in friendly fashion and trying to conceal his emotion.

'I trust your voice when I'm sitting with you like this. But I mean, I realize we can't be viewed as equals, you and I . . .'

'Why did you add that? And now you're irritable again,' said the prince, looking at Rogozhin in wonder.

'Well where that's concerned, brother, no one asks us our opinion,' the other replied. 'Where that's concerned, the decision is taken without us. We also love different in different ways, we differ in everything,' he continued quietly and after a silence. 'You say you love her out of pity. There's no such pity for her in me. And she hates me more than anything. I dream about her every night now: it's always that she's with another man, laughing at me. It's like that, brother. She'll go to the altar with me, but she never gives me a thought, it's as though she were changing a shoe. Would you believe it, I haven't seen her for five days, because I don't dare to go to her. She'll ask: "Why have you come?" She's shamed me enough . . .'

'Shamed you? What do you mean?'

'As if you didn't know! Why, it was you she ran away to "from the altar", you said it yourself just now.'

'You don't believe that she . . .'

'She shamed me with that officer in Moscow, Zemtyuzhnikov, wasn't it? I know for certain that she did, and it was after she herself had fixed the day of the wedding.'

'It cannot be!' exclaimed the prince.

'I know it for a fact,' Rogozhin stated with conviction. 'What, you think she's not like that? Don't try to tell me she's not like that, brother. That's just nonsense. She may not be like that with you, and would probably be horrified at the notion, but with me that's exactly what she's like. It's true, you know. She looks on me as the very lowest of riff-raff. With Keller, that officer, the boxer, I know for a fact that she told stories in order to make fun of me . . . And you don't know what she did to me in Moscow! And the money, all the money I've given her . . .'

'But . . . how can you marry her now? . . . What will it be like afterwards?' the prince asked in horror.

Rogozhin gave the prince a grim and terrible look and made no reply.

'I haven't been at her house for five days,' he continued, after a moment of silence. 'I'm always afraid she'll throw me out. "I'm still my own mistress," she says; "if I want to, I'll kick you out altogether and go abroad" (she's already told me that, that she'll go abroad,' he observed as if in parenthesis, and looking the prince in the eye with an air of special significance); sometimes, it's true, she just tries to chivvy me, she finds everything about me comical for some reason. Other times she just frowns and scowls, doesn't say a word; that's what I'm really afraid of. The other day, I thought: I'll never go and see her empty-handed – but that just made her laugh, and then she even got angry. She gave her room-maid Katya a shawl I'd got for her, I bet she'd never seen one like it, even though she'd lived in luxury before. And as for when the wedding is to be, I can't even mention it. What kind of a bridegroom is it who's simply too frightened to arrive? So I sit here, and when I can't bear it any more I go past her house secretly and in stealth, or hide around a corner somewhere. The other night I watched near her gate almost until daybreak – I thought there was something going on that night. But you know, she looked out of the window: "What would you have done with me, if you'd seen me deceiving you?" she said. I couldn't help myself, but said: "You know what."'

'But what does she know?'

'How would I know?' Rogozhin began to laugh angrily. 'In Moscow I couldn't catch her with anyone, though I spent a long time trying. One day I went to her and said: "You promised to go to the altar with me, you're entering an honest family, and do you know what you are now? Is that the kind of woman you are?" I said.

'You said that to her?'

'Yes.'

'Well?'

'"I don't think I'd even hire you as a lackey, let alone be your wife," she said. "Then I won't leave, and that's the end of it!" "Well, I'll just summon Keller and tell him to throw you out," she said. And I hurled myself on her and beat her black and blue right there and then.'

'It cannot be!' exclaimed the prince.

'I tell you: it happened,' Rogozhin confirmed quietly, but with glittering eyes. 'For a day and half I didn't sleep, didn't eat, didn't drink, didn't leave her room, knelt before her: "I'll die," I said, "I won't leave until you forgive me, and if you have me thrown out, I'll drown myself: because – what will I be without you now?" She was like a madwoman all that day, now weeping, now preparing to kill me with a knife, now cursing at me. She summoned Zalyozhev, Keller and Zemtyuzhnikov, pointed me out to them, and put me to shame. "Let's all go to the theatre in a company this evening, gentleman, let him sit here, if he doesn't want to leave, I'm not tied to him. And they will serve you tea here while I'm gone, Parfyon Semyonych, you must be hungry today." She returned from the theatre alone: "They're wretched cowards and scoundrels, they're afraid of you, and they try to frighten me: he really won't go away, they say, he'll cut your throat. Well, now I'm going to the bedroom, and I won't lock the door after me: that's how afraid of you I am! I want you to know and see that! Have you had tea?" "No," I say, "and I'm not going to." "I could understand it if your honour were at stake, but this doesn't suit you at all." And she did as she said she would, and didn't lock the door. In the morning she came out and laughed: "Have gone out of your mind?" she said. "You'll starve to death like this, won't you?" "Forgive me," I said. "I don't want to forgive you, I'm not going to marry you, and that's it. Have you really been sitting in this armchair all night, not sleeping?" "That's right," I said, "I haven't slept." "How clever! And you're not going to have tea or dinner again?" "I told you I won't – forgive me!" "This really doesn't suit you," she said, "if only you knew, it's like a saddle on a cow. You're not thinking of trying to frighten me, are you? What do I care if you sit here starving; that's how much you frighten me!" She lost her temper, but not for long, began nagging me again. And then I found myself wondering at her for having no malice towards me. I mean, she remembers any harm that's done to her by others, she remembers it for a long time! Then it occurred to me that she had such a low opinion of me that she couldn't even feel much malice towards me. And it's true. "Do you know," she said, "who the Pope is?" "I've heard of him," I said. "Parfyon Semyonych," she said, "you haven't studied history." "I haven't studied anything," I said. "Well," she said, "I'll give you something to read: there once was a Pope who got angry with an Emperor,[4] and the Emperor knelt outside his palace for three days without eating or drinking, barefoot, because the Pope wouldn't forgive him; what do you suppose that Emperor thought about as he knelt for those three days and what vows did he make? . . . But wait," she said, "I'll read it to you myself!" She jumped up and fetched a book: "It's poetry," she said, and began to read me a poem about how during those three days this Emperor vowed to avenge himself on the Pope. "Don't you like it, Parfon Semyonych?" "It's all true," I said, "what you read." "Aha, you say it's true, that means perhaps you're vowing that 'when she marries me I'll remind her of all this and then I'll make fun of her!'" "I don't know," I said, "perhaps that's the way I'm thinking." "What do you mean, you don't know?" "Just as I say," I said, "I don't know, that's not what I'm thinking about just now." "And what are you thinking about just now?" "That you'll get up and walk past and I'll look at you and watch you go; your dress will rustle, my heart will sink, and you'll go out of the room, I'll remember your every word and the voice you said them in, and what you said; all last night I couldn't think about anything, just kept listening to you breathing in your sleep and stirring once or twice . . ." "But don't you think and remember," she began to laugh, "about how you beat me?" "Perhaps I do," I said, "I don't know." "And what if I don't forgive you and don't marry you?" "I told you, I'll drown myself." "I think you may kill me before you do that . . ." She said it, and thought. Then she got angry and left. After an hour she came back to me, looking gloomy. "I'll marry you, Parfyon Semyonych," she said, "and not because I'm afraid of you but because I have to go to my ruin anyway. I mean, what better way is there? Sit down," she said, "they'll bring you some dinner in a moment. And if I marry you," she added, "I'll be a faithful wife to you, don't have any doubt about that and don't worry about it." Then she was silent for a bit, and said: "At least you're not a lackey; I used to think you were a complete lackey." Then she fixed the day for the wedding, but a week later she ran away from me to Lebedev. When I arrived, she said: "I'm not rejecting you completely; I just want to wait a little longer, as long as I want, because I'm still my own mistress. You can wait, too, if you like." That's how things are between us now . . . What do you think of all that, Lev Nikolayevich?'

'What do you think of it?' the prince retorted, looking sadly at Rogozhin.

'Do I look as though I could think!' he blurted out. He was about to add something else, but fell silent in hopeless anguish.

The prince got up and made to leave again.

'I won't interfere, all the same,' he said quietly, almost reflectively, as though replying to some inner, concealed thought of his own.

'Do you know what I'm going to say to you?' Rogozhin said in sudden animation, and his eyes began to glitter. 'I don't understand why you're yielding to me like this. Or have you fallen out of love with her altogether? Before you were in anguish; I mean, I could see. So why have you come here at the gallop now? Out of pity? (And his face was contorted in a malicious, mocking smile.) Heh-heh!'

'You think I'm trying to deceive you?' the prince asked.

'No, I trust you; it's just that I don't understand any of this. What's more certain than anything is that your pity is even stronger than my love!'

Something hostile, that wanted to express itself at once at any cost, ignited in his face.

'You know, it's hard to distinguish your love from rage,' the prince smiled, 'and when it passes, things may get even worse. I say this to you now, brother Parfyon . . .'

'I'll cut her throat, you mean?'

The prince started.

'You'll hate her intensely for this love you feel, and for all this torment you're accepting now. To me, the most astonishing thing is that she can be going to marry you again. When I heard of it yesterday – I could scarcely believe it, and I felt so unhappy. I mean, she has rejected you and fled from the altar twice, and that means she has a foreboding! . . . What does she want from you now? Your money? That's nonsense. In any case, I daresay you've already spent a lot of that. Is it really just in order to find a husband? Then she could easily find someone besides you. Anyone would be better than you, because to put it bluntly you may cut her throat, and she understands that only too well now, perhaps. That you love her so deeply? Yes, perhaps it's that . . . I have heard that there are those who seek just that sort of love . . . only . . .'

The prince paused and reflected.

'Why are you smiling at father's portrait again?' asked Rogozhin, observing with exceeding closeness every change, every fleeting line on the prince's face.

'Why was I smiling? Well, it crossed my mind that if this disaster had not happened to you, if this love had not taken place, then you might have become exactly like your father, and in a very short time, too. You'd have settled down silently alone in this house with your meek and obedient wife, with few and stern words, not trusting a single person, and having no need of that at all, merely making money silently and gloomily. At the very most, you'd have praised the old books now and then, and acquired an interest in crossing yourself with two fingers,[5] and that only in your old age . . .'

'Mock all you want. She told me exactly the same thing recently, also when she was looking at that portrait! Astonishing, how the two of you see eye to eye in everything now . . .'

'Has she been to see you here, then?' the prince asked with curiosity.

'Yes, she has. She looked at the portrait for a long time, asked me questions about my late father. "You would have been just like him," she smiled to me eventually. "Parfyon Semyonych, you have strong passions, passions of a kind that would have taken you straight to Siberia, to penal labour, if you hadn't also had intelligence, because you have a lot of intelligence," she said (that's what she said, would you believe it? That's the first time I heard her say such a thing!). "You would soon have given up all this tomfoolery. And as you're a completely uneducated man, you'd have started to pile up money, and, like your father, you'd have settled down in this house with its *skoptsy*; you might even have gone over to their faith yourself in the end, and you'd have loved your money so much that you'd have piled up not two but ten millions, and died of starvation on your money-sacks, because for you everything is passion, you turn everything into a passion." That's exactly what she said, almost exactly in those words. She had never spoken like that to me before! I mean, she always talks to me about nonsensical things or mocks me; whereas here she laughed to begin with, but then got very gloomy; she went all over this house, examining it, and seemed to be frightened of it. "I'll change all this," I say, "and have it decorated, or maybe I'll buy another house in time for the wedding." "No, no," she said, "don't change anything here, we'll live like this. I want to live beside your mother," she said, "when I become your wife." I took her to see my mother – she was respectful to her, as though she were her own daughter. Even before this, for two years actually, Mother had not been in full command of her reason (she's ill), but after the death of my father she became just like a little infant, never saying anything: she's lost the use of her legs and just bows from her chair to everyone she sees; I think if one didn't feed her, she wouldn't notice for three days. I took mother's right hand, folded it: "Bless her, Mother," I said, "she's going to go to the altar with me"; so she kissed Mother's hand with feeling, "I expect your mother has endured much sorrow," she said. She saw I had this book: "What have you started to read *Russian History* for?" (Yet she herself once said to me in Moscow: "You ought to educate yourself a bit, read Solovyov's *Russian History*, I mean, you don't know anything.") "It will do you good," she said, "go on, and read it. I'll write you a little list of the books you ought to read first of all; would you like me to?" And never, never before had she talked like that to me, so that she even astonished me; for the first time I breathed like a living human being.'

'I'm very glad about that, Parfyon,' said the prince, with sincere feeling, 'very glad. Who knows, perhaps God will arrange things between you.'

'That will never happen!' Rogozhin exclaimed hotly.

'Listen, Parfyon, if you love her so much, surely you want to deserve her respect? And if you want that, then surely you will hope? I said earlier that it was a wondrous puzzle to me: why was she marrying you? But although I can't solve it, I'm in no doubt that there must be a sufficient, rational reason for it. She is convinced of your love; but she must also certainly be convinced of some of your merits. I mean, it can't be otherwise! What you said just now confirms it. You say yourself that she found it possible to talk to you in a completely different language from the one she had used and spoken before. You are suspicious and jealous, and so you exaggerated all the bad things you noticed. Of course, she doesn't think as badly of you as you say. Why, otherwise it would mean that she was consciously risking drowning or the knife by marrying you. Is that possible? Who would consciously risk drowning or the knife?'

With a bitter smile Parfyon listened to the prince's heartfelt words.

'How grimly you are looking at me now, Parfyon!' broke from the prince with grim emotion.

'Drowning or the knife!' said the other, at last. 'Heh! But that's precisely why she's marrying me, because she surely expects the knife from me! Prince, have you really not grasped before now what all this is about?'

'I don't understand you.'

'Well, perhaps he really doesn't understand, heh-heh! They say of you that you're ... *you know*. She loves someone else, get that into your head! Exactly as I love her now, exactly so, she loves someone else now. And do you know who that someone else is? It's *you*! What, you didn't know?'

'Me?'

'You. She's loved you ever since that birthday soirée. Only she thinks she can't marry you, because she would put you into disgrace and ruin your entire life. "Everyone knows what sort of woman I am," she says. She always says that about herself. She told me all this straight to my face. She's afraid to ruin and disgrace you, but that means where I'm concerned it's all right, she can marry me – that's what she thinks of me, note that, also!'

'But why did she run away from you to me, and ... from me ...'

'And from you to me! Heh! All kinds of things enter her head! She's is in a kind of fever now. Now she cries to me: "I'll marry you, though I might as well be drowning myself. Hurry up with the wedding!" She's in a hurry herself, fixes the day, but when the time starts to approach – she takes fright, or other ideas come – Lord knows, I mean, you saw her: she weeps, laughs, thrashes about in fever. And what is so wondrous about the fact that she ran away from you? She ran away from you then because she herself had grasped how intensely she loves you. It was beyond her strength when she was with you. You said earlier that I tracked her down in Moscow; that's not true – she herself came running to me: "Fix the day," she said, "I'm ready!

Serve champagne! Let's go to the gypsies!" she cried! . . . And if it weren't for me, she'd have thrown herself into the water long ago; I tell you truly. She doesn't do it because I, perhaps, am more powerful than the water. She's marrying me from spite . . . If she marries me, I tell you truly, it will be *from spite*.'

'But how can you . . . how can you! . . .' exclaimed the prince and did not finish. He looked at Rogozhin with horror.

'Why don't you finish,' the other added, grinning, 'or would you like me to tell you what you're thinking to yourself at this very moment? "Well, how can she be with him now? How can she be allowed to do that?" I know what you're thinking.'

'I didn't come here for that, Parfyon, I tell you, that's not what was on my mind . . .'

'Perhaps that's so, only now you certainly have come here for that, heh-heh! Well, enough! Why are you so disconcerted? Did you really not know about it? You amaze me!'

'This is all jealousy, Parfyon, it's all an illness, you've exaggerated it all beyond all bounds . . .' muttered the prince in extreme agitation. 'What are you doing?'

'Leave that alone,' said Parfyon, quickly tearing from the prince's hands the small knife he had picked up from the table, beside the book, and putting it back in its former place.

'It was as if I knew when I was entering St Petersburg, it was as if I had a foreboding . . .' the prince continued, 'I didn't want to come here! I wanted to forget everything here, to tear it out of my heart! Well, goodbye . . . But what is it?'

As he spoke, in his absent-mindedness the prince had picked up the knife again, and again Rogozhin removed it from his hands and threw it on the table. It was a rather ordinarily shaped knife, with a deer-horn handle, not foldable, with a blade three and a half vershoks long, and of corresponding width.

Observing that the prince was directing particular attention to the fact that this knife had been torn from his hands twice, Rogozhin seized it with ill-tempered vexation, put it inside the book and flung the book on to the other table.

'Do you cut pages with it?' asked the prince, but somehow absent-mindedly, still as if under the pressure of intense reflectiveness.

'Pages, yes . . .'

'It's a garden knife, isn't it?'

'Yes, it is. Can't one cut pages with a garden knife?'

'But it's . . . brand new.'

'Well, what of it if it's new? Can't I even buy a new knife now?' Rogozhin exclaimed in a kind of frenzy, growing more irritated with every word.

The prince gave a start and looked at Rogozhin fixedly.

'Oh, just listen to us!' he began to laugh suddenly, now in complete control of himself. 'Forgive me, brother, when my head aches as it does now, and this illness . . . I become quite, quite absent-minded and absurd. I didn't mean to ask about this at all . . . can't remember what it was. Goodbye . . .'

'Not that way,' said Rogozhin.

'I've forgotten!'

'This way, this way, come on, I'll show you.'

4

They passed through the same rooms that the prince had already traversed; Rogozhin went slightly ahead, the prince following him. They entered the large hall. Here, on the walls, were several pictures, all portraits of bishops, and landscapes in which it was impossible to make anything out. Above the door into the next room hung a painting, rather strange in shape, about two and half arshins[1] in length and certainly no more than six vershoks in height. It depicted the Saviour, who had just been taken down from the cross. The prince gave it a fleeting glance, as though remembering something but, without stopping, made to pass through the doorway. He felt very unhappy, and wanted to get out of this house as soon as possible. But Rogozhin suddenly stopped in front of the picture.

'All these paintings here,' he said, 'were bought by my late papa at auctions for a couple of roubles, he liked them. A man who knew something about it examined them all here; rubbish, he said, but this one – the painting above the door, which was also bought for two roubles, is not rubbish, he said. One man offered my father three hundred and fifty roubles for it, and Savelyev, Ivan Dmitrych, a merchant, and a great art-lover, went up to four hundred, and last week he offered my brother Semyon Semyonych five hundred. I've kept it for myself.'

'Yes, it's . . . it's a copy of a work by Hans Holbein,' said the prince, who had now had time to study the painting, 'and although I'm not much of an expert, it looks like a good copy. I saw this painting when I was abroad, and can't forget it. But . . . what's wrong?'

Rogozhin suddenly turned his back on the painting and continued his earlier progress. Of course, his abrupt behaviour might have been explained by the absent-mindedness and the peculiar, strangely irritable mood that had so suddenly manifested itself in him; but the prince none the less found it somewhat odd that he so suddenly broke off a conversation he, the prince, had not begun, and that Rogozhin did not even reply to him.

'I say, Lev Nikolayevich, I've long wanted to ask you, do you believe in God or not?' Rogozhin said again, suddenly, having gone a few paces.

'That's a strange thing to ask, and . . . a strange way to look!' the prince observed involuntarily.

'Well, I like looking at that painting,' muttered Rogozhin, after a silence, as though he had forgotten his question again.

'That painting!' the prince exclaimed suddenly, under the impact of a sudden thought. 'That painting! Some people might lose their faith by looking at that painting!'

'Yes, I'm losing that, too,' Rogozhin suddenly confirmed unexpectedly. By now they had reached the front door.

'What?' the prince suddenly came to a halt. 'What's the matter? I was almost joking, but you're so serious! And why did you ask me if I believe in God?'

'Oh, for no reason, I just did. I'd wanted to ask you earlier. After all, many people don't believe nowadays. Well, is it true (you've lived abroad, I mean) – one drunken fellow said to me once that we in Russia have more people who don't believe in God than in other countries? "It's easier for us," he said, "than it is for them, because we've gone further than they have . . ."'

Rogozhin sneered sarcastically; having stated his question, he suddenly opened the door and, holding the handle, waited for the prince to go out. The prince was surprised, but did so. Rogozhin came out after him on to the staircase landing and closed the door behind him. They stood facing each other, looking as though they had forgotten where they were and what they were meant to do now.

'Goodbye, then,' said the prince, giving his hand.

'Goodbye,' said Rogozhin, shaking the hand extended to him with a grasp that was firm but entirely mechanical.

The prince took one step down, and then turned round.

'Well, concerning faith,' he began, smiling (clearly not wanting to leave Rogozhin like this) and also growing more animated under the impact of a certain memory, 'concerning faith, last week I had four different encounters in two days. In the morning I was travelling on one of the new railways and spent about four hours talking to a certain S——[2] in the carriage I was in, formed an acquaintance with him there. I'd heard a great deal about him earlier, among other things, that he was an atheist. He really is a very learned man, and I was glad that I was going to talk to a real man of learning. On top of that, he's an unusually well-bred fellow, so he spoke to me entirely as though I were his equal in knowledge and ideas. He doesn't believe in God. Only one thing struck me: that he didn't seem to be talking about that at all, and I was struck precisely because earlier, too, when I'd encountered unbelievers and no matter how many of those books I read, it always seemed to me that in their talk and in their books they avoided discussing that at all, though they made it seem as though they were. I told him this opinion of mine at the time, but must not have expressed myself clearly or must have failed to express myself at all, for he didn't understand any of it . . . In the evening I stopped to spend the night at a local hotel in which a murder had been committed just the previous night, and everyone was talking about it when I arrived. Two peasants, getting on in years, who weren't drunk, and had known each other for a long time, friends, had had tea and wanted to sleep in the same little room. But during the course of the past two days, one of them had spotted that the other was wearing a watch, a silver one, on a yellow bead chain, which he hadn't seen him with before, apparently. This man was not a thief, was even honest and, by peasant standards, not at all poor. But he liked this watch so much and was so tempted by it that at last he could endure no more: he took a knife and, when his friend had turned away, went up to him cautiously from behind, took aim, raised his eyes to heaven, crossed himself and, saying a bitter prayer to himself: "Lord, forgive me in Christ's name!", cut his friend's throat in one stroke, like a sheep's, and took the watch away from him.'

Rogozhin split his sides with laughter. He roared with mirth as though he were having some kind of fit. It was positively strange to see him laughing like this after the gloomy mood he had been in so recently.

'Now, I like that! No, that's better than anything!' he shouted convulsively, almost out of breath. 'One doesn't believe in God at all, and the other believes so much that he'll cut people's throats while saying a prayer . . . No, brother Prince, you didn't invent that! Ha-ha-ha! No, that's better than anything! . . .'

'In the morning I went out to stroll about the town,' continued the prince, as soon as Rogozhin had stopped laughing, though the laughter still quivered, convulsive and fit-like on his lips. 'I saw a drunken soldier staggering along the wooden pavement, in a completely bedraggled condition. He came up to me: "Buy a silver cross, *barin*, I'll let you have it for only two copecks; it's silver!" In his hand I saw the cross, he must have just taken it off, it was on a blue, very threadbare ribbon, but it was only a tin cross, one could see that at once, large, eight-pointed, the complete Byzantine design. I fished out a two-copeck piece and gave it to him, and put the cross on right away – and by his face I could see that he was pleased, he had swindled a stupid *barin*, and at once set off to spend the money on drink, there was no doubt about that. At that time, brother, I was under the very strong impact of all the impressions that had surged upon me in Russia; before, I had understood nothing of Russia, as if I'd grown without the power of speech, and during those five years abroad I'd remembered it as a kind of fantasy. So there I was, and

I thought: no, I won't be too quick to condemn that Christ-seller. After all, God knows what's contained in those weak and drunken hearts. An hour later, as I was returning to the hotel, I bumped into a peasant woman with a newborn baby. The woman was still young, her baby would be about six weeks old. The baby smiled at her, by the look of it, for the first time since its birth. I looked, and all of a sudden, very devoutly she crossed herself. "Why are you doing that, young lady?" I asked. (For I was always asking questions in those days.) "Well," she said, "just as a mother rejoices when she notices the first smile from her baby, so God rejoices every time he looks down from heaven and sees a sinner kneeling before him and praying with all his heart." That was what the woman told me, almost in those very same words – such a profound, such a subtle and truly religious thought, a thought in which the whole essence of Christianity was instantly expressed: the whole concept of God as our father and of God's rejoicing in man, like the rejoicing of a father in his child – the principal idea of Christ! A simple peasant woman! To be sure, a mother . . . and who knows, perhaps that woman was that soldier's wife. Listen, Parfyon, you asked me a question just now. Here is my answer: the essence of religious feeling has nothing to do with any reasoning, or misdemeanours, or crimes, or atheism; it's something different, and it will always be different; it's not that, it's something the atheists will always avoid talking about, as they'll always be talking about *something else*. The main thing, however, is that you can observe this most clearly and quickly in the Russian heart, and that's my conclusion! That's one of the most important convictions I've acquired in this Russia of ours. There are things to be done, Parfyon! There are things to be done in our Russian world, believe me! Remember how we used to meet in Moscow and talk together . . . And I didn't want to come back here now! Well, what does it matter . . . Goodbye, *au revoir*! May God be with you!'

He turned and went down the staircase.

'Lev Nikolayevich!' Parfyon shouted to him from the top of the stairs when the prince had reached the first half-landing. 'That cross you bought from the soldier, are you wearing it?'

'Yes, I am.'

And the prince stopped again.

'Bring it here and show it to me.'

Again, more strangeness! He thought for a moment, then went back up and showed him the cross, without removing it from his neck.

'Give it to me,' said Rogozhin.

'Why? Surely you're not . . .'

The prince was reluctant to part with the cross.

'I'll wear it, and I'll give you mine, for you to wear.'

'You want to exchange crosses? Very well, Parfyon, if that's what you want, I'll be glad to; we'll be brothers.'

The prince took off his tin cross, Parfyon his gold one, and they exchanged them. Parfyon said nothing. With painful surprise, the prince noticed that the earlier mistrust, the earlier bitter and almost mocking smile still seemed to linger on the face of his sworn brother, for at certain moments, at least, it was still strongly evident. At length, in silence, Rogozhin took the prince's hand and stood for a while as if hesitating about something; then he suddenly pulled the prince after him, saying in a barely audible voice: 'Come on!' They crossed the first floor landing and rang the bell of the door that faced the one from which they had emerged. It was quickly opened to them. A little old woman, hunched and all in black, her head bound with a kerchief, bowed deeply and silently to Rogozhin; he asked her some rapid question and, not stopping for an answer, led the prince further through the interior of the apartment. Again there was a sequence of dark rooms that displayed a peculiar, cold cleanliness, coldly and severely furnished with old furniture that was covered by clean, white sheets. Without any announcement, Rogozhin led the prince straight into a small room, similar to a drawing room, divided by a gleaming mahogany partition, with two doors at the sides, behind which there was probably a bedroom. In a corner of the drawing room, by the stove, in an armchair, sat a little old woman who did not look all that old, and even had a rather healthy, pleasant, round face, but was already completely grey-haired and (one could tell at first glance) had lapsed into complete childish senility. She wore a black woollen dress, with a large black kerchief at her neck, and a clean white cap with black ribbons. Her feet were supported by a footstool. Beside her was another small, clean old woman, a little older than her, also dressed in mourning and also in a white cap, who must have been some kind of poor retainer, silently knitting a stocking. They probably both spent all their time in silence. At the sight of Rogozhin and the prince, the first old woman smiled to them and inclined her head affectionately several times as a sign of pleasure.

'Mother,' said Rogozhin, kissing her hand, 'this is my great friend, Prince Lev Nikolayevich Myshkin; he and I have exchanged crosses; he was like a brother to me in Moscow at one time, and did a lot for me. Bless him, Mother, as you would bless your own son. Wait now, old one, do it like this, like this, let me set your hand . . .'

But before Parfyon could take hold of her, the old woman raised her right hand, set three of her fingers together and devoutly made the sign of the cross over the prince three times. Then she nodded to him again in affectionate tenderness.

'Well, come along then, Lev Nikolayevich,' said Parfyon. 'That was the only reason I brought you here.'

When they emerged on to the staircase again, he added:

'I mean, she doesn't understand anything of what's said, and she didn't understand my words, but she blessed you; that means she herself wanted to . . . Well, goodbye, it's time for you and I to go our separate ways.'

And he opened his door.

'But let me at least embrace you in farewell, you strange man!' exclaimed the prince, looking at him with tender reproach, and made to embrace him. But no sooner had Parfyon raised his arms than he at once lowered them again. He could not bring himself to do it, and turned away in order to avoid the prince's eyes. He did not want to embrace him.

'Don't worry! Though I took your cross, I won't cut your throat for your watch!' he muttered indistinctly, beginning a strange laugh. But all of a sudden his entire face was transformed: he turned horribly pale, his lips began to tremble, his eyes lit with fire. He raised his arms, embraced the prince tightly and, gasping for breath, said:

'Then take her, if that's what fate decrees! She's yours! I yield! . . . Remember Rogozhin!'

And turning his back on the prince, not looking at him, he hurriedly went inside and slammed the door behind him.

5

It was late now, almost half-past two, and the prince did not find General Yepanchin at home. Leaving his card, he decided to go to 'The Scales' hotel and ask if Kolya was there; if he were not there, he would leave him a note. At 'The Scales' he was told that Nikolai Ardalionovich 'went out this morning, sir, but when he left he gave advance notice that if anyone should come asking for him she should be informed that he might perhaps be back by three o'clock, sir. If he did not turn up by half-past three, it would mean he had gone to Pavlovsk by train, to Mrs Yepanchin's dacha, sir', and would be 'having his dinner there, sir.' The prince sat down to wait and, since he was there, ordered dinner.

Kolya did not appear by half-past three, nor even by four. The prince went out and set off mechanically wherever his eyes led him. There are sometimes beautiful days at the beginning of summer in St Petersburg – bright, hot and quiet. As luck would have it, this was one of those infrequent days. For a while the prince wandered aimlessly. He was not very well acquainted with the city. From time to time he would stop at crossroads, in front of certain houses, on squares, on bridges; once he went into a patisserie to rest. At times he studied the passers-by with great curiosity; but more often he noticed neither the passers-by, nor precisely where he was going. He was in a tormented state of tension and anxiety, and at the same time he felt an extraordinary need for solitude. He wanted to be alone and to give himself up to this agonizing tension quite passively, without seeking the slightest relief. With revulsion he declined to settle the questions that had flooded into his soul and heart. 'Well, none of this is my fault, is it?' he muttered to himself, almost unaware of what he was saying.

By six o'clock he found himself on the platform of the railway station at Tsarskoye Selo. Solitude had soon become unendurable to him; a new, violent impulse enveloped his heart, and for a moment the gloom in which his soul languished was illumined by bright light. He bought a ticket for Pavlovsk and impatiently hurried to be off; but, of course, he was being followed, and it was for real, not the fantasy he had perhaps been inclined to think it was. As he was almost on the point of boarding the train, he suddenly threw the ticket he had just bought to the floor and left the station again, troubled and reflective. Later, in the street, he suddenly seemed to remember something, as if he had become aware of something, something very strange that had probably been worrying him for a long time. He suddenly caught himself doing something he had been doing for a long time, but had not noticed until this moment: for several hours now, even at 'The Scales', or even before 'The Scales', perhaps, he would find himself suddenly looking for something around him. And he would forget about it for quite a while, half an hour, even, and then suddenly look round anxiously once again, searching around him.

But no sooner had he noticed this morbid and hitherto quite unconscious movement that had possessed him for so long, than there suddenly flickered through his mind another memory that interested him exceedingly: he remembered that at the moment when he noticed that he was constantly searching around him, he was standing on the pavement outside the window of a shop, examining the things displayed in it with great curiosity. Now he wanted to ascertain without fail whether he had really stood, only five minutes ago, perhaps, in front of the window of this shop, or whether he had imagined it, got something mixed up. Did this shop and these things in its window really exist? For he did feel in a particularly ill state of mind today, almost the same state of mind that had affected him before at the beginning of the fits that had accompanied his earlier illness? He knew that in the time before those fits occurred he could be extraordinarily absent-minded, often mixing up objects and people, if he looked at them without particularly close attention. But there was also a particular reason why he so very much wanted to ascertain whether he had been standing in front of the shop at that time: among the articles displayed in the shop window was something he had looked at and even valued at sixty silver copecks, he remembered that, in spite of all his absent-mindedness and anxiety. Consequently, if that shop existed and that object really was displayed there among the others, then he must have stopped because of it. That meant that this object was of such powerful interest to him that it had attracted his attention even at the very time when he was in such a severe state of disturbance after leaving the railway station. He walked, looking almost in anguish to the right, his heart pounding with uneasy impatience. But here was that shop, he had found it at last! He had only gone a quarter of a mile from the shop when it had occurred to him to go back. And here was that object costing sixty copecks; 'of course, sixty copecks, it couldn't cost more than that,' he confirmed now, laughing. But it was a hysterical laugh; he felt very wretched. He now clearly recalled that precisely here, standing in front of this window, he had suddenly turned round, exactly as earlier, when he had caught Rogozhin's eyes on him. Having made sure that he was not mistaken (of which, however, he had been quite certain before), he turned his back on the shop and quickly walked away from it. He must think all this over as soon as possible, without fail; now it was clear that he had not imagined it at the station either, that something real and certainly connected with all his earlier unease had undoubtedly happened to him. But a kind of overwhelming inner revulsion again overcame him: he did not feel like thinking anything over, and he did not do so; he began to reflect about something else altogether.

He began to reflect, among other things, about the fact that in his epileptic condition there was a certain stage almost immediately before the fit itself (if the fit came when he was awake) when, amidst the sadness, the mental darkness, the pressure, his brain suddenly seemed to burst into flame at moments, and with an extraordinary jolt all his vital forces seemed to be tensed together. The sensation of life and of self-awareness increased almost tenfold at those moments, which had a duration like that of lightning. The mind, the heart were flooded with an extraordinary light; all his unrest, all his doubts, all his anxieties were as if pacified at once, were resolved into a kind of higher calm, full of a serene, harmonious joy and hope, full of reason and the final cause. But these moments, these flashes were still merely the presentiment of that final second (never more than a second), with which the fit itself began. That second was, of course, unendurable. Reflecting about that moment afterwards, now in a condition of health, he often told himself: that after all, those gleams and lightning flashes of higher self-perception and self-awareness and consequently of 'higher existence' were nothing but an illness, a violation of the normal condition, and, if that were so, then it was not higher existence at all, but, on the contrary, must be reckoned among the very lowest. And yet he reached, at last, an exceedingly paradoxical conclusion: 'What does it matter if it's an illness, then?' he decided, at last, 'what does it matter that it's an abnormal tension, if the result itself, if the moment of sensation, recalled and examined in a condition of health, turns out to be the highest degree of harmony and beauty, yields a hitherto unheard-of and undreamed-of sense of completeness, proportion, reconciliation and an ecstatic, prayerful fusion with the highest synthesis of life?' These nebulous expressions seemed to him very clear, though too weak. But that it was really 'beauty and prayer', that it really was 'the highest synthesis of life', of that he could be in no doubt, nor could he allow any doubts. After all, these were not, were they, some visions he dreamed at that moment, as induced by hashish, opium or wine, degrading the reason and distorting the soul, abnormal and non-existent? About this he was able to form a sane judgement when the morbid condition was at an end. For these moments were simply an extraordinary intensification of self-awareness – if that condition had to be expressed in a single word – of self-awareness and at the same time of a self-perception in the highest degree direct. If in that second, that is, in the very last conscious moment before the fit, he had time clearly and consciously to say to himself: 'Yes, for this moment one could give up one's whole life!' – then, of course, that moment was in itself worth the whole of one's life. However, he did not insist on the dialectical part of his conclusion: stupefaction, mental darkness, idiocy stood before him as the vivid consequence of those 'highest moments'. He would not, of course, have argued this seriously. In the conclusion, that is, in his evaluation of that moment, without doubt, there was an error, but the reality still disturbed him. What indeed was he to do with the reality? After all, this same thing had happened before, he himself had managed to tell himself in that very second that that second, because of the boundless happiness fully experienced by him, might be worth the whole of his life. 'In that moment,' as he once said to Rogozhin, in Moscow, at the time of their meetings there, 'in that moment I somehow begin to understand the extraordinary phrase *"there should be time no longer"*.[1] Probably', he added, smiling, 'that is the very second that was not long enough for water to be spilled from the epileptic Mahomet's overturned water-jug, though in that very second he was able to survey all the habitations of Allah.' Yes, in Moscow he had met Rogozhin often and talked not only about this, but about other things as well. 'Rogozhin said earlier that I was a brother to him then; today was the first time he said that,' the prince thought to himself.

He thought about this as he sat on a bench, under a tree, in the Summer Gardens. It was about seven o'clock. The Gardens were deserted; a darkness clouded the setting sun for a moment. It was oppressive; there was something like the distant premonition of a thunderstorm. In his present contemplative state there was for him a kind of allure. He clung with his memories and mind to each external object, and this pleased him: he kept wanting to forget something, the present, the vital, but at a first glance around him he at once again recognized his gloomy thought, the thought he so much wanted to get rid of. He remembered that earlier he had talked to the waiter at the inn about a recent extremely strange murder that had produced much stir and talk. As soon as he remembered this, however, something peculiar happened to him again.

An extreme, overpowering desire, a temptation almost, suddenly froze his will entirely. He got up from the bench and walked out of the garden straight to the St Petersburg Side.

Earlier, on the Neva Embankment, he had asked some passer-by to point out the St Petersburg Side to him across the Neva. The passer-by had pointed it out; but he had not gone there at the time. And in any case there was no point in going today; he knew that. He had had the address for a long time; he could easily locate the house of Lebedev's female relative; but he knew almost for certain that he would not find her at home. 'She'll have gone to Pavlovsk, otherwise Kolya would have left some message at "The Scales", as we arranged.' Thus, if he was going there now, it was of course not in order to see her. The curiosity that tempted him was another, gloomy and tormenting. A new, sudden idea had occurred to him . . .

But for him it was really more than enough that he was on his way and knew where he was going: a moment later he was again on the move, almost not noticing the route he was taking. To reflect any further on his 'sudden idea' at once seemed to him horribly repulsive and almost impossible. With agonizingly strained attention he scrutinized everything that met his eye, stared at the sky, at the Neva. He talked to a small child he met. Perhaps his epileptic condition was growing more and more intense. A storm really did seem to be approaching, though slowly. Distant thunder was already beginning. It was becoming very oppressive . . .

For some reason he now kept remembering, as one sometimes remembers a nagging and stupidly tedious musical phrase, Lebedev's nephew, whom he had seen earlier. What was strange was that he kept remembering him in the guise of that murderer whom Lebedev had mentioned earlier when introducing his nephew. Yes, he had read about that murderer only very recently. Had read and heard a lot about such things since he had returned to Russia; he had followed it all assiduously. And earlier, in his conversation with the waiter, he had even got too interested in that very same murder of the Zhemarins. The waiter had agreed with him, he remembered that. He remembered the waiter, too; he was a fellow far from stupid, solid and cautious, though 'goodness only knows. It's hard to make out new people in a new country.' In the Russian soul, however, he began to believe passionately. Oh, many, many things that were entirely new to him had he endured in these past six months, things that to him were unguessed-at, unheard-of and unexpected! But the soul of others is darkness, and so is the Russian soul – darkness to many. There was Rogozhin, with whom he had long been associating on close, 'brotherly' terms – but did he know Rogozhin? And as a matter of fact, what chaos, what muddle, what disorder there was in all this sometimes! And what a loathsome and self-contented pimple that nephew of Lebedev's was! Though really, what am I saying? (the prince continued to muse). He didn't murder those creatures, those six people, did he? I seem to be getting things mixed up . . . how strange this is! My head seems to be spinning . . . And what a sympathetic, what a charming face Lebedev's elder daughter has, the one who stood with the baby, what an innocent, what an almost childlike expression and what almost childlike laughter! It was strange that he had almost forgotten that face and only now remembered it. Lebedev, stamping his feet at them, probably adored them all. But what was surer than anything, like two times two, was the fact that Lebedev also adored his nephew!

But then, how could he take it upon himself to judge them so finally, he who had only arrived this morning, how could he pronounce such verdicts? And Lebedev had set him a problem today: well, had he expected Lebedev to be like that? Had he known Lebedev to be like that earlier? Lebedev and Du Barry – good Lord! And in any case, if Rogozhin were to commit murder, he would not do it in such a disorderly fashion. There would be none of that chaos. A murder weapon made to order and six people dispatched in total frenzy! Did Rogozhin have a weapon made to order . . . he had . . . but . . . was it certain that Rogozhin would kill? The prince shuddered suddenly. 'Is it not a crime, is it not an act of baseness on my part to make such a hypothesis so cynically and openly?' he exclaimed, and a flush of shame suffused his entire face. He was amazed, he stood in the road like one transfixed. He at once remembered both the Pavlovsk station and the Nikolayevsk station from earlier that day, and his question to Rogozhin, straight to his face, about the *eyes*, and Rogozhin's cross, which he was wearing now, and the blessing of his mother, to whom Rogozhin himself had brought him, and the last final embrace, Rogozhin's final renunciation, earlier, on the staircase – and after that to catch himself in a ceaseless search for something around him, and that shop, and that object . . . what baseness! And after all that he was now on his way with a 'special purpose', with a special 'sudden idea'! Despair and suffering seized the whole of his soul. The prince wanted to go back to his room at the hotel immediately; he even turned round and set off; but after a moment he stopped, reflected, and turned back again along his previous route.

Indeed, he was already on the St Petersburg Side, he was close to the house; after all, he was not going there now with his former purpose, nor with his 'special idea'! And how could that be! Yes, his illness was returning, there was no doubt of it; perhaps he would not avoid a fit today. It was because of the fit that all this darkness had fallen, because of the fit that he had the 'idea'! Now the darkness was dispersed, the demon banished, no doubts existed, there was joy in his heart! And – it was so long since he had seen her, he had to see her, and . . . yes, would like to have met Rogozhin now, he would have taken him by the arm, and they would have gone together . . . His heart was pure. How could he be Rogozhin's rival? Tomorrow he himself would go and tell Rogozhin that he had seen her; after all, he had sped to her, as Rogozhin had said earlier, just in order to see her! Perhaps he would find her at home, after all, it was not certain that she was in Pavlovsk!

Yes, everything now had to be clearly formulated, so that they could all clearly read one another's thoughts, so that there were no more of these gloomy and passionate renunciations, like Rogozhin's earlier on, and it should all take place freely and . . . in the light. Rogozhin was able to withstand the light, was he not? He said that he did not love her in that way, that he had no compassion, had 'no pity of that kind'. To be sure, he had added later that 'your pity may be even stronger than my love' – but he was slandering himself. Hm, Rogozhin at his book – was that not 'pity', the beginnings of 'pity'? Did not the presence of that book prove that he was fully conscious of his attitude towards *her*? And what about his story earlier on? No, that was rather deeper than mere passion. And did her face only inspire passion? And could even that face inspire passion now? It inspired suffering, it captured the whole of one's soul, it . . . and a burning, agonizing memory suddenly passed through the prince's heart.

Yes, it was agonizing. He remembered the agony he had recently experienced when he began to notice the signs of madness in her for the first time. Then he had almost felt despair. And how could he have left her, when she left him for Rogozhin? He ought to have run after her, not waited for news. But . . . had Rogozhin really not noticed the madness in her yet? . . . Hm . . . Rogozhin saw different reasons for everything, reasons of passion! And what insane jealousy! What was he trying to say with his offer of that morning? (The prince suddenly blushed, and something seemed to shiver in his heart.)

But why remember this? Here there was insanity on both sides. And for him, the prince, to love this woman passionately was almost unthinkable, would almost amount to cruelty, inhumanity. Yes, yes! No, Rogozhin was slandering himself; he had an enormous heart that was able both to suffer and to have compassion. When he learned the whole truth and when he was convinced what a pitiful creature that damaged, half-witted woman was – would he not forgive her then for all the earlier things, all his torments? Would he not become her servant, brother, friend, Providence? Compassion would impart understanding and instruction even to Rogozhin. Compassion was the principal and, perhaps, the only law of existence for the whole of mankind. Oh, how unforgivably and dishonourably guilty he was before Rogozhin! No, it was not 'the Russian soul' that was 'darkness', but he himself had darkness in his soul, if he was able to imagine such horror. Because of a few warm and heartfelt words in Moscow, Rogozhin now called himself his brother, and he . . . But this was illness and delirium! This would all be resolved! . . . How gloomily Rogozhin had said earlier that he was 'losing his faith'. The man must be suffering intensely. He said that he 'liked looking at that painting'; not 'liked' really, but rather he felt a need to look at it. Rogozhin was not just a passionate soul; he was also a fighter: he wanted to restore his

lost faith by force. He needed it now to the point of torment . . .
Yes! To believe in something! To believe in someone! But how
strange that painting of Holbein's was . . . Ah, here is that street!
This must be the house, yes, it is, number 16, 'the house of
collegiate secretary's widow Filosova'. Here! The prince rang
the bell and asked for Nastasya Filippovna.

The lady of the house replied to him that Nastasya Filippovna
had left that morning for Darya Alexeyevna's in Pavlovsk, 'and
it may even be, sir, that she will stay there for several days'.
Filisova was a small, sharp-eyed and sharp-faced woman of
about forty, with a sly, fixed look. To her question about his
name – a question to which she intentionally gave a tinge of
mystery – the prince at first did not want to reply, but at
once returned and insistently asked that his name be given
to Nastasya Filippovna. Filisova received this insistency with
increased attention and an extraordinarily secretive air, which
was evidently meant to convey: 'Don't worry, I understand,
sir.' The prince's name had obviously made a most powerful
impression on her. The prince looked at her absent-mindedly,
turned and walked back to his hotel. But he came out with a
look that was different from the one he had when he rang
Filisova's doorbell. Again, and as if in a single moment, an
extraordinary change had come over him: as he walked, he
again looked pale, weak, suffering, agitated; his knees were
trembling, and a troubled, bewildered smile wandered across
his bluish lips: his 'sudden idea' had been abruptly confirmed
and justified, and – he again believed in his demon!

But had it been confirmed? But had it been justified? Why was
there this shivering again, this cold sweat, this darkness and
chill in the soul? Because he had seen those *eyes* again just now?
But after all, he had left the Summer Gardens solely in order to
see them! For that was what his 'sudden idea' was all about. He
had insistently wanted to see those 'eyes of earlier on', in order
to be finally convinced that he could not fail to encounter them
there, outside this house. This was his convulsive desire, and so
why was he so crushed and shocked by having actually seen
them just now? As though he had not expected them! Yes,
they were *the same* eyes (and that they were *the same ones*, of

that there was no longer any doubt!) that had glittered at him that morning, in the crowd, when he had left the train at Nikolayevsk; those same eyes (absolutely the same!) whose gaze he had caught earlier, behind his back, as he sat down on the chair at Rogozhin's. Rogozhin had denied it earlier: he had asked with a contorted, icy smile: 'Then whose eyes were they?' And the prince had felt a dreadful urge, just then, at Tsarskoye Selo station – when he had boarded the train in order to go to Aglaya, and had suddenly seen those eyes again, for the third time that day – to go up to Rogozhin and ask him, 'Whose eyes were those?'! But he had fled from the station and only regained his composure in front of the cutler's shop at the moment when he had stood valuing an object with a deer-horn handle at sixty copecks. The strange and terrible demon had finally attached itself to him and did not want to leave him any more. This demon had whispered to him in the Summer Gardens, as he sat, in oblivion, under a lime tree, that if Rogozhin had found it so necessary to follow him since morning and dog his every step, then, having learned that he was not going to Pavlovsk (which for Rogozhin, of course, would be a fateful piece of information), Rogozhin would certainly go *there*, to that house on the St Petersburg Side, and would certainly lie in wait for him, the prince, there, who that morning had given him his word of honour that he 'would not see her', and that he 'had not come to St Petersburg for that'. And yet here was the prince convulsively rushing off to that house, and what if he did encounter Rogozhin there? He had seen only an unhappy man, whose mental state was gloomy, but very understandable. This unhappy man was not even hiding now. Yes, for some reason Rogozhin had kept his mouth shut earlier and lied, but at the station he had stood there openly, almost without hiding. It was rather he, the prince, who had been hiding, not Rogozhin. And now, outside the house, he stood on the other side of the street, some fifty paces away, at an angle, on the opposite pavement, with his arms folded, waiting. Here he was entirely in view and, it seemed, deliberately wanted to be in view. He stood like an accuser and like a judge, and not like . . . Not like what?

And why had he, the prince, not gone up to him, but turned

away from him, as if he had not noticed anything, although their eyes met. (Yes, their eyes met! And they looked at each other.) Why, earlier he had wanted to take him by the arm and go *there* together with him, had he not? He had wanted to go and see him the next day and tell him he had been at her house, had he not? He had renounced his demon while on his way there, half way, when joy had suddenly filled his soul, had he not? Or was there indeed something in Rogozhin, that is, in the whole of *that day's* profile of the man, in the totality of his words, movements, actions, looks, that might justify the prince's terrible forebodings and the disturbing whisperings of his demon? Something that was self-evident, but was hard to analyse and describe, impossible to justify by sufficient reasons, but which, however, in spite of all this difficulty and impossibility, produced a total and overwhelming impression that led involuntarily to the most complete conviction? ...

Conviction – of what? (Oh, how the prince was tormented by the monstrosity, the 'humiliation' of this conviction, 'this base foreboding', and how he blamed himself!) 'Then say it, if you dare – conviction of what?' he kept saying to himself constantly, with reproach and challenge. 'Formulate it, dare to express the whole of your thought, clearly, precisely, without hesitation! Oh, how dishonourable I am!' he repeated, flushing with anger. 'How will I be able to look that man in the face for the rest of my life? Oh, what a day! O God, what a nightmare!'

There was a moment, at the end of that long and tormenting walk from the St Petersburg Side, when the prince was suddenly gripped by an irresistible desire – to go to Rogozhin's right there and then, wait for him, embrace him with shame, with tears, tell him everything and put an end to it all at once. But he was already standing outside his hotel ... How he had disliked this hotel earlier, these corridors, the whole of this building, his room, had disliked them at first sight; several times that day he had remembered with a kind of peculiar revulsion that he would have to return here ... 'But why, like a sick woman, do I believe today in every kind of premonition?' he thought with an irritable, mocking smile, stopping in the gateway. A new, unbearable rush of shame – of despair, almost – rooted him to the spot, right by the entrance to the gate. He stopped for a moment. This is how it is with people sometimes: sudden, unbearable memories, especially those connected with shame, usually make them stop for a moment where they are. 'Yes, I am a man without a heart, and a coward!' he repeated gloomily, and jerkily moved to go, but . . . stopped again.

In that gateway, dark at the best of times, it was very dark at this moment: the advancing thundercloud had devoured the evening light, and just as the prince was approaching the house, the cloud suddenly opened and released a deluge. As he jerkily resumed his progress after his momentary halt, he found himself at the very beginning of the gate, right outside the entrance from the street. And suddenly in the depths of the gateway, in the semi-darkness, right beside the entrance to the stairs, he caught sight of a man. The man seemed to be waiting for something, but then quickly flitted past and disappeared. The prince could not discern him clearly and, of course, could not possibly say for certain who he was. What was more, so many people might pass through here; there was a hotel here, and people were constantly walking or running to and fro along its corridors. But he suddenly felt utterly and totally convinced that he knew who the man was, and that the man was certainly Rogozhin. A moment later the prince rushed after him up the staircase. His heart froze. 'It will all be decided in a moment!' he said to himself with strange conviction.

The staircase, up which the prince ran from the gateway, led to corridors on the first and second floors, along which the hotel rooms were situated. This staircase, as in all houses that were built long ago, was of stone; it was dark, narrow and wound around a thick stone column. On the first half-landing there was a hollow in this column, a sort of niche, no more than one pace wide and half a pace deep. There was, however, room for a man there. In spite of the darkness, when he reached the half-landing the prince at once saw that a man was hiding there, in that niche, for some reason. The prince suddenly felt an urge to walk past and not look to the right. He took one more step, but could not help turning round.

The two eyes of earlier that day, *the same ones*, suddenly met his gaze. The man who was hiding in the niche also managed to take one step out of it. For a second they stood almost touching, facing each other. Suddenly the prince seized him by the shoulders and turned back towards the staircase, closer to the light: he wanted to see the face more clearly.

Rogozhin's eyes had begun to glitter, and a rabid smile distorted his face. His right hand was raised, and something flashed in it; the prince did not think of stopping him. The only thing he seemed to remember was shouting:

'Parfyon, I don't believe it!'

Then suddenly something seemed to open before him: an extraordinary *inner* light illumined his soul. This moment lasted for half a second, perhaps; but he clearly and consciously remembered the beginning, the very first sound of his terrible howl, that tore from his breast of its own accord and which he could not stop by any effort. After that, his consciousness was extinguished instantaneously, and utter darkness ensued.

He had had a fit of epilepsy, the affliction that had left him a very long time ago. It is well known that fits of epilepsy, the *falling sickness*, occur instantaneously. In that instant the face is suddenly distorted to an extreme degree, especially the eyes. Convulsions and spasms take possession of the whole body and all the features of the face. A terrible, unimaginable howl, unlike anything else, tears from the breast; in that howl everything human seems to disappear, and it is in no way possible, or at least very difficult, for an observer to imagine and admit that it is the same person howling. It even seems that some other person, inside that person, is doing the howling. Many people have at any rate conveyed their impression in this way, and in many the sight of a man with the falling sickness produces a total and unendurable horror that may even contain a mystical element. One must suppose that it was this sensation of sudden horror, combined with all the other terrible impressions of the moment, that suddenly froze Rogozhin to the spot and thus saved the prince from the inevitable blow of the knife that was already descending on him. Then, before he had time to realize it was a fit, seeing the prince stagger back from him and suddenly fall backwards straight down the staircase, striking the back of his head violently against the stone step, Rogozhin rushed headlong downstairs, avoided the prostrate man and, his mind almost drained to a blank, ran out of the hotel.

Convulsing and writhing in spasms the sick man's body fell down the steps, of which there were no more than fifteen, to the very foot of the staircase. Very soon, after no more than about five minutes, the prostrate man was noticed, and a crowd gathered. A large pool of blood near his head caused perplexity: had the man sustained an injury, or had there been 'some foul play'? Soon, however, some of them realized it was the falling sickness; one of the hotel valets recognized the prince as a recent guest. The confusion was, at last, very happily resolved because of a happy circumstance.

· Kolya Ivolgin, who had promised to be at 'The Scales' by four o'clock, but had instead gone to Pavlovsk, had on a sudden impulse turned down the offer of lunch at Mrs Yepanchin's, and had come back to St Petersburg and hurried to the 'The Scales', where he arrived at about seven o' clock that evening. Having learned from the note that had been left for him that the prince was in town, he rushed to see him at the address given in the note. On being informed at the hotel that the prince had gone out, he went downstairs to the buffet rooms and began to wait, having tea and listening to the organ.[2] Hearing by chance a conversation about someone who had had a fit, he rushed to the spot following a sure premonition, and recognized the prince. Proper measures were at once taken. The prince was carried to his room; though he came round, it was quite a long time before he regained full consciousness. The doctor who was summoned to examine his broken head administered a lotion and said there was not the slightest danger from the injuries. And when, an hour later, the prince had begun to be fairly well aware of what was happening around him, Kolya took him in a cab from the hotel to Lebedev's. Lebedev greeted the sick man with uncommon warmth, and with bows. For the prince's sake he also speeded up his move to the dacha: three days later they were all in Pavlovsk.

6

Lebedev's dacha was small but comfortable and even pretty. That part of it designated to be rented out was particularly lavishly decorated. On the rather spacious veranda at the entrance to the rooms from the street some orange, lemon and jasmine trees had been placed in large green tubs, creating, in Lebedev's opinion, a most flattering aspect. Some of these trees he had acquired together with the dacha and was so enchanted by the effect they made in the veranda that he had decided, thanks to an opportunity that presented itself, to buy a complement of similar trees at an auction. When all the trees had finally been brought to the dacha and set up, Lebedev ran down the veranda steps several times that day to admire his property from the street, each time mentally increasing the sum he intended to ask from his future dacha tenant. The prince, weakened, melancholy and physically broken as he was, found the dacha much to his liking. As a matter of fact, on the day of his move to Pavlovsk, that is, on the third day after the fit, the prince already had the outward appearance of being almost well again, though inwardly he felt he had not yet recovered. He was glad of everyone he saw around him in those three days, glad of Kolya, who almost never left his side, glad of the whole Lebedev family (without the nephew, who had vanished off somewhere), glad of Lebedev himself; he even received with pleasure a visit from General Ivolgin, who came to see him while he was still in town. On the day of the move itself, which took place towards evening, quite a lot of visitors gathered round him on the veranda: the first arrival was Ganya, whom the prince hardly recognized, so thin and altered had he become during all this time. Then Varya and Ptitsyn, who also had dachas in Pavlovsk, appeared. As for General Ivolgin, he was to be found at Lebedev's quarters almost permanently, and even seemed to have moved with him. Lebedev tried to prevent him from going to see the prince and keep him at his house; he treated him like an old friend; they had evidently known each other for a long time. The prince noticed that during all those three days they sometimes entered into long conversations with each other, quite often shouting and arguing, even, it seemed, on learned subjects, which, it was evident, gave Lebedev pleasure. One could suppose that he even needed the general. But right from the time of the move to the dacha, Lebedev began to observe the same precautions in relation to the prince with his own family: on the pretext of not disturbing the prince, he would not let anyone go and see him, stamped his feet, rushing at his daughters and chasing them away, even Vera with her baby, at the first suspicion that she might be going to the veranda, where the prince was, in spite of all his requests that no one be chased away.

'In the first place, they will never have any respect if they're given their freedom like that; and in the second place, it's even indecent for them . . .' he explained, at last, to a direct question from the prince.

'But why?' the prince appealed to him. 'Really, you're only tormenting me with all this supervision and watching over me. I get bored on my own, I've told you that several times, yet with your constant waving of arms and walking about on tiptoe you make my melancholy even worse.'

The prince was alluding to the fact that although Lebedev had told all the people in the house to go away on the pretext of the peace and quiet needed by the sick man, throughout these three days he himself went in to see the prince almost every minute, on each occasion opening the door, poking his head through, surveying the room, as though he wanted to check if the prince was there and had not run away, and then on tiptoe, slowly and stealthily, approaching the armchair, sometimes unwittingly giving his tenant a fright as he did so. He constantly inquired whether he needed anything, and when the prince began at last to observe to him that he would like him to leave him in peace, turned away obediently and silently, crept back on tiptoe to the door, waving his arms all the while, as though letting it be known that he had only dropped in, that he would not say a word, and that look, now he had gone out of the room, and would not come back – but ten minutes or at most a quarter of an hour later appeared again. Kolya, who had free access to the prince, by this very fact aroused in Lebedev the most profound chagrin and even a pained indignation. Kolya noticed that Lebedev stood outside the door for half an hour at a time, eavesdropping on his conversation with the prince, and of course he told the prince about it.

'It's as if I'd become your property and you were keeping me under lock and key,' the prince protested. 'At a country dacha I'd like things to be different, and please be assured that I will receive anyone I like and go out anywhere I like.'

'Without the slightest doubt,' Lebedev began to wave his arms.

The prince surveyed him fixedly from head to foot.

'I say, Lukyan Timofeyevich, have you brought your safe, the little one that hangs above the head of your bed, here?'

'No, I haven't.'

'You haven't left it there, have you?'

'It's impossible to bring it, I'd have had to break it out of the wall . . . It's strong, strong.'

'But I suppose you have another one like it here?'

'Even better, even better, that's why I bought this dacha.'

'Aha. Who was it you wouldn't let in to see me? An hour ago.'

'That was . . . that was the general, sir. To be sure, I didn't let him in, for he's not the right person for you. I respect the man profoundly, prince, he's . . . he's a great man, sir; you don't believe it? Well, you'll see, but all the same . . . you'd do best, most illustrious Prince, not to receive him, sir.'

'And why is that so, may I ask you? And why are you standing on tiptoe now, Lebedev, and why do you always come up to me as though you wanted to whisper a secret in my ear?'

'I'm vile, vile, I feel it,' Lebedev replied unexpectedly, striking his chest with emotion. 'But wouldn't the general be too hospitable for you, sir?'

'Too hospitable?'

'Yes, sir. In the first place, he wants to come and live in my house; that would be all right, sir, but he's too excitable, he wants to be one of the family right away. He and I have worked out the genealogy several times now, it turns out that we're

related. You also turn out to be a distant nephew of his on your
mother's side, he explained to me yesterday. If you're a nephew,
then you and I, most illustrious Prince, are related. That would
be nothing, sir, a small weakness, but he at once declared that
throughout the whole of his life, right from the time he was an
ensign until the eleventh of June last year, he never had less than
two hundred people sitting down at his table every day. It finally
got to the point where they didn't get up again, so that they
dined, and had supper, and drank tea for some fifteen hours out
of the twenty-four for some thirty years on end without the
slightest pause, there was hardly time to change the tablecloth.
One would get up and leave, and another would arrive, and on
feasts and public holidays there were up to three hundred people
present. And on Russian Millennium Day[1] he said he counted
seven hundred there. I mean, that's terrible, sir; stories like that
are a very bad sign, sir; one's even afraid to receive men of such
hospitality in one's house, and I thought: won't he be too
hospitable for you and me?'

'But you and he seem to be on very good terms?'

'On brotherly terms, and I take it all as a joke; so we're
relations: what's it to me – the honour is all the greater. Even in
spite of two hundred people and the Russian Millennium, I
discern in him a most remarkable man. I speak sincerely, sir.
You began to speak of secrets just now, Prince, or rather, that I
came up to you as though I wanted to tell you a secret, but as it
happens there is a secret: a certain person told me just now that
she wanted to have a very secret rendezvous with you.'

'Why secret? Not at all. I'll go and see her, today, even.'

'Not at all, not at all!' Lebedev began to wave his arms, 'and
she isn't afraid of what you're thinking, either. By the way: that
monster comes here absolutely every day to ask about your
health, did you know that?'

'You seem to call him a monster rather often. That makes me
a bit suspicious.'

'You need have no suspicion, none at all,' Lebedev deflected
quickly, 'I merely wished to explain to you that the certain
person is afraid not of him, but of something else entirely,
something else entirely.'

'What then? Hurry up and tell me,' the prince questioned with impatience, watching Lebedev's mysterious grimaces.

'That's the secret.'

And Lebedev gave a crooked smile.

'Whose secret?'

'Your secret. You yourself, most illustrious Prince, forbade me to mention in your presence . . .' Lebedev muttered and, enjoying the fact that he had roused his listener's curiosity to an almost pathological impatience, suddenly concluded: 'He's afraid of Aglaya Ivanovna.'

The prince frowned, and was silent for a moment.

'Really, Lebedev, I shall leave your dacha,' he said suddenly. 'Where are Gavrila Ardalionovich and the Ptitsyns? With you? You've lured them to your place, too.'

'They're coming, sir, they're coming. And even the general is coming, after them. I'm going open all the doors, and summon all my daughters, all of them, right now, right now,' Lebedev whispered in fear, waving his arms and lunging from one door to the next.

At that moment Kolya appeared on the veranda, entering from the street, and announced that visitors were coming, Lizaveta Prokofyevna with her three daughters.

'Should I let the Ptitsyns and Gavrila Ardalionovich in or shouldn't I? Should I admit the general or shouldn't I?' Lebedev jumped up, shocked by the news.

'But why not? Admit them all, anyone you like! I assure you, Lebedev, that you seem to have been under a misapprehension about my situation from the very start; you constantly make the same mistake. I have not the slightest reason to conceal myself or hide from anyone,' the prince laughed.

Looking at him, Lebedev also considered it his duty to laugh. In spite of his extreme agitation, it was clear that he was also extremely pleased.

The news brought by Kolya was correct; he was only a few steps ahead of the Yepanchins, in order to announce them, and the visitors suddenly appeared from both sides – the Yepanchins from the veranda, and the Ptitsyns, Ganya and General Ivolgin from the house itself.

Only now, from Kolya, had the Yepanchins learned of the
prince's illness, and of the fact that he was in Pavlovsk; before
then, the general's wife had been in a state of painful bewilderment. Two days earlier, the general had shown his family the
prince's visiting card; this card had aroused in Lizaveta Prokofyevna the total certainty that the prince would immediately
follow his card, and arrive in Pavlovsk to see them. In vain did
the girls protest that a man who had not written for half a year
was, perhaps, highly unlikely to be in such a hurry now, and
that perhaps he had enough to keep him busy in St Petersburg
without troubling about them – how could they know his
business affairs? The general's wife decidedly took offence at
these comments and was ready to wager that the prince would
appear the following day at the latest, although 'that will be too
late'. The next day she waited all morning; they waited until
dinner, until evening, and by the time twilight had quite fallen,
Lizaveta Prokofyevna grew angry about it all and quarrelled
with everyone, without, of course, mentioning the prince among
the reasons for the quarrel. Not a word was said about him on
the whole of the third day, either. When it inadvertently escaped
from Aglaya at dinner that *maman* was angry because the prince
had not arrived, to which the general at once remarked that 'it
wasn't *his* fault' – Lizaveta Prokofyevna got up and left the table
in anger. Finally, Kolya appeared towards evening with all the
news and a description of all the prince's adventures of which
he knew. As a result, Lizaveta Prokofyevna was triumphant, but
Kolya got a good telling-off all the same. 'He hangs about here
for days on end and you can't get rid of him, but he might at
least have let us know, if he didn't consider us worthy of paying
us a visit.' Kolya at once started to lose his temper at the phrase
'can't get rid of him', but postponed it for another time, and if
the phrase had not been simply too offensive would probably
have quite forgiven it: so pleased was he by Lizaveta Prokofyevna's agitation and alarm about the prince's illness. For a
long time she insisted on the necessity of immediately sending a
courier to St Petersburg in order to rouse a medical celebrity of
the first magnitude and rush him to Pavlovsk by the first train.
But her daughters dissuaded her; they did not, however, want

to be left behind by their mother when she instantly made plans to visit the sick man.

'He's on his deathbed,' said Lizaveta Prokofyevna, as she fussed about, 'and yet we have to stand on ceremony here! Is he a friend of our household or not?'

'But, as the proverb says, one should look before one leaps,' Aglaya observed.

'Well, don't come, then, and a good thing too, for otherwise Yevgeny Pavlych will arrive with no one to receive him.'

After these words, Aglaya, of course, at once set off after them all, which, as a matter of fact, she had planned to do in any case. Prince Shch., who was sitting with Adelaida, at her request, immediately agreed to accompany the ladies. Even before this, on first making the Yepanchins' acquaintance, he had been extremely interested when he heard from them about the prince. It turned out that he knew the prince, that they had recently got to know each other somewhere and had spent a couple of weeks together in some small town. This had been about three months earlier. Prince Shch. even had many things to say about the prince, and on the whole had a very sympathetic opinion of him, so that it was with genuine pleasure that he went to visit his old acquaintance. The general, Ivan Fyodorovich, was not at home on this occasion. Yevgeny Pavlovich had also not arrived yet.

Lebedev's dacha lay not more than three hundred yards from the Yepanchins'. The first unpleasant impression Lizaveta Prokofyevna received at the prince's was to find him surrounded by a whole company of visitors, not to mention the fact that in that company there were two or three people she perfectly detested; the second was one of surprise at the sight of the perfectly healthy-looking young man, fashionably dressed and laughing, who came to meet them, instead of the dying man on his deathbed she had expected to find. She even came to a halt in astonishment, much to the extreme delight of Kolya, who could, of course, have explained to her very well, even before she had left her dacha, that absolutely no one was dying here, and there was no deathbed, but did not do so, having a sly premonition of the comical wrath of the general's wife when, as he calculated, she would certainly lose her temper at finding the prince, her sincere friend, well. Kolya was even tactless enough to express his conjecture aloud, really in order to tease Lizaveta Prokofyevna, whom he constantly and sometimes very wickedly engaged in altercation, in spite of the friendship that bound them.

'Wait, dear boy, don't hurry, don't spoil your triumph!' replied Lizaveta Prokofyevna, sitting down in the armchair the prince had provided for her.

Lebedev, Ptitsyn and General Ivolgin rushed to fetch chairs for the girls. The general fetched a chair for Aglaya. Lebedev also provided a chair for Prince Shch., contriving even in the very flexure of his back to demonstrate an extraordinary degree of respect. Varya, as usual, greeted the young ladies with rapture, and in whispers.

'It's true that I almost thought I would find you in bed, Prince, so much did I exaggerate everything out of fear, and, I will not lie, I felt terribly annoyed just now at the sight of your happy face, but I swear to you, it was only for a moment, before I'd had time to reflect. I always act and talk more sensibly when I've had time to reflect; I think you do the same. But really, I would be less glad about the recovery of my own son, if I had one, than I am about yours; and if you don't believe me when I tell you that, then the shame is yours, not mine. But that wicked boy takes the liberty of playing much worse tricks on me. I think he's a protégé of yours; then I warn you that one fine morning, believe me, I shall deny myself the pleasure of enjoying the honour of his acquaintance any more.'

'But what have I done wrong?' cried Kolya. 'No matter how hard I tried to assure you that the prince was almost well again, you wouldn't have wanted to believe me, because it was far more interesting to imagine him on his deathbed.'

'Will you be with us for long?' Lizaveta Prokofyevna addressed the prince.

'The whole summer and, perhaps, longer.'

'You're alone, aren't you? Not married?'

'No, I'm not married,' the prince smiled at the naivety of the thrust.

'No need to smile; it happens. I was referring to the dacha;

why didn't you move in with us? We have a whole vacant wing, but as you wish. Is it him you're renting from? That man?' she added in an undertone, nodding at Lebedev. 'Why does he keep making faces like that?'

At that moment Vera came out of the house on to the veranda, with the baby in her arms as usual. Lebedev, who was fidgeting about by the chairs, decidedly at a loss where to put himself, but dreadfully reluctant to leave, suddenly turned on Vera, waved his arms at her to chase her away from the veranda, and even forgot himself, and began to stamp his feet.

'Is he a madman?' the general's wife added suddenly.

'No, he's . . .'

'Drunk, perhaps? Not very pleasant, the company you keep,' she snapped, taking in the other visitors with her gaze. 'Though actually, what a charming girl! Who is she?'

'That's Vera Lukyanovna, the daughter of this Lebedev.'

'Ah! . . . Very charming. I want to be introduced to her.'

But Lebedev, having heard Lizaveta Prokofyevna's praise, had already dragged his daughter out to present her.

'Orphans, orphans!' he melted as he approached. 'And that child in her arms is an orphan, her sister, my daughter Lyubov, born in the most lawful wedlock by the newly deceased Yelena, my wife, who died six weeks ago, in childbirth, by the Lord's will . . . yes, ma'am . . . she's acted as a mother, though she's only a sister and no more than a sister . . . no more, no more . . .'

'And you, sir, are nothing but a fool, excuse me for saying so. Well, that will do, you know it yourself, I think,' Lizaveta Prokofyevna snapped suddenly in extreme indignation.

'Quite true!' Lebedev bowed low, most respectfully.

'Listen, Mr Lebedev, is it true what they say about you, that you interpret the Book of Revelation?' asked Aglaya.

'Quite true . . . for fifteen years now.'

'I have heard about you. They have written about you in the newspapers, I believe?'

'No, that was another interpreter, another one, ma'am, but he died, and I'm left in his place,' Lebedev said, beside himself with delight.

'Please oblige me by doing some interpreting for me some

time, as we are neighbours. I know nothing of Revelation at all.'

'I cannot but warn you, Aglaya Ivanovna, that all this is pure charlatanry on his part, believe me,' General Ivolgin suddenly and swiftly put in, having waited on tenterhooks, desperately anxious to start a conversation somehow; he sat down beside Aglaya Ivanovna, 'Of course, a country dacha has its own principles,' he continued, 'and its own pleasures, and to receive such an extraordinary *intrus* in order to interpret Revelation is a pastime like any other, and is even a remarkably intelligent pastime at that, but I ... You seem to be looking at me in surprise? General Ivolgin, I have the honour of introducing myself. I carried you in my arms, Aglaya Ivanovna.'

'Delighted, I'm sure. I know Varvara Ardalionovna and Nina Alexandrovna,' Aglaya muttered, trying her utmost not to burst into laughter.

Lizaveta Prokofyevna flared with anger. Something that had long been accumulating within her soul suddenly demanded release. She could not abide General Ivolgin, whose friend she had once been, though very long ago.

'My dear, you're lying as usual: you never carried her in your arms,' she snapped at him in indignation.

'You've forgotten, *Maman*, he did carry me, honestly he did, in Tver,' Aglaya suddenly said, in support of the general's claim. 'We were living in Tver at the time. I was six years old then, I remember. He made me a bow and arrow, and taught me to shoot, and I killed a pigeon. Do you remember, we killed a pigeon, you and I?'

'And he brought me a cardboard helmet and a wooden sword, I remember, too!' exclaimed Adelaida.

'I remember it, too,' Alexandra confirmed. 'You also quarrelled over the wounded pigeon at the time, and you were made to stand in corners of the room; Adelaida stood in her helmet, holding her sword.'

In telling Aglaya that he had carried her in his arms, the general had said this *for its own sake*, merely in order to start a conversation, and solely because he almost always began a conversation like this with all young people if he wanted to make their acquaintance. On this occasion, however, as luck would have it, he happened to have told the truth and, as luck would have it, he himself had forgotten that truth. So that, when Aglaya suddenly confirmed that they had shot a pigeon together, his memory was instantly restored, and he remembered it all right down to the last detail, as those in their declining years not infrequently remember something from the distant past. It was hard to tell what there might be in this memory that could have had such a powerful effect on the poor and, as usual, somewhat intoxicated general; but he was suddenly extraordinarily moved.

'I remember, I remember it all!' he exclaimed. 'I was a staff-captain at the time. You were a tiny little thing, so pretty. Nina Alexandrovna . . . Ganya . . . I was . . . often received in your house. Ivan Fyodorovich . . .'

'And now look what you've come to!' the general's wife retorted. 'At any rate, it means you haven't drunk away your decent feelings, if it's had such an effect on you! But you've worn your wife out with worry. You should have been giving your children guidance, but you're in the debtors' prison. Leave this place, my dear, find somewhere to go, stand behind the door in a corner and shed a few tears, remember your earlier innocence, and perhaps God will forgive you. Off you go, now, go, I mean it seriously. There is nothing better for correcting the soul than remembering the past with contrition.'

But it was not necessary for her to repeat that she meant it seriously: the general, like all drunkards, was very sensitive and, like all drunkards who have fallen too far, found it hard to endure memories from a happier past. He got up and meekly set off towards the door, so that Lizaveta Prokofyevna at once felt sorry for him.

'Ardalion Alexandrych, dear!' she cried after him. 'Stop for a moment; we're all sinners; when you feel that your conscience is reproaching you less, come and see me, we shall sit and chat about the past. I myself am possibly fifty times more of a sinner than you are; well, and now goodbye, off you go, there's nothing more for you here . . .' she said, suddenly frightened that he would come back.

'Don't go after him just now,' the prince stopped Kolya, who was running after his father. 'Or else in a moment he'll get annoyed, and the whole moment will be spoiled.'

'That's true, leave him alone; go in half an hour,' Lizaveta Prokofyevna decided.

'That's what it means to tell the truth at least once in one's life – it's moved him to tears!' Lebedev ventured to interject.

'Well, you're a fine one to talk, my dear, if what I've heard is true,' Lizaveta Prokofyevna beleaguered him at once.

The interrelationship of all the visitors who had gathered around the prince gradually defined itself. The prince, of course, was able to appreciate and did appreciate the whole degree of sympathy extended to him by the general's wife and her daughters and, of course, told them sincerely that, before their visit, he had planned to present himself to them that very day, in spite of both his illness and the late hour. Lizaveta Prokofyevna, casting a glance at his visitors, replied that he could do that even now. Ptitsyn, a polite and extremely easy-going man, very soon got up and retired to Lebedev's wing of the house, and was very desirous of taking Lebedev with him. The latter promised to come soon; meanwhile Varya talked with the girls and stayed. She and Ganya were very glad of the general's absence; Ganya himself also soon set off after Ptitsyn. For the few minutes he had spent on the veranda in the presence of the Yepanchins he had comported himself modestly, with dignity, and was not at all disconcerted by the determined stares of Lizaveta Prokofyevna, who twice looked him over from head to foot. Really, anyone who had known him earlier would have thought him greatly changed. Aglaya found this much to her liking.

'I say, was that Gavrila Ardalionovich leaving?' she asked suddenly, as she was sometimes fond of doing, loudly and sharply, interrupting the conversation of others with her question and not addressing anyone in person.

'Yes, it was,' replied the prince.

'I hardly recognized him. He has greatly changed and ... much for the better.'

'I'm very glad for him,' said the prince.

'He was very ill,' added Varya with joyful commiseration.

'What do you mean, he's changed for the better?' Lizaveta Prokofyevna asked in angry bewilderment and almost in fright. 'Where did you get that from? There's nothing that's better. What precisely seems better to you?'

'There's nothing better than the "poor knight"!' proclaimed Kolya suddenly, who had been standing all the time beside Lizaveta Prokofyevna's chair.

'I also think so,' said Prince Shch., and began to laugh.

'I am quite of the same opinion,' Adelaida solemnly proclaimed.

'What "poor knight"?' asked the general's wife, surveying all the speakers with vexation, but, on seeing that Aglaya had flared up, added angrily: 'Some nonsense, I daresay! What "poor knight" is this?'

'It's not the first time that urchin, your favourite, has distorted other people's words!' Aglaya replied with haughty indignation.

In each of Aglaya's angry outbursts (and she was angry very often), all her evident seriousness and implacability notwithstanding, there invariably peeped through something so childish, impatiently schoolgirl-like and poorly concealed that it was sometimes impossible, looking at her, not to laugh, to the extreme annoyance of Aglaya, however, who could not understand what people were laughing at and 'how can they, how dare they laugh?' Now her sisters and Prince Shch. began to laugh, and even Prince Lev Nikolayevich smiled, also red in the face for some reason. Kolya laughed loudly and enjoyed his triumph. Aglaya lost her temper in earnest and grew twice as pretty. Her confusion greatly became her, and also her annoyance at herself for this confusion.

'He's distorted your words plenty of times,' she added.

'I base my assertion on something you yourself exclaimed!' cried Kolya. 'A month ago you were looking through *Don Quixote* and exclaimed those words, that there was nothing better than the "poor knight". I don't know who you were talking about then: Don Quixote or Yevgeny Pavlych, or someone else, but you were talking about someone, and it was a long conversation . . .'

'I think you allow yourself too many liberties with your guesses, young man,' Lizaveta Prokofyevna stopped him with annoyance.

'But am I the only one?' Kolya would not be silenced. 'Everyone said it at the time, and they're saying it now; Prince Shch. just now, and Adelaida Ivanovna, and all of them declared they were in favour of the "poor knight", so the "poor knight" must exist, and certainly so, and I think that if it weren't for Adelaida Ivanovna, we would all have known long ago who the "poor knight" is.'

'Why is it my fault?' laughed Adelaida.

'You wouldn't paint his portrait – that's why it's your fault! Aglaya Ivanovna asked you to paint the portrait of a "poor knight" and even gave you the subject of the painting, which she'd thought of herself, do you remember? You wouldn't do it . . .'

'But how could I have painted it? Who would I have painted? According to the subject, this "poor knight"

> From his face he never raised
> To anyone his visor's steel.

Whose face would it have been, then? What would I have painted: the visor? An anonymous figure?'

'I don't understand any of this, what visor?' the general's wife said in irritation, though she had begun to have a very good idea of who was being referred to under the name (one probably agreed on long before) of "poor knight". But it particularly irked her that Prince Lev Nikolayevich was also embarrassed and in the end completely covered in confusion, like a boy of ten years old. 'Well, is it going to end soon, this nonsense? Is someone going to explain this "poor knight" business, or not? Is it such a dreadful secret that one can't even begin to comprehend it?'

But they all just went on laughing.

'It's quite simple: there's a strange Russian poem,' Prince Shch. intervened at last, obviously wishing to kill this conversation and change the topic, 'about a "poor knight", it's a fragment without a beginning or an end. About a month ago, we were all laughing after dinner and, as usual, trying to think of a subject for Adelaida Ivanovna's next painting. You know, it's long been a family tradition to find subjects for Adelaida's paintings. Well, someone had the idea of the "poor knight". Who thought of it first, I don't remember . . .'

'Aglaya Ivanovna!' exclaimed Kolya.

'You may well be right, but I don't remember,' Prince Shch. went on. 'Some people laughed at this subject, others avowed that there could be nothing more lofty, but that in order for the "poor knight" to be depicted, he had to have a face; we began to go over the faces of everyone we knew, but none of them was suitable, so the matter remained there; that's all; I don't know why Nikolai Ardalionovich thought of remembering all this and bringing it up now. What seemed amusing and appropriate at the time is now quite uninteresting.'

'Because there's some new nonsense at the back of it, something sarcastic and offensive, I expect,' snapped Lizaveta Prokofyevna.

'There's no nonsense, just the most profound respect,' quite unexpectedly, in a solemn and serious voice, pronounced Aglaya, who had managed to recover herself and suppress her earlier confusion. Not only that, but by certain signs one could suppose, looking at her, that she was happy now that the joke was going further and further, and this change took place in her precisely at the moment when the prince's embarrassment, which had been all too noticeably and steadily increasing, reached a pitch of extremity.

'One moment they're laughing like scalded cats, and then suddenly they're talking about the most profound respect! They're mad! What's all this about respect? Tell me right now why out of the blue you're suddenly talking about respect?'

'The most profound respect,' Aglaya went on just as seriously and solemnly in response to the almost malicious question from her mother, 'because that poem directly portrays a man who is capable of having an ideal, and in the second place, having set himself his ideal, of believing in it, and believing in it, blindly devoting the whole of his life to it. In our time, that doesn't always happen. The poem doesn't actually say what the "poor knight's" ideal is, but it's clear that it's some kind of radiant image, an "image of pure beauty",[2] and the lovesick knight even wears a rosary round his neck instead of a scarf. It's true that there's some sort of obscure, enigmatic device, the letters A.N.B, which he inscribes on his shield . . .'

'A.N.D.' Kolya corrected.

'Well, I say A.N.B., and that's what I meant to say,' Aglaya interrupted with annoyance. 'Whatever it was, it's clear that by now it was all the same to this "poor knight" who his lady was and what she did. It was enough that he chose her and believed in her "pure beauty", and then worshipped her for ever; that was its merit, that even if later she became a thief, he would still be bound to believe in her and break a lance for her pure beauty. It seems that the poet wanted to unite in one extreme image the whole enormous concept of medieval chivalrous platonic love in a pure and lofty knight; of course, all that is an ideal. In the "poor knight" this emotion has reached its ultimate degree, asceticism; it must be admitted that to be capable of such an emotion signifies a great deal and that such emotions leave behind them a deep mark and one that is from one point of view most praiseworthy, not to mention Don Quixote. The "poor knight" is Don Quixote, but a serious, not a comical one. At first I didn't understand this, and laughed, but now I love the "poor knight", and, more than that, admire his exploits.'

Thus did Aglaya conclude and, looking at her, it was actually hard to know whether she was serious or laughing.

'Well, it's some fool and his exploits!' the general's wife decided. 'And you, mademoiselle, have been talking a lot of nonsense, a whole lecture; it's not even suitable on your part, in my opinion. At any rate, it's improper. What poem is it? Recite it, I'm sure you know it! I absolutely insist on knowing this poem. I've never been able to stand poetry, it's as though I'd had a premonition. For God's sake – Prince, have patience, it seems that you and I will have to endure this together,' she addressed Prince Lev Nikolayevich. She was extremely annoyed.

Prince Lev Nikolayevich wanted to say something, but could get nothing out because of his continuing embarrassment. Only Aglaya, who had taken so many liberties in her 'lecture', was not at all embarrassed, and even seemed pleased. She at once got up, still serious and solemn as before, looking as though she had prepared herself for this beforehand, and had only been waiting to be asked, came out to the middle of the veranda and stood facing the prince, who continued to sit in his armchair. They all looked at her with some surprise, and almost all of them, Prince Shch., her sisters and mother, gazed with an unpleasant sensation on this new mischief in the making, which had at any rate gone rather too far. It was plain, however, that what Aglaya found enjoyable was precisely the affectation with which she had ceremonially begun the reciting of the poem. Lizaveta Prokofyevna very nearly chased her back to her seat, but at the very moment that Aglaya began to declaim the well-known ballad, two new visitors, talking loudly, entered the veranda from the street. They were General Ivan Fyodorovich Yepanchin and, following him, a young man. This caused a small commotion.

7

The young man who accompanied the general was about twenty-eight years old, tall, slim, with a handsome and intelligent face, and large, dark eyes that flashed with wit and mockery. Aglaya did not even turn round to look at him and went on with her recitation of the poem, making a point of looking only at the prince, and addressing him alone. It became obvious to the prince that she was doing all this with some special purpose. But at least the new visitors made his awkward situation a little easier. At the sight of them, he got up, nodded politely to the general, gave a sign that the recitation should not be interrupted, and managed to retreat out of his armchair and behind it, where, leaning his left elbow on its back, he continued to listen to the ballad, so to speak, in a more comfortable and less 'ridiculous' position than when he had been sitting down. For her part, Lizaveta Prokofyevna twice motioned with an imperious gesture to the two men who had entered to stand still. Incidentally, the prince was extremely interested in the new visitor who accompanied the general; he correctly guessed that he must be Yevgeny Pavlovich Radomsky, of whom he had heard a great deal and had thought about more than once. The only thing he found puzzling about him was his civilian dress; he had heard that Yevgeny Pavlovich was a military man. A mocking smile strayed across the lips of the new visitor throughout the whole recitation of the poem, as though he too had heard something about the "poor knight".

'Perhaps it was his idea,' the prince thought to himself.

But it was quite different with Aglaya. Now she cloaked all the initial affectation and pomposity with which she had begun her recitation in such earnestness and such penetration to the spirit and meaning of the poetic work, articulating each word of it with such understanding, enunciating them with such lofty simplicity, that by the end of the recitation she not only drew general attention, but by her rendering of the ballad's lofty spirit justified in part, as it were, the heightened and affected grandeur with which she had so solemnly stepped into the middle of the veranda. In this grandeur one could now discern only the immensity and, perhaps, even naivety of her respect for what she had undertaken to render. Her eyes shone, and a light, barely perceptible spasm of inspiration and rapture passed over her beautiful face a couple of times. She recited:

> Once a poor knight lived in the world,
> Silent and simple his state,
> Though his mien was pale and gloomy,
> His spirit was bold and straight.

> A single vision he possessed,
> From reason kept far apart –
> And deep was its impression
> Engraved upon his heart.

Thenceforth, his soul consumed to ash,
No look on womankind he cast,
Spoke not to them until the day
That to the grave he passed.

Round his neck a rosary he wore
In place of a scarf genteel,
And from his face he never raised
To anyone his visor's steel.

Filled with a love for ever pure,
Faithful to his dream's sweet note,
F.N.B. at last in his own blood
Upon his shield he wrote.

And in the wilds of Palestine
As o'er the rocks they came,
The paladins rushed into battle,
Declaimed each lady's name,

Lumen coeli, sancta Rosa!
Cried he with zealous frown,
And like thunder did his menace
Strike the Moslems down.

Returning to his distant castle,
He lived, strictly confined,
Always silent, always sad,
As a madman he died.

Remembering the whole of this moment later on, the prince was for a long time extremely disturbed, tormented by a problem that he could not solve: how could such noble, fine emotion be combined with such open and malicious mockery? That it was mockery, of that he had no doubt; he clearly understood this and had reasons for it: during her recitation, Aglaya had taken the liberty of altering the letters *A.N.D.* to *N.F.B.* That this was not a mistake and not a mishearing on his part – of that

he could not be in any doubt (it was later proved to be so).
At any rate, Aglaya's prank – a joke, of course, though a very
harsh and thoughtless one – had been premeditated. Everyone
had been talking (and 'laughing') about the 'poor knight' for a
month now. And yet, as far as the prince could later recall, it
had turned out that Aglaya pronounced those letters not only
with the complete absence of a joking manner, or any kind of
ironic smile, or even any emphasis on those letters, in order to
convey their hidden meaning in greater relief, but, on the
contrary, with such immutable earnestness, with such innocent
and naive simplicity, that one might have supposed those
very letters were in the ballad and were printed in the book.
Something painful and unpleasant seemed to sting the prince.
Lizaveta Prokofyevna, of course, had not understood or noticed
either the change of letters or the allusion. General Ivan
Fyodorovich realized only that a poem was being declaimed. Of
the other listeners very many understood, and were surprised
at the boldness of the prank and its intention, but kept silent
and tried not to let on. But Yevgeny Pavlovich (the prince
was even ready to bet) had not only understood, but was
even trying to let on that he understood: his smile was a very
mocking one.

'What a lovely poem!' the general's wife exclaimed in genuine
rapture, as soon as the recitation was over. 'Who is it by?'

'Pushkin, *Maman*, don't put us to shame – that's shocking!'
exclaimed Aglaya.

'It's a wonder I'm not a complete fool with daughters like
you!' Lizaveta Prokofyevna retorted bitterly. 'Shameful! I want
you to give me that poem by Pushkin as soon as we get home.'

'I don't think we have a Pushkin at all.'

'We've had two tattered volumes lying around since time
immemorial.'

'We must send someone to town to buy one, Fyodor or Alexei,
by the first train – Alexei would be best. Aglaya, come here!
Give me a kiss, you recited beautifully, but – if you were sincere
in your recital,' she added, 'then I am sorry for you; if you
recited it to make fun of him, then I don't approve of your
feelings, and so really it would have been better not to recite it

at all. Do you understand? Go now, young lady, I'll talk to you later, we've sat here too long.'

Meanwhile the prince exchanged greetings with General Yepanchin, and the general introduced him to Yevgeny Pavlovich Radomsky.

'I picked him up on the way, he'd just arrived on the train; he learned that I was coming here and that all our family were here . . .'

'I learned that you were here, too,' Yevgeny Pavlovich interrupted, 'and since I long ago decided to seek not only your acquaintance, but also your friendship, I didn't want to waste any time. Are you unwell? I've only just learned . . .'

'I'm quite well and very pleased to meet you, I've heard a lot about you and have even talked about you with Prince Shch.,' replied Lev Nikolayevich, extending his hand.

Mutual courtesies were spoken, both men shook hands and looked each other fixedly in the eye. In a single moment the conversation became general. The prince noticed (and now he noticed everything quickly and eagerly, even things that were perhaps not there at all) that Yevgeny Pavlovich's civilian attire was causing universal and rather extreme surprise, to the point that all other impressions were even forgotten and effaced for a while. One might have thought there was something particularly significant about this change of clothing. Adelaida and Alexandra were questioning Yevgeny Pavlovich in puzzlement. Prince Shch., his relative, even with concern; the general spoke almost with agitation. Only Aglaya cast an inquisitive but completely calm glance at Yevgeny Pavlovich for a moment, as if she merely wanted to compare whether military or civilian dress suited him better, but a moment later turned away and did not look at him any more. Lizaveta Prokofyevna also was reluctant to ask any questions, although, perhaps, she too was somewhat concerned. It seemed to the prince that Yevgeny Pavlovich did not enjoy her favour.

'Astonished, flabbergasted!' Ivan Fyodorovich repeated in answer to all questions. 'I couldn't bring myself to believe it when I met him earlier in St Petersburg. And why just suddenly like that, that's the mystery! He himself was the first to shout that one shouldn't break the chairs.'[1]

From the conversations that arose it turned out that Yevgeny Pavlovich had announced his retirement a long time ago; but every time he had spoken with such a lack of seriousness that one could not believe him. Indeed, of serious matters he always spoke with such a jesting look that it was impossible to make him out, especially if he did not want to be made out.

'Oh, it's just a temporary retirement, for a few months, a year at the very most,' laughed Radomsky.

'But there's no need for it, from what I know of your affairs,' the general still pursued, heatedly.

'And what about visiting my estates? You advised it yourself; and I want to go abroad as well . . .'

The conversation soon changed tack, however; but in the prince's opinion their excessive and persisting unease went beyond the limits of the normal, and he felt there was definitely something peculiar behind it.

'So the "poor knight" is back on the scene again?' Yevgeny Pavlovich asked, going over to Aglaya.

To the prince's amazement, she surveyed him in a puzzled, questioning fashion, as though wishing to indicate to him that there could be no talk between them of any 'poor knight' and that she did not even understand the question.

'But it's too late, it's too late to send to town for a Pushkin, it's too late!' Kolya argued with Lizaveta Prokofyevna, straining himself to breaking point. 'For the thousandth time: it's too late.'

'Yes, it really is too late to send to town now,' Yevgeny Pavlovich inserted at this point, quickly leaving Aglaya. 'I think the shops in St Petersburg will be closed, it's getting on for nine,' he confirmed, taking out his watch.

'You've managed without it for so long, you can wait until tomorrow,' Adelaida put in.

'And anyway,' Kolya added, 'it's not done for people of high society to take much interest in literature. Ask Yevgeny Pavlych. It's much more the done thing to have a yellow *char à bancs* with yellow wheels.'

'Out of a book again, Kolya.'

'Oh, he never ever says anything that isn't out of a book,'

Yevgeny Pavlovich interjected. 'He expresses himself in whole
sentences taken from critical journals. I've long had the pleasure
of being acquainted with Nikolai Ardalionovich's conversation,
but on this occasion he's not talking out of a book. Nikolai
Ardalionovich is clearly referring to my yellow *char à bancs*
with red wheels. Only I've changed it now, you're too late.'

The prince listened closely to what Radomsky was saying
... It seemed to him that Radomsky comported himself with
excellent manners, in a cheerful way, and he especially liked it
that he spoke to Kolya on equal terms, in friendly fashion, even
though Kolya was trying to tease him.

'What's this?' Lizaveta Prokofyevna addressed Vera,
Lebedev's daughter, who stood before her holding several
books, in large format, magnificently bound and almost new.

'Pushkin,' said Vera. 'Our Pushkin. Papa told me to present
it to you.'

'What? How can that be?' Lizaveta Prokofyevna was surprised.

'Not as a gift, not as a gift! I would not have the effrontery!'
Lebedev jumped out from behind his daughter's shoulder. 'At
its purchase price, ma'am. This is our own family Pushkin,
Annenkov's edition, which one can't find nowadays – at its
purchase price, ma'am. I present it to you with reverence, wishing to sell it and thus satisfy the noble impatience of your
excellency's most noble literary feelings.'

'Well, if you're selling it, then thank you. You won't lose by
it, I daresay; only please don't cringe, sir. I have heard of you,
they say you are very well read, we shall have a talk some time;
will you bring the books to me yourself?'

'With reverence and . . . respect!' Lebedev cringed, extremely
pleased, snatching the books from his daughter,

'Well, as long as you don't lose them, you may bring them
without respect, but only on this condition,' she added, giving
him a steady look. 'I will only allow you as far as the threshold,
and don't intend to receive you today. You could send your
daughter Vera right now if you want, I like her very much.'

'Why don't you tell him about those people?' Vera said,
turning to her father impatiently. 'After all, if you don't, they'll

just come in anyway: they've started making a row. Lev Nikolay-evich,' she addressed the prince, who had already picked up his hat, 'some people came to see you a while ago, there are four of them, they're waiting outside and shouting abuse, but Papa won't let them in to see you.'

'Who are these visitors?' asked the prince.

'They say they're here on business, but they're in the sort of mood where if you don't let them in now they'll stop you in the street. You'd better let them in, Lev Nikolayevich, and then you'll be rid of them. Gavrila Ardalionovich and Ptitsyn are trying to reason with them, but they won't listen.'

'Pavlishchev's son! Pavlishchev's son! He's not worth it, he's not worth it!' Lebedev waved his arms. 'They're not worth listening to, sir; and it would be indecent for you even to bother your head about them, Prince. Really, sir! They're not worth it . . .'

'Pavlishchev's son! Good heavens!' the prince exclaimed in extreme confusion. 'I know . . . but I mean, I . . . I entrusted that matter to Gavrila Ardalionovich. Gavrila Ardalionovich told me just now . . .'

But Gavrila Ardalionovich had already emerged from the house on to the veranda; he was followed by Ptitsyn. In the nearest room there was a hubbub; the loud voice of General Ivolgin was apparently trying to shout down several other voices. Kolya ran at once towards the noise.

'This is very interesting!' Yevgeny Pavlovich observed aloud.

'So he knows what it's about!' thought the prince.

'Pavlishchev's son – who is he? And . . . how can Pavlishchev have a son?' Ivan Fyodorovich, the general, asked in bewilder-ment, surveying every face, and realizing with astonishment that he was the only person who knew nothing of this affair.

Indeed, the commotion and expectancy were universal. The prince was profoundly astonished that his completely private concern should have aroused such intense interest.

'It would be very good if you yourself were to put an end to this matter right now,' said Aglaya, approaching the prince with particular seriousness, 'and allow us all to be your witnesses. They want to sully your good name, Prince, you must vindicate yourself triumphantly, and I am terribly glad for you in advance.'

'I also want this loathsome claim brought to an end once and for all,' exclaimed the general's wife. 'Give it to them good and proper, Prince, don't have any mercy on them! This affair has been constantly dinned into my ears, and I've worried myself sick because of you. In any case, I'll be interested to take a look at them. Call them in, and we'll sit down. Aglaya has the right idea. Have you heard anything about this, Prince?' she addressed Prince Shch.

'Of course I have, and in your house, too. But I particularly want to take a look at these young men,' replied Prince Shch.

'They're nihilists, aren't they?'

'No, ma'am, they're not really nihilists,' Lebedev stepped forward, almost quivering with excitement, 'they're different, ma'am, peculiar, my nephew says they've gone further than the nihilists, ma'am. It's no good thinking you'll confound them by being a witness, your excellency; they don't get confounded, ma'am. In spite of it all, nihilists are sometimes well-versed people, even learned, but these have gone further, ma'am, because above all they're men of practical action, ma'am. It's really a kind of extension of nihilism, though not by a straight route, but by hearsay and obliquely, and they don't declare themselves in some little newspaper article, but directly in action, ma'am; it's not a question, for example, of the sense-lessness of some Pushkin or another, and doesn't concern, for example, the need to break Russia up into pieces;[2] no, ma'am, now it's considered a positive right that if someone wants some-thing very much, he should let no barriers stop him, even if it means killing eight people, ma'am. But Prince, all the same I wouldn't advise you . . .'

But the prince was already going off to open the door to the visitors.

'That's slander, Lebedev,' he said, smiling. 'Your nephew must really have upset you a great deal. Don't believe him, Lizaveta Prokofyevna. I assure you that the Gorskys and Dani-lovs are merely exceptions, and these people are simply . . . wrong . . . But I would prefer it not to be in here, in front of everyone. You will forgive me, Lizaveta Prokofyevna, but when they come in I'll show them to you and then take them away. Come in, gentlemen!'

He was more troubled by another thought that tormented him. He had a feeling that this affair had been arranged in advance, for now, for precisely this hour and time, for precisely these witnesses and, perhaps, in order to bring about his expected disgrace, and not his triumph. But he was very sad about his 'monstrous and wicked suspiciousness'. He would have died, he thought, if anyone had learned that he had such a thought in his mind, and at the moment his new visitors entered, he was sincerely ready to consider himself, of all those who were around him, the lowest of the low in a moral regard.

Five people entered: four new visitors followed by General Ivolgin, who was flushed, excited and in a most intense fit of eloquence. 'He's certainly on my side!' the prince thought with a smile. Kolya slipped through together with them all; he was talking heatedly to Ippolit, who was one of the visitors; Ippolit was listening with an ironic smile.

The prince bade his visitors be seated. They all looked so young, so far from grown up that one might well have marvelled at the occasion and the ceremonious way in which they were received. Ivan Fyodorovich Yepanchin, for example, who knew and understood nothing of this 'new affair', even grew indignant at the sight of such young people and would probably have made some kind of protest if he had not been stopped by his wife's zeal, which he found strange, with regard to the particular interests of the prince. However, he stayed partly out of curiosity, and partly out of the kindness of his heart, even hoping that he might be able to offer some help or at any rate be useful with his authority; but the bow he received from General Ivolgin as the latter entered made him indignant once again; he frowned, and decided to stay stubbornly silent.

Of the four young visitors one, however, was about thirty, the 'retired lieutenant from Rogozhin's company, the boxer, who gave beggars fifteen roubles at a time'. One could guess that he was accompanying the others to give them courage, in the capacity of a true friend and, should the need arise, to offer support. Among the rest, the first place and leading role was taken by the visitor who was known as 'Pavlishchev's son', though he introduced himself as Antip Burdovsky. He was a fair-haired young man, poorly and untidily dressed, in a frock coat with sleeves that were stained to a mirror-like gloss, a greasy waistcoat buttoned to the top, with no sign of any linen, a black silk scarf, impossibly greasy and twisted to a plait, his hands unwashed, his face covered in pimples, and, if one may express it thus, with a gaze that was both innocent and insolent. He was not short of stature, thin, about twenty-two. Not the slightest irony, not the slightest reflection was expressed in his face; on the contrary, it expressed a complete and unquestioning intoxication with his own rights, and at the same time something approaching a strange and unceasing need to be, and to feel, constantly insulted. He spoke with agitation, hurrying and stammering, seeming not quite to finish his words, as though he were inarticulate or even a foreigner, though as a matter of fact he was completely Russian in his origins.

He was accompanied, in the first place, by Lebedev's nephew, already known to the reader, and in the second, by Ippolit. Ippolit was a very young man, about seventeen, or perhaps eighteen, with an intelligent but constantly irritated expression on his face, where disease had placed its terrible marks. He was as thin as a skeleton, pale yellow, his eyes glittered, and two red spots burned on his cheeks. He coughed without cease; his every word, every breath, almost, was accompanied by a wheezing. He was clearly in a very advanced stage of consumption. It looked as though he had no more than two or three weeks left to live. He was very tired, and was the first to sink on to a chair. The others stood on ceremony somewhat as they entered, and were almost embarrassed, but looked solemn and were evidently afraid of losing their dignity in some way, which was strangely out of harmony with their reputation of being the spurners of all useless worldly trivia, prejudices and almost everything else in the world except their own interests.

'Antip Burdovsky,' 'Pavlishchev's son' announced, hurrying and stammering.

'Vladimir Doktorenko,' Lebedev's nephew introduced himself, clearly, distinctly, and as if he were boasting that he was Doktorenko,

'Keller,' muttered the retired lieutenant.

'Ippolit Terentyev,' the last one squeaked in an unexpectedly shrill voice.

They all, at last, sat down on chairs facing the prince, and all, having introduced themselves at once, frowned, and, to keep their spirits up, moved their peaked caps from one hand to another, kept preparing to speak, but then remained silent, waiting for something with a challenging look, in which one could unmistakably read: 'No, brother, it's no good, you won't pull the wool over our eyes!' One felt that as soon as one of them uttered a word they would all start talking at once, interrupting and running ahead of one another.

8

'Gentlemen, I wasn't expecting any of you,' the prince began. 'I've been ill until today, and at least a month ago I entrusted your case (he turned to Antip Burdovsky) to Gavrila Ardalionovich Ivolgin, as I informed you at the time. However, I don't object to having a face-to-face discussion, though you will agree that at such an hour . . . I suggest you come with me to another room, if it won't take long . . . My friends are here now, and believe me . . .'

'Your friends . . . as many as you like, but permit us,' Lebedev's nephew suddenly interrupted in a very sententious tone, though still not raising his voice very much, 'permit us to declare that you could have shown us a little more politeness, and not made us wait two hours in your lackeys' hall . . .'

'And, of course! . . . and I . . . and it's just what a prince would do! And it . . . you must be a general! And I'm no lackey of yours! And I, I . . .' Antip Burdovsky suddenly began to mutter in extraordinary agitation, his lips trembling, a tremor of outrage in his voice, spittle flying from his mouth, as if he had burst, or erupted, but was in such a hurry that after a dozen words it was no longer possible to understand him.

'It was just what a prince would do!' Ippolit cried in a shrill, cracked voice.

'If it had happened to me,' growled the boxer, 'that's to say, if I'd been directly concerned with this, as a man of honour, if I'd been in Burdovsky's shoes . . . I'd have . . .'

'Gentlemen, I only learned a moment ago that you were here, and that's the honest truth,' the prince repeated again.

'We're not afraid of your friends, no matter who they may be, because we are within our rights,' Lebedev's nephew declared again.

'But what right did you have, permit me to ask you,' Ippolit squeaked again, growing extremely heated now, 'what right did you have to submit Burdovsky's case to the judgement of your friends? We may not wish the judgement of your friends; it's all too easy to understand what the judgement of your friends might signify! . . .'

'But Mr Burdovsky, if you don't want to talk here,' the prince managed to interject, at last, extremely taken aback by such a beginning, 'then, as I say, let us go to another room right away. I repeat that I only heard about you a moment ago . . .'

'But you have no right, you have no right, you have no right . . . your friends . . . Look! . . .' Burdovsky began to babble again, staring about him with wild apprehension, and growing more excited the greater his suspicion and shyness became. 'You have no right!' Having said this he stopped abruptly, as though he had been cut short and, silently focusing his short-sighted, goggling eyes with their thick red veins, stared questioningly at the prince, leaning his whole torso forward. This time the prince was so astonished that he also fell silent and stared back at him, his eyes also a-goggle, and not saying a word.

'Lev Nikolayevich!' Lizaveta Prokofyevna called suddenly. 'Read this at once, this very minute, it directly concerns your business.'

She hurriedly held out to him a weekly humorous paper[1] and pointed her finger at an article. While the visitors were entering,

Lebedev had obliquely approached Lizaveta Prokofyevna, whose favour he was trying to curry, and, without saying a word, had taken this paper from his pocket and placed it straight before her eyes, indicating a marked column. What Lizaveta Prokofyevna had so far managed to read had shocked and disturbed her terribly.

'Wouldn't it be better not to read it aloud?' mouthed the prince, greatly embarrassed. 'I'd rather read it alone ... later ...'

'Then you'd better read it, read it right now, out loud! Out loud!' Lizaveta turned to Kolya, snatching the paper from the hands of the prince, who had barely managed to touch it. 'Out loud to everyone, so that everyone can hear.'

Lizaveta Prokofyevna was a hot-blooded woman, easily carried away, who suddenly and on the spur of the moment, without deliberating long about it, would sometimes raise all her anchors and launch herself upon the open sea, no matter what the weather. Ivan Fyodorovich stirred uneasily. But while in that first moment they all involuntarily stopped and waited in bewilderment, Kolya unfolded the newspaper and began to read aloud from the place indicated by Lebedev, who had leaped to his side:

'*Proletarians and Scions of Nobility, an Episode of Daylight and Everyday Robbery! Progress! Reform! Justice!*

'Strange things are taking place in our so-called Holy Russia, in our age of reforms and company initiatives, an age of national awareness and hundreds of millions exported abroad each year, an age of the encouragement of industry and the paralysis of working hands, etcetera, etcetera, the list is too long to be enumerated, gentlemen, and therefore let us come straight to the point. A strange anecdote occurred with one of the scions of our obsolete landowning gentry (*de profundis!*), one of those scions, however, whose grandfathers lost everything they had at roulette, whose fathers were forced to serve as cadets and lieutenants and usually died while facing trial for some innocent mistake in a calculation of public finances, and whose children, like the hero of our tale, either grow up as idiots, or even become involved in criminal activities, of which, however, in the interests of edification and correction, they are acquitted by our juries; or, at last, they end by embarking upon one of those incidents that amaze the public and disgrace our already sufficiently dis- honourable age. Our scion, some six months ago, shod in foreign fashion, in gaiters, and shivering in his wretched little overcoat without any lining, returned in winter to Russia from Switzer- land, where he had been treated for idiocy (*sic!*). It must be admitted that fortune was on his side, as quite apart from the interesting illness for which he had been treated in Switzerland (well, can one be treated for idiocy, imagine that?!), he could prove the verity of the Russian saying: 'some people have all the luck'! Judge for yourselves: left a babe in arms after the death of his father, a lieutenant, it is said, who died while facing trial for the sudden disappearance, at cards, of the entire funds of his company, and perhaps also for giving an excessive number of strokes of the birch to a subordinate (remember the good old days, gentlemen?), our baron was taken, out of charity, to be brought up by one of the very rich Russian landowners. This Russian landowner – let us call him P. – in the former golden age the owner of four thousand bonded serfs (bonded serfs! Do you understand such an expression, gentlemen? I do not. I will have to resort to the dictionary: "fresh is the legend, but hard to believe"),[2] was evidently one of those Russian lazy-bones and parasites who spent their idle lives abroad, in summer at the spas, and in winter at the Château des Fleurs in Paris where, in their day, they left immense sums. It could be positively stated that at least one-third of the quit-rent paid under the former system of serfdom was received by the owner of the Château des Fleurs in Paris (lucky man!). However that may be, the carefree P. brought up the *barin*'s orphaned son like a prince, hired tutors and governesses (doubtless pretty ones) for him, whom, incidentally, he brought from Paris himself. But the *barin*'s scion, the last in his line, was an idiot. The Château des Fleurs governesses were of no assistance, and until the age of twenty our protégé had not even learned to speak any language at all, including Russian. This latter circumstance was excusable, however. Finally, the fantastic notion entered P.'s feudal head that the idiot might be taught some sense in Switzerland – a fantastic notion that was, however, a logical one: a parasite and *propriétaire* would naturally imagine that even intelligence could be purchased on the market, especially in Switzerland. Five years of treatment in Switzerland with some professor went by, and thousands were spent: the idiot did not acquire intelligence, of course, but it is said that none the less he began to resemble a human being, though doubtless only just. Suddenly, P. died. There was, of course, no will; his affairs were, as usual, in disorder, there was a host of greedy heirs who could not care less about the last scions of the line being cured of the idiocy of the line, on charity, in Switzerland. The scion, though he was an idiot, none the less tried to swindle the professor, it is said, managed to have two years' treatment with him, concealing from his doctor the death of his benefactor. But the professor was himself a formidable charlatan; alarmed, at last, by the penury and above all the appetite of his twenty-five-year-old parasite, he shod him in his wretched old gaiters, gave him his tattered overcoat and, out of charity, sent him, third-class, *nach Russland* – to get him off his back, and out of Switzerland. It might appear that fortune had turned its back on our hero. But not so, gentlemen: fortune, which kills whole provinces with famine, pours out all her gifts at once on a little aristocrat, like Krylov's Cloud,[3] which sailed over the dried-up fields and emptied its contents over the ocean. Almost at the very moment he appeared from Switzerland in St Petersburg, a relative of his mother's (who was, of course, from a merchant's family) died in Moscow, a childless old bachelor, a merchant, bearded, a Schismatic, leaving an inheritance of several millions, incontestable, in ready cash, and (if only it were you and I, reader!) all to our scion, all to our baron, who had been treated for idiocy in Switzerland! Well, now it was a different kettle of fish. Around our baron in gaiters, who had started to run after a certain well-known beauty and kept woman, there suddenly gathered a whole crowd of friends and companions; there were even relatives, and above all whole crowds of well-brought-up girls hungering and thirsting for lawful wedlock – all the qualities at once, you would not find such a husband even with a lantern, and you couldn't have such a one made to order! . . .'

I . . . I don't understand this at all!' cried Ivan Fyodorovich, in the highest degree of indignation.

'Stop it, Kolya!' the prince cried in an imploring voice. There were exclamations from every side.

'Read it! Read it at all costs!' snapped Lizaveta Prokofyevna, evidently restraining herself with extreme effort. 'Prince! If it isn't read – we shall quarrel.'

There was nothing for it. Kolya, flushed, red and excited, continued the reading in an agitated voice:

'But while our precocious millionaire was, so to speak, in the empyrean, an altogether extraneous event took place. One fine morning a visitor called on him, with a calm and stern countenance and a polite but dignified and correct manner of speech, dressed modestly and decently, with an evident progressive tinge of thought, and in two words explained the reason for his visit: he was a well-known lawyer; a certain matter had been entrusted to him by a young man; he was calling in his name. This young man was no more nor less than the late P.'s son, though he bore a different name. The voluptuary P., having seduced in his youth a certain honest, poor girl, one of his house serfs, but brought up in European fashion (here the baronial rights of the now obsolete serf system were, of course, involved), and having noticed the unavoidable but imminent consequence of his liaison, quickly married her off to a man of good character who worked in trade and had even been employed in government service, and who had long loved this girl. At first he helped the newly weds; but soon her husband's good character made it impossible for him to accept this help. Some time passed, and little by little P. managed to forget both about the girl and about the son he had had by her, and then, as we know, died without having made any arrangements. Meanwhile, his son, who had been born in lawful wedlock, but had grown up under another surname and had been completely adopted by the good character of his mother's husband, who nevertheless died in his own good time, was left completely to his own resources and with an ailing, suffering mother who could not walk, in one of the remote provinces; he himself earned money by respectable daily toil, giving lessons in merchants' houses and thereby supporting himself, first at a gymnasium and then as an extra-mural student attending lectures that might be useful to him, with a future aim in mind. But how much can one earn from a Russian merchant for lessons at ten copecks an hour, and, moreover, with an ailing mother who could not walk, and who, at last, did almost nothing to make his situation any easier when she died in a remote province? Now the question is: what thoughts, in all fairness, must have gone through our scion's mind? You, of course, reader, think that he said to himself: "All my life I have had the advantage of all P.'s gifts, for my upbringing, for governesses and treatment for idiocy tens of thousands went to Switzerland; and here I am now with millions, and the good character of P.'s son, not to blame in any way for the misdemeanours of his light-minded father who had forgotten about him, is being ruined in the giving of lessons. Everything that was spent on me should really have been spent on him. Those enormous sums of money that were wasted on me are not really mine. It was just a blind mistake of fortune; they really belonged to P.'s son. They ought to have been used to help him, not me – the result of a fantastic whim of the light-minded and forgetful P. If I were really decent, sensitive and fair, I ought to have given his son half of my inheritance; but as I am above all a prudent man and understand only too well that this is not a juridical matter, I will not give half of my millions. But at any rate it would be too base and shameless (the scion forgot that it would not be prudent, either) on my part if I do not now return to him those tens of thousands that were spent on my idiocy by P. That is only what conscience and justice demand! For what would have happened to me had P. not taken me into his tutelage and concerned himself with his son instead?

'But no, gentlemen! Our scions do not think like that. No matter how the young man's lawyer, who had taken it upon himself to act for him solely out of friendship and almost against his will, almost by force, presented it to him, no matter how much he pointed out to him the obligations of honour, decency, justice, and even plain prudence, the Swiss protégé remained adamant, and what of it? All that would be nothing, but what was really unforgivable, and not excusable by any interesting illness, was that this millionaire who had only just left his professor's gaiters could not realize even then that the noble character of the young man, who was wearing himself out giving lessons, was not asking him for charity and help, but for his rightful due, though not in legal terms, and was not even asking – his friends were merely interceding on his behalf. With a majestic air, and enraptured by the opportunity now afforded to him to crush people with impunity because of his millions, our scion took out a fifty-rouble note and sent it to the decent young man in the form of an insolent handout. You don't believe it, gentlemen? You are revolted, you are insulted, you expostulate in a cry of indignation; but he did so, all the same! Of course, the money was at once returned to him, thrown back in his face, so to speak. How then is this matter to be resolved? It is not a legal matter, there remains only public opinion! In communicating this anecdote to the public, we vouch for its trustworthiness. It is said that one of our best-known humorists let slip a delightful epigram in this connection, one that deserves to take its place not only in provincial sketches of our manners, but also in metropolitan ones:

> In Schneider's coat did Lyova
> Play for five years long
> Filling up his wasted time
> With usual dance and song.
>
> Returning now in gaiters tight
> To a million he is heir,
> Says his prayers in Russian,
> But fleeces students bare.'[4]

When Kolya had finished, he quickly handed the paper to the prince and, without saying a word, rushed into a corner and hid in it, covering his face with his hands. He felt intolerably ashamed, and his childish impressionability, which had not yet managed to accustom itself to filth, was revolted beyond all bounds. It seemed to him that something extraordinary had happened, destroying everything at once, and he himself had really been the cause of it, by the mere fact of having read this aloud.

But everyone, it seemed, had felt something of this kind.

The girls felt very awkward and ashamed. Lizaveta Proko- fyevna was restraining extreme anger within herself and also, perhaps, bitterly regretting she had got involved in the matter; now she said nothing. With the prince there took place the same thing that often happens to excessively shy people in such cases: so ashamed by the actions of others, so ashamed for his visitors was he, that at that initial moment he was afraid even to look at them. Ptitsyn, Varya, Ganya, even Lebedev – they all looked somewhat embarrassed. Strangest of all, Ippolit and 'Pavlish- chev's son' also seemed to be astonished by something; Lebedev's nephew was also evidently displeased. The boxer alone sat in complete calm, twirling his moustache, with a solemn air, his eyes lowered, though not with embarrassment but, on the contrary, it appeared, from well-bred modesty, as it were, and all-too-obvious triumph. From all the signs it was clear that he had enjoyed the article greatly.

'The devil knows what this is,' Ivan Fyodorovich growled in an undertone. 'It's as though fifty lackeys had got together and written it.'

'But pe-ermit me to inquire, dear sir, how you can be so rude as to offend people by such hypotheses?'

'This, this, this for a man with any decency . . . you will agree yourself, general, that if a man with any decency . . . it's really offensive!' growled the boxer, also suddenly rousing himself for some reason, twirling his moustache and jerking his shoulders and torso.

'In the first place, I am not your "dear sir", and in the second, I do not intend to give you any explanation,' the dreadfully flushed Ivan Fyodorovich answered sharply, rose from his seat and, without saying a word, walked towards the exit from the veranda and stood on the top step with his back to the public – to the very great indignation of Lizaveta Prokofyevna, who had no thought of moving from her seat even now.

'Gentlemen, gentlemen, permit me, at last, to speak,' the prince exclaimed in melancholy and agitation. 'And do me a favour, and let us speak in such a way that we can understand one another. I don't mind the article, gentlemen, let it be; except that, gentlemen, everything that is printed in the article is untrue: I say that because you know it yourselves; it's even shameful. So I will be truly astonished if any of you has written it.'

'I knew nothing about this article until this very moment,' declared Ippolit. 'I don't approve of it.'

'Although I knew it had been written, I . . . also would not have advised it to be printed, because it's premature,' added Lebedev's nephew.

'I knew but I have the right . . . I . . .' muttered 'Pavlishchev's son'.

'What? You wrote all that yourself?' asked the prince, looking at Burdovsky with curiosity. 'It cannot be!'

'One could, however, refuse to recognize your right to ask such questions,' Lebedev's nephew intervened.

'But you see, I was only surprised that Mr Burdovsky had succeeded in . . . but . . . I mean that if you've already aired the article in public, then why did you take such offence when I began to talk about it in the presence of my friends?'

'At last!' Lizaveta Prokofyevna muttered in indignation.

'And Prince, you've even forgotten to mention,' Lebedev suddenly slipped between the chairs, unable to restrain himself, and almost in a fever, 'you've even forgotten to mention that it was only because of your good will and the unexampled kindness of your heart that you received them and listened to them, and that they have no right to make such a demand, all the more so since you've already entrusted this matter to Gavrila Ardalionovich, and that it was also because of your exceeding kindness that you acted thus, and that now, most illustrious Prince, remaining among your chosen friends, you cannot sacrifice such company for these gentlemen, sir, and could, so to speak, show all these gentlemen the door this very moment, so that I, in the capacity of master of the house, would even with exceeding pleasure, sir . . .'

'Quite right!' General Ivolgin suddenly thundered from the depths of the room.

'Enough, Lebedev, enough, enough . . .' the prince began, but a veritable explosion of indignation covered his words.

'No, I'm sorry, Prince, I'm sorry, now that really is enough!'
Lebedev's nephew almost shouted everyone down. 'Now the
matter must be set forth clearly and firmly, because it is evidently
not understood. There were legal quibbles involved, and on the
basis of these quibbles we are threatened with being kicked out
of the house! And do you really consider us such fools, Prince,
that we ourselves don't realize the extent to which our case is
not a legal one, and that if it were to be examined legally we
have no right to demand even one single rouble from you, by
law? But we realize precisely that if there is no legal right here,
there's a human right, a natural one; the right of common sense
and the voice of conscience, and even though this right of ours is
not written down in any rotten human code of law, a decent and
honest man, a right-thinking man, that's to say, is obliged to
remain a decent and honest man even on those points that aren't
written down in the law books. That is why we have come here,
unafraid of being thrown out of the house (as you threatened just
now) precisely because we *do not ask*, but *demand*, and as for the
impropriety of visiting at such a late hour (though we didn't arrive
at a late hour, but you made us wait in the lackeys' hall), that is
why, I say, we came, not at all afraid, because we supposed you
to be a man of common sense, that's to say, someone with honour and conscience. Yes, that is true, we entered not meekly, like
hangers-on and seekers, but with our heads raised, like free men,
and not with any plea, but with a free and proud demand (you
hear, not with a plea, but with a demand, mark that!). With dignity and bluntness we put before you a question: in the case of
Burdovsky, do you consider yourself right or wrong? Do you
admit that you were shown much favour and even perhaps
saved from death by Pavlishchev? If you admit it (which is
obvious), then do you intend, or do you consider it just, in all
conscience, that when you have received your millions, you
should reward Pavlishchev's needy son, even though he bears
the name Burdovsky? Yes or no? If the answer is *yes*, that is, in
other words, if you possess what you in your language call
honour and conscience, and what we, with greater precision,
designate with the name "common sense", then give us satisfaction and the matter is at an end. If you do so, it will be without

pleas or gratitude on our part, do not expect them from us, for you will be acting not for our sakes but for the sake of justice. If you are unwilling to give us satisfaction, that's to say, if your reply is *no*, then we shall leave at once, and the case is closed; but we shall say to your face, in front of all your witnesses, that you are a man of coarse intelligence and low development; that in future you will not dare to call yourself a man of honour and conscience, and that you have no right, that you want to purchase that right too cheaply. I have finished. I have put the question. Now turn us out, if you dare to. You can do that, you have the advantage of numbers. But remember that we demand and do not beg. Demand and do not beg!'

Lebedev's nephew, who was very flushed, stopped.

'We demand, we demand, we demand, and do not beg! . . .' Burdovsky began to mouth, blushing red as a lobster.

After Lebedev's nephew's words a certain general movement ensued, and a murmur of protest even arose, though all in the assembled company were evidently trying to avoid becoming involved in the affair, except perhaps for Lebedev, who was as in a kind of fever. (It was strange: Lebedev, standing near the prince, was apparently now enjoying a sense of family pride after his nephew's speech; at any rate, he was surveying the public with an odd air of satisfaction.)

'In my opinion,' the prince began rather quietly, 'in my opinion, Mr Doktorenko, in all that you have said just now, you are halfway quite correct, I would even agree that it is by far the greater half, and I would agree with you completely if you hadn't left something out in what you said. Precisely what you left out, I am unable and am in no position to express to you exactly, but for what you said to be completely correct, something is certainly lacking. But let us rather turn to the matter itself. Gentlemen, tell me, why did you publish this article? I mean, every word in it is a slander; and so, gentlemen, in my opinion, you've done something rather base.'

'If you please! . . .'

'My dear sir! . . .'

'It's . . . it's . . . it's . . .' for their part, the excited visitors uttered simultaneously.

'With regard to the article,' Ippolit interjected shrilly, 'with regard to this article I've already told you that I and the others do not approve of it! He's the one who wrote it' – he pointed to the boxer sitting next to him – 'wrote it indecently, I agree, wrote it illiterately and in the style that retired military men like him employ. He's stupid, and an opportunist, too, I tell him that to his face every day, but even so he was half right: freedom of speech is everyone's legal right, and therefore it's Burdovsky's too. As for his absurdities, let him answer for them himself. With regard to my earlier protest on behalf of us all against your friends being present, I think it necessary to explain to you, dear sirs, that I protested solely in order to declare our right, but that in reality we actually want there to be witnesses – and earlier on, before we came here, all four of us agreed on that. Whoever your witnesses are – even if they are your friends – since they cannot but concede Burdovsky's right (because it is, obviously, a mathematical one), then it's even better that these witnesses are your friends; the truth will present itself even more evidently.'

'That's true, we agreed on that,' Lebedev's nephew confirmed.

'Then why was there such noise and shouting earlier, if that was what you wanted?' the prince asked in astonishment.

'But as regards the article, Prince,' the boxer inserted, dreadfully eager to get his word in and growing pleasantly animated (one might have suspected that the presence of the ladies was having a visible and powerful effect on him), 'as regards the article, I confess that I am indeed its author, though my sick friend, whom I'm accustomed to forgive everything because of his debility, has just criticized it to shreds. But I did write it, and I published it in the journal of a true friend of mine, in the form of a correspondence. Though the poem's not really mine, and actually belongs to the pen of a well-known humorist. I merely read it to Burdovsky, and even then not all of it, and at once received his agreement to publish it, but you'll agree that I couldn't have published it without his agreement. Freedom of speech is a universal, noble and salutary right. I hope, Prince, that you're progressive enough not to deny that . . .'

'I won't deny anything, but you must admit that in your article . . .'

'I was harsh, you mean? But you see, this case involves the public interest, you must admit that, and, in any case, is it possible to turn a blind eye to such a provocative incident? So much the worse for the culprits, but the interests of society come first. As for certain imprecisions, so to speak, certain hyperboles, you must also admit that initiative is the most important thing, the aim and the intention; what's important is a salutary example, and only after that can we examine individual cases, and, lastly, there's the matter of style, the humorous angle, so to speak, and in any case – everyone writes like that, you must admit! Ha-ha!'

'But you're completely on the wrong track. I do assure you, gentlemen,' the prince exclaimed, 'you published the article on the assumption that I would on no account agree to give Mr Burdovsky satisfaction, so you could frighten me and take your revenge on me in some way. But how do you know: perhaps I may have decided to give Burdovsky satisfaction. In fact, I declare to you straight, in front of everyone now, that I *will* give him satisfaction . . .'

'There, at last, are the decent and intelligent words of a decent and intelligent man!' the boxer proclaimed.

'Good Lord!' blurted Lizaveta Prokofyevna.

'This is intolerable!' muttered the general.

'Allow me, gentlemen, allow me, I will explain the matter,' implored the prince: 'About five weeks ago, Mr Burdovsky, your attorney and solicitor, Chebarov, arrived in Z. You described him very flatteringly, Mr Keller, in your article,' the prince addressed the boxer, laughing suddenly, 'but I didn't like the look of him at all. I simply realized at once that the principal substance of this affair lies entirely in the person of this Chebarov, that it was possibly he who put you up to all this, Mr Burdovsky, taking advantage of your simplicity, and got you to start this business, if I may be frank.'

'You have no right . . . I'm . . . not simple . . . this is . . .' Burdovsky began to babble in excitement.

'You have no right to make such assumptions,' Lebedev's nephew intervened sententiously.

'This is offensive in the highest degree!' Ippolit began to

squeal. 'It's an offensive assumption, false and irrelevant to the matter in hand!'

'I'm sorry, gentlemen, I'm sorry,' the prince hurriedly apologized. 'Please, forgive me; it's because I thought it would be better if we were completely open with one another; but do as you please, do as you like. I told Chebarov that as I was in St Petersburg, I would immediately grant a friend power of attorney to conduct this case, and that I'd inform you of that, Mr Burdovsky. I will tell you straight, gentlemen, that this case seemed to me one of out-and-out fraud, precisely because Chebarov was involved in it . . . Oh, don't take offence, gentlemen! For heaven's sake don't take offence!' the prince exclaimed in alarm, once again observing the manifestation of Burdovsky's insulted embarrassment, and the excitement and protest of his friends. 'It cannot refer to you personally, if I say that I considered the case one of fraud! I mean, I didn't know any of you personally then, and did not know your names; I judged by Chebarov alone; I'm speaking generally, because . . . if only you knew how dreadfully I've been deceived since I obtained my inheritance!'

'Prince, you're are dreadfully naive,' Lebedev's nephew observed mockingly.

'And a prince and a millionaire, to boot! For all your possibly good and rather simple heart, you cannot, of course, avoid the general law,' proclaimed Ippolit.

'Perhaps, that may very well be, gentlemen,' the prince hurried, 'though I don't know what general law you are talking about; but I will continue, only don't take needless offence: I swear I've not the slightest wish to offend you. And really, what is this, gentlemen: one cannot say a single word sincerely, but you at once take offence! But for one thing I was dreadfully astonished that a 'son of Pavlishchev' existed, and existed in such a dreadful situation, as Chebarov explained to me. Pavlishchev is my benefactor and a friend of my father's. (Oh, why did you write such an untruth about my father in your article, Mr Keller? There was no embezzlement of company funds and no abuse of subordinates – of that I am positively convinced, and how could your hand raise itself to write such a slander?) And what you

wrote about Pavlishchev is quite intolerable: you call that most
noble man a voluptuary, and light-minded, so boldly, so positively, as though you really were speaking the truth, and yet he
was one of the most virtuous men in the world! He was even a
remarkable scholar; he corresponded with many respected men
of science and donated a lot of money towards learning and
research. As for his heart, his good deeds, oh, of course, you
were correct in writing that I was almost an idiot then and could
not understand anything (though I nevertheless spoke Russian
and understood it), but after all, I can appreciate all that I
remember now . . .'

'If you please!' squealed Ippolit, 'isn't this getting too sentimental? We're not children. You were going to come straight to
the point, it's getting on for ten o'clock, remember that.'

'Certainly, certainly, gentlemen' the prince agreed at once.
'After my initial suspicions, I decided that I might be mistaken
and that it was indeed possible that Pavlishchev had a son. But I
was dreadfully shocked that this son would so readily, so publicly, that is, divulge the secret of his birth and, above all, disgrace
his mother. Because even then Chebarov was threatening me with
public opinion . . .'

'What stupidity!' Lebedev's nephew began to shout.

'You have no right . . . you have no right!' exclaimed
Burdovsky.

'The son's not answerable for the debauched action of his
father, and the mother's not to blame,' Ippolit squealed, with
vehemence.

'All the more reason to be merciful to her then, it would
appear . . .' the prince said timidly.

'Prince, you are not only naive, but have possibly gone even
further,' Lebedev's nephew smirked maliciously.

'And what right did you have?' Ippolit squealed in a most
unnatural voice.

'None, none!' the prince interrupted hurriedly. 'In that you
are right, I admit, but it was involuntary, and I at once told
myself then that my personal feelings ought not to have any
influence on the matter, because if I admitted that I was obliged
to satisfy Mr Burdovsky's demands, in the name of my feelings

for Pavlishchev, then I had to satisfy them no matter what, that is, whether I respected Mr Burdovsky or did not respect him. I only mentioned this, gentlemen, because it seemed to me unnatural that a son should so publicly disclose his mother's secret . . . In a word, it was this that mainly convinced me that Chebarov must be a scoundrel and had himself egged Mr Burdovsky on, by deception, to such fraud.'

'But I say, this is intolerable!' resounded from the direction of the visitors, some of whom had even leaped up from their chairs.

'Gentlemen! But that is why I decided that the unfortunate Mr Burdovsky must be a simple man, a defenceless man, who fell easy prey to fraudsters and swindlers, so that I was all the more obliged to help him, as "Pavlishchev's son" – in the first place, as a counter-thrust to Mr Chebarov, in the second place, with my devotion and friendship, in order to guide him, and in the third place, by arranging for him to be paid ten thousand roubles, in other words all the money that, according to my calculations, Pavlishchev could have spent on me . . .'

'What? Only ten thousand?' cried Ippolit.

'Well, Prince, you're not very good at arithmetic – or perhaps you're rather too good at it, though you present yourself as a simpleton!' exclaimed Lebedev's nephew.

'I won't accept ten thousand,' said Burdovsky.

'Antip! Accept it!' the boxer prompted in a rapid and distinct whisper, leaning forwards over the back of Ippolit's chair. 'Accept it, and then later on we'll see!'

'N-now listen, Mr Myshkin,' squealed Ippolit, 'you must realize that we are not fools, not vulgar fools, as is probably the opinion of all your visitors and these ladies, who are sneering at us with such indignation, and especially that gentleman of fashion (he pointed to Yevgeny Pavlovich) whom, I of course, don't have the honour of knowing, but about whom, of course I seem to have heard a few things . . .'

'Come, come, gentlemen, you've once again failed to understand me!' the prince addressed him in agitation. 'In the first place, you, Mr Keller, estimated my fortune very inaccurately in your article: I received no millions: I have, perhaps, only an eighth or a tenth part of what you suppose me to have; in the second place, no tens of thousands were spent on me in Switzerland: Schneider received six hundred a year, and that only for the first three years; and Pavlishchev never went to Paris for pretty governesses; that's another piece of slander. In my opinion, far less than ten thousand was spent on me, but I decided on a figure of ten thousand, and, you must admit that in repaying the debt I could not possibly offer Mr Burdovsky more than that, even if I were terribly fond of him, and would be unable to do so because of a sense of tact, precisely because I was repaying a debt and not sending him a hand-out. I don't know why you don't understand that, gentlemen! But I wanted to make compensation for all this later on, with my friendship and my active interest in the fate of the unfortunate Mr Burdovsky, who had obviously been deceived, because he could not, without deception, have agreed to such a base act, as, for example, today's disclosure in Mr Keller's article about his mother . . . But really, gentlemen, why are you getting angry again? I mean, really, we shan't ever be able to understand one another at all! After all, it turned out the way I predicted, didn't it? I'm now convinced with my own eyes that my guess was correct,' the flushed and excited prince tried to persuade them, anxious to calm the agitation and not noticing that he was merely making it greater.

'What? What are you convinced of?' they set about him, almost in a frenzy.

'Oh, for pity's sake, in the first place, I myself have had plenty of time to study Mr Burdovsky, I mean, I myself can see now what he is like . . . He's an innocent man, but one whom everyone deceives! A defenceless man . . . and that's why I must spare him, and in the second place, Gavrila Ardalionovich – to whom the matter was entrusted and from whom I haven't had any news for a long time, as I was travelling for three days and was then ill for three days in St Petersburg – now suddenly, only an hour ago, at our first meeting, told me that he had seen through all of Chebarov's intentions, had proof, and that Chebarov was exactly what I supposed him to be. I mean, I know, gentlemen, that many people consider me an idiot, and Chebarov, too, because of my reputation for easily parting with money, thought it would be very easy to deceive me, relying on my feelings for Pavlishchev. But the main thing – oh, hear me through, gentlemen, hear me through! – the main thing is that it now suddenly turns out that Mr Burdovsky is not Pavlishchev's son at all! Gavrila Ardalionovich has just told me that and assures me he has obtained positive proof. Well, what do you make of that, I mean, it's impossible to believe after all the fuss there's been! And listen: the proof is positive! I still don't believe it, don't believe it myself, I assure you; I still have doubts, because Gavrila Ardalionovich has not managed to tell me all the details, but that Chebarov is a scoundrel, of that there can now be no doubt! He has swindled the unfortunate Mr Burdovsky and all of you, gentlemen, who have come so nobly to support your friend (as he is obviously in need of support, I understand that, of course!), he has swindled you all and mixed you all up in a case of fraud, because that in essence is what it is, trickery and fraud!'

'What do you mean, fraud? . . . What do you mean: "not Pavlishchev's son"? . . . How is it possible? . . .' the exclamations resounded. Burdovsky's entire company was in a state of utter disarray.

'But of course it's fraud! I mean, if Mr Burdovsky now turns out not to be "Pavlishchev's son", then Mr Burdovsky's demand will be downright fraudulent (that is, of course, if he knows the truth!), but that's the whole point, that he's been deceived, and it's for that reason I insist that he be acquitted; it's for that reason I say that he deserves pity for his naivety, and must have support; otherwise he too will emerge from this case as a fraudster. Look, I myself am already convinced that he doesn't know anything! I myself was in such a condition before I left for Switzerland, also babbled incoherent words – one wants to express oneself, and can't . . . I understand that; I find it very easy to sympathize with that, because I'm almost the same, and so I can speak! And, in any case, all the same – in spite of the fact that there is no "Pavlishchev's son" now and all of this turns out to be a mystification – all the same I am not changing my decision, and am ready to return the ten thousand, in memory of Pavlishchev. You see, before Mr Burdovsky I wanted to spend that ten thousand on a school, in memory of Pavlishchev, but now it won't matter whether it goes on a school or to Mr Burdovsky, because Mr Burdovsky, though he isn't "Pavlishchev's son", is as good as "Pavlishchev's son": because he himself has been so cruelly deceived; he sincerely believed that he *was* Pavlishchev's son! So listen, gentlemen, to what Gavrila Ardalionovich has to say, let's finish this, don't be angry, don't get excited, sit down! In a moment Gavrila Ardalionovich will explain it all to us, and I confess that I myself am exceedingly eager to learn all the details. He says, Mr Burdovsky, that he even went to Pskov to see your mother, who had not died at all, as you were made to say in the article . . . Sit down, gentlemen, sit down!'

The prince sat down and again managed to make Mr Burdovsky's company, who had leaped up from their places, resume their seats. For the last ten or twenty minutes he had been talking with a flushed face, loudly, in an impatient patter, carried away, trying to talk or shout everyone else down, and afterwards, of course, had occasion bitterly to regret some of the phrases and sentences that broke from him now. If he had not been so exercised and almost brought to the point of losing his temper he would not have permitted himself to express aloud, so touchily and hurriedly, some of his conjectures and unneeded frank disclosures. But no sooner had he sat down on his chair than his heart was transfixed to the point of agony by a burning sense of remorse. In addition to having 'offended' Burdovsky, by so publicly assuming that he too suffered from the same illness for which he had been treated in Switzerland – in addition to that, his offer of ten thousand, instead of a school, had been made, in his opinion, rudely and insensitively, like a hand-out, especially as it had been made aloud in front of people. 'I should have waited and made the offer tomorrow alone with him,' the prince thought at once, 'but I don't think it can be put right now! Yes, I'm an idiot, a real idiot!' he decided to himself in a fit of shame and extreme vexation.

Meanwhile Gavrila Ardalionovich, who had hitherto kept to one side and maintained a stubborn silence, came forward at

the prince's invitation, stood beside him and began to give a
calm and clear account of the matter that had been entrusted to
him by the prince. All conversation fell silent instantly. Everyone
listened with extreme curiosity, especially all the members of
Burdovsky's company.

9

'You will not, of course, deny,' Gavrila Ardalionovich began,
directly addressing Burdovsky who was listening to him with all
his might, eyes bulging at him in astonishment, and obviously
in a state of intense dismay, 'you will not deny – nor, of course,
will you wish to – that you were born just two years after the
lawful marriage of your esteemed mother to collegiate secretary
Mr Burdovsky, your father. The time of your birth may very
easily be proved on a factual basis, so the distortion of that fact
in Mr Keller's article, so offensive to you and your mother,
can only be explained by the playfulness of Mr Keller's own
imagination, as he thought this would strengthen the self-
evident nature of your claim and thus aid your interests. Mr
Keller says that he read you the article beforehand, though not
in its entirety . . . without any doubt, he did not read as far as
that part . . .'

'That's true, I didn't,' the boxer interrupted, 'but all the facts
were given to me by a competent person, and I . . .'

'Excuse me, Mr Keller,' Gavrila Ardalionovich stopped him.
'Permit me to speak. I assure you that we shall come to your
article in its turn, and then you will make your explanation, but
now we had better continue in proper order. Quite by chance,
with the help of my sister, Varvara Ardalionovna Ptitsyna, I
have obtained from her intimate companion, Vera Alexeyevna
Zubkova, a landowner and a widow, a certain letter from the
late Nikolai Andreyevich Pavlishchev, which he wrote to her
from abroad twenty-four years ago. Having made the acquaintance of Vera Alexeyevna, I applied, on her instructions, to
the retired colonel Timofei Fyodorovich Vyazovkin, a distant

relative and at one time a great friend of Mr Pavlishchev's. From him I succeeded in obtaining two more letters from Nikolai Andreyevich, also written from abroad. From these three letters, from the dates and the facts mentioned in them, it is proven mathematically, without the slightest possibility of refutation or even doubt, that Nikolai Andreyevich then went abroad (where he stayed for three whole years) just one and a half years before you were born, Mr Burdovsky. Your mother, as you know, never left Russia . . . At this present moment I shall not read those letters. It's late now; at all events, I am merely stating a fact. But Mr Burdovsky, if you would like to make an appointment with me for tomorrow morning and to bring your witnesses (in any number you wish) and handwriting experts, I have no doubt that you will not fail to be convinced of the obvious truth of the fact I have related. If that is so then, of course, this entire case falls to the ground, and is ended of its own accord.'

There again ensued a universal stir and deep excitement. Burdovsky suddenly rose from his chair.

'If that is so, then I have been deceived, deceived, and not by Chebarov, but long, long ago; I don't want experts, I don't want an appointment, I believe you, I refuse . . . I won't accept the ten thousand . . . goodbye . . .'

He took his peaked cap and moved back his chair in order to leave.

'If you can, Mr Burdovsky,' Gavrila Ardalionovich stopped him quietly and sweetly, 'stay for another five minutes or so. A few more exceedingly important facts have come to light concerning this case; they affect you in particular, and are at any rate interesting. In my opinion, you cannot possibly ignore them, and perhaps you yourself will feel better if the matter is completely cleared up . . .'

Burdovsky sat down in silence, his head slightly lowered and as if in intense reflection. Lebedev's nephew, who had also risen to accompany him, sat down as well; though he had not lost his head or his boldness, it was clear that he was greatly puzzled. Ippolit was frowning, sad, and seemed very astonished. At that moment, however, he began to cough so violently that his handkerchief was stained with blood. The boxer looked almost afraid.

'Ech, Antip!' he cried bitterly. 'I mean, I told you at the time . . . the day before yesterday, that you may not be Pavlishchev's son!'

There was a burst of laughter, two or three laughing louder than the rest.

'The fact you stated just now, Mr Keller,' Gavrila Ardalionovich interjected, 'is most valuable. None the less, I am completely within my rights, on the most precise evidence, to assert that although Mr Burdovsky was very well aware of the date of his birth, he was not at all aware of the circumstance of this sojourn of Pavlishchev's abroad, where Mr Pavlishchev spent the greater part of his life, only returning to Russia for short periods. In addition, the very fact of his departure at that time is not at all so remarkable in itself that people would remember it after twenty or more years, even those who knew Pavlishchev well, not to mention Mr Burdovsky, who was not even born then. Of course, it proved not impossible to make inquiries now; but I must confess that the information I received came to me quite accidentally and might easily not have come to me at all; so that for Mr Burdovsky and even for Chebarov these inquiries would have really been almost impossible, even if they had thought of making them. But then again, they might not have . . .'

'Forgive me, Mr Ivolgin,' Ippolit suddenly interrupted him irritably, 'but what is all this rigmarole – if you'll forgive me – about? The case has now been explained, we agree to believe the main fact, so why drag out these painful and hurtful proceedings any further? Perhaps you want to boast of the skill of your investigations, show off to the prince and ourselves what a good investigator, what a good detective you are? Or do you plan to excuse and justify Burdovsky on the grounds that he became involved in the matter through ignorance? But that is insolent, dear sir! Burdovsky does not need your justifications and excuses, I think you ought to know! He feels hurt, he is suffering now as it is, he is in an awkward position, you ought to have guessed that, realized it . . .'

'That will do, Mr Terentyev, that will do,' Gavrila Ardalionovich managed to interrupt, 'please calm down, do not excite yourself; you are quite ill, I believe? I sympathize with you. In that case, if you wish, I have finished, that is, I shall be compelled to give but a brief account of the facts which, in my opinion, ought to be known in their entirety,' he added, having noticed a certain universal movement resembling impatience. 'I merely wish to state, with proof, for the information of all those who have an interest in the case, that your mother, Mr Burdovsky, enjoyed Pavlishchev's attention and concern for the sole reason that she was the sister of that serf-girl with whom, in his very earliest youth, Nikolai Andreyevich Pavlishchev was so much in love that he would certainly have married her, had she not died suddenly. I have proof that this domestic fact, wholly true and genuine, is very little known, and even quite forgotten. Furthermore, I could explain how your mother, while yet but a child ten years old, was taken by Mr Pavlishchev to be brought up in place of her sister, that she was allotted a considerable dowry and that all these concerns gave rise to some extremely alarming rumours among the numerous Pavlishchev clan; it was even thought that he would marry his protégée, but in the end she married, from inclination (and this I could prove in the most precise manner), an official from the Surveyor's Office, Mr Burdovsky, in the twentieth year of his age. Here I have gathered a few most precise facts, for proof, which show that your father, Mr Burdovsky, who was not a man of business at all, having received fifteen thousand as your mother's dowry, gave up his civil service post, entered commercial undertakings, was deceived, lost his capital, could not endure the sorrow, and began to drink, which made him ill and, at last, died prematurely, in the eighth year of his marriage to your mother. After that, according to your mother's own testimony, she remained in poverty and would have perished altogether had it not been for the constant and generous assistance of Pavlishchev, who paid her an allowance of up to six hundred roubles a year. Then there is a vast amount of evidence that he loved you greatly when you were a child. From this testimony, and again as confirmed by your mother, it appears that he loved you mainly because as a child you had an air of being tongue-tied, the air of a cripple, the air of a wretched, unhappy child (and Pavlishchev, as I deduced from exact proof, all his life had a special kind of tender disposition towards all that was oppressed and insulted by nature, especially in children – a fact, in my opinion, extremely important for our case.) Lastly, I can boast of the most precise investigations about that main fact, how that extreme devotion shown towards you by Pavlishchev (by whose efforts you entered the gymnasium and studied under special supervision) gave rise, at length, little by little, to the thought among Pavlishchev's relatives and family that you were his son and that your father was simply a deceived husband. But the main thing is that this thought strengthened into a definite and universal conviction only in the latter years of Pavlishchev's life, when everyone was alarmed about the will, and when the original facts had been forgotten, and inquiries were impossible. Without doubt, this thought reached you, also, Mr Burdovsky, and took possession of you entirely. Your mother, with whom I had the honour to be personally acquainted, though she knew about all these rumours, even to this day does not know (I also concealed it from her), that you, her son, were also under the spell of that rumour. Your much respected mother, Mr Burdovsky, I found in Pskov, ill and in the most extreme poverty, into which she had fallen after Pavlishchev's death. With tears of gratitude she told me that it was only through you and through your assistance that she was alive at all; she expects many things of you in the future and ardently believes in your future success . . .'

'This is really intolerable!' Lebedev's nephew suddenly declared loudly and impatiently. 'What's all this *roman* in aid of?'

'Disgusting and indecent!' Ippolit gave a violent movement. But Burdovsky did not notice anything and did not even move.

'What's it in aid of? What's the reason for it?' Gavrila Ardalionovich wondered slyly, venomously preparing to present his conclusion. 'Well, for one thing, Mr Burdovsky is now, perhaps, quite convinced that Mr Pavlishchev loved him out of magnanimity, and not as a son. This one fact needed to be known by Mr Burdovsky, who confirmed and approved Mr Keller's action just now, after the reading of the article. I say this because I consider you a decent man, Mr Burdovsky. For another thing, it turns out that there was not the slightest thievery or fraud on the part of Chebarov; that is an important point for me, too, because just now the prince, getting excited, mentioned that I was of the same opinion about the thievery and fraud in this unfortunate case. On the contrary, there was absolute conviction on all sides, and although Chebarov really was, perhaps, a major fraudster, in this affair he appears to have been no more than a pettifogger, a scrivener, a fixer. He hoped to earn big money as a lawyer, and his calculation was not only subtle and masterly, but most correct: he based himself on the ease with which the prince parted with money, and on his feeling of grateful veneration for the late Pavlishchev; he based himself, finally (and most importantly of all), on certain chivalrous views held by the prince concerning the obligations of honour and conscience. As regards Mr Burdovsky himself, one might even say that, thanks to certain convictions of his, so egged on by Chebarov and the gang that surrounded him was he that he began the affair almost not out of interest at all, but almost as a service to truth, progress and mankind. Now, after the facts that have been reported, it should be clear to everyone that Mr Burdovsky is a man of pure conduct, in spite of all appearances, and the prince can now more swiftly and more readily than before offer him both his friendly co-operation and that active assistance of which he spoke just now when he spoke of schools and Pavlishchev.'

'Stop, Gavrila Ardalionovich, stop!' cried the prince in genuine alarm, but by now it was too late.

'I've said it, I've said it three times,' cried Burdovsky irritably, 'that I don't want money. I won't accept it . . . why . . . I don't want . . . I'm going! . . .'

And he almost ran from the veranda. But Lebedev's nephew caught him by the arm and whispered something to him. Burdovsky quickly returned and, taking from his pocket a large, unsealed envelope, threw it on the table that stood next to the prince.

'Here's your money! . . . How dare you . . . how dare you! . . . Money!'

'The two hundred roubles you dared to send him through Chebarov in the form of a handout,' explained Doktorenko.

'In the article it says fifty!' cried Kolya.

'I am to blame!' said the prince, approaching Burdovsky. 'I am very much to blame in your regard, Burdovsky, but I did not send it as a handout, believe me. I am to blame even now . . . I was to blame just now. (The prince was very upset, looked tired and weak, and his words were incoherent.) I spoke of fraud . . . but that wasn't about you, I was wrong. I said that you . . . are like me – you're ill. But you're not like me, you . . . give lessons, you support your mother. I said that you had defamed your mother, but you love her; she says it herself . . . I didn't know . . . Gavrila Ardalionovich didn't manage to tell me earlier . . . I am to blame. I dared to offer you ten thousand, but I am to blame, I shouldn't have done it like that, but now . . . it's impossible, because you despise me . . .'

'Why, this is a madhouse!' exclaimed Lizaveta Prokofyevna.

'Of course, it's a lunatic asylum!' Aglaya said, unable to restrain herself, but her words were lost in the general commotion; everyone was talking loudly now, discussing, some were arguing, some were laughing. Ivan Fyodorovich Yepanchin was in the last stages of indignation, waiting for Lizaveta Prokofyevna with a look of affronted dignity. Lebedev's nephew interjected the last word:

'Yes, Prince, one must give you your due, you certainly know how to make good use of your . . . well, your illness (to put it politely); you've managed to offer your friendship and money in such a cunning way that it would now be impossible for a decent man to accept them under any circumstances. It's either very innocent or very cunning . . . but only you know which.'

'I say, gentlemen,' exclaimed Gavrila Ardalionovich, who had meanwhile opened the package of money. 'There are only a hundred roubles here, not two hundred and fifty. I merely point it out, Prince, so there should be no misunderstanding.'

'Never mind, never mind,' the prince waved his hand at Gavrila Ardalionovich.

'No, not "never mind"!' Lebedev's nephew pounced on this. 'We find your "never mind" insulting, Prince. We do not conceal, we declare openly; yes, there are only a hundred roubles here, not two hundred and fifty, but it's all the same, isn't it . . .'

'N-no, it's not all the same,' Gavrila Ardalionovich managed to insert with an air of naive bewilderment.

'Don't interrupt me; we are not such fools as you think, Mr Lawyer,' Lebedev's nephew exclaimed with vicious irritation. 'Of course, a hundred roubles is not two hundred and fifty roubles, and it's not all the same, but it's the principle that's important; here what matters is the principle, and the fact that a hundred and fifty roubles are missing is only a detail. What's important is that Burdovsky does not accept your handout, your excellency, that he throws it in your face, and in that sense it's all the same whether it's a hundred or two hundred and fifty. Burdovsky has not accepted the ten thousand; you saw that; he wouldn't have brought the hundred roubles if he were dishonest! That hundred and fifty roubles were spent on Chebarov's expenses for his journey to see the prince. Laugh if you will at our clumsiness, at our inability to do business; you have tried with all your might to make us look ridiculous as it is; but do not dare to say that we are dishonest. My dear sir, we shall pay back that hundred and fifty roubles to the prince between us; we shall return it a rouble at a time, and return it with interest. Burdovsky is poor, Burdovsky has no millions, but Chebarov presented his bill after the journey. We had hoped to win . . . Who would have acted differently in his place?'

'Who indeed?' exclaimed Prince Shch.

'I shall go mad in here!' cried Lizaveta Prokofyevna.

'This puts me in mind,' laughed Yevgeny Pavlovich, who had stood watching for a long time now, 'of the recent famous defence of the lawyer who, pleading as an excuse the poverty of his client, who had murdered six people in one fell swoop,[1] in order to rob them, suddenly concluded his speech in the following vein: "It's natural," he said, "that it occurred to my client, being so poor, to commit this murder of six people, and indeed is there anyone in his shoes to whom it would not have occurred?" Something in that vein, only very amusing.'

'Enough!' Lizaveta Prokofyevna trumpeted suddenly, almost

quivering with wrath. 'It's time to bring this rigmarole to an end! . . .'

She was in the most dreadful agitation, she threw her head back menacingly and with a haughty, passionate and impatient challenge passed her flashing gaze over the whole company, at that moment not really distinguishing friends from enemies. This was that point of long suppressed but finally exploding anger when the central impulse becomes imminent battle, the imminent need to hurl oneself on someone as soon as possible. Those who knew Lizaveta Prokofyevna at once sensed that something extraordinary had happened to her. Ivan Fyodorovich told Prince Shch. the following day that 'she has turns like that, but even with her it seldom reaches the degree it did last night, once in about three years, but no more often than that! No more often than that!' he added, with an air of instruction.

'Enough, Ivan Fyodorovich! Leave me alone!' Lizaveta Proko-fyevna exclaimed. 'Why do you offer me your arm now? You didn't have the wit to take me away earlier; you're a husband, you're the head of the household; you should have taken me out by the ear, silly woman that I am, if I didn't obey you and leave. You might at least have shown some concern for your daughters! But now we shall find our way without you, there's enough shame here to last a whole twelve months . . . Wait, I also want to thank the prince! . . . Thank you, Prince, for the entertain-ment! And there was I sitting back to listen to the young men . . . It is baseness, baseness! It is chaos, outrage, one could not even dream of such things! And are there really many like those young men? . . . Be quiet, Aglaya! Be quiet, Alexandra! It has nothing to do with you! . . . Stop hovering about me, Yevgeny Pavlych, I'm tired of you! . . . So you're asking their forgiveness, my dear,' she caught up again, addressing herself to the prince, '"I'm to blame," you say, "for offering you money". . . and what are you laughing at, you wretched braggart?' she hurled herself suddenly on Lebedev's nephew, '"We refuse your money," you say, "we demand, we don't ask!" As though he didn't know that this idiot will go trailing to them tomorrow to offer them his friendship and money! You'll go to them, won't you? Will you or won't you?'

'I will,' the prince said in a quiet and submissive voice.

'You hear? I mean, that's what you're counting on, isn't it?' she turned to Doktorenko again. 'After all, the money's already more or less in your pocket, and you're boasting and bragging in order to throw dust in our eyes . . . No, my dear fellow, find some other fools, for I can see right through you . . . I see your game in its entirety!'

'Lizaveta Prokofyevna!' the prince exclaimed.

'Let us leave here, Lizaveta Prokofyevna, it's high time, and let us take the prince with us,' said Prince Shch., as calmly as he could, and smiling.

The girls stood to one side, almost frightened, while the general was frightened in good earnest; everyone was in a state of astonishment. Some, who stood further away, were furtively grinning and exchanging whispers; Lebedev's face displayed the last stages of ecstasy.

'You will find outrage and chaos everywhere, *madame*,' Lebedev's nephew said, though he was considerably perplexed.

'But not like this! Not like this, sir, as with you now, not like this!' Lizaveta Prokofyevna interjected gleefully, almost in hysteria. 'But will you leave me alone?' she began to shout at those who were trying to persuade her. 'No, if even you, Yevgeny Pavlych, could say just now that even the defence counsel at the trial declared that there's nothing more natural than to murder six people because of one's poverty, then the last days of mankind have come, and there's an end of it. I've never heard anything like it. Now it's all been explained to me! And this tongue-tied fellow, wouldn't he cut someone's throat (she pointed to Burdovsky, who was looking at her in extreme bewilderment)? Why, I bet he would! He may not take your money, the ten thousand, won't take it out of conscience, but he'll come at night and cut your throat, and take the money from your safe. He'll take it out of conscience! He doesn't think that's dishonourable! It's an "impulse of noble despair", it's a "negation", or the devil knows what . . . Fie! It's all topsy-turvy, they're in walking upside down land. A girl grows up in a house, suddenly in the middle of the street she jumps into a droshky: "Mama, I just got married to some Karlych or Ivanych or other,

farewell!"² Do you think that's a good way to behave? Worthy
of respect, natural? The woman question? This urchin here' (she
pointed to Kolya), 'he too was arguing the other day that this is
what the "woman question" means. Even if the mother is a fool,
you should still treat her like a human being! . . . Why did you
come in here with your noses in the air just now? "Don't dare
to come near us": we're coming in. "Give us all our rights, but
don't dare even to stammer in front of us. Give us every mark
of respect, even marks that have never been heard of, but we'll
treat you worse than the lowest lackey!" They seek the truth,
stand on their rights, but in their article they slandered him like
infidels. "We demand, we don't ask, and you won't hear any
gratitude from us, because you're doing it in order to placate
your own conscience!" What a morality: after all, if there's not
going to be any gratitude from you, the prince can tell you in
reply that he doesn't feel any gratitude towards Pavlishchev,
because Pavlishchev also did good in order to placate his own
conscience. And yet his gratitude to Pavlishchev was what you
were relying on, wasn't it? I mean, it wasn't from you that he
borrowed money, he wasn't in debt to you, so what were you
relying on if it wasn't his gratitude? How can you refuse it
yourself, then? You're madmen! They call society savage and
inhuman because it shames a girl who's been seduced. But if
you call society inhuman, you must admit that the girl suffers
at the hands of that society. And if she suffers at its hands, then
how can you drag her into the newspapers in front of that
society and demand that she should not suffer? Madmen! Conceited! They don't believe in God, they don't believe in Christ!
Why, you're so eaten up with vanity and pride that you'll end
by eating one another, I predict that to you. And isn't that
confusion, and chaos, and an outrage? And after that, as if it
weren't enough, this shameless man crawls to beg their forgiveness! Are there many like you? What are you grinning at? That
I've brought shame on myself by talking to you? Well, if I have,
I have, there's nothing to be done about it! . . . And you can
stop grinning at me, scallywag!' (she suddenly hurled at Ippolit).
'He can scarcely draw breath, yet he corrupts others. You've
corrupted that urchin of mine' (she again pointed to Kolya); 'all

he can do is rave about you, you're teaching him atheism, you don't believe in God, but you can still be given a thrashing, dear sir, and fie upon you! . . . So you're going to see them tomorrow, Prince Lev Nikolayevich, are you?' she asked the prince again, almost panting.

'I am.'

'Then I don't want to know you any more!' She was about to quickly turn and go, but suddenly came back again. 'And you're going to see this atheist, too?' she pointed to Ippolit. 'But why are you grinning at me?' she exclaimed somehow unnaturally and suddenly rushed up to Ippolit, unable to endure his sarcastic grin.

'Lizaveta Prokofyevna! Lizaveta Prokofyevna! Lizaveta Prokofyevna!' was heard at once from every side.

'*Maman*, this is shameful!' Aglaya shouted loudly.

'Don't worry, Aglaya Ivanovna,' replied Ippolit, whom Lizaveta Prokofyevna, darting over to him, had seized and for some unknown reason was firmly holding by the arm; she stood in front of him, seeming to bore into him with her frenzied gaze, 'don't worry, your *maman* will see that it's not done to attack a dying man . . . I'm ready to explain why I was laughing . . . I shall be very glad of your permission . . .'

Here he suddenly began to cough and could not stop coughing for a whole minute.

'I mean, he's really dying, yet he keeps on making speeches!' exclaimed Lizaveta Prokofyevna, releasing his arm and watching almost with horror as he wiped the blood from his lips. 'But what are you talking for? You simply must go to bed . . .'

'So it shall be,' Ippolit replied quietly, hoarsely and almost in a whisper. 'As soon as I get home today I shall go to bed . . . in two weeks' time, as I know, I shall die . . . B—n himself[3] told me last week . . . So if you will permit me, I would like to say a few words to you in farewell.'

'But have you gone mad, or what? Nonsense! You must have treatment, now is no time for talking! Go, go, go to bed! . . .' Lizaveta Prokofyvna cried in alarm.

'If I go to bed, then I won't get up again until I'm dead,' smiled Ippolit. 'I wanted to lie down yesterday, and not get up until I'm dead, but decided to put it off until the day after tomorrow, while my legs still carry me . . . so I could come here on them today . . . only I'm very tired . . .'

'But sit down, sit down, why are you standing? Here's a chair for you,' Lizaveta Ivanovna jumped up and brought a chair for him herself.

'Thank you,' Ippolit continued quietly, 'and you sit down opposite me, and we shall have a talk . . . we must have a talk, Lizaveta Prokofyevna, I insist on that now . . .' he smiled to her again. 'Just think, today is the last time I shall be out in the fresh air and among people, for in two weeks' time I shall certainly be in the earth. That means that this will be a kind of farewell to people and nature. Though I'm not very sentimental, imagine, I'm very glad that this has all come to pass here in Pavlovsk: one can at least look at a tree in leaf.'

'But this is no time for talk,' Lizaveta Prokofyevna grew more and more alarmed, 'you're all in a fever. Just now you were squeaking and squealing, and now you can hardly draw breath, you're choking!'

'I shall be better in a moment. Why do you want to deny me my last wish? . . . But you know, I have long dreamed of somehow meeting you, Lizaveta Prokofyevna; I have heard a lot about you . . . from Kolya; I mean, he's almost the only person who does not leave my side . . . You're an original woman, an eccentric woman, I have seen that for myself now . . . you know, I think I even fell in love with you a little.'

'Merciful Lord, and I really was just about to hit him.'

'Aglaya Ivanovna stopped you; I'm not wrong, am I? That's your daughter, Aglaya Ivanovna? She is so pretty that I guessed who she was at first sight, though I had never seen her before. At least let me look at a beautiful woman for the last time in my life,' Ippolit smiled with a kind of awkward, crooked smile. 'The prince is here, and your husband, and the whole company. Why do you deny me my last wish?'

'A chair!' cried Lizaveta Prokofyevna, but seized one herself and sat down facing Ippolit. 'Kolya,' she ordered, 'go with him right now, accompany him, and tomorrow I shall certainly come myself . . .'

'If you will permit it, then I should like to ask the prince for
a cup of tea ... I am very tired. You know what, Lizaveta
Prokofyevna, I think you were going to take the prince home
with you to drink tea, but stay here, let's spend the time together,
and I'm sure the prince will give us all tea. Forgive me for
ordering you around like this ... But I mean, I know you, you
are kind, the prince, too ... we are all the most kind people, to
the point of comic absurdity.'

The prince was startled, Lebedev rushed from the room as
fast as his legs would carry him, Vera ran after him.

'It's true,' the general's wife decided, sharply. 'Talk, only
quietly, and don't get carried away. You've moved me to pity
... Prince! You are not worthy to have me drink tea with you,
but so let it be, I shall stay, though I ask forgiveness of no one!
No one! Nonsense! ... However, if I scolded you, Prince, forgive
me – if, that is, you want to. However, I'm not detaining anyone,'
she suddenly addressed her husband and daughters with a look
of extraordinary anger, as though it were they who were dreadfully guilty of something in her regard. 'I can get home on my
own ...'

But they did not let her finish. They all came up and gathered
round her readily. The prince at once began to implore everyone
to stay and have tea, and apologized for not having thought of
this before now. Even the general was polite enough to mutter
something reassuring, and politely asked Lizaveta Prokofyevna
whether she was not too cold on the veranda. He even nearly
asked Ippolit how long he had been at the university, but did not.
Yevgeny Pavlych and Prince Shch. suddenly became extremely
polite and cheerful, the faces of Adelaida and Alexandra even
expressed pleasure through their continuing astonishment, in a
word, everyone was visibly pleased that the crisis with Lizaveta
Prokofyevna was over. Aglaya alone frowned and sat down in
silence, at a distance. All the rest of the company stayed too; no
one wanted to leave, not even General Ivolgin, to whom
Lebedev, however, whispered something in passing, probably
something not very pleasant, because the general at once retired
into a corner. The prince also went up to Burdovsky and company with an invitation, leaving no one out. They muttered

with a stiff look that they would wait for Ippolit, and at once withdrew to the very furthest corner of the veranda, where they all again sat down side by side. Lebedev had probably had the tea made long ago for himself, for it appeared immediately. It struck eleven o'clock.

10

Ippolit moistened his lips with the cup of tea handed to him by Vera Lebedeva, placed the cup on the little table and suddenly, as though he had begun to lose his nerve, looked around him almost in embarrassment.

'Look, Lizaveta Prokofyevna, these cups,' he said quickly in a strange patter, 'these porcelain cups, excellent porcelain, too, I think, Lebedev always keeps them in the chiffonier under glass, locked up; they're never used . . . that's the family custom, they were part of his wife's dowry . . . it's the family custom . . . and now he's used them for us, in your honour, of course, he was so pleased . . .'

He was about to add something else, but could not find the right words.

'Lost his nerve, I knew he would!' Yevgeny Pavlovich suddenly whispered in the prince's ear. 'Dangerous, don't you think? The surest sign that now, out of spite, he'll throw some eccentric tantrum so extreme that Lizaveta Prokofyevna probably won't be able to tolerate it.'

The prince gave him an inquiring look.

'You're not afraid of eccentricity?' added Yevgeny Pavlovich. 'Well, neither am I, I would even like it; all I want is for our dear Lizaveta Prokofyevna to be punished, and that it should be this evening, without fail; I don't want to leave until it's happened. You look as though you have a fever.'

'Later, don't agitate me. Yes, I'm not well,' the prince replied absent-mindedly and even impatiently. He had heard his name; Ippolit was talking about him.

'You don't believe it?' Ippolit laughed hysterically. 'I suppose that's bound to be so, but the prince will believe it at once, and won't be surprised at all.'

'You hear, Prince?' Lizaveta Prokofyevna turned round to him. 'You hear?'

There was laughter all round. Lebedev was busily showing off and hovering around Lizaveta Prokofyevna.

'He says that this poseur, your landlord ... corrected that gentleman's article, the article about you that was read just now.'

The prince gave Lebedev a look of surprise.

'Why don't you say anything?' Lizaveta Prokofyevna even stamped her foot.

'Well,' muttered the prince, continuing to study Lebedev. 'I can see now that he did correct it.'

'Is it true?' Lizaveta Prokofyevna quickly turned round to face Lebedev.

'It's the honest truth, your excellency!' Lebedev replied firmly and unshakably, putting his hand to his heart.

'It's as if he were boasting about it!' she nearly leaped up from her chair.

'I'm vile, vile!' Lebedev began to mutter, starting to beat his breast and inclining his head lower and lower.

'Oh, what do I care that you're vile! He thinks that if he says "vile" he'll get out of it. And aren't you ashamed, Prince, to associate with such wretched people, I ask you again? I shall never forgive you!'

'The prince will forgive me!' Lebedev said with conviction and tender emotion.

'Solely out of generosity,' came the sudden loud and resonant voice of Keller, who had jumped up and was addressing Lizaveta Prokofyevna directly, 'solely out of generosity and so as not to betray a compromised friend, I said nothing just now about the corrections, in spite of the fact that he proposed to kick us downstairs, as you yourself heard. In order to establish the truth, I admit that I really did turn to him, for six roubles, but not in any way for the style, but in order to learn facts that were mostly unknown to me, and because he's a competent person. About the gaiters, about the appetite at the Swiss professor's, about the fifty roubles instead of two hundred and fifty, about that entire grouping, in short: it's all his, for six roubles, but he didn't correct the style.'

'I'm bound to observe,' Lebedev interrupted him with feverish impatience and in a kind of grovelling voice, to the accompaniment of increasingly rising laughter, 'that I only corrected the first half of the article, but since when we got to the middle we didn't agree and quarrelled over a certain idea, I didn't correct the second half, ma'am, so anything that's illiterate there (and there's much that is!) cannot be ascribed to myself, ma'am . . .'

'That's all he cares about!' exclaimed Lizaveta Prokofyevna.

'Permit me to inquire,' Yevgeny Pavlovich turned to Keller, 'when the article was corrected?'

'Yesterday morning,' Keller reported. 'We had a meeting, with a promise on our word of honour to keep it a secret on both sides.'

'That was when he grovelled in front of you and assured you of his devotion! Oh, wretched people! I don't want your Pushkin, and I don't want your daughter to come visiting me!'

Lizaveta Prokofyevna was about to get up, but suddenly addressed the laughing Ippolit in irritation:

'Really, my dear fellow, was it your idea to hold me up to ridicule?'

'God forbid,' Ippolit smiled crookedly, 'but what strikes me most of all is your extreme eccentricity, Lizaveta Prokofyevna; I confess that I brought up the subject of Lebedev deliberately, I knew it would make an impression on you, on you alone, because the prince really would forgive you and has probably already forgiven you . . . has even, perhaps, found an excuse for him in his mind, that's so, Prince, isn't it?'

He was gasping for breath, and his terrible agitation was growing with each word.

'Well? . . .' Lizaveta Prokofyevna said angrily, astonished at his tone. 'Well?'

'I have already heard much about you, in this same vein . . . with much gladness . . . and have learned to respect you exceedingly,' Ippolit continued.

He said one thing, but it was as though with these words he

THE IDIOT

wanted to say quite another. He spoke with a tinge of mockery and was at the same time disproportionately agitated, looking around him suspiciously, visibly confused and lost at every word, and all this, together with his consumptive look and strange, glittering and almost frenzied gaze, continued to attract involuntary attention to him.

'It would have quite surprised me, however, as I don't know the ways of society (I admit that), that you not only remained with our company just now, something not proper for you, but that you also left these ... girls to hear the whole scandalous business, though they have already read it all in novels. Perhaps, however, I don't know ... because I am muddled, but at any rate who, but you, could remain ... at the request of a boy (yes, a boy, I again admit) to spend the evening with him and take part ... in everything and ... so that the next day you felt ashamed ... (though actually I agree that I'm not expressing myself well), I praise all that exceedingly, and I deeply respect it, though from the look on the face of his excellency, your husband, alone I can see how unpleasant he finds it all ... He-he!' he began to giggle, quite confused, and all of a sudden began to cough so violently that it was some two minutes before he could continue.

'He's even choked himself!' Lizaveta Prokofyevna said coldly and sharply, studying him with stern curiosity. 'Well, my dear boy, that's enough from you. It's time!'

'Permit me also, for my part, to observe to you, dear sir,' Ivan Fyodorovich said suddenly in irritation, having lost the last of his patience, 'that my wife is here as a guest of Lev Nikolayevich, our common friend and neighbour, and that in any case it is not for you, young man, to make judgements about the actions of Lizaveta Prokofyevna, nor to make loud pronouncements to my face about what is written on it. No, sir. And if my wife has remained here,' he continued, growing more and more irritated almost with every word, 'it was more, good sir, from astonishment and the modern interest, which everyone will understand, in such strange young people. I too remained, just as occasionally I stop in the street when I see something that may be viewed as ... as ... as ...'

'As a curiosity,' prompted Yevgeny Ivanovich.

'Excellently put, and correct,' said his excellency in relief, having become somewhat bogged down in his comparison, 'precisely: as a curiosity. But at any rate, what is most astonishing and even vexing to me, if it is grammatical so to express oneself, is that you, young man, were not even able to grasp that Lizaveta Prokofyevna has remained with you now because you are ill – if you really are dying, that's to say – so to speak, out of compassion, because of your piteous words, good sir, and that no mud can importune her name, qualities and importance in any way . . . Lizaveta Prokofyevna!' the flushed general concluded, 'if you want to go, then let us say farewell to our kind prince and . . .'

'I thank you for the lesson, general,' Ippolit interrupted seriously and unexpectedly, looking at him reflectively.

'Let us go, *Maman*, how much longer is this to continue? . . .' Aglaya said impatiently and angrily, getting up from her chair.

'Another two minutes, dear Ivan Fyodorovich, if you please,' Lizaveta Prokofyevna turned round to face her husband with dignity. 'I think he's altogether in a fever, and is simply raving; I'm convinced of that by his eyes; we can't leave him like that. Lev Nikolayevich! Could he spend the night here with you, so that he doesn't have to drag himself to St Petersburg tonight? *Cher Prince*, are you bored?' she suddenly addressed Prince Shch. for some reason. 'Come here, Alexandra, straighten your hair, my dear.'

She straightened her hair, which did not need straightening, and gave her a kiss; that was the only reason she had summoned her.

'I believed you were capable of development . . .' Ippolit began again, emerging from his reflection. 'Yes! That's what I wanted to say,' he said in relief, as though suddenly remembering: 'Burdovsky genuinely wants to protect his mother, doesn't he? But it turns out that he's disgraced her. The prince wants to help Burdovsky, is offering him his tender friendship and capital and is perhaps alone among you all in feeling no revulsion towards him, and yet here they are facing each other like real enemies . . . Ha-ha-ha! You all hate Burdovsky because, in your opinion, he has an unpleasant and graceless attitude towards his mother, that's true, isn't it? Isn't it? Isn't it? I mean, you're all dreadfully fond of the beauty and elegance of social manners, they're all you live for, aren't they? (I suspected that long ago!) Well, let me tell you then that probably not one of you has loved his mother as Burdovsky has! I know that you, Prince, sent money on the sly, via Ganya, to Burdovsky's mother, and I bet (he-he-he! he laughed hysterically), I bet that Burdovsky will now accuse you of lack of tactful manners and of disrespect for his mother, by God, I bet you, ha-ha-ha!'

Here he choked again, and began to cough.

'Well, is that all? Is that all now, have you said it all? Well, now go to bed, you have a fever,' Lizaveta Prokofyevna broke in impatiently, not taking her restless gaze off him. 'Oh, merciful Lord! He's still talking!'

'I think you're laughing, aren't you? Why are you all laughing at me? I've noticed that you're constantly laughing at me,' he suddenly addressed Yevgeny Pavlovich anxiously and irritably; the latter really was laughing.

'I merely wanted to ask you, Mr . . . Ippolit . . . forgive me, I've forgotten your surname.'

'Mr Terentyev,' said the prince.

'Yes, Terentyev, thank you, Prince, they told me earlier, but it slipped my mind . . . I wanted to ask you, Mr Terentyev, if it's true what I heard, that you believe you need only talk out of the window to the common folk for a quarter of an hour and they will instantly agree with you in everything and instantly follow you?'

'It may very well be that I said that . . .' replied Ippolit, as though remembering something. 'Yes, I certainly did!' he added suddenly, growing animated again and giving Yevgeny Pavlovich a firm look. 'But what of it?'

'Nothing at all; I merely asked in order to be informed, for the sake of completeness.'

Yevgeny Pavlovich fell silent, but Ippolit still looked at him in impatient expectation.

'Well, have you finished, then?' Lizaveta Prokofyevna

addressed Yevgeny Pavlovich. 'Hurry up and finish, sir, it's time he went to bed. Or do you not know how?' (She was in a dreadful state of vexation.)

'I must admit that I wouldn't mind adding,' Yevgeny Pavlovich continued, with a smile, 'that all I have heard from your companions, Mr Terentyev, and all you have expounded just now, and with such indubitable talent, comes down, in my opinion, to a theory of the triumph of right, over everything else and in spite of everything else, and even to the exclusion of everything else, and even, perhaps, before the analysis of what that right consists in. Perhaps I'm mistaken?'

'Of course you're mistaken, I don't even understand what you mean . . . go on.'

There was also a murmur of protest from the corner. Lebedev's nephew muttered something in an undertone.

'There's not really much more to go on with,' Yevgeny Pavlovich continued. 'I merely wished to observe that it's a short hop from there to the concept of might is right, that is, to the right of the individual fist and the individual will, as it has often turned out in the way of the world – as a matter of fact, Proudhon[1] was in favour of the principle of might is right. In the American War[2] many of the foremost liberals came out in support of the plantation owners, on the grounds that the Negroes were Negroes, inferior to the white race, and so the principle of might is right favoured the whites . . .'

'Well?'

'So, in other words, you don't deny that might is right?'

'Go on.'

'You certainly are consistent, I'll say that; I merely wished to observe that from the principle of might is right it's a short step to the right of tigers and crocodiles, and even to the right of a Danilov or a Gorsky.'

'I don't know about that; but go on.'

Ippolit was hardly listening to Yevgeny Pavlovich, to whom he seemed to be saying "well" and "go on" more from an old acquired habit in conversation than from any particular attention or curiosity.

'There's nothing more . . . that's all.'

'Actually, I'm not angry with you,' Ippolit suddenly concluded quite unexpectedly and, not really fully conscious of what he was doing, extended his hand, even with a smile. Yevgeny Pavlovich was at first astonished, but touched the hand extended to him with a most serious look, as though he were receiving forgiveness.

'I cannot help adding,' he said in the same ambiguously respectful tone, 'my gratitude to you for the consideration with which you have allowed me to speak, because, as I have seen from my numerous observations, our liberals are never able to allow anyone else to have their own opinion without replying at once to their opponents' abuse, or even worse . . .'

'That's absolutely true,' observed the general, Ivan Fyodorovich, and, putting his hands behind his back, with a look of the utmost boredom retreated to the exit from the veranda, where he yawned with vexation.

'Well, that's enough from you, sir,' Lizaveta Prokofyevna suddenly announced to Yevgeny Pavlovich. 'I'm fed up with you all . . .'

'It's time to go.' Ippolit suddenly got to his feet looking anxious and almost in alarm, gazing around him perplexedly. 'I've detained you; I wanted to tell you everything . . . I thought that everyone . . . for the last time . . . it was a fantasy . . .'

It was clear that he was returning to life in bursts, suddenly, for a few moments, emerging from something that was almost a state of delirium, suddenly remembering and speaking with full consciousness, for the most part in fragments, phrases that he had invented and learned by heart, perhaps, during the long, dreary hours of his illness, on his bed, in his solitude and insomnia.

'Well, goodbye!' he suddenly said, sharply. 'Do you think it's easy for me to say "goodbye" to you? Ha-ha!' he laughed with vexed irony at his own 'awkward' question and suddenly, as though in a fit of anger that he was not going to be able to say what he wanted to, said loudly and irritably: 'Your excellency! I have the honour of inviting you to my funeral, if you will do me such an honour, and . . . all of you, ladies and gentlemen, after the general! . . .'

He began to laugh again; but now it was the laughter of a madman. Lizaveta Prokofyevna moved towards him in alarm, and caught him by the arm. He looked at her fixedly, with the same laugh, which did not, however, continue but seemed to halt and freeze on his face.

'Do you know that I came here to see the trees? Those ones, there . . .' (He pointed to the trees in the park.) 'That's not ridiculous, is it? I mean, there's nothing ridiculous about it?' he asked Lizaveta Prokofyevna seriously, and suddenly began to reflect; then, a moment later, raised his head and began to search the crowd with interest. He was looking for Yevgeny Pavlovich, who was standing not very far away, to the right, in the same place as before – but now he had forgotten this and kept searching around. 'Ah, you're still here!' he found him, at last. 'You kept laughing just now about my wanting to speak out of a window for a quarter of an hour . . . But you know, I'm not eighteen: I've lain on that pillow so long, and have looked out of that window so long, and have thought so much . . . about everyone . . . that . . . A dead man has no age, you know. I thought about that only last week when I woke up one night . . . And do you know what you're afraid of most of all? It's our sincerity you're most afraid of, even though you despise us! That's another thing I thought as I lay on my pillow that night . . . Do you think I wanted to laugh at you just now, Lizaveta Prokofyevna? No, I wasn't laughing at you, I simply wanted to give you some praise . . . Kolya said that the prince called you a child . . . that's good . . . Yes, what was it . . . there was something else I was going to . . .'

He covered his face with his hands and fell into reflection.

'That's it: as you were saying goodnight just now, I suddenly thought: here are these people, and they will never exist any more, never! And the trees, too – there will only be a brick wall, the red one, Meyer's house . . . opposite my window . . . well, and tell them about all that . . . go on, try and tell them; here's a beautiful girl . . . I mean, you're dead, introduce yourself as a corpse, say that "a corpse can say anything" . . . and that Princess Marya Alexevna won't scold,[3] ha-ha! You're not laughing?' he looked at them all suspiciously. 'But you know, a lot of thoughts came to me on that pillow . . . you know, I've become convinced that nature is very given to mocking . . . You said just now that I'm an atheist, but you know that this nature . . . Why are you laughing again? You're terribly cruel!' he said suddenly with sad indignation, looking round at them all. 'I've not been corrupting Kolya,' he concluded in a completely different tone, serious and with conviction, as though he had suddenly also remembered this.

'No one, no one here is laughing at you, calm yourself!' Lizaveta Prokofyevna was almost in torment. 'Tomorrow a new doctor will arrive; the other one was wrong; but sit down, you can hardly stand! You're delirious . . . Oh, what are we going to do with him now!' she fussed, sitting him down in the arm-chair. A teardrop gleamed on her cheek.

Ippolit stopped, as if in shock, raised his hand, timidly reached out and touched this teardrop. He smiled a sort of childish smile.

'I . . . you . . .' he began joyfully, 'you don't know how I . . . how he always spoke of you in such rapture, Kolya there . . . I love his rapture. I have not been corrupting him! I am only leaving him . . . I wanted to leave everyone, everyone – but there was no one, no one . . . I wanted to be a man of public action, I had the right . . . Oh, how many things I wanted! I don't want anything now, I don't want to want anything, I promised myself I wouldn't want anything any more; let them, let them seek the truth without me! Yes, nature is given to mocking! Why does she,' he suddenly caught up heatedly, 'why does she create the very finest beings just in order to mock them? Was it she who made it so that the only being who was acknowledged on earth for his perfection . . . was it she who made it so that, having shown him to people, she destined him to say things on account of which so much blood was shed that if it were shed all at once people would probably have drowned in it? Oh, it's good that I am dying! I would also probably have uttered some horrible lie, nature would have betrayed me like that! . . . I haven't been corrupting anyone . . . I wanted to live for the happiness of all people, for the revelation and the proclamation of the truth . . . I looked out of the window at Meyer's wall and thought of speaking for only a quarter of an hour, and convincing everyone,

everyone, and for once in my life I've met . . . you, if not the people! And what has come of it? Nothing! What's come of it is that you despise me! That means I'm superfluous, that means I'm a fool, that means it's time I went! And I haven't been able to leave one single memory behind! Not a sound, not a trace, not a single deed, I haven't spread a single conviction![4] . . . Don't laugh at a stupid fool! Forget him! Forget it all . . . forget it, please don't be so cruel! Do you know, if this consumption hadn't happened along, I'd have killed myself . . .'

It seemed that there was much he still wanted to say, but he did not finish, flung himself into his armchair, covered his face with his hands and began to weep like a little child.

'Well, now what are we supposed to do with him?' exclaimed Lizaveta Prokofyevna, leaped over to him, seized his head and pressed it hard as hard could be against her bosom. He was sobbing convulsively. 'There, there, there! There, don't cry, there, enough, you're a good boy, God will forgive you, because of your ignorance; there, that's enough, be a man . . . What's more, you'll feel ashamed . . .'

'Back there at home,' said Ippolit, making an effort to raise his head, 'I have a brother and sisters, children, young, poor, innocent . . . *She* will corrupt them! You are a saint, you . . . yourself are a child – save them! Tear them away from that woman . . . she . . . shame . . . Oh, help them, help them, God will reward you a hundredfold, in the name of God, in the name of Christ! . . .'

'Well, Ivan Fyodorovich, tell me what I'm to do now!' Lizaveta Prokofyevna exclaimed irritably. 'Please be so good as to break your majestic silence! If you don't decide, then I think you ought to know that I shall stay the night here, you've tyrannized me long enough with your autocracy!'

Lizaveta Prokofyevna asked the question with feeling and anger, and expected an immediate reply. In such circumstances, however, those present, even if there are many of them, usually respond with silence and passive curiosity, reluctant to commit themselves, and only express their thoughts long afterwards. Among those present were also some who were ready to sit there until morning, if necessary, without saying a word, like

Varvara Ardalionovna, for example, who had been sitting all evening at a slight distance, listening all the while with intense interest, perhaps having reasons for this.

'My opinion, my dear,' said the general, 'is that what we need now, so to speak, is a sick-nurse rather than all this agitation, and, perhaps, a reliable, sober person for the night. At any rate, we must ask the prince and . . . give him some peace without delay. Then tomorrow we may examine the matter again.'

'It's twelve o'clock now, and we're leaving. Is he coming with us, or is he staying with you?' Doktorenko addressed the prince irritably and angrily.

'If you like, you can stay with him, too,' said the prince. 'There's room.'

'Your excellency,' Mr Keller darted up to the general unexpectedly and enthusiastically, 'if a reliable person is required for the night, I'm ready to make a sacrifice for a friend . . . he's such a wonderful fellow! I have long considered him a great man, your excellency! It's true that I've neglected my education, but if he criticizes me, it's as though pearls, pearls were scattered, your excellency! . . .'

The general turned away in despair.

'I'll be very glad if he stays. Of course, it's difficult for him to travel,' the prince declared in response to Lizaveta Prokofyevna's irritable questions.

'You're not asleep, are you? I mean, if you don't want him here, sir, I'll take him home with me! Merciful Lord, why, he can hardly stand on his feet! What's wrong, are you feeling ill?'

That evening, not finding the prince on his deathbed, Lizaveta Prokofyevna really had much exaggerated the satisfactory condition of his health, judging by his external appearance, but the recent illness, the painful memories that had accompanied it, the tiredness caused by the busy evening, the incident with 'Pavlishchev's son', the incident now with Ippolit – all this had really excited the prince's morbid impressionability almost to the point of fever. But, what was more, in his eyes there was now another worry, a fear, even; he stared at Ippolit warily, as though he expected something further from him.

Suddenly Ippolit got up, horribly pale and with a look of

terrible shame, amounting to despair, on his contorted face. This was mainly expressed in his eyes, which stared at the gathering with fear and hatred, and in the forlorn, crooked and abject smile on his trembling lips. He lowered his gaze at once, and dragged himself, staggering and still smiling as before, over to Burdovsky and Doktorenko, who were standing by the exit from the veranda: he was going with them.

'Well, this is what I was afraid of!' exclaimed the prince. 'It was bound to happen!'

Ippolit quickly turned to him with the most rabid hatred, and the whole of his face seemed to be trembling and speaking.

'Oh, that's what you were afraid of! "It was bound to happen," you think? Then be advised that if there is anyone I hate here,' he began to howl in a hoarse shriek, spray coming from his mouth, '(and I hate you all, you all!) – but you, you, you jesuitical, syrupy little thing, you idiot and millionaire benefactor, I hate more than anyone and anything in the world! I understood and hated you long ago, when I first heard about you, I hated you with all the hatred of my soul . . . It's you who've brought me to all this! It's you who've made me have an epileptic fit! You've reduced a dying man to shame, it's you, it's you who's to blame for my vile cowardice! I'd kill you if I had any life left to live! I don't need your charity, I won't accept it from anyone, do you hear, not from anyone, nothing! I was delirious, and don't dare to exult in your triumph! . . . I curse you all once and for all!'

At this point he choked completely.

'He's ashamed of his tears!' whispered Lebedev to Lizaveta Prokofyevna, "This was bound to happen!" Hurrah for the prince! Saw right through him . . .'

But Lizaveta Prokofyevna did not even deem him worthy of a glance. She stood, proud and straight, her head thrown back, examining 'these wretched people' with contemptuous curiosity. When Ippolit had finished, the general began to shrug his shoulders; she surveyed him wrathfully from head to foot, as though requesting him to account for this movement, and at once turned towards the prince.

'Thank you, Prince, eccentric friend of our family, for the

pleasant evening you have provided for us all. I expect your heart's now rejoicing that you've succeeded in involving us in your follies . . . Enough, dear friend of the family, thank you for letting us see what you're really like, at last.'

She straightened her mantilla indignantly, waiting for 'those people' to leave. At that moment a hired droshky, for which Doktorenko had sent Lebedev's nephew, the gymnasium student, a quarter of an hour earlier, rolled up for them. As soon as his wife had finished, the general at once put in a word as well:

'Really, Prince, I even did not expect . . . after everything, after all our friendly relations . . . and, lastly, Lizaveta Prokofyevna . . .'

'How can you, how can you, Father!' Adelaida Ivanovna exclaimed. She went quickly up to the prince and gave him her hand.

The prince smiled to her with a forlorn look. Suddenly a hot, rapid whisper seemed to scorch his ear.

'If you don't get rid of these loathsome people at once, then all my life, all my life I shall hate you!' Aglaya whispered; she was almost in a frenzy, but turned away before the prince had time to glance at her. By now, however, there was no one left for him to get rid of: they had somehow managed to get Ippolit into the droshky, and it had left.

'Well, how long is this to continue, Ivan Fyodorovich? What is your opinion? How long am I to endure such mischief from these vicious urchins?'

'Why, my dear . . . I am, of course, ready and . . . the prince . . .'

Ivan Fyodorovich did, however, offer the prince his hand, but did not succeed in an actual handshake, and ran off after Lizaveta Prokofyevna, who was noisily and angrily leaving the veranda. Adelaida, her fiancé and Alexandra took their leave of the prince with sincere affection. Yevgeny Pavlovich, the only cheerful person present, did likewise.

'It turned out the way I thought it would! It's just a pity that you had to suffer, too, poor fellow,' he whispered with a most charming smile.

Aglaya walked away without saying goodbye.

But the adventures of that evening were not yet at an end; Lizaveta Prokofyevna had to endure yet one more highly unexpected encounter.

She had not yet managed to descend the flight of steps to the road (which skirted the park), when suddenly a splendid carriage, a carriage, drawn by two white steeds, rushed past the prince's dacha. In the carriage sat two magnificent ladies. But, having gone no more than ten yards past, the carriage stopped again; one of the ladies quickly turned round, as though she had suddenly spotted some friend she wanted to see.

'Yevgeny Pavlych! Is it you?' suddenly cried a resonant, beautiful voice that made the prince start, and, perhaps, also someone else. 'Oh, how glad I am to have found you at last! I sent a special messenger to you in town; no, two! They've been looking for you all day!'

Yevgeny Pavlovich stood on the steps of the veranda as if thunderstruck. Lizaveta Prokofyevna also stood still, but not in frozen horror, like Yevgeny Pavlovich: she looked at the insolent woman just as proudly and with the same cold contempt as five minutes earlier she had looked at 'those wretched people', and at once transferred her steady gaze to Yevgeny Pavlovich.

'Good news!' the resonant voice continued. 'Don't worry about Kupfer's promissory notes; Rogozhin has bought them for thirty, I managed to persuade him. You can be assured for at least some three months yet. And we'll probably get something sorted out with Biskup and all that riff-raff, on a friendly basis! Well, so that means everything's fine. Be happy. Until tomorrow!'

The carriage moved off and quickly disappeared.

'She's crazy!' Yevgeny Pavlovich cried at last, flushed with indignation and looking around him in bewilderment. 'I've no idea what she was talking about! What promissory notes? Who is she?'

Lizaveta Prokofyevna continued to look at him for another two seconds; at last she set off quickly and abruptly for her dacha, and everyone followed her. A minute later Yevgeny Pavlovich announced himself to the prince back on the veranda again, in extreme agitation.

'Prince, in all truthfulness, do you know what this means?'

'I don't know anything about it,' replied the prince, who was now himself in a state of extreme and morbid tension.

'No?'

'No.'

'Neither do I,' Yevgeny Pavlovich suddenly began to laugh. 'I swear to you, I had nothing to do with those promissory notes, believe me, on my word of honour! . . . But what's the matter, are you feeling faint?'

'Oh no, no, I assure you, no . . .'

11

Three days went by before the Yepanchins were quite pro-pitiated. The prince, though he blamed himself for many things, as usual, and sincerely expected punishment, still at first had a complete inner conviction that Lizaveta Prokofyevna could not be seriously angry with him, but was really more angry with herself. Thus, by the third day, such a long period of hostility had put him in a very gloomy state of mind, from which there seemed to be no way out. There were other factors at work, too, but one of them stood out among the rest. Throughout all these three days it had grown progressively within the prince's morbidly sensitive imagination – and of late the prince had been finding himself guilty of two extremes: his extraordinarily 'senseless and stubborn' credulity and at the same time an 'unworthy and gloomy' suspiciousness. In short, by the end of the third day the incident with the eccentric lady who spoke to Yevgeny Pavlovich from her carriage had acquired frightening and mysterious dimensions in his mind. The essence of the mystery, apart from the other aspects of the matter, was summed up for the prince in a painful question: to wit, was he to blame for this new 'enormity', or was it merely . . . But he did not get as far as saying who it might be. As for the letters N.F.B., that, in his view, was simply an innocent prank, even a most childish prank, so that it would be shameful, and even in a certain respect almost dishonourable, to give it any sustained reflection.

However, on the very first day after the disgraceful 'soirée', for the disorders of which he had been such a primary 'cause', the prince had the pleasure that morning of receiving Prince Shch. and Adelaida: they had dropped in '*mainly* in order to inquire about his health', had done so while taking a walk, the two of them together. Adelaida had just noticed a tree in the park, a wonderful old tree, a spreading one, with long, gnarled branches, covered in young green leaves, with a hollow and a cleft; she must, she absolutely must paint a watercolour of it! And she talked of almost nothing else for the whole half hour of her visit. Prince Shch. was courteous and charming as usual, asked the prince about former times and recalled the circumstances of their first acquaintance: of the previous day's events almost nothing was said. Adelaida could not restrain herself and admitted, with a smile, that they had dropped in *incognito*; there, however, the confessions ended, though from this *incognito* it was not hard to guess that her parents, and chiefly Lizaveta Prokofyevna, were really rather particularly illdisposed towards him. But neither about her, nor about Aglaya, nor even about Ivan Fyodorovich did Adelaida and Prince Shch. utter a single word during their visit. As they left to continue their walk, they did not invite the prince to go with them. There was not even a hint of asking him to visit them; in that connection Adelaida even let slip a very characteristic remark: as she talked about one of her watercolours, she suddenly felt a very strong desire to show it to him. 'How can we do that quickly? Wait! I'll send it to you today with Kolya, if he calls, or bring it tomorrow, when I go for a walk with the prince,' she concluded, at last, her bewilderment, relieved that she had succeeded in solving this problem so neatly and conveniently for all concerned.

At last, when he was almost on the point of taking his leave, Prince Shch. suddenly seemed to remember something:

'Oh, yes,' he asked, 'you don't know, dear Lev Nikolayevich, who that lady was who shouted to Yevgeny Pavlych from her carriage, do you?'

'It was Nastasya Filippovna,' said the prince. 'Didn't you realize it was her? Though I don't know who was with her.'

'Yes, I know, I heard!' Prince Shch. interjected. 'But what was all that shouting of hers about? I confess it really is a mystery to me . . . to me and to others.'

Prince Shch. spoke with extreme and visible puzzlement.

'She was talking about some kind of promissory notes of Yevgeny Pavlovich's,' the prince replied very simply. 'They'd come into Rogozhin's hands from some moneylender or other, at her request, and Rogozhin was going to wait for Yevgeny Pavlych to redeem them.'

'I heard it, I heard it, my dear prince, but I mean, that simply could not possibly have been true! With a fortune like that . . . To be sure, he used to do such things in the old days, because of carelessness, and I even used to help him out . . . But with a fortune like that, to give promissory notes to moneylenders and worry about them – is impossible. And he can't possibly be so familiar and on such friendly terms with Nastasya Filippovna – that's the main problem. He swears he knows nothing, and I fully believe him. But the fact is, dear Prince, that I wanted to ask you, do you know anything? That is, has any rumour reached you, by some miracle?'

'No, I don't know anything, I assure you that I had no part in it whatsoever.'

'Oh, what has happened to you, Prince? I simply don't recognize you today. Do you really think I could possibly suppose you to have a part in a matter like that? . . . Well, but of course you're upset today.'

He embraced him and kissed him.

'What do you mean, a matter like what? I don't see any matter "like that".'

'Without a doubt, that lady wished to thwart Yevgeny Pavlych in some way, by endowing him in the eyes of witnesses with qualities he does not possess and cannot possess,' Prince Shch. replied rather thinly.

Prince Lev Nikolayevich was embarrassed, but continued to gaze at the prince fixedly and questioningly; the latter, however, fell silent.

'Was it not just promissory notes she was talking about, then? Was she not just talking literally yesterday?' the prince muttered, at last, in a kind of impatience.

'But look, judge for yourself, what can there be in common between her and Yevgeny Pavlych and . . . Rogozhin, of all people, too? I repeat to you, an enormous fortune, which I know all about; another fortune, which he expects from his uncle. Nastasya Filippovna simply . . .'

Prince Shch. suddenly fell silent again, evidently because he did not want to continue on the subject of Nastasya Filippovna to the prince.

'So at any rate he knows her, then?' Prince Lev Nikolayevich asked suddenly, after a moment's silence.

'I think there was something between them; he's a frivolous sort of fellow, you know! However, if there was something, it was a very long time ago, in the old days, two or three years ago, that is. After all, he was a friend of Totsky's. But there couldn't be anything of that kind now, they could never be on such familiar terms! You know yourself that she hasn't been here; she hasn't been anywhere. Many people don't even know now that she's appeared again. I've noticed the carriage for about three days, no more.'

'It's a magnificent carriage!' said Adelaida.

'Yes, the carriage is magnificent.'

As a matter of fact, both went away on most friendly and, one might say, most brotherly terms with Prince Lev Nikolayevich.

For our hero, on the other hand, this visit represented something of capital importance. We may assume that he himself had suspected many things since the previous night (and perhaps even earlier), but until their visit he had not been able to bring himself to justify his apprehensions completely. But now it was becoming clear: Prince Shch., of course, interpreted the event wrongly, but had none the less come near the truth, had realized that there was an *intrigue*. ('Perhaps he understands it perfectly,' thought the prince, 'but just doesn't want to express himself openly, and so misinterprets it on purpose.') Clearest of all was that they (and especially Prince Shch.) had dropped in on him in the hope of some kind of explanation; and, if that were so, it meant they considered that he had a part in the intrigue. In addition, if that was so and really was important, then she must have some dreadful purpose, and what could that purpose be? How dreadful! 'And how can she be stopped? There's no possibility of stopping her, if she's convinced of her purpose!' The prince knew this from experience. 'She's mad. Mad.'

But that morning there were far, far too many other insoluble matters, all coming at the same time, and all demanding an immediate solution, and the prince was very disheartened. He was somewhat diverted by Vera Lebedeva, who came to see him with Lyubochka, and, laughing, told him some long story or other. She was followed by her sister, who stood with her mouth open, and then by the gymnasium student, Lebedev's son, who asserted that 'the star Wormwood', in Revelation, which fell to earth upon the sources of the waters was, according to his father's interpretation, the network of railways that stretched across Europe. The prince did not believe that this was how Lebedev interpreted it, and they decided they would ask him about it at the earliest available opportunity. From Vera Lebedeva the prince learned that Keller had moved in with them the previous day and that all the signs were that he would not be leaving them again for a long time, as he had found company and was now on friendly terms with General Ivolgin; he had, however, announced that he would stay with them solely in order to complete his education. On the whole, the prince was beginning to like Lebedev's children more and more with each day that passed. Kolya had not been there all day: he had set off for St Petersburg very early in the morning. (Lebedev had also gone off at the crack of dawn on some small matters of his own.) But the prince was waiting with impatience for a visit from Gavrila Ardalionovich, who was due to call on him that very day without fail.

He arrived between six and seven in the evening, just after dinner. From a first glance at him it occurred to the prince that at least this gentleman must have a flawless knowledge of the whole truth – and how could he not have, when he had helpers such as Varvara Ardalionovna and her husband? But the prince's relations with Ganya were still rather peculiar. The prince had, for example, entrusted him with managing the Burdovsky affair and had particularly asked him to do so; but, in spite of this trust, and of something that had happened previously, there still remained between the two of them certain points on which, as it were, they had mutually decided to stay silent. It sometimes seemed to the prince that Ganya really did perhaps wish them both to be on terms of the most complete and friendly sincerity; for example, as soon as he entered, the prince at once had the impression Ganya was convinced that the time had come for him to break the ice on all points. (Actually, Gavrila Ardalionovich was in a hurry; his sister was waiting for him at Lebedev's; they were both in a hurry to deal with some matter or other.)

But if Ganya was really expecting a whole series of impatient questions, spontaneous confessions and friendly outpourings, then, of course, he was very mistaken. During the whole twenty minutes of his visit, the prince was pensive, almost preoccupied. As for the questions, or rather, the one principal question that Ganya was expecting, these could not possibly have arisen. Then Ganya also decided to speak with greater reserve. He spoke without cease for the whole twenty minutes, laughed, engaged in the lightest, most charming and rapid chit-chat, but did not touch upon the main question.

Ganya related, among other things, that Nastasya Filippovna had only been in Pavlovsk for some four days, but was already drawing general attention to herself. Though her carriage was almost the finest in Pavlovsk, she was staying in some Sailor Street or other, in a poky little house, with Darya Alexeyevna. Around her a whole crowd of suitors had gathered; the carriage was sometimes escorted by men on horseback. As before, Nastasya Filippovna was very selective, receiving only those whom she had chosen. Yet none the less a large company had formed around her, and she had plenty of people to turn to in case of need. One man, formally betrothed, a dacha dweller, had already quarrelled with his fiancée because of her; one old general had almost cursed his son. She often took out driving with her a certain delightful young girl, only sixteen years old, a distant relative of Darya Alexeyevna; this girl was a good singer – so that in the evenings their little house drew attention.

Nastasya Filippovna behaved with exceeding decorum, however, and although she did not dress extravagantly, dressed with
uncommon good taste, and all the ladies envied 'her taste, her
beauty and her carriage'.

'Yesterday's eccentric incident,' Ganya said, 'was of course
premeditated and should not be taken too seriously. In order to
find fault with her in anything, one would have to go out of
one's way to find some excuse, or slander her, things that
will in any case not be long in happening,' concluded Ganya,
expecting the prince to ask at this point why he thought that
yesterday's incident was premeditated, and why those things
would not be long in happening. But the prince asked no such
questions.

About Yevgeny Pavlovich, Ganya again spoke at length of his
own accord, in response to no particular questions, which was
very strange, as he had brought him into the conversation without any special reason. In Gavrila Ardalionovich's opinion,
Yevgeny Pavlovich had not known Nastasya Filippovna, even
now he only barely knew her, and then only because some four
days earlier he had been introduced to her on a walk, and he
was scarcely likely to have been at her house even once, together
with the others. With regard to the promissory notes, there
could well have been something in that (Ganya knew this for
certain); Yevgeny Pavlych's fortune was, of course, an enormous
one, but 'some matters connected with the estate really were
in disorder'. Having reached this interesting subject, Ganya
suddenly broke off. With regard to Nastasya Filippovna's eccentric behaviour of the night before, he said not a single word,
apart from the passing reference mentioned above.

At length Varya Ardalionovna arrived to fetch Ganya, stayed
for a moment, announced (also without being asked) that Yevgeny Pavlovich would be in St Petersburg that day, and possibly
the next day as well, that her husband (Ivan Petrovich Ptitsyn)
was also in St Petersburg, and also very probably on Yevgeny
Pavlovich's business, and that something really did seem to be
taking shape there. As she was leaving, she added that Lizaveta
Prokofyevna was in a hellish temper that day, but strangest of
all was that Aglaya had quarrelled with the whole family, not

just with her father and mother but even with both her sisters, and that 'it was quite disagreeable'. Having delivered this last piece of news (which was extremely important for the prince) as if in passing, brother and sister went away. About the matter of 'Pavlishchev's son' Ganechka also said not a word, perhaps out of false modesty, or perhaps 'to spare the prince's feelings' – but the prince thanked him once more none the less for the conscientious way which he had brought the matter to a conclusion.

The prince was very glad to be left alone again at last; he descended the veranda, crossed the road and entered the park; he wanted to consider a certain step and make up his mind about it. This 'step', however, was not of a kind to be considered, but was rather the sort that one simply decides upon: he suddenly had an overpowering desire to leave everything here[1] and go away, back to where he had come from, somewhere far away, into the wilds, to leave right away, and without even saying goodbye to anyone. He had a premonition that if he remained here a few days more, he would be drawn into this world irrevocably, and this world would in future be his. He had not reflected on this for ten minutes, however, when he at once decided that to run away was 'impossible', that it would almost amount to cowardice, that he was faced with such tasks that he did not even have the right to avoid their resolution or, at any rate, must exert all his energies towards resolving them. Absorbed in such thoughts he returned home, having been out walking for only a quarter of an hour. At that moment he felt completely wretched.

Lebedev was not home yet, and towards evening Keller managed to burst in, not drunk, but with outpourings and confessions. He declared straight out that he had come to tell the prince the story of his life, and that this was why he had remained in Pavlovsk. There was not the slightest possibility of driving him away: he would not have gone on any account. Keller had been getting ready to speak for a very a long time and very incoherently, but suddenly, almost from his first words, skipped to the conclusion and announced that he had to such a degree lost 'every phantom of morality' (solely because of lack of belief in the Almighty) that he had even taken to thieving. 'Can you imagine that?'

'Listen, Keller, in your place I wouldn't confess to that unless I particularly had to,' the prince began, 'however, I expect you're slandering yourself on purpose, aren't you?'

'I'm telling you, you alone, and solely in order to assist my own development! I'll tell no one else; I'll die and carry my secret to the grave! But, Prince, if you knew, if you only knew how hard it is in our time to obtain money! Where is one to get it, I ask you? There is but one answer: "Bring us our gold and diamonds, and we'll lend you money against those," in other words the very things I don't have! In the end, I got angry, waiting and waiting. "Will you lend me money against emeralds?" "Yes, I can lend you money against emeralds, too." "Well, that's splendid," I said, put on my hat and went out; the devil take you, you villains! By God, they're villains!'

'And did you have any emeralds?'

'What sort of emeralds could I ever have? Oh, Prince, what a bright and innocent, even, one might say, pastoral view of life you have!'

In the end, the prince felt not so much sorry for him as guilty about him. The thought even occurred to him: 'Couldn't one make something out of this man through someone's good influence?' For several reasons he considered his own influence most unsuitable – not out of self-depreciation, but because of a certain peculiar view of things. Gradually they got into conversation, and to a point where they did not want to part. Keller was confessing with such extraordinary readiness to such things that it was impossible to imagine how anyone could talk about such things. As he began each story, he assured the prince that he felt positive remorse and was inwardly 'full of tears', all the while telling the story as though he were proud of what he had done, and so amusingly that he and the prince ended up laughing like madmen.

'The main thing about you is that you have in you a kind of childish trust, and an extraordinary truthfulness,' the prince said, at last. 'Do you realize that by this alone you greatly redeem yourself?'

'Noble, noble, chivalrously noble!' Keller confirmed with tender emotion. 'But you know, Prince, it's all just dreams and Dutch courage, so to speak, nothing ever comes of it in reality! Why is that? I really don't know.'

'Don't despair. Now it can be definitely said that you've presented all the details of your life to me; at least it seems to me that there isn't any more to add to what you've told me, I mean, is there?'

'Nothing more to add?' Keller exclaimed with a kind of compassion. 'Oh, Prince, what a Swiss view of man you have, so to speak.'

'Is there really more?' the prince said in timid surprise. 'Then what did you expect from me, Keller, tell me, please, and why did you come here with your confession?'

'From you? What did I expect? In the first place, it's pleasant just to observe your simple-heartedness; to sit and talk with you is pleasant; at least I know that I'm in the presence of a most virtuous person, and in the second place ... in the second place ...'

He stopped short in embarrassment.

'Perhaps you wanted to borrow money?' the prince prompted very gravely and simply, even rather timidly, almost.

Keller gave a violent start; quickly, with his earlier surprise, he looked the prince straight in the eye, and banged his fist hard on the table.

'Well, that's how to flabbergast a man completely! For pity's sake, Prince: such simple-heartedness, such innocence as were unheard of even in the golden age, and then suddenly you pierce a man through like an arrow, with such profound psychology of observation. No, I'm sorry, Prince, that demands explanation, because I ... I'm simply flabbergasted! Of course my ultimate aim was to borrow money, but you asked me about money as though you didn't find anything blameworthy in it, as though it were the most natural thing in the world.'

'Yes ... with you that's just what it is.'

'And you're not angry?'

'But ... what about?'

'Listen, Prince, I stayed on here after yesterday evening, in the first place, out of special respect for the French Archbishop Bourdaloue[2] (we were cracking bottles open at Lebedev's until three in the morning), and in the second place, and mainly (and I swear by all the saints in heaven that I speak the honest truth!), I stayed on because I wanted to give you my full and sincere confession, so to speak, and by that means to further my own development; with that thought I cried myself to sleep at four o'clock in the morning. Please believe an honourable man: at the very moment I was falling asleep, full of inward and, so to speak, outward tears (because, at last, I was crying, I remember that!), a devilish thought came to me: "Well, why don't I borrow money from him, after I make my confession?" So I prepared the confession, so to speak, as it were, like some "*fines herbes* with tears*", in order to smooth the way with those tears and to soften you up so you'd fork out a hundred and fifty roubles to me. That was vile, don't you think?'

'But that's surely not true? One thing just got mixed up with another. Two thoughts coincided, that very often happens. To me, constantly. As a matter of fact, I think it's a bad thing, and, you know, Keller, I reproach myself most of all for it. What you told me just now could have been about me. I've even sometimes thought,' the prince continued with real gravity, genuinely and deeply interested, 'that all human beings are like that, so that I even began to approve of myself, because it's terribly difficult to fight those *double* thoughts; God knows how they come into being. But you will call this downright vileness! Now I'll start being afraid of those thoughts again. At any rate, I am not your judge. But all the same, in my opinion, it's impossible to call it downright vileness: what do you think? You used cunning in order to coax money out of me by means of tears, but after all, you yourself swear that your confession had a different aim, a noble, not merely a financial one; as for the money, you need it in order to go on a drinking spree, don't you? And after such a confession that's weakness, of course. But how can one give up drinking sprees in a single moment? I mean, it's impossible. So what is to be done? Is it best to leave it to your own conscience, what do you think?'

The prince gazed at Keller with intense interest. The question of double thoughts had evidently been occupying him for a long time now.

'Well, how they can call you an idiot after that, I don't understand!'

The prince blushed slightly.

'The preacher Bourdaloue, well, he wouldn't have spared a man, but you've spared a man and judged me like a human being! To punish myself and in order to show that I'm touched, I won't ask for a hundred and fifty roubles, just give me twenty-five, and leave it at that! That's all I need, at least for two weeks. Until two weeks are up I won't come asking again. I wanted to spoil Agashka a little, but she doesn't deserve it. Oh, dear Prince, may the Lord bless you!'

At last Lebedev came in, having just returned home, and, noticing the twenty-five rouble note in Keller's hands, frowned. But Keller, finding himself with money again, was already hurrying away, and immediately disappeared. Lebedev at once began to malign him behind his back.

'You're unjust, he really was genuinely repentant,' the prince observed, at last.

'But what is there in his repentance? It's just like yesterday: "I'm vile, vile," but it's all just words, sir!'

'So it was all merely words with you? And I was beginning to think . . .'

'Well, to you, only to you, I'll tell the truth, because you can see through a man: words and actions, falsehood and truth – they're all in me together, and quite sincerely. For me truth and actions are part of my genuine repentance, believe it or not, but I swear it is so, while words and falsehood constitute the devilish (and ever present) thought of how to get the better of a man, how to gain an advantage, as it were, by means of tears! It honestly is so! I wouldn't tell anyone else, they'd laugh, or spit in my face, but you, Prince, you will judge me like a human being.'

'Well, that's it, exactly what he was telling me just now,' the prince exclaimed, 'and you both seem to boast of it! You even astonish me, except that he is more sincere than you, while you have turned it into a regular craft. Well, that will do, don't frown, Lebedev, and don't put your hand on your heart. Haven't you anything to say to me? You wouldn't come to see me for no reason . . .'

Lebedev began to cringe and grovel.

'I've waited all day to ask you one question; just answer with the truth for once in your life, right from the first word: did you play any part in that carriage business yesterday?'

Lebedev again began to cringe, giggled, rubbed his hands, and even, at last, sneezed several times, but was still unable to bring himself to say anything.

'I see that you did.'

'But obliquely, only obliquely! I speak the whole truth! I only took part by letting a certain lady know beforehand that a certain company had gathered at my house and that certain persons were present.'

'I know that you sent your son *there*, he himself told me earlier, but what is all this intrigue?' the prince exclaimed in impatience.

'It's not mine, the intrigue, not mine,' Lebedev warded him off. 'There are others, others, here, and it's more fantasy, so to speak, than intrigue.'

'But what is it all about then, explain, for God's sake, can't you? Don't you understand that this concerns me directly? I mean, Yevgeny Pavlovich's name is being blackened here.'

'Prince! Most illustrious Prince!' Lebedev began to grovel again. 'Why, you won't allow me to tell the whole truth; I mean, I've already started to tell you about the truth; several times; you wouldn't allow me to continue . . .'

The prince was silent and thought for a bit.

'Well, all right; tell the truth,' he said heavily, evidently after a major struggle.

'Aglaya Ivanovna . . .' Lebedev began at once.

'Be quiet, be quiet!' the prince shouted violently, red all over with indignation, and perhaps also with shame. 'That is impossible, that's all nonsense! You've thought it all up yourself, or madmen like you have. I never want to hear about it from you again!'

Late in the evening, towards eleven o'clock, Kolya appeared

with a veritable mountain of news. The news was of two kinds, and concerned St Petersburg and Pavlovsk. He hurriedly related the most important of the St Petersburg news (mostly about Ippolit and the incident of the previous day), with the intention of returning to it later, and quickly went on to the Pavlovsk news. Three hours earlier he had returned home from St Petersburg and, not calling on the prince, had set straight off for the Yepanchins. 'Things are dreadful over there!' Of course, the carriage business had pride of place, but something of that kind must probably also have happened, something that was unknown to him and the prince. 'I didn't go spying, of course, and I didn't want to question anyone; however, they received me well, so well that I really didn't expect it; but about you, Prince, there was not a word!' Most important and interesting of all was that Aglaya had earlier quarrelled with her family about Ganya. What the details of the matter were he did not know, but it was about Ganya (imagine that!), and the quarrel was indeed a terrible one, so it must have been something important. The general had arrived late, had arrived frowning, had arrived with Yevgeny Pavlovich, who received a magnificent reception, and Yevgeny Pavlovich himself was remarkably cheerful and charming. The news of principal importance was that Lizaveta Prokofyevna, without further ado, had summoned Varvara Ardalionovna, who was sitting with the girls, and turned her out of the house once and for all, though in the most polite manner – 'I heard it from Varya herself.' But when Varya came out from Lizaveta Prokofyevna and said goodbye to the girls, they did not even know that she had been shown the door once and for all and that she was saying goodbye to them for the last time.

'But Varvara Ardalionovna came to see me at seven o'clock!' the prince said with astonishment.

'She was turned out after eight, or shortly before that. I'm very sorry for Varya, sorry for Ganya ... they certainly have perpetual intrigues, they can't get by without them. And I was never able to find out what they were thinking up, and I don't want to. But I assure you, my dear, good Prince, that Ganya has a heart. He is a man who is in many respects a wreck, but in many respects he has qualities that are worth looking for, and I shall never forgive myself for not having understood him before ... I don't know if I should continue now, after the episode with Varya. To be sure, I took a completely independent and separate position right from the beginning, but even so, it needs thought.'

'You shouldn't feel too sorry for your brother,' the prince observed to him. 'If matters have gone that far, Gavrila Ardalionovich must be dangerous in Lizaveta Prokofyevna's eyes, and thus certain hopes of his are being confirmed.'

'What? What hopes?' Kolya exclaimed in amazement. 'You don't really think that Aglaya ... it isn't possible!'

The prince was silent.

'You are a dreadful sceptic, Prince,' Kolya added some two minutes later. 'I've noticed for some time now that you're becoming an extreme sceptic; you're starting not to believe anything and to suppose everything ... I say, am I right to use the word "sceptic" in this connection?'

'I think so, though as a matter of fact I myself don't know for certain.'

'But I'll renounce the word "sceptic", for I've found another explanation,' Kolya shouted suddenly. 'You're not a sceptic, you're jealous! You're infernally jealous of Ganya over a certain proud girl!'

Saying this, Kolya jumped up and roared with laughter as he had perhaps never succeeded in laughing before. Seeing the prince blush all over, Kolya began to laugh even louder; he found the idea that the prince was jealous about Aglaya immensely appealing, but fell silent at once when he observed that the prince was genuinely upset. After that they continued to talk, with great seriousness and concern, for another hour or hour and a half.

Next day the prince spent the whole morning in St Petersburg on a certain piece of urgent business. Returning to Pavlovsk between four and five in the afternoon, he encountered Ivan Fyodorovich in the railway station. Ivan Fyodorovich seized him by the arm, looked around him as if in fear, and took the prince with him into a first-class carriage, so that they could travel together. He was burning with a desire to discuss some important matter.

'In the first place, dear Prince, don't be angry with me, and if there's been anything on my part – forget it. I would have come to see you yesterday, but didn't know how Lizaveta Prokofyevna would view it . . . My home is . . . sheer hell, an enigmatic sphinx has moved in, and I wander about and understand nothing. But as for you, you are less to blame than any of us, although, of course, much has happened because of you. You see, Prince, it's pleasant to be a philanthropist, but not very much so. You yourself have already tasted the fruits, perhaps. Of course, I love kindness, and respect Lizaveta Prokofyevna, but . . .'

The general continued for a long time in this vein, but his words were remarkably incoherent. It was evident that he was exceedingly shaken and upset by something incomprehensible to him in the extreme.

'For me there is no doubt that you are not involved in this,' he managed to get out, at last, more clearly. 'But please don't visit us for a time, I ask you as a friend, until the wind has changed. As for Yevgeny Pavlych,' he exclaimed with extraordinary fervour, 'that is all senseless slander, a slander of slanders! It's a plot, there's an intrigue there, a desire to destroy everything and make us fall out. Look, Prince, let me say this in your ear: not a single word has yet passed between Yevgeny Pavlych and myself, do you understand? We're not associated in any way – but that word may be spoken, and even soon and even, perhaps, very soon! Just to cause harm! But as for why, for what reason – I don't understand! An astonishing woman, an eccentric woman, I'm so afraid of her that I can hardly sleep. And such a carriage, with white horses, I mean, it's *chic*, it's exactly what the French call *chic*! Who gave her that carriage? My God, I must confess that the other day I thought it must be Yevgeny Pavlych! But it turns out that that couldn't have been, and if that is so, then why does she want to upset things here? That, that is the question! To keep Yevgeny Pavlych with her? But I repeat to you, and I will swear to you by all the saints, that he doesn't know her and that those promissory notes are a fabrication! And how brazenly she shouts to him across the street in that familiar way! The purest conspiracy! It's clear that it must be repudiated with contempt, and our respect for Yevgeny Pavlych be redoubled. That's how I put it to Lizaveta Proko-fyevna. Now I will tell you my most intimate thought: I am stub-bornly convinced that she did it to take personal revenge on me, you remember, for things that happened before, though I was never guilty before her in anything. The mere memory makes me blush. Now she's appeared again, just when I thought she'd vanished for ever. But where is that Rogozhin, can you tell me, please? I thought she'd become Mrs Rogozhin long ago ...'

In short, the man was thoroughly bewildered. For almost the whole hour of the journey he alone had spoken, asked questions, answered them himself, shaken the prince's hand, and at least convinced the prince of one thing, that he did not suspect him of anything. That was important for the prince. He concluded with a story about Yevgeny Pavlych's uncle, the head of some chancellery in St Petersburg – 'in an important post, seventy years old, a *bon viveur*, a gourmet, and in general a susceptible old fellow ... Ha! ha! I know he had heard about Nastasya Filippovna and was even trying to see her. I dropped in on him earlier; he wasn't receiving, is unwell, but rich, rich, he's important and ... may God let him prosper for many years, but once again it's Yevgeny Pavlych who gets everything ... Yes, yes ... but I'm still afraid! I don't know what I'm afraid of, but I'm afraid ... It's as though there were something in the air, like a bat, trouble is on the wing, and I'm afraid, afraid! ...'

And, at last, three days later, as we mentioned above, the formal reconciliation between the Yepanchins and Prince Lev Nikolayevich took place.

12

It was seven o'clock in the evening; the prince was about to go for a walk in the park. Suddenly Lizaveta Prokofyevna came to see him on the veranda.

'*In the first place*, don't even dare to think,' she began, 'that

I've come to see you in order to apologize. Rubbish! You're to blame all round.'

The prince was silent.

'Are you to blame or not?'

'As much as you are. However, neither I nor you are guilty of anything intentional. The other day I thought I was to blame, but I've now decided that I'm not.'

'So that's the way it is, is it? Well, all right; then listen and sit down, for I don't intend to stand.'

They both sat down.

'*In the second place*: not a word about the spiteful urchins! I'll sit and talk to you for ten minutes; I came to see you in order to make an inquiry (goodness knows what you thought I wanted!), but if you so much as utter one word about those impudent cheeky urchins I shall get up and go away, and then break off with you altogether.'

'Very well,' replied the prince.

'Now, permit me to ask you: did you, about two or two and half months ago, around Easter, send Aglaya a letter?'

'I d-did.'

'Whatever for? What was in the letter? Show it to me!'

Lizaveta Prokofyevna's eyes were burning; she was almost quivering with impatience.

'I haven't got the letter,' the prince said in surprise, growing horribly timid. 'If it's still intact, Aglaya Ivanovna has it.'

'Don't play games! What did you write about?'

'I'm not playing games, I'm not afraid of anything. I see no reason why I shouldn't write . . .'

'Be quiet! You'll speak afterwards. What was in the letter? Why did you blush?'

The prince thought for a moment.

'I don't know what's in your thoughts, Lizaveta Prokofyevna. I see only that you find this letter upsetting. You will agree that I could refuse to answer such a question; but in order to show you that I'm not afraid with regard to the letter, do not regret having written it, and am certainly not blushing because of it (the prince blushed almost twice as red as before), I'll read you the letter, because I think I can remember it by heart.'

So saying, the prince quoted the letter almost word for word.

'What a rigmarole! What's that nonsense supposed to mean, in your opinion?' Lizaveta Prokofyevna asked sharply, having listened to the letter with extraordinary attention.

'I don't really know, altogether; I know that my feelings were genuine. I had moments of being completely alive, and extraordinary hopes.'

'What sort of hopes?'

'It's hard to explain, only they weren't the kind of hopes you're thinking of now, perhaps . . . well, in short, they were hopes for the future and joy in the fact that perhaps I wasn't an alien *there*, not a foreigner. I was suddenly very pleased to be back in my native land. One sunny morning I picked up a pen and wrote her a letter; why to her, I don't know. I mean, sometimes one wants to have a friend beside one; and I suppose I felt like having a friend there . . .' the prince added, after a silence.

'Are you in love, then?'

'N-no. I . . . I wrote to her as to a sister; I even signed myself as a brother.'

'Hmmm; on purpose; I understand.'

'It's very hard for me to reply to these questions of yours, Lizaveta Prokofyevna.'

'I know it's hard, but I really don't care. Listen, tell me the truth, before God; are you lying to me or are you not?'

'I'm not.'

'Are you telling the truth when you say that you're not in love?'

'I think I'm telling the complete truth.'

'Listen to him: "I think"! Did the urchin deliver it?'

'I asked Nikolai Ardalionovich . . .'

'The urchin! The urchin!' Lizaveta Prokofyevna interrupted heatedly. 'I don't know of any Nikolai Ardalionovich around here! The urchin!'

'Nikolai Ardalionovich . . .'

'The urchin, I tell you!'

'No, he's not an urchin, he's Nikolai Ardalionovich,' the prince replied at last, firmly though rather quietly.

'Oh, very well, dear man, very well! I shall hold you to account for this.'

For a moment she tried to overcome her agitation, and relaxed.

'And what's the "poor knight"?'

'I really don't know; I wasn't there; it was some sort of joke.'

'That's a nice thing to discover all of a sudden! But could she really have been interested in you? She called you a "little freak" and an "idiot".'

'You might not have told me that,' the prince observed reproachfully, almost in a whisper.

'Don't be angry. She's a despotic, crazy, spoilt girl – if she falls in love with a man, she'll be sure to call him names out loud and mock him to his face; I was just the same. Only don't go preening yourself, my good man, she's not yours; I can't believe it, and it will never be! I'm telling you so that you can take the necessary steps. Look here, I want you to swear that you're not married to *that woman*.'

'Lizaveta Prokofyevna, what are you saying, for pity's sake?' the prince nearly leaped to his feet in amazement.

'But you almost married her, didn't you?'

'Yes, I almost did,' whispered the prince, hanging his head.

'Well, are you in love with *her* then, if that is so? Is that why you're here now? For that woman?'

'I haven't come here to get married,' replied the prince.

'Is there anything you hold sacred in the world?'

'Yes, there is.'

'Swear that you didn't come here in order to marry *that woman*.'

'I'll swear on anything you like!'

'I believe you; you may give me a kiss. At last I can breathe freely again; but know this: Aglaya doesn't love you, you must take the necessary steps, and she will not marry you as long as I live! Do you hear?'

'I hear.'

The prince was blushing so much that he could not look Lizaveta Prokofyevna straight in the face.

'Don't forget it, then. I have waited for you as if you were

Providence (you weren't worth it!), I have soaked my pillow with tears at night – not about you, dear man, don't worry, I have my own sorrow, another, eternal and always the same. But that's why I've been waiting for you with such impatience: I still believe that God himself has sent you to me as a friend, and as a kindred brother. I have no one to turn to except old Princess Bolokonskaya, and she too has flown away, and has also become as silly as a sheep in her old age. Now just reply *yes* or *no*: do you know why *she* shouted from her carriage the other day?'

'On my word of honour, I had no part in it and don't know anything!'

'Enough, I believe you. Now I have other thoughts about this, but even yesterday, in the morning, I was blaming Yevgeny Pavlych for it all. Yesterday morning and the whole of the day before. Now, of course, I can't help agreeing with them: obviously they were making fun of him, as if he were a fool, for some reason, because of something, for some purpose (that alone is suspicious! And it won't do, either!) – but Aglaya is not going to marry him, I tell you that! He may be a good man, but that is how it is going to be. I hesitated earlier, but now I've decided: "Put me in my coffin first and bury me in the ground, then marry off my daughter." That's what I snapped at Ivan Fyodorovich today. You see, I trust you, you see?'

'I see and understand.'

Lizaveta Prokofyevna scrutinized the prince with a penetrating gaze; it was possible that she very much wanted to know what impression the news about Yevgeny Pavlych had made on him.

'You don't know anything about Gavrila Ivolgin?'

'Well . . . I know a great deal.'

'Did you know that he sees Aglaya?'

'I didn't know that at all,' the prince said in surprise, and even with a start. 'What, you say that Gavrila Ardalionovich sees Aglaya Ivanovna? It cannot be!'

'It's very recent. His sister has been clearing the way for him here all winter, working like a rat.'

'I don't believe it,' the prince repeated firmly after some

reflection and excitement. 'If that had been so I would have certainly known about it.'

'You don't think he would have come and confessed on your bosom in tears, do you? Oh, you simpleton, simpleton! Everyone deceives you, like . . . like . . . And aren't you ashamed to confide in him? Don't you see that he has swindled you all round?'

'I know very well that he sometimes deceives me,' the prince said reluctantly, in an undertone, 'and he knows that I know . . .' he added, without finishing his sentence.

'You know and confide in him! That's all I needed to hear! However, that's how it's bound to be with you. And why should I be surprised, in any case? Merciful Lord! Has there ever been a man like you? Fie upon you! And do you know that this Ganka, or this Varka, has put her in contact with Nastasya Filippovna?'

'Who?' exclaimed the prince.

'Aglaya.'

'I don't believe it! It cannot be! What on earth for?'

He leaped up from the chair.

'I don't believe it either, though there is evidence. A self-willed girl, a fantastical girl, a crazy girl! A wicked, wicked, wicked girl! I'll go on saying it for a thousand years, that she's wicked! All my girls are like that now, even that wet hen Alexandra, but this one has really got out of hand. But I don't believe it either! Perhaps because I don't want to believe it,' she added, as if to herself. 'Why haven't you come to see me?' she suddenly turned to the prince again. 'You haven't been to see me for a whole three days!' she shouted at him again, a second time.

The prince began to tell her his reasons, but she again broke in.

'They all think you're a fool, and they deceive you! You went to town yesterday; I bet you got down on your knees and begged that scoundrel to accept your ten thousand!'

'Not at all, I didn't think of it. I didn't even see him and, what's more, he's not a scoundrel. I've had a letter from him.'

'Show me the letter!'

The prince retrieved a note from his briefcase and gave it to Lizaveta Prokofyevna. The note said:

Dear sir,

It is true that I have not the slightest right, in the eyes of others, to have any pride in myself. In the opinion of others I am too insignificant for that. But that is in the eyes of others, and not yours. I am all too convinced that you, dear sir, are possibly better than others. I disagree with Doktorenko, I part company with him in that conviction. I will never take a copeck from you, but you helped my mother, and for that I am obliged to be grateful to you, even if only through weakness. At any rate, I look upon you differently, and thought that I should tell you. And having done so, I assume that there can be no further relations between us.

                                                                Antip Burdovsky.

P.S. The outstanding sum of two hundred roubles will be paid to you in due course without fail.

'What a blockhead!' Lizaveta Prokofyevna concluded, throwing the note back. 'It's not worth reading. What are you smirking at?'

'You must admit that you also enjoyed reading it.'

'What? That rigmarole, eaten away with vanity! But don't you see that they've all gone off their heads with pride and vanity?'

'Yes, but all the same he's confessed, broken with Doktorenko, and there's even the fact that that the vainer he is, the more his vanity has cost him. Oh, what a child you are, Lizaveta Prokofyevna!'

'Do you plan to receive a slap in the face from me, at last?'

'No, not at all. Because you're pleased about the note, but you're hiding it. Why are you ashamed of your feelings? I mean, you're like that in everything.'

'Don't ever dare to cross my threshold,' Lizaveta Prokofyevna leaped up, pale with anger. 'I never want you to set foot in my house again from now on!'

'And in three days' time you'll come and invite me to your house ... Don't you feel embarrassed? Those are your best feelings, why are you ashamed of them? I mean, you're only tormenting yourself.'

'I'll invite you over my dead body! I'll forget your name! I've forgotten it!'

She stormed away from the prince.

'I've already been forbidden to visit you!' the prince cried after her.

'Wha-at? Who forbade you?'

She turned round instantly, as though she had been stabbed with a needle. The prince hesitated with his reply; he felt he had inadvertently, but badly, let the cat out of the bag.

'Who has forbidden you?' Lizaveta Prokofyevna cried furiously.

'Aglaya Ivanovna . . .'

'When? Spe-e-ak can't you?'

'She sent this morning to tell me never to dare to go and visit you.'

Lizaveta Prokofyevna stood as if turned to stone, but she was putting two and two together.

'What did she send? Whom did she send? Was it the urchin? By word of mouth?' she suddenly exclaimed again.

'I received a note,' said the prince.

'Where? Give it to me! At once!'

The prince thought for a moment, but then produced from his waistcoat pocket a careless scrap of paper, on which was written:

'Prince Lev Nikolayevich! If, after all that has passed, you intend to surprise me with a visit to our dacha, then be assured that you will not find me among those who are pleased. Aglaya Yepanchina.'

Lizaveta Prokofyevna reflected for a moment; then she suddenly rushed over to the prince, seized him by the arm and hauled him off with her.

'At once! Come along! We must go at once, this very minute!' she exclaimed in an extraordinary fit of agitation and impatience.

'But you're subjecting me to . . .'

'To what? Innocent simpleton! Even as though you weren't a man at all! Well, now I shall see it all with my own eyes . . .'

'At least let me get my hat . . .'

'Here is your atrocious little hat, come along! He couldn't even choose a fashionable one with taste! . . . She must have . . . she must have done it after what happened this morning . . . in a fever,' muttered Lizaveta Prokofyevna, hauling the prince along behind her and not letting go of his arm for a moment. 'I took your part this morning, said out loud you were a fool for not coming . . . otherwise she wouldn't have written you such a muddle-headed note! An unseemly note! Unseemly for a well-brought up, well-educated, clever, clever girl! . . . Hmm,' she continued, 'of course she was vexed that you didn't come, only she didn't reckon with the fact that one can't write such a thing to an idiot, because he'll take it literally, and so it turned out. Don't eavesdrop!' she cried, realizing she had let the truth slip out. 'She needs a clown like you, hasn't seen one for a long time, that's why she's asking for you! And I'm glad, glad that now she'll tear you to pieces! It's what you deserve. And she knows how to do it, oh, how she knows!'

PART THREE

I

People are forever complaining that we have no practical men; that there are, for example, many politicians; also many generals; various kinds of managers, as many as one might require, may presently be found wherever one looks – but practical men there are none. At least, everyone complains that there are none. It is even said that on several railways there are no decent staff; it is not possible to find even halfway tolerable staff to run a steam company, it is said. There, one hears, on some newly opened railway, coaches have collided or gone plunging down a collapsed bridge; there, they write, a train almost spent the whole winter in the midst of a snowfield: it travelled for a few hours, but got stuck in the snow for five days. Here, it is related, many thousands of poods[1] of merchandise are rotting in one place for two or three months, waiting to be dispatched, while there, it is said (though it is not even believed), an administrator, that is, some inspector or other, administered to some merchant's clerk who came bothering him about the dispatch of his goods, not a dispatch but a blow to the jaw, and, moreover, explained his administrative action by the fact that he had 'got a bit worked up'. There seem to be so many offices in the civil service that it is even terrifying to think of it; everyone has served, everyone is serving, everyone plans to serve – so why then, given such material, is it impossible to find decent staff to run a steam company?

To this an extremely simple answer is sometimes given – so simple that no one will even believe such an explanation. To be

sure, it is said, everyone in our country has worked in the service
or is currently serving, and this has already been going on
for two hundred years, on the best German example, from
grandfathers to grandsons – but civil servants are the least
practical of men, and it has got to the point where abstraction
and a lack of practical knowledge have, even quite recently, been
considered, even among civil servants themselves, as almost the
greatest virtue and recommendation. However, we ought not to
be talking about civil servants, we really intended to talk about
practical men. There is no doubt that we have always considered
timidity and a most complete lack of personal initiative to be
the principal and best indicators of the practical man – and they
are so considered even now. But why blame only ourselves – if
we construe this opinion as an accusation? Lack of originality
has always, everywhere, in the whole world, from time immemorial, been considered the primary quality and finest recommendation of the efficient, businesslike and practical man, and at
least ninety-nine per cent of men (at the very least) have always
shared this view, while only one per cent has viewed, and
continues to view, the matter differently.

At the beginning of their careers (and very often at the end of
them, too), inventors and geniuses have always been considered
in society as not much more than fools – that is really a most
routine observation, all too familiar to everyone. If, for example,
for scores of years everyone put their money into a loan bank,
depositing billions there at four per cent interest, then, of course,
when the loan bank folded and everyone was left to act on their
own initiative, the greater part of those billions would be bound
to perish in the stock-market fever and the hands of swindlers –
and this would even be demanded by decency and decorum.
Precisely by decorum; if decorous shyness and a decent lack
of originality have until now constituted for us, according to
generally received opinion, the inalienable qualities of the
businesslike and respectable man, it would be most indecorous
and even indecent to so suddenly change it all. What mother,
for example, tenderly loving her child, would not be dismayed
and sick with fear if her son or daughter were to go off the rails
by even the smallest of margins: 'No, let him be happy and live

comfortably, without originality,' thinks every mother, as she rocks her child. And our nurses, as they rock their children, have wailed and intoned from time immemorial: 'One day you'll walk about in gold, the rank of general you'll hold!' Thus, even among our nurses the rank of general was considered the acme of Russian happiness and has therefore been the most popular national ideal of peaceful, radiant bliss. And indeed, having passed the examination and served for thirty-five years – which of us would not be able to become generals and amass a certain amount in a loan bank? In this way the Russian, almost without any effort, has at last attained the designation of a businesslike and practical man. In essence only the man who is original, or in other words, the man who is restless, could fail to become a general. There may possibly be some misunderstanding here; but, on the whole, it seems that this is true and our society is quite correct in the way it defines its ideal of the practical man. None the less, we have said much that is superfluous; what we really intended to do was say a few explanatory words about the Yepanchin household, now familiar to us. Those people, or at least the more reasoning members of that household, constantly suffered from a certain family trait they almost all shared, one that was directly opposed to the virtues we were discussing just now, above. Not understanding the true situation completely (because it is difficult to understand), they still sometimes suspected that things in their household did not go as in others. In other households things went smoothly, while in theirs they went rather roughly; others simply rolled along the rails, while they kept falling *off* the rails. Others were always decorously diffident, while they were not. Lizaveta Prokofyevna, to be sure, was even very apprehensive, but this was not the decorous worldly diffidence for which they yearned. However, perhaps only Lizaveta Prokofyevna was anxious: the girls were still young – though a very shrewd and ironic bunch – while the general, though he was capable of being shrewd (though not without difficulty), in awkward situations merely said: 'Hmm!' and ended by placing all his hopes in Lizaveta Prokofyevna. So it was on her that the responsibility lay. And it was not as if, for example, this family were distinguished by any personal initiative, or fell off the rails out of any conscious inclination towards originality, which would have been quite indecent. Oh no! There was really nothing like that, that is to say, no consciously posited aim, and yet in the end it turned out that the Yepanchin household, though very respected, was none the less somehow not what all respected households ought to be. Recently Lizaveta Prokofyevna had begun to consider herself and her 'unfortunate character' to blame for everything – which made her sufferings even greater. She constantly referred to herself as a 'stupid, indecent eccentric', and suffered agonies of suspicion, was forever at a loss, unable to see a solution to the most ordinary conflicts, and was forever exaggerating all misfortunes.

Back at the beginning of our story we mentioned that the Yepanchins enjoyed widespread and real respect. Even General Ivan Fyodorovich, a man of obscure descent, was received unquestioningly everywhere with respect. He did indeed deserve respect, in the first place, as a man who was rich and 'not among the least', and, in the second place, as a man who was completely honest, though not any too clever. But a certain dullness of mind seems to be an almost indispensable quality if not of every public figure, then at least of every serious accumulator of money. Lastly, the general had decent manners, was modest, knew how to keep silent and at the same time not let anyone tread on his toes, and not just because of his general's rank, but also as a man of honour and good breeding. Most important of all was that he was a man with powerful patronage. As for Lizaveta Prokofyevna, she, as has already been explained above, was of good family, although in our country family is not paid much regard unless it is accompanied by the necessary connections. But she eventually turned out to have the connections, too; she was respected and, eventually, loved by persons of such standing that after that everyone had no option but to respect and receive her. There is no doubt that the torments of anxiety she endured about her family were groundless, had a trivial cause and were exaggerated to the point of the ridiculous: but if someone has a wart on their nose or their forehead, it really does seem that the only thing anyone in the world wants to do is to look at your wart, laugh at it and condemn you for it, even though you may have discovered America in the meanwhile. There is no doubt either that in society Lizaveta Prokofyevna really was considered an 'eccentric'; she was also unquestionably respected; but in the end, Lizaveta Prokofyevna began not to believe that she was respected – and that was where all the trouble lay. As she looked at her daughters, she was tormented by the suspicion that she was forever harming their career in some way, that her character was ridiculous, indecent and intolerable – for which, of course, she constantly accused her daughters and Ivan Fyodorovich, and quarrelled with them for whole days on end, while at the same time loving them to the point of self-forgetfulness and almost to the point of passion.

She was tormented most of all by the suspicion that her daughters were becoming 'eccentrics' like herself, and that there were no girls like them in society, nor should there be. 'They're growing into nihilists, that's the plain truth of it!' she would say to herself. During the last year, and especially in the most recent days, this melancholy thought had begun to take an increasing hold of her. 'In the first place, why don't they get married?' she kept asking herself. 'In order to torment their mother – that's become the aim of their lives, and it's all because of these new-fangled ideas, that damned "woman question"! Didn't Aglaya take it into her head six months ago to cut off her magnificent hair? (Merciful Lord, I never had hair like that in my day!) I mean, the scissors were in her hands, I got down on my knees to beg her not to! . . . Well, one must assume she did it out of spite, to torment her mother to the limit, because she's a wicked girl, self-willed, spoilt, but above all, wicked, wicked, wicked! And didn't that fat Alexandra compete with her by also cutting off her tresses, and not out of spite, not on caprice, but sincerely, like a fool, because Aglaya had convinced her that she'd sleep better without hair, and her headaches would go? And how many suitors have they had – it's five years now – how many, how many? And they were really good-looking men, sometimes even the most splendid-looking men! But what are they waiting for, why don't they marry? Just in order to vex their mother – there can be no other reason! None! None!'

At last the sun was about to rise for her motherly heart; at least one daughter, at least Adelaida, would finally be settled. 'At least that's one off our hands,' said Lizaveta Prokofyevna, when she had to express an opinion on the subject (privately she expressed herself in much gentler fashion). And how well and how properly the whole thing had been handled; people had even begun to talk of it in society with respect. A man of renown, a prince, with a fortune, a man who was good and who in addition to all that was one after her own heart – what, it seemed, could be better? But earlier, too, she had been less afraid about Adelaida than about her other daughters, though her artistic inclinations sometimes ceaselessly troubled Lizaveta Prokofyevna's doubting heart. 'But she has a cheerful character, and a lot of common sense besides – so the girl won't come to grief,' she comforted herself in the last result. It was Aglaya she worried most about. Incidentally, with regard to her eldest, Alexandra, she did not know what to think: should she be worried about her or not? Now it seemed to her that the girl had quite 'come to grief'; she was twenty-five – and so she would be left an old maid. And 'with such beauty! . . .' Lizaveta Prokofyevna even wept for her at nights, while on those same nights Alexandra Ivanovna slept the soundest sleep. 'But what is she – a nihilist or just a fool?' That she was not a fool – of that, however, even Lizaveta Prokofyevna was in no doubt: she had exceeding respect for Alexandra Ivanovna's opinions, and liked to seek her advice.[2] But that she was a 'wet hen' – of that there was no doubt: 'she's so placid that one can't shake her out of slumber! As a matter of fact, even "wet hens" aren't placid. Fie! They really do exasperate me!' Lizaveta Prokofyevna had a kind of inexplicable compassion and sympathy for Alexandra, more even than for Aglaya, whom she idolized. But her splenetic outbursts (in which, above all, her maternal concern and sympathy were manifested), her teasing, such names as 'wet hen', only made Alexandra laugh. It sometimes got to the point that the most trivial things would make Lizaveta Prokofyevna terribly angry and throw her into a rage. For example, Alexandra Ivanovna was fond of sleeping for a very long time and usually had many dreams; but her dreams were always characterized by a kind of extraordinary triviality and innocence – they would have been right for a seven-year-old child; and so, even the innocence of these dreams began to irritate her mother for some reason. Once Alexandra Ivanovna had a dream about nine hens, and it caused a regular quarrel between her and her mother, why it was hard to explain. Once, only once, she succeeded in dreaming something that seemed original – she dreamed about a monk, on his own in some dark room she was frightened to enter. The dream was at once reported in triumph to Lizaveta Prokofyevna by the two laughing sisters; but their mother got angry again and called all three of them fools. 'Hm! Placid as a fool, and I mean she's an utter "wet hen", one can't shake her out of bed in the morning, yet she's melancholy, sometimes she looks really melancholy! What is she grieving about, what?' Sometimes she would ask Ivan Fyodorovich this question, and in the way she usually did, hysterically, threateningly, expecting an immediate reply. Ivan Fyodorovich would hem and haw, frown, shrug his shoulders and decide, at last, lifting his hands in dismay:

'She needs a husband!'

'Only please God may it not be one like you, Ivan Fyodorovich,' Lizaveta Prokofyevna would explode at last, like a bomb. 'Not like you in his opinions and verdicts; not a coarse boor like you, Ivan Fyodorovich . . .'

Ivan Fyodorovich would immediately withdraw, while Lizaveta Prokyevna calmed down after her 'explosion'. Of course, towards evening of the same day she would invariably become uncommonly attentive, quiet, affectionate and respectful to Ivan Fyodorovich, her 'coarse boor Ivan Fyodorovich', her kind and charming, adored Ivan Fyodorovich, because all her life she had loved her Ivan Fyodorovich, and even been in love with him, something that Ivan Fyodorovich knew very well and because of which he had an infinite respect for his Lizaveta Prokofyevna.

But her principal and constant torment was Aglaya.

'Exactly like me, exactly, my portrait in every way,' Lizaveta Prokofyevna would say, 'the self-willed, nasty little demon! A nihilist, an eccentric, a mad girl, wicked, wicked, wicked! Oh, Lord, how unhappy she's going to be!'

But, as we have already said, a rising sun began to soften and illuminate everything for a moment. There was almost a month in which she had had a complete rest from all her anxieties. People began to talk about Adelaida's imminent wedding and also about Aglaya, and in this Aglaya had comported herself so splendidly, so calmly, so cleverly, so triumphantly, with a certain pride; but after all, that suited her so well! So affectionate, so friendly she had been towards her mother for a whole month! ('It's true, that Yevgeny Pavlovich needs to be watched very, very closely, he needs to be thoroughly investigated, and Aglaya doesn't seem to show him much more affection than she does the others!') Yet she had suddenly become such a wonderful girl – and how pretty, oh Lord, how pretty she was, better from one day to the next! And now . . .

And now this wretched little princeling had appeared, this rubbishy little idiot, and it had all been stirred up again, everything in the house had been turned upside down!

But what had happened, really?

Others would probably not have thought that anything had happened. But what distinguished Lizaveta Prokofyevna was that in the melée and muddle of the most ordinary things, because of the anxiety that was always in her, she always managed to discover something that frightened her to the point of making her ill with the most suspicious, most inexplicable fear, which was therefore very difficult to endure. How must she have felt now, when suddenly, through the confusion of her absurd and unfounded anxieties, there really did begin to peep through something that was indeed important, something that really did justify her anxieties and doubts and suspicions.

'And how did they dare, how did they dare write me that accursed anonymous letter about that *creature*, that she sees Aglaya?' thought Lizaveta Prokofyevna all the way, as she dragged the prince after her, and at home, when she had sat him down at the circular table, around which the entire household was assembled. 'How did they even dare to think of it? Why, I would have died of shame had I believed even one word of it, or had I shown Aglaya that letter! Such gibes at us Yepanchins! And all, all of it because of Ivan Fyodorych, all because of you,

Ivan Fyodorych! Oh, why didn't we go to Yelagin: I mean, I said we should go to Yelagin! It may have been Varya who wrote the letter, I know, or perhaps ... Ivan Fyodorych is to blame for all of it, all of it! That *creature* has played this trick on him, in memory of their previous relations, to make him look like a fool, just as she used to laugh at him like the fool he was, led him by the nose when he took her pearls ... And the end of it is that we're all mixed up in it, your daughters are mixed up in it, Ivan Fyodorych, girls, young ladies, young ladies of the best society, brides-to-be, they were here, stood here, heard everything, and they were also mixed up in the episode with the urchins, you ought to rejoice in that, they were also here and listened! I shall never forgive, I won't ever forgive that wretched little prince, I will never forgive him! And why has Aglaya been in a hysterical fit for three days, why has she almost quarrelled with her sisters, even with Alexandra, whose hands she has always kissed like those of her mother – so much did she respect her? Why has she been posing riddles for everyone for three days? What is Gavrila Ivolgin's role in all this? Why did she start singing paeans of praise to Gavrila Ivolgin and bursting into tears? Why is that wretched "poor knight" mentioned in that anonymous letter, when she hasn't shown the letter from the prince even to her sisters? And for what reason ... why, why did I go running to him like a scalded cat and drag him here myself? Merciful Lord, I must have taken leave of my senses, the things I've been doing now! Discussing my daughter's secrets with a young man, and ... and secrets that concern him! Merciful Lord, it's just as well he's an idiot and ... and ... a friend of the family! But can Aglaya really have fallen for a freak like that? Lord, what nonsense I'm talking! Pah! We're eccentrics ... we ought all to be displayed under glass, me first, for an entrance fee of ten copecks. I won't forgive you for this, Ivan Fedorych, I will never forgive it! And why isn't she working on him now ? She said she would, but she's not! Look, look, she's staring at him, all eyes, she doesn't say anything, doesn't go away, just stands there, yet she told him not to come calling ... He sits there all pale. And that damned, damned chatterbox Yevgeny Pavlych, he's taken over the whole conversation! Listen to his outpourings, he doesn't let one get a word in. I would have discovered it all at once, if I'd been able to open my mouth . . .'

The prince was indeed sitting, rather pale, at the circular table, apparently in a state of extreme fear combined with an intermittent rapture that was incomprehensible to him and enveloped his soul. Oh, how afraid he was to look in that direction, into that corner, from where two familiar black eyes looked at him, and at the same time how he thrilled with happiness that he was sitting here again among them, that he would hear the familiar voice – after what she had written to him. 'Lord, what will she say now?' He himself did not utter a single word and listened with strained attention to the 'outpourings' of Yevgeny Pavlovich, who had been seldom in such a happy and excited mood as he was now, this evening. The prince listened to him for a long time almost without understanding a word. Everyone had assembled, apart from Ivan Fyodorovich, who had not yet returned from St Petersburg. Prince Shch. was here too. It appeared that in a while, once they had had tea, they were going off to listen to the band. The present conversation had evidently started before the prince's arrival. Soon Kolya slid on to the veranda, having arrived from somewhere. 'So he's being received here as he was before,' the prince thought to himself.

The Yepanchins' dacha was a luxurious one, in the style of a Swiss chalet, elegantly adorned on every side with flowers and leaves. It was surrounded on all sides by a small but beautiful flower garden. As at the prince's, everyone sat on the veranda; only the veranda was somewhat more spacious and more stylishly appointed.

The theme of the conversation that had begun was not, it seemed, to the taste of many; the conversation, as might be expected, had started from an impatient quarrel and, of course, everyone would have liked to have changed the subject, but Yevgeny Pavlovich seemed to be persisting, and ignoring the effect this was making; the prince's arrival seemed to stimulate him even more. Lizaveta Prokofyevna was frowning, though she did not understand everything. Aglaya, who sat at the side, almost in the corner, did not go away, listened and was stubbornly silent.

'If you please,' Yevgeny Pavlovich was retorting heatedly, 'I have nothing against liberalism. Liberalism is not a sin; it's a necessary part of the whole, which without it would disintegrate or start to rigidify; liberalism has just as much right to exist as the most well-behaved conservatism; but it's Russian liberalism I'm attacking, and I repeat again that I attack it really because a Russian liberal is not a *Russian* liberal, but an *un-Russian* liberal. Give me a Russian liberal, and I will kiss him in front of you right now.'

'If he's willing to kiss you, you mean,' said Alexandra Ivanovna, who was in an extraordinary state of excitement. Her cheeks had grown even redder than usual.

'Just look at her,' Lizaveta Prokofyevna thought to herself, 'she spends all her time sleeping and eating, you can't budge her, and then once a year she suddenly gets up and says something that makes you simply throw up your hands in horror.'

The prince observed in passing that Alexandra Ivanovna did not like Yevgeny Pavlovich speaking so cheerfully on a serious subject, and seeming to grow vehement while at the same time apparently joking.

'I was maintaining just now, just before your arrival, Prince,' Yevgeny Pavlovich continued, 'that until now our liberals have come from only two social strata, the old landowning class (now obsolete) and the graduates of the religious seminaries. And since both of these classes have finally turned into out and out castes, into something quite distinct from the nation, and increasingly so, from generation to generation, then it follows that all that they have done and are doing is completely non-national . . .'

'What? So all that's been done – none of it's Russian?' retorted Prince Shch.

'Not national; Russian maybe, but not national; our liberals aren't Russian, and our conservatives aren't Russian, none of them . . . And you can be assured that the nation won't recognize anything that's done by the landowners and the seminarians, either now, or later . . .'

'That's a good one! How can you maintain such a paradox, if you are serious? I cannot allow such attacks on the Russian landowner; you're a Russian landowner yourself,' Prince Shch. retorted heatedly.

'But I'm not speaking about the Russian landowner in the sense in which you take it. An honourable class, if only because I belong to it; especially now that it's ceased to exist . . .'

'Has there really been nothing national in our literature, either?' Alexandra Ivanovna interrupted.

'I'm no authority on literature, but it seems to me that none of Russian literature is Russian, except perhaps for Lomonosov, Pushkin and Gogol.'

'For one thing, that's rather a lot, and for another, one of them was a commoner, while the other two were landowners,' Alexandra began to laugh.

'Indeed so, but don't crow. Because, out of all Russian writers to date, only those three managed to say something to each individual reader that was really *his*, his own, not borrowed from anyone, by that same fact those three also at once became national. Any Russian who says, writes or does something of his own, something that is inalienably *his* and that has not been borrowed, inevitably becomes national, even though he may not even speak Russian very well. To me, this is an axiom. But we weren't talking about literature, we were talking about the socialists, and it was about them that the conversation started; well, so I maintain that we don't have a single Russian socialist; we don't and never have done, because all our socialists are also from the landowners or the seminarians. All our inveterate, proclaimed socialists, both the local and the foreign, are nothing more than landowner liberals from the days of serfdom. Why are you laughing? Give me their books, give me their teachings, their memoirs, and I, who am no literary critic, will undertake to write you a most convincing literary critique, in which I shall prove with daylight clarity that every page of their books, brochures and memoirs is written by none other than a former Russian landowner. Their spite, indignation and wit are land-ownerly (even pre-Famusov!);[3] their rapture, their tears, genuine, perhaps, sincere, but – landownerly! Landownerly or seminarian . . . You're laughing again, and you're laughing, too, Prince? You don't agree either?'

They really were all laughing, and the prince smiled too.

'I can't say yet straight out whether I agree or disagree,' said the prince, suddenly smiling no more, and starting with the look of a schoolboy caught in the act, 'but I assure you that I'm listening to you with great pleasure . . .'

As he said this, he almost choked, and a cold sweat even broke out on his forehead. These were the first words uttered by him since he had sat down here. He tried to look around him, but did not dare; Yevgeny Pavlovich caught his gesture, and smiled.

'I will tell you a fact, ladies and gentlemen,' he continued in his earlier tone of voice, that is, apparently with extraordinary enthusiasm and fervour yet at the same time almost laughing, perhaps at his own words, 'a fact, an observation the discovery of which I have the honour to ascribe to myself, and even to myself alone; at any rate nothing has been said or written about this anywhere yet. In this fact is expressed the whole essence of Russian liberalism of the kind of which I speak. In the first place, what is liberalism, generally speaking, if not an attack (reasonable or erroneous – that is another question) on the existing order of things? That is so, is it not? Well, so my fact consists in the perception that Russian liberalism is not an attack on the existing order of things, but an attack on the very essence of the things in our land, the things themselves, and not just an attack on order, on the Russian social order, but on Russia itself. My liberal has got to the point where he rejects Russia itself, that is, he hates and beats his own mother. Every unhappy and unfortunate fact of Russian life arouses laughter in him, rapture, almost. He hates our national customs, Russian history, everything. If there is an excuse for him, it is perhaps that he doesn't know what he is doing, and mistakes his hatred of Russia for the most fruitful liberalism (oh, in our country you will often meet a liberal whom the others applaud and who is really, perhaps, the most absurd, the most stupid and dangerous conservative, without being aware of it himself!). Not so long ago, our liberals almost mistook this hatred of Russia for a genuine love of the fatherland, and they boasted that they saw better than others what it ought to consist of; but now they have grown more candid and have even begun to be ashamed of the words 'love of the fatherland', have even banished the concept and got rid of it as something harmful and trivial. This is an established fact, I insist on that and . . . after all, it was necessary to speak the truth one day, wholly, simply and candidly; but at the same time this fact is something of a kind that has not ever, anywhere, since time immemorial, existed or occurred in a single nation on earth, and so it may be a mere accident, and will pass, I admit. There cannot be a liberal anywhere who would hate his own fatherland. How can all this be explained in our country, then? In the same way as before – because a Russian liberal is at present not a Russian liberal; that's the only explanation there can be, in my view.'

'I take all that you have said as a joke, Yevgeny Pavlych,' Prince Shch. retorted gravely.

'I haven't seen every liberal and will not undertake to judge,' said Alexandra Ivanovna, 'but I listened to your idea with indignation: you have taken a particular instance and have elevated it into a general law, and so you've committed a slander.'

'A particular instance? Ah, ah! The word is spoken,' Yevgeny Pavlovich chimed in. 'Prince, what do you think, is it a particular instance or isn't it?'

'I must also say that I haven't seen much and haven't spent much time with . . . liberals,' said the prince, 'but it seems to me that you are possibly right to a certain extent, and that the Russian liberalism you spoke of really is sometimes inclined to hate Russia itself, and not simply the Russian order of things. Of course, it's only sometimes . . . of course, it can't be true of them all . . .'

He stopped short, and did not finish his sentence. In spite of his excitement, the conversation interested him greatly. The prince had one peculiar trait which consisted in the extraordinary naivety of the attention with which he always listened to something that was of interest to him, and of the replies he gave when people addressed him with questions. Somehow his face and even the position of his body expressed this naivety, this faith that suspected neither mockery nor humour. But although Yevgeny Pavlovich had long addressed him only with a certain special kind of ironic smile, now, in response to this reply, he gave him a very serious look, as though he had not at all expected such an answer from him.

'Yes . . . well, you are a strange fellow,' he said. 'And really, was your reply a serious one, Prince?'

'Wasn't your question a serious one?' retorted the prince in surprise.

They all began to laugh.

'Trust him,' said Adelaida. 'Yevgeny Pavlych always makes a fool of people! If you only knew the things he sometimes says, so solemnly, too!'

'In my opinion this is a painful conversation, and one that should not have been started at all,' Alexandra observed sharply. 'We were going to go out for a walk . . .'

'And let's go, it's a lovely evening!' exclaimed Yevgeny Pavlovich. 'But, in order to prove to you that on this occasion I was speaking quite seriously, and, principally, in order to prove it to the prince (you have begun to interest me exceedingly, Prince, and I swear to you that I'm not quite such a frivolous fellow as I am sure I must seem – though I am indeed a frivolous fellow!), and . . . if you will permit, ladies and gentlemen, I shall ask the prince one final question, out of my own curiosity, and then let us leave it at that. This question came into my head, as if on purpose, two hours ago (you see, Prince, I also sometimes reflect on serious matters); I resolved it, but let us see what the prince says. Just now there was talk of a "particular instance". That phrase is very significant in our country, one hears it frequently. Not long ago everyone was talking and writing about that dreadful murder of six people by that . . . young man and about the strange speech of the defence counsel, in which it was said that because of the criminal's impoverished state it must have been *natural* for him to kill those six people. That was not the literal wording, but that, I think, was the sense, or nearly so. In my personal opinion, the defence counsel who expressed such a strange idea was utterly convinced that he was saying the most liberal, most humane and progressive thing that could be said in our days. Well, so what do you think: this distortion of concepts and convictions, this possibility of such a twisted and extraordinary view of the matter, is this a particular instance or a general one?'

They all began to laugh loudly.

'A particular one; of course, a particular one,' Alexandra and Adelaida laughed.

'And permit me to remind you again, Yevgeny Pavlych,' added Prince Shch., that your joke has worn very thin.'

'What do you think, Prince?' Yevgeny Pavlovich did not listen to the end, catching Prince Lev Nikolayevich's inquisitive and serious gaze on him. 'How does it seem to you: is it a particular instance or a general one? I confess that I thought up this question for you.'

'No, it's not a particular one,' the prince said quietly but firmly.

'For heaven's sake, Lev Nikolayevich,' Prince Shch. exclaimed with some vexation, 'can't you see that he's trying to catch you out; he's positively laughing at you and is determined to tear you to pieces.'

'I thought Yevgeny Pavlych was speaking in earnest,' the prince blushed and lowered his eyes.

'Dear Prince,' Prince Shch. continued, 'remember what you and I talked about once, about three months ago; what we talked about was that it's now possible to point to so many splendid and talented defence lawyers in our newly opened courts! And about all the splendid jury verdicts there have been! How pleased you were, and how pleased I was at the time about your pleasure . . . we said we could be proud . . . But this clumsy defence, this strange argument is, of course, an accident, an individual case among thousands.'

Prince Lev Nikolayevich thought for a bit, but with an air of being thoroughly convinced, though he spoke quietly and even almost timidly, replied:

'All I wanted to say is that the distortion of ideas and concepts (as Yevgeny Pavlych expressed it) is encountered very often, and it's far more of a general than a particular instance, unfortunately. Even to the point where if this distortion were not such a general instance, there might perhaps not be as many unspeakable crimes like these . . .'

'Unspeakable crimes? But I assure you that crimes of precisely this kind, and, perhaps, even more dreadful, took place earlier, and have always taken place, and not only in our country, but everywhere else as well, and, in my opinion, will go on being repeated for a very long time yet. The difference is that in our country earlier there was less public accountability, whereas now people have begun to talk aloud and even write about them, and that is why it seems as though these criminals have only just appeared. That's where your mistake lies, Prince, I assure you,' Prince Shch. smiled mockingly.

'I know that earlier, too, there were many crimes, and just as dreadful; I've recently visited prisons, and I managed to get acquainted with several criminals and accused men. There are criminals even more terrible than this one, men who have murdered ten people without any remorse whatsoever. But what I've noticed is that the most hardened and unrepentant murderer knows he is a *criminal*, that is, believes in his conscience that he has acted wrongly, even though he has no remorse. And they are all of them like that; but you see, those people Yevgeny Pavlych started to talk about don't even want to consider themselves criminals and privately consider that they had a right to do what they did, and . . . even did the right thing, I mean, it's almost like that. It's there, in my opinion, that the dreadful difference lies. And note that they are all young men, that is, precisely of an age at which one is most vulnerable and prone to fall victim to the distortion of ideas.'

Prince Shch. was no longer laughing, and listened to the prince with a puzzled look. Alexandra Ivanovna, who had long wanted to make some observation, fell silent, as though some peculiar thought had stopped her. As for Yevgeny Pavlovich, he looked at the prince in genuine surprise, and on this occasion now without the slightest of ironical smiles.

'But why are you so surprised at him, my dear sir,' Lizaveta Prokofyevna intervened unexpectedly. 'Did you think he was more stupid than you, and couldn't argue as you do, is that what it is?'

'No, ma'am, I was not concerned with that,' said Yevgeny Pavlovich. 'It's just that, well, how did it come about that you, Prince (forgive me asking), if you see things like that and argue that way, how was it (forgive me again) that in that strange business . . . the incident that took place the other day . . . involving Burdovsky, I think . . . how was it that you didn't notice any distortion of ideas and moral convictions there? I mean, it's exactly the same! It seemed to me at the time that you hadn't noticed it.'

'Well I'll tell you this, my dear,' Lizaveta Prokofyevna said vehemently, 'we noticed everything, sitting here boasting in front of him, and today he got a letter from one of them, the main, the pimply one, you remember, Alexandra? In the letter he asks his forgiveness, though in his own manner, and declares that he has broken with that companion of his who egged him on at the time – you remember, Alexandra? And that he has more faith in the prince now. Well, but we haven't yet had a letter like that, so we can't turn up our noses at him here.'

'And Ippolit has also just moved into our dacha!' cried Kolya.

'What? Is he here already?' the prince said in alarm.

'He arrived just after you left with Lizaveta Prokofyevna; I brought him over!'

'Oh, I'll bet you,' Lizaveta Prokofyevna boiled up suddenly, completely forgetting that she had just been praising the prince, 'I'll bet you he went to see him in his garret yesterday and begged forgiveness of him on his knees to get that malicious little snake to consent to move over here. Did you go there yesterday? Why, you confessed it yourself earlier. Did you or not? Did you get down on your knees?'

'Of course he didn't,' cried Kolya, 'but quite the opposite: Ippolit seized the prince's hand yesterday and kissed it twice, I saw it myself, and that was the end of the whole discussion, except that the prince simply said that Ippolit would feel better at the dacha, and Ippolit agreed to come there at once, as soon as he felt better.'

'You oughtn't to say that, Kolya . . .' muttered the prince, getting up and grabbing his hat, 'why are you telling them that . . .'

'Where are you going?' Lizaveta Prokofyevna stopped him.

'Don't worry, Prince,' the excited Kolya continued. 'Don't go and bother him, he's fallen asleep after the journey; he's very happy; and you know, Prince, in my opinion, it would be far better if you didn't meet today; even put it off until tomorrow, or else he'll get embarrassed again. Yesterday morning he said that he hadn't felt so well and strong for a whole six months; he's even coughing much less.'

The prince noticed that Aglaya had suddenly left her place and gone over to the table. He did not dare to look at her, but he felt with all his being that at that moment she was looking at him and was, perhaps, looking sternly, that there was certainly indignation in her black eyes, and her face was flushed.

'Well, Nikolai Ardalionovich, I think you ought not to have brought him here, if this is the same consumptive boy who burst into tears that time and invited us to his funeral,' observed Yevgeny Pavlovich. 'He spoke so eloquently that night about the wall of the house next door that he must surely be pining away for it, you may be certain of that.'

'What you say is true: he'll fall out with you, fight with you and go away, that's the whole story!'

And with dignity Lizaveta Prokofyevna moved up her sewing-basket, forgetting that everyone was getting up to go out for a walk.

'I remember he used to boast a lot about that wall,' Yevgeny Pavlovich interjected again. 'Without that wall he won't be able to die eloquently, and he very much wants to die eloquently.'

'So what, then?' muttered the prince. 'If you're not willing to forgive him, he'll die without you ... Now he's come for the sake of the trees.'

'Oh, as far as I'm concerned I forgive him everything; you can tell him that.'

'That's not what I meant,' the prince replied quietly and almost reluctantly, continuing to look at one point on the floor, and without raising his eyes. 'What I meant was that you must agree to accept forgiveness from him, too.'

'How am I involved here? In what way am I guilty before him?'

'If you don't understand, then . . . but I mean, you do understand; that time he wanted to . . . bless you all and receive
blessing from you, that's all . . .'

'Dear Prince,' Prince Shch. interjected somewhat cautiously,
exchanging glances with some of those present, 'paradise on
earth is not attained easily; but you rely on paradise a little too
much; paradise is a difficult thing, Prince, far more difficult
than it seems to your splendid heart. Let's stop this, for otherwise I think we shall indeed all get embarrassed again, and
then . . .'

'Let's go and listen to the band,' Lizaveta Prokofyevna said
sharply, getting up from her place in anger.

Everyone else rose, too.

2

The prince suddenly went up to Yevgeny Pavlovich.

'Yevgeny Pavlovich,' he said with strange fervour, seizing him
by the arm, 'be assured that I consider you the most noble and
best of men, in spite of everything; be assured of that . . .'

Yevgeny Pavlovich even took a step backwards in surprise.
For a moment he restrained himself from an irresistible fit of
laughter; but, taking a closer look, he noticed that the prince
was somehow not himself, or at least in some peculiar condition.

'I'll wager, Prince,' he exclaimed, 'that you wanted to say
something else and, perhaps, not to me at all . . . But what is
wrong with you? You're not feeling ill, are you?'

'Possibly, very possibly, and that was a very subtle observation, that perhaps it wasn't you I wanted to approach!'

Having said this, he smiled a strange and even absurd smile,
but then suddenly, as if working himself into a passion,
exclaimed:

'Don't remind me of my action three days ago! I have felt very
ashamed these past three days . . . I know that I'm to blame . . .'

'But . . . but what did you do that was so dreadful?'

'I see that you, perhaps more than anyone else, are ashamed

of me, Yevgeny Pavlovich; you're blushing, that is the mark of a noble heart. I'm going right now, rest assured.'

'But what's he talking about? Is this how his fits begin?' Lizaveta Prokofyevna turned to Kolya in alarm.

'Don't pay any attention, Lizaveta Prokofyevna, I'm not having a fit; I'm going right now. I know that I'm . . . afflicted by nature. I was ill for twenty-four years, until the age of twenty-four. So accept what I say now as coming from someone who is ill. I am going right now, right now, rest assured. I am not blushing – because after all it would be strange to blush over this, would it not? – but in company I am superfluous . . . I don't say it out of vanity . . . I've been thinking things over these past three days and have decided that I have a duty to inform you sincerely and honourably at the earliest opportunity. There are ideas, there are lofty ideas of which I must not start to speak, because I'll be bound to make you all laugh; Prince Shch. reminded me of that just now . . . I have no decent gestures, no sense of proportion; my words are different, and my thoughts do not conform, and that's a humiliation for those thoughts. And so I don't have the right . . . what's more, I'm hypersensitive, I . . . I'm convinced that in this house no one can hurt me or love me more than I deserve, but I know (I mean, I know for certain) that after twenty years of illness there cannot fail to be some sort of residue, so that people will be bound to laugh at me . . . sometimes . . . it's true, isn't it?'

He seemed to be waiting for a reply and a resolution, looking around him. They all stood in painful bewilderment at this unexpected, morbid and, it would seem, at any rate unmotivated outburst. But the outburst formed the pretext for a strange episode.

'Why are you saying this here?' Aglaya suddenly exclaimed. 'Why are you saying it to them? Them! Them!'

She seemed to be in the last degree of indignation: her eyes were blazing. The prince stood before her mute and speechless and suddenly turned pale.

'There's no one here who is worthy of such words!' Aglaya burst out. 'None of them, none of them here are worthy of your little finger, nor your heart! You are more honourable than them all, nobler than them all, better than them all, kinder than them all, cleverer than them all! There are people here who are unworthy to bend down and pick up the handkerchief you've dropped . . . Why do you humiliate yourself and make yourself lower than them all? Why have you twisted everything in yourself, why is there no pride in you?'

'Merciful Lord, who would have thought it?' Lizaveta Prokofyevna threw up her hands.

'The poor knight! Hurrah!' Kolya cried in rapture.

'Be quiet! . . . How dare they insult me here in your home!' Aglaya suddenly hurled at Lizaveta Prokofyevna, now in that hysterical condition when no limits are any longer observed and when all obstacles are set aside. 'Why does everyone, every single person, torment me? Why do they all make my life a misery because of you, Prince? I will not marry you, not for anything! Understand that, never, and not for anything! Understand it! How could one possibly marry someone as absurd as you? Take a look at yourself in the mirror, the way you're standing now! . . . Why, why do they tease me, saying I'm going to marry you? You must know the answer! You're in the conspiracy with them!'

'No one has ever teased you!' Adelaida muttered in alarm.

'No one has ever had anything like that in their minds, nothing like that has been said!' exclaimed Alexandra Ivanovna.

'Who's been teasing her? When did they tease her? Who could have said that to her? Is she raving, or isn't she?' Lizaveta Prokofyevna addressed them all, trembling with anger.

'Everyone's been saying it, every single person, for a whole three days! I will never, never marry him!'

Having shouted this out, Aglaya dissolved into bitter tears, covered her face with her handkerchief, and flopped into a chair.

'But he hasn't asked you yet . . .'

'I haven't asked you, Aglaya Ivanovna,' the prince suddenly blurted out.

'Wha-at?' Lizaveta Prokofyevna drawled suddenly in surprise, indignation and horror. 'What on e-e-arth?'

She was unwilling to believe her ears.

'I meant . . . I meant,' the prince began to tremble, 'I merely

wanted to explain to Aglaya Ivanovna . . . to have the honour
of explaining that I have never had the intention of . . . having
the honour of asking for her hand . . . even some day . . . I'm
not to blame for this in any way, I swear to God, I'm not to
blame, Aglaya Ivanovna! I've never wanted to, and it has never
been in my mind, I will never want to, you'll see: rest assured!
Some cruel person has slandered me to you! You mustn't worry!'

As he said this, he approached Aglaya. She took away the
handkerchief with which she had been covering her face, gave
a quick glance at him and his frightened figure, made sense of
his words and suddenly burst into loud laughter, straight in his
face – such cheerful and irrepressible laughter, such absurd
and mocking laughter that Adelaida was the first to lose her
self-restraint, especially when she also cast a glance at the prince;
she rushed to her sister, embraced her and began to laugh the
same irrepressible, schoolgirlish, cheerful laughter. As he looked
at them, the prince suddenly also began to smile and with a
joyful and happy expression began to repeat:

'Well, thank God, thank God!'

Now Alexandra too could no longer restrain herself, and she
began to laugh at the top of her voice. It seemed that there
would be no end to the laughter of all three.

'Let's go for our walk, let's go for our walk!' cried Adelaida.
'All of us together, and the prince must come, too; there's no
reason for you to leave, you dear man! What a dear man he is,
Aglaya! Don't you think so, Mama? What's more, I absolutely,
absolutely must give him a kiss and a hug for . . . for his being
so candid with Aglaya just now. *Maman*, dear, will you allow
me to give him a kiss? Aglaya! Allow me to give *your* prince a
kiss!' cried the mischievous girl, and she really did jump over to
the prince and give him a kiss on the forehead. He seized
her hands and pressed them tightly, so that Adelaida almost
exclaimed, gave her a look of infinite delight and suddenly,
swiftly brought her hand to his lips and kissed it three times.

'But let's be off!' called Aglaya. 'Prince, you shall escort me.
May he do that, *Maman*? A suitor who has refused me? After
all, you've refused me for ever, haven't you, Prince? But that's
not the way, that's not the way to give your arm to a lady, don't

you know how to take a lady by the arm? That's the way, come along now, we shall go ahead of them all, do you want to walk ahead of them all, *tête-à-tête*?'

She spoke without cease, still laughing in gusts.

'Thank God! Thank God!' Lizaveta Prokofyevna kept repeating, not knowing herself why she was so happy.

'Exceedingly strange people!' thought Prince Shch., for perhaps the hundredth time since he had begun to associate with them, but ... he liked these strange people. Regarding the prince, it was possible that he did not like him very much; as they all went out to take their walk, Prince Shch. had a somewhat frowning and worried look.

Yevgeny Pavlovich, it seemed, was in a most cheerful frame of mind. All the way to the station he amused Alexandra and Adelaida, who laughed with a rather excessive readiness at his jokes, to a point where he fleetingly began to suspect that they might not be listening to him at all. This thought made him suddenly burst out laughing, with extreme and complete sincerity (such was his character!). The sisters, who were, as a matter of fact, in a most festive mood, kept casting looks at Aglaya and the prince, who were walking in front; it was plain that the younger sister had posed them a major riddle. Prince Shch. kept trying to talk to Lizaveta Prokofyevna about irrelevant matters, perhaps in order to divert her, and had bored her dreadfully. She seemed quite distraught, replied inappropriately, and sometimes did not reply at all. But Aglaya Ivanovna's riddles were not yet at an end that evening. The last one fell to the lot of the prince alone. When they had gone about a hundred paces from the dacha, Aglaya said to her stubbornly silent *chevalier* in a quick half-whisper:

'Look to the right.'

The prince cast a glance.

'Look more closely. Do you see that bench, in the park, over there where those three big trees are ... the green bench?'

The prince replied that he saw it.

'Don't you like that spot? I sometimes come and sit here early, at about seven in the morning, when everyone is still asleep.'

The prince muttered that it was a beautiful spot.

'And now leave me, I don't want to walk arm in arm with you any more. Or rather, walk arm in arm with me, but don't say a word to me. I want to think in private . . .'

The warning was in any case unnecessary: the prince would probably not have uttered a single word all the way, even without being instructed. When he heard about the bench, his heart began to beat horribly. A moment later he pulled himself together and, with shame, drove away the absurd thought.

As everyone knows and as everyone at least asserts, the public that assembles in the Pavlovsk pleasure gardens on weekdays is more 'select' than on Sundays and holidays, when 'all kinds of people' come visiting from the city. The ladies' dresses are not festive, but they are elegant. It is the accepted custom to meet by the bandstand. The band is perhaps the finest of our park bands, and plays the latest things. Propriety and decorum are exceedingly well observed, in spite of a certain general air of homeliness, and even intimacy. Acquaintances, all of whom are dacha-dwellers, meet to take a look at one another. Many do this with genuine pleasure and come only for this purpose; but there are also those who come only to listen to the band. Scandals are extremely rare, though they do happen, even on weekdays. But such things are inevitable, after all.

On this occasion the evening was a beautiful one, and there was quite a large crowd. All the seats near the band were taken. Our company settled down on chairs a little to the side, near the left-hand exit from the park. The crowd and the band enlivened Lizaveta Prokofyevna somewhat and diverted the young ladies; they contrived to exchange glances with some of the people they knew, and nodded politely to one or two of them from afar; they managed to examine the dresses, observe some strange eccentricities, discuss them, and smile mockingly. Yevgeny Pavlovich also did a lot of bowing to people he knew. Aglaya and the prince, who were still together, had already drawn some attention. Soon several young men of their acquaintance came to talk to the mother and the young ladies; two or three of them stayed to converse; they were all friends of Yevgeny Pavlovich. Among them was a young and very handsome officer, very cheerful, very talkative; he hurried to talk to

Aglaya and did his utmost to draw her attention. Aglaya was very kind to him, and smiled and laughed a great deal. Yevgeny Pavlovich asked the prince's permission to introduce this friend to him; the prince barely understood what was required, but the introduction went ahead and the two of them bowed and shook hands with each other. Yevgeny Pavlovich's friend asked a question, but the prince seemed not to reply to it, or mumbled something to himself so strangely that the officer gave him a very fixed look, then glanced at Yevgeny Pavlovich, realized at once why the latter had arranged this introduction, smiled a slightly sardonic smile, and turned again to Aglaya. Only Yevgeny Pavlovich noticed that Aglaya suddenly blushed at this.

The prince had not even noticed that others were talking and paying their compliments to Aglaya; from time to time he even almost forgot that he was sitting beside her. Sometimes he felt like going away somewhere, vanishing completely, and he would really have liked a gloomy, deserted place where he could be alone with his thoughts, and no one would know where he was. Or at least be at home, on the veranda, but with no one else there, neither Lebedev nor Lebedev's children; to throw himself on his sofa, bury his head in the pillow and lie like that for a day, a night, another day. At times he dreamed of the mountains, and one particular spot in the mountains which he always liked to remember, and where he had been fond of going when he had lived there, looking down from there at the village, the barely visible white thread of the waterfall below, the white clouds, the old abandoned castle. Oh, how he would have liked to be there now and think of only one thing – oh! all his life about that one thing – it would be enough for a thousand years! And to be forgotten, forgotten here entirely. Oh, that was what was needed, it would be better if no one knew him at all and this whole vision were simply something in a dream. But wasn't it all the same, whether it was in a dream or waking? Sometimes he suddenly began to stare at Aglaya and keep his gaze on her for five minutes at a time; but his look was very strange: it was if he were gazing at an object that was a mile away from him, or as if at a portrait, rather than Aglaya herself.

'Why are you looking at me like that, Prince?' she asked suddenly, breaking off her cheerful conversation and laughter with those around her. 'I'm afraid of you; I keep thinking you want to reach out and touch my face with your finger. Don't you think that's what he looks like, Yevgeny Pavlych?'

The prince listened, in apparent surprise at being addressed, then took it in, though perhaps not quite understanding, did not reply, but seeing that she and everyone else were laughing, suddenly opened his mouth and began to laugh himself. The laughter grew louder all round; the officer, who was apparently a humorous fellow, simply exploded with laughter. Aglaya suddenly whispered angrily to herself:

'An idiot!'

'Good Lord! Can she really ... a man like that ... has she really gone quite mad?' Lizaveta Prokofyevna ground out between her teeth.

'It's a joke. It's the same joke as with the "poor knight" that time,' Alexandra whispered firmly in her ear. 'That's all it is! She's tearing him to pieces again. Only this joke has gone too far; it must be put a stop to, *Maman*! Earlier she was carrying on like an actress and frightening us out of pure mischief . . .'

'It's a good thing she picked on an idiot like him,' Lizaveta Prokofyevna parried back in a whisper. Her daughter's remark had come as a relief to her, all the same.

But the prince had heard himself being called an idiot, and he gave a start, though not because of that. He forgot the 'idiot' at once. In the crowd, however, not far from the place where he was sitting, somewhere at the side – he could not have pointed to the exact spot – a face, a pale face, with dark, curly hair, a familiar, very familiar smile and gaze – fleeted into view and disappeared. It was very possible that it was merely something he had imagined; of the whole vision all that remained to him was the impression of a crooked smile, a pair of eyes and the fancy light green tie the fleeting gentleman was wearing. Whether this gentleman had vanished in the crowd or slipped through into the park, the prince could also not have determined.

A moment later, however, he suddenly began to look around

him quickly and anxiously; this first vision might be the harbinger and predecessor of a second vision. That must be certain. Had he really forgotten about a possible encounter when they set off for the park? To be sure, when he entered the park he seemed to be quite unaware that he was going there – such was his state of mind. If he had been able to be more attentive, he would have noticed a quarter of an hour earlier that Aglaya was also looking around her, apparently in some unease, from time to time, as though she were searching for something. Now that his own unease had become very noticeable, Aglaya's agitation and anxiety had increased, and as soon as he looked back, she too looked round. The resolution of their anxious feelings soon ensued.

From the same side exit from the park, near which the prince and the whole Yepanchin company were sitting, a crowd of at least ten people suddenly appeared. At the head of the crowd were three women; two of them were wonderfully pretty, and there was nothing strange in the fact that so many admirers were moving in their train. But about both admirers and women there was something peculiar, something not quite like the rest of the public that had gathered to hear the band. Almost everyone noticed them at once, but for the most part tried to pretend they did not see them at all, and only a few of the young people smiled at them as they spoke to one another in low voices. Not to see them at all was impossible: they were openly displaying themselves, talking loudly, laughing. One might have supposed that among them were many who were intoxicated, though some of them seemed to be dressed in smart and elegant costumes; but there were also people who looked very strange indeed, in strange clothes, with strangely excited faces; among them were several military men; there were some who were not young at all; there were those who were comfortably dressed, in wide and elegantly cut clothes, with rings and cuff-links, in magnificent coal-black wigs and side-whiskers and with particularly noble, though somewhat fastidious, expressions on their faces, but who are avoided like the plague in society. Among our suburban gatherings, of course, there are those people who are distinguished by their extraordinary propriety and who have a particularly good reputation; but even the most cautious man cannot constantly protect himself against a brick falling from the house next door. That brick was now preparing to fall on the decorous audience that had gathered to hear the band.

In order to cross from the park to the rostrum where the band was playing, one had to go down three steps. At these steps the crowd came to a halt; they could not bring themselves to go down, but one of the women moved forward; only two of her retinue were so bold as to follow her. One was a middle-aged man of rather modest aspect, respectable in appearance, but with the air of a loner, that is, the kind of person who never knows anyone and whom no one else knows either. The other, who never left his lady's side, was a perfect vagabond, of most ambiguous aspect. No one else followed the eccentric lady; but as she descended the steps she did not even glance back, as though it were really all the same to her whether anyone followed her or not. She was laughing and talking loudly, as before; she was dressed with exquisite and opulent taste, but with rather more extravagance than was proper. She set off past the band to the other end of the rostrum, where a carriage was waiting for someone by the side of the road.

The prince had not seen *her* for more than three months now. Ever since his recent arrival in St Petersburg he had intended to visit her; but a secret premonition was perhaps preventing him from doing so. At any rate, he was quite unable to guess the effect that a future meeting with her would have on him, though sometimes, in fear, he tried to imagine it. One thing was clear to him – that the meeting would be a painful one. Several times during those six months he had remembered the initial sensation this woman's face had caused in him, when he had seen it only in her portrait; but even in that impression, he recalled, there had been too much that was painful. That month in the provinces, when he had seen her almost every day, had had a terrible effect on him, to the point that he sometimes even tried to drive away the memory of that still recent time. In the very face of this woman there was always something tormenting for him: the prince, as he talked to Rogozhin, had ascribed this sensation to one of infinite compassion, and this was the truth: even in the portrait, this face had called forth from his heart the whole suffering of pity; this impression of suffering, and even of suffering for this creature, never left his heart, did not leave him even now. Oh no, it was even stronger. But the prince was dissatisfied with what he had told Rogozhin; and only now, in this moment of her sudden appearance, he realized, perhaps intuitively, what had been lacking in his words to Rogozhin. What had been lacking were the words that could have expressed horror – yes, horror! Now, at this moment, he sensed it fully; he was certain, was completely convinced, for particular reasons of his own, that this woman was insane. If, loving a woman more than anything in the world, or anticipating the possibility of such a love, one were suddenly to see her on a chain, behind an iron grille, under the warder's stick – such an impression would be somewhat similar to what the prince felt now.

'What's wrong?' Aglaya whispered quickly, surveying him and tugging him innocently by the arm.

He turned his head towards her, looked at her, glanced at her dark eyes which for some reason were glittering at that moment, tried to smile at her, but suddenly, as though he had forgotten her for a moment, moved his eyes away to the right again, and once more began to observe his extraordinary vision. At that moment Nastasya Filippovna was walking right past the young ladies' chairs. Yevgeny Pavlovich was still telling Alexandra Ivanovna something that was obviously very amusing and interesting, in a quick and animated voice. The prince remembered that Aglaya suddenly said in a half-whisper: 'What a . . .'

A vague and unfinished remark; she instantly restrained herself and added no more, but this was already enough. Nastasya Filippovna, who was walking past as if she had not noticed anyone in particular, suddenly turned round in their direction and seemed only now to be aware of Yevgeny Pavlovich.

'B-bah! So this is where he is!' she exclaimed, suddenly stopping. 'No messengers can find him, and there he sits as if on purpose, where you'd never dream . . . Why, I thought you were over there . . . at your uncle's!'

Yevgeny Pavlovich flushed, gave Nastasya Filippovna a furious look, but quickly turned away from her again.

'What? Don't you know? He still doesn't know, imagine! He's shot himself! This morning your uncle shot himself! They told me this afternoon, at two o'clock; and half the city knows by now; three hundred and fifty thousand roubles of state funds are missing, they say, though others say it's five hundred thousand. And there was I thinking he was going to leave you an inheritance; he's blown the lot. He was a most dissolute old character . . . Well, goodbye, *bonne chance*! So you're not going to be there? You certainly took your retirement at the right time, you cunning fellow! But that's nonsense, of course you knew, you knew in advance: perhaps you even knew yesterday . . .'

Although in her brazen pestering, in her advertising of their acquaintance and an intimacy that did not exist, there was certainly a purpose, and of this there could be no doubt, Yevgeny Pavlovich first thought of somehow getting away and at all costs ignoring the woman who was insulting him. But Nastasya Filippovna's words had struck him like thunder; hearing of his uncle's death, he turned as pale as a handkerchief, and turned to face his informant. At that moment Lizaveta Prokofyevna quickly got up from her seat, made everyone else get up as well, and almost ran from the seat. Only Prince Lev Nikolayevich remained seated for a moment, as though undecided, and Yevgeny Pavlovich continued to stand, unable to gather his wits. But the Yepanchins had not managed to go twenty paces when a terrible scandal broke out.

The officer, Yevgeny Pavlovich's great friend, who had been talking to Aglaya, was in the highest degree of indignation.

'You need to use the whip, otherwise you'll get nowhere with that creature!' he said almost loudly. (He had apparently been Yevgeny Pavlovich's *confidant* earlier, too.)

Nastasya Filippovna turned round to him in an instant. Her eyes flashed; she rushed up to the young man, whom she did not know at all, who stood two paces from her, holding a thin plaited riding crop, tore it out of his hands and lashed her insulter across the face with it. All this happened in a single moment . . . The officer, beside himself, rushed at her; around Nastasya Filippovna there was no longer a retinue; the decorous middle-aged gentleman had already managed to make himself scarce altogether, while the tipsy gentleman was standing to one side and laughing fit to burst. A moment later, of course, the police would have appeared, and that moment would have cost Nastasya Filippovna dear, had not unexpected help arrived: the prince, who had come to a halt two paces away, managed to seize the officer's arms from behind. Tearing his arm free, the officer gave him a powerful shove in the chest; the prince went flying back some three paces and fell into a chair. But now Nastasya Filippovna had two more defenders. Before the attacking officer stood the boxer, the author of the article familiar to the reader, and a fully paid-up member of the old Rogozhin gang.

'Keller! Retired lieutenant,' he introduced himself with a swagger. 'If it's hand-to-hand fighting you want, captain, then, replacing the weaker sex, I am at your service; I am trained in all the arts of English boxing. Don't push, captain; I sympathize about the *bloody* insult, but I cannot allow you to exercise the right of the fist upon a woman in public. But if, as befits a most hon-our-able man, you wish to fight in a different manner, then – you do, of course, understand what I mean, captain . . .'

But by now the captain had recovered his wits, and was no longer listening to him. At that moment Rogozhin, who had appeared from the crowd, caught Nastasya Filippovna by the arm and led her off with him. For his part, Rogozhin looked dreadfully shaken – pale and trembling. As he led Nastasya Filippovna away, he managed to laugh maliciously in the officer's face and, with the look of a gloating shopkeeper, say:

'Hah! Caught it, didn't you? Your face all covered in blood! Hah!'

Having gathered his wits and now quite aware of whom he was dealing with, the officer politely (covering his face with a handkerchief, however) turned to the prince, who had already risen from his chair:

'Prince Myshkin, whose acquaintance I had the pleasure of making?'

'She's a madwoman! Insane! I assure you!' the prince replied in a trembling voice, for some reason stretching out his shaking hands to him.

'Of course, I have no such inside information, but I must have your name.'

He nodded and walked away. The police arrived exactly five seconds after the last of the *dramatis personae* had disappeared. As a matter of fact, the scandal had lasted no more than two minutes. Several members of the public got up from their seats and left, others merely moved from one seat to another; still others were very pleased about the scandal; others yet again began intense discussions, taking a keen interest in it all. In short, the matter ended in the usual way. The band began to play again. The prince went off after the Yepanchins. If it had occurred to him or if he had managed to look to the left, as he sat on his chair after being pushed away, he would have seen Aglaya, some twenty paces from him; she had stopped to observe the scandalous scene and was not heeding the cries of her mother and sisters as they walked on, summoning her to catch up with them. Prince Shch. ran up her and at last persuaded her to leave. Lizaveta Prokofyevna remembered that Aglaya returned to them in such excitement that it was unlikely she had even heard their summoning cries. But exactly two minutes later, as soon as they entered the park, Aglaya said quietly in her usual indifferent and capricious voice:

'I wanted to see how the comedy would end.'

3

The incident in the pleasure gardens affected both mother and daughters almost with horror. In dismay and agitation, Lizaveta Prokofyevna almost literally ran all the way home with her daughters. According to her view of the world, too much had taken place and been revealed in that incident, so that in spite of all the disorder and alarm, determined thoughts were already being born within her mind. Everyone realized, however, that something peculiar had happened and that it was possibly just as well that some extraordinary secret was about to be revealed. In spite of Prince Shch.'s earlier assurances and explanations,

Yevgeny Pavlovich had now been 'brought to the surface', exposed, unmasked and 'publicly disgraced in his relations with that creature'. That was how Lizaveta Prokofyevna, and even both elder daughters, saw it. The result of this conclusion was the amassing of yet more riddles. Though the girls were privately somewhat indignant about their mother's excessive alarm and all-too-conspicuous flight, in the initial period of turmoil they could not bring themselves to upset her with questions. For some reason, moreover, it appeared to them that their sister, Aglaya Ivanovna, perhaps knew more about this matter than either they or their mother did. Prince Shch. also looked as black as night, and very pensive. Lizaveta Prokofyevna said not a word to him all the way, but he never even seemed to notice. Adelaida tried to ask him what uncle they had been talking about just then and what had happened back in St Petersburg, but he muttered in reply to her, with the sourest of expressions, something very vague about some kind of inquiries, and that it was all totally absurd, of course. 'There's no doubt about that!' replied Adelaida, and after that asked no further questions. Aglaya had become unusually quiet and the only comment she made on the way was that they were running too fast. Once she turned round and saw the prince, who was trying to catch them up. Having noticed his efforts to catch up with them, she smiled mockingly, and did not look round at him any more.

At last, almost at the dacha itself, they met Ivan Fyodorovich coming towards them, having just returned from St Petersburg. The first thing he did was to inquire about Yevgeny Pavlovich. But his wife walked sternly past him, not replying and without even so much as a glance at him. From the looks on the faces of his daughters and Prince Shch. he guessed at once that there was a storm in the house. But quite apart from this, his own face reflected some unusual perturbation. He at once took Prince Shch. by the arm, stopped him at the entrance to the house and almost in a whisper exchanged some words with him. By the troubled look of both, when they later went out to the veranda and through to Lizaveta Prokofyevna's room, one might have thought they had both heard some extraordinary piece of news. Little by little they all gathered in Lizaveta Prokofyevna's room upstairs, and on the veranda only the prince remained, at last. He sat in the corner, as though he were expecting something, though not knowing why; it did not occur to him to leave, seeing the turmoil in the house; he seemed to have forgotten the entire universe, and looked as though he was prepared to sit it out for two years on end, no matter where he was put. From upstairs he occasionally heard echoes of anxious conversation. He himself could not have said how long he sat there. It was getting late, and twilight had fallen. Suddenly Aglaya appeared on the veranda; she looked calm, though somewhat pale. Catching sight of the prince, whom she was 'obviously not expecting' to meet here, sitting on a chair, in a corner, Aglaya smiled as though in bewilderment.

'What are you doing here?'

Embarrassed, the prince muttered something, and jumped up from his chair; but Aglaya at once sat down beside him, and he too sat down again. She cast a sudden but attentive glance at him, then looked out of the window, as if without anything particular in mind, then back at him again. 'Perhaps she feels like laughing,' thought the prince. 'But no, after all, then she would have laughed.'

'Perhaps you'd like some tea, I'll have some made,' she said, after a silence.

'N-no . . . I don't know . . .'

'But how can one not know that? Oh yes, listen: if someone challenged you to a duel, what would you do? I wanted to ask you that earlier.'

'But . . . who . . . no one would challenge me to a duel.'

'Well, but what if they did? Would you be very afraid?'

'I think I would be very . . . afraid.'

'Do you mean it? Then you're a coward?'

'N-no; perhaps not. A coward is someone who's afraid and runs away; but someone who's afraid and doesn't run away is not a coward,' smiled the prince, after some thought.

'And you wouldn't run away?'

'Perhaps not,' he laughed, at last, in response to Aglaya's questions.

'Although I'm a woman, I would never run away,' she

observed, almost offended. 'Actually, I think you're laughing at me and putting on airs in your usual way, to make yourself more interesting; tell me: do they usually fire at twelve paces? And some at ten? That would mean one of them would certainly be killed or wounded, wouldn't it?'

'I don't think people are very often hit in duels.'

'No? But Pushkin was killed.'

'That was possibly an accident.'

'It wasn't an accident at all; it was a duel to the death, and he was killed.'

'The bullet struck so low that D'Anthès[1] was probably aiming somewhere higher, at the chest or the head; but no one aims so low, and so the bullet most likely struck Pushkin by accident, as the result of a slip. People who are experts have told me that.'

'Well, a soldier I talked to once told me that when they're drawn up to fire, they're specially instructed by the regulations to aim halfway down the man, that's how they put it: "halfway down the man". So that means they're ordered to shoot not at the chest and not at the head, but precisely halfway down the man. I later asked an officer, and he told me that it's quite true.'

'It's probably because they fire from a long distance.'

'Can you shoot?'

'I never have.'

'You mean you don't know how to load a pistol?'

'No. That is, I know how to, but I've never loaded one myself.'

'Well, that means you don't know how to, because to do it you need practice! Listen then, and remember it: number one, buy good pistol powder, not damp (they say it shouldn't be damp, but very dry), the fine sort, you have to ask for it, and not the sort they use to fire cannons. They say you have to make the bullet yourself. Have you got pistols?'

'No, and I don't want any,' the prince began to laugh.

'Oh, what nonsense! You must buy one without fail: a good one, they say French or English are the best. Then take a pinch of powder, perhaps two pinches, and put it in. The more you use, the better. Stuff it in with felt (they say it has to be felt, for some reason), you can get it from a mattress, or sometimes doors are upholstered with felt. Then, when you've stuffed the felt in, insert the bullet – do you hear, the bullet comes after, and the powder first, otherwise it won't fire. Why are you laughing? I want you to practise shooting several times each day and you must learn how to hit the target. Will you do it?'

The prince laughed; Aglaya stamped her foot in vexation. Her serious air during this conversation somewhat surprised the prince. He had a vague feeling that there was something he ought to find out, something he ought to ask – at any rate, something more serious than how to load a pistol. But all of that had flown out of his mind, excepting the one circumstance that she was sitting before him, and he was looking at her, and it would have been a matter of almost total indifference to him no matter what she had been talking about.

From upstairs on to the veranda, at last, came Ivan Fydorovich himself; he was setting off somewhere with a frowning, preoccupied and determined look.

'Ah, Lev Nikolayevich, it's you ... Where are you off to now?' he asked, in spite of the fact that Lev Nikolayevich had no thought of moving from his chair. 'Come along, then, there's something I'd like to tell you.'

'Goodbye,' said Aglaya, extending her hand to the prince.

By now it was quite dark on the veranda, and the prince would not have been able to distinguish her face very clearly. A moment later, as he and the general were leaving the dacha, he suddenly blushed terribly and clenched his right hand tightly.

It turned out that Ivan Fyodorovich was going his way; Ivan Fyodorovich, in spite of the late hour, was hurrying to have a talk with someone about something. But meanwhile he began to talk to the prince, quickly, anxiously, rather incoherently, often mentioning Lizaveta Prokofyevna in the conversation. If the prince had been able to be more attentive at that moment, he would have realized that Ivan Fyodorovich wanted, among other things, to worm something out of him, too, or, rather, directly and openly ask him about something, but was not succeeding in getting to the main point. To his shame, the prince was so distracted that at first he even heard nothing, and when the general stopped in front of him with some burning question, he was forced to confess that he understood none of it.

The general shrugged his shoulders.

'You're all turning into a strange bunch of people, from every aspect,' he began again. 'I tell you that I really do not understand the ideas and anxieties of Lizaveta Prokofyevna. She's in a hysterical fit, crying and saying that they've shamed and disgraced us. Who? How? With whom? When and why? I confess I am guilty (that I admit), very guilty, but the solicitations of that ... troublesome woman (who behaves outrageously into the bargain) can only be curtailed, at last, by the police, and I intend to see someone this very day, and warn them. It can all be done quietly, modestly, in a kindly fashion, even, on a friendly basis and without any scandal. I also agree that the future is fraught with events and that there is much that is unexplained; there is also an intrigue at work here; but if no one knows anything here, no one can explain anything there; if I haven't heard, you haven't heard, he hasn't heard, and another hasn't heard anything either, then who, in the end, has heard, I ask you? How can this be explained, in your opinion, except by the fact that half of it's a mirage, does not exist, in the manner of moonlight, for example ... or other ghostly visions.'

'*She* is insane,' muttered the prince, suddenly remembering, with pain, all that had happened earlier.

'That's it in a nutshell, if it's her you're talking about. The same idea, more or less, visited me yesterday, and I fell asleep peacefully. But now I see that there are those here who see the matter more correctly, and I don't believe that she's insane. She's a cantankerous woman, I grant, but also a subtle one, and not merely clever. That outburst of hers about Kapiton Alexeich today proves it. There's some trickery on her part, or at any rate some sort of Jesuitical cunning, for special aims of her own.'

'Who is this Kapiton Alexeich?'

'Oh, Good Lord, Lev Nikolayevich, you're not listening at all. I started out by telling you about Kapiton Alexeich; I got such a shock that my arms and legs are trembling even now. That's why I got delayed in town today. Kapiton Alexeich Radomsky, Yevgeny Pavlych's uncle ...'

'Well!' exclaimed the prince.

'Shot himself this morning, at dawn, at seven o'clock. A

respected old fellow, seventy years old, an Epicurean – and exactly as she said – it was public money, a whacking sum!'

'But where did she . . .'

'Find out about it? Ha-ha! Well, as soon as she appeared, a whole staff formed itself round her, didn't it? You know the kind of people who visit her now and seek "the honour of her acquaintance". Naturally she could have heard something about it from those who came to see her, because now the whole of St Petersburg knows, and half of Pavlovsk, if not the whole of it. But what a subtle observation of hers that was about the uniform, as they told it to me, that is, about Yevgeny Pavlych going into retirement ahead of time! What a devilish hint! No, that doesn't indicate insanity. Of course, I refuse to believe that Yevgeny Pavlych could have known about the disaster in advance, that is, at seven o'clock on such-and-such a date, and so on. But he could have had a premonition of it all. And there was I, and there were we all, Prince Shch., too, reckoning that the old man would leave him an inheritance! Dreadful! Dreadful! Please note, however, that I'm not accusing Yevgeny Pavlych of anything – I hasten to explain that to you – but all the same, it is suspicious. Prince Shch. is very shocked. It's all turned out rather strangely.'

'But what's suspicious about Yevgeny Pavlych's behaviour?'

'Nothing! He's conducted himself in a most noble manner. I wasn't hinting at anything. His own fortune is, I believe, intact. Lizaveta Prokofyevna, of course, doesn't want to hear anything . . . But the main thing is that all these family disasters, or, rather, all these petty squabbles, one doesn't even know what to call them . . . To tell the truth, you, Lev Nikolayevich, are a friend of the family, and imagine, it's only now just emerging, though without precise details, that more than a month ago Yevgeny Pavlych apparently had a confidential talk with Aglaya and received a formal refusal from her.'

'That's impossible!' the prince exclaimed heatedly.

'Well, do you know anything about it? Look, my dear fellow,' the general said in startled surprise, rooted to the spot like one thunderstruck, 'perhaps I put my foot in it by telling you, and it was improper and indecent of me, but I mean, it's because you

... you ... that's the sort of man you are. Perhaps you know something definite?'

'I don't know anything ... about Yevgeny Pavlych,' muttered the prince.

'And neither do I! You know, brother, they really do want to dig a hole in the ground and bury me, and they don't want to reflect that it's hard for a man and I won't come through it. There was such a scene just now, dreadful! I'm talking to you as I would to my own son. The worst of it is that Aglaya seems to laugh at her mother. The part about her apparently having refused Yevgeny Pavlych a month ago and with them having had a confidential talk, a rather formal one, was told to me by the sisters, as a sort of guess ... a reliable guess, however. But I mean, she's such a self-willed and fantastical creature that it defies description! All the generous feelings, all the brilliant qualities of heart and mind – that is all, perhaps, in her, but it is accompanied by caprice, mockery – in a word, a devilish character, and with fantasies as well. She laughed in her mother's face just now, at her sisters, at Prince Shch., not to speak of me, she hardly ever stops laughing at me, but I, well, I love her, you know, I even love her laughter – and, I think, that little devil loves me specially for it, that is, more than all the others, I think. I'll bet she's already made a laughing-stock of you about something or another. I caught the two of you in conversation just now after the storm earlier, upstairs; she was sitting with you as if nothing had taken place.'

The prince blushed dreadfully, and clenched his right hand, but continued to remain silent.

'My dear, good Lev Nikolayevich!' the general said suddenly with feeling and ardour, 'I ... and even Lizaveta Prokofyevna herself (who has, however, begun to abuse you again, and me, too, because of you, I don't understand why), we love you all the same, love you sincerely and respect you, even in spite of everything, of all appearances, that is. But you must admit, dear friend, you must admit that it was baffling and vexing to suddenly hear that cold-blooded little devil (for she faced her mother with an air of the most profound contempt for all our questions, and above all for mine, because I, damn it, was stupid enough to think that I could be stern with her, as I was the head

of the household – well, it was a stupid thing to do), that cool
and composed little devil suddenly explaining with a smile that
the "madwoman" (that was how she put it, and I find it strange
that she should have used the same word as you: "didn't you
guess it before?", she said), that the madwoman had "taken it
into her head to marry me at all costs to Prince Lev Nikolayevich,
and is doing her best to get Yevgeny Pavlych out of our house"
. . . that's all she said; she gave no further explanation, laughed
to herself as we gaped in astonishment, then slammed the door
and left. Later they told me about the turn of events between
her and you this afternoon and . . . and . . . listen, dear Prince,
you're not a man who takes offence easily and you're very
sensible, I've noticed that about you, but . . . please don't be
angry: she is laughing at you. Laughing like a child, and so
please don't be angry at her, but it is certainly so. Don't read
anything into it – she's simply making fun of both you and of
all of us, from idleness. Well, goodbye! You know our feelings,
don't you? Our sincere feelings for you? Those feelings are
devoted, and they will never change, never . . . but . . . I must be
off this way now, so *au revoir*! I've seldom been quite so down
in the dumps (is that how they say it?) as I am now . . . A grand
life one has at one's dacha, doesn't one?'

Remaining alone at the crossroads, the prince looked about
him, quickly crossed the street and went up close to the lighted
window of one of the dachas, unfolded a small piece of paper
he had been tightly clutching in his right hand during the whole
of his conversation with Ivan Fyodorovich, and read, catching
the faint ray of light:

Tomorrow at seven o'clock in the morning I shall be on the green
bench, in the park, and shall wait for you. I have decided to speak
to you about a certain extremely important matter that affects
you directly.

P.S. I hope you won't show this note to anyone. Although I am
ashamed to write you such an admonition, I considered that you
merit it, and wrote it – blushing with embarrassment at your
absurd character.

P.P.S. It's the same green bench I showed you earlier today. You ought to be ashamed! I had to write this too.

The note had been written in a hurry and folded carelessly, most probably before Aglaya had come out on to the veranda. In a state of indescribable agitation, bordering on terror, the prince again tightly clutched the piece of paper in his hand and quickly darted away from the window, from the light, like a frightened thief; but in this movement he suddenly collided head on with a gentleman who was standing right behind him.

'I've been following you, Prince,' said the gentleman.

'Is it you, Keller?' exclaimed the prince in surprise.

'I'm looking for you, Prince. I waited for you outside the Yepanchins' dacha – I couldn't go in, of course. I followed you when you went off with the general. At your service, Prince – Keller is at your disposal. Ready to make any sacrifice and even to die, should it be necessary.'

'But . . . why?'

'Well, there will certainly be a challenge. That Lieutenant Molovtsov, I know him, not personally, of course . . . he won't tolerate an insult. Of course, he's inclined to view people like us, Rogozhin and myself, I mean, as riff-raff, and, perhaps, rightly so, so you're the only one who needs to respond. You'll have to pay for the bottles,[2] Prince. He's been making inquiries about you, I heard, and tomorrow his friend will certainly call on you, and is perhaps waiting there now. If you'll do me the honour of choosing me as your second, I'm ready to take the red cap;[3] that's why I've been looking for you.'

'So you're talking about a duel, too!' the prince suddenly began to laugh, to Keller's extreme surprise. He laughed mightily. Keller, who had really almost been on tenterhooks until he had obtained satisfaction, offering himself as a second, almost took offence as he beheld the prince's merry laughter.

'But Prince, you seized him by the arms earlier on. That's hard for a well-bred man to tolerate, and in public, too.'

'Well, he pushed me in the chest!' the prince exclaimed, laughing. 'There's no reason for us to fight! I shall apologize to him, and that will be the end of it. But if we're to fight, then we shall fight! Let him take a shot at me; why, I even want him to. Ha-ha! I know how to load a pistol now. Do you know that I've just been taught how to load a pistol? Do you know how to load a pistol, Keller? You have to buy the powder first, the pistol sort of powder, not the damp sort and not the large-grained sort that's used for firing cannons; and then you have to put the powder in first, get felt from a door somewhere, and only then insert the bullet, and you mustn't put the bullet in before the powder, because if you do it won't fire. Ha-ha! Isn't that a splendid reason, friend Keller? Ah, Keller, you know, I'm going to hug and kiss you in a moment. Ha-ha-ha! How did you manage to suddenly pop up in front of him like that earlier? Come and see me as soon as you can, and we'll drink champagne. We'll all get drunk! Do you know that I have twelve bottles of champagne, in Lebedev's cellar? Lebedev sold them to me the other day "on the occasion", the first day after I moved in, and I bought them all! I'll get the whole gang together! I say, you're not going to get any sleep tonight, are you?'

'I'll sleep like I do every other night, Prince.'

'Well, pleasant dreams! Ha-ha!'

The prince walked across the road and vanished into the park, leaving the somewhat puzzled Keller in reflection. He had never seen the prince in such a strange mood before, and could not even have imagined it before now.

'Perhaps it's a fever, for he's a nervous sort of fellow, and all this has had its effect, but of course he won't get cold feet. Fellows like him never get cold feet, my God they don't!' Keller thought to himself. 'Hmm, champagne! Interesting news, I'll be bound. Twelve bottles, sir, a round dozen; not bad, a decent garrison. And I'll bet that Lebedev won the champagne in a wager from someone else. Hmm ... he's a rather agreeable fellow, this prince; yes, I like men like him; but there's no time to be lost and ... if there's champagne, now is the time ...'

That the prince was almost in a fever was, of course, true.

For a long time he roamed around the dusky park, and eventually 'found himself' walking along an avenue. In his consciousness there remained a memory of having already passed along this avenue before, from the bench to an old tree,

tall and conspicuous, about a hundred paces away, some thirty
or forty times, to and fro. He could not have remembered what
he had thought in that hour, at least, that he had spent in the
park, even if he had wanted to. However, he caught himself in
a certain thought that made him shake with sudden laughter;
though there was nothing to laugh about, he kept wanting to
laugh. He imagined that the proposal for a duel might not have
come into being in Keller's head alone, and that, consequently,
the episode about the loading of a pistol might not have been
an accident ... 'Bah!' He stopped suddenly, illuminated by
another idea. 'She came down to the veranda, when I was sitting
in the corner, and was terribly surprised when she found me
there, and – laughed so much ... she began to talk about tea;
and yet, I mean, she had this piece of paper in her hands then,
so she must have known that I was sitting on the veranda, so
why was she surprised? Ha-ha-ha!'

He grabbed the note out of his pocket and kissed it, but then
stopped at once, and reflected.

'How strange! How strange!' he said a moment later, even
with a kind of sadness: at moments of intense joy he always
felt sad, he did not know why. He looked intently about him
and was surprised that he had come here. He felt a great
tiredness, approached the bench, and sat down on it. All around
there was deep silence. The band had finished its concert in the
park. There was probably no one there, now; of course, it was
at least half-past eleven. The night was quiet, warm, light – a
St Petersburg night in early June, but in the dense, shadowy
park, in the avenue where he sat, it was almost completely
dark.

If anyone had told him at that moment that he had fallen in
love, was passionately in love, he would have rejected the idea
with astonishment and, perhaps, even with indignation. And if
anyone had added to this that Aglaya's note was a love letter,
the assignation of a lovers' tryst, he would have burned with
shame for that man, and might possibly have challenged him to
a duel. All of this was completely sincere, and he never once
doubted or had the slightest 'ambiguous' thought about the
possibility of this girl loving him, or even of the possibility of

him loving this girl. He would have considered monstrous the possibility that anyone might love him, 'a man like him'. He fancied that it was simply mischief on her part, if there really was anything in it; but he was really quite indifferent to the mischief, and found it only natural; he was preoccupied and troubled by something else entirely. He fully believed what the agitated general had let slip earlier to the effect that she was laughing at everyone, and particularly at him, the prince. He felt not the slightest sense of injury at this; in his opinion, that was how it was bound to be. The main thing for him was that tomorrow he would see her again, early in the morning, would sit beside her on the green bench, listen to her tell him how to load a pistol, and gaze at her. He did not want any more than that. The question of what she intended to tell him and what this important matter was that affected him personally also flickered through his mind once or twice. What was more, in the real existence of this 'important matter', on account of which he was being summoned, he did not doubt for a single moment, but almost gave no thought to the important matter now, to the point where he did not even feel the slightest prompting to think about it.

The crunch of quiet footsteps on the gravel of the avenue made him lift his head. A man whose face it was hard to make out in the darkness approached the bench and sat down beside him. The prince quickly moved closer to him, almost touching him, and discerned the pale face of Rogozhin.

'I knew you were wandering around here somewhere, it didn't take me long to track you down,' Rogozhin muttered through his teeth.

It was the first time they had met since their encounter in the corridor at the inn. Shaken by Rogozhin's sudden appearance, the prince was for a long time unable to gather his thoughts, and an agonizing sensation rose up again in his heart. Rogozhin was evidently aware of the effect he was producing; but although he too was disconcerted at first, he spoke as though with an air of studied familiarity. However, the prince soon had the impression that there was nothing studied about it, and not even any particular embarrassment; if there was a certain awkwardness in his gestures and conversation, it was merely external; in his soul this man could never change.

'How did you . . . know where I was?' the prince inquired, in order to say something.

'I heard from Keller (I dropped in at your place) that you'd gone to the park; well, I thought, so that's the way it is.'

'What do you mean, "that's the way it is"?' the prince anxiously picked up on the phrase that had slipped out.

Rogozhin smiled wryly, but gave no explanation.

'I got your letter, Lev Nikolaich; there's no point in all this . . . you're wasting your time . . . But I come to you now from *her*: she wants to see you without fail; there is something she absolutely must tell you. She asks you to go there this evening.'

'I'll come tomorrow. I'm going home now; will you . . . come to my place?'

'Why? I've told you everything; good night.'

'Are you sure you won't come?' the prince asked him quietly.

'You're an amazing fellow, Lev Nikolaich, one can't help marvelling at you.'

Rogozhin smiled a caustic smile.

'Why? Why do you have such hatred for me now?' the prince interjected sadly and with feeling. 'I mean, you yourself know that all the things you thought are not true. And actually, I had a pretty good idea that the hatred you had for me hadn't passed yet, and do you know why? Because you made an attempt on my life, that's why your hatred doesn't pass. I tell you, the only Rogozhin I remember is the one with whom I exchanged crosses as a brother that day; I wrote that to you in my letter yesterday, so that you'd stop thinking about all that delirium and not begin to talk to me about it. Why are you avoiding me? Why are you hiding your hands from me? I tell you, I view all the things that happened that day as sheer delirium: I know exactly what you went through that day, as though it had been myself. The thing you imagined did not exist and could not exist. Why should there be any hatred between us?'

'What hatred could you ever feel?' Rogozhin laughed again in response to the prince's sudden, heated address. He really was standing in a way that suggested he was avoiding him, having taken a couple of steps back and hiding his hands.

'It's not right for me to visit you at all now, Lev Nikolaich,' he added, slowly and sententiously, in conclusion.

'Do you hate me that much, then?'

'I don't like you, Lev Nikolaich, so why should I come and see you? Ach, Prince, you're like a child, when you want a toy, you take it out and play with it, but you don't understand the real world. You're saying exactly what you said in your letter, and do you think I don't believe you? I believe your every word and know that you have never deceived me and will never deceive me in the future; but I still don't like you. Look, you write that you've forgotten it all and that you only remember your brother Rogozhin, with whom you exchanged crosses, and not the Rogozhin who raised the knife against you that day. But how do you know what my feelings are? (Rogozhin smiled wryly again.) Why, I may have never once felt remorse since that day, and yet you've already sent me your brotherly forgiveness. I might have been thinking of something quite different that evening, while about that . . .'

'You forgot even to think!' the prince interjected. 'And no wonder! And I'll bet you got straight on the train that day and came down here to Pavlovsk to hear the band, and followed her and spied on her exactly as you did today. Not much of a surprise there! Why, if you hadn't been in such a state that day that you were only capable of thinking about one thing, then you might not have raised the knife against me. I had a premonition right from the morning of that day, when I looked at you; do you know what you looked like then? Perhaps it was when we were exchanging crosses that this thought began to stir in me. Why did you take me to see the old woman that day? Did you think that would stay your hand? But you can't possibly have thought that, you merely felt it, as I did . . . We felt the same thing. Had you not raised your hand against me (which God turned away), how would I appear to you now? I mean, I did suspect you of it, the same sin, we felt the same! (And don't frown! Oh, what are you laughing at?) "I felt no remorse!" Why, you wouldn't have been able to feel remorse even if you'd wanted to, for you don't like me. And even if I were as innocent as an angel before you, you would still not be able to endure me as long as you thought that it wasn't you but me whom she loved. That must be what jealousy is. Except that – this is what I've been thinking about all week, Parfyon, and I'll tell you: do you know that it's possible she loves you now more than anyone, so that the more she torments you, the more she loves you. She won't tell you that, and you have to be able to see it. After all, why is she marrying you? Some day she'll tell you that. Some women even want to be loved like that, and that's precisely her character! For your love and your character must overwhelm her! Do you know that a woman is capable of tormenting a man with cruelty and mockery without feeling a pang of conscience, because every time she looks at you she thinks: "Now I'll torment him to death, but later I'll make it up to him with love" . . .'

Having listened to the prince, Rogozhin began to laugh.

'But I say, Prince, haven't you ended up in something of that sort yourself? If what I've heard about you is true?'

'Why, what could you have heard?' the prince quivered suddenly, and stopped in extreme embarrassment.

Rogozhin went on laughing. He had listened to the prince not without interest and, perhaps, not without enjoyment, either; the prince's joyful and ardent enthusiasm struck him and cheered him greatly.

'Well, even if I didn't hear it, I can see for myself now that it's true,' he added. 'I mean, when have you ever spoken as you did just now? Why, it was if it was someone else talking, not you. Had I not heard something of the sort about you, I wouldn't have come here to the park, at midnight.'

'I don't understand you at all, Parfyon Semyonych.'

'She explained to me about you long ago, but earlier on I saw you sitting with the other girl at the bandstand. She swore to me, yesterday and today she swore that you were head over heels in love with Aglaya Yepanchina. It's all the same to me, Prince, and it's not my business, either; if you've fallen out of love with her, she hasn't yet fallen out of love with you. I mean, you know perfectly well that she really wants you to marry that other one, she's given her word on it, heh-heh! She says to me:

"Until then, I won't marry you – they go to church first, and then we go to church." What's going on there I don't understand and have never understood: either she loves you beyond all bounds, or . . . if she loves you, then why does she want to get you married to someone else? She says: "I want to see him happy" – that means she loves you.'

'I told you and wrote to you that she's . . . not in her right mind,' said the prince, listening to Rogozhin's words in torment.

'God knows! It may be that you're the one who's mistaken . . . however, she did name the day of our wedding this afternoon, after I brought her back from the band concert: we'll go to the altar in three weeks' time, and possibly even earlier, she says; she swore a vow, took down the icon, kissed it. So now, Prince, it's all up to you, heh-heh!'

'This is all delirium! What you say about me will never, never be! Tomorrow I shall come and see you both . . .'

'But how can she be mad?' observed Rogozhin. 'How can everyone else consider that she's in her right mind for everyone else, while only you believe she's insane? How can she write the letters they're receiving there? If she's mad, then they'd be able to see that from the letters.'

'What letters?' the prince asked in alarm.

'She sends letters there, to *the other one*, who reads them. Didn't you know? Well, then you'll find out; she'll probably show them to you herself.'

'I don't believe it!' the prince exclaimed.

'Ach! Well, Lev Nikolaich, it's easy seeing you've only gone a little way along this path, and you're merely at the beginning. Just you wait: you'll be keeping your own private police force, patrolling day and night yourself and knowing every step that's taken, if only . . .'

'Stop it, and don't ever say that again!' exclaimed the prince. 'Listen, Parfyon, I was walking here before you arrived just now, and I suddenly began to laugh, I don't know why, the only reason I can think of is that tomorrow is my birthday, as if it were preordained. It's nearly twelve now. Let's go and celebrate the day! I have wine, let's drink wine, wish for me what I don't know what to wish for myself, and it must be you who wishes

it, while I shall wish you complete happiness. Otherwise, return
my cross to me! I mean, you didn't send my cross back to me
the next day, did you? Are you wearing it now?'

'Yes, I am,' Rogozhin said quietly.

'Well, let's go. I don't want to celebrate my new life without
you, because my new life has started! Didn't you know, Parfyon,
that my new life started today?'

'Now I can see for myself that it has; I'll tell *her*. You're not
yourself at all, Lev Nikolaich.'

4

As he approached his dacha with Rogozhin, the prince noticed
with extreme astonishment that a noisy and numerous company,
brightly illuminated, had assembled on the veranda. This merry
company was laughing and singing loudly; it even seemed to be
arguing, to the point of shouting; at a first glance one might
have supposed that everyone was having a most hilarious time.
And indeed, when he went up the steps to the veranda, he saw
that everyone was drinking, and drinking champagne, and had
apparently been doing so for quite a long time now, with the
result that many of the revellers had managed to become most
pleasantly animated. The guests were all familiar to the prince,
but it was strange that they had all gathered at once, as if by
invitation, though the prince had not invited anyone, and had
only just remembered it was his birthday, by chance.

'You must have told someone you were going to serve champagne, so they all came flocking round,' muttered Rogozhin,
ascending the veranda after the prince. 'We know how it is; you
just have to whistle to them . . .' he added, almost with hatred,
recalling of course his own recent past.

They all greeted the prince with shouts and birthday wishes,
and surrounded him. Some were very noisy, others much calmer,
but all hurried to congratulate him, having heard about his
birthday, and each one waited his turn. The presence of certain
persons engaged the prince's interest, Burdovsky, for example;

but most surprising of all was the fact that Yevgeny Pavlovich had suddenly turned up among this company the prince could almost not believe it, and felt something almost approaching fear at the sight of him.

In the meanwhile Lebedev, flushed and almost in ecstasy, came running up with explanations; he was rather well *primed*. From his chatter it turned out that everyone had gathered quite naturally, and even by accident. Ahead of everyone else, towards evening, Ippolit had arrived and, feeling much better, had requested that he be allowed to wait for the prince on the veranda. He had made himself comfortable on the sofa; then Lebedev came down to join him, and after that the entire household, including General Ivolgin and his daughters. Burdovsky had arrived with Ippolit, as his escort. Ganya and Ptitsyn, it seemed, had dropped in not long ago, as they were passing (their appearance coincided with the incident in the park); then Keller appeared, told them about the birthday and demanded champagne. Yevgeny Pavlovich had arrived only half an hour before. Kolya had also vociferously insisted on champagne and a festive celebration. Lebedev had readily served the wine.

'But it's mine, it's mine!' he babbled to the prince, 'it's all on me, to celebrate and congratulate you, and there'll be refreshments, *zakuski*,[1] and my daughter is attending to it; but, Prince, if you only knew the subject that's currently being discussed. Do you remember Hamlet's "To be or not to be"? A contemporary subject, sir, a contemporary one! Questions and answers . . . And Mr Terentyev is in the highest degree of . . . he doesn't want to go to sleep! Oh, he's only had the merest sip, the merest sip of champagne, it won't harm him . . . Approach, O Prince, and decide! They've all been waiting for you, they've all been waiting for your pleasant wit . . .'

The prince noticed the charming, affectionate gaze of Vera Lebedeva, who had also hurried to thread her way through the crowd towards him. Past all the rest of them, he extended a hand to her first; she blushed with pleasure and wished him 'a happy life *starting this very day*'. Then she ran at full tilt to the kitchen, where she prepared the *zakuski*; but even before the prince's arrival – as soon as she had a moment to tear herself away from her work – she appeared on the veranda and listened with all her attention to the heated arguments about the most abstract matters, strange to her, which flowed ceaselessly on among the tipsy guests. Her younger sister had fallen asleep in the next room, on a trunk, with her mouth open, but the boy, Lebedev's son, was standing beside Kolya and Ippolit, and the look on his animated face alone was enough to show that he was ready to stand here, enjoying and listening, for another ten hours on end if need be.

'I've been specially waiting for you, and I'm awfully glad you've arrived in such a happy mood,' Ippolit said quietly when the prince went over to shake his hand, immediately after Vera.

'And how do you know that I'm so "happy"?'

'One can see it in your face. Say good evening to the gentlemen and come and sit with us here as soon as you can. I've been especially waiting for you,' he added, placing significant emphasis on the fact that he had been waiting. To the prince's observation as to whether it might not be harmful for him to sit up so late, he replied that he was surprised at himself for having wanted to die three days earlier, and that he had never felt better than this evening.

Burdovsky jumped up and muttered that he was 'on hand . . .', that he was 'escorting' Ippolit, and that he was also glad; that in the letter he had 'written rubbish', but was now 'just glad . . .' Without finishing his sentence, he shook the prince's hand firmly and sat down on his chair.

After all the others, the prince went over to Yevgeny Pavlovich, who at once took him by the arm.

'I just want to say a couple of words in your ear,' he whispered in an undertone, 'about something extremely important; let's go over there for a moment.'

'A couple of words,' another voice whispered in the prince's other ear, and another hand took him by the arm from the other side. With surprise, the prince observed a dreadfully dishevelled figure, flushed, winking and laughing, in whom at that same moment he recognized Ferdyshchenko, who had appeared from Lord only knows where.

'Do you remember Ferdyshchenko?'

'Where did you spring from?' exclaimed the prince.

'He apologizes!' exclaimed Keller, running up. 'He's been hiding, he didn't want to come out and see you, he was hiding in the corner there, he apologizes, Prince, he feels he's to blame.'

'But for what, for what?'

'I met him, Prince, I met him just now and brought him here; he's my rare friend; but he apologizes.'

'I'm very glad, gentlemen; now in you go, sit down with everyone else, I'll be there in a moment,' the prince freed himself, at last, hurrying over to Yevgeny Pavlovich.

'It's entertaining here at your place,' the latter observed, 'and I've enjoyed the half hour I've spent waiting for you. Listen, dearest Lev Nikolayevich, I've arranged everything with Kurmyshev and have dropped by to reassure you; you have nothing to worry about, he has taken the matter very, very sensibly, all the more so, in my opinion, as he himself was more to blame.'

'Who is this Kurmyshev?'

'Why, the fellow you seized by the arms today . . . He was so furious that he was going to send someone to you tomorrow with a demand for satisfaction.'

'Oh come, what nonsense!'

'Of course it was nonsense, and it would probably have ended with nonsense; but there are these people around . . .'

'Perhaps there's another reason why you dropped by, Yevgeny Pavlych?'

'Oh, of course, there's another reason,' the latter burst out laughing. 'Dear Prince, tomorrow morning at the crack of dawn I'm going to St Petersburg on this unhappy business (about my uncle, you know); imagine: it's all true, and everyone knows it except me. It all came as such a shock to me that I haven't been able to go *there* (to the Yepanchins); I shan't be there tomorrow, either, as I'll be in St Petersburg, you understand? I may be away for several days – in a word, my affairs have started to go to pot. Though the matter is not one of great importance, I thought I should tell you something about it in the most candid way I can, without wasting time, before my departure, I mean. Now if it's all right with you I shall sit and wait until the guests disperse; what's more, I have nowhere else to go: I'm so agitated that I can't sleep. Finally, though it's wrong and indecent to hound a man so blatantly, I will tell you blatantly: I've come to seek your friendship, my dear Prince; you're a most exemplary fellow, for you don't tell lies at every step, or perhaps ever at all, and I'm in need of a friend and adviser in a certain matter, for I am now decidedly one of the unfortunate . . .'

He again began to laugh.

'The only thing is,' the prince thought for a moment, 'that you want to wait until they disperse, but I mean, Lord only knows when that will be. Wouldn't it be better for us to go down to the park now; I'm sure they can wait; I'll make my excuses.'

'No, no, I have my reasons for not having them suspect us of having an urgent conversation with a purpose; there are people here who are very interested in our relationship – didn't you know that, Prince? And it will be far better if they see that our relationship is perfectly normal, friendly, and not simply a matter of urgent expediency – you understand? They'll disperse in an hour or two; I'll only take up about twenty minutes, well, half an hour of your time . . .'

'By all means, please – I am only too glad, and you don't need to explain anything; and thank you very much for your kind words about our friendly relationship. You must forgive me for being so absent-minded today; you know, I somehow can't concentrate on anything right now.'

'I can see, I can see,' muttered Yevgeny Pavlovich, with a slight smile. He was in a very jovial mood this evening.

'What can you see?' the prince started.

'Oh, have no suspicion, dear Prince,' Yevgeny Pavlovich continued to smile, but without replying directly to the question, 'have no suspicion that I've simply come to hoodwink you and find something out of you in passing, eh?'

'That you've come to find something out from me, of that there can be no doubt,' the prince began to laugh, at last – and you may even have decided to hoodwink me a little. But after all, so what, I'm not afraid; what's more, it's somehow all the same to me now, can you believe it? And . . . and . . . and as I'm above all convinced that you're an excellent fellow, then perhaps we shall end by being on friendly terms. I like you very much, Yevgeny Pavlych, you're . . . a very, very decent man, in my view!'

'Well, at any rate it's most delightful to have dealings with you, irrespective of what they're about,' concluded Yevgeny Pavlovich. 'Come, I'll drink a glass to your health; I'm awfully glad I came and made a nuisance of myself. Ah!' he stopped suddenly. 'Has that Mr Ippolit moved in to stay with you?'

'Yes.'

'I mean, he's not going to die just yet, I think?'

'But why?'

'Oh, no reason; I've spent half an hour with him here . . .'

Ippolit had been waiting for the prince all this time, ceaselessly watching him and Yevgeny Pavlovich as they talked at one side of the veranda. As they walked over to the table, he became feverishly enlivened. He was anxious and excited; the sweat stood out on his forehead. In addition to a kind of wandering, constant anxiety, there was in his glittering eyes a kind of vague impatience; his gaze moved aimlessly from one object to another, from one face to another. Although so far he had been taking part in the general noisy conversation, his animation was a feverish one; to the actual conversation he was inattentive; his arguing was incoherent, mocking and carelessly paradoxical; he did not finish his sentences, abandoning topics that only a minute before he himself had begun to talk about with vehement ardour. The prince learned with surprise and concern that Ippolit had been allowed to drink two full glasses of champagne that evening without hindrance, and that the glass before him, already begun, was now the third. But he only learned this later; at the present moment he was not very observant.

'You know, I'm terribly glad that your birthday's today!' cried Ippolit.

'Why?'

'You'll see; please hurry up and sit down; in the first place, because all your . . . people are here together. I somehow guessed there would be a lot of people; for the first time in my life my guess proved correct! But it's a pity I didn't know it was your birthday, or I'd have brought a present . . . Ha-ha! But perhaps

I have brought a present, after all! Will it be long until daylight?'

'It will be dawn in less than two hours,' observed Ptitsyn, looking at his watch.

'But what's the point of dawn now, when one can read outside without it?' someone commented.

'Because I want to see the rim of the sun. Is it possible to drink to the health of the sun, Prince, what's your view?'

Ippolit asked his questions abruptly, addressing everyone without ceremony, as though he were giving commands, but seemingly unaware of this.

'Let's drink, certainly; but you ought to calm down, Ippolit, eh?'

'You're always talking about sleeping; Prince, you're my nanny! As soon as the sun appears and "resounds" in the sky (who was it who said in a poem: "in the sky the sun resounded"?[2] It's nonsense, but it's good!) – then we shall sleep. Lebedev! After all, the sun is the spring of life,[3] isn't it? What's the meaning of the "springs of life" in Revelation? Have you heard of the "star Wormwood", Prince?'

'I've heard that Lebedev thinks the "star Wormwood" is the network of railways that spread over Europe.'

'No, sir, permit me, sir, that's not fair, sir!' cried Lebedev, jumping up and waving his arms, as though trying to stop the universal laughter that had broken out. 'Permit me, sir! With these gentlemen . . . all these gentlemen,' he turned round suddenly to face the prince, 'What I mean is, that in certain respects, sir . . .' and he rapped on the table twice, without ceremony, which made the laughter grow even louder.

Although Lebedev was in his usual 'evening' condition, on this occasion he was very excited and irritated by the long and 'learned' argument that had preceded this remark, and in such instances he generally treated his opponents with infinite and wholly undisguised contempt.

'That's not so, sir! Prince, half an hour ago we made an agreement not to interrupt; not to laugh while someone was speaking; to let him say all he had to say freely, and only then let the atheists raise their objections if they want to; we appointed the general as moderator, sir! Otherwise, what would happen, sir? That way anyone could lose the thread of his argument, in the middle of a lofty idea, sir, in the middle of a profound idea, sir . . .'

'But continue, continue: no one's making you lose *your* thread!' voices rang out.

'Continue, but don't ramble.'

'What's this "star Wormwood"?' someone inquired.

'I have no idea!' replied General Ivolgin, resuming his recent appointment as moderator with an air of importance.

'I really love all these arguments and states of irritation, Prince, learned ones, of course,' Keller muttered meanwhile, squirming about on his chair in genuine rapture and impatience. 'Learned and political ones,' he said suddenly and unexpectedly to Yevgeny Pavlovich, who was sitting almost next to him. 'You know, I'm awfully fond of reading the newspaper reports of proceedings in the English houses of parliament, that is, not in the sense of what's discussed there (I'm not a politician, you know), but in the sense of how the members talk to one another, how they behave as politicians, so to speak: "the noble viscount sitting opposite", "the noble count who shares my view", "my noble opponent, who has astonished Europe with his proposal", that's to say, all those pretty expressions, all that parliamentarism of a free people – that's what's fascinates people like me! I'm captivated, Prince. I've always been an artist in the depths of my soul, I swear to you, Yevgeny Pavlych.'

'So what follows from that?' Ganya said heatedly from another corner of the room. 'I suppose you think the railways are accursed, that they bring ruin to mankind, that they're a plague fallen to earth in order to pollute the "springs of life"?'

Gavrila Ardalionovich was in a particularly excited mood that evening, and it was a cheerful, almost triumphant mood, or so it seemed to the prince. He had, of course, been making fun of Lebedev, egging him on, but soon he himself grew heated.

'Not the railways, no, sir!' Lebedev retorted, losing his temper at the same time, and experiencing a boundless pleasure. 'Of themselves, the railways will not pollute the springs of life, but all of it as a whole, sir, is accursed, the whole spirit of our recent centuries, as a general scientific and practical totality, perhaps really is accursed, sir.'

'Definitely accursed or only perhaps?' Yevgeny Pavlovich inquired. 'I mean, that's important in this case.'

'Accursed, accursed, definitely accursed!"' Lebedev confirmed with passion.

'Don't go over the top, Lebedev, you're much kinder in the mornings,' Ptitsyn observed, smiling.

'But at night I'm more candid! At night I'm more sincere and more candid!' Lebedev addressed him heatedly. 'I'm more straightforward and more definite, more honest and more decent, and although I may make myself vulnerable as a result, I don't care, sir; I challenge you all now, all of you atheists: how are you going to save the world and where have you found the right road for it – you men of science, industry, associations, wages and the like? How? With credit? What is credit? Where will credit take you?'

'I say, you are an inquisitive chap!' observed Yevgeny Pavlovich.

'Well, it's my opinion that anyone who isn't interested in such questions is a high society loafer, sir!'

'Still, it may lead to a universal solidarity and a balancing of interests,' observed Ptitsyn.

'And that's all, that's all it will do! Without accepting any moral foundation, apart from the satisfaction of personal egoism and material necessity! Universal peace, universal happiness – from necessity! Isn't that how it is, may I dare to inquire, my dear sir?'

'Yes, but the universal need to live, drink and eat, and the most complete, indeed scientific conviction, that one cannot satisfy that need without universal association and a solidarity of interests, is, I think, an idea strong enough to serve as a point of support and a "spring of life" for future ages of mankind,' observed Ganya, who was by now seriously excited.

'The need to drink and eat, that's to say, the instinct for self-preservation . . .'

'But is the instinct for self-preservation such a small thing?

After all, the instinct for self-preservation is the normal law of mankind . . .'

'Who told you that?' cried Yevgeny Pavlovich suddenly. 'A law – that's true, but as normal as the law of destruction, and, perhaps, of self-destruction, too. Does the whole normal law of mankind consist of self-preservation alone?'

'Aha!' exclaimed Ippolit, quickly turning to Yevgeny Pavlovich and studying him with wild curiosity; but having seen that he was laughing, he also began to laugh, nudged Kolya, who was standing beside him and once again asked him the time, even pulled Kolya's silver watch towards him, casting an avid look at its hands. Then, as though oblivious to everything, he stretched out on the sofa, threw his hands behind his head and began to look at the ceiling; half a minute later he was sitting at the table again, sitting up straight and listening to the chatter of Lebedev, who was now excited beyond all bounds.

'A perfidious and mocking idea, an insidious idea!' Lebedev seized avidly on Yevgeny Pavlovich's paradox, 'an idea expressed with the aim of provoking your opponents to a fight – but an idea that is true! Because you, a high society mocker and cavalry officer (though not without talent!) don't know yourself the degree to which your idea is a profound one, a true one! Yes, sir. The law of self-destruction and the law of self-preservation are equally strong in mankind! The devil rules equally over mankind until the end of a time that is not yet known to us.[4] You laugh? You don't believe in the devil? Disbelief in the devil is a French idea, a frivolous idea. Do you know who the devil is? Do you know what his name is? Without even knowing his name, you laugh at his form, like Voltaire, at his hoofs, tail, horns, which you've invented; for the impure spirit is a great and terrible spirit, though not with the hoofs and horns that you've invented for him. But we are not concerned with him just now! . . .'

'How do you know we're not concerned with him just now?' Ippolit cried all of a sudden, and began to laugh convulsively.

'A clever and allusive thought!' Lebedev interjected, 'but again we're not concerned with that, for our question is whether the "springs of life" have not grown feeble with the growth of . . .'

'The railways?' cried Kolya.

'Not the lines of railway communication, young but excitable puppy, but the whole tendency of which the railways may serve, so to speak, as a picture, as an artistic expression. They speed, they thunder, they rattle and hurry for the happiness of mankind, we are told! "Mankind is becoming too noisy and industrious, there's not enough spiritual calm," complains one thinker who has withdrawn from the melée. "Perhaps, but the rattle of wagons bearing grain for starving mankind may be better than spiritual calm," another thinker who is always travelling about triumphantly replies, and walks away in vanity. I, loathsome Lebedev, don't believe in those wagons that bear grain for mankind! For the wagons that bear grain to the whole of mankind without any moral basis for their action may most cold-bloodedly exclude an important part of mankind from the enjoyment of what they bear, something that has already happened . . .'

'You mean the wagons can exclude them cold-bloodedly?' someone interposed.

'It's already happened,' Lebedev confirmed, not deeming the question worthy of attention. 'We have already had Malthus,[5] the friend of mankind. But a friend of mankind with a shaky moral foundation is a devourer of mankind, not to speak of his vanity; for if you offend the vanity of any one of those countless friends of mankind, he will instantly be ready to set fire to the world and all its four corners out of petty revenge – as a matter of fact, just like any one of us, if truth be told, like myself, who am most loathsome of all, for I would probably be the first to bring the kindling, and then run away. But again we're not concerned with that!'

'Well, what are we concerned with, then?'

'We've heard enough of this!'

'We are concerned with the following anecdote from ages past, for I feel a need to tell a story from ages past. In our time, in our fatherland, which I hope you love as much as I do, gentlemen, as I for my part am even ready to shed every drop of my blood . . .'

'Continue! Continue!'

'In our fatherland, just as in Europe, universal, ubiquitous and terrible famines have visited mankind according to calculations and, as far as I remember, no more than once every quarter of a century, in other words, once every twenty-five years. I shall not argue over the precise figure, but they are comparatively quite rare . . .'

'Comparatively with what?'

'With the twelfth century and with the centuries that neighbour it on either side. For then, as the scribes write and confirm, universal famines in mankind visited it every two years or at least every three years, so that given such a state of affairs man even resorted to cannibalism, though keeping it a secret. One such cannibal, approaching old age, announced of his own accord and without any compulsion that throughout his long and poverty-stricken life he had killed and eaten personally and in the deepest secret sixty monks and several lay infants – about six of them, but no more, that is, very few compared to the number of clerics he had eaten. As for lay adults, as it turned out, he never set a finger on any of them with this purpose.'

'This is impossible!' cried the general, in his capacity of moderator, in a voice that sounded almost offended. 'I often reason and argue with him, gentlemen, and always about ideas like that; but more often than not he comes up with such absurdities that one's ears even start to fall off, for there's not one copeck's worth of plausibility in it all!'

'General! Remember the siege of Kars, and I assure you, gentlemen, that my story is the unvarnished truth. For my part I will observe that although almost every real fact has its own immutable laws, such facts nearly always seem improbable and implausible. And the more real the fact, the more implausible it sometimes is.'

'But could anyone possibly eat sixty monks?' people laughed all round.

'Though he didn't eat them all at once – that is obvious – he may have done so in the course of fifteen or twenty years, which is quite understandable and natural.'

'Natural?'

'Natural!' Lebedev ground out with pedantic obstinacy. 'And what is more, a Catholic monk is by his nature gullible and inquisitive, and it would be all too easy to lure him into a forest or into some secluded place and there deal with him in the manner described above – but I won't dispute that the number of eaten persons seemed inordinate, even to the point of intemperance.'

'Perhaps it is indeed true, gentlemen,' the prince observed suddenly.

Until now he had listened to the disputants in silence, and had not engaged in the conversation; often, after the universal explosions of laughter, he had laughed with all his heart and soul. It was plain that he was very glad everyone was so cheerful, so noisy; even that they were drinking so much. Perhaps he might not have said a word all evening, but suddenly he took it into his head to speak. He spoke with great seriousness, so that everyone suddenly turned towards him with curiosity.

'I refer, gentlemen, to the fact that there were such frequent famines in those days. Even I have heard about that, though I have a poor knowledge of history. But it appears that it must have been so. When I ended up in the Swiss Alps, I marvelled greatly at the ruins of the old feudal castles built on the slopes of the mountains, on steep rocks, and at least half a mile up as the crow flies (that means several miles by the mountain paths). Everyone knows what a castle is: it's a whole mountain of stones. A terrible labour, impossible! And of course it was built by all those poor people, the vassals. What was more, they had to pay all kinds of taxes and support the clergy. How could they feed themselves and cultivate the land? There were few of them in those days, most of them must have died of hunger, and there was literally nothing to eat. I sometimes even used to think: how was it that these people had not died off altogether or something else happened to them, how could they stand their ground and endure? That there were cannibals and, possibly, a great many of them, Lebedev is doubtless right to assert; the only thing I don't understand is why he brought the monks into it, and what he means to imply by that.'

'It's probably that in the twelfth century monks were all there was to eat, because only monks were fat,' observed Gavrila Ardalionovich.

'A most splendid and most accurate perception!' cried Lebedev. 'For he never laid a finger on lay persons. Not a single lay person, as against sixty ecclesiastics, and that is a terrible thought, a historical thought, a statistical thought, indeed, and it is from such facts that history is built for those in the know; for it may be concluded with numerical precision that ecclesiastics were at least sixty times happier and freer than the rest of mankind then. And were, perhaps, sixty times fatter than the whole of the rest of mankind . . .'

'An exaggeration, an exaggeration, Lebedev!' they laughed all around.

'I agree that it's a historical thought, but what are you leading up to?' the prince continued to inquire. (He spoke with such seriousness and such an absence of any kind of joking or fun poked at Lebedev, at whom everyone was laughing, that his tone unwittingly became comical when set against the tone of the rest of the company; a little more of it and they would have started to make fun of him too, but he did not notice this.)

'Can't you see that the fellow's insane, Prince?' Yevgeny Pavlovich leaned over to him. 'They told me here earlier that he's lost his wits over the matter of being a lawyer and making lawyer's speeches, and that he wants to take the law exam. I expect he'll produce a wonderful parody.'

'What I'm leading up to is a an earth-shattering conclusion,' Lebedev was thundering, meanwhile. 'But first of all let us examine the psychological and legal position of the accused. We see that the accused, or, so to speak, my client, in spite of all the impossibility of finding any other edible object, several times in the course of his curious career revealed a desire to repent, and declined to consume ecclesiastics. We see this clearly from the facts: it is mentioned that he did indeed eat five or six infants, a relatively trifling figure, but none the less significant in another respect. It is evident that, tormented by terrible pangs of conscience (for my client is a religious and conscientious man, as I shall prove), and in order to reduce his sin as much as possible, as a kind of experiment, on six occasions he exchanged his monkish diet for secular fare. That this was a kind of experiment is again beyond doubt; for had it been merely for the sake of gastronomic variety, the figure of six would have been too trifling: why only six, and not thirty? (I am taking it half and half.) But if it was only an experiment, conducted out of sheer despair in the face of blasphemy and ecclesiastical outrage, then the figure of six becomes all too comprehensible; for six experiments, in order to satisfy the pangs of conscience, would be more than sufficient, as the experiments could not possibly be successful, after all. And then, in the first place, as I perceive it, an infant is too small, that's to say, not large enough in size, as over a certain period of time the number of lay infants would have to be three, nay, five times greater than the number of monks, so that the sin, if it were reduced on the one hand, would at last be increased on the other, if not in the matter of quality, then in the matter of quantity. In arguing thus, gentlemen, I do, of course, descend into the heart of a twelfth-century criminal. Where I myself, a man of the nineteenth century, am concerned, I should argue differently, I would have you know, so there is no need for you to grin at me, gentlemen, and as for you, General, it's actually quite unseemly. In the second place, an infant, in my personal view, is not nutritious, perhaps even too sweet and sickly, so that, while not satisfying one's hunger, it leaves only pangs of conscience. Now the conclusion, the finale, gentlemen, the finale, in which is contained the solution of one of the greatest questions of those bygone days and of our own! The criminal ends up denouncing himself to the clerics and consigning himself to the hands of the government. The question is, what torments awaited him in those days, what wheels, what stakes and bonfires? For who was it who impelled him to denounce himself? Why not simply stop at the figure of sixty, preserving the secret to his last breath? Why not simply give up monks, and live in repentance as a hermit? Why not, indeed, become a monk himself? Now there is the solution! So there must have been something more powerful than stakes and bonfires, more powerful even than the habit of twenty years! There must have been an idea more powerful than all the disasters, crop failures, tortures, plagues, leprosy and all the hell that mankind would not have been able to endure without that one idea that bound and directed the heart and fructified the springs of life! Show me anything resembling such a power in our age of seaminess and railways ... what I ought to say is steam engines and railways, but I say seaminess and railways, for I am drunk but tell the truth! Show me an idea that binds the mankind of today with even half the power there was in those centuries. And then you have the effrontery to tell me that the springs of life have not been weakened, been polluted under this "star", this net that has entangled human beings. And do not try to intimidate me with your prosperity, your wealth, the infrequency of famine and the swiftness of the paths of communication! The wealth is greater, but the power is less; there is no binding idea left; everything has grown soft, everything has stewed to mush! We have all stewed to mush, all, all of us! ... But enough, we're not concerned with that now, but with the circumstance, most worthy and respected Prince, that we should, shouldn't we, see to the *zakuski* that have been prepared for the guests?'

Lebedev, who had almost brought some of his listeners to the point of genuine indignation (it should be observed that bottles were being opened ceaselessly all the while), instantly reconciled all his opponents by this unexpected conclusion to his speech. He himself called such a conclusion 'a skilful lawyer's twist to the case'. Cheerful laughter rose once more, the guests grew animated; everyone got up from the table in order to stretch their limbs and stroll about the veranda. Only Keller found Lebedev's speech not to his liking, and was in a state of extreme excitement.

'He attacks enlightenment, he preaches the fanatical cruelty of the twelfth century, putting on airs, and not because he doesn't know any better: where did he find the money to buy a house, may one ask?' he said aloud, stopping all whom he encountered.

'I've seen a real interpreter of Revelation,' the general was saying in another corner to other listeners, among them Ptitsyn, whom he had buttonholed – 'the late Grigory Semyonovich Burmistrov: now he was a man who, so to speak, set hearts on fire. To begin with he would put on his spectacles and open a

large, ancient book in a black leather binding, well, and he also
had a grey beard, and two decorations for charitable work. He
would begin sternly and severely, generals bowed before him,
and ladies fell into a swoon, well – and this chap ends with
zakuski! I've heard a few things, but never anything like that!'

As he listened to the general, Ptitsyn smiled and seemed to be
about to reach for his hat, but was apparently unable to make
up his mind, or kept forgetting his intention. Even before the
guests rose from the table, Ganya suddenly stopped drinking
and pushed his glass away; an expression of gloom passed over
his face. When the guests rose, he went over to Rogozhin and
sat down beside him. One might have thought they were on the
most friendly of terms. Rogozhin, who had initially also quietly
been preparing to leave, was now sitting motionless, his head
lowered and as if he too had forgotten that he had intended to
go away. All that evening he had not had a single drop of wine,
and was very pensive; from time to time he merely raised his
eyes and surveyed everyone present. And now it appeared that
he was waiting for something here, something extremely important for him, and had determined not to leave until then.

The prince had drunk only two or three glasses, and was
merely cheerful. Half getting up from the table, he met Yevgeny
Pavlovich's gaze, remembered the talk they were going to have
together, and smiled in friendly fashion. Yevgeny Pavlovich
nodded to him and suddenly pointed to Ippolit, whom he was
watching intently at that moment. Ippolit was asleep, stretched
out on the sofa.

'Tell me, why has this urchin wormed his way into your
company, Prince?' he said suddenly with such open annoyance,
and even hatred, that it surprised the prince. 'I'll wager he's up
to no good!'

'I've noticed,' said the prince. 'At least, you seem to be very
interested in him today, Yevgeny Pavlych; am I right?'

'And you may add: in my own particular circumstances I have
enough to think about, so that I myself am surprised at not
having been able to take my eyes off his loathsome physiognomy
all evening!'

'He has a handsome face . . .'

'There, there, look!' cried Yevgeny Pavlovich, tugging the prince's arm. 'There! . . .'

The prince again stared at Yevgeny Pavlovich in surprise.

5

Ippolit, who towards the end of Lebedev's dissertation had suddenly fallen asleep on the sofa, now suddenly woke up, as though someone had nudged him in the side, shuddered, lifted himself on one elbow, looked about him and turned pale; in a kind of fear, even, he gazed around; but something almost like horror was expressed in his face when he remembered everything and put it all together.

'What, they're leaving? It's over? Has the sun risen?' he asked anxiously, seizing the prince's arm. 'What time is it? For God's sake: the time? I overslept. Was I asleep for long?' he added, with a look almost of despair, as though he had missed something on which, at the least, his entire fate depended.

'You were asleep for seven or eight minutes,' replied Yevgeny Pavlovich.

Ippolit gave him an avid glance and pondered for several moments.

'Ah . . . is that all! So I . . .'

And he deeply and avidly drew breath, as though having cast off an extreme burden from himself. He had realized, at last, that nothing was 'over', that dawn had not yet broken, that the guests had risen from the table only for the *zakuski*, and that it was only Lebedev's chatter that was at an end. He smiled, and a consumptive flush, in the form of two bright spots, began to play on his cheeks.

'And you were actually counting the minutes I was asleep, Yevgeny Pavlych,' he interjected mockingly, 'you haven't been able to tear yourself away from me all evening, I saw . . . Ah! Rogozhin! I dreamt about him just now,' he whispered to the prince, frowning and nodding at Rogozhin, who was sitting at the table. 'Ah, yes,' he suddenly veered off again, 'where is the orator, where is Lebedev? So Lebedev has finished, has he? What was he talking about? Is it true, Prince, that you once said the world will be saved by beauty? Gentlemen,' he cried loudly to them all, 'the prince says that the world will be saved by beauty! But I say that he has such whimsical notions merely because he's presently in love. Gentlemen, the prince is in love; earlier, as soon as he came in, I was convinced of that. Don't blush, Prince, I shall feel sorry for you. What sort of beauty will save the world? Kolya told me about it . . . Are you a zealous Christian? Kolya said you call yourself a Christian.'

The prince studied him attentively and did not reply to him.

'Aren't you going to reply to me? Perhaps you think I'm very fond of you?' Ippolit added suddenly, as though he were venting his spleen.

'No, I don't think so. I know that you don't like me.'

'What? Even after yesterday? I was sincere with you yesterday, wasn't I?'

'Even yesterday I knew that you don't like me.'

'You mean, because I envy you, is that it, envy you? You've always thought that, and you think it now, but . . . but why am I talking to you about this? I want some more champagne; pour me some, Keller.'

'You can't have any more, Ippolit, I won't let you . . .'

And the prince moved the glass away from him.

'Oh, very well, then . . .' he agreed at once, as though reflecting. 'I suppose they'll say . . . but what the devil do I care what they'll say? Don't you think? Don't you think? Let them say what they like afterwards, don't you think, Prince? And what do any of us care what will happen *afterwards*? . . . However, I'm only half-awake. What a horrible dream I had, I've only remembered it now . . . I don't wish you such dreams, Prince, though perhaps I really don't like you. As a matter of fact, if one doesn't like someone, why wish him ill, don't you think? Why do I keep asking questions, I'm constantly asking questions! Give me your hand; I shall shake it firmly, like this . . . But you stretched out your hand to me, didn't you? So you know that I'm shaking it sincerely . . . I suppose I shan't have any more to drink. What time is it? Actually, don't bother, I know what time it is. It's time! Now's the time. What's going on over there, are they serving *zakuski*? So that means this table is free? Splendid! Gentlemen, I . . . but none of these gentlemen is listening . . . I intend to read aloud a certain article, Prince; the *zakuski* are, of course, more interesting, but . . .'

And suddenly, quite unexpectedly, he pulled from his top side pocket a large, official-sized package, stamped with a large red seal. He placed it on the table in front of him.

This unexpected event had an effect on the company, which was not primed for it or, rather, was *primed*, but not for that. Yevgeny Pavlovich even jumped upright in his chair; Ganya swiftly moved over to the table; Rogozhin too, but with a kind of peevish annoyance, as though he understood what was going on. Lebedev, who happened to be standing in the vicinity, approached with small, inquisitive eyes and looked at the package, trying to guess what was afoot.

'What's that you've got there?' the prince asked, uneasily.

'With the first rim of the sun I shall lie down, Prince, I told you; word of honour: you'll see!' exclaimed Ippolit, 'but . . . but . . . do you really think I'm not capable of unsealing this package?' he added, looking round with a kind of challenge and as if addressing them all indifferently. The prince noticed that he was trembling all over.

'None of us thinks that,' the prince replied for them all, 'and why do you think that anyone has such a thought and what . . . what's this strange idea you have of reading? What have you got there, Ippolit?'

'What's he got there? What's happened to him this time?' people asked all round.

They all approached, some still munching their *zakuski*; the package with its red seal drew them all like a magnet.

'It's something I wrote yesterday, just after I promised I'd come and stay with you, Prince. I spent all yesterday writing it, carried on into the night and finished it this morning; in the night, towards morning, I had a dream . . .'

'Wouldn't it be better to do it tomorrow?' the prince broke in timidly.

'Tomorrow "there shall be time no longer"!' Ippolit laughed

hysterically. 'However, don't worry, it will only take me forty minutes to read it, well – or an hour ... And you see how interested everyone is; they've all come over here; they're all looking at my seal, and you see, if I hadn't sealed the article in a package, there would have been no effect! Ha-ha! That's the meaning of mystery! Shall I unseal it or not, gentlemen?' he cried, laughing his strange laughter, his eyes glittering. 'A secret! A secret! Do you remember, Prince, who proclaimed that "there shall be time no longer"? It's proclaimed by the great and mighty angel in the book of Revelation!'

'You'd better not read it!' Yevgeny Pavlovich exclaimed suddenly, but with such an air of alarm, unexpected in him, that many thought it strange.

'Don't read it!' cried the prince, putting his hand on the package.

'What's all this reading about? We're having *zakuski* now,' someone observed.

'An article? For a journal, is it?' someone else inquired.

'It's probably boring, isn't it?' added a third.

'Just what have you got there?' the others inquired. But the prince's frightened gesture seemed to frighten Ippolit, too.

'Then ... I shouldn't read it?' he whispered to him, almost warily, with a twisted smile on his blue lips. 'I shouldn't read it?' he muttered, looking round at the whole audience, all the eyes and faces, and seeming again to clutch at them all, as if pouncing on them, with his earlier expansiveness. 'Are you ... afraid?' he turned to the prince again.

'Of what?' asked the latter, his expression altering more and more.

'Does anyone have a twenty copeck piece?' Ippolit suddenly leapt up from his chair as though he had been yanked to his feet. 'Any coin will do.'

'Here!' Lebedev gave him one instantly; the thought flashed through his mind that the sick Ippolit had gone mad.

'Vera Lukyanovna!' Ippolit asked hurriedly. 'Take it and throw it on the table: heads or tails? If it's heads, then I'll read it!'

Vera cast a frightened look at the coin, at Ippolit, and then at her father, and rather awkwardly, with her head thrown back as though in the conviction that she must not look at the coin, threw it on the table. It was heads.

'I'll read it!' whispered Ippolit, as though crushed by the decision of fate; he could not have turned paler if a death sentence had been read aloud to him. 'Though actually,' he started suddenly, after half a minute's silence, 'what is this? Did I really cast lots just now?' He looked round at them all with the same intrusive candour. 'But I mean, this a remarkable psychological phenomenon!' he exclaimed suddenly, addressing the prince, in sincere amazement. 'It's . . . it's an unfathomable phenomenon, Prince!' he confirmed, growing animated and as if coming to his senses. 'Write it down, Prince, remember it, after all, I believe you're collecting materials on the death penalty . . . They told me, ha-ha! Oh God, what senseless absurdity!' He sat down on the sofa, put both elbows on the table and clutched at his head. 'I mean, it's even shameful! . . . But what the devil do I care if it's shameful,' he raised his head almost immediately. 'Gentlemen! Gentlemen, I'm unsealing the package,' he proclaimed with sudden determination. 'However . . . I . . . I shan't force anyone to listen! . . .'

With hands trembling from excitement he unsealed the package, took from it several sheets of notepaper covered with small handwriting, placed them in front of him and began to smooth them out.

'But what is this? What has he got there? What's going to be read out?' some muttered gloomily; others said nothing. But all sat down and watched with curiosity. Perhaps they really were expecting something unusual. Vera seized hold of her father's chair, almost in tears with fright; Kolya was almost in the same state of fright. Lebedev, who had already sat down, suddenly got to his feet, reached for the candles and moved them closer to Ippolit, so he would have more light to read by . . .

'Gentlemen, this . . . you'll see in a moment what it is,' Ippolit added for some reason, and suddenly began his reading: '"My Necessary Explanation"! Epigraph: *Après moi le déluge* . . . Pah, the devil take it!' he exclaimed, as though he had burned himself – 'Could I seriously have written such a stupid epigraph?

'. . . Look, gentlemen! . . . I assure you that all this may, in the last analysis, be the most dreadful rubbish! It merely contains some of my thoughts . . . If you think that there's . . . anything mysterious or . . . forbidden . . . about it . . . in short . . .'

'Why don't you read it without the preamble,' Ganya interrupted.

'Too much talk,' inserted Rogozhin, who had said nothing all this time.

Ippolit suddenly gave him a look and, when their eyes met, Rogozhin bared his teeth at him with bitter spleen, and slowly articulated some strange words:

'That's not the way to go about this business, lad, not the way . . .'

No one understood what Rogozhin meant, of course, but his words made a rather strange impression on them all; a single common idea touched each of them obliquely. On Ippolit, however, the words had a terrible effect: he began to tremble so violently that the prince stretched out his hand in order to support him, and he would probably have cried out, had not his voice, as it appeared, suddenly choked. For a whole minute he was unable to get a word out and, breathing heavily, looked steadily at Rogozhin. At last, gasping and with extreme effort, he said:

'So it was you . . . you were the one . . . you?'

'What do you mean, I was the one? What did I do?' Rogozhin answered, bewildered, but Ippolit, flaring up and in an almost rabid fury that suddenly gripped him, harshly and violently exclaimed:

'*You* were in my room last week, at night, at nearly two o'clock in the morning, that day when I came to see you in the morning, *you*!! Confess, it was you?'

'Last week, at night? Have you gone out of your mind, lad?'

The 'lad' again fell silent for a moment, putting his index finger to his forehead, as if trying to work something out: but in his pale, still terror-distorted smile there suddenly flickered something almost cunning, even triumphant.

'It was you!' he repeated, at last, almost in a whisper, but with extreme conviction. '*You* came to see me and sat silently in my room on a chair, by the window, for a whole hour; more; between one and three in the morning; then you got up and left when it was getting on for three . . . It was you, you! Why you were trying to frighten me, why you came to torment me, I don't know, but it was you!'

And in his gaze there suddenly flickered an infinite hatred, in spite of the fact that he was still trembling with fear.

'In a moment, gentlemen, you will learn all this, I . . . I . . . listen . . .'

Again, in terrible haste, he reached for his sheets of paper; they had come loose and had fallen apart, he tried to put them together; they trembled in his trembling hands; it was a long time before he could recover his composure.

At last, the reading began. At first, for about five minutes, the author of the unexpected *article* still gasped for breath and read incoherently and unevenly; but then his voice became firmer and began fully to express the sense of what was being read. Only sometimes did a rather violent cough interrupt him; half way through the article he grew very hoarse; an extreme animation, which mastered him more and more as he continued to read, attained its highest degree towards the end, as did the painful impression on his listeners. Here is the whole of that 'article':

'MY NECESSARY EXPLANATION
'*Après moi le déluge*

'Yesterday morning the prince came to see me; among other things, he tried to persuade me to move to his dacha. I somehow knew that he would be bound to insist on this, that he would blurt straight out to me that at the dacha "it will be easier for me to die among people and trees", as he puts it. But today he did not say "die", but "it will be easier to live", which is, however, almost the same thing for me, in my position. I asked him what he meant with these perpetual "trees" of his, and why he kept going on to me about them – and with astonishment learned from him that I myself had apparently said at that soirée that I had come to Pavlovsk to look at trees for the last time. When I observed to him that it was all the same whether I died under trees or looking out of the window at my bricks, and that there was no reason to make such a big thing out of two weeks, he at once agreed with me; but the green leaves and the pure air, in his opinion, could not fail to bring about some sort of physical change in me, and my agitation and *my dreams* would change, too and, perhaps, be relieved. I again observed to him, laughing, that he talked like a materialist. He replied to me with that smile of his that he had always been a materialist. Since he never lies, those words must signify something. His smile is pleasant; I have now studied him more closely. Now I don't know whether I like him or don't like him; I don't have time to bother about that now. My five-month-old hatred of him, I must observe, has begun to abate altogether during the past month. Who knows, perhaps the main reason I came to Pavlovsk was in order to see him. But . . . in that case, why did I leave my room? The man who has been condemned to death must not leave his corner; and if I had not made a final decision now, and decided, on the contrary, to wait until the last hour, then, of course, I would not have left my room on any account, and would not have accepted an invitation to go and stay with him to "die" in Pavlovsk.

'I must hurry and finish this explanation by tomorrow without fail. That means I will not have time to read it over and correct it; I shall read it over tomorrow when I read it to the prince and the two or three witnesses I intend to find at his place. As there will not be one word of falsehood in it, nothing but the truth, final and solemn, I'm already curious what sort of impression it will make on me at the moment when I begin to read it over. As a matter of fact, I ought not to have written the words: "the final and solemn truth"; it's not worth telling lies for two weeks, because it's not worth living for two weeks; that's the best proof that I will write the truth and nothing but. (NB Must not forget the thought: am I not insane at this moment, or rather moments? I was told positively that consumptives in the last stages of the disease sometimes go insane for a while. Check this tomorrow during the reading, from effect on listeners. This question must be resolved with complete exactitude, otherwise I can't proceed with anything.)

'It seems to me that I have just written something terribly stupid; but I don't have the time to correct it, as I said; what is more, I promise myself that I won't correct a single line of this manuscript, even if I notice that I contradict myself every five lines. At the reading tomorrow I want to determine whether the logical flow of my thought is correct; whether I notice my own mistakes, and whether all I have thought about in this room during the past six months is true or just mere raving.

'If even two months ago I had had to say farewell to my room altogether and say farewell to Meyer's wall, then I am sure I would have been sad. But now I don't feel anything, and yet tomorrow I am leaving this room and the wall, *for ever*! So my conviction that for two weeks it's not worth feeling sorry or giving oneself up to any kind of sensation at all has got the better of my nature and may now be in command of all my feelings. But is that true? Is it true that my nature has now been completely vanquished? If they were to put me to torture now, I would probably cry out, and not say that it wasn't worth crying out and feeling pain because I only have two weeks left to live.

'But is it true that I have only two weeks left to live, and no more? That day in Pavlovsk I lied: B-n told me nothing and never saw me; but about a week ago they brought a student called Kislorodov[1] to my room; by conviction he's a materialist, an atheist and a nihilist, and that's precisely why I summoned him; I needed a man who would finally tell me the naked truth, without mollycoddling and without ceremony. This he did, and not only with eagerness and without ceremony, but even with evident enjoyment (which I think is going too far). He blurted straight out to me that I only had about a month left; perhaps a little more, if the circumstances were good, but I might die far sooner than that. In his opinion, I might die suddenly, even tomorrow, for example: such things have occurred, and just the other day a young lady, suffering from consumption and in a position similar to my own, in Kolomna, was setting off for the market to buy provisions when she suddenly felt ill, lay down on the sofa, uttered a sigh, and died. All this Kislorodov told me even with a certain bravura that consisted of callousness and indiscretion, and as though in this he were doing me an honour, indicating that he considered me to be the same kind of all-denying, superior being as himself, for whom dying is naturally of no account. In the end the facts were quite clear: a month and no more! I am quite certain he isn't wrong about it.

'It surprised me greatly when the prince guessed the other day that I was having "bad dreams"; he said *literally* that in Pavlovsk "my agitation and *my dreams*" would alter. And why dreams? Either he's a medic or else a man of extraordinary intellect who can guess his way to the truth of very many things. (But that he is, after all, an idiot, of that there can be no doubt.) As if on purpose, just before his arrival I had a pretty dream (as a matter fact, of a kind I now have hundreds of). I fell asleep – I think, an hour before his arrival – and dreamed I was in a room (but not my own). A room larger than my own, with a higher ceiling, better furnished, light; a cupboard, a chest of drawers, a sofa and my bed, large and wide and covered with a green silk quilt. But in this room I observed a horrible creature, some kind of monster. It was like a scorpion, but not a scorpion, more loathsome and far more horrible, precisely because there are no such creatures in nature, and because it had appeared in my room *on purpose*, and in this there was some kind of secret. I studied it very closely: it was brown and covered with a shell-like skin, a reptile, some eight inches long, two fingers thick around the head, tapering off towards the tail, so that the very tip of the tail was no more than a fifth of an inch thick. At two inches from the head two legs stuck out from its body, at an angle of forty-five degrees, one on each side, each four inches in length, so that the whole creature, if looked on from above, presented the aspect of a trident. The head I could not make out, but I saw two feelers, not long, like two strong needles, and also brown. There were two similar feelers at the tip of the tail and on the end of each leg, making eight feelers in all. The creature was running around the room very quickly, supporting itself with its legs and tail, and as it ran both its body and its legs wriggled like small serpents, at an extraordinary speed, in spite of the shell, and this was most loathsome to watch. I was dreadfully afraid that it would sting me; they had told me it was poisonous, but what tormented me most was: who had sent it into my room, what did they want to do to me and what was the secret

behind it? The creature hid under the chest of drawers or the
cupboard, crept away into the corners. I squatted up on a chair
and squeezed my legs underneath me. It quickly ran obliquely
right across the room and vanished somewhere near my chair. I
looked around me in terror, but as I was sitting with my legs
tucked underneath me, I hoped it would not climb up on to the
chair. Suddenly I heard from behind me, almost next to my
head, a kind of crackling rustle; I turned round and saw that the
reptile was climbing up the wall and was almost level with my
head, even touching my hair with its tail, which was twirling and
wriggling with incredible speed. I leaped up, and the creature
vanished. I was afraid to lie down on the bed in case it had
crawled under the pillow. Into the room came my mother and
some friend of hers. They began to try to catch the loathsome
thing, but were calmer than I, and not even afraid. But they
knew nothing. Suddenly the reptile crawled out again; this time
it crawled very quietly and as if with some special intention,
wriggling slowly, which was even more repulsive, obliquely
across the room again, towards the door. At this point my
mother opened the door and called Norma, our dog – an enormous Newfoundland, black and shaggy; she died five years ago.
She rushed into the room and stood over the loathsome thing
as if rooted to the spot. The reptile stopped too, but still wriggling and clacking the ends of its legs and tail against the floor.
Animals are not capable of feeling mystical terror, if I am not
mistaken; but at that moment it seemed to me that in Norma's
terror there was something apparently very unusual, almost
mystical, and that therefore she also had a foreboding, as I did,
that there was something very fateful about the beast and that
it contained some secret. She slowly backed away from the
reptile, which was crawling quietly and cautiously towards her;
it apparently intended to rush at her suddenly and sting her.
But, in spite of all her terror, Norma looked dreadfully fierce,
though she was trembling in every limb. All of a sudden she
slowly bared her terrible teeth, opened her enormous red jaws,
positioned herself, found the right posture, plucked up her
courage and suddenly grabbed the reptile in her teeth. The
reptile must have jerked violently, trying to slip away, for Norma

caught it again, in flight this time, and twice took it right into her jaws, still in flight, as though swallowing it. The shell crackled in her teeth; the creature's tail and legs, sticking out of her jaws, moved with horrible speed. Suddenly Norma gave a plaintive yelp: the loathsome thing had managed to sting her tongue. With a yelp and a howl she opened her mouth in pain, and I saw that the chewed-up reptile was still moving across it, emitting from its half-crushed body a large quantity of white fluid, similar to the fluid of a crushed cockroach ... At that point I woke up, and the prince came in.'

'Gentlemen,' said Ippolit, suddenly tearing himself away from his reading, and even almost in shame, 'I haven't read this over, but it seems to me that I really have written much that is superfluous. This dream . . .'

'Is of that order,' Ganya hurried to put in.

'There's too much that's personal in it, I agree, too much about myself, really . . .'

As he said this, Ippolit looked tired and limp, wiping away the sweat from his forehead with a handkerchief.

'Yes, sir, too damn interested in yourself,' hissed Lebedev.

'Gentlemen, I'm not forcing anyone, again I say it: whoever doesn't want to listen may leave.'

'He's kicking people out . . . of someone else's house,' Rogozhin muttered barely audibly.

'And what if we all got up and left?' Ferdyshchenko said suddenly, not having had the boldness to speak out until now, however.

Ippolit suddenly lowered his eyes and reached for the manuscript; but at that same second he again raised his head and, with glittering eyes, and two red spots on his cheeks, said, as he stared at Ferdyshchenko:

'You don't like me at all!'

Laughter rang out; as a matter of fact, though, most people did not laugh. Ippolit turned horribly red.

'Ippolit,' said the prince, 'put your manuscript away and give it to me, and go to bed now, in my room. We shall talk before you sleep, and also tomorrow; but with the proviso that you never take out these sheets again. Would you like that?'

'How could that be possible?' Ippolit looked at him in decided astonishment. 'Gentlemen!' he cried, again growing feverishly animated. 'A stupid episode, in which I didn't know how to conduct myself. I shall not interrupt my reading again. Whoever wants to listen – listen . . .'

He took a quick gulp of water from the glass, quickly leaned his elbows on the table to protect himself from their gazes, and began to continue the reading again with dogged tenacity. His shame soon passed, however . . .

'The idea' (he continued to read) 'that it was not worth living for a few weeks began to really overpower me, I think, a month ago, when I still had four weeks left to live, but really over-whelmed me only three days ago, when I returned from that soirée in Pavlovsk. The first moment that this thought penetrated me completely and directly was on the veranda at the prince's, at the very same moment when it occurred to me to sample life for the last time, and I wanted to see people and trees (all right, I did say that), got excited, insisted on the rights of Burdovsky, my "neighbour", and wished they would all spread their arms wide, take me into their embrace, and ask me to forgive them for something, and I them; in a word, I ended up an untalented fool. And it was in those hours that my "last conviction" flared up in me. I am astonished now how I could have lived for a whole six months without that "conviction"! I knew positively that I had consumption, and that it was incurable; I did not deceive myself and had a clear understanding of the matter. But the clearer my understanding, the more frantically did I want to live; I clung to life and wanted to live at whatever cost. I agree that I might have been angry at the dark, deaf and blind fate that proposed to crush me like a housefly and, of course, not knowing why; but why did I not leave it there, at anger? Why did I really *start* to live, knowing that it was already too late for me to start; make an attempt, knowing that it was already too late for me to make an attempt? And all the while I was even unable to read books, and gave up reading; what was the point of reading, what was the point of learning anything for six months? That thought made me abandon a book on more than one occasion.

'Yes, that wall of Meyer's could tell many stories! I have written many things on it. There was not a stain on that dirty wall that I didn't know by heart. Accursed wall! And yet it is dearer to me than all the trees in Pavlovsk, or rather would be dearer than them all if everything was not all the same to me now.

'I recall now with what avid interest I began to follow *their* lives; I had had no such interest earlier. Impatiently and cursing, I would sometimes wait for Kolya, when he himself was so ill that he could not leave his room. I went so deeply into every trivial detail, took such an interest in any kind of rumour that I believe I became a gossip-monger. I did not understand, for example, how these people, possessing so much life, were not able to make themselves rich (as a matter of fact, I don't understand it even now). I knew one poor fellow of whom it was later told to me that he had died of hunger, and, I remember, this drove me into a fury: if it had been possible to bring that poor fellow back to life, I think I would have killed him. Sometimes I felt better for whole weeks on end, and I was able to go out in the street; but in the end the street began to make me so angry that I deliberately spent whole days locked in my room, though I could have gone out like everyone else. I could not endure that poking, bustling, eternally preoccupied, gloomy and anxious mass of human beings that scurried about me on the pavements. Why their eternal dolefulness, their eternal anxiety and bustle; their eternal gloomy spite (for they are spiteful, spiteful, spiteful)? Whose fault is it that they are unhappy and don't know how to live, each with sixty years of life ahead of them? Why did Zarnitsyn allow himself to die of hunger when he had sixty years ahead of him? And each of them shows his rags, his toiling hands, is angry and shouts: "We work like oxen, we toil, we're as hungry as dogs and are poor! Others don't work and don't toil, but they're rich!" (The eternal refrain!) Beside them, running and bustling from morning to night, is some miserable weakling "of noble birth", Ivan Fomich Surikov – in our building, he lives on the floor above us – eternally with worn-out elbows, with missing buttons, running errands for other people, carrying out various commissions, and again from morning to night. Talk to him: "I'm poor, destitute and wretched, my wife has died, there was no money to buy medicine, and in winter our baby froze; my eldest daughter is a kept woman..." – eternally snivelling, eternally complaining! Oh, I never had any sympathy for those fools in the past, and I have none now – I say that with pride! Why is he not a Rothschild? Whose fault is it that he has not a mountain of gold imperials and napoleons, such a mountain, a mountain as high as the helter-skelter at a Shrovetide fair? If he's alive, then everything should be within his power! Whose fault is it that he doesn't understand that?

'Oh, now it's all the same to me, now I have no time to be angry, but then, then, I repeat, I literally gnawed my pillow at nights and tore my quilt with fury. Oh, how I dreamed then, how I wished, deliberately wished that I, eighteen years old, hardly clothed, hardly covered, could be suddenly turned out into the street and left completely alone, without shelter, without employment, without a crust of bread, without relations, without a single person I knew in the most enormous city, hungry, beaten (so much the better!), but healthy, and then I would have shown...

'What would I have shown?

'Oh, do you really suppose I don't know how I've degraded myself as it is with this "Explanation" of mine? Well, who will not consider me a weakling with no knowledge of life, who's forgotten he is no longer eighteen; has forgotten that to live as I have lived these past six months means to live to an age where one has grey hair! But let them laugh and say it's all fairytales. I have filled my nights full of them; I can remember them all now.

'But do I really have to retell them all now – now, when the time for fairytales has passed for me? And tell whom? I mean, I used to console myself with them when I clearly saw that I was even forbidden to study Greek grammar, as I once had the idea of doing: "I'll die before I get to the syntax," I thought as I read the first page, and threw the book under the table. It's still lying there; I've forbidden Matryona to pick it up.

'Let those into whose hands my "Explanation" falls, and who

have the patience to read it through, take me for a madman, or even a schoolboy, or most probably of all a man condemned to death, to whom it has naturally begun to seem that all human beings apart from himself attach far too little value to life, have become far too accustomed to wasting it, avail themselves of it far too lazily, far too unscrupulously, and are therefore unworthy of it, every one of them! And what of it? I declare that my reader will be mistaken and that my conviction has nothing to do with my death sentence. Ask them, just ask them what they all, every one of them, understand by happiness. Oh, you may be sure that Columbus was happy not when he had discovered America but when he was discovering it; be assured that the highest point of his happiness was perhaps just three days before the discovery of the New World, when in despair the mutinying crew very nearly turned the ship towards Europe, back again! What mattered now was not the New World, even though it might have vanished. Columbus died almost without having seen it and not really knowing what he had discovered. What matters is life, nothing but life – its revelation, constant and eternal, while the discovery matters not at all! But what's the point of talking? I suspect that all I am saying now is so similar to the most commonly used phrases that I will probably be taken for a first-grade schoolboy presenting his essay on "the sunrise", or it will perhaps be said that I wanted to express something, but in spite of all my desire to do so was unable to . . . "develop my thought". But, on the other hand, I would add that in every human idea that possesses genius or is new, or even simply in every serious human idea that is conceived in someone's head, there always remains something that cannot be conveyed to other people, even though whole volumes were written and your idea explained for thirty-five years; there will always remain something that is on no account willing to come out of your skull and will remain with you for ever; so that you will die without perhaps ever having conveyed to anyone the most important part of your idea. But if I have also been unable to convey everything that has tormented me these last six months, then at least people will understand that, having attained my present "final conviction", I may have paid very dearly for it; it was this that I considered necessary, for certain reasons of my own, to set forth in my "Explanation".

'But, anyway, to continue.'

6

'I will not lie: reality has been trying to catch me on its hook these past six months, and has sometimes distracted me to the point where I forgot about my death sentence or, rather, was unwilling to think about it, and even engaged in practical activities. By the way, about my circumstances at the time. When, about eight months ago, I really became very ill, I broke off all my social contacts and abandoned all the friends I'd had. As I had always been a rather gloomy person, my companions found it easy to forget me; of course, even without that, they would have forgotten me. My circumstances at home, "in the household", that is, were also those of a recluse. Some five months ago I locked myself away and completely separated myself from the family's rooms. I was always obeyed, and no one dared to enter my room, except at a predetermined hour to tidy it and bring me my dinner. My mother trembled at my orders and did not even dare to whimper on those rare occasions when I decided to admit her. She was constantly spanking the children to stop them making a noise and disturbing me; I complained often enough about their shouting; they must be very fond of me now! I think I also tormented "faithful Kolya", as I nicknamed him, rather a lot. Latterly he tormented me, too: it was all quite natural, human beings are created in order to torment one another. But I noticed that he tolerated my irritability, as if he had promised himself in advance that he would spare the invalid. That was naturally a source of irritation to me; but it seems that he had taken it into his head to imitate the prince in "Christian meekness", which was really rather ridiculous. He's a young and hotheaded boy, and imitates everything, of course; but it sometimes seemed to me that it was time he developed his own ideas. I'm very fond of him. I also tormented Surikov, who lived

above us and ran other people's errands from morning to night;
I constantly attempted to prove to him that he himself was to
blame for his poverty, and at last he took fright and stopped
coming to see me. He is a very meek person, the meekest of
creatures (NB They say that meekness is an awe-inspiring force;
I must ask the prince about that, it's something he said); but
when in March I went upstairs to see the baby that had been
"a-froze", to use his own word, and inadvertently smiled over
the dead body of his infant, as I had once again begun to explain
to Surikov that "he himself was to blame", that weakling's lips
suddenly began to tremble and, seizing me by the shoulder with
one hand, with the other he showed me the door and quietly,
that's to say, almost in a whisper, he said to me: "Go, sir!" I
went out, and I really liked that, liked it at the time, even at the
very moment he was showing me out; but for a long time
afterwards his words produced a painful effect on me, a strange,
contemptuous pity for him, which I did not want to feel at all.
Even at the moment of such an insult (I mean, I feel that I
insulted him, though I didn't mean to), even at such a moment
this man was unable to lose his temper! His lips did not tremble
with anger at all, I swear to it: he seized me by the arm and
uttered his magnificent "Go, sir" quite without anger. Of dignity
there was even a great deal, even an amount that was wholly
inappropriate for him (so that, to tell the truth, there was much
that was comical here), but there was no anger. Perhaps he just
suddenly began to despise me. Since then, two or three times
when I've met him on the stairs, he has suddenly begun to doff
his hat to me, something he never used to do, without stopping
as he used to, and instead running past, in embarrassment. If he
did despise me, then it was in his own way: he "*meekly* despised
me". Though perhaps he doffed his hat simply out of fear, to
the son of his creditor, as he constantly owed my mother money
and was quite unable to climb his way out of debt. And that
may even be the most probable explanation. I was on the point
of remonstrating with him, and I know for certain that he would
have begun to apologize to me within ten minutes; but I judged
it better not to trouble him.

'At this same time, that is, around the time that Surikov

PART THREE, CHAPTER 6 463

"a-froze" the baby, about the middle of March, I suddenly began to feel much better for some reason, and this went on for about two weeks. I began to go out, most often towards twilight. I loved the March twilight, when the frost was beginning to bite and the gas was being lit; I sometimes walked a long way. Once I was overtaken on Shestilavochnaya Street[1] in the dark by some "gentleman", I could not make him out properly; he was carrying something wrapped in paper and was dressed in a *kurguz*[2] and a disgraceful old overcoat – far too thin for the season. When he drew level with a street lamp, some ten paces ahead of me, I noticed something fall out of his pocket. I hurried to pick it up – and just in time, because a person in a long caftan suddenly popped up; but, seeing the object in my hands, he did not begin to argue, glanced fleetingly at my hands and slipped past. This object was a large, old-fashioned morocco leather pocket book, tightly stuffed; but somehow I knew at first sight that whatever else this pocket book contained, it was not money. The passer-by who had lost it was already walking some forty paces ahead of me, and soon disappeared from view in the crowd. I broke into a run and began to shout to him; but as all I could shout was "Hey!", he did not even turn round. Suddenly he darted off to the left, through the gateway to a tenement building. When I ran inside the gateway, where it was very dark, there was no one there. The tenement was enormous, one of those Leviathans built by speculators, for small flats; those tenements sometimes contain up to a hundred rooms. As I ran in through the gateway, I had the impression that in the rear right-hand corner of the enormous courtyard a man was walking along, though in the darkness I could hardly discern anything. Having run as far as the corner, I saw the entrance to a staircase; the staircase was narrow, extremely dirty and not lit at all; but further up I could hear a man still ascending the steps at a run, and I set off up the staircase, calculating that somewhere a door would be opened for him, and I would catch him up. So it transpired. The flights of stairs were very short but their number was infinite, and I became dreadfully out of breath; a door was opened and closed again on the fifth floor, I guessed this while still three floors below. While I ran up, got my breath back on the landing and looked for the bell, several minutes passed. At last the door was opened to me by a woman who was blowing up the samovar in a tiny kitchen; she heard out my questions in silence, understood nothing, of course, and silently opened the door to the next room, also small, horribly low-ceilinged, with poor-quality, essential furniture and an enormous, wide bed draped with curtains, on which lay "Terentyich" (as the woman called him), drunk, it seemed to me. On the table a candle-end was burning down in an iron holder, and there was a half-shtof[3] of vodka, almost empty. Terentyich mumbled something to me as he lay there and waved towards the next door, but the woman had left, so there was nothing left for me but to open that door. I did so, and entered the next room.

'This room was even more cramped than the last one, so that I did not even know where to turn round; the narrow, single bed in the corner took up a dreadful amount of space; the other furniture consisted of three plain chairs, piled with all sorts of rags, and the very plainest of wooden kitchen tables in front of an old oilcloth sofa, making it almost impossible to pass between the table and the bed. On the table burned another tallow candle in an iron holder like the one in the other room, and on the bed squealed a tiny baby, no more than three weeks old, perhaps, to judge by its crying; it was being "changed", swaddled that is, by a sick, pale woman, who looked young, was in a marked state of undress, and was, perhaps, only just beginning to get up again after giving birth; but the child would not quiet down and went on crying in expectation of the skinny breast. On the sofa slept another child, a three-year-old girl, covered, it appeared, by a tail-coat. By the table stood a gentleman in a very frayed frock coat (he had taken off his topcoat, and it lay on the bed) and was undoing some blue paper in which were wrapped about two pounds of white bread and two small sausages. On the table there was a pot of tea, and some pieces of black bread lying strewn about. From under the bed an open travelling box projected, and two bundles of rags stuck out.

'In a word, there was terrible disorder. It seemed to me from the first that both of them – the gentleman and the lady – were decent folk, but reduced by poverty to that degrading condition in which disorder finally overcomes all attempts to fight it, and even leads people to the bitter necessity of taking a kind of bitter and almost vengeful sense of satisfaction in it, one that increases with each day.

'As I entered, this gentleman, who had come in just before me and was unpacking his provisions, was discussing something quickly and heatedly with his wife; the latter, though she had not yet finished her nappy-changing, had already begun to whimper; the news must have been bad, as usual. The face of this gentleman, who looked about twenty-eight, was swarthy and thin, framed by black side-whiskers, with a chin shaven till it shone, and it seemed to me rather decent and even pleasant; it was gloomy, with a gloomy gaze, but also with a morbid tinge of pride that was too easily offended. When I went in, a strange scene took place.

'There are people who take exceeding pleasure in their own irritable touchiness, especially when it reaches the final limit (which always happens very quickly); at that moment they even find it more enjoyable to be offended than not to be offended. These irritable people always suffer dreadful torments of remorse afterwards, if they are intelligent, of course, and able to reflect that they got ten times more worked up than was necessary. This gentleman looked at me for some time in amazement, and his wife with fear, as though there were something wondrously strange about someone entering their room; but suddenly he pounced on me with almost rabid fury; I had not yet managed to mutter a couple of words, but he, especially since he saw that I was decently dressed, must have considered himself to have been terribly insulted by the fact that I had dared to glance into his corner with such lack of ceremony and see the whole untidy mess of which he himself was so ashamed. Of course, he was glad of the chance to take out on someone else all the anger he felt at all his failures. For one moment I even thought he was going to hurl himself on me and engage me in fisticuffs; he had turned pale, as in a woman's hysterical fit, and gave his wife a dreadful fright.

' "How dare you come in here! Get out!" he cried, trembling and even finding it hard to get the words out. But suddenly he saw his pocket-book in my hands.

' "I think you dropped this," I said as calmly and coolly as I was able. (That, as a matter of fact, was the right way to go about it).

'He stood before me in total dismay, and for some time seemed unable to take anything in; then he quickly grabbed at his side pocket, opened his mouth wide in horror, and slapped his forehead.

' "Good Lord! Where did you find it? How?"

'I explained in the briefest of terms and even more coolly, if that were possible, how I had picked up the pocket-book, how I had run and called after him and how, at last, by guesswork and almost by feel, had followed him up the stairs.

' "Oh God!" he exclaimed, turning to his wife. "It contains all our documents, it contains my last deeds, it contains all . . . Oh, dear sir, do you know what you have done for me? I would have been lost!"

'Meanwhile I had reached for the door handle, in order to leave without replying; but I was out of breath myself, and suddenly my agitation burst out in such a violent fit of coughing that I could hardly maintain my balance. I saw the gentleman rush about in all directions in order to find me a vacant chair, grab the rags, at last, from one chair, throw them on the floor and hurriedly offer me the chair, carefully making me sit down. But my cough continued and did not subside for about another three minutes. When I recovered myself, he was sitting beside me on another chair, from which he had also probably thrown the rags to the floor, studying me intently.

' "I think you're . . . suffering from something?" he said in the tone of voice that doctors usually employ when approaching a patient. "I'm a medic," (he did not say "doctor"), for some reason indicating the room to me, as though protesting against his present situation. "I can see that you . . ."

' "I have consumption," I said as shortly as I could, and stood up.

'He at once also leaped to his feet.

' "It may be that you're exaggerating, and . . . if you took remedies . . ."

'He was very disconcerted and seemed unable to regain his composure; the pocket-book stuck out of his left hand.

' "Oh, don't trouble yourself," I broke in again, reaching for the door handle, "B-n examined me last week (I brought B-n into it again here), and in my case the diagnosis is certain. I'm sorry . . ."

'I was again about to open the door and leave my embarrassed and grateful doctor, who was crushed with shame, but just then the damned cough again seized hold of me. At this, my doctor insisted that I should sit down again and rest; he turned to his wife, and she, without leaving her place, quietly said some words of thanks and friendship to me. As she did so she became very embarrassed, and a blush even began to play on her dry, pale-yellow cheeks. I stayed, but with a look that indicated every second that I was dreadfully afraid of disturbing their privacy (which was the right note to strike). My doctor's remorse had begun to torment him now, I could see that.

' "If I . . ." he began, breaking off for a moment and changing the subject. "I'm so grateful to you and so guilty before you . . . I . . . you see . . ." he again indicated the room. "At the present moment I'm in such a situation . . ."

' "Oh," I said, "it's not hard to see; it happens every day; I expect you've lost your job and have come here to St Petersburg in order to explain yourself and seek another post?"

' "How did you . . . find out?" he asked with surprise.

' "It's obvious at first sight," I replied, mockingly in spite of myself. "Many people come here from the provinces with high hopes, run about, and live like this."

'He suddenly began to talk heatedly, his lips trembling; he began a plaintive discourse, and, I confess, it caught my interest; I sat with him for almost an hour. He told me his story, a very common one, as a matter of fact. He had been a doctor in a province, held a government post, but then all sorts of intrigues had begun, in which even his wife had become involved. He had stood on his pride, lost his temper; a change in the provincial government took place which worked to the advantage of his enemies; he was undermined, and complaints were made about him; he lost his post and used the last of his means on travelling to St Petersburg in order to explain himself; in St Petersburg it took him a long time to obtain a hearing, of course, and then when he obtained one he was met with a refusal, then lured with promises, then threatened with rigorous measures, then told to write an explanation, then had the explanation rejected, was then told to file a petition – in a word, he had been running about for five months now, had spent all his savings; he had pawned his wife's last rags, and now a child had been born and, and . . . "today I got the final rejection of the petition I filed, and I have almost no bread, there is nothing, my wife has given birth. I, I . . ."

'He jumped up from his chair and turned away. His wife was weeping in the corner, the baby was beginning to shriek again. I took out my notebook and began to write in it. When I had finished and got up, he was standing before me, staring with timid curiosity.

'"I've written your name down," I told him, "well, and all the rest: place of work, the name of your governor, the dates, the months. I have a friend, was at school with him, Bakhmutov, and his uncle is Pyotr Matveyevich Bakhmutov, State Councillor,[4] who works as director . . ."

'"Pyotr Matveyevich Bakhmutov!" my medic exclaimed, almost beginning to tremble. "But I mean, he's the one on whom almost everything depends!"

'Indeed, in the story of my medic and its dénouement, which I accidentally brought about, everything came together and was settled as though it had been arranged that way deliberately, just as in a novel. I told those poor folk that they should try not to place any hopes in me, that I myself was a poor high-school student (I deliberately exaggerated my lowliness; I had finished my studies long ago and was no longer a high-school student) and that there was no need for them to know my name, but that I would go right now to Vasily Island and see my friend Bakhmutov, and as I knew for a fact that his uncle, a State Councillor, a bachelor with no children, revered his nephew and was passionately fond of him, seeing in him the last scion of his family, "perhaps my friend will be able to do something for you and for me, of course, through his uncle . . ."

' "All I need is to be allowed to explain myself to his excellency! If only I might be granted the honour of explaining in my own words!" he exclaimed, trembling as in a fever, his eyes glittering. He actually said: "be granted the honour". Repeating once more that the project would probably fall through and would all be a nonsense, I added that if tomorrow morning I did not come and see them, that would mean that the project was at an end, and there was no point in them expecting anything. They saw me out with bows, they were almost beside themselves. Never will I forget the expressions on their faces. I took a cab and set off at once for Vasily Island.

'For several years at high school I was in perpetual conflict with this Bakhmutov. We considered him an aristocrat, or at any rate that was what I called him; he dressed well, arrived in his own carriage, did not boast at all, was always an excellent companion, was always exceptionally cheerful and even sometimes rather witty, though he was not very clever, in spite of always being top of the class; I was never top in anything. All his comrades liked him, except me. Several times during those several years he approached me; but each time I snubbed him morosely and irritably. I had not seen him now for about a year; he was at the university. When, some time before nine, I entered his rooms (to great ceremony: I was announced), he greeted me at first with astonishment, not at all kindly, even, but then at once became more cheerful and, looking at me, suddenly burst out laughing.

' "But wherever did you get the idea of coming to see me, Terentyev?" he exclaimed with his habitual charming familiarity, sometimes cheeky, but never offensive, which I so loved in him and for which I so hated him. "But what is this?" he cried in alarm. "You're so ill!"

'The cough had begun to torment me again, I fell on to a chair and could hardly catch my breath.

' "Don't let it trouble you, I've got T.B.," I said. "I've come to ask you for a favour."

'He sat down in astonishment, and I at once set forth to him

the doctor's entire story and explained that since he had a great
deal of influence on his uncle, he might be able to do something.

'"I'll do it, I'll do it without fail, and I'll tackle Uncle
tomorrow; I'll really be glad to, and you've told it all so well . . .
But all the same, Terentyev, wherever did you get the idea of
turning to me?"

'"So much depends upon your uncle, and since moreover
we've always been enemies, Bakhmutov, and as you're a decent
fellow, I thought that you wouldn't refuse an enemy," I added
with irony.

'"In the way that Napoleon turned to England!"[5] he
exclaimed, bursting into laughter. "I'll do it, I'll do it! Why, I'll
go right now, if I can!" he added quickly, seeing me get up from
my chair seriously and sternly.

'And indeed, in the most unexpected fashion, this matter was
arranged between us with the best possible result. A month and
a half later our medic got another post, in another province,
received a travelling allowance, and even a cash advance. I
suspect that Bakhmutov, who had developed a great habit of
visiting him (while I deliberately stopped doing so and received
the doctor almost coolly whenever he dropped in on me) –
Bakhmutov, I suspect, even persuaded the doctor to borrow
money from him. I saw Bakhmutov a couple of times during
those six weeks, we met for the third time when we were seeing
the doctor off. Bakhmutov held the farewell party at his house,
in the form of a dinner with champagne, which the doctor's
wife also attended; however, she very soon left to go back to
her baby. This was in early May, it was a clear evening, the
enormous disc of the sun was sinking into the Gulf. Bakhmutov
accompanied me home; we walked across Nikolayevsky Bridge;
we had both had quite a lot to drink. Bakhmutov talked about
his delight that the affair had ended so well, thanked me for
something, explained how good he felt now after doing a good
deed, assured me that all the credit belonged to me and that
those many people who nowadays taught and preached that the
individual good deed was of no significance were wrong. I was
also very anxious to talk for a while.

'"Whoever attacks individual 'charity'," I began, "attacks

the nature of man and despises his personal dignity. But the organization of 'public charity' and the question of personal freedom are two different questions and are not mutually exclusive. Individual kindness will always remain, because it is a need of the personality, a living need for the direct influence of one personality on another. In Moscow there used to live an old man, a 'general', that is, a State Councillor, with a German name; all his life he had traipsed around prisons and criminals; every party of convicts on its way to Siberia knew in advance that 'the old general'[6] would visit them at Sparrow Hills. He did his work with great seriousness and devotion; he arrived, walked along the ranks of the convicts, who surrounded him, stopped before each one, asked each about his needs, hardly ever gave anyone a lecture, called them all 'dear friends'. He gave money, sent necessary items – foot-bindings, foot-rags, linen, sometimes brought edifying books and distributed them to each man who could read, in the full conviction that they would be read en route and that those who could read would read them aloud to those who could not. About crime he rarely asked any questions, though he would listen if a criminal began to talk. All the criminals were on an equal footing as far as he was concerned, there were no distinctions. He talked to them like brothers, but towards the end they began to view him as a father. If he noticed a female convict with a baby in her arms, he would approach, fondle the baby and snap his fingers at it to make it laugh. These things he did for many years, right up to his death; eventually he was famous all over Russia and all over Siberia, among the criminals, that is. One man who had been in Siberia told me that he himself had witnessed how the most hardened criminals remembered the general, and yet the general, when he visited the gangs of convicts, was rarely able to give more than twenty copecks to each man. It's true that he wasn't remembered with much affection, or even very seriously. Some 'unfortunate wretch', who had killed twelve people, or put six children to the knife solely for his own amusement (there were such men, it is said), would suddenly, apropos of nothing, perhaps only once in twenty years, sigh and say: 'Well, and how's the old general now, is he still alive?' He would even, perhaps, smile as he said

it – and that would be all. How can you know what seed had
been cast into his soul for ever by this 'old general', whom
he had not forgotten in twenty years? How can you know,
Bakhmutov, what significance this communication between one
personality and another may have in the fate of the personality
that is communicated with? . . . I mean, we're talking about the
whole of a life, and a countless number of ramifications that are
hidden from us. The very finest player of chess, the most acute
of them, can only calculate a few moves ahead; one French
player, who was able to calculate ten moves ahead, was
described in the press as a miracle. But how many moves are
here, and how much is there that is unknown to us? In sowing
your seed, sowing your 'charity', your good deeds in whatever
form, you give away a part of your personality and absorb part
of another; a little more attention, and you are rewarded with
knowledge, with the most unexpected discoveries. You will,
at last, certainly view your deeds as a science; they will take
over the whole of your life and may fill it. On the other hand,
all your thoughts, all the seeds you have sown, which perhaps you have already forgotten, will take root and grow;
the one who has received from you will give to another. And
how can you know what part you will play in the future resolution of the fates of mankind? If this knowledge, and a whole
lifetime of this work, exalts you, at last, to the point where
you are able to sow a mighty seed, leave a mighty idea to the
world as an inheritance, then . . ." And so on, and so on. I talked
a lot that day.

'"And to think that one such as you is refused life!" Bakhmutov exclaimed to someone in heated reproach.

'At that moment we stood on the bridge, leaning on the
railings, and looking at the Neva.

'"Do you know what occurs to me?" I said, leaning over the
railings even more.

'"Surely not to throw yourself into the water?" exclaimed
Bakhmutov, almost in fear. Perhaps he had read my thought in
my face.

'"No, at present I have only one reflection, the following:
here I am now with two or three months left to live, perhaps

four; but, for example, when I have only two months left, and
if I should terribly want to do one good deed that would require
much work, much running about and fuss, like the business
with our doctor, then in that case I suppose I would have to
refuse it because of the lack of time remaining to me and try to
find some other 'good deed', a lesser one, which was within my
means (if I'm so intent on doing good deeds). You must admit
that it's an amusing thought!"

'Poor Bakhmutov was very worried about me; he accompanied me all the way to my building, and was so tactful that he
never once launched into commiserations, and said practically
nothing the whole way. On saying goodbye to me, he fervently
shook my hand and asked to be allowed to visit me. I replied to
him that if he came to see me as a "comforter" (because even if
he said nothing, he would still come as a comforter, I explained
that to him), then by that very fact he would remind me of death
even more each time he came. He shrugged his shoulders, which
I had not really expected.

'But on that evening and that night the first seed of my "final
conviction" was sown. I seized eagerly on this new thought,
eagerly analysed it in all its ramifications, in all its aspects (I
couldn't sleep all night), and the more I immersed myself in it,
the more I absorbed it, the more afraid I was. At last a terrible
fear descended on me, and stayed with me over the days that
followed. Sometimes, thinking about that constant fear of mine,
I would swiftly freeze in the face of a new terror: could I not
infer from this new fear that my "final conviction" had taken
root in me too profoundly, and that it could not but arrive at a
resolution? But I had not sufficient determination to resolve it.
Three weeks later it was all over, and the resolution manifested
itself, but as a result of a very strange circumstance.

'At this point in my explanation, I jot down all those numbers
and dates. To me, of course, it will all be the same, but *now*
(and, perhaps, only at this moment), I want those who will judge
my action to be able to see clearly the logical chain of deductions
from which my "final conviction" emerged. I wrote just now,
above, that the ultimate determination I lacked in order to fulfil
my "final conviction" came to me, it seems, not from any logical

deduction at all, but from some strange jolt, a certain strange
circumstance that was not, perhaps, connected with the previous
course of events in any way. About ten days ago Rogozhin
dropped in to see me about some business of his, the nature of
which it I don't need to go into here. I had never seen Rogozhin
before, but had heard a very great deal about him. I gave him
all the information he wanted, and he soon left, and since he
had only come for information, the matter between us would
have ended there. But he had begun to interest me too much,
and all that day I was under the influence of strange thoughts,
so much so that I determined to go and see him the next day
myself, to return the visit. Rogozhin was obviously displeased,
and even "delicately" hinted that there was no point in continuing our acquaintance; but all the same, I spent a very interesting
hour there, as, probably, did he. There was such a contrast
between us that it could not fail to affect us both, me especially:
I was a man already counting his days, while he was living the
fullest and most spontaneous of lives, in the present, without
any concern for "final" conclusions, numbers or anything else
that did not concern . . . that did not concern . . . that did not
concern what he was mad about; I hope that Mr Rogozhin will
forgive me that expression, if only because I am an inferior
littérateur who is unable to express his own ideas. In spite of all
his lack of courtesy, it seemed to me that he was a man of
intelligence and able to understand many things, though he took
little interest in anything that did not affect him directly. I made
no allusion to him about my "final conviction", but it somehow
seemed to me that, while listening to me, he guessed what it
was. He said nothing, he is a dreadfully taciturn fellow. I hinted
to him as I left that in spite of all the difference between us
and all our opposing qualities, *les extrémités se touchent*[7] (I
translated it into Russian for him), so perhaps he himself is not
as far from my "final conviction" as it seems. To this he replied
with a very morose and sour grimace, got up, found my cap for
me himself, making it look as if I were leaving of my own accord,
and quite simply showed me out of his gloomy house with the
pretence that he was seeing me off out of politeness. His house
shocked me; it's like a cemetery, but he likes it, I think, which

is, however, understandable: a full and spontaneous life such as the one he leads is too full in itself to require furnishings.

'This visit to Rogozhin tired me greatly. Moreover, I had not been feeling well since morning; towards evening I grew very weak and lay down on the bed, from time to time experiencing a high fever, and at some moments even delirium. Kolya stayed with me until eleven o'clock. However, I remember all that he talked about and all that we talked about. But when at certain moments my eyes closed, I kept seeing Ivan Fomich receiving millions in cash. He really did not know where to put it all, racked his brains over it, trembled with fear lest someone stole it, and, at last, decided to bury it. I finally advised him that instead of gratuitously burying such a heap of gold, he should have the whole pile melted down to make a gold coffin for the "frozen" child, and dig up the child for that purpose. Surikov seemed to receive my mocking gibe with tears of gratitude, and at once proceeded to put the plan into action. In the dream I spat, and left him. Kolya assured me, when I had quite recovered consciousness, that I had not been asleep at all, and that I had spent the whole time talking to him about Surikov. At some moments I was in a state of extreme anguish and perturbation, and when Kolya left, he was anxious. When I myself got up in order to lock the door behind him, I suddenly remembered the painting I had seen that day at Rogozhin's, in one of the most gloomy chambers of his house, above the door. He himself had shown it to me as we passed; I must have stood before it for about five minutes. It had no artistic merit; but it produced in me a strange sense of unease.

'Depicted in the painting is Christ, who has just been taken down from the cross. I think that painters have usually been in the habit of depicting Christ, both on the cross and when taken down from it, still with a nuance of extraordinary beauty in the face; this beauty they seek to preserve in him even during his most terrible torments. But in Rogozhin's painting there was no trace of beauty; this really was the corpse of a man who had endured endless torments even before the cross, wounds, tortures, beating from the guards, beating from the mob while he carried the cross and fell beneath it, and, at last, the agony of

the cross which lasted six hours (by my calculations, at least).
To be sure, it is the face of a man who has *just* been taken down
from the cross, that is, retaining very much that is still alive and
warm; nothing has yet had time to go stiff, so that on the face
of the dead man one can even see suffering, as though he were
experiencing it even now (this is very well captured by the artist);
but on the other hand, the face is not spared at all; here there is
only nature, and this is truly what the corpse of a man, whoever
he may be, must look like after such torments. I am aware that
the Christian Church established in the first centuries that Christ
did not suffer figuratively but actually, and that therefore his
body must have been wholly and completely subject to the laws
of nature on the cross. In the painting, the face has been horribly
lacerated by blows, swollen, with terrible, swollen and bloody
bruises, the eyes open, the pupils narrow; the large, open whites
of the eyes gleam with a deathly, glassy sheen. But strangely, as
one looks at this corpse of a tortured man, a peculiar and
interesting question arises: if this is really what the corpse looked
like (and it certainly must have looked just like this) when it was
seen by all his disciples, his chief future apostles, by the women
who followed him and stood by the cross, indeed by all who
believed in him and worshipped him, then how could they
believe, as they looked at such a corpse, that this martyr would
rise from the dead? Here one cannot help being struck by the
notion that if death is so terrible and the laws of nature so
powerful, then how can they be overcome? How can they be
overcome when they have not been conquered even by the one
who conquered nature in his own lifetime, to whom it submitted,
who cried: "*Talitha cumi*"[8] – and the damsel arose, "*Lazarus,
come forth*",[9] and the dead man came forth? Nature appears,
as one looks at that painting, in the guise of some enormous,
implacable and speechless animal or, more nearly, far more
nearly, though strangely – in the guise of some enormous
machine of the most modern devising, which has senselessly
seized, smashed to pieces and devoured, dully and without
feeling, a great and priceless being – a being which alone was
worth the whole of nature and all its laws, the whole earth,
which was, perhaps, created solely for the emergence of that

being! It is as though this painting were the means by which this idea of a dark, brazen and senseless eternal force, to which everything is subordinate, is expressed, and is involuntarily conveyed to us. Those people who surrounded the dead man, though not one of them is visible in the painting, must have felt a terrible anguish and perturbation that evening, which had smashed all their hopes and almost all their beliefs in one go. They must have parted in the most dreadful fear, though each of them also took away within him an enormous idea that could never now be driven out of them. And if this same teacher could, on the eve of his execution, have seen what he looked like, then how could he have ascended the cross and died as he did now? This question also involuntarily presents itself as one looks at the painting.

'All this appeared to me in fragments, perhaps in the midst of real delirium, sometimes even in images, for a whole hour and a half after Kolya's departure. Is it possible for an image to contain that which has no image? For at times I seemed to see, in some strange and impossible form, that infinite force, that blind, dark and speechless creature. I remember someone taking me by the arm, a candle in his hands, and showing me some sort of enormous and repulsive tarantula, assuring me that this was that same dark, blind and all-powerful creature, and laughing at my indignation. In my room, in front of the icon, a small lamp is always lit for the night – a dim and paltry light, and yet one can make out everything, and under the lamp it is even possible to read. I think that at first it was some time before one in the morning; I could not sleep at all and lay with my eyes open; suddenly the door of my room opened, and Rogozhin came in.

'He came in, shut the door, looked at me without saying anything and quietly went over to the chair in the corner that stands almost under the lamp. I was very surprised and watched in expectation; Rogozhin leaned his elbows on the small table and began to stare at me in silence. Some two or three minutes passed like this, and I remember that his silence offended me and annoyed me greatly. Why would he not speak? That he had come so late seemed strange to me, of course, but I remember that I was not really, in the end, all that surprised by it. Even the contrary: though I hadn't expressed my idea clearly to him that morning, I knew that he understood it; and of course, this idea was of such a kind that one might come to talk about it once again, even though it was very late. I had a fair idea that he would come in order to do this. We had parted that morning on rather hostile terms, and I even remember that a couple of times he looked at me rather mockingly. It was this same mockery that I read in his stare now, and it was this that offended me. But from the very first, of the fact that this really was Rogozhin, and not an apparition, not delirium, I had no doubt at all. It did not even enter my mind.

'Meanwhile he continued to sit and look at me with that same ironic smile. I angrily turned round in bed, also leaned my elbows on my pillow, and deliberately resolved not to say anything either, even if we spent the whole time sitting like that. For some reason I categorically wanted him to begin first. I think about twenty minutes passed like that. Suddenly the thought presented itself to me: what if this was not Rogozhin, but an apparition?

'Neither in my illness nor ever before have I ever seen a ghost; but it had always seemed to me, while yet a boy, and even now, that is, recently, that if I ever saw a ghost I would die on the spot, even in spite of the fact that I do not believe in ghosts. But when the thought came to me that this was not Rogozhin, but only a ghost, I remember I was not frightened at all. Not only that, it even made me angry. It was also strange that the resolution of the question "was it Rogozhin himself, or a ghost?" somehow did not interest me or trouble me, as I think it ought to have; I believe I was thinking about something else at the time. I was, for example, far more interested to know why Rogozhin, who in the morning had been wearing a domestic dressing gown and slippers, was now wearing a tailcoat, a white waistcoat and a white tie. I also had the fleeting thought that if this was a ghost and I was not afraid of it, then why should I not get up, go over to it and ascertain this for myself? Perhaps, however, I did not dare and was afraid. But no sooner had I thought that I was afraid, than ice seemed to pass through my whole body; I felt a chill in my spine, and my knees trembled. At that very instant, as though having guessed that I was afraid, Rogozhin unbent the arm he had been leaning on, straightened up and opened his mouth, as though preparing to laugh; he was looking at me intently. Rabid fury took possession of me to the point where I decidedly wanted to throw myself upon him, but as I had vowed that I would not be the first to speak, I remained on the bed, particularly as I was still not certain whether it was Rogozhin or not.

'I don't remember for certain how long this went on; neither can I remember whether I lost consciousness at times, or not. Only that, at last, Rogozhin got up, surveyed me just as slowly and attentively as before, when he had come in, but stopped smiling and quietly, almost on tiptoe, went over to the door, opened it, closed it behind him and went out. I did not get up from the bed; I don't remember how long I continued to lie there with my eyes open, thinking all the time; God knows what I was thinking about; I also don't remember losing consciousness. The next morning I woke up to a knocking at the door after nine. I have an arrangement that if I haven't opened the door by nine, or shouted for tea, Matryona must knock. When I opened the door to her, the thought at once presented itself to me: how could he have come in when the door was locked? I made inquiries and was convinced that it was impossible for the real Rogozhin to come in, because all our doors are locked at night.

'It was this peculiar incident, which I have described in such detail, that was the reason for my "deciding" so completely. Thus, my final decision was made possible not by logic, not by a logical conviction, but by revulsion. It's impossible to remain in a life that takes such strange forms, which offend me. That apparition had humiliated me. I am not able to submit to a dark force that takes the form of a tarantula. And only when, at twilight now, I at last experienced within myself the final moment of complete decision, did I feel better. It was only the first part of the moment; the second part of it was when I went to Pavlovsk, but that has already been explained enough.'

7

'I had a small pocket pistol, I obtained it when I was a boy, at that silly age when one suddenly becomes fond of stories about duels and the assaults of bandits, or about myself being challenged to a duel and standing nobly facing the pistol. A month before, I examined it and got it ready. In the drawer where it lay I found two bullets, and enough powder in the horn for three charges. It's a hopeless pistol, one can't aim straight with it and it only has a range of about fifteen paces; but of course, one can remove one's skull with it if one puts it to one's temple.

'I proposed to die in Pavlovsk, going into the park at sunrise in order not to upset anyone at the dacha. My "Explanation" would explain the whole affair sufficiently to the police. Those who are interested in psychology, and anyone else, may conclude from it whatever they please. However, I should not like this manuscript to be put in the public domain. I ask the prince to retain one copy for himself and to entrust another copy to Aglaya Ivanovna Yepanchina. Such is my wish. I bequeath my skeleton to the Medical Academy for the benefit of science.

'I recognize no judges over me and know that I am now beyond the power of any court. Not long ago I was amused by the proposition: what if I were to suddenly take it into my head to kill anyone I liked, perhaps ten people at once, or commit some atrocity, something considered the most atrocious thing in the world, then what a quandary the court would be faced with, given my two or three weeks left to live and the fact that ordeals and torture are no longer part of our legal system? I would die comfortably in their hospital, in warmth and with an attentive doctor, and, perhaps, far more comfortably than at home. I don't know why people in my position don't have the same idea, if only for a joke. But perhaps they do, however; even among us, there is no shortage of cheerful people.

'But even if I recognize no judges over me, I none the less know that I shall be judged when I am a deaf and voiceless defendant. I do not want to go without leaving a word in my defence – a word that is free, and not compelled – not in order to justify myself – oh no! I have no need to ask anyone's forgiveness for anything – but simply because I myself wish it.

'Here, to start with, is a strange thought: who, by what right, in the name of what motive, would take it into his head to question my right to these two or three weeks I have left? What business is it of any court? Just who requires me not only to be condemned to death, but also to wait on my best behaviour for my sentence to be carried out? Does anyone really want that? For the sake of morality? I also realize that if, in the flower of health and strength, I were to take my own life, which "might be of benefit to my neighbour", etcetera, morality might reproach me, according to the old rigmarole, for having disposed of my life without permission, or for something else which only it knows. But now, now when my sentence has been read out to me? What kind of morality is it that even demands, in addition to one's life, one's last gasp as one surrenders the last atom of life, listening to the comfortings of the prince, who in his Christian arguments will not fail to arrive at the happy thought that, really, it is even for the best that you should die? (Christians like him always arrive at that idea: it's their favourite hobby-horse.) And what is their aim with their ridiculous "Pavlovsk trees"? To sweeten the final hours of my life? Do they really not understand that the more I forget myself, the more I give myself up to this last phantom of life and love with which they want to shield me from my Meyer's wall and all that is so openly and simply written on it, the more unhappy they make me? What use to me are your nature, your Pavlovsk Park, your sunrises and sunsets, your blue sky and your all-satisfied faces, when the whole of this feast, which has no end, began by considering me alone superfluous? What is there for me in all this beauty, when at each minute, each second, I'm now compelled to be aware that even this tiny housefly buzzing around me in the sunbeam now, even it is a participant in all this feast and chorus, knows its place, loves it and is happy, while I alone am an outcast, and it's only because of my cowardice that I've been unwilling to realize that before now! Oh, after all, I know how the prince and all of them would like to bring me to the point where, instead of all these "perfidious and hate-filled" speeches, I would

sing, for the sake of good behaviour and triumphant morality
the renowned and classical stanza of Millevoix:[1]

> O, puissent voir votre beauté sacrée
> Tant d'amis sourds à mes adieux!
> Qu'ils meurent pleins de jours, que leur mort soit pleurée,
> Qu'un ami leur ferme les yeux!

'But believe me, believe me, innocent people, that even in this
well-behaved stanza, in this academic blessing to the world in
French verse there is so much hidden bile, so much irreconcilable
rhymed hatred, that even the poet himself has, perhaps, fallen
into the trap and mistaken that hatred for tears of emotion, and
so died, peace to his ashes! You should be aware that there is a
limit to the shame of the awareness of one's own insignificance
and weakness, beyond which a man cannot go, and at which
point he begins to take an enormous pleasure in his very shame
... Well, of course, humility is a mighty force in that sense, I
admit that – though not in the sense in which religion takes
humility as a force.

'Religion! I admit the existence of eternal life, and have perhaps always admitted its existence. Let us allow that the spark
of consciousness was lit by the will of a higher power, let us
allow that it looked round at the world and said: "I am!", and
let us allow that it was suddenly instructed by that higher power
to destroy itself, because for some reason – and the reason was
not even explained – that was just how it was up there, let us
allow that, I admit all that, but there still remains the eternal
question: why is my meekness demanded in all this? Could I not
simply be devoured without being required to praise what has
devoured me? Will someone up there really be offended that I'm
unwilling to wait for two weeks? I don't believe that; and it's
far more probable to suppose that my insignificant life, the life
of an atom, was required in order to complete some universal
harmony of the whole, some plus and minus, some sort of
contrast, etcetera, etcetera, in just the same way as every day
the sacrifice of the lives of large numbers of creatures is required,
without whose death the rest of the world would not be able to

carry on (though one must observe that this in itself is not a very generous notion). But let us allow that it is so! I agree that otherwise without, that is, our constant devouring of one another, it would be quite impossible to organize the world; I'm even ready to admit that I understand nothing of that organization; but on the other hand, I do know this for certain: if I've been allowed to perceive that "I am", what does it matter to me that mistakes have been made in the organization of the world, and that without those mistakes it could not carry on? If that is so, who is going to judge me, and for what? Whatever you say, all of this is impossible and unjust.

'And yet never, in spite of all my wish to do so, was I able to imagine that there was no life to come, or no Providence. The most likely thing is that all of that exists, but that we don't understand anything of the life to come or its laws. But if that is so difficult, and even quite impossible to understand, then must I really answer for the fact that I'm unable to make sense of the unfathomable? To be sure, they say – and the prince, of course, concurs with them – that here obedience is necessary, that one must obey without arguing, out of sheer decorum, and that I will certainly be rewarded for my meekness in the world to come. We greatly belittle Providence by ascribing our own conceptions to it, out of annoyance that we cannot understand it. But again, if it's impossible to understand it, then, I repeat, it's also difficult to answer for what man has not been given to understand. And if that is so, then how can I be judged for not having been able to understand the true will and laws of Providence? No, let us leave religion alone.

'And in any case, enough. When I reach these lines, the sun will probably rise and "begin to resound in the sky", and its enormous, immeasurable power will pour down on all that is beneath it. Let it be so! I shall die looking straight at the source of strength and life, and I shall not want this life! If I'd had the power not to be born, I would probably not have accepted existence on such ridiculous terms. But I still have the power to die, though what I'm giving back are days that are already numbered. Not much power in that, and not much of a mutiny, either.

'A final explanation; I'm by no means dying because I haven't the strength to endure these three weeks; oh, I'd have strength enough, and if I'd wanted it, I'd have been sufficiently consoled by the mere awareness of the injury that's being done to me; but I'm not a French poet, and don't want such consolations. Finally, there is also a temptation: nature has so circumscribed my activity so much by its three-week sentence that suicide may possibly be the only action I can still begin and end of my own free will. What of it, perhaps I want to take advantage of my last chance to *act*? A protest is sometimes no small thing . . .'

The 'Explanation' was at an end; at last, Ippolit stopped talking . . .

There is, in extreme cases, that stage of final, cynical frankness, when a highly strung person, goaded and driven beyond himself, no longer fears anything and is ready for any scandal, is even glad of it; lashes out at people, all the while with the vague but firm intention of jumping off a belfry a moment later and thereby resolving at a stroke all misunderstandings, should there be any. Another sign of this condition is usually the approaching exhaustion of physical strength. The extreme, almost unnatural tension that had been keeping Ippolit afloat until now had reached its last degree. Viewed in isolation, this eighteen-year-old boy, exhausted by illness, appeared weak, like a trembling leaf torn from a tree; but as soon as he looked round at his listeners – for the first time in the whole of the last hour – the most haughty, the most contemptuous and offensive disgust was at once expressed in his gaze and smile. His challenge was a swift one. But his listeners were also most indignant. They were all getting up from the table with bustle and annoyance. Tiredness, wine and tension were increasing the disorder and, as it were, the sordidness of the general impression, if one may put it that way.

Suddenly Ippolit leaped from his chair, as though he had been yanked upright.

'The sun has risen!' he exclaimed, catching sight of the gleaming tops of the trees, and pointing them out to the prince as though they were a miracle. 'It's risen!'

'Did you think it wouldn't, then?' observed Ferdyshchenko.

'Another whole day of this damned heat,' Ganya muttered with careless annoyance, holding his hat, stretching and yawning. 'This drought will probably go on for a month, and then where shall we be . . . Shall we go, Ptitsyn?'

Ippolit listened with an astonishment that intensified to the point of stupefaction; suddenly he grew terribly pale and began to shake all over.

'You are very clumsily feigning your indifference in order to insult me,' he said, turning to Ganya, staring at him intently. 'You're a scoundrel!'

'Well, have you ever damn well seen the like, letting himself go like that!' Ferdyshchenko bawled. 'What phenomenal weakness!'

'He's simply a fool,' said Ganya.

Ippolit mustered his strength a little.

'I realize, gentlemen,' he began, trembling as before, and halting at every word, 'that I may have deserved your personal retaliation, and . . . regret that I have bored you with my raving (he pointed to the manuscript), though as a matter of fact, I regret not having bored you completely . . .' (he smiled stupidly) 'have I bored you, Yevgeny Pavlych?' he suddenly shot the question at him. 'Have I bored you or not? Speak!'

'It was a bit long-winded, though as a matter of fact . . .'

'Tell me everything! Don't lie, at least once in your life!' Ippolit commanded him, trembling.

'Oh, it's really all the same to me! Do me a favour, I beg you, and leave me alone,' Yevgeny Pavlovich turned away with distaste.

'Good night, Prince,' Ptitsyn approached the prince.

'But he's going to shoot himself in a moment, what are you thinking of? Look at him!' Vera exclaimed, rushing over to Ippolit in extreme alarm and even seizing him by the arms. 'I mean, he said he would shoot himself when the sun rose, what are you thinking of?'

'He won't shoot himself!' several voices, including Ganya's, muttered gloatingly.

'Gentlemen, watch out!' cried Kolya, also seizing Ippolit by the arm. 'Just look at him! Prince! Prince, what are you thinking of?'

Vera, Kolya, Keller and Burdovsky crowded round Ippolit; all four caught hold of his arms.

'He has the right, the right!' muttered Burdovsky, though he also looked quite lost.

'With your permission, Prince, but what are your instructions?' Lebedev approached the prince, drunk and resentful to the point of insolence.

'What instructions?'

'No, sir; with your permission, sir, I am the master of the house, sir, though I don't wish to appear lacking in respect for you . . . Let's say that you're the master of the house, too, but I don't want this in my own home . . . That's what it is, sir . . .'

'He won't shoot himself; the urchin's playing the fool,' General Ivolgin shouted unexpectedly, with indignation and aplomb.

'Hurrah for the general!' Ferdyshchenko chimed in.

'I know he won't shoot himself, General, most esteemed General, but all the same . . . for I am the master of the house, after all.'

'Listen, Mr Terentyev,' said Ptitsyn suddenly, having said goodbye to the prince, and extending his hand to Ippolit. 'I believe you said something in your notebook about your skeleton and that you're bequeathing it to the Academy? You were talking about your own skeleton, yours and no one else's, in other words, you are bequeathing your own bones?'

'Yes, my bones . . .'

'It's best to be sure. Otherwise, it's possible for mistakes to happen: they say there was such an incident once.'

'Why are you teasing him?' the prince exclaimed suddenly.

'You've reduced him to tears,' added Ferdyshchenko.

But Ippolit was not crying at all. He began to get up from his chair, but the four people who surrounded him suddenly grabbed him, all together, by the arms. Laughter rang out.

'That's what he was leading up to, to make us grab him by the arms; that's why he read his notebook, too,' observed

Rogozhin. 'Goodbye, Prince. Ach, we've been sitting long enough; my bones are aching.'

'If you really intended to shoot yourself, Terentyev,' Yevgeny Pavlovich began to laugh, 'then if I were in your place, after compliments like those I would purposely refrain from shooting myself, just in order to tease them.'

'They can't wait to see me shoot myself!' Ippolit hurled at him.

He spoke as though he were attacking someone.

'They're annoyed that they're not going to see it.'

'So you think they're not going to see it?'

'I'm not trying to egg you on; on the contrary, I think it very possible that you'll shoot yourself. The main thing is not to lose your temper . . .' Yevgeny Pavlovich drawled in a patronizing manner.

'Only now do I see that I made a terrible mistake in reading them that notebook!' Ippolit said quietly, looking at Yevgeny Pavlovich with such a trusting gaze that it was as though he were asking a friend for friendly advice.

'It's a ridiculous situation, but . . . truly, I don't know what to advise you,' Yevgeny Pavlovich replied, smiling.

Ippolit stared at him sternly, not taking his eyes away, and said nothing. It was possible to guess that from time to time he was entirely oblivious of his surroundings.

'No, sir, with your permission, sir, what a manner of speech that is, I mean to say, sir,' said Lebedev. ' "I'll shoot myself in the park," he says, "so as not to upset anyone"! He thinks he won't upset anyone if he goes down and takes a couple of paces into the garden.'

'Gentlemen . . .' the prince began.

'No, sir, with your permission, highly esteemed Prince, sir,' Lebedev interjected, 'as your highness can see that this is not a joke, and as at least half of your guests are of the same opinion and are certain that now, after the words he has uttered here, he is certainly bound to shoot himself from considerations of personal honour, then I am the master of the house, sir, and declare before witnesses that I expect you to be of assistance!'

'But what do we have to do, Lebedev? I am ready to assist you.'

'It's like this, sir: he must give up his pistol at once, the one he was boasting about to us, along with all its accessories. If he does so, then I agree to allow him to spend the night in this house, in view of his invalid state, under my supervision, of course. But tomorrow he must definitely go on his way; forgive me, Prince! If he doesn't give up the gun, I shall immediately, at once, take him by the arms, I shall take one arm, the general will take the other, and I shall have the police informed forthwith, and then the matter will pass to the inspection of the police, sir. Mr Ferdyshchenko, as he is a friend, will go down to the station, sir.'

A hubbub ensued; Lebedev was already becoming excited beyond all limits; Ferdyshchenko was preparing to go for the police; Ganya kept vehemently insisting that no one was going to shoot himself, Yevgeny Pavlovich was silent.

'Prince, have you ever hopped off a belfry?' Ippolit whispered to him suddenly.

'N-no . . .' the prince replied innocently.

'Did you really think that I didn't foresee all this hatred?' Ippolit whispered again, his eyes beginning to flash, looking at the prince as though he really was expecting a reply from him. 'Enough!' he suddenly shouted at the whole audience. 'I'm to blame . . . more than anyone else! Lebedev, here is the key (he took out a purse and from it a steel ring with three or four small keys), here, this one, the last but one . . . Kolya will show you . . . Kolya! Where's Kolya?' he exclaimed, looking at Kolya without seeing him. 'Yes . . . he'll show you; he packed the bag with me earlier. Take him through, Kolya; in the prince's study, under the table . . . my bag . . . with this key, underneath, in a little box . . . my pistol and the powder-horn. He packed them himself, Mr Lebedev, he'll show you; but provided that first thing, early tomorrow morning, when I return to St Petersburg, you give me back the pistol. Do you hear? I'm doing this for the prince; not for you.'

'That's better!' Lebedev grabbed the key and, smiling poisonously, ran into the adjacent room.

Kolya stopped, and was about to make some remark, but Lebedev hauled him off after him.

Ippolit looked at the laughing guests. The prince noticed that his teeth were chattering, as in the most violent fever.

'What scoundrels they all are!' Ippolit whispered again to the prince in frenzy. Whenever he spoke to the prince, he leaned forward and whispered.

'Let them be; you're very weak . . .'

'In a moment, in a moment . . . I'll go in a moment.'

Suddenly he embraced the prince.

'Perhaps you think I'm insane?' He looked at him, beginning to laugh strangely.

'No, but you . . .'

'In a moment, in a moment, be quiet; don't say anything; wait . . . I want to look into your eyes . . . Stand like that, I'm going to look. I'm going to say farewell to Man.'

He stood and looked motionlessly and silently at the prince, for about ten seconds, very pale, his temples wet with sweat, and clutching rather strangely at the prince with one hand, as though afraid to let him go.

'Ippolit, Ippolit, what's the matter with you?' exclaimed the prince.

'In a moment . . . enough . . . I'm going to lie down. I'll drink one mouthful to the health of the sun . . . I want to, I want to, leave me alone!'

He quickly seized a glass from the table, darted away, and in a single instant approached the descent from the veranda. The prince was about to run after him, but it so happened that, as if on purpose, at that same instant Yevgeny Pavlovich stretched out his hand to him in farewell. One second passed, and suddenly a universal cry resounded on the veranda. This was followed by a moment of extreme confusion.

This is what had happened:

Right at the top of the steps that led down from the veranda, Ippolit stopped, holding the glass in his left hand and putting his right hand into the right-hand pocket of his coat. Keller avowed later that Ippolit had been keeping that hand in his right pocket earlier, while he was talking to the prince, and had seized him by the shoulder and collar with his left hand, and Keller maintained that it was this right hand in the pocket that had caused the first stirrings of suspicion in him. Whatever the truth of the matter, a certain uneasiness had made him run after Ippolit. But he had not had time to catch him up. All he saw was something gleam suddenly in Ippolit's right hand, and at that same second a small pocket pistol appeared right next to his temple. Keller rushed to seize him by the hand, but at that same second Ippolit had pulled the trigger. The sharp, dry click of the trigger was heard, but no shot followed. When Keller put his arms round him, he fell into them as though unconscious, perhaps imagining that he was already dead. The pistol was now in Keller's hands. Ippolit was lifted up, a chair was placed under him, he was made to sit in it, and everyone crowded round, everyone shouted, everyone asked questions. They had all heard the click of the trigger and seen the man alive, not even scratched. Ippolit sat, not understanding what was happening, and looking round at all with a senseless gaze. At that moment, Lebedev and Kolya came running in.

'Didn't it go off?' some people asked.

'Perhaps it wasn't even loaded?' others guessed.

'It was loaded!' proclaimed Keller, examining the pistol, 'but . . .'

'Did it really not go off?'

'There was no firing cap at all,' announced Keller.

It is hard to describe the pitiful scene that followed. The initial and universal alarm began to be replaced by laughter; some people even began to laugh loudly, taking a malicious pleasure in this. Ippolit sobbed as in a hysterical fit, wrung his hands, went rushing up to them all, even to Ferdyshchenko, seized him with both arms and swore to him that he had forgotten – 'I forgot by complete accident, not on purpose' – to insert the firing cap, that 'the caps are all here, in my waistcoat pocket, about ten of them' (he showed them to everyone), that he had not inserted one earlier, fearing the gun might go off in his pocket by accident, that he had always reckoned on having time to insert in when he needed to, and had suddenly forgotten. He rushed over to the prince, to Yevgeny Pavlovich, implored Keller to give him back the pistol, said that he would now show them all that 'my honour, my honour . . .' that now he was 'dishonoured for ever'.

He collapsed at last, truly unconscious. He was carried into the prince's study, and Lebedev, who had quite sobered up now, immediately sent for a doctor, while he himself, together with his daughter, son, Burdovsky and the general, remained by the sick man's bed. When the unconscious Ippolit had been carried out, Keller stood in the middle of the room and proclaimed for all to hear, rapping out each word separately, in a state of total inspiration:

'Gentlemen, if any of you ever again, out loud, in my presence, expresses any doubt that the cap was forgotten on purpose, and tries to assert that the unhappy young man was merely indulging in playacting – then you'll have me to deal with.'

But he received no reply. The guests, at last, dispersed in a throng and hurriedly. Ptitsyn, Ganya and Rogozhin set off together.

The prince was very surprised that Yevgeny Pavlovich seemed to have changed his plans and was leaving without having a proper talk.

'I mean, you wanted to talk to me, when they'd all gone home, didn't you?' he asked him.

'That's correct,' said Yevgeny Pavlovich, suddenly sitting down in a chair and seating the prince beside him, 'but now I have temporarily changed my plans. I'll confess to you that I am somewhat upset, as you are, too. My thoughts have been thrown off balance; moreover, what I want to talk to you about is very important to me, and for you also. You see, Prince, just once in my life I want to do something completely honourable, that is, completely without any ulterior motive, well, but I think that now, at this moment, I'm not capable of doing anything completely honourable, and neither, perhaps, are you . . . so . . . and . . . well, and we can talk later. Perhaps the matter will even gain in clarity both for you and for me, if we wait for two or three days, which I shall spend in St Petersburg.'

Here he again got up from his chair, which made it appear

strange that he had sat down at all in the first place. To the prince it also seemed that Yevgeny Pavlovich was unhappy and irritated, and there was a hostility in his gaze that had certainly not been there before.

'Incidentally, are you going to see the patient now?'

'Yes . . . and I'm afraid,' the prince said quietly.

'Don't be afraid; he'll probably live for at least another six weeks, and may even recover his health here. But the best thing would be if tomorrow you told him to go.'

'Perhaps I really did force his hand by . . . not saying anything; he may have thought I also doubted that he'd shoot himself. What do you think, Yevgeny Pavlych?'

'Nothing of the kind. You're too soft-hearted, don't trouble yourself about it. I've heard, but have never actually seen it in real life, of a man deliberately shooting himself in order to be praised for it, or out of spite for not being praised for it. Above all, I would never have believed there could be such an open admission of feebleness!'

'Do you think he'll try to shoot himself again?'

'No, not after this he won't. But beware of these home-grown Lacenaires[2] of ours! I repeat, crime is too common a refuge for such untalented, impatient and greedy nonentities.'

'He's not really a Lacenaire, is he?'

'The essence is the same, though their *emplois* may be different. You'll see if this gentleman is not capable of knocking off ten people just for a "joke", exactly as he read aloud to us just now in his "Explanation". Now those words of his won't let me get any sleep.'

'Perhaps you're worrying too much.'

'You are extraordinary, Prince; don't you believe he's capable of killing ten people *now*?'

'I'm afraid to answer you; it's all very strange; but . . .'

'Well, as you please, as you please!' Yevgeny Pavlovich concluded irritably. 'What's more, you're a very brave man; just don't end up one of the ten yourself.'

'The most likely thing is that he won't kill anyone,' said the prince, looking at Yevgeny Pavlovich reflectively.

The latter burst into malicious laughter.

'*Au revoir*, it's time I was off! But did you notice that he wanted to leave a copy of his confession to Aglaya Ivanovna?'

'Yes, I did and . . . I'm thinking about it.'

'I'm sure you are, if those ten people are on your mind,' Yevgeny Pavlovich laughed again, and went out.

An hour later, some time between three and four, the prince went down into the park. He had tried to fall asleep in the house, but could not, because of the violent beating of his heart. In the house, however, everything had been dealt with and made as quiet as it could be in the circumstances; the patient had fallen asleep, and the doctor who arrived declared that there was no particular danger. Lebedev, Kolya and Burdovsky had stretched out in the patient's room, so they could take it in turns to keep watch; thus, there was no reason for apprehension.

But the prince's anxiety kept growing from one minute to the next. He roamed about the park, absent-mindedly looking around him, and stopped in surprise when he reached the platform in front of the pleasure gardens and saw the row of empty benches and the music stands for the band. He was shocked by this place, and for some reason it seemed horribly ugly. He turned back and straight along the road he had walked the previous day with the Yepanchins into the pleasure gardens, reached the green bench that had been assigned to him for the rendezvous, sat down on it and suddenly burst out laughing loudly, which at once caused him extreme indignation. His depression continued; he felt like going away somewhere . . . He knew not where. Above him in a tree a bird was singing, and he began to look for it between the leaves; suddenly the bird fluttered up from the tree, and at that same moment he for some reason recalled the 'housefly' in the 'sun's hot beam', about which Ippolit had written that 'even it knew its place and was a participant in the general chorus, while he alone was just an outcast'. This sentence had struck him earlier, and he remembered it now. A long-forgotten memory began to stir in him and all of a sudden acquired clarity.

It had happened in Switzerland, in the first year of his treatment, in the first few months, in fact. At the time, he had still been a complete idiot, not even able to talk properly, sometimes unable to understand what was being asked of him. One bright, sunny day he went into the mountains, and for a long time walked with a certain tormenting thought in his mind, but one that simply would not take shape. Before him was the brilliant sky, below him the lake, all round a radiant and unending horizon, which had no termination and no limit. For a long time he gazed, and was racked by torment. Now he remembered how he had stretched out his arms into that radiant, unending blue and had wept. What tortured him was that he was completely alien to all this. What feast was this, what permanent, great holiday, which had no end and to which he had been drawn long ago, always, ever since childhood, and which there was no way he could join. Each morning the same radiant sun ascended; each morning there was a rainbow on the waterfall; each evening the snowy, highest mountain, there, in the distance, on the edge of the sky, burned with a purple flame; each 'little housefly that buzzed about him in the sun's hot ray was a participant in all this chorus: it knew its place, liked it and was happy'; each blade of grass was growing and was happy! And everything had its path, and everything knew its path, left with a song and arrived with a song; he alone knew nothing, understood nothing, neither people, nor sounds, was alien to everything and an outcast. Oh, of course, he had not been able to say it in so many words at the time, or express his question; he suffered his torment like a deaf mute; but now it seemed to him that he *had* said all this at the time, all these same words, and that Ippolit had taken what he had said about the 'housefly' from him, from his words and tears at the time. He was sure of this, and for some reason this thought made his heart beat faster . . .

On the bench he fell into oblivion, but his anxiety continued even in his sleep. Just before drowsing off, he remembered that Ippolit was going to kill ten people, and smiled wryly at the absurdity of supposing such a thing. All around him was a beautiful, clear quietness, with only the rustle of the leaves, which seemed to make it all even quieter and more secluded. He had a great many dreams, all anxious ones, which made him start awake every minute. At last a woman came to him; he knew her, knew her to the point of torment; he was always able to name her and point her out – but it was strange – she now seemed to have a face that was not at all the one he had always known, and he was agonizingly reluctant to accept her as that woman. In that face there was so much remorse and horror that it seemed she was a terrible criminal who had just committed a dreadful crime. A tear trembled on her pale cheek; she beckoned to him with her hand and put a finger to her lips, as though warning him to be quiet when he followed her. His heart froze; not for anything, not for anything was he willing to see her as a criminal; but he felt that something dreadful was about to happen, that would have a bearing on his entire life. She seemed to want to show him something, quite close to here, in the park. He got up in order to follow her, and suddenly someone's radiant, fresh laughter rang out beside him; someone's hand was suddenly in his; he seized that hand, pressed it hard and woke up. Before him stood Aglaya, laughing loudly.

8

She was laughing, but she was also indignant.

'He's asleep! You were asleep,' she exclaimed in scornful surprise.

'It's you!' the prince muttered, not yet quite awake, recognizing her with astonishment. 'Ah, yes! That rendezvous . . . I've been asleep here.'

'I saw.'

'Are you the only person who woke me? Has no one been here, except you? I thought there was . . . another woman here . . .'

'There was another woman here?!'

At last he completely woke up.

'It was just a dream,' he said reflectively. 'Strange, to have such a dream at such a moment . . . Sit down.'

He took her by the hand and seated her on the bench; he sat down beside her and fell into reflection. Aglaya did not begin a conversation, but merely surveyed her interlocutor with a fixed look. He also gazed at her, but only from time to time, as though he did not see her before him at all. She began to blush.

'Ah, yes!' the prince started. 'Ippolit shot himself!'

'When? At your house?' she asked, though without much surprise. 'But he was alive last night, I believe? How on earth could you sleep here after all that?' she exclaimed, growing suddenly animated.

'But you see, he isn't dead, the pistol misfired.'

At Aglaya's insistence, the prince had to tell immediately, and in great detail, the entire story of the preceding night. She constantly hurried him in his narrative, but interrupted him with ceaseless questions, which were nearly all irrelevant. Among other things, she listened with great interest to what Yevgeny Pavlovich had said, and several times even asked him to repeat it.

'Well, that's enough, we must hurry,' she concluded when she had heard it all. 'We can only stay here for another hour, until eight o'clock, for at eight I must be home without fail, so that they don't find out I've been here, but I'm here on a matter of business; there is much that I need to tell you. Only you've quite disconcerted me now. As for Ippolit, I think that his pistol was bound to misfire, that would be most like him. But are you sure that he really wanted to shoot himself and that there was no deception there?'

'No deception at all.'

'That's more likely. He wrote that you would bring me his confession, didn't he? Why haven't you brought it?'

'But I mean, he isn't dead. I'll ask him for it.'

'You must bring it without fail, and there's no need to ask him. He'll certainly be very pleased, because he probably tried to shoot himself so I would read his confession afterwards. Please, I ask you not to laugh at my words, Lev Nikolaich, because it could very well be so.'

'I'm not laughing – I too am certain that it could very well be so.'

'You're certain? Do you really also think that?' Aglaya said suddenly in great astonishment.

She asked her questions quickly, spoke rapidly, but sometimes seemed to lose the thread and often did not finish what she was saying; she was in a constant hurry to warn him about something; in general, she was in a state of extraordinary anxiety, and although she was putting a very brave face on it, even with a kind of challenge, she was also perhaps a little frightened. She was wearing the most ordinary, simple dress, which suited her very well. She frequently started and flushed, and sat on the edge of the bench. The prince's agreement with her assertion that Ippolit had shot himself so that she would read his confession had surprised her very much.

'Of course,' explained the prince, 'he wanted us all, not only you, to praise him . . .'

'How do you mean, praise him?'

'Well, it's . . . How can I say it? It's very hard to say. It's just that he probably wanted us all to surround him and tell him that we love and respect him very much, and wanted us all to implore him to remain alive. It's very possible that he had you in mind more than anyone else, because he mentioned you at a moment like that . . . though perhaps he didn't even know himself that he had you in mind.'

'That I really do not understand at all: he had me in mind, and didn't know that he had me in mind. Though as a matter of fact, I think I do understand: you know, when I was a girl of thirteen I thought of poisoning myself about thirty times, and then writing all about it in a letter to my parents, and also imagined how I would lie in my coffin, with everyone weeping over me and blaming themselves for having been so cruel to me . . . Why are you smiling again?' she added quickly, frowning. 'What do you think about to yourself when you daydream? Perhaps you imagine you're a field-marshal, and have beaten Napoleon?'

'Well, yes, to be quite honest, I do think about that, especially when I'm falling asleep,' the prince began to laugh. 'Only it's not Napoleon, but always the Austrians I'm beating.'

'I really don't feel like joking with you, Lev Nikolaich. I will see Ippolit; please let him know. But as for you, I think you behave very badly, because it's very ill-mannered to examine and judge a man's soul in the way that you judge Ippolit. You have no tenderness: only truth, and so you're not fair.'

The prince reflected.

'I think it's you who are being unfair to me,' he said. 'I mean, I don't see anything bad in him having thought like that, because everyone's inclined to think like that; what's more, it may be that he didn't think at all, just wanted it . . . he wanted to meet people for the last time, to earn their respect and love; after all, those are very fine feelings, it's just that it in this case it didn't work out somehow; there was the fact of his illness, and something else as well! And besides, with some people everything works out fine, while with others it all goes as wrong as it possibly can . . .'

'I suppose you added that last bit about yourself?' Aglaya remarked.

'Yes, that's right,' replied the prince, not noticing any *schadenfreude* in the question.

'But all the same, if I were I in your place I should never have fallen asleep; it's as though wherever you poke your nose in, you fall asleep; that's very ill-bred of you.'

'But you see, I hadn't slept all night, and then I walked and walked, went to where the music was . . .'

'What music?'

'Where the band played yesterday, and then I came here, sat down, thought and thought, and fell asleep.'

'Oh, so that's how it was, was it? That alters things in your favour . . . And why did you go to the music?'

'I don't know, I just did . . .'

'All right, all right, later; you keep interrupting me, and what does it matter to me if you went to the music? Who is this woman you were dreaming about?'

'I was dreaming . . . about . . . you've seen her . . .'

'I understand, I understand perfectly. She's someone you're very much in . . . What was she like in your dream, what did she look like? Though actually, I don't want to know,' she snapped suddenly, with annoyance. 'Don't keep interrupting me . . .'

She waited a little, as though plucking up her courage or trying to drive away her annoyance.

'This is the reason I asked you to come here: I want to propose that you become my friend. Why did you stare at me like that suddenly?' she added almost with anger.

The prince really was studying her very closely at that moment, having noticed that she had again begun to blush dreadfully. In such instances, the more she blushed, the more angry she seemed to become with herself, which was plainly expressed in her flashing eyes; usually a moment later she would transfer her anger to the person she was talking to, no matter whether he was to blame or not, and begin to quarrel with him. Aware of her awkwardness and bashfulness, and feeling it, she usually kept her conversation to a minimum and was more taciturn than the other sisters, sometimes even too much so. And when, especially in a ticklish case like this, she really had to speak, she would begin the conversation with extreme hauteur, and as if with a kind of challenge. She could always sense in advance when she was starting to blush, or was on the point of starting to do so.

'Perhaps you don't want to accept my proposal?' she cast a haughty look at the prince.

'Oh yes, I do, only it's quite unnecessary . . . that is, I never thought it was necessary to make such a proposal,' the prince said in embarrassment.

'But what did you think, then? Why would I have asked you to come here? What is on your mind? Actually, I think you probably consider me a silly little fool, as they all do at home?'

'I didn't know that they consider you a silly little fool, I . . . I don't.'

'You don't? That's very clever on your part. Very cleverly expressed.'

'In my opinion you are even, perhaps, very clever sometimes,' continued the prince, 'you suddenly said something very clever earlier on. You said of my doubts about Ippolit: "You have only truth, and so you're unfair." I shall remember that and think about it.'

Aglaya suddenly flushed with pleasure. All these changes took place in her with extreme frankness and extraordinary rapidity. The prince was also delighted, and even burst out laughing with joy as he looked at her.

'Then listen,' she began again. 'I've waited a long time to tell you all this, waited ever since you wrote me that letter, and even earlier . . . Half of it you already heard from me yesterday: I consider you a most honest and truthful man, more honest and truthful than anyone else, and if they say of you that your mind . . . that is, that you're sometimes ill in your mind, then that is unfair; I've decided that, and have had arguments about it, because although you are indeed ill in your mind (please don't be angry, I'm speaking from a higher point of view), the part of your mind that's important is better than any of theirs, and it's of a sort they've never even dreamed of, because there are two parts of the mind: one that's important and one that's not important. Isn't that true? It is, isn't it?'

'Perhaps it is,' the prince barely got out; his heart was trembling and thumping dreadfully.

'I knew you would understand,' she continued solemnly. 'Prince Shch. and Yevgeny Pavlych don't understand anything about those two parts of the mind, and Alexandra doesn't either, but imagine: *Maman* understood.'

'You're very like Lizaveta Prokofyevna.'

'What? Really?' Aglaya was astonished.

'As God is my witness, you are.'

'I thank you,' she said, after some thought. 'I'm very glad I'm like *Maman*. You must respect her very much, then?' she added, quite unaware of the naivety of the question.

'Very much, very much, and I'm glad you realized it straight away.'

'And I'm glad, too, because I have noticed that people sometimes . . . laugh at her. But listen, this is the main thing: I've thought about it for a long time and have finally chosen you. I don't want them to laugh at me at home; I don't want them to consider me a silly little fool; I don't want them to tease me. I understood all that at once, and rejected Yevgeny Pavlych point-blank, because I don't want them to keep trying to marry me off! I want . . . I want . . . well, I want to run away from home, and I've chosen you to help me.'

'Run away from home?' exclaimed the prince.

'Yes, yes, yes, run away from home!' she exclaimed suddenly, burning with extraordinary anger. 'I don't want, I don't want to be made to blush there eternally. I don't want to blush, either in front of them, or Prince Shch., or Yevgeny Pavlych, or anyone, and I've chosen you. To you I want to say everything, everything, even about the most important things, when I want to; for my part, and you must hide nothing from me. I want to talk about everything with at least one human being as I talk to myself. They suddenly began saying that I was waiting for you and that I loved you. That was even before your arrival, and I didn't show them the letter; but now everyone's saying it. I want to be bold and not be afraid of anything. I don't want to go traipsing around their ballrooms, I want to be of some use. I've wanted to go away for a long time now. I've been corked up with them for twenty years, and all that time they've been trying to marry me off. When I was only fourteen I thought of running away, though I was a silly fool. Now I've worked it all out and have been waiting for you so I can ask you everything about abroad. I've never seen a single Gothic cathedral, I want to stay in Rome, I want to see all the learned cabinets,[1] I want to study in Paris; all this last year I've been preparing myself and studying and have read an enormous number of books; I've read all the forbidden books. Alexandra and Adelaida are always reading books, they're allowed to, but I'm not given all of them, I'm supervised. I don't want to quarrel with my sisters, but I told my mother and father long ago that I want to change my social position entirely. I've decided to train to be a teacher, and I'm relying on you, because you said you love children. Can we both train to be teachers together, if not now, then in the future? Together we shall be of some use; I don't want to be a general's daughter . . . Tell me, are you a man of great learning?'

'Oh, not at all.'

'That's a pity, and I thought . . . why did I think that, then? But even so, you shall guide me, because I've chosen you.'

'This is absurd, Aglaya Ivanovna.'

'I want to run away from home, I want to!' she exclaimed, and again her eyes began to flash. 'If you won't agree, I'll marry Gavrila Ardalionovich. I don't want to be considered a fallen woman at home and accused of God knows what.'

'Are you in your right mind?' the prince nearly leaped up from his seat. 'What do they accuse you of, who accuses you?'

'At home, all of them, my mother, my sisters, my father, Prince Shch., even your nasty Kolya! Even if they don't say it outright, it's what they think. I said it to their faces, my mother and my father. *Maman* was ill all day; and the next day Alexandra and Papa told me that I didn't understand that I was talking nonsense and using such words. And I snapped at them straight that I understand everything now, all the words, that I'm not a little girl now, that two years ago I deliberately read two novels by Paul de Kock,[2] in order to find out everything. When she heard that, *Maman* nearly fainted.'

A strange thought suddenly fleeted through the prince's mind. He looked fixedly at Aglaya, and smiled.

He could not believe that before him sat the same haughty girl who had once so proudly and overbearingly read Gavrila Ardalionovich's letter aloud to him. He could not understand how in such an overbearing, stern beauty, there could be such a child, who perhaps even now really did not understand *all the words*.

'Have you always lived at home, Aglaya Ivanovna?' he asked. 'I mean, you've never been to school anywhere, haven't studied at an institute?'

'I've never been anywhere; I've stayed at home, corked up as in a bottle, and I shall marry straight from the bottle, too; why are you laughing again? I notice that you also seem to laugh at me and take their side,' she added, frowning sternly. 'Don't make me angry, I don't know what's wrong with me as it is . . . I'm convinced that you came here in the full certainty that I'm in love with you and have called you to a tryst,' she snapped irritably.

'I really was afraid of that yesterday,' the prince blurted out ingenuously (he was very embarrassed), 'but today I'm convinced that you . . .'

'What?' exclaimed Aglaya, and her lower lip suddenly began to tremble. 'You were afraid that I . . . you dared to think that I . . . Good Lord! I dare say you thought I summoned you here in order to draw you into my net so that they'd catch us here and force you to marry me . . .'

'Aglaya Ivanovna! Are you not ashamed? How could such a sordid thought arise in your pure, innocent heart? I bet you don't believe a single word you are saying and . . . don't even know what you're saying!'

Aglaya sat with her eyes stubbornly lowered, as though she herself were frightened by what she had said.

'I'm not ashamed at all,' she muttered. 'How do you know that my heart is innocent? How did you dare to send me a love letter that time?'

'A love letter? My letter – a love letter? That letter was a most respectful one, that letter poured from my heart at the most difficult moment of my life! I remembered you then as a kind of light[3] . . . I . . .'

'Oh, very well, very well,' she suddenly interrupted, though not in the same tone at all, but in complete remorse and almost fear, even bent forward to him, but trying not to look at him directly, made to touch him on the shoulder, to plead more convincingly with him not to be angry. 'Very well,' she added, dreadfully ashamed, 'I feel that I used a very stupid expression. I just did it . . . in order to test you. Pretend I never said it. And if I've offended you, then forgive me. You said it was a very sordid thought: I said it on purpose, to wound you. Sometimes I myself am afraid of the things I feel like saying, and then suddenly I say them. You said just now that you wrote that letter at the most difficult moment of your life . . . I know what moment it was,' she said quietly, again looking at the ground.

'Oh, if you only knew all of it!'

'I do know all of it!' she exclaimed, with fresh agitation. 'You'd been living for a whole month in the same apartment with that fallen woman you ran away with . . .'

She did not blush now, but turned pale as she said this, and suddenly got up from her seat, as though in oblivion, but at once, recovering herself, sat down again; her lip continued to tremble for a long time. The silence lasted for about a minute. The prince was dreadfully shocked at the suddenness of her outburst and did not know what to ascribe it to.

'I don't love you at all,' she said suddenly, as though snapping the words out.

The prince did not reply; again they were silent for about a minute.

'I love Gavrila Ardalionovich . . .' she said rapidly, but so it was hardly audible, and leaning her head forward even more.

'That isn't true,' the prince said, also nearly in a whisper.

'So I'm lying, am I? It is true; I gave him my word the day before yesterday, on this same bench.'

The prince was alarmed, and reflected for a moment.

'It isn't true,' he repeated, firmly. 'You're making it up.'

'Remarkably polite. You may as well know that he's mended his ways; he loves me more than his life. He burned his hand in front of me, just to prove to me that he loves me more than his life.'

'Burned his hand?'

'Yes, his hand. Believe it or don't believe it – it's all the same to me.'

The prince again fell silent. There was no joking in Aglaya's words; she was angry.

'What did he do, bring a candle with him, if it happened here? Otherwise I can't imagine . . .'

'Yes . . . he did. What's so improbable about that?'

'A whole candle, or one in a holder?'

'Well, yes . . . no . . . half a candle . . . a candle-end . . . a whole candle – it's all the same, stop it! . . . And he brought matches, if you want to know. Lit the candle and held his finger in the flame for a whole thirty minutes; is that impossible?'

'I saw him yesterday; his fingers are unharmed.'

Aglaya suddenly burst into laughter, just like a child.

'Do you know why I lied just now?' she suddenly turned to the prince with the most childish trustfulness, and still with the laughter trembling on her lips. 'Because when one lies, if one skilfully inserts something not quite ordinary, something eccentric, well, you know, something that's really too unusual or even doesn't happen at all, one's lie becomes far more plausible. That's something I've noticed. Only with me it didn't work, because I didn't know how . . .'

Suddenly she frowned again, as though recovering herself.

'If that day,' she addressed the prince, looking at him seriously and even sadly, 'if that day I recited that poem about the "poor knight" to you, it was because though I wanted to . . . praise you for one thing, I also wanted to put you to shame for your behaviour and to show you that I knew everything . . .'

'You're very unfair to me . . . to that unhappy woman of whom you said such dreadful things just now, Aglaya.'

'Because I know everything, everything, that's why I said those things! I know that six months ago you offered her your hand in marriage in front of everyone. Don't interrupt, you see, I speak without comment. After that she ran off with Rogozhin, then you lived with her in some village or in the city, and she left you for someone else. (Aglaya blushed dreadfully.) Then she went back to Rogozhin again, who loves her like . . . like a lunatic. Then you, who are also a very clever man, went galloping off after her, as soon as you learned that she'd returned to St Petersburg. Yesterday evening you rushed to defend her, and just now you were dreaming about her . . . You can see that I know everything; I mean, you came here because of her, because of her, didn't you?'

'Yes, I did,' the prince replied quietly, inclining his head sadly and reflectively, and not suspecting the flashing gaze with which Aglaya glanced at him, 'I came here because of her, just in order to find out . . . I don't believe she'll be happy with Rogozhin, although . . . in a word, I don't know what I could do for her, or how I could help her, but I came.'

He started, and looked at Aglaya; she was listening to him with hatred.

'If you came without knowing why, that means you must love her very much,' she said quietly, at last.

'No,' replied the prince, 'no, I don't. Oh, if you only knew with what horror I remember the time I spent with her!'

A shudder even passed through his body at these words.

'Tell me everything,' said Aglaya.

'There's nothing that your ears should not hear. Why I wanted to tell this precisely to you, and you alone – I don't know; perhaps because I really did love you very much. This unhappy woman is deeply convinced that she is the most fallen, the most depraved creature in the whole world. Oh, don't shame her, don't cast your stone. She has tortured herself too much with the consciousness of her own undeserved shame! And what is she guilty of, oh my goodness? Oh, every moment she cries in a frenzy that she acknowledges no guilt, that she is a victim of other people, the victim of a libertine and a villain; but whatever she may say to you, I think you should know that she herself is the first not to believe it and that, on the contrary, she believes with all her conscience that she . . . she herself is to blame. When I tried to dispel this gloom, she entered upon such sufferings that my heart will never heal when I remember that dreadful time. It was as though my heart had been pierced through once and for all. She ran away from me, do you know why? In order to prove to me that she is base. But the most dreadful thing of all is that she herself may not have been aware that it's only me she wanted to prove this to, and she ran away because she had a consuming inner desire to commit some shameful act, so that she could say to herself right there and then: "Now you've committed another shameful act, so that means you're a base creature!" Oh, perhaps you will not understand this, Aglaya! Do you know that this constant awareness of her shame may contain for her a kind of dreadful, unnatural pleasure, as if it were a revenge on someone. Sometimes I managed to lead her to a point where she saw the light around her again, as it were; but she would immediately fly into a rage again, and she reached a point where she bitterly accused me of setting myself high above her (when this was not even in my thoughts!), and told me directly, at last, when I proposed marriage, that she did not require from anyone condescending sympathy, or help, or "being raised to anyone's level". You saw her yesterday; do you really suppose she's happy with that company, that that is any kind of society for her? You don't know how cultured she is, and the things she's able to understand! She really used to astonish me sometimes!'

'Did you read her such . . . sermons then, too?'

'Oh no,' the prince continued reflectively, not noticing the tone of the question, 'I was silent nearly all the time. I often wanted to speak, but truly I didn't know what to say. You know, in some situations it's best not to say anything at all. Oh, I loved her; Oh, I loved her very much . . . but later . . . later . . . later she guessed everything.'

'What did she guess?'

'That I was only sorry for her, and that I . . . didn't love her.'

'How do you know that she didn't fall in love with that . . . landowner she went away with?'

'No, I know it all; she was just laughing at him.'

'And she never made a laughing-stock of you?'

'N-no. She laughed out of malice; oh, she reproached me terribly, in anger – and herself suffered at the same time! But . . . later . . . Oh, don't remind me, don't remind me of it!'

He covered his face with his hands.

'But do you know that she writes me letters almost every day?'

'So it's true!' the prince exclaimed in alarm. 'I'd heard, but still didn't want to believe it.'

'Who did you hear it from?' Aglaya roused herself fearfully.

'Rogozhin told me yesterday, only not very clearly.'

'Yesterday? Yesterday morning? When yesterday? Before the music or after?'

'After; in the evening, between eleven and twelve.'

'A-ah, well, if it was Rogozhin . . . But do you know what she wrote to me about in those letters?'

'Nothing would surprise me; she's mad.'

'Here are those letters.' (Aglaya took from her pocket three letters in three envelopes and threw them in front of the prince.) 'For a whole week now she's been imploring, coaxing, flattering me in order to make me marry you. She . . . well yes, she is clever even though she's mad, and it's true what you say, she is far cleverer than me . . . she writes to me that she's in love with me, that every day she seeks a chance to see me, even if only from afar. She writes that you love me, that she knows this, has noticed it for a long time, and that you and she used to talk about me there. She wants to see you happy; she's sure that only I can constitute your happiness . . . She writes such wild things . . . such strange things . . . I haven't shown the letters to anyone, I've been waiting for you; do you know what this means? Can't you guess?'

'It's madness; it's proof of her insanity,' the prince said quietly, and his lips began to tremble.

'You're not crying, are you?'

"No, Aglaya, no, I'm not crying,' the prince said, with a look at her.

'But what am I to do now? What would you advise me? I mean, I can't go on getting these letters!'

'Oh, leave her, I beg you!' exclaimed the prince. 'What can you do in that dark morass? I'll make every effort to see that she doesn't write to you any more.'

'If you do that, then you're a man without a heart!' exclaimed Aglaya. 'Surely you can see that it's not me she's in love with, but you, she loves you alone! Can it really be that you've noticed everything about her, but haven't noticed that? Do you know what those letters mean? They mean jealousy; they mean more than jealousy! She . . . do you think she's really going to marry Rogozhin, as she writes in these letters? She'd kill herself the very next day, as soon as we were joined in wedlock!'

The prince shuddered; his heart froze. But he looked at Aglaya in astonishment: it felt strange to him to admit that this child had long ago become a woman.

'As God is my witness, Aglaya, I'd give my life in order to return her peace of mind to her and make her happy, but . . . I cannot love her now, and she knows it!'

'Then sacrifice yourself, that would be in character with you! I mean, you're such a great benefactor, aren't you? And don't call me "Aglaya" . . . You called me simply "Aglaya" earlier, too . . . You must restore her to life, you must go away with her again, to pacify and calm her heart. Why, after all, you love her!'

'I can't sacrifice myself like that, though there was one occasion when I did and . . . perhaps I want to now. But I know *for certain* that with me she would be ruined, and that's why I am leaving her. I was supposed to see her today at seven; I may not go now. In her pride she'll never forgive me for my love – and we shall both be ruined! It's unnatural, but in this situation everything is unnatural. You say she loves me, but is it really love? Can there be such love after what I've already endured? No, in this situation there's something else, and it's not love!'

'How pale you've gone!' Aglaya said in sudden alarm.

'It's all right; I didn't sleep much; I feel weak, I . . . we really did use to talk about you then, Aglaya . . .'

'So it's true? You really *were able to talk to her about me* and . . . and how could you fall in love with me when you'd only seen me once?'

'I don't know. In the dark morass I was living in then I dreamed . . . imagined, perhaps, a new dawn. I don't know how it was that I thought about you first. What I wrote you at the time was the truth, that I didn't know. All that was just a dream, caused by the horrible situation I was in . . . Later I began to study; I didn't intend to return here for three years . . .'

'So you came back for her?'

And something in Aglaya's voice began to tremble.

'Yes, I did.'

Some two minutes of gloomy silence passed on both sides. Aglaya got up from her chair.

'If you say,' she began in a voice that lacked steadiness, 'if you yourself believe that this . . . woman of yours . . . is insane, then you must see that I can have nothing to do with her insane fantasies . . . I ask you, Lev Nikolaich, to take these three letters and throw them back at her from me! And if,' Aglaya exclaimed suddenly, 'if she has the temerity to send me another line, then tell her that I'll complain to my father and that she'll be hauled off to a lunatic asylum . . .'

The prince leaped to his feet, observing Aglaya's sudden fury with alarm; and suddenly a kind of mist seemed to fall before him . . .

'You can't feel like that . . . It's not true!' he muttered.

'It's true! True!' exclaimed Aglaya, almost out of her mind.

'What is true? What?' a frightened voice rang out beside them.

Before them stood Lizaveta Prokofyevna.

'It's true that I'm going to marry Gavrila Ardalionovich! That I love Gavrila Ardalionovich and am going to run away from this house with him tomorrow!' Aglaya hurled at her. 'Do you hear? Is your curiosity satisfied? Are you satisfied with that?'

And she ran off home.

'No, my dear sir, don't go away now,' said Lizaveta Prokofyevna, stopping the prince. 'Please be so good as to come with me and explain yourself . . . What torments I must suffer, and I haven't slept all night as it is . . .'

The prince followed her.

9

On entering her house, Lizaveta Prokofyevna stopped in the first room; she could walk no further and dropped on to a couch, completely drained of strength, even forgetting to invite the prince to sit down. It was a rather large drawing room, with a round table in the middle, a stove, a great quantity of flowers on the chiffoniers by the windows, and another door, a glass one, set in the rear wall. Adelaida and Alexandra came in at once, looking questioningly and with bewilderment at the prince and their mother.

At the dacha the girls usually got up at about nine o'clock; Aglaya alone, during the past two or three days, had got into the habit of getting up somewhat earlier and going out to walk in the garden, though not at seven, but rather at eight, or even a little later. Lizaveta Prokofyevna, who really had not slept at all because of her various worries, rose at about eight o'clock with the express purpose of meeting Aglaya in the garden, supposing her to have already risen; but neither in the garden nor in the bedroom did she find her. At this point she became quite worried and woke her daughters. From the maid they learned that Aglaya Ivanovna had gone out into the park before seven. The girls smiled at this new, fantastical caprice of their fantastical sister and observed to their mama that Aglaya might be angry with her if she went into the park to look for her, and that she was probably sitting now with a book on the green bench she had talked about three days earlier and because of which she had almost quarrelled with Prince Shch. for not having found anything remarkable about the location of that bench. Having intercepted the tryst, and hearing her daughter's strange words, Lizaveta Prokofyevna was dreadfully alarmed, for many reasons; but, bringing the prince back with her, regretted having started the whole thing: 'Why couldn't Aglaya have met the prince in the park and talked to him, if this was a rendezvous they had fixed in advance?'

'Don't get the idea, dear Prince,' she braced herself at last, 'that I've dragged you back here to interrogate you ... After last night, my good man, I might not have wanted to meet you again for a long time ...'

She stopped short, somewhat tentatively.

'But all the same, you'd very much like to know how Aglaya and I met today?' the prince concluded very calmly.

'Well, of course I would!' Lizaveta Prokofyevna flared up at once. 'I'm not afraid of plain language. Because I'm not offending anyone and did not wish to offend anyone ...'

'For pity's sake, it's natural that you should want to know, and there's no offence involved in it; you are her mother. Aglaya Ivanovna and I met today by the green bench at exactly seven o'clock this morning, in consequence of the invitation she made yesterday. She sent word to me yesterday evening by means of a note, saying that she needed to see me and talk to me about an important matter. We met and talked for a whole hour about matters that concern Aglaya Ivanovna alone; that was all.'

'Of course that was all, my dear, and there can be no doubt of it,' Lizaveta Prokofyevna pronounced with dignity.

'Splendid, Prince!' said Aglaya, suddenly entering the room. 'I thank you with all my heart for considering me incapable of degrading myself here by lying. That will do, *Maman*, or do you plan to interrogate him further?'

'You know that I haven't had occasion to blush before you until now ... though I daresay you might have been pleased if I had,' Lizaveta Ivanovna replied in didactic tones. 'Goodbye, Prince; and forgive me for having upset you. And I hope you will remain assured of my unaltering respect for you.'

The prince at once bowed in both directions, and left without saying anything. Alexandra and Adelaida grinned and whispered about something between themselves. Lizaveta Prokofyevna gave them a stern look.

'We were just saying, *Maman*,' Adelaida laughed, 'that the prince took his leave so wonderfully: sometimes he's a complete sack of potatoes, and then suddenly, he's like . . . like Yevgeny Pavlych.'

'Fine manners and dignity are taught by the heart, not by the dancing master,' Lizaveta Prokofyevna concluded sententiously, and went back to her room upstairs, without even giving Aglaya a glance.

When the prince returned to his quarters, at about nine o'clock, they were clearing up and sweeping the floor after the disorder of the night before.

'Thank goodness, we managed to finish before you got here!' Vera said happily.

'Good morning; my head is spinning a little; I slept badly; I'd like to sleep for a bit.'

'Here on the veranda, like yesterday? Very well. I'll tell them all that you're not to be disturbed. Papa has gone off somewhere.'

The maid went out; Vera set off after her, but turned back and anxiously approached the prince.

'Prince, have pity on that unhappy . . . boy; don't make him leave today.'

'On no account will I do that; let him stay here as long as he likes.'

'He won't do anything now, and . . . don't be too stern with him.'

'Certainly not. Why would I be?'

'And . . . don't laugh at him; that's the main thing.'

'Oh, of course not!'

'It's stupid of me to mention this to a man such as yourself,' Vera began to blush. 'But even though you're tired,' she laughed, half turning round in order to leave, 'your eyes look so lovely at this moment . . . they're happy.'

'Are they really?' the prince asked cheerfully, and burst into delighted laughter.

But Vera, who was as straightforward and unceremonious as a boy, suddenly seemed to grow embarrassed, blushed even harder and, continuing to laugh, hurriedly left the room.

'How . . . wonderful she is,' thought the prince, and at once forgot about her. He went down to a corner of the veranda where there was a couch with a small table in front of it, sat down, covered his face with his hands and sat there for about ten minutes; all of a sudden he hurriedly and anxiously lowered his hand into his side pocket and took out three letters.

But again the door opened, and Kolya came in. The prince seemed glad of having to put the letters back in his pocket and being able to postpone the moment of reading them.

'Well, quite an incident!' said Kolya, seating himself on the couch and coming straight to the point, as boys like him usually do. 'How do you regard Ippolit now? Without respect?'

'No, why do you say that . . . but, Kolya, I'm tired. What's more, it's just too sad to start talking about that again . . . But how is he?'

'He's sleeping, and will sleep for another two hours yet. I understand: you couldn't sleep in the house, went walking in the park . . . the excitement, of course . . . I don't wonder!'

'How do you know that I went walking in the park and couldn't sleep in the house?'

'Vera just told me. She tried to persuade me not to go in; I simply had to, for a moment; I've been keeping watch by his bedside for the past two hours; now I've put Kostya Lebedev on duty. Burdovsky has gone. So go to bed, Prince; good night . . . I mean, good morning! Only, you know, I was struck!'

'Of course . . . all this . . .'

'No, Prince, no; I was struck by his confession. Especially the part where he talks about providence and the life to come. There's a gi-gant-ic thought there!'

The prince cast an affectionate look at Kolya who had, of

course, dropped in to have a talk about the gigantic thought as soon as possible.

'But the main thing, the main thing is not the thought alone, but the whole background! Had it been written by Voltaire, Rousseau, Proudhon, I would have read it, and noted it, but wouldn't have been so struck. But a man who knows for certain that he only has ten minutes left, and can talk like that – I mean, that's pride! I mean, it's the loftiest independence of personal dignity, it's sheer bravado . . . No, it's gigantic strength of spirit! And after that, to maintain that he didn't put the firing cap in on purpose – that is base, unnatural! But you know, he deceived us last night, he pulled the wool over our eyes: I certainly never helped him to pack his bag, and I never saw the pistol; he packed everything himself, so he threw me off guard. Vera says you're letting him stay here; I swear there will be no risk, particularly as we're all with him constantly.'

'And which of you was there last night?'

'Myself, Kostya Lebedev and Burdovsky; Keller was there for a bit, and then he went to Lebedev's rooms to sleep, because we had nowhere for him to lie down. Ferdyshchenko also slept at Lebedev's, he left at seven o'clock. The general is always at Lebedev's, now he's gone, too . . . Lebedev may come and see you soon; I don't know why, but he was looking for you, he asked for you twice. Should I let him in or not, if you're going to bed? I'm also going to bed. Oh yes, there was one thing I meant to tell you; the general surprised me just now: Burdovsky woke me so I could take my turn at keeping watch, it was almost six a.m.; I went out for a moment and suddenly encountered the general, who was still so intoxicated that he didn't recognize me: stood before me like a post; then fairly hurled himself on me when he came to: "How's the patient?" he said. "I was going to find out about the patient . . ." I delivered my report, and we talked about this and that. "That's all very well," he said, "but the main reason I've come is in order to warn you; I have grounds for supposing that it's out of the question to talk freely in the presence of Mr Ferdyshchenko and that one must . . . exercise restraint." Do you understand, Prince?'

'Really? As a matter of fact, though . . . it doesn't concern us.'

'Yes, of course, we're not freemasons! Why, I was even astonished that the general came specially to wake me during the night because of it.'

'Ferdyshchenko has left, you say?'

'He left at seven; looked in to see me on his way; I was keeping watch. He said he was going to finish what was left of the night at Vilkin's – there's a drunkard of that name, Vilkin, who lives here. Well, I'm going! And here is Lukyan Timofeich . . . The prince wants to sleep, Lukyan Timofeich; about turn!'

'Just one moment of your time, much esteemed Prince, on a certain matter that in my view is important,' Lebedev, who had entered, said stiffly and in a meaningful undertone, bowing in solemn fashion. He had only just returned, had not yet been to his rooms, and was still holding his hat in his hands. His face had a worried expression, and it bore a singular and unusual nuance of personal dignity. The prince invited him to sit down.

'You've asked for me twice? Perhaps you're still worried about what happened yesterday . . .'

'About that boy yesterday, you mean, Prince? Oh no, sir; yesterday my thoughts were in disarray . . . but today I don't intend to contrecarrate¹ a single one of your proposals.'

'Contreca . . . what did you say?'

'I said: contrecarrate; the word is a French one, like a large number of other words that have entered the body of the Russian language; but I don't particularly insist on it.'

'Why are you so solemn and formal today, Lebedev, and talking like a book?' the prince smiled.

'Nikolai Ardalionovich!' Lebedev turned to Kolya with a voice that was almost one of tender emotion. 'As it's incumbent on me to inform the prince of a matter that regards . . .'

'Well yes, of course, of course, it's not my business! *Au revoir*, Prince!' said Kolya, withdrawing at once.

'I like the boy for his quick grasp of things,' Lebedev pronounced, watching him go. 'He's a lively lad, though a troublesome one. Esteemed Prince, last night or at dawn today I experienced a severe misfortune . . . I still hesitate to assert the exact time.'

'What was it?'

'The loss of four hundred roubles from my side pocket, much esteemed Prince; I was robbed!' Lebedev added with a sour smile.

'You lost four hundred roubles? That's a pity.'

'And especially for a poor man, nobly living by his own toil.'

'Of course, of course; how did it come about?'

'As a consequence of wine, sir. I come to you as to my providence, much esteemed Prince. I received the sum of four hundred silver roubles at five o'clock yesterday afternoon from one of my debtors and returned here by train. I had my wallet in my pocket. Changing out of my civil service coat into my frock coat I transferred the money to the frock coat, intending to keep it upon my person, with the plan of disbursing it against a certain request . . . I was expecting my agent to arrive.'

'Incidentally, Lukyan Timofeich, is it true that you put an advertisement in the papers saying that you lend money against items of gold and silver?'

'Through an agent; my own name is not given, nor any address. Since I have practically no capital and in view of the growth of my family, you must admit it's an honest percentage . . .'

'Yes, yes; I merely wished to inquire; forgive me for interrupting.'

'The agent didn't show up. At the same time they brought the unfortunate fellow; I was already somewhat tipsy, having dined; those guests arrived, we drank . . . tea, and . . . I got a bit merry, to my ruin. And when, late in the evening, that Keller walked in and made the announcement about your ceremonial day and the arrangements concerning the champagne, then dear and much esteemed Prince, being in possession of a heart (something you've probably noticed, for I deserve it), being in possession of a heart, I will not say a sensitive one, but a grateful one, in which I take pride – I, for the greater ceremony of the meeting that was in preparation, and in expectation of personally congratulating you, decided to go and change my old rags for the civil service coat I had taken off on my return, and did so, as you, Prince, probably noticed, as you saw me in the civil service coat all evening. As I was changing, I left the wallet in my pocket . . .

Truly, when God wishes to punish a man, he first of all deprives him of reason. And only today at half-past seven, on waking up, I leaped out of bed like a man half insane, the first thing I did was to reach for my frock coat – one empty pocket! There was no trace of my wallet.'

'Oh, how unpleasant!'

'Yes sir, unpleasant indeed; and with unfailing tact you have found just the right expression,' Lebedev added, not without craftiness.

'Though actually . . .' the prince began to grow alarmed, reflecting, 'I mean, this is serious . . .'

'Serious indeed – Prince, you've discovered another word to describe . . .'

'Oh, that will do, Lukyan Timofeich, what is there to discover here? The words are not the important thing . . . Do you suppose it might have dropped out of your pocket when you were drunk?'

'It might have. Anything is possible when one's drunk, as you sincerely expressed it, dear Prince! But please take account of this, sir: if I'd shaken the wallet out of my pocket when I was changing my frock coat, the shaken object ought to be lying right there on the floor. Where is that object, sir?'

'Did you put it away somewhere, perhaps, in a drawer, in the desk?'

'I've looked through everything, rummaged everywhere, even though I didn't put it away anywhere and didn't open any drawer, I remember that clearly.'

'Have you looked in the safe?'

'That was the first thing I did. sir, and even several times today . . . And how could I have put it away in the safe, truly much esteemed Prince?'

'I will confess, Lebedev, that this alarms me. So someone must have found it on the floor?'

'Or snatched it from my pocket! Two alternatives, sir.'

'It alarms me greatly, because who . . . That is the question!'

'Without any doubt, there lies the main question; you are wonderfully adept at finding words and ideas for defining situations, Prince.'

'Oh, Lukyan Timofeich, stop your mockery, this is no time for it . . .'

'Mockery?' exclaimed Lebedev, throwing up his hands.

'Oh, very well, very well, I'm not angry, there is something else at the bottom of this . . . It's the people I'm afraid for. Whom do you suspect?'

'A most difficult question, and one that is . . . most complex! The maid I cannot suspect; she was sitting in her kitchen. Nor can I suspect my children . . .'

'Of course not.'

'So it must be one of the guests, sir.'

'But is that possible?'

'Completely and in the highest degree impossible, but it must certainly be so. I am, however, prepared to admit and am even convinced that if there was a theft, it was committed not in the evening, when everyone was at the gathering, but during the night or even towards morning, by one of those who passed the night here.'

'Oh my goodness!'

'I naturally exclude Burdovsky and Nikolai Ardalionovich; they did not even come into my rooms, sir.'

'Of course not, and even if they had! Who did pass the night in your part of the house?'

'Counting me, there were four of us in two adjoining rooms: myself, the general, Keller and Mr Ferdyshchenko. So it was one of us four, sir!'

'Three, you mean; but who, then?'

'I counted myself for the sake of fairness and decency; but you will agree, Prince, that I could not have robbed myself, though there have been such cases in the world . . .'

'Oh, Lebedev, how tedious this is!' the prince exclaimed impatiently. 'Get on with it, why are you spinning it out? . . .'

'So there remain three, sir, and in the first place, Mr Keller, an unreliable, drunken man, and in some respects a liberal, where the pocket is concerned, that is, sir; otherwise his inclinations are more of the antique chivalrous than of the liberal kind. He started off by sleeping in the sick man's room, and only during the night moved through to us, under the pretext that the bare floor was too hard to sleep on.'

'Do you suspect him?'

'I did, sir. When at about eight o'clock I leaped up like a man half insane, clutching my forehead, I instantly woke the general, who was sleeping the sleep of the just. Taking into consideration the strange disappearance of Ferdyshchenko, which in itself aroused suspicion in us, we both at once decided to search Keller, who was lying there like . . . like . . . almost like a doornail, sir. We searched him all over: not a centime in his pockets, and there wasn't one of his pockets that didn't have holes in it. There was a blue check cotton handkerchief, in an indecent condition, sir. There was also a love letter from some chambermaid or other, with threats and a demand for money, and excerpts from the feuilleton with which you're already familiar, sir. The general decided that he was innocent. In order to make our inquiries more complete, we woke him up, which involved a lot of pushing and shoving; he could hardly understand what was afoot; his mouth hung open, he was drunk, he had an absurd and innocent, even stupid, expression on his face – he wasn't himself, sir!'

'Well, I'm glad!' the prince sighed in relief. 'I was so afraid for him!'

'Afraid? So you already had grounds for that?' Lebedev narrowed his eyes.

'Oh no, I wasn't thinking,' the prince hesitated. 'That was a dreadfully silly thing to say. Be a good fellow, Lebedev, and don't tell anyone . . .'

'Prince, Prince! Your words are safe in my heart . . . in the depths of my heart! It's as quiet as the grave in there, sir!' Lebedev said rapturously, pressing his hat to his heart.

'Very well, very well! . . . So it's Ferdyshchenko? That is, I mean, you suspect Ferdyshchenko?'

'Who else?' said Lebedev quietly, looking fixedly at the prince.

'Well yes, of course . . . who else . . . that is, again, what clues are there?'

'There are clues, sir. For one thing, his disappearance at seven o'clock this morning, or even earlier, during the hour before that.'

'I know, Kolya told me that he dropped in to see him and said he was going to spend what was left of the night at ... I've forgotten whose place it was, a friend of his.'

'Vilkin, sir. So Nikolai Ardalionovich has already spoken to you?'

'He said nothing about a theft.'

'He doesn't know, for I'm keeping the matter secret at present. So, he goes to Vilkin's; it would seem a sensible thing for a drunkard to go and see someone like himself, also a drunkard, even though it was the crack of dawn and he had no reason, wouldn't it, sir? But it's here that the trail begins: as he goes away, he leaves an address ... Now, Prince, observe the question: why did he leave the address? ... Why did he purposely go and see Nikolai Ardalionovich, making a detour, sir, and tell him he was "going to sleep the rest of the night at Vilkin's"? And who was going to be interested in the fact that he was going away, and to Vilkin's, moreover? What was the point of making it public? No, here there is subtlety, sir, thievish subtlety! It means: "Look, I'm purposely not concealing my tracks, so what kind of thief am I after that? Would a thief publicize the time when he was going to leave?" Excessive concern to divert suspicion and, so to speak, erase his footprints in the sand ... Do you take my meaning, much esteemed Prince?'

'I do, I take your meaning very well, but that's not enough, you know.'

'The second clue, sir: the trail turns out to be false, and the address given is not correct. An hour later, at eight o' clock, that is, I was already knocking at Vilkin's door; he lives on Fifth Street[2] here, sir, and I even know him, sir. There was no sign of Ferdyshchenko. Though I managed to get from the maid, who's completely deaf, sir, that about an hour earlier someone actually had knocked at the door, and even rather violently, and he'd broken the doorbell. But the maid hadn't opened up, not wanting to wake Mr Vilkin, or perhaps she just didn't want to get up herself. That happens, sir.'

'And those are all the clues you have? It's not enough.'

'Prince, but who else can I suspect, think about it?' Lebedev concluded with emotion, and something sly showed through for a moment in his smile.

'I think you ought to look through your rooms and all the drawers again!' the prince said worriedly after some reflection.

'I have, sir!' Lebedev sighed with even more emotion.

'Hm! . . . and why, why did you have to change that frock coat?' exclaimed the prince, banging the table in vexation.

'A question out of an old comedy, sir. But, most kind-natured Prince! You're taking my misfortune much too much to heart. I am not worth it. That is, I alone am not worth it; but you are suffering for the criminal, too . . . for the worthless Mr Ferdyshchenko!'

'But yes, yes, you really have worried me,' the prince interrupted him absent-mindedly and with displeasure. 'Well then, what do you intend to do . . . if you're so certain that it's Ferdyshchenko?'

'Prince, much esteemed Prince, but who else, sir?' Lebedev writhed with growing emotion. 'I mean, the absence of anyone else who comes to mind and, so to speak, the complete impossibility of suspecting anyone except Mr Ferdyshchenko, why, that is, so to speak, yet another clue that speaks against Mr Ferdyshchenko, the third clue! For again, who else could it be? I mean, I can't very well go suspecting Mr Burdovsky now, can I, heh-heh-heh!'

'Really, what nonsense!'

'Nor the general either, really, could I, heh-heh-heh!'

'What rubbish!' the prince said almost angrily, turning about impatiently in his seat.

'You're right, it's rubbish! Heh-heh-heh! And the fellow made me laugh, the general, I mean, sir! This morning we were hot on the trail to Vilkin's, sir . . . and I must observe to you that the general was even more shocked than I was when, after the loss, I had no scruples about waking him up: his face even changed, he turned red, turned pale and, at last, suddenly entered a state of such fierce and righteous indignation that I'd never have expected such a degree of it, sir. A most noble man! He lies constantly, out of weakness, but he's a man of the loftiest feelings, doesn't spend a lot of time thinking, but inspires the most complete trust with his innocence. I've already told you, much esteemed Prince, that not only do I have a soft spot for him, I even love him, sir. Suddenly he stops in the middle of the street, throws open his frock coat, and exposes his chest: "Search me", he says, "you searched Keller, so why don't you search me?" His arms and legs were trembling, he even turned quite pale, fearsome looking. I began to laugh and said: "Listen, general," I said, "if someone else were to say that about you, I'd remove my head with my own hands, put it on a large dish and take it to all who doubted: "Look," I'd say, "you see this head, well, I'll vouch for him with my own head, and not only that, but I'll walk into the flames as well. That's how much I'm prepared to vouch for you." At this, he threw himself into my embrace, right in the middle of the street, sir, burst into tears, trembling and pressing me so hard against his chest that I nearly choked: "You're the only friend I have left in my misfortunes! A man of feeling, sir!" Well, of course, right there in the roadway he told me a relevant anecdote about how once in his youth he'd been suspected of stealing five hundred thousand roubles and how the very next day he had rushed into the flames of a burning house and dragged from them the count who had suspected him and Nina Alexandrovna, who was still a spinster at the time. The count embraced him, and that was how he came to marry Nina Alexandrovna, and the next day they found a safe containing the missing money in the ruins of the fire; it was an iron safe, of English manufacture, with a secret lock, and had somehow fallen through the floor, so that no one noticed it, and it was only found because of the fire. A complete lie, sir. But when he began to talk about Nina Alexandrovna, he even began to whimper. Nina Alexandrovna is a most noble person, though she's angry with me.'

'You don't know her?'

'Not really, sir, though with all my soul I should like to, if only so I could justify myself to her. Nina Alexandrovna has a grudge against me, she thinks I'm trying to debauch her husband with drunkenness. But not only am I not debauching him, I'm actually reining him in; I may even be keeping him away from the most pernicious company. What's more, he's a friend to me, sir, and I will confess to you that I never leave his side now, sir, so that it's even like this, sir: wherever he goes, I go with him, because the only way you can have any effect on him is by means of emotion. He doesn't even visit his captain's widow at all now, though he secretly yearns for her, and even sometimes moans for her, especially in the morning when he gets up and puts his boots on, I don't know why it's at that time, precisely. He has no money, sir, that's the trouble, and he can't present himself to her without money, sir. He hasn't asked you for money, has he, much esteemed Prince?'

'No, he hasn't done that.'

'He's too ashamed. He'd like to: he even confessed to me that he wanted to trouble you, but he's bashful, sir, as you lent him some money quite recently, and in any case he supposes that you wouldn't lend him more. He poured this out to me as a friend.'

'And you don't lend him any?'

'Prince! Much esteemed Prince! Not only money, but for that man I would, so to speak, even give my life . . . no, as a matter of fact, I don't want to exaggerate; not my life, but if it were, so to speak, a fever, a boil or even a cough, then as God's my witness I'd be willing to endure it, if it were for a matter of great urgency; for I consider him a great, but ruined man! That's what, sir; not only money, sir!'

'So you do lend him money?'

'N-no, sir; I've never lent him money, sir, and he knows that I won't, sir, but it's solely in the interests of bringing him to abstinence and reform. Now he wants to go to St Petersburg with me; I mean, I'm going to St Petersburg, sir, in order to catch Mr Ferdyshchenko while his trail's still hot, for I know for certain that he's already there. My general is fairly raring to go, sir; but I suspect that in St Petersburg he'll slip away from me, in order to visit his captain's widow. I confess that I'll even deliberately let him go, as we've agreed to split up as soon as we get there, to make it easier to catch Mr Ferdyshchenko. So I'll let him go, and then suddenly, like snow on his head, I'll catch him at the captain's widow's; purely in order to shame him as a family man and as a human being in general.'

'Only don't cause a row, Lebedev, for God's sake don't cause a row,' the prince said in a low voice, extremely anxious.

'Oh no, sir, it's purely in order to shame him and to see what kind of physiognomy he adopts; for one may conclude much from a man's physiognomy, much esteemed Prince, and especially a man like that! Oh, Prince! Though my own misfortune is great, even now I cannot help thinking about him and the correction of his moral nature. I have an urgent request to make of you, much esteemed Prince, and I will even confess that it is the real reason why I've come, sir; you are acquainted with their household and have even stayed in it, sir; so if, most kind-natured Prince, you could bring yourself to help me in this, purely for the sake of the general and his happiness . . .'

Lebedev even put his hands together, as in prayer.

'What do you mean? How can I help you? I do assure you that I very much want to understand you completely, Lebedev.'

'Only in that certitude did I come to you! One could influence him through Nina Alexandrovna; observing and, so to speak, keeping an eye on his excellency constantly, in the bosom of his own family. But unfortunately I don't know her, sir . . . in addition, Nikolai Ardalionovich, who worships you, so to speak, from the bosom of his young soul, might perhaps be able to assist you . . .'

'N-no . . . Nina Alexandrovna in this affair . . . God forbid! Or Kolya . . . As a matter of fact, I don't think I really understand you yet, Lebedev.'

'But there's absolutely nothing to understand!' Lebedev even leaped up from his chair. 'Nothing but feeling, feeling and tenderness – that's all the medicine that our patient needs. You will allow me, Prince, to consider him ill?'

'That certainly displays your tact and intelligence.'

'I'll explain to you with an example taken, for clarity's sake, from practical reality. You see what this man is like, sir: now he has only a weakness for this captain's widow, to whom he cannot present himself without money and at whose home I today intend to catch him, for his own good, sir; but, let us suppose that it was not merely the captain's widow, but that he had even committed a real crime, oh, you know, some most dishonourable misdeed (although he's quite incapable of it), why, even then, I say, the only way to reach him is by noble, so to speak, tenderness, for he is a most feeling man, sir! Believe me, he wouldn't be able to hold out for five days, he'd blab, start weeping and confess to everything – and especially if one were to act deftly and nobly, through his family's and your own supervision of all his, as it were, moves and manoeuvres . . . Oh most kind-hearted Prince!' Lebedev jumped up, in a kind of inspiration, 'I mean, I'm not maintaining that he will with certainty . . . I'm prepared, as it were, to shed every drop of my blood for him right now, though you must admit that his intemperance and drunkenness, and the captain's widow, and all of it together, could lead him to anything . . .'

'I am, of course, always ready to help towards such an end,' said the prince, getting up, 'only, I will confess to you, Lebedev, I'm dreadfully anxious; tell me, I mean, you still . . . in a word, you yourself say that you suspect Mr Ferdyshchenko.'

'But who else is there? Who else is there, most sincere Prince?' Lebedev again put his hands together in emotion, sweetly smiling.

The prince frowned and got up from his seat.

'You see, Lukyan Timofeich, it would be terrible to make a mistake here. This Ferdyshchenko . . . I don't want to speak ill of him . . . but this Ferdyshchenko . . . though who knows, perhaps it was him! . . . I mean that perhaps he really is more capable of it than . . . than anyone else.'

Lebedev's sharpened his eyes and pricked up his ears.

'You see,' the prince said, becoming embarrassed, and frowning more and more, pacing up and down the room and trying not to look at Lebedev, 'I've been informed . . . I was told about Mr Ferdyshchenko, that he is, above all, the sort of man in whose presence one should restrain oneself and not say anything . . . superfluous – you understand? What I'm getting at is that he may indeed have been more capable than anyone else . . . but we mustn't make a mistake, you understand?'

'And who told you this about Mr Ferdyshchenko?' Lebedev fairly hurled at him.

'Oh, someone whispered it to me; actually, I don't believe it myself . . . I'm terribly annoyed at having had to tell you this, I assure you, I don't believe it myself . . . it's some nonsense or other . . . Ugh, what a stupid thing I did!'

'You see, Prince,' Lebedev even began to tremble all over, 'it's important, it's very important now, that is, not with regard to Mr Ferdyshchenko, but with regard to how this information got to you.' (As he said this, Lebedev ran to and fro after the prince, trying to keep up with him.) 'This is what I want to tell you now, Prince: this morning the general, when we were going to see that Vilkin fellow, after he had told me about the fire and boiling with anger, of course, suddenly began to hint the same thing to me about Mr Ferdyshchenko, but so incoherently and vaguely that I found myself asking him certain questions and as a result was quite convinced that all this information was nothing but one of his excellency's inspirations . . . He really does it out of sheer good nature. For he lies solely because he can't restrain his emotions. Now look, sir: if he lied, and I'm sure that he did, then how could you have heard about it? You must understand, Prince, that for him it was just the inspiration of the moment – so who, then, was it who told you? It's important, sir, it's . . . it's very important, sir and . . . so to speak . . .'

'Kolya told me about it just now, and he was told this morning by his father, whom he met at six o'clock, or slightly later, in the passage, when he went out for some reason.'

And the prince recounted all the details to him.

'Well, there we are, sir, that's what's called a clue, sir,' Lebedev laughed inaudibly, rubbing his hands. 'It's as I thought, sir! That means his excellency deliberately interrupted his sleep of the just, between six and seven, in order to go and wake up his beloved son and tell him of the extreme danger of having anything to do with Mr Ferdyshchenko! What a dangerous man Mr Ferdyshchenko must be after that, and what must the general's fatherly concern have been, heh-heh-heh! . . .'

'Look here, Lebedev,' the prince said in embarrassment, at last, 'look here, act quietly! Don't cause a row! I beg you, Lebedev, I implore you . . . If you'll be reasonable, then I'll co-operate, but no one must know of it; no one must know!'

'Be assured, most kind-natured, most sincere and most noble Prince,' Lebedev exclaimed in positive inspiration, 'be assured that all this will die within my most honourable heart! With quiet steps,[3] sir, together! With quiet steps, sir, together! I'll give every drop of my blood ... Most illustrious Prince, I am base in soul and spirit, but ask anyone, even a scoundrel, whom he would rather deal with, a scoundrel like himself or a most noble man like yourself, most sincere Prince? He will reply: "with a most noble man", and there is the triumph of virtue! *Au revoir*, much esteemed Prince! With quiet steps ... with quiet steps and ... together, sir.'

IO

The prince understood, at last, why he went cold each time he touched these three letters, and why he was postponing the moment of reading them until late in the evening. When earlier, in the morning, he had fallen into the oblivion of a heavy slumber on his couch, still unable to bring himself to open any of these three envelopes, he again had a bad dream, and again that same 'criminal' woman came to him. Again she looked at him with glittering tears on long eyelids, again called him to follow her, and again he woke up, as before, remembering her face with torment. He wanted to go to *her* at once, but could not; at last, almost in despair, he opened the letters and began to read.

Those letters also resembled a dream. Sometimes one has terrible dreams, impossible and unnatural; waking up, you remember them clearly and are astonished at a strange fact: you remember above all that your reason did not desert you throughout the entire duration of your dream; you even remember that you acted with extreme cunning and logic during all this long, long time, when you were surrounded by murderers, when they practised cunning on you, concealed their intention, addressed you in a friendly manner, while they already had their weapons ready and were only waiting for a sign; you remember how cunningly, at last, you deceived them, hid from them; then you guessed that they knew all of your deceit by heart and were merely not letting on that they knew where you had hidden; but you practised cunning and deceived them again, all this you remember clearly. But then why at the same time was your reason able to reconcile itself to such obvious absurdities and impossibilities, of which, by the way, your dream was full? One of your murderers turned before your very eyes into a woman, and from a woman into a small, cunning, loathsome dwarf – and you allowed all this instantly, as a *fait accompli*, almost without the slightest perplexity, and precisely at this time, when, on the other hand, your reason was in the most violent state of exertion, displaying extreme strength, cunning, guesswork, logic? Why also, waking from your dream and completely entering reality, do you feel almost every time, and sometimes with an impression that is extraordinarily strong, that together with the dream you are leaving something that, for you, is unresolved? You laugh at the absurdity of your dream and at the same time feel that in the interweaving of these absurdities there is some idea, but an idea that is now a reality, something that is part of your real life, something that exists and has always existed in your heart; it is as though what your dream has told you is something new, prophetic, something you have been waiting for; your impression is a strong one, it is a joyful or a tormenting one, but of what it consists, and what was told to you – all that you can neither understand nor remember.

Almost the same thing happened after those letters. But before he had even opened them, the prince felt that the very fact of their existence and possibility was like a nightmare. How could *she* have brought herself to write to *her*, he asked himself, as he roamed about alone in the evening (sometimes not even conscious of where he was walking). How could she write *about that*, and how could such a crazy dream be born within her head? But this dream had already come true, and for him the most surprising thing was that while he was reading those letters he himself almost believed in the possibility and even the justification of this dream. Yes, of course, it was a dream, a nightmare and a madness; but in it there was something tormentingly real and true to the point of suffering, something that justified the dream, and the nightmare and the madness.

For several hours on end he seemed to be in a kind of delirium from what he had read, kept remembering fragments, paused on them, thought about them. Sometimes he even felt like telling himself that he had had a premonition of all this and had guessed it in advance; it even seemed to him that he had read it all before, some time long, long ago, and all that he had grieved about, all that had caused him suffering and fear – all that was contained in those letters he had read long ago.

'When you open this letter,' (thus did the first missive begin) 'you will look first of all at the signature. The signature will explain everything to you, and so there is no need for me to justify myself, and no point in explaining. Were I in any way equal to you, you might be insulted by such insolence; but who am I, and who are you? We are two opposites, and I am so much out of your rank that I could not possibly insult you, even if I wanted to.'

Further on, in another passage, she wrote:

'Do not consider my words the sick rapture of a sick mind, but to me you are – perfect! I have seen you, I see you every day. For I do not judge you; not through my reason did I arrive at the thought that you are perfection; I have simply come to believe it. But I am guilty of a sin before you: I love you. After all, one should not love perfection; perfection should only be viewed as perfection, shouldn't it? And yet I am in love with you. Though love makes people equal, do not be upset, I have not placed myself on an equal level with you, not even in my most secret thought. I wrote: "do not be upset"; how could you be upset? . . . If it were possible, I would kiss the imprints of your feet. Oh, I do not put myself on an equal level with you . . . Look at the signature, quick, look at the signature!'

'I notice, however,' (she wrote in another letter) 'that I am associating him with you without having once yet asked if you love him? He fell in love with you having seen you only once. He remembered you as "a light"; those were his own words, I heard them from him. But I understood without any need for words that you are a light for him. I lived beside him for a whole month and understood then that you also love him; for me, you and he are the same.'

'What is this?' (she writes again) 'Yesterday I walked past you, and you seemed to blush? It cannot be, I must have imagined it. Even if one were to take you into the filthiest den of thieves and show you vice revealed, you could not blush; you could not possibly be angry because of an insult. You can hate all those who are vile and base, but not for yourself, but for others, for those whom they insult. But no one could insult you. You know, I think you must even love me. For me, you are the same as for him: a radiant spirit; an angel cannot hate, it cannot help loving. Can one love everyone, all human beings, all one's neighbours? I have often asked myself that question. Of course not, and it would even be unnatural. In an abstract love of humanity it is nearly always only oneself whom one loves. But for us that is impossible, while you are a different matter: how could you not love anyone at all, when you cannot compare yourself to anyone, and when you are above all insult, above all personal anger? You alone can love without egoism, you alone can love not for your own sake, but for the sake of the one whom you love. Oh, how bitter it would be for me to learn that you feel shame or anger because of me! That would be your downfall: you would at once be on an equal level with me . . .

'Yesterday, after meeting you, I came home and devised a painting. Artists always paint Christ according to the gospel legends; I would paint him differently: I would depict him alone – after all, his disciples did leave him alone sometimes. I would leave with him only one small child. The child is playing beside him; perhaps telling him some story in his childish language. Christ is listening to him, but now falls into reflection; his hand remains unconsciously, forgetfully, on the child's radiant little head. He is looking into the distance, at the horizon; a thought as enormous as the whole world rests in his gaze; his face is sad. The child has fallen silent, rests his elbows on his knees, and, propping his cheek in his hand, raises his head and reflectively, as children sometimes reflect, looks at him with an intent gaze. The sun is setting . . . That is my painting! You are innocent, and in your innocence lies all your perfection. Oh, just remember that! What do you care about my passion for you? You are mine now, all my life I will be near you . . . I shall soon be dead.'

Finally, in the very last letter, she wrote:

'For God's sake do not worry about me; do not think, either, that I am abasing myself by writing to you like this, or that I am one of those creatures that enjoy abasing themselves, even though they do it out of pride. No, I have my consolations; but it is hard for me to explain that to you. It would even be hard for me to say it clearly to myself, though I suffer torment because of it. But I know that I cannot abase myself even in a fit of pride. And of self-abasement I am incapable, because of the purity of my heart. So, therefore, I am not abasing myself at all.

'Why do I want to unite the two of you: is it for you or for myself? For myself, of course, it would bring the solution to all my difficulties, I told myself that long ago . . . I heard that your sister, Adelaida, said of my portrait one day that with such beauty one could turn the world upside down. But I have renounced the world; do you find it comical to hear that from me, meeting me in lace and diamonds, with drunkards and scoundrels? Don't pay any attention to that, I hardly exist any more, and I know it; God knows what lives in me instead of me. I read it every day in two dreadful eyes that constantly look at me, even when they are not before me. Those eyes are *silent* now (they are always silent), but I know their secret. His house is dark and tedious, and there is a secret in it. I am certain that hidden in a drawer he has a razor wrapped in silk, like that Moscow murderer; he also lived in the same house as his mother and also bound a razor in silk, to cut someone's throat. All the time I was in their house it seemed to me that somewhere, under a floor-board, by his father, perhaps, was hidden a corpse, covered with an oilcloth, like that Moscow fellow, and also surrounded by bottles of Zhdanov fluid,[1] I could even show you the spot. He keeps his silence; but I know he loves me so much that he cannot possibly prevent himself from hating me. Your wedding and my wedding – together: that is what he and I have arranged. I have no secrets from him. I would kill him out of fear . . . But he will kill me first . . . he began to laugh just now and said I was raving; he knows that I am writing to you.'

And there was much, much more of the same kind of delirium

in those letters. One of them, the second, was on two sheets of closely written, large format notepaper.

At last the prince left the sombre park, in which he had been wandering for a long time, as he had done yesterday. The light, transparent night seemed even lighter than usual; 'is it really still so early?' he thought. (He had forgotten to take his watch.) Somewhere he thought he heard distant music: 'it must be in the pleasure gardens,' he thought again, 'they haven't gone there today, of course.' Having grasped this, he saw that he was standing right outside their dacha; he had known that in the end he would be bound to finish here, and, with sinking heart, stepped on to the veranda. No one came to greet him, and the veranda was deserted. He waited for a moment and opened the door into the drawing room. 'They've never kept this door locked,' flashed through his head, but the drawing room was also deserted; it was almost completely dark there. He stood in the middle of the room, perplexed. Suddenly a door opened and Alexandra Ivanovna came in, holding a candle. Seeing the prince, she was surprised, and stopped before him, as though asking a question. Evidently, she was merely passing through the room, from one door to another, certainly not expecting to find anyone there.

'How did you get in here?' she said quietly, at last.

'I . . . dropped by . . .'

'*Maman* is not quite well, and neither is Aglaya. Adelaida is going to bed, and I am, too. We've been at home alone all evening. Papa and the Prince are in St Petersburg.'

'I've come . . . I've come to see you . . . now . . .'

'Do you know what time it is?'

'N-no . . .'

'It's half-past twelve. We always go to bed at one.'

'Oh, I thought it was . . . half-past nine.'

'It doesn't matter!' she began to laugh. 'But why didn't you come earlier? They were probably expecting you.'

'I . . . thought . . .' he mouthed, as he walked away.

'*Au revoir*! Tomorrow I'll make them all laugh.'

He walked along the road that skirted the park, to his dacha. His heart was thumping, his thoughts were in a muddle, and everything around him seemed like a dream. And suddenly, just as before, when on both occasions he had woken from the same apparition, that apparition appeared to him again. That woman walked out of the park and stood before him, as though she had been waiting for him here. He shuddered and stopped; she seized his hand and pressed it hard. 'No, this is not an apparition!'

And here, at last, she stood before him face to face, for the first time since they had parted; she was saying something to him, but he gazed at her in silence; his heart overflowed and began to ache with pain. Oh, never afterwards was he able to forget this meeting with her and always remembered it with the same pain. She sank to her knees before him, right there in the street, like one demented; he stepped back in alarm, but she caught his hand in order to kiss it, and, just as before, in his dream, tears now shone on her long eyelashes.

'Get up, get up!' he said in a frightened whisper, trying to make her rise. 'Get up, quickly!'

'Are you happy? Happy?' she kept asking. 'Just tell me one thing, are you happy now? Today, right now? With her? What did she say?'

She did not rise, she did not listen to him; she questioned him in a hurry, and hurried to speak, as though she were being pursued.

'I'm going tomorrow, as you told me to. I shall not . . . I mean, I'm seeing you for the last time, the last! Now, this is the very last time!'

'Calm yourself, get up!' he said quietly in despair.

She scrutinized him avidly, seizing his hands.

'Farewell!' she said at last, got up and quickly walked away from him, almost running. The prince saw Rogozhin suddenly appear at her side, grip her by the arm and lead her away.

'Wait, Prince,' cried Rogozhin, 'I'll be back in five minutes.'

Five minutes later he really did come back; the prince was waiting for him in the same place.

'I've put her in the carriage,' he said. 'There's been a barouche waiting on the corner there since ten o'clock. She had a feeling that you'd spend the whole evening with the other one. I told her in detail the things you wrote to me earlier. She won't write to the other one any more; she's promised; and, in accordance with your wishes, she'll be leaving here tomorrow. She wanted to see you, for the last time, even though you refused; we've been waiting right here at this spot for you to come back, look, over there, on that bench.'

'She took you with her herself?'

'So what?' Rogozhin grinned. 'I saw what I knew to be true. You've read the letters, evidently?'

'Have you really read them?' asked the prince, shocked by this thought.

'You bet I have; she showed me all the letters herself. Do you remember the part about the razor, heh-heh!'

'She's insane!' exclaimed the prince, wringing his hands.

'Who knows, perhaps she isn't,' Rogozhin said quietly, as if to himself.

The prince did not reply.

'Well, goodbye,' said Rogozhin. 'I mean, I'm going tomorrow, too; don't hold it against me! But listen, brother,' he added, quickly turning round. 'Why didn't you answer her question? "Are you happy, or aren't you?"'

'No, no, no!' exclaimed the prince, with boundless sorrow.

'I didn't think you'd say "yes"!' Rogozhin laughed maliciously, and left without looking back.

PART FOUR

I

About a week had passed since the meeting of two characters from our story on the green bench. One bright morning, at about half-past ten, Varvara Ardalionovna Ptitsyna, who had gone out to visit some friends, returned home in great and sorrowful reflection.

There are people of whom it is difficult to say something that would present them at once and entirely, in their most typical and characteristic aspect; they are those people who are usually called 'ordinary', 'the majority', and who really do constitute the overwhelming majority of any society. In their novels and stories, writers mostly try to select social types and to present them vividly and pictorially – types who are extremely seldom encountered in reality as a whole, but who are none the less almost more real than reality itself. Podkolyosin[1] in his typical aspect is, perhaps, even an exaggeration, but he is by no means an empty fiction. How many intelligent people, learning about Podkolyosin from Gogol, at once began to discover that dozens, indeed hundreds of their good friends and acquaintances were terribly like Podkolyosin? Even before Gogol came along, they had known that these friends were like Podkolyosin; it was merely that they didn't yet know this was their name. In reality, bridegrooms very seldom jump out of windows just before their wedding, because, not to mention other drawbacks, it is rather an awkward thing to do; none the less, how many bridegrooms, even worthy and intelligent men, have been ready to admit just before going to the altar that in the depths of their conscience they are Podkolyosins. And not all husbands cry at every step: '*Tu l'as voulu, Georges Dandin!*'[2] But good heavens, how many millions and billions of times has this *cri de cœur* been echoed by husbands the world over after their honeymoon, or, who knows, even on the day after their wedding?

And so, without entering upon more serious explanations, we shall merely say that in reality the typical qualities of human beings are, as it were, watered down, and all these Georges Dandins and Podkolyosins really do exist, hurrying and scurrying before us daily, though in a somewhat diluted condition. With the reservation, finally, that the whole of Georges Dandin in his entirety, as Molière created him, may also be encountered in reality, though rarely, we shall now conclude our argument, which is beginning to resemble a critical review in a journal. None the less, we are still faced with the question: what is the novelist to do with people who are commonplace, completely 'ordinary', and how are they to be presented to the reader so as to make them at least somewhat interesting? It is simply not possible to avoid them altogether in the narrative, for ordinary people are always, and overwhelmingly, an essential link in the chain of everyday events; thus, by avoiding them, we upset the realm of the plausible. To fill novels solely with types or even simply, for interest's sake, with strange and imaginary people would be implausible, and indeed uninteresting. In our opinion, a writer ought to try to find interesting and instructive nuances even among the ordinary. When, for example, the very essence of certain ordinary characters consists precisely in their habitual and invariable ordinariness or, even better, when, in spite of all the extreme efforts of these characters to emerge at all costs from the rut of custom and routine, they still end up remaining invariably and eternally bound to routine, then such characters even acquire a kind of typicality of their own – an ordinariness that is on no account willing to remain what it is, and wants at all costs to become original and independent, while not possessing the slightest means of independence.

Also belonging to this category of 'commonplace' or 'ordinary' people are some of the characters of our narrative, who have so far (I admit) been insufficiently explained to the reader.

Such, in particular, are Varvara Ardalionovna Ptitsyna, her spouse Mr Ptitsyn and Gavrila Ardalionovich, her brother.

Indeed, there is nothing more vexing, for example, than to be wealthy, of decent family, of decent appearance, not badly educated, not stupid, even kind-hearted, and at the same time to possess no talent, no special quality, nor even any eccentricity, not a single idea of one's own, to be decidedly 'just like everyone else'. Wealth, perhaps, but not the wealth of a Rothschild; an honourable family, but not one that has ever distinguished itself in any way; a decent appearance, but really not very expressive; a decent education, but no idea about how to put it to use; intelligence, but an absence of *one's own ideas*; a heart, but a lack of generosity, etcetera, etcetera, in every respect. There is an extremely large number of such people in the world, and even far more than it may seem; they are divided, like all human beings, into two main categories: those who are limited and those who are 'far more intelligent'. The first category is the happier one. For the limited 'ordinary' person there is, for example, nothing easier than to imagine himself to be an unusual and original person, and to take enjoyment in this without hesitation. Some of our young ladies need only have their hair cut short, put on blue spectacles and call themselves nihilists in order to be instantly persuaded that, having donned the spectacles, they have at once begun to possess their own 'convictions'. Some men need only feel a drop of some universally human and good-natured feeling within their hearts in order to be instantly persuaded that no one feels as they do, that they are in the vanguard of public enlightenment. Others need only accept some idea by word of mouth or read a page of something without beginning or end in order instantly to believe that this is 'their own idea' and has been conceived within their own brains. In such cases, the insolence of naivety, if one may be permitted to express it thus, attains an astonishing dimension; it is all of it incredible, but is constantly encountered. This insolence of naivety, this undoubting trust the stupid man has in himself and in his own talent, is splendidly presented by Gogol in the remarkable type of Lieutenant Pirogov.[3] Pirogov does not even doubt that he is a genius, even superior to any genius; so little does he doubt that he never once asks himself any question about it; as a matter of fact, questions do not exist for him. In the end, the great writer was forced to give him a thrashing in order to satisfy the outraged moral sensibilities of his readers, but seeing that the great man merely shook himself and ate a cream pie to fortify himself after his ordeal, he simply threw up his hands in amazement and walked out on his readers. I have always mourned the fact that Gogol bestowed such a lowly rank on the great Pirogov, for Pirogov is so self-satisfied that, as the epaulettes thicken and spiral on him with age and promotion, he finds nothing easier than to imagine himself a commander-in-chief; and not even imagine it, but simply not doubt it at all: if he were to be made a general, then why not a commander-in-chief? And how many such men later commit dreadful blunders on the battlefield? And how many Pirogovs have there been among our littérateurs, our scholars and propagandists? I say 'have been', but, of course, they exist even now . . .

One of the dramatis personae of our narrative, Gavrila Ardalionovich Ivolgin, belonged to the second category; he belonged to the category of men who are 'far more intelligent', though completely inflamed, from head to toe, with the desire to be original. As we noted above, however, this category is far more unhappy than the first. The fact of the matter is that the *intelligent* ordinary man, even though he may imagine himself in passing (and, indeed, throughout the whole of his life) to be a man of genius, and most original, none the less retains within his heart a worm of doubt, which sometimes leads to the intelligent man ending in total despair; for if he submits, it is not until he has been entirely poisoned by a vanity that has been driven inward. However, we have in any case taken an extreme instance: for the overwhelming majority of this *intelligent* category of men, matters do not proceed at all so tragically; their livers may deteriorate towards the sunset of their lives, perhaps, but that is all. Even so, before surrendering and resigning themselves, these men sometimes continue to play the fool for an extremely long time, all the way from their youth to the age of submission, and all from a desire to be original. Strange instances are even encountered: from a desire for originality an honest man may be prepared to resolve upon a base action; it sometimes even happens that one of these unfortunates is not only honest, but is kind, the Provider of his household, maintaining and nourishing by his toils not only his own family, but others, too, and what do we see? All through his life he can have no rest! For him, the thought that he has performed his duties as a human being so well is not at all a calming or a consoling one; even the contrary – it is this thought that irritates him: 'This,' he says, 'is what I have wasted all my life on, this is what has bound me hand and foot, this is what has prevented me from discovering gunpowder! Had it not been for this, I would certainly have discovered either gunpowder or America – I don't really know which, but I would certainly have discovered one of them!' Most typical of all for these gentlemen is that throughout their lives they can never ascertain for certain just what it is they need to discover and just what it is that, all their lives, they are on the point of discovering: gunpowder or America? While their sufferings, their longing for discovery, would truly have been enough for Columbus or Galileo.

Gavrila Ardalionovich was making some beginnings along these lines; but so far they were only beginnings. For a long time yet he would go on playing his pranks. A deep and uninterrupted awareness of his own lack of talent and, at the same time, an irresistible desire to be persuaded that he was a man of the greatest independence of mind had badly wounded his heart, almost since his boyhood. He was a young man with envious and impetuous desires and, it appeared, someone who had been born with over-excited nerves. The impetuous quality of these desires he took to be their strength. In his passionate desire to excel, he was sometimes ready to take the most reckless leap; but no sooner had the matter gone as far as that reckless leap than our hero always turned out to be too intelligent to take it. This mortified him. He might even possibly have resolved, had the occasion offered itself, to commit some extremely base action, just in order to attain something of his dream: but, as if on purpose, as soon as he got to the point, he always turned out to be too honest to commit a really base action. (He was,

however, always ready to agree to an act of lesser baseness.) It
was with revulsion and hatred that he viewed the poverty and
decline of his household. He treated even his mother in a condescending, contemptuous manner, in spite of the fact that he
himself understood very well that his mother's reputation and
character were, for the time being, the principal support of his
career. On starting work in General Yepanchin's office, he
immediately said to himself: 'If I'm to act like a villain, then I
might as well act like a villain in every respect, as long as it does
me some good,' and – almost never acted like a villain in every
respect. And indeed, why did he imagine he had to act like a
villain? As for Aglaya, at the time he had simply been afraid of
her, but did not curtail his attentions, protracted them, just in
case, though he never seriously believed that she would ever
yield to him. Later, during his episode with Nastasya Filippovna,
he suddenly imagined that *everything* could be attained by
means of money. 'If I'm to act like a villain, then I should act
like a villain,' he kept repeating to himself every day with the
same self-satisfaction, but also with a certain amount of fear: 'If
I'm to act like a villain, then I really might as well take it to the
limit,' he kept encouraging himself. 'In such cases the routine,
run-of-the-mill fellow gets cold feet, but that's not going to
happen to us!' On losing Aglaya, crushed by circumstances, he
fell into very low spirits and actually returned to the prince the
money that had been thrown to him that day by the madwoman,
to whom it had likewise been given by a madman. Later he
regretted this return of the money a thousand times, though he
constantly indulged in vain boasting about it. He actually wept
for three days, while the prince was in St Petersburg, but during
those three days he also managed to conceive a hatred of the
prince for regarding him with too much compassion, while his
return of the money was something that 'not everyone could
have brought himself to do'. But the noble confession that all
his anguish was nothing but perpetually crushed vanity caused
him horrible torment. Only a long time later did he take a good
look round and realize what a serious turning matters might
have taken for him with a creature as strange and innocent as
Aglaya. Remorse gnawed at him; he relinquished his post and

sank into anguish and despondency. He was living at Ptitsyn's, supported by him, with his father and mother, and openly despised Ptitsyn, though at the same time listened to his advice and had sufficient sense almost always to ask for it. Gavrila Ardalionovich was angry, for example, that Ptitsyn had no plans to become a Rothschild, and that he did not even set himself this goal. 'If you're a money-lender, then take it to its limits, squeeze people, make a mint of money out of them, be a man of character, be a King of the Jews!' Ptitsyn was modest and quiet; he merely smiled, but on one occasion considered it necessary to have a serious talk with Ganya, and even did so with a certain dignity. He pointed out to Ganya that he was doing nothing dishonest and that Ganya should not call him a Yid; that if money had such a high price, it was not his, Ptitsyn's, fault; that he was acting truthfully and honestly and, in reality, was only an agent in 'these' matters, and, at last, that thanks to his punctilious ways of doing business he was already well known, in a most positive sense, to the most eminent people, and his business was expanding. 'I shall never be a Rothschild, and I have no reason to be one,' he added, laughing, 'but I'll have a house on Liteinaya, perhaps even two, and I'll make do with that.' 'Though who knows, perhaps I'll even have three houses!' he thought to himself, but never said this aloud, and concealed the dream. Nature loves and fawns upon such people: it will probably reward Ptitsyn with not three but four houses, and all because he already knew from childhood that he would never be a Rothschild. On the other hand, however, nature will certainly not go beyond four houses, and in Ptitsyn's case that is where the matter will end.

Gavrila Ardalionovich's sister was quite a different sort of person. She too had powerful desires, but they were more stubborn than impetuous. She had a great deal of common sense when matters reached a head, nor did it abandon her before that point was reached. True, she too was one of those 'ordinary' people who dream of being original, but on the other hand she very soon came to realize that there was not a single drop of any particular originality in her, and was not too upset about it – who could tell, perhaps because of an odd sort of pride. She had taken her first practical step with great determination by marrying Mr Ptitsyn; but, in doing so, she never once said to herself: 'If I'm to act like a villain, then I might as well really act like a villain, just as long as I reach my goal', as Gavrila Ardalionovich would not have failed to put it in such a case (and very nearly did so even in her presence, when as her elder brother he had uttered his approval of her decision). Even quite the contrary: Varvara Ardalionovna got married after making thoroughly sure that her future husband was a modest, pleasant, almost progressively educated man who would never commit any major act of vileness. With regard to minor acts of vileness, Varvara Ardalionovna did not inquire, viewing them as trifles; where were such trifles not to be found? She was not in search of the ideal, after all! What was more, she knew that by marrying she was also providing a corner for her mother, father and brothers. Seeing her brother in misery, she felt like helping him, in spite of all their earlier domestic perplexities. Ptitsyn would sometimes urge Ganya, in a friendly way, of course, to join the civil service. 'Here you sit despising generals and their rank,' he would sometimes say to him jokingly, 'but just watch, all of "them" will end as generals in their turn; if you live that long, you'll see.' 'But where do they get the idea that I despise generals and their rank?' he would think to himself sarcastically. In order to help her brother, Varvara Ardalionovna determined to widen the circle of her actions: she ingratiated herself with the Yepanchins, something in which she was aided by her childhood memories: both she and her brother had played with the Yepanchins as children. Let us observe here that if, in visiting the Yepanchins, Varvara Ardalionovna had been pursuing some unusual dream, she might perhaps have instantly left behind the category of people in which she included herself; but she was not doing so; indeed, what was involved here was in fact a rather considerable degree of calculation on her part: she took her bearings from the character of this family. As for Aglaya's character, she studied it untiringly. She made it her task to bring them both, her brother and Aglaya, back together again. Perhaps she really did achieve something; perhaps she also fell into errors, relying, for example, too much on her brother and expecting from him things he could never by any stretch of the imagination have provided. At any rate, she acted rather skilfully at the Yepanchins: did not mention her brother for weeks, was always exceedingly truthful and sincere, conducted herself simply, but with dignity. As for the depths of her conscience, she was not afraid to look into them and did not reproach herself for anything at all. It was this that gave her strength. Only sometimes did she notice that she lost her temper, perhaps, that she had a great deal of personal pride and even crushed vanity; she noticed this at certain moments, in particular almost every time she left the Yepanchins.

And now here she was returning from their house, as we have already said, in sorrowful reflection. This sorrow also contained elements of some bitter and mocking kind. Ptitsyn was living in Pavlovsk, in an unprepossessing but spacious wooden house that stood on a dusty street, and would soon pass into his full ownership, with the result that he was already, in his turn, beginning to sell it to someone. As she climbed the front steps, Varvara Ardalionovna heard an extraordinary din coming from the top of the house and discerned the shouting voices of her brother and Papa. Entering the drawing room and seeing Ganya pacing to and fro about the room, pale with rabid fury, and almost tearing his hair out, she frowned and sank with a weary look on to a sofa, not removing her hat. Very well aware that if she said nothing more for a minute or so and did not ask her brother why he was pacing about so furiously, he would certainly lose his temper, Varya hurried, at last, to articulate in the form of a question:

'Still the same as before?'

'What do you mean?' exclaimed Ganya. 'The same as before? No, the devil knows what's happening now, but it's not the same as before! The old man's started foaming at the mouth . . . mother's bawling. I swear to God, Varya, say what you want, but I'll kick him out of the house or . . . or leave myself,' he added, probably in recollection of the fact that one cannot really kick people out of someone else's house.

'You have to make allowances,' muttered Varya.

'Allowances for what? For whom?' Ganya flared up. 'For his

loathsome tricks? No, I don't care what you say, but this is impossible. Impossible, impossible, impossible! And his behaviour: he's the one at fault, and yet he swaggers even more! "I can't be bothered to use the gate, take the fence down! . . ." Why are you sitting there like that? You look terrible!'

'I look the way I always do,' Varya replied with displeasure.

Ganya cast a more intent glance at her.

'Have you been there?' he asked suddenly.

'Yes.'

'Listen, they're shouting again! How shameful, and at a time like this!'

'What time? There's nothing special about it.'

'Have you discovered anything?'

'Nothing that wasn't expected, at any rate. I discovered that it's all true. My husband was closer to the truth than either of us; as he predicted right from the start, so it's turned out. Where is he?'

'He's not in. What's turned out?'

'The prince is the official fiancé, the matter is decided. The elder sisters told me. Aglaya has given her consent; they've even stopped trying to conceal it. (I mean, there's been so much secretiveness until now.) Adelaida's wedding has been delayed again, so that both weddings can be held together, on the same day – such poetry! Just like verses. Why don't you write some wedding verses, rather than waste your time pacing about the room like that? This evening Belokonskaya will be at their house; she's come for the occasion; there'll be guests. He'll be presented to Belokonskaya, though he knows her already; I think they're going to make an announcement. The only thing they're afraid of is that he'll drop or break something in front of all the guests when she comes in, or fall down; that's the sort of thing he might do.'

Ganya listened to what she had to say with great attention, but, to his sister's surprise, this shattering news seemed not to shatter him very much at all.

'Well, I suppose we had that coming,' he said, having thought for a bit. 'So that's the end of it, then!' he added with a strange, ironic smile, slyly watching his sister's face and continuing to move to and fro about the room, though far more slowly now.

'Good that you can take it like a philosopher; I'm truly glad,' said Varya.

'It's a weight off one's shoulders; off yours, at any rate.'

'I think I've served you sincerely, without arguing and without making a nuisance of myself; I haven't ever asked you what sort of happiness you intended to seek with Aglaya.'

'Was I seeking . . . happiness with Aglaya?'

'Oh, please don't embark on philosophy! Of course you were. Of course, we've endured enough: been made fools of. I will confess to you that I've never been able to take this matter seriously; only got involved in it "just in case", relying on her absurd character, but mainly in order to please you; it was ninety per cent likely to come to nothing. I still to this day don't know what you were trying to achieve.'

'Now you and your husband will hound me into the civil service; you'll read me lectures about tenacity and will-power, not ignoring small mercies and so forth, I know it all by heart,' Ganya began to laugh.

'He has some new plan on his mind!' thought Varya.

'How is it over there – are they pleased, the parents?' Ganya asked suddenly.

'N-no, I don't think they are. Though actually, you may draw your own conclusions; Ivan Fyodorovich is pleased; the mother is afraid; even earlier, she looked on him with revulsion as a fiancé, everyone knows that.'

'That's not what I meant; he's impossible and unthinkable as a fiancé, that's clear. I'm asking about what's happening now, what are things like over there now? Has she given her formal consent?'

'She hasn't said "no" yet – that's all; but that couldn't be any different. You know how extraordinarily shy and bashful she is: as a child she used to creep into a cupboard and stay there for two or three hours at a time, just so as not to meet the guests; she's grown up into a hulking great girl, but I mean, she's just the same even now. You know, I somehow think there really is something serious there, even on her part. They say she laughs at the prince from morning to night as hard as she can, so as not to let on, but she probably manages to say something to him every day on the sly, for he positively walks on air, glows . . . They say he's dreadfully absurd. I've even heard it from them. I also fancied that they were laughing at me to my face, the older ones.'

At length, Ganya began to frown; Varya was probably expatiating on this subject deliberately, in order to find out what he really thought. But again there was shouting from upstairs.

'I'll throw him out!' Ganya shouted, as though glad to vent his exasperation.

'And then he'll go round all the houses, dragging us into disgrace, like yesterday.'

'What – what do you mean? What do you mean: like yesterday? Did he . . .' Ganya said suddenly in horrible alarm.

'Oh, good heavens, don't you know?' Varya collected herself.

'What . . . you don't mean he was over there?' exclaimed Ganya, blazing with shame and rabid fury. 'Good God, but you've come from there! Did you discover anything? Was the old man there? Was he there or wasn't he?'

And Ganya rushed to the door; Varya hurled herself at him and seized him with both hands.

'What are you doing? Where are you going?' she said. 'If you let him out of the house now he'll do something even worse, he'll go and see everyone! . . .'

'What did he do there? What did he say?'

'Oh, they couldn't tell me, they didn't understand what he said; he just frightened them all. He went to see Ivan Fyodorovich, but he wasn't at home; demanded to see Lizaveta Prokofyevna. Began by asking her for a job, working in the office there, and then began to complain about us, about me, my husband, you especially . . . he said a great many things.'

'Couldn't you find out?' Ganya trembled, almost hysterically.

'But how could I? He himself hardly knew what he was saying, and perhaps they didn't tell me it all.'

Ganya clutched at his head and ran to the window; Varya sat down by the other window.

'Aglaya's ridiculous,' she observed suddenly. 'She stopped me and said: "Please give your parents my special, personal regards;

I shall probably find an opportunity to meet your father in a few days' time." And she said it so seriously. Dreadfully strange . . .'

'Wasn't she mocking? Wasn't she?'

'That's the whole thing, she wasn't; that's what makes it so strange.'

'Does she know about the old man or doesn't she, what do you suppose?'

'I have no doubt at all that they know nothing at the house; but you've given me an idea: perhaps Aglaya does know. She alone knows, for her sisters were also surprised when she asked me to give her greetings to my father. And why precisely to him? If she knows, then the prince must have told her!'

'It's not hard to guess who told her! A thief! That's all we needed. A thief in our own family, "the head of the family".'

'Oh, that's rubbish!' cried Varya, completely losing her temper. 'A drunken escapade, nothing more. And who thought it up? Lebedev, the prince . . . they're fine ones to talk, surely; towering intellects both. I wouldn't buy their stories for the price of a table-leg!'

'The old man's a thief and a drunkard,' Ganya continued biliously, 'I'm a beggar, my sister's husband's a money-lender – a fat lot for Aglaya to covet, and no mistake! Very nice, I must say!'

'That sister's husband, the money-lender, is your . . .'

'Provider, is it? Please don't stand upon ceremony . . .'

'What are you so angry for?' Varya collected herself. 'You don't understand anything, you're like a schoolboy. Do you think all this will have damaged you in Aglaya's eyes? You don't know what she's like; she'd reject the most peerless of fiancés, and happily run away and starve to death with some student in a garret – that's her dream! You've never been able to understand how interesting you'd have become in her eyes if you'd managed to endure your surroundings with firmness and pride. The prince caught her on his hook because, for one thing, he wasn't trying to catch her at all, and secondly, because everyone thinks he's an idiot. The very fact that she upsets her family because of him – that's what she likes now. A-ach, you don't understand anything!'

'Well, we'll see whether I understand or not,' Ganya muttered enigmatically. 'Only I wouldn't like her to find out about the old man. I thought the prince would restrain himself, and not tell her. He also held Lebedev in check; he wouldn't even tell me everything when I pressed him . . .'

'So you can see for yourself that it's not only him, everyone knows. And what do you want now? What do you hope for? Why, even if there was any hope left, this would just lend you an air of martyrdom in her eyes.'

'Well, she'd also be afraid of a scandal, in spite of all the romanticism. Everything up to a certain limit, and everyone up to a certain limit, you're all the same.'

'Aglaya afraid?' Varya flared up, giving her brother a contemptuous look. 'What a base little soul you have! You don't deserve anything. Even if she is ridiculous and eccentric, she's a thousand times more noble than any of us.'

'Oh, very well, very well, don't lose your temper,' Ganya muttered again, complacently.

'It's mother I feel sorry for,' continued Varya. 'I'm afraid that this episode of father's will reach her ears, oh, I'm so afraid!'

'It probably *has* reached her ears,' observed Ganya.

Varya made to get up, in order to set off upstairs and see Nina Alexandrovna, but stopped and gave her brother an attentive look.

'But who could have told her?'

'Ippolit, it must have been. He probably considered it a first-rate satisfaction to report it to mother as soon as he moved here.'

'But how does he know, tell me, please? The prince and Lebedev decided not to tell anyone. Not even Kolya knows anything.'

'Ippolit? He found out for himself. You can't imagine what a sly creature he is; what a gossipmonger he is, what a nose he has for sniffing out anything bad, anything that savours of scandal. Well, you may believe it or not, but I'm convinced he's got Aglaya eating out of his hand! And if he hasn't, then he will. Rogozhin has also been in touch with him. How is it that the prince doesn't notice it? And now he wants to set a trap for me! He considers me his personal enemy, I saw through that long ago, and why, what is there for him in it, I mean, he's going to die – I don't understand it! But I'll put a stop to his game; you'll see, it won't be him who sets a trap for me, I'll set one for him.'

'But why did you get him to come here, if you hate him so much? And is he worth setting traps for?'

'It was you who advised me to get him to come here.'

'I thought he'd be useful; but do you know, he has also fallen in love with Aglaya, and has been writing to her? They were asking me . . . he very nearly wrote a letter to Lizaveta Prokofyevna.'

'He's not a danger in that sense!' said Ganya, beginning to laugh maliciously. 'Though there's no doubt that something is up. It's very possible that he's in love, because he's a little brat! But . . . he wouldn't write the old woman anonymous letters. He's a malicious, petty, self-satisfied mediocrity! . . . I'm convinced, I know for certain that he presented me to her as an intriguer, that was how he got started. I admit that like a fool I let the cat out of the bag to him at the beginning; I thought he'd support my interests out of pure revenge on the prince; he's such a sly creature! Oh, I've seen through him completely now. As regards that theft, he heard about it from his mother, the captain's widow. If the old man resolved to commit such a deed, he did it for the captain's widow. All of a sudden, for no apparent reason, he informed me that "the general" had promised his mother four hundred roubles, just like that, for no apparent reason, without any ceremony. At that point, I understood everything. And the way he looked me in the eye, with a kind of enjoyment; he probably also told his mother, purely for the satisfaction of breaking her heart. And why doesn't he die, tell me, if you please? I mean, he pledged himself to die in three weeks, and yet he's put on weight here! He's isn't coughing so much; he himself said last night that he hadn't coughed blood for two days . . .'

'Throw him out.'

'I don't hate him, I despise him,' Ganya said proudly. 'Well yes, yes, I suppose I do hate him, I suppose I do!' he exclaimed suddenly with particular fury. 'And I shall tell him that to his face, even when he's about to die, on his deathbed! If you'd

read his confession – my God, what naive brazenness! He's
Lieutenant Pirogov, he's Nozdrev[4] in a tragedy, but above all,
he's a little brat! Oh, with what pleasure I'd have thrashed him
then, precisely in order to give him a surprise. Now he's taking
his revenge on everyone because he didn't succeed that time . . .
But what's that? There's noise there again! But really, what on
earth is going on? I really can't stand it any more! Ptitsyn!' he
exclaimed to Ptitsyn, who was entering the room, 'what is this,
what are things coming to in our house? It's . . . it's . . .'

But the noise was rapidly coming closer, the door suddenly
flew open, and old Ivolgin, wrathful, purple, shaken, beside
himself, also lunged at Ptitsyn. The old man was followed by
Nina Alexandrovna, Kolya and, bringing up the rear, Ippolit.

2

It was now five days since Ippolit had moved into Ptitsyn's
house. This had happened more or less naturally, without many
words and without any falling-out between him and the prince;
not only did they not quarrel, but apparently they even parted
as friends. Gavrila Ardalionovich, who had been so hostile to
Ippolit at the soirée, himself came to visit him, on the third
day after the event, no less, probably guided by some sudden
thought. For some reason Rogozhin also began to visit the
patient. At first the prince thought that it might even be better
for the 'poor boy' if he were to move out of his house. But even
during his move, Ippolit was already saying that he would be
moving to Ptitsyn, 'who is so kind that he's giving me a corner
in his home', and, as if deliberately, never once said that he was
moving to Ganya's, though it was Ganya who had insisted that
he be received into the household. At the time, Ganya noticed
this, and touchily locked it away within his heart.

He was right when he told his sister that the patient was
recovering. Ippolit really did feel somewhat better than before,
and this could be seen from a first glance at him. He entered the
room in leisurely fashion, behind all the others, with a mocking

and ill-natured smile. Nina Alexandrovna entered in a state of considerable alarm. (She had changed much in the past six months, grown thinner; having given her daughter away in marriage and moved in to live with her, she had almost stopped involving herself outwardly in the affairs of her children.) Kolya was worried, and seemed somewhat perplexed; there was of course much that he did not understand about 'the general's madness', as he put it, as he did not know the particular reasons for this fresh turmoil in the house. But it was clear to him that his father was now becoming so involved in squabbles, at every hour and in every place, and had suddenly changed so much, that it was as if he had become quite a different person from before. It also made him uneasy that during the past three days the old man had even quite given up drinking. He knew that his father had parted company with Lebedev and the prince, and had even quarrelled with them. Kolya had just returned to the house with a half-*shtof* of vodka, acquired with his own money.

'Truly, Mama,' he had already assured Nina Alexandrovna upstairs, 'truly, it's better for him to have a drink. It's three days since he touched it; so he must be miserable. Truly, it's better; I used to bring it to him when he was in the debtors' prison . . .'

The general opened the door so violently that it nearly flew off its hinges, and stood on the threshold, almost quivering with indignation.

'My dear sir!' he began to shout at Ptitsyn in a thunderous voice. 'If you have really decided to sacrifice your own father, or at least the father of your wife, a man who has distinguished himself in the service of his sovereign, to a milksop and atheist, then I shall cease to set foot in your house from this time on. You must choose, sir, and choose immediately: either me or this . . . screw! Yes, screw! It slipped out of my mouth, but he's – a screw! For he bores into my soul like a screw, and without any respect . . . like a screw!'

'Not a corkscrew?' Ippolit put in.

'No, not a corkscrew, for you see before you a general, not a bottle. I have medals, medals of distinction. . .and you have not a fig. Either he or I, sir! You must decide right now, this very moment!' he shouted again at Ptitsyn in a frenzy. At this point Kolya brought up a chair for him, and he subsided on to it almost in exhaustion.

'Really, it would be better if you . . . took a nap,' the dumbfounded Ptitsyn began to mutter.

'He's still making threats!' Ganya said to his sister in a half whisper.

'A nap?' cried the general. 'I am not drunk, my dear sir, and you are insulting me. I see,' he continued, getting to his feet again, 'I see that everyone here is against me, everything and everyone. Enough! I am going away . . . But I'll have you know, my dear sir, I'll have you know . . .'

They did not let him finish and sat him down again, began entreating him to calm himself. Ganya went off to a corner in a fury. Nina Alexandrovna trembled and wept.

'But what have I done to him? What's he complaining about?' exclaimed Ippolit, baring his teeth in a grin.

'I suppose you think you've done nothing?' Nina Alexandrovna observed suddenly. 'You are the one who ought to be particularly ashamed . . . of tormenting the old man in such an inhuman fashion . . . and in your position, too . . .'

'For one thing, what is my position, madam? I respect you very much, you in particular, personally, but . . .'

'He's a screw!' shouted the general. 'He bores into my soul and heart! He wants me to believe in atheism! I'll have you know, milksop, that I was showered with honours before you were even born; but you are just an envious worm, torn in half, with a cough . . . and dying of malice and unbelief . . . And why has Gavrila brought you here? Everyone is against me, from strangers to my own son!'

'Oh, that will do, now he's playing his tragedy!' cried Ganya. 'Things might be a bit better if you'd stop disgracing us all over town!'

'What, I disgrace you, milksop? You? I can only bring you honour, not dishonour you!'

He leaped to his feet, and this time could not be restrained; but Gavrila Ardalionovich had also plainly thrown caution to the winds.

'Get out of here with your talk about honour!' he cried with malice.

'What did you say?' the general boomed, turning pale and taking a step towards him.

'That I have only to open my mouth for . . .' Ganya howled suddenly, but did not finish. Both stood facing each other, extremely shaken, especially Ganya.

'Ganya, stop it!' cried Nina Alexandrovna, rushing forward to restrain her son.

'A lot of nonsense, on every side!' snapped Varya angrily. 'That will do, Mama,' she said, seizing her.

'I spare him only for mother's sake,' Ganya announced in a tragic tone.

'Speak!' roared the general in a perfect frenzy. 'Speak, on pain of a father's curse . . . speak!'

'Well now, your curse, you really frighten me with that! And who's to blame for the fact that you've been going around like a madman for eight days now? Eight days, you see, I've been keeping count . . . Just mind you don't drive me to the limit: I'll say it all . . . Why did you drag yourself to the Yepanchins yesterday? And he calls himself the old man, the grey hair, the paterfamilias! Very fine, I must say!'

'Be quiet, Ganka!' shouted Kolya. 'Be quiet, you fool!'

'But what about me, how have I insulted him?' insisted Ippolit, but still, as it were, in the same mocking tone. 'Why does he call me a screw, you heard him? He was the one who pestered me; arrived just now and started talking about some Captain Yeropegov. I've absolutely no desire for your company, General; I've avoided it before, as you well know. What do I care about your Captain Yeropegov, come now, admit it! I didn't come all the way here for Captain Yeropegov. I merely expressed aloud to him my opinion that perhaps this Captain Yeropegov never existed at all. Then he let all hell break loose.'

'He never existed, beyond any shadow of doubt!' snapped Ganya.

But the general stood like a man dumbfounded, and merely gazed around him senselessly. His son's words had shocked him with their exceeding frankness. For a moment or two he was even unable to find any words. And, at last, only when Ippolit burst into laughter at Ganya's reply and shouted: 'Well, there you are, you heard him, even your own son says Captain Yeropegov didn't exist!' the old man babbled, utterly disconcerted:

'Kapiton Yeropegov, not Captain . . . Kapiton . . . retired lieutenant-colonel, Yeropegov . . . Kapiton.'

'And there wasn't any Kapiton, either!' Ganya had completely lost his temper now.

'Wh . . . what do you mean there wasn't?' muttered the general, and the colour rushed to his face.

'Oh, that's enough!' Ptitsyn and Varya tried to calm them.

'Shut up, Ganka!' Kolya cried again.

But the intervention seemed to jog the general's memory.

'What do you mean, there wasn't? How could he not have existed?' he assailed his son threateningly.

'Because he didn't. He didn't exist, and that's that, and it's quite impossible! There. Back off, I tell you.'

'And this is my son . . . this is my own son, whom I . . . Oh Lord! Yeropegov, Yeroshka Yeropegov didn't exist!'

'There, first it's Kapitoshka, and now it's Yeroshka!' Ippolit put in, turning the screw.

'Kapitoshka, sir, Kapitoshka, not Yeroshka! Kapiton, Kapitan Alexeyevich, Kapiton, rather . . . lieutenant-colonel . . . retired . . . married Marya . . . Marya Petrovna Su . . . Su . . . friend and companion-at-arms . . . Sutugova, all the way, even from the time we were cadets. I shed my blood for him . . . deflected the bullet . . . but he was killed. Wasn't any Kapitoshka Yeropegov, indeed! Didn't exist!'

The general was shouting excitedly, but in such a way that one might have supposed the matter concerned one thing, and the shouting another. To be sure, on another occasion he would, of course, have endured things far more offensive than the news of the complete non-existence of Kapiton Yeropegov, would have shouted, caused a scene, been beside himself with rage, but even so, in the end he would have retired upstairs to his room to take a nap. But now, because of the exceeding strangeness of the human heart, it so transpired that it was precisely an insult such as the doubt in the existence of Yeropegov that was destined to fill the cup to overflowing. The old man turned pale, raised his arms, and shouted:

'Enough! My curse ... away from this house! Kolya, fetch my bag, I'm going ... away!'

He went out, hurrying and in a state of exceeding wrath. After him rushed Nina Alexandrovna, Kolya and Ptitsyn.

'Well, what have you done now?' said Varya to her brother. 'He's probably going to go trailing over there again. The disgrace, the disgrace!'

'And don't go thieving!' cried Ganya, almost choking with fury; suddenly his gaze encountered Ippolit; Ganya almost began to shake. 'And you, my dear sir,' he cried, 'ought to remember that you are, after all, in someone else's house, and ... enjoying hospitality, and should not be provoking an old man who has obviously lost his mind ...'

Ippolit also seemed to shudder in a kind of convulsion, but in an instant regained control.

'I don't quite agree with you that your papa has lost his mind,' he replied calmly. 'On the contrary, it seems to me that his mind has even been growing stronger of late, truly it does; you don't believe it? He's become so cautious, suspicious, tries to find out everything, weighs every word ... I mean, he started telling me about this Kapitoshka with a purpose; imagine, he wanted to suggest to me ...'

'Oh, what the devil do I care what he wanted to suggest to you! I would ask you not to scheme and not to be evasive with me, sir!' screeched Ganya. 'If you also know the real reason why the old man is in such a state (and you've been spying on me these past five days so much that you probably do), then you really ought not to be provoking the ... poor man, and tormenting my mother by exaggerating the affair, because the whole affair is rubbish, just a drunken episode, no more, not even proven in any way, and I wouldn't give the price of a table-leg for it ... But you have to wound and spy because you're ... you're ...'

'A screw,' Ippolit said with a sarcastic smile.

'Because you're trash, for half an hour you tormented people, thinking to frighten them into supposing you were going to shoot yourself with your pistol, which was unloaded, and with which you made such a cowardly spectacle of yourself, you failed suicide, you burst spleen . . . on two legs. I gave you hospitality, you put on weight, stopped coughing, and yet you repay . . .'

'Two words only, if you will be so good, sir; it's Varvara Ardalionovna I'm staying with, not you; you have given me no hospitality, and I even think that you're enjoying Mr Ptitsyn's hospitality yourself. Four days ago I asked my mother to find an apartment in Pavlovsk for me and to move here herself, because I really do feel better here, although I haven't put on any weight, and still have my cough. Mother informed me last night that the apartment is ready, and I hasten to inform you on my part that, having thanked your dear mother and sister, I shall be moving to my quarters this very day, something I decided last night. I'm sorry, I interrupted you; I believe you still had much to say.'

'Oh, if that's how it is . . .' Ganya began to tremble.

'If that's how it is, then allow me to sit down,' added Ippolit, very calmly sitting down on the chair the general had been seated on. 'I mean, I'm still sick, you see; well, now I am ready to listen to you, all the more so as this is our last conversation and even, perhaps, our last meeting.'

Ganya suddenly felt ashamed.

'Believe me when I say I shall not lower myself to settling scores with you,' he said, 'and if you . . .'

'You needn't be so snooty,' Ippolit broke in. 'I, for my part, on the very first day I moved here, vowed to myself that I wouldn't deny myself the pleasure of telling you everything in no uncertain terms, and even in the frankest manner, when we said farewell. I intend to fulfil my vow in a moment – after you've finished, of course.'

'And I request you to leave this room.'

'You'd do better to talk; I mean, you'll regret not having spoken your mind.'

'Stop it, Ippolit, all this is horribly shameful, please be so good as to stop it!' said Varya.

'Anything to please a lady,' Ippolit laughed, getting up. 'Very well, Varvara Ardalionovna, for you I'm prepared to shorten it, but only shorten it, because some sort of explanation between myself and your dear brother has become absolutely necessary, and I can't possibly bring myself to go while leaving misunderstandings behind me.'

'Quite simply, you're a scandalmonger,' exclaimed Ganya, 'and so you can't bring yourself to go without starting some scandal.'

'There, you see,' Ippolit observed dispassionately, 'you really can't control yourself, can you? Truly, you'll regret not having spoken your mind. Once again I give you the floor. I'm waiting.'

Gavrila Ardalionovich was silent, and looked at him contemptuously.

'No, you're not. You plan to assert your character – as you wish. For my part, I shall be as brief as possible. Two or three times today I have heard a reproach concerning hospitality; that is unfair. In inviting me to stay with you, you yourself were trying to catch me in your net; you counted on me taking revenge on the prince. You had also heard that Aglaya Ivanovna had expressed sympathy for me and had read my confession. Calculating, for some reason, that I would therefore wholly consign myself to your interests, you hoped that in me you might perhaps find an accomplice. I shall not explain myself in more detail! I demand on your part neither admission nor confirmation; it's enough for me to leave you with your conscience, as I think that now we understand each other very well.'

'But you're creating Lord only knows what out of a most ordinary matter!' exclaimed Varya.

'I told you: a scandalmonger and a little brat,' said Ganya.

'With your permission, Varvara Ardalionovna, I shall continue. The prince, of course, I can neither love nor respect; but he is certainly a kind man, though also a . . . ridiculous one. There would have been absolutely no reason for me to hate him, however; I did not let on to your dear brother when he himself tried to incite me against the prince; I simply calculated that I'd be able to laugh when the dénouement arrived. I knew that your brother would let the cat out of the bag to me and miss his cue in the highest degree. So indeed it was . . . I am ready now to

spare him, but solely out of respect for you, Varvara Ardalionovna. But, having made it clear to you that it is not so easy
to make me swallow the bait, I must also make it clear to you
why I so much wanted to make a fool of your dear brother. I
may as well tell you, then, that I did it out of hatred, I admit it
openly. In the process of dying (for I shall die none the less, even
though I have put on weight, as you assert), in the process of
dying I felt I would go to an incomparably more peaceful paradise were I to make a fool of at least one representative of that
countless category of men who have persecuted me all my life,
whom I have hated all my life and of whom your brother serves
as such a graphic example. I hate you, Gavrila Ardalionovich,
solely because – and to you this may seem surprising – *solely
because* you are the type and incarnation, the personification
and acme of the most brazen, the most vulgar and loathsome
ordinariness! You are a pompous commonplace, an unswerving
commonplace of Olympian calm; you are the routine of the
routine! Not one even slightly original idea is ever destined to
come into being either in your mind or in your heart. But you
are infinitely envious; you're firmly convinced that you're the
greatest genius, yet doubt still sometimes visits you at dark
moments, and you're filled with anger and envy. Oh, there are
still dark patches on your horizon; they will pass when you
become completely stupid, which will not be long now; and yet
a long and varied path still lies ahead of you, though I wouldn't
say it's a cheerful one, and I'm glad of that. In the first place, I
predict to you that you will never win a certain lady . . .'

'Oh, this is intolerable!' exclaimed Varya. 'Will you stop this,
you repulsive, malicious creature?'

Ganya turned pale, trembled, and was silent. Ippolit stopped,
looked at him with beady satisfaction, transferred his gaze to
Varya, smiled ironically, bowed and walked out, not adding a
single word.

Gavrila Ardalionovich might justifiably have complained of
his fortune and failure. For some time Varya could not bring
herself to speak to him, did not even give him a glance as he
strode past her with long steps; at last he went to the window
and stood with his back to her. Varya thought of the Russian

saying: 'a stick with two ends'.[1] Noise was coming from upstairs again.

'Are you going?' Ganya turned to her suddenly, hearing her get up. 'Wait; just look at this.'

He walked over and threw on to the chair in front of her a small piece of paper, folded to make a little note.

'Merciful Lord!' exclaimed Varya, throwing up her hands.

The note contained just seven lines:

'Gavrila Ardalionovich! Being now persuaded of your kind disposition towards me, I have resolved to ask your advice in a certain matter that is important to me. I should like to meet you tomorrow morning at exactly seven o'clock, on the green bench. It is not far from our dacha. Varvara Ardalionovna, who must accompany you without fail, knows this place very well. A. E.'

'Well, what is one to make of her after that?' Varvara Ardalionovna threw up her hands.

No matter how far Ganya felt from wanting to brag at that moment, he could not help showing his triumph, especially after Ippolit's humiliating predictions. A complacent smile began to shine openly on his face, and even Varya beamed with delight.

'And on the very day they're announcing the engagement! Well, what can one make of her after this?'

'What do you think she's going to talk about tomorrow?' asked Ganya.

'It doesn't matter, the main thing is that she wants to see you again for the first time in six months. Now listen to me, Ganya: whatever happens there, however it turns out, remember that it's *important*! It is very important! Don't go boasting again, don't put your foot in it, but don't be cowardly either, mind that! Do you think she hasn't realized why I've been trailing over there this last six months? And imagine: she didn't say a word about it to me today, didn't let on. I mean, I smuggled myself in to see them, the old woman didn't know I was there, otherwise she'd have probably shown me the door. I took the risk of going there for you, in order to find out, no matter what . . .'

There was more shouting and noise from above; several people were coming down the stairs.

'We mustn't allow this now, not on any account!' Varya exclaimed, frightened and in haste. 'There mustn't be even the shadow of a scandal! Go and apologize!'

But the paterfamilias was already out in the street. Kolya followed him, lugging the bag. Nina Alexandrovna stood on the front steps, crying; she wanted to run after them, but Ptitsyn held her back.

'You'll only make him worse doing that,' he told her. 'He has nowhere to go, they'll bring him back in half an hour, I've already spoken to Kolya; let him play the fool for a bit.'

'What's all the swagger, where are you off to?' cried Ganya from the window. 'You've nowhere to go, anyway!'

'Come back, Papa!' cried Varya. 'The neighbours will hear.'

The general stopped, turned round, extended his arm and exclaimed:

'My curse upon this house!'

'And he has to say it in a theatrical voice!' muttered Ganya, closing the window with a bang.

The neighbours were indeed listening. Varya ran out of the room.

When Varya was out the way, Ganya took the note from the table, kissed it, clicked his tongue and performed an *entrechat*.

3

At any other time, the fuss with the general would not have led to anything. In the past there had been similar instances of sudden eccentricity, though they had been rather infrequent, because, on the whole, he was a very quiet man, and one with inclinations that were almost good. He had gone to battle, perhaps, a hundred times against the disorderliness that had overmastered him in recent years. He would suddenly remember that he was a 'paterfamilias', make it up with his wife, and weep sincerely. He respected Nina Alexandrovna to the point of adoration for the fact that she had forgiven him so often and in silence, and loved him even in his degrading aspect of buffoon. But the magnanimous struggle with disorderliness did not usually last for long; the general was also very much 'a man of impulse', though in his own way; as a rule, he was unable to endure the idle life of a penitent he led in his own family, and ended in revolt; fell into a passion, for which even he reproached himself at those very moments, but could not hold himself in check: picked a quarrel, began to talk with grandiose eloquence, demanded for himself a boundless and impossible respect, and finally vanished out of the house, sometimes even for a long time. During the past two years he had known about the affairs of his family only in vague terms, or by hearsay; he had ceased to enter into them in more detail, feeling not the slightest inclination to do so.

But on this occasion there was something unusual about the 'fuss with the general'; there was something that everyone seemed to know, and something that everyone seemed afraid to talk about. The general had presented himself 'formally' to the family, or to Nina Alexandrovna, rather, only three days before, but somehow without reconciliation and without penitence, as had always happened at earlier 'presentations', and, on the contrary – with extraordinary irritability. He was garrulous, agitated, talked to all who encountered him with vehemence, as if attacking them, but always about subjects so varied and surprising that it was in no way possible to ascertain what was really upsetting him. At odd moments he was cheerful, but was more often sunk in reflection, though without knowing himself precisely upon what; would suddenly start talking about something – the Yepanchins, the prince and Lebedev – and suddenly break off and stop talking altogether, replying to further questions only with a stupid smile, not even noticing, however, that people were asking him something, but he was merely smiling. He had spent the past night moaning and groaning, and had worn out Nina Alexandrovna, who for some reason had stayed up all night warming poultices for him; towards morning he had suddenly dozed off, slept for four hours and woken up in a most violent and disorderly fit of morbid depression, which had ended in the quarrel with Ippolit and the 'curse upon this house'. They also noticed that throughout those three days he kept constantly lapsing into the most intense vaunting of ambition and, as a consequence, into extreme touchiness. Kolya, for his part, persisted, assuring his mother that all this was simply due to a craving for drink, and perhaps for Lebedev, too, with whom the general had become extremely friendly of late. However, three days earlier he had suddenly quarrelled with Lebedev and parted from him in dreadful rage, and there had even been some sort of scene with the prince. Kolya had asked the prince for an explanation, and began, at last, to suspect that there was something that even the latter did not appear to be willing to tell him. If, as Ganya assumed with very good reason, some particular conversation between Ippolit and Nina Alexandrovna had taken place, it was strange that this malicious gentleman, whom Ganya had so directly called a scandalmonger, had not taken pleasure in bringing Kolya to reason in a similar manner. It might very well be that he was not a malicious 'brat' as Ganya had called him, while talking to his sister, but was a malicious person of some other sort; and it was also hardly likely that he would have told Nina Alexandrovna his observations solely in order to 'break her heart'. Let us not forget that the causes of human actions are usually infinitely more complex and more various than we are in the habit of explaining them afterwards, and are seldom clearly outlined. Sometimes it is best for the narrator to confine himself to a simple exposition of events. This is how we shall proceed with the rest of our account of the present catastrophe with the general; for no matter how hard we may try, we are confronted by the decided necessity of allotting to this secondary character in our story rather more attention and space than we had hitherto proposed.

These events followed one after the other, in this order:

When Lebedev, after his trip to St Petersburg in order to seek the whereabouts of Ferdyshchenko, returned that very same day, together with the general, he said nothing particular to the prince. If the prince had not at that time been very abstracted and preoccupied with other experiences of importance to him, he might soon have noticed that during the two days that followed Lebedev not only failed to present him with any explanations, but even, on the contrary, seemed for some reason to be avoiding him. Having at last paid heed to this, the prince was surprised to recall that during those two days, whenever he chanced to meet Lebedev, he never found him in anything but the most radiant disposition, and almost always in the general's company. The two friends were never parted for a moment. The prince sometimes heard loud and rapid conversations, wafted to him from upstairs, jovial and cheerful argument; once, very late at night, there came to him the sounds, ringing out suddenly and unexpectedly, of a martial bacchanalian song, and he at once recognized the general's hoarse bass. But the song that had rung out was not sustained, and suddenly fell silent. Then for about an hour there continued a violently animated and, by all the signs, drunken conversation. It was possible to guess that the friends who had been enjoying themselves upstairs were now embracing, and someone, at last, began to weep. Then suddenly there followed a violent quarrel, which also soon and swiftly died away. All during this time, Kolya was in a peculiarly worried state of mind. For the most part, the prince was not at home and sometimes returned to his quarters very late; he was always informed that Kolya had been looking for him and asking for him all day. But when they met, Kolya was not able to tell him anything in particular, apart from the fact that he was decidedly 'unhappy' with the general and his present conduct: 'They trail about, get drunk at an inn not far from here, embrace each other and shout at each other in the street, make each other worse and can't be parted.' When the prince observed to him that earlier, too, the same thing had happened almost every day, Kolya really did not know what to say to this or how to explain the cause of his present anxiety.

As the prince was leaving the house at about eleven the next morning, after the bacchanalian singing and the quarrels, the general suddenly appeared before him, extremely agitated, almost shaken.

'I have long sought the honour and the opportunity of meeting you, much-esteemed Lev Nikolayevich, long, very long,' he muttered, squeezing the prince's hand with extreme firmness, almost so it hurt. 'Very, very long.'

The prince asked him to sit down.

'No, I won't, and in any case I'm detaining you, I'll . . . another time. I think on this occasion I can congratulate you on . . . the fulfilment . . . of your heart's desire.'

'What heart's desire?'

The prince was embarrassed. Like many others in his situation, he thought that absolutely no one had seen, guessed or realized anything.

'Be assured, be assured! I shall not disturb the most delicate feelings. I have experienced it myself and know myself how it is when someone else's . . . so to speak, nose . . . as the saying has it . . . goes poking where it's not wanted. I experience that every morning. I've come to see you on another matter, an important one. On a very important matter, Prince.'

The prince again asked him to sit down, and sat down himself.

'Just for a second, perhaps? I've come for advice. Of course, I live without practical aims, but since I respect myself and . . . the business mentality in which Russians are, on the whole, so deficient . . . I wish to place myself, and my wife, and my children, in a position . . . in a word, Prince, I seek advice.'

The prince warmly praised his intention.

'Well, that's all rubbish,' the general interrupted quickly, 'that's not what I've come to see you about, it's something else, important. In fact, I've resolved to explain to you, Lev Nikolayevich, as a man of whose sincerity of approach and nobility of feeling I am certain, as . . . as . . . You are not surprised by my words, Prince?'

The prince watched his guest, if not with particular surprise, then with exceeding attention and curiosity. The old man was rather pale, his lips sometimes quivered slightly, his hands seemed to be unable to find a quiet place for themselves. He had been sitting for only a few minutes, but had already managed a couple of times to suddenly get up from his chair for some reason and then suddenly sit down again, evidently not paying the slightest attention to his own manoeuvres. There were books on the table; he picked up one of them, continuing to talk, took a glance at the opened page, closed the book at once and put it back on the table, seized another book, which this time he did not open, but held all the rest of the time in his right hand, constantly waving it in the air.

'Enough!' he exclaimed suddenly. 'I see that I've caused you a lot of nuisance.'

'But not at all, for goodness' sake, please continue, on the contrary, I am all ears and want to try to guess . . .'

'Prince! I wish to put myself in a position of respect . . . I wish to respect myself and . . . my rights.'

'A man with such a wish is already worthy of respect by that very fact alone.'

The prince uttered his clichéd phrase in the firm certainty that it would have a positive effect. He somehow guessed instinctively that some emptily resonant but pleasant phrase, spoken at the right time, might suddenly subdue and reconcile the soul of such a man, especially in a position like the one in which the general found himself. At any rate, a visitor of this kind must be sent away with a lightened heart, and that was the task in hand.

The phrase flattered, touched and greatly pleased the general; he was suddenly deeply moved, instantly changed his tone and launched into long and rapturous explanations. But no matter how hard the prince tried, no matter how closely he listened, he was literally unable to understand a single word. The general spoke for about ten minutes, heatedly and quickly, as if he could not manage to express his jostling crowd of thoughts; by the end of it, tears had begun to glisten in his eyes, but even so, it was merely phrases without beginning or end, unexpected words and unexpected thoughts, swiftly and unexpectedly breaking through and skipping out one after the other.

'Enough! You understand me and I am at ease,' he concluded suddenly, getting up. 'A heart like yours cannot fail to understand one who suffers. Prince, you are the ideal of nobility! What are others before you . . . But you are young, and I give you my blessing. What I've actually come to see you about is to ask you to grant me an appointment for an important conversation, and that is my chief hope. I seek nothing but friendship and the heart, Prince; I have never been able to cope with the demands of my heart.'

'But why not right now? I'm ready to listen . . .'

'No, Prince, no!' the general broke in heatedly, 'not now! Now is merely a dream! This is too, too important, too important! This appointment will be an hour of final destiny. It will be *my* hour, and I would not wish that we could be interrupted at such a sacred moment by the first person to walk in, the first insolent fellow, and there are not a few such insolent fellows,' he bent forwards to the prince with a strange, mysterious and almost frightened whisper, 'the sort of insolent fellow who is not worth the heel . . . of your boot, beloved Prince! Oh, I do not say: of my boot! Note particularly, that I haven't mentioned my boot; for I respect myself too much to be able to say that in plain terms; it is simply that you alone are capable of understanding that, rejecting my heel in this instance, I am perhaps displaying an exceeding pride in my own dignity. No other person would understand apart from you, and *he* is at the head of the "other persons". *He* doesn't understand anything, Prince; he is quite, quite incapable of understanding! One must have a heart, in order to understand!'

Towards the end, the prince almost began to feel afraid, and granted the general an appointment the following day at the same hour. The general left in cheerful spirits, greatly consoled and almost reassured. At seven o'clock that evening the prince sent to ask Lebedev to come and see him for a moment.

Lebedev appeared with exceeding haste, 'considering it an honour', as he at once began to say as he entered; there seemed to be no trace of the fact that for three days he had more or less hidden himself away, and had plainly avoided meeting the prince. He sat down on the edge of the chair, with grimaces, with smiles, with laughing and peeping little eyes, with a rubbing of hands and an air of the most naive expectation of hearing something of capital importance, long awaited and guessed by all. Again, this jarred on the prince; it became plain to him that they had all begun to expect something of him, that they were all glancing at him, as if they wanted to congratulate him on something, with hints, smiles and winks. Keller had already dropped in for a moment several times, also with an evident desire to congratulate: on each occasion he began ecstatically

and vaguely, did not finish any of his sentences, and quickly
retired into the background. (Of recent days he had been off
somewhere drinking rather a lot, building a bad reputation in
some billiard hall or other.) Even Kolya, in spite of his sadness,
also began vague conversations with the prince.

The prince directly and rather irritably asked Lebedev what
he thought about the general's present condition and why he
was so troubled. In a few words, Lebedev told him about the
scene that had earlier taken place.

'Everyone has his troubles, Prince, and . . . especially in our
strange and troubled times, sir; that's how it is, sir,' Lebedev
replied with a certain dryness, and fell touchily silent, with the
air of a man who was sorely deceived in his expectations.

'What a philosophy!' the prince smiled ironically.

'Philosophy is necessary, sir, it's very necessary in our times,
sir, in a practical sense, but it's neglected, sir, that's what, sir.
For my part, much esteemed Prince, though I was honoured by
your confidence in me regarding a certain point that's known
to you, sir, it was only up to a certain degree, and by no means
any further than the circumstances relating to that point alone,
sir . . . I understand that, and have no complaint at all.'

'Lebedev, you seem to be angry about something.'

'Not at all, not in the slightest, much esteemed and radiant
Prince, not in the slightest!' Lebedev exclaimed rapturously,
putting his hand to his heart. 'On the contrary, I perceived at
once that neither on account of my position in the world, nor
the development of my mind and heart, nor my accumulation
of wealth, nor my earlier behaviour, nor indeed my knowledge
– on account of nothing do I deserve your honorific confidence,
which extends far beyond my hopes; and that if I can serve you,
then it is as a slave and a hireling, not otherwise . . . I'm not
angry, sir, I'm sad.'

'Lukyan Timofeich, for heaven's sake!'

'Not otherwise! That's how it is now, that's how it is in the
present instance, too! Encountering you and following you in
heart and thought, I said to myself: I am not worthy of friendly
communication, but in my capacity as landlord of these lodgings, perhaps, I might at the proper time, by the expected term,

so to speak, receive an instruction, or at least a notification, in view of certain imminent and expected . . .'

As he said this, Lebedev fairly bored his sharp little eyes into the prince, who was staring at him in amazement; the prince still entertained the hope of satisfying his own curiosity.

'I understand nothing of this whatsoever,' the prince exclaimed, almost in anger, 'and – you are the most dreadful schemer!' he suddenly burst out in the most sincere laughter.

In a flash, Lebedev also burst out laughing, and his beaming gaze expressed in no uncertain terms the fact that his hopes had brightened and had even been redoubled.

'And do you know what I will say to you, Lukyan Timofeich? Now don't be angry with me, but I'm surprised at your naivety, and not yours alone! You're expecting something from me, I mean now, at this very moment, with such naivety that I even feel guilty and ashamed before you for having nothing with which to satisfy you; but I swear to you that I have decidedly nothing, do you believe me?'

The prince again began to laugh.

Lebedev assumed a dignified air. It was true that he was sometimes too naive and importunate in his curiosity; but at the same time he was a rather cunning and sneaky individual, and in some cases just too insidiously silent; by his constant rebuffs, the prince had almost made an enemy of him. The prince had been rebuffing him, however, not because he despised him, but because the subject of his curiosity was a delicate one. The prince had, only a few days earlier, looked upon certain dreams of his own as a crime, while Lebedev construed the prince's refusals as mere personal loathing of him and a lack of trust, went away with a wounded heart and felt jealous, where the prince was concerned, not only of Kolya and Keller, but even of his own daughter, Vera Lukyanovna. Even at this very moment he might have sincerely wished to inform the prince of a certain piece of news that the prince would have found extremely interesting, but fell gloomily silent and did not do so.

'How, then, exactly, may I be of service to you, much esteemed Prince, since you did, after all . . . summon me just now?' he said quietly at last, after a silence.

'Well, it was about the general,' the prince began, after a moment's reflection, 'and . . . about this theft of yours, which you told me about . . .'

'What theft would that be, sir?'

'There you go again, as if you didn't understand me even now! Oh, good heavens, Lukyan Timofeich, how you playact all the time! The money, the money, the four hundred roubles you lost that day, from your wallet, and which you came here to tell me about, as you were setting off for St Petersburg – now do you understand?'

'Oh, you mean the four hundred roubles!' Lebedev said in elongated tones, as though he had only guessed now. 'I thank you, Prince, for your sincere concern; it's very flattering to me, but . . . I found the money, sir, and long ago now.'

'You found it! Oh, thank God!'

'A most noble exclamation on your part, for four hundred roubles is certainly not an unimportant matter for a poor man who lives by heavy toil, and has a numerous family of motherless orphans . . .'

'But that's not what I meant! Of course I'm glad you found the money,' the Prince quickly corrected himself, 'but . . . how did you find it?'

'Extremely simply, sir, I found it under the chair on which I'd hung my frock coat, so obviously the wallet must have slipped out of my pocket on to the floor.'

'How can that be, under the chair? It's impossible, I mean, you told me that you'd looked in every corner; so how could you have missed that most important place?'

'The thing is that I did look there, sir! I very, very clearly remember that I looked there, sir! I crept about on all fours, felt that place with my hands, having pushed back the chair, not quite believing my own eyes: and I saw that there was nothing there, just a smooth, empty place, like the palm of my hand here, sir, and yet I went on feeling about. Such fear always affects a man, sir, when he really wants to find something very badly . . . in the case of important and regrettable losses, sir: he sees that there's nothing there, just an empty place, and yet he'll look there more than a dozen times.'

'Yes, I suppose so; only how could it have happened? . . . I still don't understand,' muttered the prince, thrown off balance. 'Before, you said, it wasn't there, and you looked in that place, and then it suddenly turned up?'

'Yes, it did, sir.'

The prince gave Lebedev a strange look.

'And what about the general?' he asked suddenly.

'Er, how do you mean, the general, sir?' Lebedev did not understand again.

'Oh, good heavens! I mean what did the general say when you found the wallet under the chair? After all, you had both been looking for it together earlier.'

'Yes, we had sir. But on this occasion I confess that I kept my silence, sir, and preferred not to inform him that the wallet had already been found by myself, on my own.'

'But . . . wh-why? And was the money all there?'

'I opened the wallet; it was all there, right to the last rouble, sir.'

'You might have come and told me,' the prince observed reflectively.

'I was afraid to disturb you in person, Prince, in view of your personal and, perhaps, extreme, so to speak, cogitations; and in addition, I myself pretended that I had not found anything. I opened the wallet, examined it, then closed it and put it back under the chair again.'

'But what on earth for?'

'I just d-did, sir; out of further curiosity, sir,' Lebedev giggled suddenly, rubbing his hands.

'So it lies there now, and has been there since the day before yesterday?'

'Oh no, sir; it has lain there but twenty-four hours. You see, I partly wanted the general to find it, sir. Because if I had found it, at last, then why would the general not notice an object, so to speak, casting itself upon his gaze, sticking out from under the chair. I lifted that chair several times and moved its position, so that the wallet was completely visible, but the general didn't notice anything, and so it went on, for a whole twenty-four hours. It's plain to see that he's very absent-minded now, and you can't make him out; he talks, tells stories, laughs, guffaws, and then all of a sudden gets dreadfully angry with me, I don't know why, sir. At last we began to leave the room, and I left the door open on purpose; he hesitated, was about to say something, was probably alarmed by a wallet with all that money in it, but suddenly got dreadfully angry and didn't say anything, sir; we hadn't gone two paces along the street when he turned his back on me and went off in a different direction. We didn't meet again until evening, at the inn.'

'But even so, you took the wallet from under the chair?'

'No, sir; that same night it went missing from there, sir.'

'So where is it now, then?'

'Why, it's here, sir,' Lebedev suddenly began to laugh, getting up from his chair and looking pleasantly at the prince. 'It suddenly turned up here, in the lining of my own frock coat. Here, be so good as to take a look – feel, sir.'

Indeed, in the left flap of the frock coat, right at the front, in full view, there was a sack-like bulge, and as one felt it one could guess instantly that inside was a leather wallet which had fallen down through a hole in the pocket.

'I took it out and looked at it, sir, it was all there, sir. I put it back again, and I've been walking around like that since yesterday morning, carrying it in my lining; it even knocks against my legs.'

'And you don't notice it?'

'No, sir, heh-heh! And imagine, much esteemed Prince – though the subject is unworthy of such special attention from you – my pockets are always sewn up tight, and then suddenly in one night a hole like that! I began to examine it with more interest – it seemed that someone had cut the pocket with a penknife; it's almost beyond belief, isn't it, sir?'

'And . . . the general?'

'All day he's been angry, both yesterday and today; dreadfully out of temper, sir; now cheerful and Bacchic even to the point of flattery, now sensitive even to the point of tears, and then he'll suddenly get angry, so much that I'm even afraid, sir, honest to God, sir; Prince, after all I'm not a military man, sir. Yesterday we were sitting in the inn, and my coat-lining

happened to be on view, as it were, plain as plain could be; he
squinted at it, got angry. Now he won't even look me in the eye,
sir, hasn't done for a long time, only when he's very tipsy or
sentimental; but yesterday he did look at me a couple of times
in a way that simply sent a chill down my spine. As a matter of
fact, I intend to find the wallet tomorrow, but before that I'm
going out for a nice little evening with him.'

'Why are you tormenting him like that?' exclaimed the Prince.

'I'm not tormenting him, Prince, I'm not,' Lebedev retorted
heatedly. 'I love him sincerely, sir . . . and I respect him, sir; and
now, well, believe it not, he has become even dearer to me, sir;
I have begun to value him even more, sir!'

Lebedev said all this with such sincere gravity that the prince
became indignant.

'You're fond of him, yet you torment him like that! For
heaven's sake, by the very act of restoring your lost item, under
the chair and into your frock coat, by that action alone he is
plainly demonstrating to you that he doesn't want to play tricks
on you, and is open-heartedly asking your forgiveness. Do you
hear: he's asking forgiveness! He is placing his trust in the
delicacy of your feelings; he believes in your friendship towards
him. Yet you wreak such deep humiliation . . . on such a very
honourable man!'

'Very honourable, Prince, very honourable!' Lebedev interjected, his eyes sparkling. 'And you alone, most noble Prince,
are in a position to make such a true remark! For that I am
devoted to you even to the point of adoration, sir, though I'm
rotted through with various vices! It's settled! I shall find the
wallet right now, this instant, and not tomorrow; here, I take it
out before your eyes, sir; here it is; and here is the money, all
present and correct; here, take it, most noble Prince, take it and
keep it until tomorrow. I'll take it tomorrow or the day after,
sir; but you know, Prince, it's obvious that it must have been
lying under a stone in my garden somewhere, that first night it
went missing, sir; what do you think?'

'Listen, be careful, and don't tell him straight out that you've
found the wallet. Just let him see very plainly that there's nothing
in the lining of your coat now, and he'll understand.'

'Do you think that's best, sir? Wouldn't it be better to tell him that I've found it, sir, and pretend I hadn't realized it was there until now?'

'N-no,' the prince reflected. 'N-no, it's too late now; that would be more risky; truly, you'd do better not to say anything at all! And be nice to him, but . . . don't lay it on too thick, and . . . and, you know . . .'

'I know, Prince, I know, that is, I know that I probably won't be able to carry it off; for in a case like this one needs to have a heart like yours. And what's more, he's irritable and easily provoked, he's begun to treat me far too condescendingly sometimes; now he snivels and embraces me, and now he suddenly starts to humiliate me and make contemptuous fun of me; well, now I'll deliberately show him my lining, heh-heh! *Au revoir,* Prince, for I'm obviously detaining you and disturbing, so to speak, your most interesting emotions . . .'

'But, for God's sake, keep it secret, as before!'

'With quiet steps, sir, with quiet steps, sir!'

But although the matter was at an end, the prince was even more worried now than he had been before. Impatiently he awaited next day's meeting with the general.

4

The hour of the appointment was from eleven to twelve, but the prince was quite unexpectedly late. Returning home, he found the general waiting for him. At first glance he observed that the general was displeased, possibly for the very reason that he had had to wait. Apologizing, the prince hurriedly seated himself, but somehow felt strangely timid, as though his visitor was made of porcelain, and he was constantly afraid of breaking him. He had never felt timid with the general earlier, and indeed it had never entered his mind to feel so. The prince soon perceived that this was quite a different man from the day before; instead of confusion and distraction there were glimpses of an extraordinary self-control; one might conclude that here was a man who had finally resolved upon something. His calm was, however, more apparent than real. But at any rate, his visitor's manner was decently familiar, though with a dignified reserve, and initially he even treated the prince with a certain air of condescension: all of this precisely in the way that people who are proud, but have been unfairly insulted, sometimes behave. He spoke mildly, though not without a certain note of disgruntlement.

'Your book, the one I borrowed from you yesterday,' he nodded meaningfully at the book he had brought and which lay on the table. 'Thank you.'

'Ah, yes; did you read that article, General? How did you like it? It's interesting, isn't it?' The prince was relieved at having the chance to begin the conversation on a side-topic.

'It may be interesting, but it's crude and, of course, it's rubbish. Probably lies every step of the way, too.'

The general spoke with aplomb, even affecting a slight drawl.

'Oh, but it's such an uncontrived story; the story of an old soldier who was an eyewitness to the French occupation of Moscow; several parts of it are splendid. What's more, any memoirs by eyewitnesses are a treasure, no matter who the eyewitness happens to be. Don't you think so?'

'If I'd been the editor I would never have published it; and as for memoirs by eyewitnesses, people are more prepared to believe a coarse liar who is entertaining than they are a man of worth and merit. I know some writings about the year 1812 that . . . Prince, I've made my decision, Prince, I'm leaving this house – Mr Lebedev's house.'

The general gave the prince a meaningful look.

'You have your own lodgings in Pavlovsk, at the home of your . . . daughter . . .' the prince said quietly, not knowing what to say. He remembered that, after all, the general had come for advice concerning an urgent matter on which his fate depended.

'At my wife's, sir; in other words, in my own home, and that of my daughter.'

'Forgive me, I . . .'

'I'm leaving Lebedev's house because, dear Prince, I've broken with that man; I broke with him last night, and I regret it was not sooner. I demand respect, Prince, and I wish to receive it even from those persons to whom, so to speak, I give my heart. Prince, I often give my heart and am almost invariably deceived. That man was unworthy of my gift.'

'There's a lot of disorderliness in him,' the prince observed cautiously, 'and certain features . . . but in the midst it all one may observe a heart, and a mind that's cunning and sometimes even entertaining.'

The refinement of the prince's expressions, and his deferential tone, visibly flattered the general, though he still sometimes glanced with sudden mistrust. But the prince's tone was so natural and sincere that it was impossible to have any doubts.

'That there are good qualities in him,' the general interjected. 'I was the first to declare when I was almost about to give that individual my friendship. After all, I have no need of his house and his hospitality, as I possess a household of my own. I'm not trying to justify my own defects; I'm intemperate; I drank wine with him and now, perhaps, I regret that. But after all, it was not merely for drinking (Prince, you must forgive the coarseness of expression on the part of a man who's exasperated), not merely for that that I associated with him, was it? I was, in fact, as you say, attracted by his qualities. But everything has its limits – even qualities; and if he suddenly, to my face, has the insolence to assert that in the year 1812, still a lad, in his childhood, he lost his left leg and buried it in the Vagankov Cemetery, in Moscow, that goes beyond all limits and shows lack of respect, displays effrontery . . .'

'Perhaps it was only a joke, to make you laugh.'

'I understand, sir. An innocent lie to make one laugh, even though it may be a crude one, does not insult the human heart. A man may lie, if you will, from simple friendship, in order to afford enjoyment to his partner in conversation; but if disrespect shows through, if precisely by such disrespect, perhaps, the intention is to show that the friendship is a burden, then all that's left to a decent man is to turn away and end the friendship, thus showing the insulter his proper place.'

The general even reddened as he spoke.

'But Lebedev couldn't have been in Moscow in 1812; he's too young for that; it's absurd.'

'That, for one thing; but supposing he could have been born then: how can he assert to my face that a French chasseur pointed his cannon at him and blew off his leg, just like that, for fun; that he picked up that leg and took it home, then buried it in the Vagankov Cemetery, and then he put a gravestone over it with on one side the inscription: "Here lies the leg of Collegiate Assessor Lebedev", and on the other: "Rest, dear ashes, until the joyous morn", and that he has a service held over it every year (which is blasphemy), and makes a trip to Moscow for that purpose every year. As proof he invites me to Moscow in order to show me the grave, and even that same French cannon in the Kremlin, captured from the enemy; he says it's the eleventh from the gate, a French falconet of the old make.'

'And yet both his legs are fine, and in full view!' the prince laughed. 'I assure you, it's an innocent joke; don't be angry.'

'You must allow me to have my opinion about that, sir; with regard to his legs being in full view – it may not be so improbable, after all; he says it's a Chernosvitov leg.'[1]

'Ah, yes, they say it's possible to dance with one of those.'

'I know that for a fact, sir. The first thing Chernosvitov did when he'd invented his leg was to pop over and show it to me. But the Chernosvitov leg was invented later, far later ... And what's more, he claims that even his deceased wife, throughout the duration of their entire marriage, never knew that he, her husband, had a wooden leg. "If you," he said, when I pointed out all the absurdities to him, "if you were one of Napoleon's pageboys in 1812, you may at least permit me to bury my leg in the Vagankov Cemetery."'

'But were you really ...' the prince began, and grew embarrassed.

The general gave the prince a decidedly haughty look, which was almost one of mockery.

'Do go on, Prince,' he drawled with particular smoothness, 'please do. I am a tolerant man, you may say it all: admit that you find preposterous even the very idea of seeing a man in his present state of humiliation and ... uselessness, and of hearing

at the same time that this man was a personal witness of ...
great events. *He* hasn't managed to ... tell you any tales about
me yet, has he?'

'No; I've heard nothing from Lebedev – if it's Lebedev you're
talking about ...'

'Hm, I thought the contrary. Actually, the conversation we
had yesterday was about that ... strange article in the *Archive*.
I commented on its absurdity, and as I myself was a personal
witness ... You're smiling, Prince, you're looking at my face?'

'N-no, I ...'

'I may look young,' the general drew out his words, 'but I'm
rather older than I appear. In 1812 I was about ten or eleven. I
don't really know my age. In the army service list it's less; all
my life it's been a weakness of mine to understate my age.'

'I assure you, General, that I in no way find it strange that
you were in Moscow in 1812 and ... of course, you're able to
report ... just like everyone else who was there. Indeed, one of
our autobiographers[2] begins his book by relating that as a babe
in arms in Moscow in 1812 he was fed with bread by the French
soldiers.'

'There, you see,' the general approved tolerantly. 'My own
case, of course, stands out from the ordinary, but it doesn't contain anything unusual. Very often the truth seems impossible. A
pageboy! It does sound strange, of course. But the episode with
the ten-year-old boy may perhaps be explained precisely by his
age. It wouldn't have happened to a fifteen-year-old, and that is
unquestionably so, because as a fifteen-year-old I would not have
run away from our wooden house on Staraya Basmannaya on the
day of Napoleon's entrance to Moscow, leaving my mother,
who was too late to leave Moscow, and trembling with fear. At
fifteen I'd have been afraid, but at ten I was afraid of nothing
and pushed my way through the crowd right up to the front
steps of the palace just as Napoleon was getting off his horse.'

'Without a doubt, that was an excellent observation of yours,
that at ten years old it's possible not to be afraid ...' the prince
confirmed timidly, tormented by the thought that he might blush
at any moment.

'Without any doubt all, and it all happened as simply and

naturally as can only be the case in real life. Were a novelist to take up the matter, he'd weave fables and fantasies.'

'Oh, that is true!' exclaimed the prince. 'That thought struck me, too, and even recently. I know of a genuine case of murder for the sake of a watch, it's in the newspapers just now. If an author had invented it, the experts on our national life would have instantly shouted that it was incredible; yet as one reads it in the papers as a fact, one feels it's precisely from such facts that one comes to learn about Russian reality. That was a splendid observation of yours, General!' the prince concluded with ardour, hugely relieved at being able to divert attention from the obvious blush on his face.

'Isn't it so? Isn't it?' exclaimed the general, his eyes even sparkling with pleasure. 'A boy, a child, not understanding the danger, makes his way through the crowd in order to see the glitter, the uniforms, the retinue and, at last, the great man, about whom so much had been trumpeted to him. For at the time, for several years on end, people had done nothing but shout about him. The world was filled with that name; I, so to speak, sucked it in with my mother's milk. Napoleon, as he walked by at two paces from me, happened to discern my gaze; I was dressed in the clothes of a young nobleman, my family dressed me well. I was the only one like that, in that crowd, so you will admit . . .'

'Without a doubt, that must have struck him and proved to him that not everyone had left, and that even some noblemen with their children had remained.'

'Precisely, precisely! He was anxious to attract the boyars! When he cast his aquiline gaze at me, my eyes must have sparkled in response to it. "*Voilà un garçon bien éveillé! Qui est ton père?*"[3] I at once replied to him, almost choking with excitement: "A general who died in the fields of his fatherland." "*Le fils d'un boyard et d'un brave pardessus le marché! J'aime les boyards. M'aimes-tu, petit?*"[4] To this swift question I replied just as swiftly: "The Russian heart is able to discern a great man even in its fatherland's enemy!" Though really, I can't remember if those were his actual words . . . I was a child . . . but that was probably the gist of it! Napoleon was struck, he thought for a moment and said to his retinue: "I like the pride of this boy! But if all Russians think like this child, then . . ." He didn't finish, and entered the palace. I at once joined the retinue and ran after him. The members of the retinue were already stepping aside for me and looking on me as a favourite. But all that just fleeted past . . . I remember only that, as he entered the first hall, the emperor suddenly stopped in front of a portrait of Empress Catherine, looked at it for a long time and, said, at last: "She was a great woman!" – and walked past. Two days later everyone in the palace and the Kremlin knew me, and called me "*le petit boyard*". I only went home to sleep. At home they were almost beside themselves. Another two days later, Napoleon's page, Baron de Bazancourt,[5] died after failing to endure the campaign. Napoleon remembered me. I was taken and brought to the palace without explanation, was given the uniform of the deceased, a boy of about twelve, and when they had led me to the emperor, wearing the uniform, and he had nodded at me, they told me that I had been granted favour and been made a page of his majesty. I was pleased, I really did feel an ardent sympathy for him, and had done for a long time . . . well, and also there was the resplendent uniform, which is something that means a great deal to a child . . . I went about in a dark-green coat with long, narrow tails; gold buttons, red trimmings on the sleeves with gold braid, a high, stiff, open collar, embroidered in gold, embroidery on the tails; white, close-fitting buckskin breeches, silk stockings, shoes with buckles . . . and during the emperor's outings on horseback, and if I was part of the retinue, high hessian boots. Although the situation was none too good, and enormous calamities were already being anticipated, etiquette was observed as far as possible, and one could even say that it was observed with more punctilio the more strongly those calamities were sensed to be imminent.'

'Yes, of course,' the prince muttered, with an almost perplexed look. 'Your memoirs would be . . . extremely interesting.'

The general was, of course, merely repeating what he had told Lebedev the day before, and so had it off pat; but now once again he looked at the prince out of the corner of his eye, with mistrust.

'My memoirs,' he said with redoubled pride, 'write my memoirs? That has not tempted me, Prince! If you want to know, my memoirs are already written, but . . . they lie in my desk. Let them appear when my eyes are sprinkled with earth, and no doubt they will be translated into other languages, not because of their literary merit, but because of the importance of the most tremendous facts of which I was an eyewitness, although I was a child; but *tant pis*: as a child, I penetrated to the most intimate, so to speak, bedchamber of the great man! At nights I heard the groans of that "giant in misfortune", he could have no pangs of conscience about groaning and weeping in front of a child, though I already understood that the cause of his sufferings was the silence of the Emperor Alexander.'

'Yes, after all, he did write letters . . . with peace proposals,' the prince confirmed.

'We don't actually know just what the proposals were, but he wrote them every day, every hour, and in letter after letter! He was terribly wrought up. One night, when I was alone with him, I rushed to him in tears (oh, I loved him!): "Please, please ask Emperor Alexander for forgiveness!" I shouted to him. You see, I should have expressed it as: "Make peace with Emperor Alexander!", but, like a child, I naively came out with all that was on my mind. "Oh, my child!" he replied – he was pacing up and down the room – "Oh, my child!" – at the time he seemed not to notice that I was ten, and even liked to hold conversations with me. "Oh, my child, I am ready to kiss the feet of Emperor Alexander, but for the King of Prussia and the Emperor of Austria, oh, for those men nothing but eternal hatred, and . . . in any case . . . you know nothing of politics!" He suddenly seemed to remember who he was talking to, and fell silent, but his eyes continued to flash long after that. Well, were I to describe all those facts – and I was a witness of the very greatest facts – were I to publish them now, all those critics, all those literary vanities, all that envy, partisanship and . . . no, sir, your humble servant!"

'With regard to partisanship you are, of course, correct, and I agree with you,' the prince replied quietly, after a moment's silence. 'I also very recently read Charasse's book on the

Waterloo campaign.[6] It's obviously a serious book, and the
specialists assert that it's written with an exceptional knowledge
of the subject. But on every page his joy in Napoleon's humiliation shows through, and were it possible to dispute the existence of the slightest sign of talent in Napoleon with regard to
his other campaigns as well, then one feels that Charasse would
be extremely glad about it; but that is not a good thing in a
serious work of this kind, for it shows partisan spirit. Were you
kept very busy in your service with . . . the emperor?'

The general was delighted. With its seriousness and simplicity,
the prince's remark dispelled the last remnants of his mistrust.

'Charasse! Oh, I was so indignant! I wrote to him at the time,
but . . . actually, I can't remember now . . . You ask if I was kept
very busy in my service? Oh no! I was called a pageboy, but I
didn't take it seriously then. What's more, Napoleon very soon
lost all hope of bringing the Russians closer to him, and, of
course, would have forgotten about me, too, whom he had
brought close to him for political reasons, had . . . had he not
become personally fond of me, I boldly say that now. As for
myself, my heart was drawn to him. My service made few
demands: I sometimes had to present myself at the palace and
. . . accompany the emperor on horseback when he went out
riding, that was all. I was not a bad rider. He used to ride out
before dinner, the retinue was composed of Davoust, myself,
Mameluke Rustan . . .'[7]

'Constant,'[8] the prince suddenly let slip.

'N-no, Constant wasn't there at that time; he was taking a
letter to . . . to the Empress Josephine; but in his place there
were two orderlies, a few Polish Uhlans . . . well, that was
the whole retinue, apart from the generals, of course, and the
marshals, whom Napoleon took with him in order to inspect
the terrain, the disposition of the troops, to consult with them
. . . Most often Davoust would be with them, as I remember
now: an enormous, stout, cool-headed man in spectacles, with
a strange look in his eyes. It was with him that the emperor
most often took counsel. The emperor valued his thoughts. I
remember that they had already spent several days in consultation; Davoust would come both in the morning and in the

evening, often they even engaged in arguments; at last Napoleon
seemed to begin to agree with him. They were alone together in
the study, with myself as a third person, almost unnoticed by
them. Suddenly Napoleon's gaze happened to fall on me, and a
strange thought fleeted in his eyes. "Child!" he said to me
suddenly. "How do you suppose: if I accept Orthodoxy and
free your serfs, will the Russians follow me?" "Never!" I
exclaimed in indignation. Napoleon was struck. "In the eyes of
this child, shining with patriotism," he said, "I have read the
opinion of the entire Russian people. Enough, Davoust! This is
all fantasies! Let me hear your other plan."

'Yes, but that first plan contained a powerful idea!' said the
prince, visibly interested. 'So you ascribe that plan to Davoust?'

'Well, at any rate they discussed it together. Of course, it was
a Napoleonic idea, an aquiline idea, but the other plan was also
an idea . . . That was the famous "*Conseil du lion*", as Napoleon
himself called Davoust's plan. It consisted in them barricading
themselves inside the Kremlin with all the troops, building barracks, digging fortifications, positioning cannon, slaughtering
as many horses as possible and salting their flesh; obtaining or
plundering grain, and holding out all winter until the spring;
and in spring, breaking through the Russian lines. This plan
strongly attracted Napoleon. Every day we rode round the
Kremlin walls, he would indicate where we should demolish,
where we should build, where we should construct the lunettes,
the ravelins, the blockhouses – one glance, then swiftness and
thrust! At last, it was all decided; Davoust pressed for a final
decision. Again they were alone together, and I was the third
person present. Again Napoleon paced up and down the room,
his arms folded. I couldn't take my eyes off his face, and my
heart was thumping. "I'm going," said Davoust. "Where to?"
asked Napoleon. "To salt the horses," said Davoust. Napoleon
shuddered; his fate was being decided. "Child!" he said to me
suddenly. "What do you think of our plan?" Of course, he
asked the question in the way that, on occasion, a man of the
greatest intellect, will at the last moment resort to heads or tails.
Instead of Napoleon, I turned to Davoust and spoke like one
inspired: "Go home, General!" The plan was ruined. Davoust

shrugged his shoulders and, as he went out, said in a whisper: "*Bah! Il devient superstitieux!*"[9] And next day the order for a retreat was given.'

'This is all extremely interesting,' the prince said, in very hushed tones. 'If that's how it all really happened . . . that's to say, I mean . . .' he hurried to correct himself.

'Oh, Prince!' exclaimed the general, intoxicated with his own story to a point where he might now be unable to hold back even the most extreme indiscretions. 'You say: "It all happened!" But there was more, I assure you, there was much more! All that is just wretched political facts. But I repeat to you, I was a witness of that great man's nocturnal tears and groans; but absolutely no one saw that, except me! Towards the end, it's true, he didn't weep at all, there were no tears, he merely groaned sometimes; but his face seemed more and more clouded by darkness. It was as though eternity were already spreading her dark wing over him. Sometimes, at night, we spent whole hours alone, in silence – the Mameluke Rustan would be snoring in the next room; that man slept awfully soundly. "But he's loyal to me and to the dynasty," Napoleon would say of him. On one occasion it all became too terribly painful, and he suddenly noticed the tears in my eyes; he gave me a look of tender emotion: "You feel sorry for me!" he exclaimed. "You, a child, and perhaps there's another child who will feel sorry for me – my son, *le roi de Rome*; all the others, they all hate me, and my brothers will be the first to sell me into slavery!" I began to sob and rushed to him; at that point he himself broke down; we embraced, and our tears mingled. "Write, write to the Empress Josephine!" I sobbed to him. Napoleon gave a shudder, thought, and said to me: "You have reminded me of another heart that loves me; I thank you, *mon ami*!" He sat right down and wrote the letter to Josephine with which Constant was dispatched the next day.'

'You did well,' said the prince. 'Amidst cruel thoughts, you led him to kind feeling.'

'Exactly, Prince, and how well you explain it, in keeping with your own heart!' the general exclaimed rapturously, and, strangely, genuine tears began to glisten in his eyes. 'Yes, Prince, yes, it was a great spectacle! And you know, I almost followed him to Paris and, of course, would have shared with him "the sultry island of confinement",[10] but alas! Our fortunes diverged! We went our separate ways: he to the sultry island, where once, at a moment of dreadful sorrow, he perhaps remembered the tears of the poor boy who had embraced him and forgiven him in Moscow; as for myself, I was sent to the Cadet Corps, where I found nothing but drilling, the vulgarity of my companions and . . . Alas! Everything had turned to ashes! "I do not wish to remove you from your mother and will not take you with me!" he told me on the day of the withdrawal. "But I would like to do something for you." He was already mounting his horse. "Write me something in my sister's album, as a keepsake," I said, timidly, for he was very gloomy and distraught. He turned round, asked for a pen, and took the album. "How old is your sister?" he asked me, as he held the pen. "Three," I replied. "*Petite fille alors.*" And he scribbled in the album:

> "*Ne mentez jamais!*
> *Napoléon, votre ami sincère.*"[11]

Such advice, and at such a moment, you will agree, Prince!'
'Yes, it was full of portent . . .'
'That page, in a gold frame, under glass, hung in my sister's drawing room all her life, in the most conspicuous place, right up until her death – she died in childbirth; where it is now, I do not know . . . but, oh, goodness me! It's two o'clock already! How I've detained you, Prince! It's unforgivable.'
The general rose from his chair.
'Oh, on the contrary!' mumbled the prince. 'You've entertained me so much, and . . . after all . . . it's so interesting. I'm so grateful to you!'
'Prince!' said the general, again pressing the prince's hand until it hurt and staring at him with glittering eyes, as though he had suddenly recollected himself and was stunned by some sudden thought. 'Prince! You're so kind, so open-hearted that I even feel sorry for you sometimes. I look on you with tender emotion; oh, God bless you! May your life begin and blossom . . . in love. My own is finished! Oh, forgive me, forgive me!'
He quickly left, covering his face with his hands. Of the

sincerity of his agitation the prince could have no doubt. He
also understood that the old man had left intoxicated by his
own success; but he still had a foreboding that he was one
of that category of liars who, though they lie to the point of
sensuality and even self-forgetfulness, at the very highest point
of their intoxication none the less have a private suspicion that
they are not believed, and cannot be believed. In his present
position the old man might recollect himself, be inordinately
ashamed, suspect the prince of excessive compassion for him,
feel insulted. 'Was it not bad of me to lead him to such a pitch
of inspiration?' the prince worried, and suddenly could not
restrain himself, but burst into the most hilarious laughter, that
lasted for some ten minutes. He began to reproach himself for
this laughter; but instantly realized that there was nothing to
reproach himself for, as he felt infinitely sorry for the general.

His forebodings were realized. That very evening he received
a strange note, short but determined. The general informed him
that he was parting from him for ever, that he respected him
and was grateful to him, but even from him would not accept
'marks of compassion, lowering the dignity of a man who is
already wretched'. When the prince heard that the old man had
locked himself up in the home of Nina Alexandrovna, he almost
felt reassured about him. But we have already seen that the
general had caused some sort of trouble at Lizaveta Prokofyevna's, too. Here we cannot report the details, but will observe
briefly that the essence of the encounter consisted in the general's
having frightened Lizaveta Prokofyevna, and brought her to
indignation by bitter allusions to Ganya. He had been shown
the door, in disgrace. That was why he had passed such a night
and such a morning, gone off his head completely, and run out
into the street almost insane.

Kolya still did not understand the matter completely, and
even hoped to save the day by taking a stern line.

'Well, where are we going to go trailing off to now, do you
suppose, General?' he said. 'You don't want to go to the prince,
you've quarrelled with Lebedev, you've no money, I never have
any: so here we are without a bean, in the middle of the street.'

'It's more pleasant to sit with the beans than to be without one,'[12] muttered the general. 'With that . . . pun I used to arouse delight . . . in the officers' mess . . . in forty-four . . . in eighteen . . . forty-four, yes! . . . I don't remember . . . Oh, don't remind me, don't remind me! "Where is my youth, where is my freshness?" As that fellow said . . . who said that, Kolya?'

'That's from Gogol, in *Dead Souls*,[13] Papa,' replied Kolya, looking out of the corner of his eye at his father, in apprehension.

'*Dead Souls*! Oh yes, dead ones! When you bury me, write on my grave: "Here lies a dead soul"! "Disgrace pursues me!" Who said that, Kolya?'

'I don't know, Papa.'

'Yeropegov didn't exist! Yeroshka Yeropegov!' he exclaimed in a frenzy, coming to a standstill in the street. 'And this from my son, my own son! Yeropegov, the man who was a brother to me for eleven months, for whom I fought a duel . . . Prince Vygoretsky, our captain, said to him over a bottle: "Where did you get your St Anne's,[14] Grisha, tell me that?" "On the battlefields of my fatherland, that's where I got it!" I shouted: "Bravo, Grisha!" Well, then there was a duel, and then he married . . . Marya Petrovna Su . . . Sutugina and was killed on the battlefields . . . The bullet bounced off the cross on my chest and straight into his forehead. "I shall never forget!" he cried and fell on the spot. I . . . I served honourably, Kolya; I served nobly, but disgrace – "disgrace pursues me!" You and Nina will come to my graveside . . . "Poor Nina!" That was what I used to call her, Kolya, a long time ago, back in the early days, and she loved me so . . . Nina, Nina! What have I done to your fate? How can you love me, patient soul? Your mother has the soul of an angel, Kolya, do you hear, of an angel!'

'I know that, Papa. My good Papa, let us go home to Mama! She was running after us! Well, why have you stopped? As if you didn't understand . . . Oh, why are you crying?'

Kolya himself was crying, and he kissed his father's hands.

'You're kissing my hands, mine!'

'Yes, yours, yours. Well, what's so surprising? Oh, why are you bawling out in the street, yet you call yourself a general, a military man, oh, come along!'

'God bless you, dear boy, for being respectful to a disgraceful

– yes! A disgraceful old man, your father . . . and may you have such a boy . . . *le roi de Rome* . . . Oh, "a curse, a curse upon this house".'

'But what's going on here, really?' Kolya suddenly began to fume. 'What's happened? Why don't you want to go home now? Why have you lost your mind?'

'I shall explain, I shall explain to you . . . I'll tell you every-thing; don't shout, they'll hear . . . *le roi de Rome* . . . Oh, I feel sick, I feel sad! *"Nurse, where is your grave?"*[15] Who said that, Kolya?'

'I don't know, I don't know who said it! Let's go home right now, right now! I'll beat Ganya black and blue if I have to . . . where are you going now?'

But the general dragged him to the front steps of a nearby house.

'What are you doing? These aren't our front steps!'

The general sat down on the steps, still drawing Kolya towards him by the hand.

'Bend down, bend down!' he muttered, 'I'll tell you everything . . . disgrace . . . bend down . . . your ear, your ear; I'll tell it in your ear . . .'

'But what on earth?' Kolya said, in terrible alarm, yet turning his ear all the same.

'*Le roi de Rome* . . .' whispered the general, also apparently trembling all over.

'What do you mean? . . . Where do you get this *le roi de Rome* business from? . . . What?'

'I . . . I . . .' the general began to whisper again, clutching the shoulder of 'his boy' tighter and tighter. 'I . . . want . . . to tell you . . . everything, Marya, Marya . . . Petrovna Su-su-su . . .'

Kolya tore himself free, seized the general by the shoulders and looked at him like one demented. The old man had gone purple, his lips turned blue, slight convulsions ran across his face. Suddenly he bent forward and began to subside gently on to Kolya's arm.

'A stroke!' Kolya exclaimed to the whole street, having real-ized at last what was wrong.

5

If truth be known, Varvara Ardalionovna, in conversation with her brother, had slightly exaggerated the accuracy of her news about the prince's proposal to Aglaya Yepanchina. Perhaps, like the shrewd woman she was, she had foreseen what was bound to happen in the near future; perhaps, upset by the way in which the dream had dispersed in smoke (a dream in which, however, she had not believed), she, being human, could not resist the satisfaction of pouring even more poison into her brother's heart by exaggerating the calamity, even though she loved him sincerely and with compassion. But at any rate, she could not have received such accurate information from her friends, the Yepanchins; there were only hints, unspoken words, silences, enigmas. And, perhaps, Aglaya's sisters had intentionally let something slip, in order to learn something from Varvara Ardalionovna themselves; and lastly, it might have been that they did not wish to deny themselves the female satisfaction of teasing their friend a little, even though she was a childhood friend: for they could not have failed to discern at least a small margin of her intentions.

On the other hand, the prince, though he was quite truthful in assuring Lebedev that he could tell him nothing and that nothing particular had happened to him, was also, perhaps, in error. Indeed, with all of them something very strange seemed to take place: nothing had happened, and yet at the same time it was as if a great deal had happened. It was this last that Varvara Ardalionovna, with her unerring feminine instinct, had guessed.

Just how it came to pass, however, that everyone at the Yepanchins suddenly had the same unanimous thought that something of capital importance had happened to Aglaya, and that her fate was being decided – that is very difficult to set down in order. But no sooner had that thought flashed, instantly, to them all, than they all instantly maintained that they had long ago discerned it and foreseen it all; that it had all been clear ever since the 'poor knight', and even earlier, except that then they had as yet been unwilling to believe anything so absurd. This was what the sisters claimed; of course, Lizaveta Proko- fyevna had also foreseen it all before anyone else, and for a long time her heart had 'ached', but now – whether that was so or not – the thought of the prince was suddenly something she could not abide, mostly for the reason that she was bewildered. There was a pressing question here that had to be resolved at once; however, not only was it impossible to resolve, but Liza- veta Prokofyevna could not even formulate it to herself quite clearly, no matter how she tried. The matter was a difficult one: was the prince a good thing or not? Was all this a good thing or not? If it was not (which was indubitably so), then why was it not? And if, perhaps, it was a good thing (which was also possible), then again, why was it? The paterfamilias himself, Ivan Fyodorovich, was, of course, initially astonished, but later suddenly made the admission that after all, to be quite honest, he too had fancied something of the kind; it had seemed to recede, but then it had returned. He at once fell silent under the withering gaze of his spouse, but did so in the morning, and in the evening, alone with his spouse and compelled to speak again, suddenly and, as if with especial courage, expressed a few unexpected thoughts: 'After all, really, what does it matter? . . .' (Silence.) 'Of course, it's all very strange, if it's true, and I don't dispute that, but . . .' (Another silence.) 'But on the other hand, if one looks at the matter directly, then the prince is, after all, quite honestly, a most splendid young fellow, and . . . and, and – well, at last, our name, our family name, all this will have the appearance, as it were, of keeping up our family name, which has fallen, in the eyes of society, that is, if one looks at it from that point of view, because . . . of course, society; society is society; but the prince is not without a fortune, though it's not much of one. He has . . . and . . . and . . .' (Prolonged silence and decided anticlimax.) Having heard her husband out, Lizaveta Prokofyevna passed beyond endurance.

In her opinion, all that had happened was 'unforgivable and even criminal nonsense, a fantastic tableau, stupid and pre- posterous!' First of all there was the fact that 'this wretched little prince was a sickly idiot, secondly, a fool with no knowledge of society and no place in it: to whom could one show him off, even were one to get him in? He was some kind of impossible democrat, didn't even have a civil service rank, and . . . and . . . what would Belokonskaya say? And was this, was this the kind of husband we imagined and intended for Aglaya?' The last argument was, of course, the main one. The mother's heart trembled at this thought, was bathed in blood and tears, though at the same time something stirred within that heart, which suddenly said to her: 'But why isn't the prince the kind of man you want?' Well, it was these objections of her own heart that were most troublesome of all for Lizaveta Prokofyevna.

For some reason, the sisters found the thought of the prince appealing; it did not even seem very strange to them; in a word, they might suddenly even have come over to his side completely. But they both decided to keep quiet. Once and for all, it was noticed in the household that the more stubborn and insistent Lizaveta Prokofyevna's objections and rebuttals on any general and controversial point concerning the family became, the more this began to serve them all as a sign that perhaps she really agreed with them on that point. But Alexandra Ivanovna could not, in the end, remain completely silent. Having long acknowledged her as her adviser, the mother now kept constantly summoning her and demanding her opinions, and above all, her recollections, with phrases like: 'How did all this happen? Why did no one see it? Why did no one say anything? What was the social standing of this wretched "poor knight"? Why was she alone, Lizaveta Prokofyevna, doomed to worry about them all, take note of everything, and foresee it, while everyone else merely twiddled their thumbs?" etcetera, etcetera. At first Alexandra Ivanovna was cautious, observing merely that her father's ideas on the matter seemed rather close to the mark. That the choice of Prince Myshkin as the husband of one of the Yepanchin girls might seem very satisfactory in the eyes of society. Gradually, becoming more heated, she even added that the prince was not at all a 'fool' and had never been one, and with regard to his standing, then after all God only knew what would be the criterion of the social standing of a decent man with us in Russia in a few years' time: obligatory success in the civil service, as previously, or something else? In response to all this the mother at once snapped that Alexandra was 'a freethinker, and all this is that accursed woman question of theirs'. Half an hour later she set off for town, and from there to Kamenny Island, in order to catch Belokonskaya, who just so happened to be in St Petersburg at that time, though was soon to leave. Belokonskaya was Aglaya's godmother.

'Old woman' Belokonskaya listened to all Lizaveta Proko-fyevna's fevered and despairing confessions and was in no way touched by the bewildered mother of the family, even gave her a mocking look. She was a dreadful despot; in friendship, even the oldest, she could not endure equality, and looked upon Lizaveta Prokofyevna decidedly as her protegée, just as she had done thirty-five years earlier, and could on no account be reconciled with the abruptness and independence of her character. She observed, among other things, that they had all been behaving as they usually did 'over there, running too far ahead of themselves and making a mountain out of a molehill'; that no matter how closely she listened, she could not be persuaded that anything serious had really happened to them; that it might be better to wait until something came of it; that the prince, in her opinion, was a decent young man, though an invalid, eccentric and of far too low a social class. Worst of all, he was openly keeping a mistress. Lizaveta Prokofyevna realized only too well that Belokonskaya was somewhat angry about Yevgeny Pavlovich's lack of success, as it had been she who recommended him. She returned home to Pavlovsk in an even greater state of irritation than the one in which she had left, and everyone immediately received a piece of her mind, mainly because they had 'lost their senses', that absolutely no one conducted their affairs in such a way, only them: 'Why were you in such a hurry? What happened? No matter how hard I look, I can on no account conclude that anything has really happened at all! Just wait until it does! Ivan Fyodorovich may fancy anything he pleases, but one shouldn't make mountains out of molehills,' etcetera, etcetera.

So it turned out that what they needed to do was calm themselves, look on the matter coolly, and wait. But alas, the calm did not last even ten minutes. The first blow was coolly inflicted by the news of what had happened during the mother's absence on Kamenny Island. (Lizaveta Prokofyevna's journey had taken place on the morning after the prince had arrived at nearly one hour after midnight instead of just after nine.) To their mother's impatient questioning the sisters replied in great detail, telling her that, in the first place, 'it seemed that nothing had happened in her absence', that the prince had arrived, that Aglaya did not appear for a long time, and when she finally did, after nearly half an hour, she at once suggested to him that they play a game of chess; that the prince did not even know how to play chess, and Aglaya had immediately beaten him; had become very gleeful and put the prince dreadfully to shame for his inability to play, so that he made a sorry sight. Then she suggested that they play a game of cards – 'fools'. But here quite the reverse transpired; the prince turned out to be as good at 'fools' as a professor, playing masterfully; Aglaya even cheated, exchanging cards and stealing tricks from him before his very eyes, yet each time he left her a 'fool'; some five times in succession. Aglaya flew into a dreadful rage and even quite forgot herself; said such hurtful and insolent things to the prince that he even stopped laughing and turned quite pale when she told him at last that she would not set foot in this room while he was sitting there, and that it was downright shameless on his part to come visiting them, especially at night, almost at one in the morning, *after all that had happened*. Then she slammed the door and went out. The prince went away as from a funeral, in spite of all their comforting words. Suddenly, a quarter of an hour later, Aglaya came running downstairs to the terrace with such haste that she had not even dried her eyes, which were full of tears; she had run down because Kolya had arrived with a hedgehog. They all began to examine the hedgehog; to their questions Kolya explained that the hedgehog was not his, and that he was passing with his companion, another gymnasium student, Kostya Lebedev, who had remained out on the street and was too shy to come in, as he was carrying an axe; that they had bought both hedgehog and axe from a passing muzhik. The muzhik had sold them the hedgehog and taken fifty copecks for it, but as for the axe, they had persuaded him to sell it, as it was a chance for him to do so, and it was a very good axe. At this point Aglaya suddenly began to insist in no uncertain terms that Kolya sell her the hedgehog at once, got quite beside herself, and even called Kolya 'dear'. For a long time Kolya resisted, but then at last gave in and summoned Kostya Lebedev, who really did come in with the axe and was very embarrassed. But then it suddenly turned out that the hedgehog was not theirs at all, but belonged to a third boy, Petrov, who had given them both money to buy Schlosser's *History*[1] from a fourth boy, who, being in need of money, was selling it at a low price; that they had gone there to buy Schlosser's *History*, but had not been able to resist the temptation and had bought the hedgehog, so that consequently both hedgehog and axe belonged to the third boy, to whom they were now taking them instead of Schlosser's *History*. But Aglaya was being so insistent that in the end they decided to sell her the hedgehog. As soon as Aglaya got the hedgehog, she at once put it, with Kolya's help, into a wicker basket, covered it with a napkin and began to ask Kolya to take it at once, without delay, to the prince, on her behalf, asking him to accept it as 'a token of her deepest respect'. Kolya agreed, with delight, and promised that he would deliver it, but at once began to ply her with questions in return: 'What does a present of a hedgehog mean?' Aglaya replied to him that it was none of his business. He retorted that he was convinced there was an allegory in it. Aglaya got angry and snapped at him that he was an urchin, and nothing more. Kolya at once replied to her that were it not for the fact that he respected the woman in her and, over and above that, his own convictions, he would have shown her directly that he knew how to reply to an insult like that. In the end, however, Kolya went off enthusiastically to deliver the hedgehog, with Kostya Lebedev running after him; Aglaya could not restrain herself, and, when she saw that Kolya was swinging the basket about too much, shouted after him from the veranda: 'Please, Kolya, don't drop it, dear!' – every bit as though she had not just been scolding him; Kolya stopped and also, with the greatest of willingness, shouted, as though he had not been scolding her: 'No, I shan't drop it, Aglaya Ivanovna. You may put your mind quite at ease!' – and ran off again at full tilt. After that, Aglaya burst into hilarious laughter, ran back to her room extremely pleased with herself, and spent all the rest of the day in a very cheerful mood.

This news completely stunned Lizaveta Prokofyevna. One might have wondered why. But such, apparently, was the mood that had assailed her. Her alarm was aroused in an extreme degree, and the main thing was the hedgehog: what was the meaning of the hedgehog? What was agreed here? What was implied here? What sort of signal was it? Was it some kind of telegram? What was more, poor Ivan Fyodorovich, who happened to be present at the interrogation, completely spoiled it all with his answer. In his opinion, there was no telegram here, and the hedgehog was 'just a hedgehog, that's all – it probably also meant friendship, the forgetting of injuries and reconciliation, in a word, it was all a prank, but at all events an innocent and excusable one'.

Let us note in parenthesis that his guess was correct. The prince, returning home from Aglaya derided and banished, had already been sitting for about half an hour in the most gloomy despair, when Kolya suddenly appeared with the hedgehog. At once the sky grew bright again; the prince rose from the dead, as it were, questioned Kolya, hung on his every word, re-questioned him a dozen times, laughed like a child and kept squeezing the hands of both boys, who were laughing and looking at him brightly. So it emerged that Aglaya had forgiven him and the prince could go and see her again that very same evening, and for him that was not only the main thing, but even everything.

'What children we are still, Kolya! And . . . and . . . how good it is that we're children!' he exclaimed with rapture, at last.

'It's quite simple, she's in love with you, Prince, and that's all!' Kolya replied with imposing authority.

The prince flushed, but this time said not a word, and Kolya merely laughed and clapped his hands; a moment later the prince also burst out laughing, and then after that looked at his watch every five minutes, to see how much time had passed and how much remained until evening.

But her mood got the better of her: Lizaveta Prokofyevna at last could restrain herself no more, and abandoned herself to a moment of hysteria. In spite of all the objections of her spouse and daughters, she at once sent for Aglaya in order to ask her a final question and receive from her a clear and final answer. 'In order to get this over with now, and off our shoulders, so that we don't have to mention it again! Otherwise,' she declared, 'I shall not survive until evening!' And only at that point did they all realize what confusion the matter had reached. Apart from feigned surprise, indignation, laughter and mockery of the prince and all who asked her questions, they obtained nothing from Aglaya. Lizaveta took to her bed and came out for tea at the time when the prince was expected. She awaited the prince with trepidation, and when he appeared she almost had a fit of hysterics.

But the prince entered timidly, almost as though he were feeling his way, smiling strangely, peering into everyone's eyes as if he were asking them all a question, because Aglaya was again not in the room, which at once alarmed him. That evening there were no outsiders, only members of the family. Prince Shch. was still in St Petersburg in connection with the business concerning Yevgeny Pavlovich's uncle. 'If only he were here and would say something,' Lizaveta Prokofyevna lamented about him. Ivan Fyodorovich sat with an exceedingly worried demeanour; the sisters were grave and, as if on purpose, said nothing. Lizaveta Prokofyevna did not know how to start the conversation. At last, she suddenly poured energetic abuse on the railway system, and looked at the prince with an air of decided challenge.

Alas! Aglaya did not appear, and the prince was lost. Barely able to mouth his words, and perplexed, he began to express the opinion that the repair of the railway was an extremely useful thing, but Adelaida suddenly began to laugh, and the prince was crushed again. It was at this very moment that Aglaya entered calmly and grandly, made a ceremonious bow to the prince, and solemnly took the most conspicuous place at the circular table. She gave the prince a questioning look. Everyone realized that the resolution of all their bewilderment had begun.

'Did you receive my hedgehog?' she asked firmly and almost angrily.

'Yes, I did,' replied the prince, blushing and with sinking heart.

'Then please explain at once what you think of it? It is necessary for Mama's peace of mind, and for that of the entire household.'

'Listen, Aglaya...' the general suddenly began to grow uneasy.

'This, this goes beyond all limits!' Lizaveta Prokofyevna was suddenly alarmed for some reason.

'There are no limits here, *Maman*,' the daughter replied sternly and at once. 'I sent the prince a hedgehog today and wish to know his opinion. Well, Prince?'

'Er, what sort of opinion, Aglaya?'

'About the hedgehog.'

'Er... I think, Aglaya Ivanovna, that you want to know how I received ... the hedgehog ... or, rather, how I looked ... upon this sending ... of a hedgehog, well ... in that case, I suppose that ... in a word...'

He lost his breath, and was silent.

'Well, you haven't said much,' Aglaya waited for about five seconds. 'Very well, I agree to leave the hedgehog; but I'm very glad that at last I'm able to put an end to all the misunderstandings that have accumulated. Permit me, at last, to learn from you yourself and in person: do you seek me as a match, or not?'

'Oh, merciful Lord!' Lizaveta Prokofyevna blurted out.

The prince gave a shudder and started back; Ivan Fyodorovich froze; the sisters frowned.

'Do not lie, Prince, tell the truth. Because of you I am being pursued with strange questions; so, do these questions have any foundation? Well?'

'I have not sought you as a match, Aglaya Ivanovna,' said the prince, growing suddenly animated, 'but ... you know yourself how I love you and how I believe in you ... even now...'

'What I asked you was: are you asking for my hand in marriage, or not?'

'I am,' his heart sinking, the prince replied.

There followed a general and violent commotion.

'This is all wrong, *mon cher ami*,' said Ivan Fyodorovich, intensely agitated, 'it's . . . it's almost impossible, if that is true, Glasha . . . Forgive me, Prince, forgive me, my dear fellow! . . . Lizaveta Prokofyevna!' he turned to his spouse for help, 'we ought to . . . go into this . . .'

'I refuse, I refuse!' Lizaveta Prokofyevna began to wave her arms about.

'Then permit me to speak, *Maman*; after all, I myself am of some significance in this matter: an extremely important moment in my fate is being decided (Aglaya actually used this expression), and I want to find out for myself and am, moreover, glad that it's happening when everyone is present . . . So permit me to ask you, Prince, if you "nourish such intentions", then how exactly do you intend to provide my happiness?'

'Truly, I don't know how to answer you, Aglaya Ivanovna: in such a case . . . in such a case what can one reply? And in fact, is any reply . . . needed?'

'You seem embarrassed and out of breath; rest for a little and gather new strength; drink a glass of water; and gather new strength; drink a glass of water; though you'll be served tea presently.'

'I love you, Aglaya Ivanovna, I love you very much; I love only you and . . . please don't joke about it, I love you very much.'

'But, however, this is an important matter; we are not children, and one must look at every aspect . . . Now try to explain, what does your fortune consist of?'

'Tut-tut-tut, Aglaya. What are you thinking of? It's wrong, wrong . . .' Ivan Fyodorovich muttered in alarm.

'Disgraceful!' Lizaveta Prokofyevna whispered loudly.

'She's taken leave of her senses!' Alexandra whispered, also loudly.

'Fortune . . . You mean money?' The prince was astonished.

'Precisely.'

'I have . . . I now have one hundred and thirty-five thousand roubles,' muttered the prince, starting to blush.

'Is that all?' Aglaya said in loud and open astonishment, not blushing at all. 'Though actually, it's all right; especially if one's economical . . . Do you intend to join the civil service?'

'I had it in mind to take the examination to qualify as a domestic tutor . . .'

'Very appropriate; of course, that will increase our wealth. Do you plan to be a gentleman of the bedchamber?'

'A gentleman of the bedchamber? I certainly didn't envisage that, but . . .'

But here the two sisters could not restrain themselves from bursting into laughter. Adelaida had long ago noticed in the twitching features of Aglaya's face the signs of swift and uncontainable laughter, which she was so far managing to hold back with all her might. Aglaya began to cast threatening glances at her laughing sisters, but in a second she too could hold out no longer and dissolved in the maddest, almost hysterical laughter; at last she leaped to her feet and ran out of the room.

'I knew she was simply doing it as a joke, and nothing else!' exclaimed Adelaida. 'right from the beginning, from the hedgehog.'

'No, this I will not allow, I will not allow it!' Lizaveta Prokofyevna suddenly boiled over with anger and quickly turned to follow Aglaya. The sisters at once ran after her. In the room only the prince and the paterfamilias were left.

'This, this . . . could you have imagined anything like it, Lev Nikolaich?' the general exclaimed abruptly, apparently not knowing himself what he wanted to say. 'No, seriously, seriously?'

'I see that Aglaya Ivanovna was laughing at me,' the prince replied sadly.

'Wait, brother; I'll go, and you wait . . . so . . . can you at least explain, Lev Nikolaich, you at least, how all this happened, and what it all means, in all its, as it were, entirety? Brother, you must admit: I am her father; in spite of everything, I am, after all, her father, so I don't understand any of this; then will you at least explain?'

'I love Aglaya Ivanovna; she knows that and . . . has known it for a long time, I think.'

The general shrugged his shoulders.

'Strange, strange . . . and you love her very much?'

'Yes.'

'I find all this strange, strange. I mean, it's such a surprise and a shock that . . . You see, dear fellow, it's not the size of your fortune (though I expected you would have a little more), but . . . my daughter's happiness . . . are you able to . . . provide it . . . her happiness? And . . . and . . . what is this: is it a joke, or is it serious on her part? I don't mean yours, but hers?'

The voice of Alexandra Ivanovna was heard outside the door: Papa was being summoned.

'Wait, brother, wait! Wait and think it over, and I'll be back in a moment . . .' he said hastily, and rushed off in response to Alexandra's summons, almost in fear.

He found his spouse and daughter in each other's embrace and showering each other with tears. They were tears of happiness, tender emotion and reconciliation. Aglaya was kissing her mother's hands, cheeks, lips; they were nestling warmly against each other.

'Well now, look at her, Ivan Fyodorych, that's what she's really like now!' said Lizaveta Prokofyevna.

Aglaya turned her small, happy and tear-stained face away from her mother's bosom, glanced at her papa, burst into loud laughter, jumped over to him, tightly embraced him and kissed him several times. Then she rushed back to her mother and completely hid her face in her bosom, so that no one would see, and at once began to cry again. Lizaveta Prokofyevna covered her with the end of her shawl.

'Now, what, what are you doing to us, you cruel little girl, after this, that's what I want to know!' she said, but joyfully now, as though she had suddenly found it easier to breathe.

'Cruel! Yes, cruel!' Aglaya suddenly chimed in. 'Rotten! Spoilt! Tell it to papa. Oh, but of course he's here. Papa, you're here? Listen!' she burst out laughing through tears.

'*Chère amie*, my idol!' the general kissed her hand, beaming all over with happiness. (Aglaya did not take her hand away.) So you love this . . . young man? . . .'

'Not at all! I cannot stand . . . your young man, I can't stand him!' Aglaya suddenly boiled over, raising her head. 'And if you dare again, Papa ... I mean it seriously; you hear; I mean it seriously!'

And she really did mean it seriously: she had even gone quite red, and her eyes glistened. Her papa stopped short in alarm, but Lizaveta Prokofyevna made a sign to him behind Aglaya's back, and he took it to mean: 'Don't question her.'

'If that is so, my angel, then of course it's as you wish, you may do as you please, he is waiting there alone; ought I not to hint to him discreetly that he should go?'

The general winked at Lizaveta Prokofyevna in his turn.

'No, no, that is really not necessary; especially if you do it "discreetly": go out to him yourself; I'll come out after you, in a moment. I want to apologize to that ... young man, because I insulted him.'

'And insulted him well and truly,' Ivan Fyodorovich confirmed, in a serious tone.

'Well, then ... you'd better stay here, and I'll go first, alone; you'll follow me at once, and arrive the very next second; it will be best that way.'

She had already gone as far as the door, but suddenly turned back.

'I shall burst into laughter! I shall die of laughter!' she said sadly.

But at that same second she turned round and ran towards the prince.

'Well, what is it, then? What do you think?' Ivan Fyodorovich said quickly.

'I'm afraid to say it,' Lizaveta Prokofyevna replied, also quickly, 'but, in my opinion, it's clear.'

'And I think the same way. It's as clear as daylight. She loves him.'

'Not only that, she's in love!' replied Alexandra Ivanovna. 'But think who with!'

'God bless her, if that is her fate!' Lizaveta Prokofyevna crossed herself devoutly.

'It must be,' the general confirmed, 'and fate cannot be avoided!'

And they all went into the drawing room, where another surprise awaited them.

Not only did Aglaya not burst out laughing when she went in to see the prince, as she had feared, she even said to him, almost timidly:

'Forgive a stupid, wicked, spoilt girl' (she took him by the hand) 'and be assured that we all have a boundless respect for you. And if I have dared to mock your beautiful ... kind simplicity, then forgive me as you would a child for a prank; forgive me for persisting with an absurdity that cannot, of course, have the slightest consequences ...'

Aglaya spoke these last words with particular emphasis.

Her father, mother and sisters all arrived in the drawing room in time to see and hear all this, and all were struck by the 'absurdity that cannot have the slightest consequences', and even more by Aglaya's serious mood as she talked about that absurdity. They all exchanged questioning glances; but the prince, it seemed, had not understood these words and was in the highest stage of happiness.

'Why do you say that,' he muttered, 'why do you ask ... forgiveness?'

He even wanted to say that he was unworthy of being asked for forgiveness. Who knows, perhaps he had even noticed the significance of the words about 'an absurdity that cannot, of course, have the slightest consequence', but, like the strange man he was, even rejoiced, perhaps, in those words. Unquestionably, for him the acme of bliss was represented by the mere fact that he would again be able to come and see Aglaya again without hindrance, that he would be allowed to talk to her, sit with her, go for walks with her, and, who knows, perhaps, would be satisfied with that for the rest of his life! (It was this very satisfaction that seemed to frighten Lizaveta Prokofyevna in private; she had a good idea of what he was about; many things frightened her which she herself was unable to express.)

It is hard to imagine the degree to which the prince grew animated and exuberant that evening. So cheerful was he that merely to look at him made one feel cheerful – that was how Aglaya's sisters put it later. He talked effusively, and this had not occurred with him since the morning when, half a year earlier, he had made his first acquaintance with the Yepanchins; for after his return from St Petersburg he had been noticeably and intentionally silent and had recently, in everyone's presence, let it slip to Prince Shch. that he had to restrain himself and keep silent, because he did not have the right to degrade an idea by setting it forth himself. He was almost the only person to talk all that evening, and told many things; clearly, with delight and in detail, he replied to questions. But nothing resembling polite conversation showed through in his words. They were all very serious, even sometimes abstruse ideas. The prince even set forth some of his own views, his own secret observations, so that it would all have even been comical, had it not been so 'well set forth', as all the listeners later agreed. The general, though he was partial to serious conversational subjects, shared with Lizaveta Prokofyevna the opinion that it was all rather too learned, so that towards the end of the evening they even became melancholy. In the end, however, the prince went so far as to tell some most ridiculous anecdotes, at which he was the first to laugh, making the others laugh, too, more at his laughter than at the anecdotes themselves. As for Aglaya, she hardly spoke all evening; on the other hand, she listened to Lev Niko-layevich intently, and even not so much listened to him, as looked at him.

'How she looks at him, can't take her eyes off him; hangs on his every word; she catches them all, catches them all!' Lizaveta Prokofyevna said to her spouse later on. 'But tell her she loves him, and she'll cry blue murder!'

'What can one do – it's fate!' the general shrugged his shoulders, and for a long time after kept repeating the word for which he had developed a liking. We should add that, as a man of business, there was also much in the present situation of all these things that he found exceedingly distasteful, especially in the vagueness of the matter; but for the present he also decided to remain silent and look . . . into Lizaveta Prokofyevna's eyes.

The family's joyful mood did not last long. The very next day Aglaya quarrelled with the prince again, and so it went on without cease, for all the days that followed. For hours on end she held the prince up to ridicule and almost turned him into a buffoon. True, they did sometimes sit for an hour or two in their small domestic garden, in the arbour, but it was noticed that the prince almost invariably spent these occasions reading aloud a newspaper or a book to Aglaya.

'You know,' Aglaya told him once, interrupting the newspaper, 'I've noticed that you're awfully ill-informed; you don't know anything properly, if one asks you for information: you don't know who it was, what year it happened in, or under the terms of what treaty. You're quite pathetic.'

'I told you, I'm not very educated,' replied the prince.

'Well, what am I to think of you after that? How can I respect you after that? Carry on reading; though actually, no, don't, please stop reading.'

And again that same evening they obtained a fleeting glimpse of something on her part that was very puzzling to them all. Prince Shch. was back from St Petersburg, and Aglaya was very affectionate to him, asking many questions about Yevgeny Pavlovich. (Prince Lev Nikolayevich had not arrived yet.) Suddenly Prince Shch. somehow permitted himself to allude to 'the new and imminent upheaval in the household', in response to a few words let slip by Lizaveta Prokofyevna to the effect that it might perhaps be necessary to postpone Adelaida's wedding again, so that both weddings could take place together. One simply cannot imagine how Aglaya flared up at 'all these stupid suppositions'; and, among other things, she blurted out that 'she did not yet intend to take the place of anyone's mistresses'.

These words shocked them all, especially the parents. Lizaveta Prokofyevna insisted, in secret consultation with her husband, that the prince would really have to explain himself concerning Nastasya Filippovna.

Ivan Fyodorovich swore that it was all merely an 'outburst', caused by Aglaya's 'shyness'; that if Prince Shch. had not begun to talk about the wedding there would have been no outburst, because Aglaya herself knew, knew for certain, that this was all a slander spread by unkind people and that Nastasya Filippovna was going to marry Rogozhin; that not only did the prince have no liaison with her, he had nothing to do with her; and, indeed, never had done, if the whole truth were to be told.

But in spite of it all, the prince showed no sign of being upset, and continued in his blissful state. Oh, of course, he too sometimes noticed something, as it were, gloomy and impatient in Aglaya's glances; but his faith was more in something else, and the gloom vanished of itself. Once having placed his trust, nothing could make him hesitate further. Perhaps he was even too calm; that, at any rate, was how it seemed to Ippolit, when he met him by chance in the park one day.

'Well, wasn't it true what I told you that time, that you're in love?' he began, coming up to the prince of his own accord and making him stop. The prince offered his hand to him and congratulated him on 'looking so well'. The invalid did indeed seem quite exuberant, as is often the case with consumptives.

He had approached the prince in order to make some caustic remark about how happy the prince looked, but at once lost the thread, and began to talk about himself. He started to complain, complained about many things, at great length, and rather incoherently.

'You wouldn't believe,' he concluded, 'how irritable, petty, selfish, vain and commonplace they all are over there; would you believe, they only took me in on condition that I died as soon as possible, and now they're all mad at me because I'm not dying and, on the contrary, feel better. It's a farce! I'll wager that you don't believe me!'

The prince did not feel like contradicting.

'I even sometimes think of coming back and moving in with you again,' Ippolit added casually. 'So you don't think they're capable of taking someone in on condition that he dies, and as soon as possible?'

'I thought they invited you with other considerations in mind.'

'Heh! You know, you're not at all as simple as you're made out to be! Now's not the time, but I could tell you a few things about that Ganechka and his hopes. They're undermining you, Prince, pitilessly undermining you, and ... I even feel sorry for you, because you're so calm. But alas – you can't be any different!'

'That's a fine thing to feel sorry for me about!' the prince began to laugh. 'Tell me, in your opinion, would I be happier if I were less calm?'

'It's better to be unhappy and *know*, than to be happy and live ... as a fool. You appear not to believe for one moment that you have a rival, and ... in that quarter?'

'Your remark about rivalry is a little cynical, Ippolit; I'm sorry, but I don't have the right to answer you. As for Gavrila Ardalionovich, then you yourself must admit that he can hardly remain calm after all he has lost, if you have the slightest knowledge of his affairs. I think it's better to see it from that point of view. He'll manage to change; he has his whole life ahead of him, and life is rich ... though actually ... actually,' the prince was suddenly perplexed, 'about this undermining ... I don't even know what you're talking about; we'd better drop this conversation, Ippolit.'

'Let's leave it for now; after all, you're required to be gracious. Yes, Prince, you have to touch it with your finger in order not to believe it again, ha-ha! And do you have a very great deal of contempt for me now, what do you think?'

'Why? Because you've suffered, and are suffering, more than us?'

'No, because I'm unworthy of my suffering.'

'The person who's able to suffer more must for that reason be worthy of suffering more. When Aglaya Ivanovna read your confession, she wanted to see you, but ...'

'She's putting it off ... it's out of the question for her, I understand ...' Ippolit cut in, as though trying to steer the conversation away from that subject as quickly as possible. 'Incidentally, they say that you yourself read all that rubbish to her out loud; it really was written ... and enacted ... in a state of delirium. And I really don't understand the degree of – I won't say cruelty (that would humiliate me) – but childish vanity and vindictiveness one would have to have in order to reproach me for that confession and use it against me as a weapon! Don't worry, it's not you I'm talking about.'

'You know, I'm sorry that you repudiate that notebook, Ippolit, what you wrote in it is sincere, and, you know, even its

most ridiculous aspects (Ippolit frowned intensely) are redeemed
by suffering, for to confess to them also involved suffering
and ... perhaps, great courage. The thought that moved you
certainly had a noble foundation, I see that more and more
clearly, I swear to you. I'm not judging you, I'm telling you this
in order to express my opinion, and I'm sorry I kept silent that
evening ...'

Ippolit flushed. The thought flickered through his mind
that the prince was dissembling and trying to catch him out;
but studying the prince's face more closely, he could not help
believing in his sincerity; his own face cleared.

'And yet all the same one must die!' he said quietly, nearly
adding: 'someone like me!' 'And can you imagine how that
Ganechka wears me out; he has devised, by way of a rebuttal,
the notion that perhaps three or four of those who listened to
my notebook that evening may die before me! He thinks that's
a consolation, ha-ha! For one thing, they're not dead yet; and
even if those people did die, then what consolation would there
be in that, tell me? He judges by his own lights; actually, he has
even gone further, now he simply hurls abuse, says that in such
cases a decent man dies in silence and that in all of this there's
nothing but egoism on my part! How do you like that? No, on
the contrary, what egoism on *his* part! What exquisite, or rather,
what bovine crudity there is in their egoism, an egoism they
simply cannot manage to perceive in themselves! ... Have you
ever read about the death of a certain Stepan Glebov,[2] in the
eighteenth century, Prince?

'What Stepan Glebov was that?'

'He was impaled on the stake in the time of Peter the Great.'

'Oh, good Lord, yes, I know! He was impaled for fifteen
hours, in the freezing cold, in his fur coat, and died with great
nobility of soul; of course, I've read about him ... well?'

'God may grant a death like that to some people, but not to
us! Perhaps you think I'm not capable of dying like Glebov?'

'Oh, not at all!' The prince was embarrassed. 'I simply meant
that you ... well, not that you wouldn't be like Glebov, but ...
that you ... that in those days you'd have been more like ...'

'Let me guess: Osterman, not Glebov – is that what you mean?'

'What Osterman?' the prince was astonished.

'Osterman, the diplomat Osterman, Peter the Great's Osterman,' muttered Ippolit, suddenly losing the thread. A certain bewilderment followed.

'Oh, n-n-no! That's not what I meant,' the prince said slowly, after a silence. 'I don't think you've ever been an ... Osterman ...'

Ippolit frowned.

'Actually, you see, the reason I say that,' the prince suddenly interjected again, evidently wishing to correct himself, 'is because the people of that time (I swear to you, this has always struck me) were apparently not at all like we are today, it was a different race from that of our own era,[3] truly, almost a different breed ... In those days people were carried by a single idea, whereas now they're more nervous, more developed, more sensitive, as if they were carried along by two or three ideas at the same time ... the man of today is broader – and, let me tell you, that's what prevents him from being the unified individual he was in those times ... I ... I ... that was all I meant, not ...'

'I understand; you're now trying to console me after disagreeing with me so naively, ha-ha! You're a complete child, Prince. However, I notice that you always treat me like ... like a china cup ... It's all right, it's all right, I'm not angry. At any rate, as it happens, we've had a very amusing conversation; you're sometimes a complete child, Prince. As a matter of fact, I'll have you know that I might perhaps want to be something better than an Osterman; it wouldn't be worth rising from the dead to be an Osterman ... Though in fact, I see that I ought to die as soon as possible, or else I could end up ... Leave me. *Au revoir!* Oh, very well, you tell me, give me your opinion: what would be the best way for me to die? ... The way that would be ... the most virtuous one, I mean? Go on, tell me!'

'Pass us by, and forgive us our happiness!' said the prince in a quiet voice.

'Ha-ha-ha! As I thought! I was definitely expecting something like that! I say ... I say ... Well, well! These eloquent folk! *Au revoir, au revoir!*'

6

Of the evening gathering at the Yepanchins' dacha, at which
Belokonskaya was expected, Varvara Ardalionovna had also
given her brother a completely faithful account; the guests were
indeed expected on the evening of that day; but again she
had put it all rather more harshly than was warranted by the
occasion. To be sure, the event had been arranged very hurriedly,
and even with a certain quite unnecessary agitation, for the sole
reason that in that household 'everything was done as no one
else does it'. It could all be explained by Lizaveta Prokofyevna's
'wish to be in no doubt no longer', and by the ardent fluttering of
both parental hearts concerning the happiness of their favourite
daughter. Moreover, Belokonskaya was indeed soon about to
leave; and as her protection really did mean a great deal in
society, and as they hoped she would be favourably inclined
towards the prince, the parents were counting on 'society'
accepting Aglaya's future husband straight from the hands of
the omnipotent 'old woman', and so, if there was anything
strange about it all, under such patronage it would seem far less
strange. In this lay the nub of the matter, for the parents were
quite unable to decide for themselves if there was anything
strange about it, and if there was, then precisely how much
about it was strange? Or was there nothing strange about it
at all? The frank and friendly opinion of authoritative and
competent people would have been useful at the present juncture
when, thanks to Aglaya, nothing had yet been finally decided.
At all events, sooner or later the prince had to be brought into
society, of which he had not the slightest conception. In short,
it was planned to 'show him off'. The projected soirée was,
however, of a simple kind; only 'friends of the family' were
expected, in the smallest of numbers. In addition to Belokonskaya, a certain lady was expected, the wife of a most important
barin and dignitary. As for young people, they were really only
counting on Yevgeny Pavlovich; he was to attend, escorting
Belokonskaya.

Of the fact that Belokonskaya would be there, the prince

heard almost three days before the evening in question; of the formal soirée he learned only the day before. He had, of course, noticed the troubled look of the members of the household and had even, from certain allusive and worried things they said to him, perceived that they were anxious about the impression he might make. But the Yepanchins, every single one of them, it appeared, had formed the notion that he, because of his simplicity, was quite unable to realize that they were so worried about him. Thus, when they looked at him, they all felt inwardly sad. As a matter of fact, he really attached almost no importance to the forthcoming event; he was preoccupied by something else entirely: Aglaya was becoming more capricious and gloomy by the hour – this was crushing him. When he learned that Yevgeny Pavlovich was also expected, he was very pleased and said that he had long wished to see him. For some reason these words were not to anyone's liking; Aglaya emerged from her room in annoyance, and only late in the evening, some time before midnight, when the prince was already leaving, did she seize the occasion to say a few words to him alone, as she was accompanying him to the door.

'I should like it if you would not come to see us during the daytime tomorrow, but arrive in the evening, when these . . . guests will be here. You do know that there are going to be guests, don't you?'

She spoke impatiently and with heightened severity; it was the first time she had mentioned this 'evening'. For her, too, the thought of the guests was almost intolerable; everyone had noticed this. It was possible that she felt a dreadful desire to quarrel with her parents about it, but pride and modesty prevented her from speaking. The prince at once realized that she too was anxious about him (and did not want to admit that she was), and suddenly felt afraid himself.

'Yes, I'm invited,' he replied.

She plainly found it hard to continue.

'May one talk to you seriously about something? Just once in your life?' she suddenly grew exceedingly angry, not knowing why, but unable to hold herself back.

'You may, and I'll listen; I'm very glad,' the prince mumbled.

Aglaya was again silent for a moment and began with visible loathing:

'I didn't want to argue with them about it; sometimes one can't make them listen to reason. I have always loathed the principles that *maman* sometimes adheres to. I'm not talking about papa, there's no point in asking him for anything. *Maman* is, of course, a decent woman; dare to suggest anything base to her, and you'll see. Well, but before that . . . trash – she bows and scrapes! I'm not just talking about Belokonskaya: a rubbishy old woman with a rubbishy character, but clever and knows how to keep people in hand – at least she has that in her favour. Oh, the baseness of it! And it's absurd: we've always been middle-class people, the most middle-class there could possibly be; so why try to climb into that high society set? My sisters are trying to get there, too; it's Prince Shch. who's turned their heads, all of them. Why are you glad that Yevgeny Pavlovich will be there?'

'Listen, Aglaya,' said the prince, 'I have the impression that you're very anxious about me, in case I flunk . . . this gathering tomorrow.'

'About you? Anxious?' Aglaya flushed to the roots of her hair. 'Why would I be anxious about you, even if you were to . . . even if you were to disgrace yourself completely? And how can you use such words? What does "flunk" mean? It's a rubbishy word, a vulgar one.'

'It's . . . a schoolboy expression.'

'Oh yes, a schoolboy expression! A rubbishy expression! I expect you intend to use expressions like that all the time tomorrow. Look for some more at home, in your dictionary: you'll certainly produce an effect! What a pity that you seem to be able to make a good entrance; where did you learn that? Will you be able to accept a cup of tea and drink it decently when everyone's watching you?'

'I think I shall.'

'That's too bad; otherwise I'd have had a good laugh. You must at least break the Chinese vase in the drawing room! It's worth a great deal of money, please, break it; it was a present, mama will go out of her mind and start weeping in front of everyone – it's so dear to her. Wave your hands about, the way you always do, knock it over and break it. Deliberately sit beside it.'

'On the contrary, I shall try to sit as far from it as possible: thank you for warning me.'

'That means you're already afraid that you'll wave your hands about a lot. I bet you'll start talking about some "topic", something serious, learned and exalted, won't you? How . . . proper that will be!'

'I think that would be stupid . . . if it wasn't appropriate.'

'Listen, once and for all,' Aglaya broke down, at last. 'If you start talking about anything like the death penalty, or the economic condition of Russia, or "beauty saving the world", then . . . I shall be delighted and laugh a great deal, but . . . I warn you now: never show yourself to my gaze again! Do you hear? I'm serious! This time I really am serious!'

She was indeed *serious* in delivering her threat, and there was even something unusual in her words and gaze that the prince had never observed before and really did not resemble a joke at all.

'Well, you've seen to it that now I shall certainly "start talking", and even . . . perhaps . . . break the vase. Earlier I wasn't anxious at all, but now I am anxious about everything. I'm sure I shall flunk.'

'Then don't say anything. Sit still and be silent.'

'That won't be possible; I am sure I'll start talking out of fear, and break the vase out of fear. Perhaps I'll fall on the slippery floor, or do something else of that sort, for that's happened to me in the past; I shall have dreams about it all night; why did you have to mention it?'

Aglaya gave him a glum look.

'You know what: I'd do best not to come at all tomorrow! I'll report sick, and that will be an end of it!' he decided, at last.

Aglaya stamped her foot and even turned pale with anger.

'Good Lord! Have you ever seen anything like it? He won't come when it's being specially arranged for him and . . . Oh God! A rare pleasure it is to have to do with such a . . . muddled fellow as you!'

'Oh, very well, I'll come, I'll come!' the prince interrupted quickly. 'And I give you my word of honour that I shall sit through the whole evening without uttering a word. I shall certainly do that.'

'You'll do well. Just now you said: "I'll report sick"; really, where do you get such expressions? What is it that makes you want to use such words when you talk to me? Are you teasing me?'

'I'm sorry; it's another schoolboy expression; I won't use it again. I completely realize that you're . . . anxious about me . . . (now don't be angry!), and I'm awfully glad about that. You wouldn't believe how apprehensive I am now, and – how I rejoice in your words. But all this fear, I swear to you, is just trivial nonsense. Quite honestly, Aglaya! But the joy will remain. I'm awfully glad you're such a child, such a good, kind child! Oh, how lovely you can be, Aglaya!'

Aglaya would have lost her temper, of course, and was already on the point of doing so, but suddenly, in a single moment, she was wholly seized by an emotion that was unexpected even to herself.

'And you won't reproach me for the crude things I said . . . at some . . . later date?' she asked him suddenly.

'No, of course not, of course not! And why have you flared up again? There you go, looking gloomy again! You've started to look very gloomy, Aglaya, as you never did before. I know the reason why . . .'

'Be quiet, be quiet!'

'No, it's better to say it. I've long wanted to say it; I've already said it, but . . . that wasn't enough, for you didn't believe me. In spite of everything, a certain creature stands between us . . .'

'Be quiet, be quiet, be quiet, be quiet!' Aglaya suddenly broke in, gripping him tightly by the hand and looking at him almost in horror. At that moment she was called for; almost in relief, she let go of him and ran away.

The prince spent the whole night in a fever. Strangely, for several nights in a row now he had had a fever. On this occasion, in a state of semi-delirium, the thought came to him: what if tomorrow, in everyone's presence, he had a fit of epilepsy? After all, he had had fits in his waking hours before, had he not? This thought made his blood run cold; all night he kept imagining himself at some wondrous and unheard-of gathering, among some strange kind of people. The main thing was that he 'began talking'; he knew that he should not talk, but he talked all the time, he was trying to talk them round to something. Yevgeny Pavlovich and Ippolit were also among the guests, and seemed to be on exceedingly friendly terms.

He woke up before nine, with a headache, disorder in his thoughts, strange impressions. For some reason he terribly wanted to see Rogozhin; see him and talk to him a great deal – about what, precisely, he himself did not know; then he was on the point of absolutely making up his mind to go and see Ippolit for some purpose. There was something troubled in his heart, so troubled that although the events he encountered that morning made an exceedingly strong impression on him, it was none the less an ill-defined one. One of those events was a visit from Lebedev.

Lebedev presented himself quite early, just after nine, almost completely drunk. Though the prince had recently become rather unobservant, it had not escaped his attention that ever since General Ivolgin had moved out of their household three days earlier, Lebedev had been behaving very badly. He suddenly became exceedingly grease-stained and mud-bespattered, his tie was knocked to one side, and the collar of his frock coat was torn. In his rooms he even stormed about and raged, and this could be heard across the small courtyard; Vera had once arrived in tears and told some story about it. Appearing now, he began to talk very strangely, striking himself on the chest and blaming himself for something . . .

'I have received. . . . received retribution for my betrayal and baseness . . . I have received a slap in the face!' he concluded, at last, tragically.

'A slap in the face! From whom? . . . And at such an early hour?'

'An early hour?' Lebedev smiled sarcastically. 'In this case the time is of no consequence . . . even for physical retribution . . . no, the retribution I received was moral . . . moral, not physical!'

He suddenly sat down, without ceremony, and began to tell a story. His story was very incoherent; the prince began to frown, and was on the point of going away, but suddenly several words struck him. He froze with astonishment . . . Strange were the things Mr Lebedev was telling.

At first what seemed to be involved was some letter or other; Aglaya Ivanovna's name was mentioned. Then suddenly Lebedev began to accuse the prince himself; one was given to understand that he had been insulted by the prince. At first, so he said, the prince had honoured him with his confidence in matters concerning a certain 'personage' (Nastasya Filippovna); but had then broken with him and driven him away in disgrace, and even to such an insulting degree that on the last occasion he had apparently refused to answer 'an innocent question about imminent changes in the household'. With drunken tears, Lebedev admitted that 'after that, he was simply unable to endure any more, particularly as he had learned a great deal . . . a very great deal . . . from Rogozhin, from Nastasya Filippovna, and from Nastasya Filippovna's friend, and from Varvara Ardalionovna . . . herself, sir . . . and from . . . from none other than Aglaya Ivanovna, even, sir, can you imagine, sir, through the mediation of Vera, sir, through my beloved daughter Vera, my only daughter . . . yes, sir . . . though actually, she's not my only daughter, for I have three of them. And who was informing Lizaveta Prokofyevna by means of letters, even in the deepest secret, sir, heh-heh! Who was writing to her about all the associations and . . . movements of the Nastasya Filippovna personage, heh-heh-heh! Who, who is this anonymous person, permit one to ask?'

'You don't mean it was you?' exclaimed the prince.

'The very same,' the drunkard replied with dignity, 'and at half-past eight this morning, only half an hour . . . no, sir, three quarters of an hour ago, I informed the most noble mother that I had a certain event to tell her about . . . a significant one. I informed her in a note, delivered by a maid, at the back door, sir. She received me.'

'You were in there, seeing Lizaveta Prokofyevna just now?' the prince asked, scarcely able to believe his ears.

'I was, and I received a slap in the face . . . a moral one. She returned the letter, even hurled it at me, without opening it . . . and threw me out upon my ear . . . though only morally, not physically . . . though *almost* physically, not far from it!'

'What letter did she hurl at you without opening it?'

'But haven't I . . . heh-heh-heh! Why, but I haven't told you yet! And I thought I'd already told you . . . I received a certain little letter, for delivery, sir . . .'

'From whom? To whom?'

But some of Lebedev's 'explanations' were extremely difficult to make sense of, or even partially understand. The prince did, however, manage to ascertain that the letter had been brought early that morning, through a servant girl, to Vera Lebedeva, for delivery to an address . . . 'the same as before . . . the same as before, to a certain personage and from the same person, sir . . . (for one of them I describe as a "person", sir, and the other only as a "personage", sir, for the sake of disparagement and distinction; for there is a great difference between an innocent and most highly noble general's daughter and . . . a *camellia*, sir), and so, the letter was from the "person", sir, whose name begins with the letter A . . .'

'How is that possible? To Nastasya Filippovna? Nonsense!' exclaimed the prince.

'It was, it was, sir, and if not to her, then to Rogozhin, sir . . . and there was even one to Mr Terentyev, for delivery, one day, sir, from the person whose name begins with A,' Lebedev winked and smiled.

As Lebedev often moved from one subject to another, and forgot what he had begun to talk about, the prince fell silent, in order to let him say what he had to say. But even then, it was all extremely vague: had the letters been sent through him, or through Vera? If he maintained that it was a matter of indifference whom they had been sent to – 'if not to Rogozhin, then to Nastasya Filippovna' – this only meant it was more likely they had not passed through his hands, if there had been any letters at all, that is. As for the question of how this letter had reached him now, it was still decidedly obscure; the most likely thing to suppose was that he had somehow purloined it from Vera . . .

quietly stolen it and taken it to Lizaveta Prokofyevna with some
plan. This the prince at last grasped and realized.

'You've gone out of your mind!' he cried, exceedingly
perturbed.

'Not entirely, much esteemed Prince,' Lebedev replied, not
without malice. 'It's true that I was going to hand it over to you,
give it into your very own hands, in order to oblige ... but
considered it better to oblige over there and declare it all to the
most noble mother ... as I had once informed her of it already,
by letter, anonymously; and when I wrote this morning on a
slip of paper, in advance, asking to be received, at twenty
minutes past eight, I also signed myself "your secret correspondent"; I was admitted at once, instantly, even with considerable
haste, by the back entrance ... to the most noble mother.'

'Well? ...'

'It's as I said, sir, she almost gave me a thrashing, sir; that is,
just a little one, sir, so it could be said that she *almost* gave me
a thrashing, sir. And then she hurled the letter at me. It's true
that she really wanted to keep it – I saw that, observed it –
but she changed her mind and hurled it: "If they've entrusted
someone like you to deliver it, then deliver it ..." She even felt
insulted. Really, if she was too embarrassed to say it to my face,
then she must have felt insulted. She does have a hot temper!'

'And where is the letter now?'

'I still have it with me, here it is, sir.'

And he handed the prince Aglaya's note to Gavrila Ardalionovich, which the latter had shown his sister with triumph that
same morning, two hours later.

'This letter can't remain in your possession.'

'But it's for you, for you! I've brought it for you, sir!' Lebedev
interjected with ardour. 'Now I'm yours again, all yours, from
head to heart, your servant, sir, after my transitory betrayal, sir!
Punish my heart, but spare my beard, as Sir Thomas More
said ...[1] in England and Great Britain, sir. *Mea culpa, mea
culpa*, as the Roman Pope says ... that's to say, he's the Pope
of Rome, but I call him the Roman Pope.'

'This letter must be dispatched at once,' the prince began to
fuss, 'I'll deliver it.'

'But wouldn't it be better, wouldn't it be better, most noble Prince, wouldn't it be better, sir . . . to do this, sir!'

Lebedev performed a strange, obsequious grimace; he suddenly began to writhe horribly in his chair, as though he had suddenly been pricked by a needle and, slyly winking, made some motions with his hands, demonstrating something.

'What on earth?' the prince asked sternly.

'You could open it first, sir!' he whispered obsequiously, and as if in confidence.

The prince leapt up with such fury that Lebedev took to flight; but, having run as far as the door, he paused to see if there might be mercy.

'Oh, Lebedev! Is it possible, is it possible to descend to such base immorality as you have done?' exclaimed the prince, sorrowfully. Lebedev's features brightened.

'I'm base, base!' he drew closer at once, with tears, beating his breast.

'I mean, that's a loathsome thing to do!'

'Indeed, a loathsome thing, sir. That's the right word, sir!'

'And what is this habit of yours of . . . acting so strangely? I mean, you're . . . simply a spy! Why did you write an anonymous note and upset . . . such a very kind and noble woman? Why, tell me, doesn't Aglaya Ivanovna have the right to write to anyone she pleases? So you went over there today in order to complain? What did you hope to achieve? What moved you to inform?'

'Solely out of pleasant curiosity and . . . in order to oblige a noble soul, yes, sir!' muttered Lebedev. 'But now I'm all yours, all of me again! Even if you hang me!'

'Did you present yourself to Lizaveta Prokofyevna as you are now?' the prince inquired with revulsion.

'No sir . . . fresher, sir . . . and even more decent, sir; it was after my humiliation that I attained . . . this state, sir.'

'Very well, then leave me, please.'

However, this request had to be repeated several times before the visitor decided, at last, to leave. Having got the door wide open, he again turned back, tiptoed to the middle of the room and began to make signs with his hands once more, demonstrating the gesture of opening a letter; but he did not dare to express his advice in words; and thereupon he left, smiling quietly and sweetly.

All this had been extremely painful to hear. From it all there emerged one principal and glaring fact: that Aglaya was greatly anxious, greatly uncertain, and for some reason greatly tormented ('by jealousy,' the prince whispered to himself). It also turned out that she was, of course, also being harassed by unkind people, and it was really very strange that she placed such trust in them. Of course, in that inexperienced but hot and proud little head certain curious plans were ripening, which were possibly also fatal and . . . resembled nothing on earth. The prince was extremely alarmed and, in his perplexity, did not know what to do. There was something he must certainly forestall, that he could feel. He looked again at the address on the sealed letter: oh, he had no doubts or anxieties there, because he trusted her; something else about this letter worried him: he did not trust Gavrila Ardalionovich. And yet, none the less, he had been on the point of deciding to deliver this letter to him himself, in person, and had already left the house for that purpose, but had changed his mind en route. Almost right outside Ptitsyn's house, as if on purpose, Kolya turned up, and the prince charged him with the task of delivering the letter into his brother's hands, as if it came directly from Aglaya Ivanovna herself. Kolya did not ask any questions and delivered it, so Ganya had no idea that the letter had passed through so many stations. Returning home, the prince asked to see Vera Lukyanovna, told her what was necessary and reassured her, because until now she had been looking for the letter and been crying. She was horrified when she learned that her father had taken the letter away. (The prince learned from her later that she had more than once served both Rogozhin and Aglaya Ivanovna in secret; she had never even dreamed that anything harmful to the prince could have been involved in it.)

At length, the prince became so upset that when, about two hours later, a messenger from Kolya arrived with the news that his father was ill, he was at first unable to comprehend what had happened. But it was this event that restored him, for it came as a powerful distraction. He remained at Nina Alexandrovna's (where the sick man had, of course, been taken) almost until evening. He was almost of no use at all, but there are people whom it is for some reason pleasant to see beside one at moments of crisis. Kolya was terribly shocked, wept hysterically, but, none the less, constantly ran errands: ran for a doctor and managed to find three, ran to the pharmacy, to the barbershop. The general was revived, but not brought back to consciousness; the doctors said that 'at any rate, the *Pazient* is in danger'. Varya and Nina Alexandrovna did not leave the sick man's bedside; Ganya was distraught and shaken, but did not want to go upstairs and was even afraid of seeing the sick man; he wrung his hands and, in an incoherent conversation with the prince, succeeded in getting out the words: 'what a misfortune, and as if on purpose, at such a time!' The prince thought he knew what 'time' he was referring to. As for Ippolit, the prince had not found him at Ptitsyn's house. Towards evening Lebedev came running, having slept like a log all day after the morning's 'explanation'. Now he was almost sober, and wept real tears over the sick man, as though this were his own brother. He blamed himself aloud, without, however, explaining what had happened, and kept pestering Nina Alexandrovna, constantly assuring her that it was 'he, he who was the cause of it, and no one but he . . . solely out of pleasant curiosity . . . and that "the deceased" (as he for some reason kept stubbornly calling the still living general) was even a man of the greatest genius!' He made a particular point of earnestly insisting on this 'genius', as though some extraordinary healing power might at that moment proceed from it. Nina Alexandrovna, beholding the sincerity of his tears, said to him quietly at last, without any reproach and even almost with affection: 'Well, God be with you, now don't cry, God will forgive you!' Lebedev was so shaken by these words and their tone that he was unwilling to leave Nina Alexandrovna all that evening (and all the days that followed, until the general's death, he spent at their house almost from morning till night). During the day there twice arrived a messenger from Lizaveta Prokofyevna to obtain information about the sick man's health. And when that evening, at nine o' clock, the prince arrived in the Yepanchins' drawing room, now full of guests, Lizaveta Prokofyevna at once began to ask him questions about the sick man, with compassion and in detail, and replied with dignity to Belokonskaya when she inquired who the sick man was and who Nina Alexandrovna was. This greatly pleased the prince. He himself, while explaining things to Lizaveta Prokofyevna, spoke 'beautifully', as Aglaya's sisters expressed it later: 'modestly, quietly, without superfluous words, without gestures, with dignity; made a beautiful entrance; was dressed superbly', and not only did not 'fall on the slippery floor', as he had feared the day before, but plainly even made an agreeable impression on everyone.

For his part, having sat down and looked around him, he at once noticed that this entire gathering in no way resembled the phantoms with which Aglaya had frightened him the day before, or the nightmares he had had during the night. For the first time in his life he saw a corner of what is given the intimidating name of 'society'. As a result of certain special intentions, considerations and personal inclinations, he had long been keen to penetrate this charmed circle of people, and so took a powerful interest in his first impressions. These first impressions of his were even ones of enchantment. It somehow suddenly seemed to him that all these people had been born to be together; that there was no 'soirée' at the Yepanchins' that evening, that these were all just 'good friends' and that he himself had long been their devoted friend and like-minded associate and had returned to them after a recent separation. The charm of refined manners, simplicity and apparent sincerity was almost magical. It could not even have entered his thoughts that all this sincerity and nobility, wit and lofty personal dignity were, perhaps, merely a splendid artistic manufacture. Most of the guests, in spite of their imposing external appearance, were even rather empty people, but unaware in their self-satisfaction that many of their good aspects were simply a manufacture, for which they were moreover not to blame, for they had attained it unconsciously and by inheritance. This the prince was unwilling even to suspect, charmed under the spell of his first impressions. He saw, for example, that this old man, this important dignitary, who was old enough to be his grandfather, even broke off his conversation in order to listen to him, such a young and inexperienced man, and not only listened to what he had to say, but apparently valued his opinion, was so kind to him, so sincerely good-natured, and yet they were strangers who were meeting for the very first time. It was perhaps the refinement of this courtesy that had the most powerful effect on the prince's excited susceptibility. He had been too much predisposed, suborned in advance, perhaps, to a favourable impression.

Yet all these people – though, of course, they were 'friends of the family' and of one another – were, however, far from being such friends either of the family or of one another as the prince took them to be when he had just been presented and introduced to them. Here there were people who would never and on no account acknowledge the Yepanchins as in any way their equals. Here there were even people who hated one another; old Belokonskaya had all her life 'despised' the wife of 'the little old dignitary', and she, in her turn, was far from being fond of Lizaveta Prokofyevna. This 'dignitary', her husband, had for some reason been a patron of the Yepanchins since their youth, and took the presiding place here, too, was such an immensely important person in Ivan Fyodorovich's eyes that he could feel nothing but reverence and awe in his presence, and would even have sincerely despised himself had he for one moment considered him his equal, and not Olympian Jove. There were people here who had not met one another for several years and felt for one another nothing but indifference, if not repugnance, but who met now as though they had seen one another only the day before in the most friendly and pleasant company. However, the gathering was a small one. Apart from Belokonskaya and the 'little old dignitary', really an important person, and apart from his spouse, there was here, in the first place, a certain very solid military general, a baron or count, with a German name – a man of extreme taciturnity, with a reputation for an amazing knowledge of government matters and even almost a reputation for scholarship – one of those Olympian administrators who know everything 'except perhaps Russia itself', a man who once in five years made a statement 'remarkable for its profundity', but of the kind, however, that at once become proverbs and are learned of in the most exalted circles; one of those high officials who, after exceedingly long service (even to the point of eccentricity), usually die covered with rank and honours, in the best positions, and with large sums of money, though without large achievements and even with a certain hostility to achievements. This general was Ivan Fyodorovich's immediate superior in the service, and was also regarded by him, because of the ardency of his grateful heart, and even because of a certain vanity, as his benefactor, though the general in no way considered himself Ivan Fyodorovich's benefactor, and took a perfectly unconcerned attitude towards him, though gladly availed himself of his numerous and varied merits, and would have lost no time in replacing him with another official, had this been required by any considerations, even those that were not exalted at all. Here there was also a certain important, middle-aged *barin*, apparently even a relative of Lizaveta Prokofyevna, though this was decidedly untrue; a man of good rank and calling, a man of wealth and breeding, solidly built and in very good health, a great talker and even possessing the reputation of a man of discontent (though in the most permissible sense of the word), a man of spleen (though in him even this was pleasant), with the ways of an English aristocrat and English tastes (regarding, for example, rare roast beef, horse harness, lackeys, etcetera). He was a great friend of the 'dignitary', kept him entertained, and moreover, Lizaveta Prokofyevna for some reason cherished a certain strange notion that this middle-aged gentleman (a man somewhat frivolous and to some extent an admirer of the fair sex) would suddenly take it into his head to make Alexandra happy by his proposal. This highest and most solid stratum of the gathering was followed by a stratum of younger guests, though they also shone with most exquisite qualities. In addition to Prince Shch. and Yevgeny Pavlovich, this stratum also comprised the well-known and charming Prince N., a former seducer and conqueror of female hearts throughout the whole of Europe, now a man of about forty-five, still of handsome appearance, with a wonderful ability as a raconteur, a man with a fortune that was, however, in some disarray, and who, from habit, lived mostly abroad. Here, lastly, there were people who apparently constituted even a third distinct stratum and who did not of themselves belong to the 'secret circle' of the company, but who, like the Yepanchins, could for some reason occasionally be encountered in that 'secret' circle. Because of a certain tact, which they adopted as a principle, on the rare occasions when they held formal gatherings, the Yepanchins liked to mix the most exalted company with people of a lower stratum, chosen representatives of 'the middle sort of people'. The Yepanchins were even praised for this and it was said of them that they knew their place and were people of tact, and the Yepanchins were proud of this opinion of themselves. One of the representatives of this 'middle sort of people' that evening was a certain colonel of the engineers, a serious man, very close friend of Prince Shch., who had introduced him to the Yepanchins, a man, however, silent in company and who wore on the large index finger of his right hand a large and conspicuous ring, which had in all probability been awarded to him. There was even, lastly, a literary man and poet, of German origin, but a Russian poet, and, moreover, completely decent, so that he could without misgivings be introduced into good society. He was of fortunate, though for some reason slightly repulsive, appearance, about thirty-eight, always impeccably dressed, belonged to a German family, bourgeois to the highest degree, but in the highest degree respectable; knew how to take advantage of various opportunities, nudge his way into the patronage of exalted people and remain in their good books. Once upon a time he had translated some important work by some important German poet, had known how to dedicate his translation in verse, had been able to boast of his friendship with a certain famous but dead Russian poet (there is an entire stratum of writers who are exceedingly fond of attaching themselves in print to the friendship of great but dead writers) and had been introduced to the Yepanchins very recently by the wife of the 'little old dignitary'. This lady had the reputation of being a patroness of literary men scholars and she actually even obtained a pension for one or two authors through the mediation of highly placed persons with whom she had influence. For influence of

a kind she did possess. She was a lady of about forty-five (thus
a very young wife for such a little old man as her husband), a
former beauty, who liked even now, because of a mania typical
of many ladies of forty-five, to dress rather too extravagantly;
she was of inconsiderable intellect, and her knowledge of literature was most dubious. But in her, the patronage of literary men
was just as much of a mania as dressing extravagantly. Many
works and translations had been dedicated to her; two or three
writers, with her permission, had published their own letters,
which they had written to her on extremely important subjects
. . . And it was all this company that the prince took for the very
purest coinage, the purest gold, unalloyed. As a matter of fact,
all these people were also, as if on purpose, in the happiest of
moods that evening, and most content with themselves. Each
single one of them knew that they were doing the Yepanchins a
great honour by their visit. But, alas, the prince had no inkling
of such subtleties. He had no inkling, for example, of the fact
that the Yepanchins, cherishing the plan of such an important
step as the resolution of their daughter's destiny, would not
have dared not to present him, Prince Lev Nikolayevich, for the
inspection of the little old dignitary, the acknowledged patron
of their family. As for the little old dignitary, though he would
have even endured quite calmly the news of a dreadful misfortune that might have befallen the Yepanchins, he would certainly
have taken offence had the Yepanchins secured their daughter's
betrothal without his counsel and, so to speak, without his
leave. Prince N., that charming, that unquestionably witty man,
of such lofty sincerity, was in the highest degree convinced
that he was something like a sun, rising that night above the
Yepanchins' drawing room. He considered them infinitely
inferior to him, and it was precisely this simple and noble
thought that engendered in him the very charming familiarity
and friendliness with which he treated the Yepanchins. He knew
very well that this evening he must be sure to tell some story,
for the fascination of the company, and was preparing for this
even with a certain amount of inspiration. Prince Lev Nikolayevich, hearing this story later, acknowledged that he had never
heard anything like it, this brilliant humour and remarkable

gaiety and naivety, which were almost touching on the lips of such a Don Juan as Prince N. And yet, had he known how old and threadbare that same story was; how it was known off by heart and how it had already been done to death and had bored everyone in every drawing room, only at the innocent Yepanchins' making its appearance again as a novelty, as the sudden, sincere and brilliant recollection of a brilliant and handsome man! Even, at last, the minor German poet, though he had conducted himself with uncommon courtesy and modesty, he too almost considered himself to be doing this house an honour by his visit. But the prince did not notice the reverse side of it all, did not observe any undercurrent. This was a form of trouble Aglaya had not foreseen. She looked extremely pretty that evening. All three young ladies were smartly dressed that evening, though not very extravagantly, and their hair was even done up in a special way. Aglaya sat with Yevgeny Pavlovich, conversing and joking with him in an uncommonly friendly manner. Yevgeny Pavlovich was conducting himself a little more solidly and respectably than at other times, also, perhaps, out of regard for the dignitaries. He had, as a matter of fact, long been well known in society; though a young man, he was already at home there. That evening he arrived at the Yepanchins' with a crêpe band round his hat, and Belokonskaya had praised him for it: in similar circumstances, perhaps not every worldly nephew might have worn a crêpe band for such an uncle. Lizaveta Prokofyevna was also pleased with this, but on the whole she seemed rather worried. The prince noticed that Aglaya looked at him attentively a couple of times and, it appeared, was pleased with him. Little by little he was becoming terribly happy. His earlier 'fantastic' thoughts and misgivings (after his conversation with Lebedev) now seemed to him, in sudden, but frequent recollections, an unrealizable, impossible and even ridiculous dream! (And in any case, his first, though unconscious, desire and inclination, earlier and throughout the whole day had been somehow to contrive it so that he could not believe in that dream!) He spoke little, and then only in response to questions, and, at last, fell altogether silent, sat and listened, though plainly drowning in gratification. Little by little, there began to take shape within him, too, something akin to inspiration, ready to flare up at the first opportunity . . . When he began to talk, it was entirely by chance, also in response to a question and, it seemed, also without any special intention at all . . .

7

Lost in the pleasurable contemplation of Aglaya gaily talking to Prince N. and Yevgeny Pavlovich, the elderly, gentlemanly, anglophile *barin*, who had been entertaining the 'dignitary' in another corner and animatedly telling him about something, uttered the name of Nikolai Andreyevich Pavlishchev. The prince quickly turned in their direction and began to listen.

The matter under discussion was the present-day order of things, and the disorderly state of things on some landowners' estates in the province of —. The anglophile's stories must have contained something amusing, as the elderly gentleman began at last to laugh at the storyteller's bilious ardour. He spoke smoothly, rather peevishly drawing out his words, with gentle emphases on the vowels, about how he had been compelled, precisely by this new order of things, to sell a magnificent estate of his in the province of — and even, though he was not particularly in need of money, at half price, and at the same time to keep an estate that was ruined, unprofitable and the subject of a process at law, and even had to pay extra for it. 'In order to avoid another lawsuit over Pavlishchev's estate as well, I ran away from them. I mean, one or two more such inheritances, and I'll be ruined. As a matter of fact, though, I'd have got three thousand desyatinas[1] of excellent land there!'

'This . . . Ivan Petrovich is a relative of the late Nikolai Andreyevich Pavlishchev, isn't he . . . I mean, you were looking for his relatives, weren't you?' Ivan Fyodorovich said to the prince in a low voice, having suddenly turned up beside him, noticing the extreme attention with which he was following the conversation. Until now he had been entertaining his superior, the general, but had long observed Lev Nikolayevich's extreme isolation, and begun to worry; he wanted to bring him into the conversation to a certain extent and thus for a second time show him off and introduce him to the 'higher ups'.

'Lev Nikolayevich was the ward of Nikolai Andreyevich Pavlishchev, after the death of his own parents,' he interposed, encountering Ivan Petrovich's gaze.

'Ve-ry pleased,' observed the latter, 'and I even remember you very well. Earlier, when Ivan Fedorych introduced us, I recognized you at once, and even by your face. Truly, you've changed little in appearance, though I only saw you when you were a child, you were about ten or eleven. There's something in your features that reminds me . . .'

'You saw me when I was a child?' asked the prince, with some surprise.

'Oh, it was very long ago,' continued Ivan Petrovich, 'in Zlatoverkhovo, where you were staying with my cousins at the time. In the old days I used to visit Zlatoverkhovo quite often – don't you remember me? It's ve-ry possible that you don't . . . In those days you had . . . you had a kind of illness then, so that I was once even astonished by you . . .'

'I don't remember anything!' the prince repeated fervently.

After a few more words of explanation, supremely calm on the part of Ivan Petrovich and oddly agitated on the part of the prince, it came to light that the two ladies, elderly spinsters, relatives of the late Pavlishchev, who lived on his Zlatoverkhovo estate and to whom the prince had been entrusted for his upbringing, were, in their turn, cousins of Ivan Petrovich. Like everyone else, Ivan Petrovich was almost unable to think of any reasons why Pavlishchev should have taken such pains over the little prince, his foster child. 'Why, I even forgot to take any interest in it at the time,' but all the same, it turned out that he had an excellent memory, because he could remember how strict his elderly cousin, Marfa Nikitishna, had been with the little ward, 'so that I even quarrelled with her once about her system of upbringing, because using the birch rod again and again on a sick child – I mean, it's . . . you must admit . . .' – and how kind, on the other hand, the younger cousin, Natalya Nikitishna,

had been to the poor boy. 'Now both of them,' he explained
further, 'live in the province of — (though I don't know if they
are alive now), where they acquired from Pavlishchev a very
decent little estate. I believe Marfa Nikitishna intended to enter
a convent; however, I cannot confirm it; it may have been
someone else I heard about . . . yes, it was about a doctor's wife
the other day . . .'

As the prince listened to this, his eyes gleamed with delight
and tender emotion. With uncommon fervour he announced, in
his turn, that he would never be able to forgive himself for not
having taken the opportunity, during the six months of his
travels around the inner provinces, of seeking out and visiting
his former educators. 'Every day he intended to go there, but
was always distracted by circumstances . . . but now he had
promised himself . . . come what may . . . even if only to the
province of — . . . So you know Natalya Nikitishna? What a
beautiful, what a saintly soul! But Marfa Nikitishna, too . . .
forgive me, but I think you are mistaken about Marfa Nikitishna! She was strict, but . . . I mean, it was impossible for her not
to lose patience . . . with an idiot such as I was then (hee-hee!). I
mean, I was a complete idiot, you would not believe (ha-ha!).
However . . . however, you saw me in those days and . . . How
is it that I don't remember you, tell me, please? So you . . .
oh, my goodness, are you then really a relative of Nikolai
Andreyevich Pavlishchev?'

'I as-sure you,' smiled Ivan Petrovich, looking the prince over.

'Oh, but I didn't say it because I . . . doubted it . . . and,
anyway, how could one doubt it (heh-heh!) . . . in the slightest?
. . . I mean, even in the slightest! (Heh-heh!) No, I just meant
that Nikolai Andreyevich Pavlishchev was such an excellent
man! The most generous of men, truly, I assure you!'

The prince was not so much out of breath as, so to speak,
'choking with a noble heart', as Adelaida put it the following
morning, in conversation with her future husband, Prince Shch.

'Oh, my goodness!' Ivan Petrovich burst out laughing! 'Why
can't I be the relative of a gen-er-ous man?'

'Oh, my goodness!' exclaimed the prince, embarrassed,
hurrying and growing more and more animated. 'I . . . I've said

something stupid again, but . . . it's bound to be like that, because I . . . I . . . actually, that again isn't what I meant! And what is there in me, tell me please, compared with such interests . . . compared with such enormous interests! And in comparison with such a most generous man – because I mean, quite honestly, he was the most generous of men, wasn't he? Wasn't he?'

The prince was even trembling all over. Why he had suddenly become so anxious, why he had fallen into such an obsequious rapture, for no apparent reason and, it seemed, quite out of proportion to the subject they were discussing – it would have been hard to determine. It was really that he was in that kind of a mood, and at that moment he was even almost experiencing, towards someone and for something, the most fervent and emotional gratitude – perhaps it was even towards Ivan Petrovich, but also, almost, towards all the guests in general. He was positively 'bursting with happiness'. At last, Ivan Petrovich began to stare at him far more intently; very intently did the 'dignitary' also examine him. Belokonskaya shot an angry look at the prince and pursed her lips. Prince N., Yevgeny Pavlovich, Prince Shch., the girls – they all broke off their conversation and listened. Aglaya seemed to be alarmed, while Lizaveta Proko-fyevna was simply terrified. They were behaving oddly, mother and daughter: it was they, after all, who had proposed and decided that it would be better for the prince to sit the evening out in silence; but no sooner did they catch sight of him in a corner, in the most complete isolation and perfectly happy with his lot, than they at once became anxious. Indeed, Alexandra had wanted to go over to him and carefully, across the whole room, attach him to their company, that is, to the company of Prince N., beside Belokonskaya. And then, as soon as the prince began to talk, they grew even more anxious.

'That he was a most excellent man, in that you are correct,' Ivan Petrovich pronounced imposingly, and not smiling now. 'Yes, yes . . . he was a splendid man! Splendid and worthy,' he added, after a short silence. 'Worthy, even, one might say, of every respect,' he added even more imposingly after a third pause, 'and . . . and it is very agreeable to see on your part . . .'

'Wasn't it this Pavlishchev that there was some episode about

'. . . a strange one . . . with an *abb*é . . . an *abb*é . . . I've forgotten
which *abb*é it was, but everyone was talking about it at the
time,' the 'dignitary' said, as if recollecting.

'It was Abbé Goureau, the Jesuit,' Ivan Petrovich reminded
him, 'yes, sir, there are most excellent and most worthy men,
sir! Because say what you like, he was a man of good family,
with a fortune, a chamberlain and if he had . . . continued to
serve . . . And then he suddenly gave up the service, and everything, in order to go over to Catholicism, and became a Jesuit,
and more or less openly, too, with a kind of delight. Truly, he
died at the right time . . . yes; everyone said it at the time . . .'

The prince was beside himself.

'Pavlishchev . . . Pavlishchev went over to Catholicism? That
cannot be!' he exclaimed in horror.

'Well, "that cannot be",' Ivan Petrovich mumbled sedately,
'is putting it a little strongly, you must admit, my dear Prince
. . . However, you have such a high opinion of the deceased . . .
indeed, he was the kindest of men, to which I ascribe, in the
main, that wily old fox Goureau's success. But really, speaking
personally, don't ask me how much fuss and bother I later
experienced on account of that matter . . . and precisely with
that selfsame Goureau! Imagine,' he suddenly addressed the
elderly gentleman, 'they even wanted to advance claims in connection with the will, and at the time I even had to resort to the
most, er, energetic measures . . . because they were masters of
the craft! Ex-tra-ord-inary! But, thank God, it happened in
Moscow, I at once went to see the count, and we . . . put some
sense into them . . .'

'You can't imagine how you have upset and shocked me!' the
prince exclaimed again.

'I am sorry; but it really is all nonsense and would have ended
in nonsense, as usual; I'm convinced of it. Last summer,' he
turned again to the elderly gentleman, 'Countess K. also entered
some Catholic convent abroad; our people don't seem to be able
to hold out, once they submit to those . . . sly-boots . . . especially
abroad . . .'

'I think it's all caused, I think, by our . . . weariness,' the
elderly gentleman mumbled authoritatively. 'Well, and their

manner of preaching . . . it's elegant, unique . . . and they know how to frighten people. They also frightened me in Vienna, in thirty-two, I assure you; only I didn't submit, and ran away from them, ha-ha!'

'I heard, my dear, that you ran away from Vienna to Paris with the society beauty Countess Levitskaya, leaving your post, and it wasn't the Jesuit you ran away from,' Belokonskaya suddenly retorted.

'Well, but I mean, it was from the Jesuit, that's how it turned out, it was the Jesuit I was running away from!' the elderly gentleman interjected, bursting into laughter at the pleasant recollection. 'You seem very religious, and that is so rarely encountered in a young man nowadays,' he turned affectionately to Prince Lev Nikolayevich, who was listening with his mouth open and was still shocked; the elderly gentleman apparently wanted to find out more about the prince; for several reasons he had been begun to interest him greatly.

'Pavlishchev was a brilliant intellect and a Christian, a true Christian,' the prince declared suddenly. 'How could he have submitted to a faith that is . . . unchristian? Catholicism is the same thing as an unchristian faith!' he added suddenly, his eyes beginning to flash, and he stared ahead of him, somehow taking them all in with his eyes.

'Well, that is too much,' muttered the elderly gentleman, giving Ivan Fyodorovich a look of surprise.

'How is that, Catholicism an unchristian faith?' Ivan Petrovich turned round on his chair. 'What sort of faith is it, then?'

'It's an unchristian faith, that is number one!' the prince began to speak again, in extreme excitement and with excessive sharpness. 'That is number one, and number two is that Roman Catholicism is even worse than atheism itself, that is my opinion! Yes! That's my opinion! Atheism merely preaches zero, but Catholicism goes further: it preaches a distorted Christ, slandered and desecrated by it, the opposite of Christ! It preaches the Antichrist, I swear to you, I assure you! That is my personal and long-established conviction, and it has been a source of torment to me . . . Roman Catholicism believes that without universal state power the Church will not endure upon earth,

and cries: '*Non possumus!*'[2] In my view, Roman Catholicism is
not even a faith, but is decidedly a continuation of the Western
Roman Empire, and in it everything, beginning with faith, is
subordinated to that idea. The Pope seized the earth, an earthly
throne, and took up the sword; ever since then it has all gone
like that, except that to the sword they've added lies, slyness,
deception, fanaticism, superstition and evil-doing, and played
with the people's most sacred, truthful, simple, fiery emotions,
exchanging everything, everything for money, for base, earthly
power. And isn't that the teaching of the Antichrist? How could
atheism have failed to originate from them? Atheism originated
from them, from Roman Catholicism itself! First of all, atheism
took its origin in them: could they believe in themselves? It
gained strength from the revulsion that was felt for them; it is
the result of their lies and spiritual impotence! Atheism! So far,
in our land it's only the upper classes who do not believe, as
Yevgeny Pavlovich put it so splendidly the other day, having
lost their roots; but there, in Europe, now, enormous masses of
the ordinary people are starting not to believe – it used to be
because of darkness and lies, but now it's because of fanaticism,
hatred of the Church and Christianity!'

The prince stopped to draw breath. He had been talking
terribly fast. He was pale and gasping. They all exchanged
glances; but at last the elderly gentleman openly burst into
laughter. Prince N. took out his lorgnette and examined the
prince steadily. The little German poet crept out of the corner
and moved closer to the table, smiling an ominous smile.

'You very much ex-ag-ger-ate,' Ivan Petrovich drawled with
a certain degree of boredom, and even as if he had something on his conscience. 'In the Church over there, there are
also representatives who are worthy of all respect and are
vir-tu-ous . . .'

'I wasn't talking about individual representatives of the
Church. I was talking about the essence of Roman Catholicism,
it is Rome of which I speak. Can a Church completely disappear?
I never said that!'

'Agreed, but that is all well known and even – superfluous,
and . . . belongs to theology . . .'

'Oh no, oh no! Not just to theology, I assure you, it doesn't! It concerns us far more closely than you suppose. That is the whole of our error, that we cannot yet see that this matter is not just a purely theological one! I mean, socialism is also a result of Catholicism and the essence of Catholicism! It also, like its brother atheism, originated in despair, opposed to Catholicism in a moral sense, in order to replace the lost moral power of religion, in order to assuage the thirst of a spiritually thirsting humanity and to save it not by Christ, but by coercion! It is also freedom by coercion, it's unification by the sword and by blood! "Do not dare to believe in God, do not dare to have property, do not dare to have individuality, *fraternité ou la mort*, two million heads!"[3] By their works ye shall know them[4] – it is written! And do not suppose that all this has been so innocent and innocuous for us; oh, we need to rebuff it, and soon, soon! Our Christ must shine out as a rebuff to the West, the Christ we have preserved and whom they have not known! Not slavishly swallowing the Jesuits' hook, but carrying our Russian civilization to them, we must now stand before them, and let no one among us say that their preaching is elegant, as someone said just now . . .'

'But permit me, permit me,' Ivan Petrovich began to grow dreadfully perturbed, looking round him, and even starting to lose his nerve. 'All your ideas are, of course, praiseworthy and full of patriotism, but it is all in the highest degree exaggerated, and . . . we had even better drop the subject . . .'

'No, it isn't exaggerated, it's rather understated; understated indeed, because I'm not able to express myself properly, but . . .'

'But per-mit me!'

The prince fell silent. He sat straight up in his chair and, motionless, looked at Ivan Petrovich with a fiery stare.

'I think the incident with your benefactor has shaken you too much,' the elderly gentleman observed, kindly and not losing his calm. 'You are ignited . . . perhaps because of your seclusion. If you lived with people more, and you would, I hope, be gladly accepted in society as a remarkable young man, then you would, of course, calm your animation and see that all this is far more simple . . . and moreover such rare instances . . . occur, in my view, partly because of our satiety and partly because of . . . boredom.'

'Precisely, precisely so!' exclaimed the prince. 'A most magnificent idea! Precisely "because of boredom, because of our boredom", not because of satiety, on the contrary, because of thirst . . . not satiety, you are wrong there! Not only thirst, but even inflammation, a feverish thirst! And . . . and do not suppose that this is on such a small scale that it may merely be laughed at; excuse me, but one must be able to have prescience! No sooner do our people reach a shore, no sooner do they come to believe that it is a shore, than they rejoice in it so much that they at once go to the last extreme; why is that? I mean, here you are being astonished at Pavlishchev, you ascribe it all to his insanity or kindness, but that is wrong! And it is not us alone, but the whole of Europe that is astonished by our passionate Russian temperament: in our country, if a man goes over to Catholicism, he unfailingly becomes a Jesuit, and one of the most clandestine sort, at that; if he becomes an atheist, he will at once begin to demand the eradication of belief in God by coercion, that is, by the sword! Why is that, why such instant frenzy? Do you really not know? It's because he has found the fatherland he failed to espy here, and is filled with joy; he has found a shore, a soil, and has rushed to kiss it! You see, it is not from vanity alone, not from mere sordid vain emotions that Russian atheists and Russian Jesuits proceed, but from a spiritual pain, a spiritual thirst, a yearning for something more exalted, for a firm shore, a motherland in which they have ceased to believe, because they have never known it! It is so easy for a Russian to become an atheist, easier than for anyone else in the whole world! And our people do not simply become atheists, they unfailingly *believe* in atheism, as in a new creed, never noticing that they have come to believe in a zero. That is what our thirst is like! "He who has no soil beneath him has no God either." That expression is not my own. It's the expression of a merchant, an Old Believer, whom I met when I was travelling. He, it's true, didn't express it like that, he said: "He who has renounced his native land has renounced his God as well." I mean, just think, highly educated people in our country have even taken up flagellantism[5] . . .

Though, as a matter of fact, in that case is flagellantism any worse than nihilism, Jesuitism or atheism? It is even, perhaps, a bit deeper than them! But that is the length to which their yearning has gone! ... Reveal the shore of the New World to Columbus's thirsting and inflamed fellow-travellers, reveal the Russian World to a Russian, let him find that gold, that treasure hidden from him in the earth! Show him in the future the renewal of all mankind and its resurrection, perhaps by Russian thought alone, by the Russian God and Christ, and you will see what a mighty and truthful, wise and meek giant will grow before an amazed world, amazed and frightened, because they expect from us only the sword, the sword and coercion, because they cannot imagine us, judging by their own standards, without barbarism. And that is how it has been hitherto, and that is how it will increasingly continue! And . . .'

But here a certain event took place, and the orator's speech was cut short in the most unexpected manner.

All this feverish tirade, all this flow of impassioned and agitated words and rhapsodic ideas, jostling, as it were, in a kind of turmoil and skipping from one to the other, all this foretold something dangerous, something peculiar in the mood of the young man who had so suddenly boiled over, apparently for no reason. Of those who were present in the drawing room, all who knew the prince marvelled fearfully (and some with embarrassment) at his outburst, which was so little in harmony with his customary and even timid reserve, his rare and peculiar tact on certain occasions, and his instinctive sense of the higher proprieties. They could not understand what had caused it: it was surely not the news of Pavlishchev's death. In the ladies' corner he was being viewed as a madman, and Belokonskaya confessed later that 'one more minute and she would have wanted to run away'. The 'elderly gentlemen' were almost dumbfounded at first; the general-superior looked with stern displeasure from his chair. The engineer-colonel sat completely immobile. The little German even turned pale, but went on smiling his false smile, casting glances at the others: how would the others respond? However, all this and the 'whole scandal' might have been resolved in the most ordinary and natural way,

perhaps, even within a minute; Ivan Fyodorovich, who was
extremely surprised, but had recovered himself earlier than the
rest, also began to try to stop the prince several times; not having
achieved success, he was now making his way towards him,
with firm and decisive ends in view. Another minute, and if it
had been necessary, then he would, perhaps, have resolved
to take the prince outside, under the pretext that he was ill,
which perhaps really was true and which Ivan Fyodorovich was
privately very inclined to believe . . . But the matter took a
different turn.

Right at the outset, as soon as the prince walked into the
drawing room, he had sat down as far as possible from the
Chinese vase with which Aglaya had so tried to frighten him.
Can one credit that after Aglaya's words of the day before there
had installed itself in him a kind of ineffaceable conviction, a
kind of extraordinary and impossible presentiment he would
unfailingly and on the next day break that vase, no matter how
he tried to avoid the disaster? But it was so. During the course
of the evening, other strong, but radiant impressions began to
rush into his soul; we have already spoken of that. He forgot
his presentiment. When he heard talk of Pavlishchev, and Ivan
Fydorovich led him over to Ivan Petrovich and introduced him
again, he changed his seat for one closer to the table, ending up
in an armchair beside the enormous, beautiful Chinese vase that
stood on a pedestal almost next to his elbow, very slightly
behind it.

As he spoke his last words, he suddenly got up from his
seat, gave an incautious wave of his hand, made some kind of
movement with his shoulder, and . . . a universal cry rang out!
The vase swayed slightly, as if at first uncertain whether to fall
on the head of one of the elderly gentlemen, but suddenly
inclined in the opposite direction, towards the little German,
who only just leaped out of the way in horror, and crashed
to the floor. The noise, the shouting, the precious fragments
scattered over the carpet, the alarm, the amazement – oh, it is
hard, and indeed almost unnecessary, to portray what the prince
felt then! But we cannot fail to mention another strange sensation that struck him at precisely that moment and suddenly

manifested itself to him out of the throng of all the other strange
and troubled sensations: it was not the shame, not the scandal,
not the suddenness that struck him most of all, but the realized
prophecy! Just what was so gripping about this idea he would
not have been able to explain to himself; he merely felt that he
had been stricken to the heart, and stood in a state of fear that
was almost mystical. Another moment, and everything around
him seemed to expand, instead of horror there were light and
joy, ecstasy; he began to lose his breath, and . . . but the moment
passed. Thank God, it wasn't that! He got his breath back and
looked around him.

For a long time he seemed not to understand the turmoil that
was seething around him, or rather, he understood completely
and saw everything, but stood like a man isolated, not taking
part in any of it, who, like the invisible man in the fairy-tale,
had made his way into the room and was observing people who
had nothing to do with him, but who interested him. He saw
them clearing away the fragments, heard rapid conversations,
saw Aglaya, pale and looking strangely at him, very strangely:
in her eyes there was almost no hatred at all, there was not a
hint of anger; she was looking at him with such a frightened but
sympathetic expression, but at the others with such a flashing
gaze . . . his heart suddenly began to sweetly ache. At last, he
saw with strange amazement that they had all settled down
again and were even laughing, as though nothing had happened!
Another minute, and the laughter increased; now they were
laughing as they stared at him, at his dumbfounded speech-
lessness, but laughing in a friendly, cheerful way; many of them
began to talk to him and talked to him so kindly, led by Lizaveta
Prokofyevna: she laughed as she spoke, saying something very,
very good-natured. Suddenly he felt Ivan Fyodorovich pat him
on the shoulder in a friendly manner; Ivan Petrovich was also
laughing; but even better, even more attractively and sympa-
thetically was the elderly gentleman laughing; he took the prince
by the arm and, squeezing it slightly, striking it lightly with the
palm of his other hand, prevailed upon him to recover himself,
as though he were a frightened little boy, which pleased the
prince terribly, and, at last, made him sit down right beside him.

The prince studied his face with pleasure, but was still unable to begin to speak, for some reason, he had lost his breath; the old man's face appealed to him so very much.

'What?' he muttered at last. 'Do you really forgive me? And . . . you, Lizaveta Prokofyevna?'

The laughter intensified; tears came to the prince's eyes; he could not believe it, and was enchanted.

'Of course, it was a lovely vase. I can remember it being here for the past fifteen, yes . . . fifteen years,' Ivan Petrovich ventured.

'Well, it's not a disaster, is it? Man, too, comes to his end, and here we are making a fuss about a clay pot!' Lizaveta Prokfyevna said loudly. 'Did you really get such a fright, Lev Nikolaich?' she added, even with fear. 'Enough, my dear fellow, enough; indeed, you frighten me.'

'Do you forgive me for *everything*? For *everything*, not only the vase?' the prince started to get up from his seat, but the elderly gentleman at once pulled him by the arm. He would not let him go.

'*C'est très curieux et c'est très sérieux*,' he whispered across the table to Ivan Petrovich, though rather loudly; the prince might even have heard it.

'So I haven't offended any of you? You won't believe how happy that thought makes me; but that's how it should be! Could I offend anyone here? If I thought that I could, I'd be offending you again.'

'Calm yourself, *mon ami*, that's an exaggeration. And you've no reason to thank us so; it's a fine sentiment, but an exaggerated one.'

'I'm not thanking you, I'm merely . . . admiring you, and just looking at you makes me happy; perhaps I'm saying stupid things, but – I need to speak, I need to explain . . . even if only out of self-respect.'

Everything about him was jerky, troubled and feverish; it was very possible that the words he was uttering were often not the ones he wanted to say. With his gaze he seemed to be asking: was it all right for him to speak? His gaze alighted on Belokonskaya.

'Never mind, my dear, continue, continue, only do not gasp so,' she observed. 'You began quite out of breath just now, and look where it got you; but don't be afraid to speak; these gentlemen have seen stranger sights than you, you will not astonish them, and God knows, you're not so complicated, after all, it's simply that you broke that vase and gave them a fright.'

The prince, smiling, heard what she had to say.

'It was you, wasn't it,' he suddenly addressed the elderly gentleman, 'it was you who saved the student Podkumov and the civil servant Shvabrin from exile three months ago?'

The elderly gentleman even blushed slightly and muttered that he should try to calm himself.

'It was you I heard about, did I not,' he at once turned to Ivan Petrovich, 'in the province of —, that after a fire you gave your muzhiks free timber with which to rebuild their village, though they'd already been freed and had given you trouble?'

'Well, that's an ex-ag-ger-ation,' muttered Ivan Petrovich, though he assumed a pleasantly dignified air; on this occasion he was quite correct in its being an 'exaggeration': it was merely a false rumour that had reached the prince.

'And you, Princess,' he turned suddenly to Belokonskaya with a radiant smile, 'did not you, six months ago, receive me in Moscow like your own son, on the strength of a letter from Lizaveta Prokofyevna, and indeed, as if I were your own son, give me some advice which I shall never forget. Do you remember?'

'Why are you in such a frenzy?' Belokonskaya said with annoyance. 'You're a good man, but a ridiculous one; they give you tuppence and you thank them as though they'd saved your life. You think it's praiseworthy, but it's actually repugnant.'

She was on the point of losing her temper completely, but suddenly burst out laughing, and this time her laughter was good-natured. Lizaveta Prokofyevna's face brightened too; even Ivan Fyodorovich beamed.

'I was saying that Lev Nikolaich is a man . . . a man . . . in a word, if only he wouldn't gasp, as the Princess observed . . .' muttered the general in a joyful rapture, repeating Belokonskaya's words, which had made an impression on him.

Only Aglaya was rather sad; but her face still glowed, perhaps with indignation.

'He is, truly, very charming,' the elderly gentleman muttered again to Ivan Petrovich.

'I came in here with torment in my heart,' the prince continued, in a kind of growing confusion, more and more quickly, with increasing strangeness and animation, 'I . . . I was afraid of you, and afraid of myself. Most of all, myself. Returning here, to St Petersburg, I vowed to myself that I would without fail see the first people in our land, the seniors, the long-established, to whom I myself belong, among whom I myself am one of the first in line. After all, I'm now sitting with princes like myself, am I not? I wanted to get to know you, and that was necessary; very, very necessary! . . . I have always heard so much about you that is bad, more than is good, about the pettiness and exclusiveness of your interests, about your backwardness, your poor education, your ridiculous habits – oh, I mean, they write and say so much about you! I came here today with curiosity, with confusion: I needed to see for myself and be personally convinced: is the whole of this upper stratum of Russian people really not fit for anything, has it lived out its time, exhausted its age-old life and is it capable only of dying, but still in a petty, envious struggle with the people . . . of the future, getting in their way, not noticing that it's dying? Before, I didn't fully share that opinion, because we have never had an upper class, except at the court, according to how one dressed at court, or . . . by accident, and now that has vanished completely, hasn't it, hasn't it?'

'Oh, that's not true at all,' Ivan Petrovich burst into caustic laughter.

'Oh no, he's begun to chatter again,' Belokonskaya could not restrain herself from saying.

'*Laissez-le dire*, he's even trembling all over,' the elderly gentleman warned again in a low voice.

The prince was well and truly beside himself.

'And what did I see? I saw people who are elegant, open-hearted, intelligent; I saw an elder statesman who was kind and attentive to a boy like me; I saw people who are capable of understanding and forgiving, good-natured Russian people, almost as good-natured and warm-hearted as those whom I met back there, almost as good as them. So you may imagine how happily I was surprised! Oh, permit me to say this! I had heard a great deal and was very much of the conviction that in society all is style, all is decrepit formality, while the essence has dried up; but I mean, now I can see for myself that it cannot be so in our country; it may be like that in other countries, but not in ours. You can't all be Jesuits and swindlers, can you? I heard Prince N. relating something just now: wasn't that open-hearted, inspired humour, wasn't it genuine good nature? Can such words come from the lips of a man who is ... dead, with a withered heart and talent? Would corpses treat me as you have treated me? Isn't that material ... for the future, for hope? Could men like him fail to understand, and fall behind?'

'I beg you again, calm yourself, my dear fellow, we'll talk about all this another time, and I shall be delighted to ...' the 'dignitary' smiled thinly.

Ivan Petrovich grunted and turned round in his armchair; Ivan Fyodorovich began to stir; the general, who was his superior, was conversing with the dignitary's wife, no longer paying the slightest attention to the prince; but the dignitary's wife frequently listened and looked.

'No, you know, it's better if I speak!' the prince continued with another feverish burst, addressing the elderly gentleman in a somehow peculiarly trusting and even confidential manner. 'Yesterday Aglaya Ivanovna forbade me to talk, and even named the topics about which I mustn't talk; she knows that I'm ridiculous when I do! I'm nearly twenty-seven, yet I know I'm like a child. I don't have the right to express my thoughts, I've long said that; only in Moscow, with Rogozhin, have I talked frankly ... He and I read Pushkin together, read the whole of it; he didn't know any of it, not even Pushkin's name ... I'm always afraid that my ridiculous appearance will compromise my thoughts and the *main idea* of what I'm trying to say. I don't have the right gestures. I always make the gesture that has the opposite meaning to what I'm saying, and that makes people laugh, and humiliates my idea. I also have no sense of proportion, and that's the principal thing; that's even the principal thing before anything else . . . I know it's better for me to sit and keep quiet. When I take a firm stand and keep quiet, I even seem very reasonable, and what's more, I reflect. But now it's better for me to speak. I began to talk because you look at me so nicely; you have a nice face! Yesterday I promised Aglaya Ivanovna that I'd keep quiet all evening.'

'*Vraiment?*' the elderly gentleman smiled.

'But there are moments when I think I'm wrong to think that way: after all, sincerity is worth more than gestures, is it not?'

'Sometimes.'

'I want to explain everything, everything, everything! Oh yes! You suppose I'm a utopian? An ideologist? Oh no, all my ideas are very simple, I swear . . . You don't believe it? You smile? You know, I'm base sometimes, for I lose my faith; earlier I thought as I was coming here: "Well, how shall I talk to them? What shall I say to begin with, so that they at least understand something?" How afraid I was, but for you I was more afraid, terribly, terribly! And yet how could I be afraid, was it not shameful to be afraid? What of it if for every advanced person there's such an abyss of backward and mean-spirited ones? That's the reason for my joy now, that I'm convinced there is no abyss at all, but it's all living material! There's no need to be embarrassed about the fact that we're ridiculous, is there? I mean, it really is so, we are ridiculous, frivolous, with bad habits, we're bored, we don't know how to look, we don't know how to understand, for we're all the same, all of us, you and I, and they! You're not insulted if I tell you to your faces that you're ridiculous, are you? And if you *are* insulted, then you're promising material, aren't you? You know, in my opinion, being ridiculous is sometimes even a good thing, and better than that: we can forgive one another more quickly, and acquire humility more quickly; after all, we can't understand everything at once, we can't begin directly from perfection! In order to achieve perfection, we must first of all fail to understand a great many things! And if we understand too quickly, we may not understand very well. I am saying this to you, you who have already been able to understand so much and . . . not understand. Now I am not afraid for you; you're not angry that someone who is only a boy should say such things to you, are you? You're laughing, Ivan Petrovich. You're thinking: I was afraid for *them*, I'm *their* advocate, a democrat, an orator of equality?' he began to laugh hysterically (at every moment he kept laughing, a short and ecstatic laugh). 'I'm afraid for you, for all of you and for all of us together. After all, I myself am a prince from a long line, and I am sitting with princes. I'm saying this in order to save us all, so that our class shall not disappear for nothing, in the darkness, without having realized anything, pouring abuse on everything and having lost everything. Why should we disappear and yield our place to others, when it's possible for us to remain in the advance guard and in charge? Let us be in the advance guard, and let us be in charge. Let us become servants in order to be leaders.'

He began to try to get up from his armchair, but the elderly gentleman kept constantly holding him back, and looking at him with growing unease.

'Listen! I know that talking isn't good enough: better simply to give an example, better simply to begin . . . I've already made a beginning . . . and – and can one really be unhappy? Oh, what are my grief and my trouble if I am able to be happy? You know, I cannot understand how one can walk past a tree and not be happy that one's seeing it? To talk to someone and not be happy that one loves him! Oh, it's just that I can't express it . . . and how many things there, at every step, so lovely that even the man at his wit's end will find them lovely! Look at a child, look at God's dawn, look at the grass growing, look into the eyes that look back at you and love you . . .'

By now he had stood for a long time, speaking. The elderly gentleman was looking at him in alarm. Lizaveta Prokofyevna, who had realized before anyone else what was the matter, exclaimed: 'Oh, my God!', and threw up her arms. Aglaya quickly ran up to him, managed to take him in her arms and, with horror, with a face distorted with pain, heard the wild cry of the unhappy one of whom it is said that 'the spirit tare him; and he fell on the ground, and wallowed foaming'.[6] The sick man lay on the carpet. Someone quickly managed to put a cushion under his head.

This was something no one had expected. After a quarter of an hour, Prince N., Yevgeny Pavlovich and the elderly gentleman made an attempt to revive the soirée, but after another quarter of an hour all the guests had already dispersed. Many words of sympathy were spoken, many complaints, a few opinions. Ivan Petrovich expressed himself, among other things, to the effect that 'the young man is a Slav-o-phile, or something of that kind, but actually it isn't dangerous'. The elderly gentleman did not express any opinion at all. To be sure, somewhat later, on the second and third day, they all got rather angry; Ivan Petrovich even took umbrage, but only slightly. The general who was his superior was somewhat cool towards Ivan Fyodorovich for a time. The family's 'patron', the dignitary, also for his part mumbled something by way of exhortation to the paterfamilias, though he still expressed the flattering assurance that he was very, very interested in Aglaya's destiny. He really was a some-what kindly man; but among the reasons for his curiosity about the prince, during the course of the evening, was the old episode of the prince and Nastasya Filippovna; he had heard a few things about this episode and was even very interested, would even have liked to ask some detailed questions.

Belokonskaya, as she left the soirée, said to Lizaveta Prokofyevna:

'Well, he is both good and bad; but if you want to know my opinion, he's more bad. You can see for yourself what sort of a man he is, a sick man!'

Lizaveta Prokofyevna finally decided in private that as a fiancé the prince was 'impossible', and overnight vowed to herself that 'while she was alive, the prince would not be husband to Aglaya'. With this decision in her mind, she rose the next morning. But that same morning, at twelve, over breakfast, she lapsed into a remarkable self-contradiction.

To a certain – it should be noted – extremely cautious question from her sisters, Aglaya suddenly replied coldly but overbear-ingly, almost snapping the words out:

'I've never given him any kind of promise and never in my life have I considered him my fiancé. He's as little a part of my life as of anyone else's.'

Lizaveta Prokofyevna suddenly flared up.

'I didn't expect this of you,' she said, upset. 'He's an impossible fiancé, I know, and thank God it's turned out like this; but I didn't expect such words from you! I thought you'd say something quite different. I'd have chased away all those guests last night, but would have let him stay, that is the kind of man he is! . . .'

At this point she stopped, alarmed by what she had said. But if she had only known how unjust she was being to her daughter at that moment! Everything was already decided in Aglaya's head; she was also biding her time until the hour at which it must all be decided, and every hint, every incautious touch cut her heart like a deep wound.

8

For the prince, too, that morning began with the influence of painful forebodings; they might have been explained by his morbid condition, but he was extremely, indefinably sad, and for him that was more tormenting than anything else. Before him, it was true, stood vivid, painful and wounding facts, but his sadness went farther than anything he could remember or grasp; he realized that on his own he would be unable to calm himself. Little by little there took root in him the expectation that today something special and final was going to happen to him. The fit that had assailed him the evening before was a slight one; apart from hypochondria, a certain heaviness in the head, and pain in the limbs, he felt no other derangement. His mind was working rather distinctly, though his soul was sick. He rose rather late and at once clearly remembered the soirée of the previous evening; though not quite distinctly, he none the less recollected being taken home half an hour after his fit. He learned that a messenger from the Yepanchins had come to inquire about his health. At half past eleven, another had arrived; this he found pleasant. Vera Lebedeva was one of the first to come and visit him and tend to him. At the first moment she saw him, she suddenly began to cry, but when the prince at once calmed her – she burst out laughing. He was somehow suddenly struck by this young woman's strong compassion for him; he seized her hand and kissed it. Vera flushed.

'Oh, what are you doing, what are you doing?' she exclaimed in fright, taking her hand away quickly.

Soon she went away, in a kind of strange embarrassment. Among other things, she managed to tell him that at the crack of dawn her father had run round to 'the deceased', as he called the general, to find out if he had died during the night, and that she had heard it said that he would soon die. Before midnight Lebedev himself came home and went to see the prince, but really 'just for a moment, to find out about your precious health', etcetera, and also to make a visit to the 'little cupboard'. He did nothing but moan and groan, and the prince soon dismissed him, but he none the less tried to ask one or two questions about the prince's fit, though it was plain that he already knew every detail about it. He was followed by Kolya, who also dropped in just for a moment. Kolya really was in a hurry and in a state of intense and gloomy anxiety. He began by requesting from the prince, forthrightly and insistently, an explanation of everything that had been concealed from him, adding that he had already found out almost everything the day before. He was intensely and profoundly shaken.

With all the sympathy of which he was possibly capable, the prince related the entire matter, establishing all the facts with complete exactitude, and the poor boy was struck as by a thunderbolt. He was unable to utter a word, and began silently to cry. The prince sensed that this was one of those impressions that remain permanently, and form a turning-point in a youngster's life for ever more. He hurried to convey to him his view of the matter, adding that, in his opinion, perhaps, the old man's approaching death was caused by the horror that had remained in his heart after his misdeed, and that not everyone was capable of this. Kolya's eyes flashed when he heard what the prince had to say.

'They're good-for-nothings, Ganka, and Varya, and Ptitsyn! I shan't quarrel with them, but from this moment on our paths diverge! Ah, Prince, since yesterday I have felt a great many things that are new; this is my lesson! As for mother, I also now consider her my direct responsibility; although she's provided for at Varya's, it's not the same thing . . .'

He leaped to his feet, remembering that he was expected, quickly asked about the condition of the prince's health and, hearing the reply, suddenly added with haste:

'Isn't there something else, too? I heard, yesterday . . . (actually, I don't have the right), but if you should ever need a faithful servant in any matter, he stands before you. I don't think either of us is quite happy, wouldn't you agree? But . . . I do not inquire, I do not inquire . . .'

He went away, and the prince began to reflect even more: they were all predicting misfortune, they had all already drawn their conclusions, they all looked as though they knew something, and something he did not know; Lebedev was plying him with questions, Kolya was directly hinting, and Vera was crying. At last he waved his arm in impatience: 'Damned morbid hypersensitivity,' he thought. His face brightened when, after one o'clock, he saw the Yepanchins coming to visit him, 'for a moment'. They really had just dropped in for a moment. Lizaveta Prokofyevna, having risen from breakfast, announced that they were all going out for a walk at once, and all together. The announcement was made in the form of an order, curtly, stiffly and without explanations. They all went out, that is, the mother, the girls and Prince Shch. Lizaveta Prokofyevna set off straight in the opposite direction from the one they took each day. They all realized what was wrong, and were all silent, fearing to irritate the mother, while she, as though hiding from reproaches and ripostes, walked ahead of them all, not looking round. At last, Adelaida observed that there was no need to run when out on a walk and that it was impossible to keep up with their mother.

'Now look,' Lizaveta turned to them suddenly, 'we're passing by his house now. Whatever Aglaya may think and whatever may happen later, he's not a stranger to us, and is now also ill and unhappy; I for one shall visit him. Whoever wants to come with me may do so, and whoever doesn't want to may walk on by; the way is not barred.'

They all went in, of course. The prince, as was proper, hurried once more to apologize for yesterday's vase and . . . scandal.

'Well, that doesn't matter,' replied Lizaveta Prokofyevna, 'I don't mind about the vase, it's you I mind about. So you do now perceive that there was a scandal: that's what "the morning after . . ." means, but that doesn't matter either, for anyone can see now that you can't be held responsible. Well, *au revoir*; if you feel strong enough, go for a walk and then sleep again for a while – that's my advice. And if you feel like it, then come and visit us as before; you may rest assured that in spite of everything you're still a friend of our family; a friend of mine, at any rate. For myself at least I can answer . . .'

They all responded to the challenge and confirmed their mama's sentiments. They went away, but in this simple haste to say something kind and encouraging there lay much that was cruel, something that Lizaveta Prokofyevna did not realize. In the invitation to visit 'as before' and the words 'of mine, at any rate' – there again sounded a note of prognostication. The prince began to try to remember Aglaya; to be sure, she had smiled to him wonderfully on entering and on saying farewell, but had said not a word, not even when everyone had declared their assurances of friendship, though she had given him a couple of fixed looks. Her face was paler than usual, as though she had slept badly during the night. The prince decided he would go and see them without fail that same evening 'as before', and glanced feverishly at his watch. Exactly three minutes after the Yepanchins had left, Vera entered.

'Lev Nikolayevich, Aglaya Ivanovna has just given me a message to pass to you in secret.'

The prince began to tremble badly.

'A note?'

'No, sir, by mouth; she only just had time. She asks you very much not to go out at all for a single moment today until seven in the evening, or even until nine, I didn't hear it all properly.'

'But . . . why? What does it mean?'

'I really don't know; only she told me to be sure to tell you.'

'Is that what she said: "be sure to"?'

'No, sir, she didn't say it directly: she was turning away, and she hardly had time to get the words out, seeing as how I myself had rushed up to her. But from her face it was plain that she was telling me to be sure I did it. She gave me such a look that my heart froze . . .'

A few more questions, and although the prince learned nothing further, he became even more anxious. Remaining alone, he lay down on the sofa and began to think again. 'Perhaps they have guests until nine, and she's afraid that I'll start playing pranks in front of them again,' he concluded to himself at last, and again began impatiently to wait for the evening, and to look at his watch. But the denouement followed long before evening and also in the form of another visit, a denouement in the form of a new, tormenting riddle: just half an hour after the Yepanchins' departure Ippolit entered his room, so tired and exhausted that, entering without saying a word, as if unconscious, he literally fell into an armchair and instantly sank into unendurable coughing. He coughed until he spat up blood. His eyes glittered and red spots glowed on his cheeks. The prince muttered something to him, but he did not reply and for a long time, still not replying, merely continued to make a defensive gesture with his arm, as a sign that he should not be disturbed. At last he came to.

'I'm leaving!' he articulated at last in a hoarse voice.

'I'll see you home if you like,' said the prince, half getting up from his chair, and stopped short, remembering the recent prohibition on going out.

Ippolit began to laugh.

'It's not you I'm leaving,' he continued, with a constant gasping, and a slight cough. 'On the contrary, I considered it necessary to come and see you, and on business . . . in the absence of which I wouldn't have troubled you. I'm going *there*, and this time, it seems, in earnest. *Kaput!* I'm not here for sympathy, believe me . . . I lay down at ten this morning, intending not to get up at all until *then*, but I changed my mind and got up again in order to come and see you ... so that means I had no alternative.'

'It hurts me to see you like this; you ought to have summoned me, rather than put yourself through all this effort.'

'Well, that will do. You've shown enough pity to satisfy the requirements of social politeness ... Oh yes, I forgot: how's your health?'

'I'm all right. Yesterday I wasn't ... very ...'

'I heard, I heard. The Chinese vase met its end; what a pity I wasn't there! But let me get down to business. Number one: today I had the pleasure of seeing Gavrila Ardalionovich at a rendezvous with Aglaya Ivanovna, at the green bench. I marvelled at the degree to which a man may possess a stupid appearance. Commented on this to Aglaya Ivanovna herself after Gavrila Ardalionovich's departure ... Nothing seems to surprise you, Prince,' he added, looking mistrustfully at the prince's untroubled face. 'It is said that not being surprised at anything is a token of great intelligence; in my opinion, it could equally well serve as a token of great stupidity ... Though actually, I'm not referring to you, forgive me ... I'm very unfortunate in my choice of words today.'

'I knew yesterday that Gavrila Ardalionovich ...' the prince stopped short, apparently embarrassed, though Ippolit was annoyed at his lack of surprise.

'You knew! Now that is news! Though actually, perhaps, don't tell me ... And you were a witness of the rendezvous this morning?'

'You would have seen that I was not there, if you were there yourself.'

'Well, perhaps you were crouching behind a bush somewhere. Actually, I'm glad, for you, of course, for otherwise I'd have thought that Gavrila Ardalionovich was the preferred suitor!'

'I would ask you not to speak of that to me, Ippolit, and especially not in such words.'

'Particularly as you already know everything.'

'You're wrong. I hardly know anything, and Aglaya Ivanovna knows for a fact that I don't know anything. Even about this

rendezvous I knew absolutely nothing . . . You say there was a
rendezvous? So, very well, let us leave it there . . .'

'But how is this, you knew, and yet you did not know? You
say: all right, let us leave it there? Well, no, don't be so trusting!
Especially if you don't know anything. That's why you're trusting, because you don't know. And do you know what those two
individuals, the brother and the sister, are counting on? You do,
perhaps, suspect something in that direction? . . . Very well,
very well, I'll leave it there . . .', he added, noticing the prince's
impatient gesture, 'but I came to see you on business of my own
and that's what I want to . . . explain. The devil take it, one
can't even die without explanations; it's dreadful, all the explaining I'm doing. Do you want to listen?'

'Go on, I'm listening.'

'Actually, as a matter of fact, I've changed my mind again: I
shall none the less start with Ganechka. Can you imagine, I too
had an appointment at the green bench this morning. However,
I won't tell lies: it was I who insisted on the rendezvous, thrust
it upon her, promised to reveal a secret. I don't know whether I
got there too early (I think I actually did), but no sooner had I sat
down beside Aglaya Ivanovna than I saw Gavrila Ardalionovich
and Varvara Ardalionovna appear, arm in arm, as if they were
out for a walk. They both seemed very surprised to see me; it
wasn't what they'd been expecting, and they were even rather
embarrassed. Aglaya Ivanovna blushed and, believe it or not,
even lost her head rather, whether it was because I was there, or
simply because she'd spotted Gavrila Ardalionovich, for he's a
very handsome fellow, after all, but she merely blushed crimson
and brought the matter to a conclusion in a single second, most
comical to watch, it was: she half got up, replied to Gavrila
Ardalionovich's bow and Varvara Ardalionovna's fawning
smile, and suddenly snapped: 'I've only come here to express to
you my personal pleasure for your sincere and friendly feelings,
and if I should ever be in need of them, then believe me . . .' At
that point she bowed, and they both went away – whether in
triumph or feeling foolish, I don't know; Ganechka, of course,
felt foolish; he couldn't make any sense of it all and blushed like
a lobster (sometimes his face has an extraordinary expression!),

but Varvara Ardalionovna, it seems, realized that they'd better quickly show a clean pair of heels, and that this was really more than enough for them to take from Aglaya Ivanovna, and hauled her brother away. She's cleverer than he is and will now be exulting, I'm sure. As for myself, I'd gone there to speak to Aglaya Ivanovna, in order to arrange a meeting with Nastasya Filippovna.'

'With Nastasya Filippovna!' the prince exclaimed.

'Aha! You seem to be losing that *sang froid* of yours, and are starting to be surprised? I'm very glad that you want to resemble a human being. In return for which I'll amuse you. That's what one gets for doing good deeds for young and high-minded girls: today I got a slap in the face from her!'

'A m-moral one?' the prince inquired, almost involuntarily.

'Yes, not a physical one. I don't think anyone would raise their hand against someone like me, not even a woman would strike me now; not even Ganechka would! Though there was a moment yesterday when I thought he was going to let fly at me . . . I bet I know what you're thinking now? You're thinking: "All right, we can't thrash him, but he could be smothered in his sleep with a cushion or a wet rag – he really ought to be . . ." It's written all over your face, at this very second.'

'I've never thought that!' the prince said with revulsion.

'I don't know, I dreamed last night that I was being smothered with a wet rag by . . . a certain person . . . well, I'll tell you who: imagine – Rogozhin! How, do you suppose, can a person be smothered with a wet rag?'

'I don't know.'

'I've heard it's possible. Very well, let's leave it. Well, so why am I a scandal-monger? Why did she call me a scandal-monger today? And take note of the fact that she'd already heard me out to the last word and had even asked me to repeat things . . . But that's what women are like! It was for her that I entered into association with Rogozhin, an interesting man; for the sake of her interests, too, I've arranged a personal meeting with Nastasya Filippovna. Was it because I wounded her pride when I hinted that she was glad of Nastasya Filippovna's "leavings"? But I constantly told her that it was in her own interests, I don't deny it, I wrote her two letters in that vein, and today a third, the rendezvous ... I began this morning by telling her that it was degrading to her ... And what's more, the word "leavings" is not really mine, but someone else's; at least, everyone was using it at Ganechka's; and she herself repeated it. Well, so what kind of scandal-monger am I where she's concerned? I see, I see: you find it dreadfully amusing now, as you look at me, and I bet you're applying those silly verses to me:

> And perhaps, upon my sad decline
> Love will gleam with parting smile.[1]

'Ha-ha-ha!' He suddenly dissolved in hysterical laughter, and began to cough. 'Take note,' he wheezed through the coughing, 'that's Ganechka for you: talks about "leavings", but now wants to avail himself of the very same thing!'

For a long time the prince said nothing; he was in a state of horror.

'You spoke of a meeting with Nastasya Filippovna?' he muttered at last.

'Oh my, is it really true that you don't know that today there's to be a meeting of Aglaya Ivanovna and Nastasya Filippovna, for which Nastasya Filippovna has been specially sent for from St Petersburg, through Rogozhin, at the invitation of Aglaya Ivanovna and by my efforts, and is now to be found, together with Rogozhin, not at all far from you, at her former house, the house of that lady, Darya Alexeyevna ... a very ambiguous lady, her friend, and that today, thence, to that ambiguous house, Aglaya Ivanovna is going to guide her steps for a friendly conversation with Nastasya Filippovna and the resolution of various problems. They're going to do some arithmetic. You didn't know? Honestly?'

'It's unbelievable!'

'Well, if that's how you see it, very well, it's unbelievable; anyway, how could you know? Though here, if a fly moves, everyone knows about it – that's the sort of place it is! But at least I've warned you, and it's possible that you may be thankful to me for it. Well, *au revoir* – in the next world, probably. Oh, and one more thing: though I've behaved like a scoundrel to you, because . . . why should I lose what belongs to me, tell me, please? For your benefit, eh? I mean, I dedicated my confession to her (you didn't know that?). And how did she receive it? Heh-heh! But I certainly haven't behaved like a scoundrel to her, and I'm really not guilty of anything in her regard; while she's dragged me into disgrace and led me up the garden path . . . Though actually, I'm not guilty in your regard, either; even if I mentioned those "leavings" just now, and all the rest of it, I'm now telling you the day, the hour, and the address of the meeting, and I'm letting you in on the whole of this game . . . out of spite, of course, and not out of generosity. Farewell, I'm as garrulous as a stutterer or a consumptive; watch out then, take precautions, and do so quickly, if you deserve to be called a man. The meeting will take place this evening, that's certain.'

Ippolit moved towards the door, but the prince shouted to him, and he stopped in the doorway.

'So in your opinion, Aglaya Ivanovna will come to see Nastasya Filippovna today?' asked the prince. Red spots had emerged on his cheeks and forehead.

'I don't know exactly, but probably, yes,' replied Ippolit, half looking round him, 'and actually it can't be otherwise. After all, Nastasya Filippovna can't go and see *her*, can she? And not at Ganechka's either; he almost has a dead man in his house. What about the general, eh?'

'For that reason alone it's out of the question!' the prince interjected. 'I mean, how could she go out, even if she wanted to? You don't know the . . . customs in that house: she can't possibly go off on her own to see Nastasya Filippovna; that's nonsense!'

'Look, you see, Prince: no one jumps out of windows, but if there's a fire, then even the finest gentleman and lady in the land will jump out of the window. If there's an emergency, then there's nothing for it, and our young lady will set off to see Nastasya Filippovna. But do they never let them go anywhere, your young ladies?'

'No, that's not what I meant . . .'

'Well then, all she needs to do is go down the front steps and walk straight on, even if she never goes home again. There are times when it's all right to burn one's boats, and when it's even all right not to go home again; there's more to life than just breakfasts and dinners and Prince Shchs. I think you take Aglaya Ivanovna for a young lady or a schoolgirl; I've already mentioned that to her; I think she agreed with me. Wait until seven or eight o'clock . . . If I were you I'd send someone there to keep watch and catch her the moment she goes down the front steps. I say, you could even send Kolya; he'd gladly do some spying, be assured, for you, that is . . . for after all, everything's relative, isn't it? . . . Ha-ha!'

Ippolit went out. The prince had no need to ask anyone to do any spying, even if he had been capable of asking for such a thing. Aglaya's telling him to stay at home was now almost explained: perhaps she wanted to drop in and visit him. Perhaps, it was true, she really did not want him to turn up there, and that was why she had told him to stay at home . . . That was also possible. His head was spinning; the whole room was going round. He lay down on the sofa and closed his eyes.

One way or another, the matter was decisive, final. No, the prince did not consider Aglaya a young lady or a schoolgirl; he felt now that he had long feared something of precisely this kind; but why did she want to see him? A chill traversed the whole of his body; once again he was in a fever.

No, he did not consider her a child! Some of the looks she had given him, some of the things she had said to him of late, had filled him with horror. Sometimes it seemed to him that she was too self-controlled, too restrained, and he remembered that this alarmed him. To be sure, during all these recent days he had tried not to think of this, had driven the painful thoughts away, but what was concealed within that soul? This question had long tormented him, though it was a soul he trusted. And now everything was to be resolved and revealed this very day. A horrifying thought! And again – 'that woman'! Why did it always seem to him that at the very last moment that woman would appear and tear his entire destiny apart, like a rotten thread? He was now ready to swear that he had always felt this, even though he was almost in semi-delirium. If he had tried to forget about *her* of late, it was solely because he was afraid of her. Well: did he love this woman or did he hate her? It was a question he had asked himself several times that day; in this respect his heart was unsullied: he knew whom he loved . . . He was not so much afraid of the meeting of the two, of its strangeness, the reason for this meeting, a reason unknown to him, of its resolution, no matter what that might be – it was Nastasya Filippovna herself he was afraid of. He remembered later, after several days, that in those fevered hours he had almost constantly imagined her eyes, her gaze, heard her words – strange words, though little remained in his memory after those hours of fever and anguish. He hardly remembered, for example, Vera bringing him his dinner and his eating it, did not remember whether or not he had slept afterwards. All he knew was that he had begun to distinguish clearly all the events of that evening from the moment when Aglaya suddenly came out to him on the terrace and he jumped up from the sofa and walked into the middle of the room to greet her: it was a quarter past seven. Aglaya was all on her own, dressed simply and apparently in haste, in a light 'burnous' cloak. Her face was pale, as it had been earlier, but her eyes glittered with a dry and brilliant lustre; he had never known such an expression in her eyes. She surveyed him attentively.

'You're all ready,' she observed quietly and almost calmly, 'dressed and hat in hand; so you were given advance warning, and I know by whom: Ippolit?'

'Yes, he told me . . .' the prince muttered like a man more dead than alive.

'Then let us go: you know that you must escort me there. You're strong enough to go out, I think, are you not?'

'Yes I am, but . . . is this really possible?'

He broke off in an instant and could not get another word out. This was his only attempt at stopping the reckless girl, and thereafter he followed her like a slave. No matter how troubled his thoughts were, he none the less realized that she would go *there* without him, and so he must follow her in any case. He could guess the strength of her determination; it was not for him to stop this wild impulse. They walked in silence, hardly spoke a word all the way. He merely noticed that she knew the way well, and when he wanted to take a detour down a side-street, because it was less crowded there, and suggested this to her, she listened as though straining her attention, and abruptly replied: 'It's all the same!' When they had almost gone right up to Darya Alexeyevna's house (a large, old wooden house), an elegant lady came down the front steps, and with her a young girl; both got into a magnificent barouche that was waiting by the steps, loudly laughing and talking, never once even glancing at those who were approaching, as though they had not noticed them. No sooner had the carriage driven off than the door immediately opened a second time, and the waiting Rogozhin admitted the prince and Aglaya, closing the door behind them.

'There's no one in the house now but the four of us,' he observed aloud, and gave the prince a strange look.

In the very first room they came to, Nastasya Filippovna was waiting, also dressed very simply and all in black; she rose to greet them, but did not smile, and did not even give the prince her hand.

Her fixed and anxious gaze impatiently fastened on Aglaya. They both sat down at a distance from each other: Aglaya on the sofa in a corner of the room, Nastasya Filippovna by the window. The prince and Rogozhin did not sit down, and were not invited to sit down. With bewilderment, and almost with pain, the prince again cast a glance at Rogozhin, but Rogozhin kept smiling his former smile. The silence continued for a few more moments.

At last a kind of ominous emotion passed across Nastasya Filippovna's face; her gaze became stubborn, hard and almost hateful, and did not leave her guest for a single moment. Aglaya was plainly embarrassed, but did not quail. Entering, she barely glanced at her rival and, for the present, sat with her eyes lowered, as if in reflection. Once or twice, as if by chance, she glanced round the room; revulsion was unmistakably portrayed in her features, as though she were afraid of being besmirched by simply being here. She mechanically adjusted her garments, and even once anxiously changed her seat, moving to the corner of the sofa. She was not really conscious of all her movements;

but the fact that they were unconscious increased their offensiveness. At last she looked Nastasya Filippovna firmly and directly in the eye, and at once clearly read all that flashed in her rival's embittered gaze. Woman understood woman; Aglaya shuddered.

'You know, of course, why I asked to see you,' she uttered at last, but very quietly, and even pausing once or twice during this short sentence.

'No, I have no idea,' Nastasya Filippovna replied, coolly and abruptly.

Aglaya blushed. Perhaps it suddenly seemed to her dreadfully strange and improbable that she was now sitting with 'that woman', in the house of 'that woman', and required her answer. At the first sounds of Nastasya Filippovna's voice a kind of shiver passed through her body. All this was, of course, very closely observed by 'that woman'.

'You understand everything . . . but you purposely make it seem that you don't,' Aglaya almost whispered, staring moodily at the floor.

'Why would I do that?' said Nastasya Filippovna, with the merest hint of an ironic smile.

'You want to take advantage of my position . . . that I'm in your house,' Aglaya continued, absurdly and awkwardly.

'That position is your fault, not mine!' Nastasya Filippovna flared up suddenly. 'I didn't ask to see you, you asked to see me, and I still don't know why!'

Aglaya raised her head with hauteur.

'Keep your tongue in check; I didn't come here to fight you with that weapon of yours . . .'

'Ah! But you've come to "fight", though, haven't you? That's funny, I thought you were . . . cleverer than that . . .'

They looked at each other, not trying to conceal their hostility now. One of these women was the same one who, not so long ago, had written the other such letters. And now all that had been dispersed by their very first meeting and very first words. But what was remarkable about that? At that moment, it seemed, not one of the four people in that room found it strange. The prince, who yesterday would not have believed in the possibility of this even in a dream, now stood there looking and listening, as if he had long had a presentiment of it. A most fantastic dream had suddenly turned into the most vivid and sharply defined reality. At that moment, one of these women so despised the other and so desired to tell her about it (perhaps she had only come there in order to do this, as Rogozhin expressed it the following day), that, no matter how fantastic that other woman might be, with her deranged mind and sick soul, no preconceived plan would, it seemed, have stood firm against her rival's poisonous, purely feminine contempt. The prince was certain that Nastasya Filippovna would not mention the letters of her own accord; by her flashing glance he guessed what those letters might cost her now; but he would have forfeited half of his life for Aglaya not to mention them now, either.

But Aglaya suddenly seemed to pull herself together, and at once regained her self-possession.

'You've misunderstood me,' she said. 'I didn't come to . . . quarrel with you, though I don't like you. I . . . I've come to talk to you . . . as one human being to another. When I asked to see you, I had already decided what I would talk to you about, and I shall adhere to that decision, even though you may not understand me at all. That will be the more unfortunate for you, not me. I wanted to reply to what you wrote to me, and to reply in person, as that seemed to me more opportune. Here, then, is my reply to all your letters: I began to feel sorry for Prince Lev Nikolayevich on the very day that I made his acquaintance, and when I later learned of all that happened at your soirée. I felt sorry for him, as he is such a simple-hearted man who, because of his simplicity, believed that he could be happy . . . with a woman . . . of that character. What I feared would happen to him did indeed happen: you were unable to love him, you tormented and abandoned him. You couldn't love him because you're too proud . . . no, not proud, I was wrong, but because you're vain . . . not even that: you are self-loving to the point of . . . insanity, of which your letters to me may serve as proof. You couldn't love him, such a simple man, and you even, perhaps, privately despised and ridiculed him, could love only your own disgrace and the constant thought that you were disgraced and that you'd been humiliated. If your disgrace had been less, or none at all, you'd be more unhappy than you are . . .' (With pleasure Aglaya uttered these words, which tripped out all too swiftly, but had long been prepared and considered by her, when she had not even dreamed of the present meeting; with a poisonous gaze she watched their effect on Nastasya Filippovna's face, which was contorted with turmoil.) 'You remember,' she continued, 'he wrote me a letter at that time; he says that you know about that letter and have even read it? From this letter I understood everything, and understood it correctly; he recently confirmed this to me himself, that is, all the things I'm telling you now, word for word, even. After the letter I began to wait. I guessed that you'd be bound to come here, because you can't live without St Petersburg: you're still too young and pretty for the provinces . . . As a matter of fact, those are not my words, either,' she added, blushing dreadfully, and from that moment on the colour did not leave her face, all the way until the very end of her speech. 'When I saw the prince again, I felt dreadfully hurt and offended on his behalf. Don't laugh; if you laugh, you're unworthy of understanding this . . .'

'You can see that I'm not laughing,' Nastasya Filippovna said, sadly and sternly.

'Though actually, it's all the same to me, you may laugh as much as you wish. When I began to question him about it myself, he told me that he had stopped loving you a long time ago, that even the memory of you was a torment to him, but that he felt sorry for you and that when he remembered you, his heart was as if "pierced for ever"; I must also say to you that I have never in my life met a man resembling him in noble simplicity and unlimited trustfulness. I guessed after his words that anyone who wanted to could deceive him, and that whoever deceived him he would later forgive, and that was why I fell in love with him . . .'

Aglaya paused for a moment, as if shocked, as if she herself did not believe she was capable of uttering that word; but at the same time an almost boundless pride began to flash in her gaze; it seemed that it was all the same to her now, even though 'that woman' at once began to laugh at the confession that had burst from her.

'I've told you everything, and now, of course, you will understand what it is I want from you?'

'Perhaps I do understand; but tell me yourself,' Nastasya Filippovna replied quietly.

Anger blazed in Aglaya's face.

'I wanted to learn from you,' she said firmly and clearly, 'by what right you interfere in his feelings for me? By what right you have dared to write letters to me? By what right you keep declaring, to him and me, that you love him, after you yourself abandoned him and ran away from him so insultingly and . . . disgracefully?'

'Neither to him nor to you did I declare that I love him,' Nastasya Filippovna articulated with an effort, 'and . . . you are right, I ran away from him . . .' she added, barely audibly.

'What do you mean, "neither to him, nor to you"?' exclaimed Aglaya. 'What about your letters? Who asked you to engage in matchmaking and try to persuade me to marry him? Is that not a declaration? Why do you thrust yourself upon us? I thought at first that you wanted, on the contrary, to instil revulsion in me towards him by meddling in our affairs, so that I would give him up, and only later realized the truth: you simply imagined that by all these affectations you were performing a lofty deed . . . Well, how could you have loved him, if you love your own vanity so? Why did you not simply go away from here, instead of writing me absurd letters? Why are you not now marrying the noble man who loves you so and has done you an honour by offering you his hand? It's all too clear why: if you marry Rogozhin, what would become of the insult to you? You would even receive too much honour! Yevgeny Pavlych said of you that you've read too many *poemy*[2] and are "too educated for your . . . position"; that you're a bookish woman and one with lily-white hands; add your vanity, and there are all your reasons . . .'

'And don't you have lily-white hands?'

All too swiftly, all too nakedly had matters reached such an unexpected point because Nastasya Filippovna, setting off for

Pavlovsk, still had dreams of something, though, of course, she assumed a bad, rather than a good outcome; as for Aglaya, she was decidedly carried away by impulse in a single moment, as though falling downhill, and could not restrain herself in the face of the dreadful pleasure of revenge. Nastasya Filippovna even found it strange to see Aglaya like this; she looked at her as if unable to believe it, and for an initial moment was decidedly at a loss. Whether she was a woman who had read too many *poemy*, as Yevgeny Pavlovich supposed, or was simply insane, as the prince was convinced, at any rate that woman – who sometimes had such cynical and insolent ways – was actually far more modest, tender and trusting than one might have thought. To be sure, there was much in her that was bookish, dreamy, closed off in itself and fantastic, but on the other hand much that was strong and deep . . . The prince understood this; suffering was expressed in his face. Aglaya observed it and began to quiver with hatred.

'How dare you address me like that?' she said quietly, with indescribable haughtiness, in reply to Nastasya Filippovna's comment.

'You must have misheard me,' Nastasya Filippovna said with surprise. 'How did I address you?'

'If you wanted to be an honest woman, why didn't you just leave your seducer, Totsky . . . without theatrical perform-ances?' Aglaya said suddenly, for no apparent reason.

'What do you know of my position, that you dare to judge me?' Nastasya Filippovna said with a start, turning horribly pale.

'All I know is that you didn't go off and work, you went off with the wealthy Rogozhin, in order to play the fallen angel. I'm not surprised that Totsky wanted to shoot himself to get away from a fallen angel!'

'Stop it!' Nastasya said quietly with revulsion and as if through pain. 'You understand me about as well as Darya Alexeyevna's housemaid, who took legal proceedings against her fiancé the other day. She'd have understood better than you . . .'

'She's probably an honest girl, and lives by her own toil. Why do you, of all people, view a housemaid with such contempt?'

'It's not toil I view with contempt, but you, when you speak of toil.'

'If you wanted to be honest, you should have been a washerwoman.'

Both rose and looked at one another palely.

'Aglaya, stop it! I mean, it isn't fair!' exclaimed the prince, like a man who was lost. Rogozhin no longer smiled, but was listening, his lips compressed and his arms folded.

'There, look at her,' said Nastasya Filippovna, trembling with animosity, 'look at that young lady! And I considered her an angel! Have you come to see me without your governess, Aglaya Ivanovna? . . . Well, would you like . . . would like me to tell you now directly, without embellishment, why you have come to see me? You're afraid, that's why you've come here.'

'Afraid of you?' asked Aglaya, beside herself with naive and insolent amazement that the other should speak to her like this.

'Of course! You're afraid of me if you've resolved to come and see me. One doesn't have contempt for someone one's afraid of. And to think that I respected you, even until this very moment! And do you know why you're afraid of me, and what your principal aim is now? You wanted to personally ascertain whether he loves me more than you, because you are horribly jealous . . .'

'He has already told me that he hates you . . .' Aglaya barely managed to mouth.

'Perhaps; perhaps I'm not worthy of him, but . . . but I think you are lying! It's not possible that he hates me, and he could not have said that! I am, however, prepared to forgive you . . . with regard to your position . . . yet all the same I thought better of you; thought that you were cleverer, and even prettier, I swear! . . . Well then, take your treasure . . . there he is, looking at you, can't recover his wits, take him, but on one condition: go away at once! This very minute! . . .

She fell into an armchair and burst into tears. But suddenly something new began to gleam in her eyes, she gave Aglaya a fixed and stubborn look, and got up.

'Or would you like me to . . . com-*mand* him, do you hear? I need only com-*mand* him, and he will immediately desert you and stay with me for good, and marry me, and you may run home alone? Is that what you want, is that it?' she shouted like a madwoman, perhaps herself almost not believing that she could utter such words.

'Would you like me to send Rogozhin away? Did you think I was going to marry Rogozhin for your pleasure? I'll shout now, in front of you: "Go away, Rogozhin!", and to the prince I'll say: "Remember what you promised?" Good Lord! Why have I lowered myself like this before them? But wasn't it you, Prince, who assured me that you would follow me, no matter what happened to me, and would never abandon me; that you love me and forgive me everything and res . . . respe . . . Yes, you said that, too! And I, merely to set you free, ran away from you, and now I don't want to! Why has she treated me as if I were a loose woman? Am I a loose woman? Ask Rogozhin, he'll tell you! Now that he has exposed me to disgrace, and in your eyes, too, will you also turn aside from me, and lead her away, arm in arm? Then curse you after that, for you were the only one I trusted. Go away, Rogozhin, you're not wanted!' she shouted, almost crazed, releasing the words from her bosom with effort, her face contorted and her lips parched, obviously not believing one iota of her own fanfaronade, but at the same time wanting to prolong the moment, if only by a second, and deceive herself. The outburst was so violent that she might perhaps have died, or at least that was how it seemed to the prince. 'There he is, look!' she shouted, at last, to Aglaya, pointing to the prince. 'If he doesn't come up to me now, doesn't take me and doesn't leave you, then take him, I'll give him up, I don't need him! . . .'

Both she and Aglaya paused as if in expectation, and both looked at the prince like women insane. It is possible, however, that he did not understand the full strength of this challenge, indeed that may even be stated for certain. All he saw before him was a desperate, reckless face which, as he had once let slip to Aglaya, had 'pierced his heart for ever'. He could endure no longer and addressed Aglaya with entreaty and reproach, pointing to Nastasya Filippovna:

'How can you do this? I mean, she is . . . so unhappy!'

But that was all he managed to get out, rendered speechless

by Aglaya's terrible gaze. In that gaze was expressed so much suffering and at the same time so much infinite hatred, that he threw up his hands, exclaimed and rushed to her, but it was already too late! She had not been able to endure even a moment of his hesitation, had covered her face with her hands, exclaimed: 'Oh my God!' – and rushed out of the room, Rogozhin following her in order to undo the bolt on the front door for her.

The prince, too, went running, but on the threshold he was seized by two arms. Nastasya Filippovna's desolate, contorted face stared at him point-blank, and her bluish lips moved, asking:

'After her? After her? . . .'

She fell senseless into his arms. He lifted her up, carried her into the room, put her down in an armchair and stood over her in dull expectancy. On the small table stood a glass of water; Rogozhin, returning to the room, seized it and sprinkled water in her face; she opened her eyes and for about a minute did not comprehend anything; but suddenly looked round, started, exclaimed and rushed over to the prince.

'Mine! Mine!' she cried. 'Has the proud young lady gone? Ha-ha-ha!' she laughed hysterically. 'Ha-ha-ha! I was giving him up to that young lady! But why? Why on earth? I'm insane! Insane! . . . Go away, Rogozhin! Ha-ha-ha!'

Rogozhin gave them a fixed look, did not say a word, took his hat and went away. Ten minutes later the prince was sitting beside Nastasya Filippovna, never taking his eyes off her and stroking her head and face, with both hands, like a little child. He laughed in response to her laughter and was ready to cry at her tears. He said nothing, but listened fixedly to her jerky, ecstatic and incoherent babbling, hardly understood anything, but quietly smiled, and as soon as it seemed to him that she was beginning to pine or weep again, to reproach or complain, he would at once begin to stroke her head again and tenderly pass his hands across her cheeks, comforting and coaxing her like a child.

9

Two weeks have passed since the event related in the last chapter, and the position of the *dramatis personae* of our narrative has changed so greatly that it would be extremely difficult for us to proceed to the sequel without particular explanations. And yet we feel that we must confine ourselves to the plain exposition of the facts, as far as possible without particular explanations, and for a very simple reason: because we ourselves, in many instances, are hard put to it to explain what happened. Such a forewarning on our part must seem very strange and unclear to the reader: how can one relate things in respect of which one has neither a clear conception nor a personal opinion? In order not to place ourselves in an even more false position, we had better attempt to explain ourselves by example, and, perhaps, the gracious reader will understand why precisely we are hard put to it, the more so as this example will not be a digression, but, on the contrary, a direct and immediate sequel to the narrative.

Two weeks later, that is to say, at the beginning of July now, and throughout these two weeks, the story of our hero, and especially the latest episode of that story, turns into a strange, highly entertaining, almost incredible and at the same time almost perfectly clear anecdote, spreading little by little through every street adjacent to the dachas of Lebedev, Ptitsyn, Darya Alexeyevna and the Yepanchins, in short, through almost the entire town and even through its environs. Almost the whole of society – local residents, dacha-dwellers, visitors to the bandstand – began to tell the same story, in a thousand different variations, of how a prince, creating a scandal in an honest and well-known household, having rejected a girl from that household, who was already his fiancée, had been carried away by a certain *lorette*,[1] had severed all his previous ties and, in spite of everything, in spite of threats, in spite of the public's universal indignation, intended to marry the disgraced woman in a few days' time here in Pavlovsk, openly, publicly, head held high and looking them all straight in the eye. So embellished with scandals did the story become, so numerous were the well-known and important personages involved in it, so many were the various fantastic and mysterious nuances attached to it, while on the other hand it presented itself in such incontrovertible and graphically visible facts, that the universal curiosity and gossip were, of course, very excusable. The most subtle, cunning and at the same time plausible interpretation remained in the hands of a few serious gossip-mongers, from that stratum of rational people who always, in every society, hurry to be the first to explain an event to others, something in which they find their calling and, not infrequently, their consolation. In their interpreting of the matter, a young man, of good family, a prince, almost wealthy, an imbecile, but a democrat who was mad about the contemporary nihilism uncovered by Mr Turgenev,[2] almost unable to speak Russian, had fallen in love with one of General Yepanchin's daughters and had got so far as to be received in the household as her fiancé. But like that French seminarist, about whom an anecdote was recently published and who deliberately allowed himself to be ordained to the cloth of the priesthood, and deliberately himself requested such ordination, completed all the rites, all the genuflections, kisses, vows, etcetera, only to publicly declare the following day in a letter to his bishop that, as he did not believe in God, he considered it dishonourable to deceive the people and make a living from it free of charge, and therefore cast away the cloth he had received the day before, and published his letter in the liberal newspapers – it was averred that the prince had played false in a manner similar to this atheist. It was said that he had deliberately waited for the formal guest night at the home of his fiancée's parents, at which he was presented to a great many important personages, in order, out loud and in everyone's presence, to declare his views, curse at the respected dignitaries, reject his fiancée publicly and with insults, and, while resisting the servants who were leading him out, break a handsome Chinese vase. To this it was added, as a contemporary characterization of *mores*, that the muddle-headed young man really loved his fiancée, the general's daughter, but had rejected her solely out of nihilism and for the sake of the impending scandal, so as not

to deny himself the pleasure of marrying a lost woman in front
of the whole world and thus to prove that in his conviction there
were neither lost nor virtuous women, but only free ones; that
he did not believe in the old social divisions, but put his faith
solely in the 'woman question'. That finally, in his eyes, a lost
woman even stood somewhat higher than one who was not lost.
This explanation seemed most plausible, and was accepted by a
majority of the dacha-dwellers, especially as it was confirmed
by daily facts. To be sure, a large number of things were still in
want of explanation: it was said that the poor girl loved her
fiancé – according to some, her 'seducer' – so much that she
went running to him the very next day after he had rejected her
and was now with his mistress; others, on the other hand,
maintained that he had deliberately enticed her to his mistress's,
solely out of nihilism, that is to say, in order to shame her
and insult her. Whatever the truth of the matter, interest in the
event grew daily, all the more so now there remained not the
slightest doubt that the scandalous wedding really was going to
take place.

And thus, were we to be asked for an explanation – not with
regard to the nihilistic qualities of the event, but simply with
regard to the degree to which the wedding that had been fixed
fulfilled the prince's actual wishes, what precisely those wishes
were at the present moment, how precisely one might define our
hero's state of mind at the present moment, etcetera, etcetera,
in similar vein, then, we must confess, we should be thoroughly
hard put to it to reply. All we know is that the wedding really
was fixed and that the prince himself had authorized Lebedev,
Keller and some acquaintance of Lebedev's, whom the latter
had introduced to the prince for this occasion, to take upon
themselves all the arrangements connected with the affair, both
ecclesiastical and economic; that they had been told not to spare
on money, that Nastasya Filippovna was in a hurry and insisting
upon the wedding; that Keller had been chosen as the prince's
best man, at Keller's own ardent request, while Burdovksy –
who accepted this appointment with enthusiasm – was to give
Nastasya Filippovna away, and that the day of the wedding was
fixed for the beginning of July. But apart from these most

precise contingencies, we know of several additional facts that
decidedly perplex us, for the specific reason that they contradict
the facts that precede them. We strongly suspect, for example,
that, having authorized Lebedev and the others to take upon
themselves all the arrangements, the prince nearly forgot that
very same day that he had a master of ceremonies, a best man
and a wedding, and that if he had given his instructions rather
quickly, entrusting the arrangements to others, it was solely so
that he need not think about them himself and might even,
perhaps, rather quickly forget about them. In that case, what
was he thinking about himself, what was he trying to remember
and what was he striving for? There can also be no doubt
that here no coercion was exerted upon him (on the part, for
example, of Nastasya Filippovna), that Nastasya Filippovna
really did desire an early wedding and that it was she who had
thought of the wedding, and not the prince at all; but the prince
freely gave his consent; even rather absent-mindedly, and as if
he had been asked to do some rather ordinary thing. Before us
there are very many such strange facts, but not only do they not
elucidate, but, in our opinion, even obscure the interpretation
of the affair, no matter how many of them are brought forward;
but, be that as it may, let us present one more example.

Thus, we know for certain that throughout those two weeks
the prince spent whole days and evenings with Nastasya Filippovna; that she took him with her on walks, to the bandstand;
that he drove about with her each day in her barouche; that he
would begin to worry about her if for but an hour he did not
see her (so that, by all the signs, he loved her sincerely); that he
listened to her with a quiet and modest smile, whatever it was
she talked to him about, for hours on end, and saying hardly
anything himself. But we also know that during those same
days, several times and even many times, he would suddenly set
off for the Yepanchins, not trying to conceal this from Nastasya
Filippovna, which almost drove her to despair. We know that
at the Yepanchins, while they remained in Pavlovsk, he was not
received, and was persistently refused an interview with Aglaya
Ivanovna; that he would go away without saying a word, and
on the following day go to see them again, as if he had completely

forgotten the refusal of the day before, and, of course, obtain a fresh refusal. We also know that an hour after Aglaya Ivanovna ran out of Nastasya Filippovna's house, perhaps even under an hour, the prince was already at the Yepanchins', of course in the certainty of finding Aglaya there, and that his appearance at the Yepanchins' then produced an exceeding perturbation and fright in the house, because Aglaya had not yet returned and it was only from that they first heard that she had gone with him to see Nastasya Filippovna. It was related that Lizaveta Prokofyevna, the daughters and even Prince Shch. had at the time treated the prince with exceeding harshness and hostility, and that they had also then, in heated expressions, denied him acquaintance and friendship, especially when Varvara Arda-lionovna suddenly presented herself to Lizaveta Prokofyevna and announced that Aglaya Ivanovna had already been in her house for about an hour, in a dreadful state, and seemed not to want to go home. This last news shocked Lizaveta Prokofyevna most of all, and was quite true: emerging from Nastasya Filip-povna's, Aglaya really would rather have died than appear now in front of her people at home, and therefore rushed to see Nina Alexandrovna. As for Varvara Ardalionovna, she at once, for her part, found it necessary to inform Lizaveta Prokofyevna of all this, without delay. Both mother and daughters, they all at once went rushing to Nina Alexandrovna, followed by the paterfamilias himself, Ivan Fyodorovich, who had just come home; Prince Lev Nikolayevich also dragged himself along after them, in spite of his expulsion and their harsh words; but, on Varvara Ardalionovna's instructions, he was not admitted to Aglaya there, either. The end of the matter was, however, that when Aglaya saw her mother and sisters weeping over her and not reproaching her at all, she rushed into their embraces and at once returned home with them. It was related, though the rumours were not completely accurate that here too Gavrila Ardalionovich had been dreadfully unlucky; that, having seized the occasion, when Varvara Ardalionovna ran off to see Lizaveta Prokofyevna, he, alone with Aglaya, had decided to start telling her of his love; that, listening to him, Aglaya, in spite of all her anguish and tears, suddenly burst out laughing and put to him a strange question: would he, as proof of his love, burn his finger on the candle forthwith? Gavrila Ardalionovich, it is said, was dumbfounded by the proposal and was so taken aback and expressed such bewilderment on his face that Aglaya burst out laughing at him, almost in hysterics, and fled from him upstairs to Nina Alexandrovna, where her parents found her. This anecdote reached the prince through Ippolit, the following day. Now bedridden, Ippolit purposely sent for the prince in order to convey this news to him. How this rumour reached Ippolit, we do not know, but when the prince heard about the candle and the finger, he laughed so much that he even surprised Ippolit; then he suddenly began to tremble, and dissolved in tears . . . In general during those days he was greatly anxious and uncommonly perturbed, in a vague and tormented way. Ippolit affirmed straight out that he did not consider him in his right mind; but this could not yet by any means be said affirmatively.

Presenting all these facts and refusing to explain them, we do not at all wish to justify our hero in the eyes of our readers. Not only that, but we are also quite prepared to share the indignation he aroused even in his friends. Even Vera Lebedeva was indignant with him for some time; even Kolya was indignant; even Keller was indignant, until he was chosen as best man, not to mention Lebedev, who even began to intrigue against the prince, also out of indignation, and even a very sincere one. But of this we shall speak later. In general, we completely and in the highest degree sympathize with several emphatic and even psychologically profound comments by Yevgeny Pavlovich, which he expressed to the prince directly and without ceremony in friendly conversation, on the sixth or seventh day after the events at Nastasya Filippovna's. We should observe, incidentally, that not only the Yepanchins themselves but all who belonged directly or indirectly to the house of the Yepanchins found it necessary to completely sever all relations with the prince. Prince Shch., for example, even turned away when he met the prince, and did not bow to him. But Yevgeny Pavlovich was not afraid of compromising himself by visiting the prince, in spite of the fact that he had again begun to spend every day at the Yepanchins and was even received with visibly increased cordiality. He came to see the prince the very next day after the departure of all the Yepanchins from Pavlovsk. As he entered, he already knew of all the rumours that had spread among the public, and had even, perhaps, contributed to this himself. The prince was terribly pleased to see him, and at once began to talk about the Yepanchins; such an open-hearted and direct beginning made Yevgeny Pavlovich feel completely unconstrained, and so he proceeded to the matter in hand without prevarication.

The prince was not yet aware that the Yepanchins had left; he was shocked, turned pale; but a moment later he shook his head in embarrassment and reflection, and admitted that 'it was bound to be like that'; then he swiftly inquired: 'Where did they go?'

Yevgeny Pavlovich, meanwhile, observed him fixedly, and all this, the swiftness of the questions, their simple-hearted nature, the embarrassment and at the same time a kind of strange candour, the frankness and the excitement – it all surprised him not a little. However, he told the prince everything amiably and in detail: there was much that the prince did not yet know, and this was the first bulletin from the house. He confirmed that Aglaya really was ill and had not slept for three nights in a row, in a fever; that now she felt better and was out of all danger, but was in a nervous, hysterical condition . . . 'It's just as well that there is perfect peace in the house! They are trying not to refer to the past even among themselves, not only in Aglaya's presence. The parents have already discussed a trip abroad, in the autumn, immediately after Adelaida's wedding; Aglaya received the first mention of that without saying anything.' He, Yevgeny Pavlovich, might also perhaps go abroad. Even Prince Shch. might go for a month or two, with Adelaida, if business allowed. The general himself would stay put. They had all now moved to Kolmino, their estate, some twenty versts from St Petersburg, where there was a spacious manor house. Belokonskaya had not yet gone to Moscow and was even remaining on purpose. Lizaveta Prokofyevna had strongly insisted that it was not possible to stay in Pavlovsk after all that had taken place; he, Yevgeny Pavlovich, informed her each day about the rumours that were passing about the town. They had also not considered it possible to move to the dacha on Yelagin Island.

'Well, and really,' added Yevgeny Pavlovich, 'you must admit, how could they have gone . . . especially knowing what was happening here in your house, hour by hour, Prince, and after your daily visits *there*, in spite of their refusals . . .'

'Yes, yes, yes, you are right, I wanted to see Aglaya Ivanovna . . .' the prince began to shake his head again.

'Oh, dear Prince,' Yevgeny Pavlovich suddenly exclaimed with animation and sadness, 'how could you have allowed . . . all that took place then? Of course, of course, it was all so unexpected for you . . . I can see that you must have been bewildered and . . . could not have stopped the crazy girl, it was beyond your powers! But even so you must have understood the degree to which that girl had strong and serious . . . feelings towards you. She did not want to share with another, and you . . . and you could abandon and break such a treasure!'

'Yes, yes, you are right; yes, I am to blame,' the prince began again in dreadful anguish, 'and you know: I mean, only she, only Aglaya looked on Nastasya Filippovna in that way . . . I mean, no one else did.'

'But that is just what is so outrageous, that there was nothing serious in it!' exclaimed Yevgeny Pavlovich, decidedly carried away. 'Forgive me, Prince, but . . . I . . . I have thought about this, Prince; I have thought it over a great deal; I know everything that took place earlier, I know everything that happened six months ago, and – none of it was serious! It was all just a cerebral infatuation, a picture, a fantasy, a vapour, and only the frightened jealousy of a completely inexperienced girl could have taken it for something serious!'

Here Yevgeny Pavlovich, now completely without ceremony, gave vent to all his indignation. Rationally and clearly and, we repeat, even in extreme psychological detail, he unfolded before the prince a picture of all the latter's former relations with Nastasya Filippovna. Yevgeny Pavlovich always had a gift for words; but now he even attained eloquence. 'Right from the start,' he proclaimed, 'you began with a lie; what began with a lie was bound also to end with a lie; that is a law of nature. I do

not agree, and am even indignant, when anyone – oh, whoever
it may be – calls you an idiot; you are too intelligent for such an
appellation; but you are strange enough not to be like everyone
else, you will admit. I have decided that the foundation of all
that has taken place was formed, in the first instance, by your,
so to speak, inborn inexperience (observe that word, Prince:
"inborn"), and then by your extraordinary open-heartedness;
further, by a phenomenal absence of a sense of proportion
(something you yourself have admitted on several occasions) –
and, lastly, by an enormous, rushing mass of cerebral convictions which you, with all your extraordinary honesty, have
persisted in taking for genuine, natural and spontaneous convictions! You will agree, Prince, that in your relations with Nastasya Filippovna there was from the very outset something
conventionally democratic (I express myself in abbreviated
form), so to speak, a fascination with the "woman question"
(to express myself even more briefly). I mean, I know in detail
of that strange and scandalous scene that took place at Nastasya
Filippovna's, when Rogozhin brought his money. If you like, I
will take you apart on my fingertips, will show you yourself as
in a mirror, in such detail do I know what it was all about and
why it turned out as it did! You, a young man in Switzerland, thirsted for the motherland, yearned for Russia as a land
unknown but promised; read many books about Russia, books
that were excellent, perhaps, but for you harmful; you made
your appearance in the first flush of a thirst for activity, so to
speak, threw yourself into activity! And then, that very same
day, you were told the sad and heartrending story of an insulted
woman – it was told to you, a knight, a virgin – and about
a woman! That same day you saw this woman; you were
entranced by her beauty, a fantastic, demonic beauty (I mean, I
agree she's a beauty). Add to this your nerves, add your epilepsy,
add our St Petersburg thaw, which shakes the nerves; add the
whole of that day, in a city unknown to you and almost fantastic
for you, a day of encounters and scenes, a day of unexpected
acquaintances, a day of the most unexpected reality, a day of
the three Yepanchin beauties, and among them Aglaya; add
tiredness, vertigo, add Nastasya Filippovna's drawing room and

the tone of that drawing room, and . . . what else could you have expected of yourself at the moment, what do you suppose?'

'Yes, yes; yes, yes,' the prince shook his head, beginning to blush, 'yes, after all, that is almost how it was; and you know, I really had hardly slept the previous night, on the train, and all the night before that, and I was very disoriented . . .'

'Well yes, of course, what else am I driving at?' Yevgeny Pavlovich continued, growing heated. 'It is clear that you, so to speak, in the intoxication of your enthusiasm, rushed at the opportunity of publicly declaring the magnanimous thought that you, an ancestral prince and a man of purity, did not consider dishonourable a woman who had been disgraced not through her own fault but through the fault of a disgusting high society profligate. Oh, Lord, but how understandable that is! But that is not the point, dear Prince, the point is whether there was truth there, whether there was truth in your emotion, whether there was nature there or just a cerebral enthusiasm? What do you suppose: the woman in the temple, a woman of just the same kind, was forgiven, but I mean, was it said to her that she had done well, was worthy of all kinds of honour and respect? Did your own common sense not suggest to you, after three months, what was really at stake? And even assuming that she is innocent now – I shall not insist, because I do not want to – but could all her adventures ever justify such intolerable, devilish pride, such shameless, such greedy egoism on her part? Forgive me, Prince, I'm getting carried away, but . . .'

'Yes, that may all be true: perhaps you are indeed right . . .' the prince began to mutter again. 'She is indeed very given to anger, and you're right, of course, but . . .'

'She's worthy of compassion? Is that what you mean, my good Prince? But for the sake of compassion and for the sake of her satisfaction was it justifiable to disgrace another girl, one who was high-minded and pure, to degrade her in those arrogant, those hate-filled eyes? But to what lengths will compassion take you after that? I mean, it's an incredible exaggeration! And was it justifiable, since you loved the girl, to degrade her like that in front of her rival, to turn your back on her for the sake of the other, in front of the other's eyes, after you'd made her an honest proposal? ... And I mean, you did make her a proposal, you made it to her in front of her parents and her sisters! After that, are you an honourable man, Prince, allow me to ask you? And ... did you not deceive the divine girl, assuring her that you loved her?'

'Yes, yes, you are right, oh, I do feel that I'm to blame!' said the prince in inexpressible anguish.

'But is that sufficient?' exclaimed Yevgeny Pavlovich in indignation. 'Is it enough simply to exclaim: "Oh, I'm to blame!" You're to blame, yet you persist! And where then was your heart, that "Christian" heart of yours? I mean, you saw her face at that moment: well, was she suffering less than the *other*, than *your* other, her rival in love? How could you see that and allow it? How?'

'But ... you see, I didn't allow it ...' muttered the unhappy prince.

'What do you mean, didn't allow it?'

'I swear to God, I didn't allow anything. I still don't understand how it all happened ... I – ran after Aglaya Ivanovna that day, and Nastasya Filippovna fell in a swoon; and after that they won't admit me to see Aglaya Ivanovna.'

'It doesn't matter! You should have run after Aglaya, even though the other one was lying in a swoon!'

'Yes ... yes, I should have ... I mean, she would have died! She would have killed herself, you don't know her, and ... I would have told Aglaya Ivanovna everything later, and ... Look , Yevgeny Pavlovich, I can see that you apparently don't know everything. Tell me, why will they not admit me to Aglaya Ivanovna now? I would explain everything to her. Look: at the time neither of them talked about what was important, not about that at all, and that is why things turned out with them as they did ... I am quite unable to explain it to you; but perhaps I'd be able to explain it to Aglaya ... Oh, my goodness, my goodness! You talk of her face at the moment she ran out that day ... Oh, my goodness, I remember it! Let us go, let us go!' He suddenly pulled at Yevgeny Pavlovich's sleeve, hurriedly jumping up from his seat.

'Where?'

'Let us go to Aglaya Ivanovna, let us go at once! . . .'

'But I mean, she's not in Pavlovsk, I told you, and why go to her?'

'She'll understand, she'll understand!' muttered the prince, putting his hands together in supplication. 'She'll understand that all this is not important, that the important thing is something quite, quite different!'

'What do you mean, quite different? But you're going to marry that woman all the same, aren't you? So you persist . . . Are you going to marry her, or aren't you?'

'Well, yes . . . I'm going to marry her; yes, I'm going to marry her!'

'So why is it not the important thing?'

'Oh no, it's not, it's not! It, it doesn't matter that I'm going to marry her, it's nothing!'

'What do you mean, it doesn't matter and it's nothing? That's nonsense, too, isn't it? You're going to marry the woman you love, in order to ensure her happiness, and Aglaya Ivanovna sees it and knows it, so how can it not matter?'

'Happiness? Oh, no! I'm simply going to marry her; that's what she wants; and what's so special about the fact that I'm going to marry her? I . . . Well, but it doesn't matter! Only she would certainly have died. I can see now that this proposed marriage of hers to Rogozhin was madness! I now understand everything I didn't understand before, and you see: when they were both standing facing each other, I couldn't bear to look at Nastasya Filippovna's face . . . You don't know, Yevgeny Pavlovich (he lowered his voice mysteriously), I've never told this to anyone, never, not even to Aglaya, but I cannot bear Nastasya Filippovna's face . . . You spoke the truth just now about that soirée at Nastasya Filippovna's; but there was one more thing there that you left out, because you do not know: I was looking at her face! Even that morning, in the portrait, I couldn't bear it . . . Vera, now, Vera Lebedeva, she has quite different eyes; I . . . I'm afraid of *her* face!' he added in extreme terror.

'You're afraid?'

'Yes; she's insane!' he whispered, turning pale.

'Do you know that for certain?' Yevgeny Pavlovich asked with intense curiosity.

'Yes, I do; now I'm certain of it; now, in these last few days I've discovered it for certain!'

'Then what are you doing to yourself?' Yevgeny Pavlovich exclaimed in alarm. 'So you're going to marry her out of some kind of fear? It's all quite incomprehensible . . . I suppose you don't even love her?'

'Oh no, I love her with all my soul! I mean she's . . . a child; now she's a child, a complete child! Oh, you don't know anything!'

'And at the same time you've been assuring Aglaya Ivanovna of your love?'

'Oh yes, yes!'

'But why? Do you want to love them both?'

'Oh yes, yes!'

'For heaven's sake, Prince, what are you saying, pull yourself together!'

'Without Aglaya I . . . I absolutely must see her! I . . . shall soon die in my sleep; I thought I was going to die in my sleep last night. Oh, if Aglaya only knew, knew everything . . . I mean, absolutely everything. Because here one must know everything, that is of paramount importance! Why can we never learn *everything* about another, when it's vital, when that other is to blame . . . Though, as a matter of fact I don't know what I'm saying, I'm confused; you gave me a dreadful shock . . . And does she really have the same face now as she had when she ran out of the room? Oh yes, I'm to blame! It's most probable that I'm to blame for it all! I don't know what it is, exactly, but I'm to blame for it . . . There is something here that I can't explain to you, Yevgeny Pavlovich, and I don't have the words, but . . . Aglaya Ivanovna will understand! Oh, I've always believed that she'd understand.'

'No, Prince, she won't understand! Aglaya Ivanovna loved like a woman, like a human being, and not like . . . an abstract spirit. Do you know what, my poor Prince? It's highly likely that you've never loved either the one or the other!'

'I don't know . . . perhaps, perhaps; in many respects you're right, Yevgeny Pavlovich. You're extremely clever, Yevgeny Pavlovich; oh, I'm starting to get a headache again, let's go to her! For God's sake, for God's sake!'

'But she's not in Pavlovsk, I tell you, she's in Kolmino.'

'Then let's go to Kolmino, let's go there right now!'

'That's im-poss-ible!' drawled Yevgeny Pavlovich, getting up.

'Listen, I'll write her a letter; please take her a letter!'

'No, Prince, no! Spare me such errands, I can't do that.'

They parted. Yevgeny Pavlovich went away with some strange convictions: in his opinion, too, it appeared that the prince was to some extent not in his right mind. And what was the meaning of this *face* he feared and loved so much! And yet after all, at the same time perhaps he really would die without Aglaya, so that perhaps Aglaya would never learn the degree to which he loved her! Ha-ha! And what was this about loving two women at once? With two different kinds of love? That was interesting . . . the poor idiot! And what was going to become of him now?

10

But the prince did not die before his wedding, either awake or 'in his sleep', as he had predicted to Yevgeny Pavlovich. Perhaps he did indeed sleep badly and have bad dreams; but during the daytime, with other people, he seemed good-natured and even content, though sometimes rather pensive, but this only when he was alone. The wedding was being hurried up; it was fixed for about a week after Yevgeny Pavlovich's visit. In the presence of such haste even the prince's best friends, if such he had, must have been disappointed in their attempts to 'save' the unfortunate madcap. Rumours were circulating that General Yepanchin and his spouse, Lizaveta Prokofyevna, were in part to blame for Yevgeny Pavlovich's visit. But even if, from the infinite goodness of their hearts, they might have wished to save the madman from the abyss, they were of course bound to limit themselves to this one feeble attempt; neither their position, nor even, perhaps, their hearts' disposition (as was natural) would have been suited to more serious efforts. We have mentioned that even those who surrounded the prince had to some extent risen against him. Vera Lebedeva, however, restricted herself to tears wept in solitude, and also to staying at home more and calling in to see the prince less often than before. Kolya was at this time in the midst of burying his father; the old man had died from a second stroke, some eight days after the first. The prince involved himself greatly in the family's grief, and initially spent several hours each day with Nina Alexandrovna; attended the funeral and went to the church. Many noticed that the public at the church whispered involuntarily as they greeted the prince and watched him leave; the same thing happened in the streets and in the park: whenever he walked or drove past there was talk, people would mention his name, point at him, and the name of Nastasya Filippovna would be heard. She was also sought at the funeral, but did not attend it. Also absent from the funeral was the captain's widow, whom Lebedev had managed to catch and prevent from coming. The funeral service made a powerful and painful impression on the prince. While they were in the church, he whispered to Lebedev in response to some question that it was the first time he had ever attended an Orthodox funeral service, and that the only other service of the kind he could recall was in some country church of his childhood.

'Yes, sir, it's as though it weren't the same man lying there, in the coffin, sir, whom we appointed chairman so very recently, you remember, sir?' Lebedev whispered to the prince. 'Who are you looking for, sir?'

'Oh, it doesn't matter, I had the impression . . .'

'Not Rogozhin, is it?'

'Is he here?'

'In the church, sir.'

'I *thought* I saw his eyes,' the prince muttered in perplexity. 'But, well . . . why is he here? Was he invited?'

'It never even crossed their minds, sir. I mean, he's not an acquaintance of theirs at all, sir. You see, there's all sorts of people here, sir, the public, sir. But why are you so surprised? I often encounter him now: I've met him about four times this last week here in Pavlovsk.'

'I haven't seen him once ... since that time,' muttered the prince.

As Nastasya Filippovna had also never once told him that she had met Rogozhin 'since that time', the prince now concluded that Rogozhin was for some reason deliberately staying out of sight. All that day he was immersed in intense reflection; while Nastasya Filippovna was unusually cheerful all that day and evening.

Kolya, who had made his peace with the prince before his father's death, suggested to him that he invite Keller and Burdovsky to be best men at the ceremony (as the matter was urgent and would brook no delay). He vouched for Keller, saying that the latter would conduct himself decently, and might even be 'useful', while Burdovsky's merits went without saying, he was a quiet and modest fellow. Nina Alexandrovna and Lebedev remarked to the prince more than once that if the wedding were decided upon, then why hold it in Pavlovsk, in the season of dachas and fashion, and why so publicly? Would it not be better to hold it in St Petersburg, or even at the house? To the prince the tendency of these apprehensions was all too clear; but he replied briefly and simply that such was Nastasya Filippovna's unalterable wish.

On the next day Keller also came to see the prince, having been informed that he was to be best man. Before entering, he stopped in the doorway and, as soon as he saw the prince, raised his right hand with index finger straightened, and shouted as if it were a vow:

'I won't drink!'

After that, he went up to the prince, firmly pressed and shook both his hands and declared that, of course, when he first heard about the wedding his attitude was one of hostility, that he had proclaimed it at the billiard hall, and for no other reason than that he had hoped and waited, with the impatience of a friend, to see the prince married to none other than the Princesse de Rohan;[1] but now he himself could see that the prince's cast of mind was at least a dozen times more noble than the rest of them 'taken together'. For what he wanted was not splendour, wealth nor even honour, but merely – the truth! The sympathies of elevated persons were all too well known, but the prince was too elevated by his education not to be an elevated person, all in all! 'But the dregs and the various riff-raff judge differently; in the town, in the houses, at the gatherings, at the dachas, at the bandstand, in the taverns, at the billiard halls, all the hue and cry is about nothing but the impending event. I've even heard that they're going to assemble a *charivari* below your windows, and this, so to speak, on your first night! Prince, if you require the pistol of an honest man, then I'm ready to exchange half a dozen honourable shots before you rise the next morning from your honeymoon couch.' He also advised, to guard against the danger of a great influx of thirsty people on their emergence from the church, the preparation of a fire-hose in the yard; but Lebedev was opposed to this: 'If they see a fire-hose,' he said, 'they'll reduce the house to splinters.'

'That Lebedev fellow is conducting an intrigue against you, Prince, by God he is! They want to make you a ward of court, can you imagine it, in everything, your free will and your money, that is, in the two things that distinguish us from the quadrupeds! I've heard it, I've heard it for a fact! It's the sheer unadulterated truth!'

The prince remembered having heard something of this kind himself, but had not, of course, paid any attention. Even now he merely burst out laughing and at once forgot again. Lebedev had been busying himself for some time; this man's calculations always came into being as if by inspiration, and because of excessive zeal grew more complex and ramified, departing from their original starting-point in all directions; that was why he had had little success in life. When later, almost on the day of the wedding, he came to the prince to confess (he had an unfailing habit of always coming to confess to those against whom he was conducting an intrigue, especially if he was not having much success), he announced to him that he had been born a Talleyrand, but for some unknown reason had remained a mere Lebedev. Thereupon he revealed his whole game, which the prince found extremely interesting. In his own words, he had begun by seeking the patronage of elevated persons from whom he could receive support if need be, and went to see General Ivan Fyodorovich. General Ivan Fyodorovich was taken aback, wished the 'young man' very well, but declared that 'for all his wish to save him, it would not be proper for him to act in this matter'. Lizaveta Prokofyevna was willing neither to hear him nor to see him; Yevgeny Pavlovich and Prince Shch. simply waved him away. But he, Lebedev, had not let his spirits sag, and had taken counsel with a certain astute legal expert, a venerable little old man, his great friend and almost his bene- factor; the latter concluded that it was a completely practicable matter, as long as there were competent witnesses of mental derangement and complete insanity, and also, most importantly, the patronage of elevated persons. Lebedev was not discouraged, and one day even brought a doctor, also a venerable little old man, a dacha-dweller, with the St Anne's ribbon,[2] to see the prince, for the sole purpose of inspecting, as it were, the lie of the land, making the prince's acquaintance and for the time being unofficially, but, as it were, in a friendly context, to inform him, Lebedev, of his conclusion. The prince remembered this visit by the doctor; he remembered that Lebedev had kept insisting the day before that he was unwell, and when the prince determinedly refused any medicine, had suddenly appeared with the doctor, on the pretext that they had both just come from Mr Terentyev, who was very poorly, and that the doctor had something to tell the prince about the sick man. The prince commended Lebedev and received the doctor with exceeding cordiality. They at once conversed about the sick Ippolit; the doctor asked the prince to relate in more detail the suicide scene of that day, and the prince completely carried him away with his account and explanation of the event. They began to talk about the St Petersburg climate, about the prince's own illness, about Switzerland, about Schneider. The exposition of Schneider's system of treatment and the prince's stories so inter- ested the doctor that he stayed for two hours; during this time he smoked the prince's excellent cigars, while courtesy of Lebedev there appeared a most splendid liqueur, brought in by Vera, whereupon the doctor, a married man with a family, launched into particular compliments in front of Vera, which aroused deep indignation in her. They parted friends. Emerging from the prince's quarters, the doctor told Lebedev that were such men were to be made wards of court, who would be found to be their guardians? As for the tragic account, on Lebedev's part, of the nearly impending event, the doctor shook his head slyly and craftily, and, at last, observed that, quite apart from the fact that 'one can never tell who will marry whom', as far as he had heard, 'the seductive lady, in addition to her inordinate beauty, which alone would be capable of turning the head of a man with a fortune, also possessed capital, both from Totsky and from Rogozhin, pearls and diamonds, shawls and furniture, so that not only did the impending choice fail to express on the part of the dear prince, as it were, any particular, glaring stupidity, it even bore witness to the cunning of an astute worldly intellect and calculation, and therefore led to an opposite conclusion, one that was perfectly favourable to the prince . . .' This thought had also struck Lebedev; this was what he was left with, and now, he added to the prince, 'Now you will see nothing from me but devotion and the shedding of my blood; that's what I came to tell you.'

During these final days Ippolit also provided the prince with diversion; he sent for him very often. They were waiting close by, in a small cottage; the small children, Ippolit's brother and sister, were at least glad of the dacha, because they could escape away from the sick man into the garden; as for the poor captain's widow, she remained constantly at his command and was quite his victim; the prince had daily to separate them and reconcile them, and the sick man continued to call him his 'nurse', at the same time apparently not daring not to despise him for his role of conciliator. He bore an exceeding grudge against Kolya, as the latter almost never came to see him, remaining at first with his dying father, and then with his widowed mother. At last, he set as the target of his mockery the prince's imminent marriage to Nastasya Filippovna, and ended by insulting the prince and eventually driving him wild with anger: the prince stopped visiting him. Two days later the captain's widow dragged herself along in the morning and in tears begged the prince to call on them, otherwise *he* would devour her. She added that he wanted to reveal a great secret. The prince left. Ippolit wanted to make his peace, began to cry and after his tears, of course, grew even more hostile and embittered, though he was afraid to show it. He was very poorly, and everything about him showed that now he was soon going to die. As for the secret, there was none, apart from urgent pleas, expressed in a voice panting with agitation (possibly artificial), so to speak, to 'beware of Rogozhin'. 'He's the kind of man who won't give up what belongs to him; he's not like you or me, Prince: if he wants something, he really will stop at nothing . . .' etcetera, etcetera. The prince began to question him more closely, wishing to obtain some facts; but facts there were none, only personal emotions and impressions. To his exceeding satisfaction, at length, Ippolit ended by giving the prince a dreadful fright. At first the prince was unwilling to answer some of his strange questions, and merely smiled at the advice to 'even flee abroad; there are Russian priests everywhere, and you can get married there'. But, at last, Ippolit ended with the following thought: 'You see, it's just that I'm afraid for Aglaya Ivanovna: Rogozhin knows how much you love her; a love for a love; you've taken Nastasya Filippovna away from him, and he will kill Aglaya Ivanovna; though she isn't yours now, all the same it will be distressing for you, won't it?' He attained his goal: when he left him, the prince was not his own man.

These warnings about Rogozhin came the day before the wedding. That same evening, for the last time before the wedding, the prince had a meeting with Nastasya Filippovna; but Nastasya Filippovna was not in a position to be able to reassure him, and had even of late, on the contrary, been intensifying his confusion more and more. Previously, several days earlier, that is, at her meeting with him, she had made every attempt to cheer him up, being dreadfully alarmed by his melancholy look; had even tried to sing to him; but most often had told him all the humorous stories she could remember. The prince had almost always pretended to laugh a great deal, and sometimes really did laugh at the brilliant wit and radiant emotion with which she sometimes told her stories when she got carried away, something that often happened. And when she saw the prince's laughter, saw the effect she had on him, she was delighted and began to feel proud of herself. But now her sadness and pensiveness were growing almost by the hour. His opinions concerning Nastasya Filippovna were established, and of course, had they not been, everything about her would now have seemed to him mysterious and incomprehensible. But he sincerely believed that she could still recover. He had been perfectly truthful in telling Yevgeny Pavlovich that he loved her sincerely and completely, and in his love for her there really was something like an inclination towards some pitiful and ailing child whom it is difficult and even impossible to leave to its own devices. He had not explained his feelings about her to anyone and did not even like to talk about them, unless it was impossible to avoid that subject of conversation; when he and Nastasya Filippovna were alone together they never talked about 'feelings', as though they had both promised each other not to. In their usual cheerful and animated conversation anyone could take part. Darya Alexey-evna said later that throughout this entire period she simply feasted her eyes and rejoiced as she looked at them.

But it was this same view of Nastasya Filippovna's emotional and mental state that relieved him, to some extent, of many other perplexities. She was now a completely different woman from the one he had known some three months earlier. He did not even reflect now, for example, on why then she had run away from marrying him, with tears, with curses and reproaches, yet now insisted on a wedding as soon as possible. 'It must be that she's not afraid now, as she was then, that marrying me would be a disaster for her,' thought the prince. Such a swiftly revived confidence in herself could not, in his view, be natural to her. Again, that confidence could not have proceeded merely from her hatred for Aglaya: Nastasya Filippovna was able to feel rather more deeply than that. Was it perhaps out of apprehension at her fate with Rogozhin? In a word, all these reasons could have played a part along with others; but what was clearer to him than anything else was that her poor, sick mind had not been able to take the strain. All this, though in a way it relieved him from perplexity, gave him no rest or peace throughout this time. Occasionally it was as if he were trying not to think about anything; he apparently viewed the marriage as a sort of unimportant formality; he placed very little value on his own fate. As for objections and conversations like the one he had had with Yevgeny Pavlovich, in those he would have been quite unable to reply, feeling himself to be quite incompetent, and therefore abstained from any conversations of that kind.

He did, however, notice that Nastasya Filippovna knew and understood all too well what Aglaya meant to him. It was merely that she did not say anything, but he saw her 'face' when sometimes she encountered him at that time, right at the beginning, when he was getting ready to go to the Yepanchins. When the Yepanchins left, she positively beamed. However unobservant and slow-witted he might be, he began to be troubled by the thought that Nastasya Filippovna was going to create some kind of scandal in order to drive Aglaya out of Pavlovsk. The noise and clamour in all the dachas about the wedding was, of course, in part kept going by Nastasya Filippovna in order to irritate her rival. Since it was hard to meet the Yepanchins, one day Nastasya Filippovna, making the prince get into her barouche, instructed the coachman to drive right past the windows of their dacha. This was a dreadful surprise for the prince; as usual, he realized what was happening only when it was already too late to mend matters and when the barouche had already driven right past the windows. He did not say anything, but was ill for two days afterwards; Nastasya Filippovna did not repeat the experiment. In the last days before the wedding she began to reflect a great deal; she always ended by conquering her sadness and becoming cheerful again, but somehow more quietly, not so noisily, not so happily cheerful as before, in the so recent past. The prince redoubled his attention. He found it curious that she would never talk to him about Rogozhin. Only once, some five days before the wedding, a message arrived from Darya Alexeyevna asking him to go there without delay, as Nastasya Filippovna was feeling very ill. He found her in a condition that resembled total insanity: she was screaming, trembling, shouting that Rogozhin was hiding in the garden, in their house, that she had just seen him, that he was going to kill her at night ... cut her throat! She was unable to calm herself for the whole of that day. But that same evening, when the prince looked in to see Ippolit for a moment, the captain's widow, who had just returned from the city, where she had gone on some trivial business of hers, told him that Rogozhin had called in to see her that day in St Petersburg and had asked her questions about Pavlovsk. To the prince's question as to precisely when Rogozhin had called in, the captain's widow mentioned almost the very hour at which Nastasya Filippovna was supposed to have seen him that day, in her garden. The matter was explained as a simple mirage; Nastasya Filippovna had gone to see the captain's widow in order to make more detailed inquiries, and had her mind put exceedingly at rest.

On the eve of the wedding the prince left Nastasya Filippovna in great animation: arrived from the dressmaker's in St Petersburg were the fine garments, the wedding dress, the head-dresses, etcetera, etcetera, she was to wear the next day. The prince had not expected that she would be excited by these fine garments; he himself praised them all, and his praise made her even happier. But she let something slip: she had already heard that there was indignation in the town and that some rakes really were arranging a *charivari*, with music and even poetry, specially written, and that this almost had the approval of the rest of society. And so now more than ever she wanted to hold her head high before them, eclipse them all with the taste and expensive allure of her garments – 'let them shout, let them whistle, if they dare!' The thought of this alone made her eyes flash. She also had another secret dream, but she did not talk of it aloud: she dreamed that Aglaya, or at least one of her emissaries, would be in the crowd, incognito, in the church, watching and observing, and she was preparing herself for that. She parted from the prince entirely preoccupied with these thoughts, at about eleven that evening; but it had not yet struck midnight when a messenger came running to the prince from Darya Alexeyevna's, telling him to 'come quickly, she is very bad'. The prince found his bride locked in her bedroom, in tears, in despair, in hysterics; for a long time she could hear nothing that was said to her through the locked door, at last opened it, admitted the prince alone, locked the door behind him and fell before him on her knees. (Such at least was the account given by Darya Alexeyevna, who had managed to peep round the corner.)

'What am I doing? What am I doing? What am I doing to you?' she kept exclaiming, convulsively embracing his legs.

For a whole hour the prince sat with her; what they talked of, we do not know. According to Darya Alexeyevna's account, they parted an hour later, reconciled and happy. The prince sent someone to inquire again that evening, but Nastasya Filippovna was already asleep. In the morning, before she awoke, two more emissaries from the prince came to see Darya Alexeyevna, and a third emissary was charged with informing the prince that 'around Nastasya Filippovna there is now a whole swarm of dressmakers and *coiffeuses* from St Petersburg, that there is not a trace of last night's trouble, that she is busy, as only a beauty like her can be busy before her wedding, with her costume, and that now, at this very moment, an extraordinary congress is in session to decide precisely which diamonds she should wear, and how they should be worn.' The prince was completely reassured.

The entire anecdote about this wedding was told in the following manner, and, it seems, with accuracy, by competent persons:

The wedding ceremony was fixed for eight o'clock in the evening; Nastasya Filippovna was ready by seven. From six o'clock, crowds of people who had come to gape gradually began to assemble around Lebedev's dacha, but especially outside Darya Alexeyevna's house; from seven o' clock the church also began to fill. Vera Lebedeva and Kolya were in the most dreadful state of apprehension for the prince; however, their hands were full at home: they were making the arrangements for the reception and hospitality in the prince's rooms. As a matter of fact, almost no kind of gathering was proposed for after the altar ceremony; apart from the persons indispensable during the performance of nuptials, Lebedev had invited the Ptitsyns, Ganya, the doctor with the St Anne's ribbon and Darya Alexeyevna. When the prince inquired of Lebedev why he had taken it into his head to invite the doctor, who was 'almost a total stranger', Lebedev replied complacently: 'He has a medal, he's a respected man, sir, it's for appearance, sir' – and this made the prince laugh. Keller and Burdovsky, in tailcoats and gloves, looked very proper; though Keller still kept causing the prince and his principals some anxiety by certain open tendencies towards battle, viewing in a most hostile manner the crowd of people who had gathered near the house in order to gape. At last, at half-past seven, the prince set off for the church, in a carriage. We should observe, by the way, that he himself had been expressly unwilling to omit a single one of the accepted habits and customs; all was done publicly, manifestly, openly and 'properly'. In the church, somehow managing to pick his way through the crowd, to the accompaniment of the constant whispering and exclamations of the public, under the leadership of Keller, who cast menacing glances to right and to left, the prince concealed himself for a time in the altar, while Keller set off to fetch the bride, finding at the front steps of Darya Alexeyevna's house a crowd not only twice or three times more dense than the one at the prince's, but even perhaps three times more unconstrained in its familiarity. Ascending the front steps, he heard such exclamations that he could no longer endure and was about to turn to the public with the intention of delivering a suitable speech, but was fortunately stopped by Burdovsky and Darya Alexeyevna herself, who came running down the steps; they seized hold of him and led him inside by force. Keller was irritable and in a hurry. Nastasya Filippovna rose, took one more glance at herself in the mirror, observed with a 'crooked' smile, as Keller recounted it later, that she was 'as pale as a corpse', bowed devoutly to the icon and went out on to the front steps. A hubbub of voices greeted her appearance. To be sure, for an initial moment there were laughter, applause, whistles, almost; but a moment later, other voices rang out:

'What a beautiful woman!' came the cry from the crowd.

'She isn't the first, and she won't be the last!'

'Marriage covers everything up, fools!'

'No, you won't find a ravishing beauty like that anywhere. Hurrah!' cried those who were close.

'A princess! For such a princess I would sell my soul!' shouted some clerk or other. '"My life I'd give for just one night! . . ."'[3]

Nastasya Filippovna really did emerge as pale as a handkerchief; but her large, black eyes flashed at the crowd like burning coals; it was this gaze that the crowd could not withstand; indignation turned into ecstatic shouts. The doors of the carriage had already been opened, Keller had already given the bride his arm, when suddenly she screamed and rushed straight down the steps into the mass of people. All who were with her froze in astonishment, the crowd parted before her, and five, six paces from the steps Rogozhin suddenly appeared. It was his gaze that Nastasya Filippovna had caught in the crowd. She ran to him like a madwoman and seized him by both hands.

'Save me! Take me away! Wherever you want, right now!'

Rogozhin almost caught her in his arms and practically lifted her into the carriage. Then, in a single instant, he took from his purse a hundred-rouble note and proffered it to the coachman.

'To the station, and if you get to the train on time, there's another hundred roubles for you!'

And he jumped into the carriage after Nastasya Filippovna and closed the doors. The coachman did not hesitate for a moment, and lashed the horses on their way. Later, Keller put the blame on the unexpectedness of it all: 'Another minute and I'd have recovered myself, I would not have allowed it!' he explained, as he described what had taken place. He and Burdovsky took another carriage that happened to be there and were about to speed off in pursuit, but while already on the road reflected that 'in any case it's too late! We can't bring them back by force!'

'And in any case, the prince doesn't want it!' the shaken Burdovsky decided.

And Rogozhin and Nastasya Filippovna got to the station on time. As he got out of the carriage, Rogozhin, almost as he was about to board the train, managed to stop a girl who was passing, dressed in an old but decent dark mantilla, a silk kerchief thrown over her head.

'I'll give you fifty roubles for your mantilla!' He suddenly held out the money to the girl. Before she had time to be astonished, and was still trying to grasp what was happening, he suddenly thrust the fifty-rouble note into her hand, took off her mantilla and kerchief and threw them over Nastasya Filippovna's head and shoulders. Her exceedingly fine attire was all too noticeable, and would have drawn attention in the railway carriage; only later did the girl understand the reason for the purchase, at such a profit to herself, of her old clothes, which were worth nothing.

The rumour of this episode reached the church with extraordinary alacrity. As Keller made his way towards the prince, a large number of people who were quite unknown to him rushed forward to ask questions. There was loud talk, shaking of heads, even laughter; no one left the church, everyone was waiting to see how the groom would receive the news. He turned pale, but received the news quietly, saying in a voice that was barely audible: 'I was afraid of this; but even so, I didn't think it would happen . . .' – and then, after a short silence, added: 'As a matter of fact . . . in her condition . . . it is quite in the order of things.' Keller himself later called this response 'unexampled philosophy'. The prince left the church, to all appearances calm and cheerful; that, at least, is what many people observed and described later. It seemed that he very much wanted to get home and be alone as soon as possible; but this he was not allowed to do. He was followed into the room by several of those who had been invited, among them Ptitsyn, Gavrila Ardalionovich and with them the doctor, who was also not intending to leave. In addition, the whole house was literally besieged by the idle public. Even from the terrace the prince could hear Keller and Lebedev enter into a fierce argument with several people who were quite unknown, though apparently people of rank, and who aspired to enter the veranda at all costs. The prince approached the disputants, inquired what the matter was and, politely moving Lebedev and Keller aside, delicately turned to one stout and grey-haired gentleman who was standing on the steps of the porch at the head of several other aspirants, and asked him to do him the honour of conferring a visit upon him. The gentleman was at first embarrassed, but complied all the same; he was followed by a second, a third. From the entire crowd there emerged some seven or eight visitors who did indeed

enter, trying to do so in as relaxed a manner as possible; but
there proved to be no more candidates, and soon, in the crowd
itself, voices began to condemn the upstarts. The entrants were
shown to their seats, conversation began, tea was served – all of
this done with exceeding decorum and modesty, somewhat to
the surprise of the entrants. There were, of course, some
attempts to enliven the conversation and bring it round to the
'proper' topic; some immodest questions were asked, and some
'bold' comments were made. The prince replied to them all so
simply and cheerfully, and at the same time with such dignity,
with such trust in the decency of his guests, that the immodest
questions died away of their own accord. Little by little the
conversation began to grow almost serious. One gentleman,
attaching himself to something that someone said, suddenly
swore, in exceeding indignation, that he would not sell his
estate, no matter what happened there; that, on the contrary,
he would wait and see what transpired, and that 'enterprises are
better than money'; 'that, my dear sir, is the basis of my economic system, you may as well know, sir.' As he was addressing
the prince, the prince praised him with ardour, in spite of the
fact that Lebedev was whispering in his ear that this gentleman
had not a stick of property to his name and had never owned
any estate. Almost an hour went by, the tea was drunk, and
after tea the guests at last began to feel guilty about staying any
longer. The doctor and the grey-haired gentleman warmly took
their leave of the prince; and indeed, all said their farewells
warmly and noisily. Good wishes were pronounced, and
opinions such as 'there is no point in grieving and perhaps it's
even all for the best,' etcetera. There were, it was true, attempts
to ask for champagne, but the older of the guests restrained the
younger. When they had all dispersed, Keller leaned over to
Lebedev and told him: 'You and I would have started shouting,
got into a fight, disgraced ourselves, and they'd have called the
police; but he, just look at him, he's acquired new friends, and
what friends, too; I know them!' Lebedev, who was rather
'primed', sighed and said: '"Thou hast hid these things from
the wise and prudent, and hast revealed them unto babes."⁴ I
have said that about him before, but now I add that God has

preserved the babe, too, saved him from the abyss, him and all his saints!'

At last, at about half-past ten, they left the prince alone, as he had a headache; last to leave was Kolya, who helped him to change out of his wedding clothes into his ordinary ones. They parted on warm terms. Kolya did not expatiate on the event, but promised to come back early the next day. In fact, he later testified that the prince had not warned him of anything at their last farewell, and so must have been hiding his intentions even from him. Soon in the entire house almost no one remained: Burdovsky returned to Ippolit's; Keller and Lebedev had gone off somewhere. Only Vera Lebedeva remained for a while yet in the rooms, hastily restoring them from their festive aspect to the one that was usual. As she was leaving, she cast a glance towards the prince. He was sitting at the table, leaning on it with both elbows and covering his face with his hands. She quietly went over to him and touched him on the shoulder; the prince looked at her in bewilderment and almost for a minute seemed to be trying to remember something; but having remembered it and worked it all out, he suddenly entered a state of extreme agitation. It was all, however, resolved with an urgent and ardent plea to Vera, that the following morning, when the first train was due to leave, at seven o'clock, she should knock on the door of his room. Vera promised to do so; the prince began to entreat her ardently not to tell anyone of it; this she promised, too, and, at last, when she had now fully opened the door in order to go out, the prince stopped her a third time, took her by the hands, kissed them, then kissed her on the forehead and with a certain 'peculiar' expression managed to say to her: 'Until tomorrow!' That, at least, was how Vera told it later. She left in great trepidation for him. In the morning she recovered her spirits somewhat when, after seven, as they had arranged, she knocked at his door and informed him that the train to St Petersburg would be leaving in a quarter of an hour; it seemed to her that when he opened the door to her he was quite cheerful, and even smiling. He had hardly undressed for the night, but had slept, all the same. In his opinion, he might return that same evening. It thus transpired that she was the only person whom he had found it possible and necessary to tell at that moment that he was setting off for the city.

11

An hour later he was already in St Petersburg and, just after nine in the morning, ringing the bell of Rogozhin's house. He chose the front entrance, and it was a long time before the door was opened to him. At last, the door to the rooms of old Mrs Rogozhin opened, and an elderly, pleasant-looking maidservant appeared.

'Parfyon Semyonovich is not at home,' she announced from the door. 'Who are you looking for?'

'Parfyon Semyonovich.'

'His honour's not at home, sir.'

The maidservant looked the prince over with intense curiosity.

'Tell me at least, did he spend the night at home? And . . . was he alone when he returned yesterday?'

The maidservant continued to look, but did not make any reply.

'Was . . . Nastasya Filippovna here with him yesterday . . . in the evening?'

'Will you permit me to ask who you are, sir?'

'Prince Lev Nikolayevich Myshkin, he and I are very well acquainted.'

'His honour's not at home, sir.'

The maidservant lowered her eyes.

'And is Nastasya Filippovna?'

'I don't know anything about that, sir.'

'Wait, wait! When will he return?'

'We don't know that either, sir.'

The door closed.

The prince decided to call back in an hour's time. Glancing into the courtyard, he met the yardkeeper.

'Is Parfyon Semyonych at home?'

'Yes, he is, sir.'

'Then why was I just told that he's not at home?'

'Is that what they told you at his rooms?'

'No, it was his mother's maidservant, I rang at Parfyon Semyonovich's front door, but no one opened up.'

'Perhaps he did go out, then,' the yardkeeper decided. 'He doesn't tell anyone, you know. And sometimes he takes the key away with him, and his rooms are locked for three days at a time.'

'You know for certain that he was at home yesterday?'

'He was. But sometimes he goes in by the front entrance, and you don't see him.'

'What about Nastasya Filippovna, was she with him yesterday?'

'That we don't know, sir. She doesn't come visiting very often; I think I'd have known if she'd visited.'

The prince left and walked up and down the pavement for some time in reflection. The windows of the rooms occupied by Rogozhin were all closed; the windows of the part of the house occupied by his mother were almost all open; it was a hot and cloudless day; the prince crossed the street to the opposite pavement and stopped to take another glance at the windows: not only were they closed, but in almost all of them white shades were lowered.

He stood for a minute or so and – it was strange – suddenly fancied that the edge of one shade was raised and that Rogozhin's face flickered into view, flickered and vanished at that same instant. He waited a while, and had already decided to go and ring the doorbell again when he thought the better of it, and put it off for an hour. 'Well, who knows, perhaps I just imagined it . . .'

Above all, he was now in a hurry to get to Izmailovsky Regiment, to the apartment that had recently been Nastasya Filippovna's. He knew that, having moved out of Pavlovsk three weeks earlier, at his request, she had settled in Izmailovsky Regiment at the home of an old close friend of hers, a schoolmaster's widow, a respectable woman with a family, who rented out a good furnished apartment which was practically her main source of income. The most likely thing was that Nastasya Filippovna, moving back to Pavlovsk, had kept the apartment on; it was at least most probable that she had spent the night in that apartment, where, of course, Rogozhin had taken her yesterday. The prince took a cab. On the way it occurred to him that this was where he ought to have begun, because it was unlikely that she would have come straight to Rogozhin's at night. Here he remembered the words of the yardkeeper, who had said that Nastasya Filippovna did not often come visiting. If it was not often, then why would she be staying at Rogozhin's now? Trying to keep his spirits up with these consolations, the prince arrived at last in Izmailovsky Regiment, more dead than alive with fear.

To his complete and utter astonishment, no one at the schoolmaster's widow's house had heard anything of Nastasya Filippovna either that day or the previous one, and instead came running out to stare as if at something strange and wonderful. All the schoolmaster's widow's numerous family – all little girls, with one year in between each of them – from fifteen all the way down to seven – came spilling out after their mother and surrounded the prince, their mouths agape. They were followed by their thin, sallow aunt, in a black dress, and, at last, the grandmother of the family appeared, a little old woman in spectacles. The schoolmaster's widow asked the prince very insistently to come in and sit down, which he did. He at once realized that they knew perfectly well who he was, and that they were quite aware that yesterday his wedding should have taken place, and that they were dying to ask him both about the wedding and about that wondrous fact that here he was asking them about the woman who ought to be nowhere but together with him, in Pavlovsk, but were too tactful to do so. In brief outline he satisfied their curiosity regarding the wedding. There were cries of astonishment, exclamations and groans, so that he was obliged to tell them almost the whole of the rest of the story, in broad outline, of course. At last, this council of most wise and excited ladies determined that he must unfailingly and before all else go and knock on Rogozhin's door and ascertain some definite facts from him about it all. And if Rogozhin was

not at home (which he must find out for sure) or was unwilling
to say anything, then he must go to Semyonovsky Regiment,[1] to
the home of a certain lady, a German and a friend of Nastasya
Filippovna's, who lived with her mother: it was possible that
Nastasya Filippovna, in her excitement and wish to conceal
herself, had spent the night with them. The prince stood up
completely crushed; they said later that he 'went awfully pale';
indeed, his legs were almost giving way under him. At last,
through a dreadful jabbering of voices, he discerned that they
were agreeing to act in concert with him, and asking for his
address in the city. It turned out that he had no address; they
advised him to stay at a hotel somewhere. The prince thought
for a moment and then gave the address of his old hotel, the one
where some five weeks earlier he had had a seizure. Then he set
off for Rogozhin's again. This time not only did Rogozhin's
door remain shut, but so did the door to the old woman's
apartment. The prince went down to find the yardkeeper, and
after some difficulty, found him out in the courtyard; the yardkeeper was busy with something and hardly replied, hardly even
looked at him, but none the less stated positively that Parfyon
Semyonovich 'went out very early this morning, travelled to
Pavlovsk and will not be home today'.

'I'll wait; perhaps he'll be back by evening?'

'And perhaps he won't be back for a week. Who can tell
with him?'

'So he did spend last night here, then?'

'Spend the night, yes he spent the night . . .'

This was all suspicious, and one could smell a rat somewhere.
In this interval of time the yardkeeper had very possibly managed to obtain new instructions: earlier he had even been talkative, but was now simply turning away. However, the prince
decided to call back once more a couple of hours later, and even
watch the house, if necessary, but there was still some hope
with the German lady, and so he dashed off to Semyonovsky
Regiment.

But at the German lady's house he could not even make
himself understood. From a few fleeting phrases he managed to
guess that some two weeks earlier the beautiful German lady

had quarrelled with Nastasya Filippovna, so that all these recent days she had not heard anything of her, and was now exerting all her energies to let it be known that she was not interested in hearing anything of her, 'even though she had married all the princes in the world'. The prince hurried to leave. Among other things, the thought came to him that perhaps, as before, she had gone to Moscow, and that Rogozhin would of course have followed her, or perhaps even gone with her. 'I must at least find some kind of trace of her!' He remembered, however, that he had to stay at an inn, and hurried to Liteinaya; there he was at once given a room. The waiter inquired if he wished to have a meal; absent-mindedly he replied that he did, and, when he regained his wits, was dreadfully annoyed with himself, as the meal detained him for more than half an hour; only later did he realize that there had been nothing to stop him leaving it uneaten. In that dim and stifling corridor a strange sensation took hold of him, a sensation that agonizingly strove to realize itself in some kind of thought; but as yet he was unable to guess what this new, insistent thought consisted of. At last, not himself, he left the inn; his head was spinning, but – where was he to go now? He rushed to Rogozhin's.

Rogozhin had not returned; when he rang the bell, no one opened; he rang at the door of old Mrs Rogozhin; the door opened and he was informed that Parfyon Semyonovich was not at home and might perhaps not be back for some three days. What upset the prince was that, as before, he was examined with such intense curiosity. This time he did not find the yardkeeper at all. As earlier, he crossed to the opposite pavement, looked at the windows and walked about in the tormenting, stifling heat for about half an hour, perhaps even more; this time nothing stirred; the windows were not opened, the white shades were motionless. It finally occurred to him that earlier he had probably just been imagining things, that the windows, by all appearances, were so dim and so long unwashed that it would have been hard to make anything out even if someone really had looked through the panes. Rejoicing in this thought, he drove back to Izmailovsky Regiment and the schoolmaster's widow's house.

There he was already expected. The schoolmaster's widow
had already been to three or four places, and had even called at
Rogozhin's house: not a trace. The prince listened without
saying anything, entered the room, sat down on a sofa and
began to look at them all, as though he did not understand what
they were saying to him. It was strange: at one moment he was
extremely observant, at another suddenly became absent-
minded to the point of absurdity. The whole family later
declared that he was an 'astonishingly' strange person that day,
so that 'perhaps it was all obvious even then'. At last he got up
and asked them to show him Nastasya Filippovna's rooms. They
were two large, light, high-ceilinged rooms, very respectably
furnished and not cheap. All these ladies said later that the
prince examined every object in the rooms; that on the small
table he spotted a book from the lending library, the French
novel *Madame Bovary*;[2] that he commented on it, and turned
down the corner of the page at which the book was open; that
he asked to be allowed to take the volume with him and right
there and then, impervious to their objections that it was a
library book; and that he put it in his pocket. That he sat
down by the open window and, seeing a card-table covered in
chalk-marks, asked who played cards. They told him that every
evening Nastasya Filippovna played card-games with Rogozhin:
'fools', *préférence*, 'millers', whist, trumps – all the games, and
that the cards had appeared only very recently, after their move
back from Pavlovsk to St Petersburg, as Nastasya Filippovna kept
complaining she was bored, and Rogozhin sat for whole evenings
in silence, unable to talk about anything, and she often wept; and
that suddenly the next evening Rogozhin had produced a pack of
cards from his pocket, at which Nastasya Filippovna burst into
laughter, and they began to play. The prince asked where were
the cards they had played with. But the cards were not there;
Rogozhin always brought them in his pocket, a new pack every
day, and later took it away with him again.

These ladies advised him to go back to Rogozhin's and knock
there again rather loudly, not right now, but in the evening:
'Perhaps he'll be there then.' The schoolmaster's widow meanwhile volunteered to go and see Darya Alexeyevna in Pavlovsk:

perhaps they would know something? They asked the prince to come back and visit them again at about ten that evening, in any case, to agree on plans for the following day. In spite of all their consoling and reassurances, the prince's soul was gripped by complete despair. In inexpressible anguish, he reached his inn on foot. The summer-bound, dusty, stifling St Petersburg crushed him as in a vice; he had been jostled in the midst of the sullen or drunken crowds, had stared purposelessly into faces, had walked far further than he ought to have done, perhaps; it was already almost evening when he entered his room. He decided to rest a little and then go back to Rogozhin's, as they had advised him, sat down on the sofa, leaned both his elbows on the table, and began to think.

Lord knows how long, and Lord knows what he thought about. Many were the things he feared, and he felt, in distress and agony, that he was horribly afraid. Vera Lebedeva entered his mind; then it occurred to him that perhaps Lebedev knew something about this matter or, if he did not, then he would be able to find out both more quickly and more easily than he, the prince. Then he remembered Ippolit, and that Rogozhin visited Ippolit. Then he remembered Rogozhin; recently at the funeral service, then in the park, then – suddenly here in the corridor, when Rogozhin had hidden in the corner that day and had waited for him with the knife. It was Rogozhin's eyes he remembered now, those eyes that had stared from the darkness then. He shuddered: the earlier insistent thought suddenly entered his mind.

It was partly that if Rogozhin were in St Petersburg, then although he might hide for a while, in the end he would most likely be certain to come to him, the prince, with good or bad intent, more or less as he had done then. At any rate, if Rogozhin wanted to come and see him, then there was nowhere for him to come but here, back to this same corridor. The address Rogozhin did not know; so it might very well occur to him that the prince was staying at the same inn as before; he would at least try to find him here . . . if he really needed him. And who could tell, perhaps he would need him?

Thus did he reflect, and for some reason this thought seemed perfectly plausible to him. Had he begun to examine it more deeply, he would have been quite unable to account for it: why, for example, would Rogozhin suddenly need him so much and why was it even impossible that they should not meet at all? The thought was a painful one: 'If he's all right, he won't come,' the prince continued to reflect. 'It's if he's not all right that he'll come; and I'm sure he isn't all right . . .'

Of course, with a conviction like this he ought to have waited for Rogozhin at home, in his room at the inn; but it was as if he could not endure this new thought, and he leaped up, grabbed his hat and ran. In the corridor it was now almost completely dark: 'What if he suddenly emerges from that corner and stops me by the staircase?' flickered through his mind as he approached the familiar spot. But no one emerged. He went downstairs and out through the gateway, stepped on to the pavement, looked in astonishment at the dense crowd of people pouring out on to the street at sunset (as always in St Petersburg in holiday time), and walked in the direction of Gorokhovaya. Fifty paces from the inn, at the first intersection, in the crowd, someone suddenly touched him on the shoulder and said in a low voice, right by his ear:

'Lev Nikolayevich, come with me, brother, you're needed.'

It was Rogozhin.

Strange: the prince suddenly began, babbling and almost not finishing his words, to tell how he had expected to see him just now, at the inn.

'I was there,' Rogozhin replied unexpectedly, 'let's go.'

The prince was astonished at the reply, but he was astonished at least two minutes later, when he had worked it out. Having worked out the reply, he was frightened and began to look closely at Rogozhin. The latter was already walking almost half a step ahead, looking straight ahead of him and not casting a glance at anyone he encountered, letting them all go past, with mechanical caution.

'But why didn't you ask for me in my room . . . if you were at the inn?' the prince asked suddenly.

Rogozhin stopped, looked at him, thought for a moment and, as if he had not understood the question at all, said:

'I tell you what, Lev Nikolayevich, you go straight on, right up to the house, you know? And I'll walk on the other side. But make sure we get there together . . .'

Having said this, he crossed the street, mounted the opposite pavement, looked to see if the prince was making his way, and, observing that the prince was standing still, staring at him, waved his arm in the direction of Gorokhovaya and set off, turning round to look at the prince every moment or so and inviting him to follow. He was plainly encouraged to see that the prince had understood him and was not coming to over to him from the other pavement. It occurred to the prince that Rogozhin needed to look out for someone and not miss him on the way, and that this was why he had crossed to the opposite pavement. 'Only why didn't he say who it was he needed to look out for?' They continued like this for some five hundred paces. And suddenly the prince began to shiver for some reason; although Rogozhin was looking round less frequently, he had not stopped doing so; the prince lost patience, and beckoned to him. Rogozhin at once came across the street towards him.

'Is Nastasya Filippovna at your house?'

'Yes, she is.'

'And was it you who looked at me from behind the shade earlier?'

'I . . .'

'Then why did you . . .'

But the prince did not know what to ask next, or how to finish the question; moreover, his heart was pounding so violently that he even found it hard to speak. Rogozhin also said nothing, and looked at him as before, as if in reflection.

'Well, I'm going,' he said suddenly, again preparing to cross over, 'and you walk alone. Let's go along the street separately . . . it'll be better for us that way . . . on opposite sides . . . you'll see.'

When, at last, they turned from their two different pavements into Gorokhovaya and began to approach Rogozhin's house, the prince's legs again started to give way under him, so that it was quite difficult for him to walk at all. It was by now about ten in the evening. The windows on the old woman's side of the

house were open, as earlier, while Rogozhin's were closed, and
in the twilight the white, lowered shades in them were becoming
even more noticeable. The prince approached the house from
the opposite pavement; while Rogozhin, from his pavement,
mounted the front steps and waved at him with his arm. The
prince crossed over to him and up the steps.

'Not even the yardkeeper knows I'm back. I told him earlier
that I was going to Pavlovsk, and I said the same thing at
mother's, too,' he whispered with a cunning and almost
contented smile. 'We'll go in, and no one will hear.'

There was now a key in his hands. Going up the stairs, he
turned and shook his finger at the prince to make him go more
quietly, quietly unlocked the door into his rooms, let the prince
in, cautiously followed him, locked the door from inside and
put the key in his pocket.

'Come on,' he said in a whisper.

Ever since the pavement on Liteinaya he had begun to speak
in a whisper. In spite of all his outward calm, he was in a kind
of deep, inner anxiety. When they entered the hall, right beside
the study, he went over to the window and mysteriously
beckoned to the prince:

'You see, when you rang my doorbell earlier, I guessed at
once that it was you; I went over to the door on tiptoe and heard
you talking to Pafnutyevna, well, at first light I'd given her
instructions: if you, or anyone from you, or anyone at all, were
to come knocking on my door, then she was to say nothing
about me at all, not under any circumstances; and especially if
you yourself came asking for me, and told her your name. But
later, when you had gone, it occurred to me: what if he's down
there now keeping a lookout, or watching from the street? I
went over to this window, moved the shade aside, and there you
were, looking right at me . . . That's what happened.'

'But where's . . . Nastasya Filippovna?' the prince got out,
struggling for breath.

'She's . . . here,' Rogozhin said slowly, as if waiting for a
moment before replying.

'But where?'

'Come on . . .'

He was still speaking in a whisper and without hurrying, slowly, and in a somehow strangely reflective tone, as before. Even when he talked about the shade, he seemed to be trying to say something else, in spite of all the expansiveness of his narrative.

They went into the study. A certain change had taken place in that room since the prince had been there last: a green damask silk curtain had been stretched the width of the entire room, with an entrance at either end, separating the study from an alcove in which Rogozhin's bed had been set up. The heavy curtain was lowered, and the entrances were closed. But it was very dark in the room; the 'white' summer nights of St Petersburg were beginning to grow darker, and had it not been for the full moon, it would have been hard to discern anything in Rogozhin's dark rooms. To be sure, it was still possible to make out faces, though very indistinctly. Rogozhin's face was pale, as usual; his eyes gazed fixedly at the prince, with an intense brilliance, but somehow motionlessly.

'Why don't you light a candle?' said the prince.

'No, there's no need,' replied Rogozhin and, taking the prince by the arm, bent him down towards a chair; he himself sat opposite, moving his chair up so that it almost touched the prince's knees. Between them, slightly to one side, was a small round table. 'Sit down, let's sit for a while!' he said, as though trying to persuade the prince not to move. For about a minute they said nothing. 'I knew you'd be staying at that inn,' he said, as people sometimes do when proceeding to the main conversation, beginning with irrelevant details that have nothing directly to do with the matter in hand. 'When I entered that corridor, I thought: perhaps he's sitting there waiting for me now, just as I'm waiting for him, at this very moment. Did you go to the schoolteacher's widow?'

'Yes,' the prince barely managed to get out, as his heart was pounding violently.

'I thought about that, too. There'll be talk, I thought . . . and then again I thought: I'll bring him here for the night, so that this night, together . . .'

'Rogozhin! Where is Nastasya Filippovna?' the prince

whispered suddenly and got up, shaking in every limb. Rogozhin also got up.

'There,' he whispered, nodding at the curtain.

'She is sleeping?' whispered the prince.

Again Rogozhin gave him a fixed look, as earlier.

'Oh, come on, then! . . . Only, you . . . well, come on!'

He raised the curtain a little, stopped and turned back to face the prince.

'Go in!' he nodded beyond the curtain, inviting him to pass through. The prince did so.

'It's dark here,' he said.

'One can see,' muttered Rogozhin.

'I can just see . . . a bed.'

'Then go closer,' Rogozhin suggested quietly.

The prince stepped even closer, one step, another, and came to a halt. He stood taking a good look for a minute or two; all the time that they stood by the bed, neither said anything; the prince's heart was beating so violently that it seemed one could hear it in the room, in the room's deathly silence. But by now he had grown accustomed to the dark, and could make out the whole of the bed; someone was asleep on it, in a perfectly motionless slumber; not the slightest rustle was audible, not the slightest breath. The sleeper was covered from the head downward with a white sheet, but the limbs somehow showed through indistinctly; all one could see, from the raised shape, was that a human being lay stretched out there. All around in disorder, on the bed, at its foot, on the armchairs beside it, on the floor, even, clothes that had been taken off were scattered, an extravagant white silk dress, flowers, ribbons. On a small table, by the head-board, diamonds scattered from a removed necklace gleamed. At the foot of the bed, some kind of lace garment had been crumpled into a ball, and on the white lace, peeping out from under the sheet, one could see the tip of a bare foot; it looked as though it had been chiselled from marble and was horribly motionless.[3] The prince stared, feeling that the more he stared, the more deathly and quiet the room became. Suddenly a fly that had woken up began to buzz, flew around above the bed and settled down by the headboard. The prince shuddered.

'Let's go out,' Rogozhin touched him on the arm.

They went out, sat down again in the same chairs, again facing each other. The prince was trembling more and more violently, and did not lower his questioning gaze from Rogozhin's face.

'I see you are trembling, Lev Nikolayevich,' Rogozhin said quietly at last, 'almost as much as you do when you have your disorder, you remember, it happened in Moscow? Or it happened just before a fit. And I can't think what I would do with you now . . .'

The prince listened closely, straining all his powers in order to understand, and still questioning with his gaze.

'It was you?' he got out at last, nodding towards the door curtain.

'It was . . . me . . .' Rogozhin whispered, and lowered his eyes.

They said nothing for about five minutes.

'Because,' Rogozhin began to continue suddenly, as if he had never broken off, 'because if you were to have your illness, and a fit, and shrieking, then someone might hear it from the street or the courtyard, and they'd guess that people are spending the night in this apartment; they'd start knocking, they'd come in . . . because they all think I'm not at home. I haven't even lit a candle, so that no one will guess in the street or the courtyard. Because when I'm not here, I take the keys with me, and no one can get in to tidy up for three or four days at a time, that's how I've arranged it. So that as now, no one will find out that we're here overnight . . .'

'Wait,' said the prince, 'earlier I asked both the yardkeeper and the old woman whether Nastasya Filippovna had spent the night here . . . So they must already know.'

'I know that you asked them. I told Pafnutyevna that Nastasya Filippovna called in yesterday and left for Pavlovsk, also yesterday, staying only ten minutes with me here. They don't know that she spent the night here – no one does. Last night we entered just as quietly as you and I did today. As we were on the way here I thought she might not come in quietly – not at all! She whispered, walked on tiptoe, gathered her dress up around her so as not to make any rustling, carried the folds in her hands, even wagged her finger at me on the staircase – all because she was afraid of you. On the train she was out of her mind, all because of fear, and wanted to come here to stay the night with me; at first I thought of taking her to the schoolmaster's widow's apartment – not at all! "He'll find me there as soon as it gets light," she said. "No, you must hide me, and tomorrow we'll go to Moscow at daybreak," though then she wanted to go to Oryol for some reason. And she went to bed, still saying we'd go to Oryol . . .'

'Wait; what will you do now, Parfyon, what are your plans?'

'I'm worried about you, you're still trembling. We'll stay the night here, together. There's only that bed here, so I thought I'd take the cushions off the two sofas, and set them up here beside the curtain, for you and me, so we can be together. Because if they come in, they'll start looking round or searching, they'll see her at once and carry her out. They'll begin to question me, and I'll tell them it was me, and they'll take me away immediately. So let her lie here beside us, beside you and me . . .'

'Yes, yes!' the prince agreed.

'That means there'll be no confession and we won't let them take her out.'

'N-not on any account!' the prince decided. 'No, no, no!'

'That's what I've decided, not on any account, my lad, and I won't let anyone have her! We'll pass the night quietly. I only went out of the house for an hour, this morning, otherwise I've been with her all the time. Well, and then I went to get you this evening. The only other thing I'm afraid of is that it's so hot, and there'll be a smell. Can you smell anything?'

'Perhaps, I don't know. By morning there probably will be a smell.'

'I've covered her with oilcloth, good American oilcloth, and on top of the oilcloth a sheet, and I've put four unstoppered bottles of Zhdanov fluid beside her, they stand there now.'

'Is that what they did . . . in Moscow?'

'Because of the smell, brother. But I mean, the way she lies there . . . Towards morning, when it gets light, take a look. What's the matter, aren't you even able to stand up?' asked

Rogozhin in anxious surprise, seeing that the prince was trembling so much that he could not get up.

'My legs are weak,' the prince muttered. 'It's because of fear, I know that . . . When the fear passes, I'll get up . . .'

'No, wait, I'll make up a bed, and then you can lie down . . . and I'll lie down too . . . and I'll listen . . . because, lad, I don't know yet . . . I don't know everything yet, lad, so I'm telling you in advance, so you know all about it in advance . . .'

Muttering these indistinct words, Rogozhin began make up the bed. It was evident that he had thought up this idea of the bed perhaps as early as that morning. During the night now past he had slept on a sofa. It was not possible for two people to lie side by side on a sofa, but he was determined that they should lie side by side, and so now, with great effort, he dragged cushions of various sizes from both sofas the entire length of the room, right to the very entrance to the curtain. Somehow the bed was arranged; he went up to the prince, took him tenderly and rapturously by the hand, brought him to his feet and led him to the bed; but it turned out that the prince was able to walk by himself; so 'the fear was passing'; and yet he still continued to tremble.

'Because, brother,' Rogozhin began suddenly, making the prince lie down on the left and best cushion, and stretching out himself on the right-hand side, without undressing, and putting both hands behind his head, 'it's hot now and of course, there'll be a smell . . . I'm afraid to open the windows; but my mother has some pots of flowers, a lot of flowers, and they give off a pleasant smell; I thought of moving them in here, but Pafnutyevna would put two and two together, because she's inquisitive.'

'Yes, she is,' the prince confirmed.

'Perhaps if I were to buy some, and put bouquets and flowers all round her? But, friend, I think I'll feel sorry for her, seeing her all covered in flowers!'

'Listen . . .' said the prince, seeming to grow confused, seeming to search around for just what it was he wanted to ask, and as if at once forgetting again. 'Listen, tell me, what did you kill her with? That knife? The same one?'

'The same one.'

'Wait again! Parfyon, I also want to ask you . . . there are many things I want to ask you about, everything . . . but you had better tell me first, before anything else, so that I know: were you going to kill her before my wedding, before we went to the altar, in the church porch, with the knife? Were you?'

'I have no idea . . .' Rogozhin replied stiffly, as though he were even somewhat taken aback by the question, and could make no sense of it.

'You never took the knife to Pavlovsk with you?'

'I never took it. All I can tell you about that knife is this, Lev Nikolayevich,' he added, after a silence. 'I took it out of the locked drawer this morning, because it all happened this morning, between three and four. It was in that book of mine all the time . . . And . . . and there's another thing I find strange: the knife only seemed to go in to a depth of three . . . or . . . maybe four inches . . . right under her left breast . . . and only about half a tablespoonful of blood flowed out onto her chemise; there was no more than that.'

'That, that, that,' the prince suddenly raised himself on one elbow in dreadful agitation, 'that, that I know, I've read that . . . it's called an internal haemorrhage . . . Sometimes there's not even a drop. It's if the blow goes straight into the heart . . .'

'Wait, do you hear?' Rogozhin quickly broke in, sitting down on the bedding in fear. 'Do you hear?'

'No!' the prince got out just as quickly, and in just as much fear, staring at Rogozhin.

'Footsteps! Do you hear? In the hallway . . .'

They both began to listen.

'Yes, I can hear,' the prince whispered firmly.

'Footsteps?'

'Yes, footsteps.'

'Shall we bolt the door?'

'Yes . . .'

They bolted the door, and they both lay down again. For a long time they said nothing.

'Ah, yes!' the prince suddenly began to say under his breath, in his earlier agitated and hurried whisper, as though he had regained control of his thought, and was horribly afraid of losing it again, and even leaped up from the bed. 'Yes ... I mean, I wanted ... those cards! Cards ... They say you used to play cards with her?'

'I did,' said Rogozhin after a certain silence.

'Then where are they ... the cards?'

'The cards are here ...' said Rogozhin, after an even longer silence. 'Here ...'

He took from his pocket a used pack of cards, wrapped in a piece of paper, and held it out to the prince. The prince took it, but almost in bewilderment. A new, sad and cheerless feeling constricted his heart; he suddenly realized that at that moment, and for a long time now, he had not been saying what he should have been saying, nor doing what he should have been doing, and that these cards he held in his hands, and had been so pleased about, could be of no help now. He rose to his feet and threw up his hands. Rogozhin lay motionless, seeming neither to hear nor to see his movement; but his eyes gleamed brightly through the darkness and were completely open and motionless. The prince sat down on a chair and began to stare at him in fear. About half an hour went by; suddenly Rogozhin began to shout and laugh loudly and jerkily, as though he had forgotten that they must talk in whispers:

'That officer, that officer ... remember how she whipped that officer, at the bandstand, remember, ha-ha-ha! And the cadet ... the cadet ... the cadet darted up ...'

The prince jumped up from his chair in new alarm. When Rogozhin quieted down (and he quieted down suddenly), the prince quietly bent towards him, settled down beside him with violently pounding heart, breathing heavily, and began to study him closely. Rogozhin did not turn his head towards him and even seemed to have forgotten him. The prince watched and waited; time passed, it began to get light, from time to time Rogozhin would suddenly start muttering, loudly, abruptly and incoherently; he began to shout and laugh; then the prince would reach out his trembling hand to him and quietly touch his head, his hair, stroke them and stroke his cheeks ... more than that there was nothing he could do! He himself again began to tremble, and again his legs seemed to give way beneath him. Some completely new sensation tormented his heart with infinite anguish. Meanwhile it had grown completely light; at last, he lay down on the cushion, as though now wholly in the grip of helplessness and despair, and pressed his face against Rogozhin's pale and motionless face; tears streamed from his eyes on to Rogozhin's cheeks, but it is possible that by then he no longer felt his own tears and knew nothing of them . . .

At any rate, when many hours later the door opened and people entered, they found the murderer completely unconscious and in a fever. The prince sat motionless beside him on the cushions and quietly, each time the sick man exploded into shouting or delirium, hurried to pass his trembling hand over his hair and cheeks, as though caressing and calming him. But by now he understood none of the questions that were asked him, and did not recognize the people who had entered the room and surrounded him. And if Schneider himself had appeared now from Switzerland to take a look at his former pupil and patient, then even he, remembering the condition in which the prince had sometimes been during the first year of his treatment in Switzerland, would now have waved his hand and said, as then: 'An idiot!'

12

Conclusion

The schoolmaster's widow, having gone post-haste to Pavlovsk, went straight to see Darya Alexeyevna, who was still upset from the previous day, and, having told her everything she knew, gave her no end of a fright. Both ladies at once decided to enter into contact with Lebedev, who was also agitated, in his capacity of the tenant's friend landlord of his lodgings. Vera Lebedeva told him everything she knew. On Lebedev's advice, all three decided to set off for St Petersburg for the most speedy prevention of 'what may very well happen'. Thus it transpired that on the following morning, at about eleven o' clock, Rogozhin's apartment was opened in the presence of the police, Lebedev, the ladies and Rogozhin's brother, Semyon Semyonovich Rogozhin, who lodged in the wing. The success of the matter was expedited above all by the statement of the yardkeeper, who testified that he had seen Parfyon Semyonovich and a guest the night before, entering by the front porch and as if by stealth. After this statement, and when no one answered the doorbell, there was no hesitation in breaking down the door.

For two months Rogozhin endured an inflammation of the brain, and when he recovered – an investigation and a trial. He gave straight, precise and completely satisfactory statements on all matters, as a result of which the prince was eliminated from the investigation. Rogozhin was taciturn during his trial. He did not contradict his skilful and eloquent lawyer, who argued clearly and logically that the crime that had been committed was the result of an inflammation of the brain that had begun long before the crime in consequence of the accused man's distressing experiences. But he did not add anything on his own behalf in confirmation of this view and, as he had done previously, clearly and precisely, confirmed and recalled each smallest detail of the incident that had occurred. He was condemned, with remission for extenuating circumstances, to fifteen years of penal labour in Siberia, and heard out his sentence grimly, silently and 'thoughtfully'. His entire enormous fortune, apart from a certain comparatively rather small portion, spent on the initial carousing, went to his brother, Semyon Semyonovich, much to the latter's great satisfaction. Rogozhin's old mother is still alive, and sometimes seems to remember her favourite son Parfyon, but not clearly; God has saved her mind and heart from an awareness of the horror that visited her melancholy house.

Lebedev, Keller, Ganya, Ptitsyn and many other characters of our story live as before, have changed little, and there is almost nothing for us to tell about them. Ippolit passed away in dreadful agitation and somewhat earlier than he had expected, some two weeks after Nastasya Filippovna's death. Kolya was deeply shaken by what had happened; he has drawn close to his mother

once and for all. Nina Alexandrovna is afraid for him, considering him too reflective for his years; it may be that he will become
a good man. Incidentally, partly as a result of his efforts, the
future destiny of the prince was also settled; a long time before,
out of all the persons whose acquaintance he had recently made,
Kolya had chosen Yevgeny Pavlovich Radomsky; he was the
first to convey to him all the details of the event that had taken
place to which he was privy, and the prince's present situation.
He was not mistaken: Yevgeny Pavlovich took the warmest
interest in the fate of the unfortunate 'idiot', and in consequence
of his efforts and care the prince ended up back abroad, in
Schneider's clinic in Switzerland. Yevgeny Pavlovich, having
himself gone abroad – with the intention of staying in Europe
for a very long time and openly calling himself 'a completely
superfluous man in Russia' – quite often, at least once every few
months, visits his sick friend at Schneider's; but increasingly
Schneider frowns and shakes his head; he hints at a complete
derangement of the mental organs; he does not yet speak in
the affirmative of incurability, but permits himself the most
melancholy allusions. Yevgeny Pavlovich takes this very much
to heart, and he does have a heart, something he has already
proved by receiving letters from Kolya and even sometimes
replying to those letters. But in addition to this, yet another
strange feature of his character has announced itself; and as it
is a good feature, we shall hasten to delineate it: after each
of his visits to Schneider's clinic Yevgeny Pavlovich sends, in
addition to the one to Kolya, another letter to a certain person
in St Petersburg, with a most detailed and sympathetic account
of the state of the prince's illness at the present moment. In
addition to the most respectful expression of devotion, in these
letters there sometimes begin to appear (with ever-increasing
frequency) some open statements of views, conceptions, emotions – in a word, there begins to manifest itself something
resembling friendly and intimate feelings. This person, who is in
correspondence (though a rather infrequent one) with Yevgeny
Pavlovich and who has earned so much of his attention and
respect, is Vera Lebedeva. We have been quite unable to ascertain exactly how such relations could have been established

between them; they were established, of course, in connection with the whole episode with the prince, when Vera Lebedeva was so afflicted with sorrow that she fell ill, but as to the details of how their acquaintance and friendship came about – we do not know. We have mentioned these letters primarily because some of them contained information about the Yepanchin family and, especially, about Aglaya Ivanovna Yepanchina. In one rather incoherent letter from Paris, Yevgeny Pavlovich imparted the information that after a brief and extraordinary attachment to a certain émigré, a Polish count, she married him, against the wishes of her parents, who if they did in the end grant their consent, then only because the matter was threatening to become a scandal of exceptional proportions. Then, after a silence that lasted almost half a year, Yevgeny Pavlovich informed his correspondent, again in a long and detailed letter, that during his latest visit to Professor Schneider in Switzerland he had there run into all of the Yepanchins (with the exception, naturally, of Ivan Fyodorovich, who remains in St Petersburg on business) and Prince Shch. The meeting was a strange one; they all greeted Yevgeny Pavlovich with a kind of rapture; for some reason Adelaida and Alexandra even considered themselves grateful to him for his 'angelic care for the unhappy prince'. Lizaveta Prokofyevna, beholding the prince in his sick and degraded condition, began to weep with all her heart. Evidently all was now forgiven him. Meanwhile, Prince Shch. spoke a few well-turned and sensible truths. It seemed to Yevgeny Pavlovich that he and Adelaida were not yet friends, but that the future held out the inevitable prospect of the submission of the passionate Adelaida to the intelligence and experience of Prince Shch. In addition, the lessons endured by the family also had a fearful effect on her, especially the latest incident with Aglaya and the émigré count. Everything that had set the family a-tremble about surrendering Aglaya to this count had been realized within the space of half a year, with the addition of surprises such as they had not even dreamed of. The count turned out not to be a count at all, and if he really was an émigré, then one with an obscure and ambiguous past. He had captivated Aglaya with the extraordinary nobility of a soul tormented by suffering for his fatherland, and captivated her to such a degree that even before she married him she became a member of some foreign committee for the restoration of Poland and, moreover, ended up in the Catholic confessional of some famous *pater*, who had taken possession of her mind to the point of frenzy. The count's colossal fortune, of which he had presented Lizaveta Prokofyevna and Prince Shch. with almost incontrovertible proof, turned out to be completely imaginary. Nor was that all, for some six months after the nuptials the count and his friend, the famous confessor, succeeded in plunging Aglaya into an all-out quarrel with her family, so that now they had not seen her for several months . . . In a word, there would have been much to tell, but Lizaveta Prokofyevna, her daughters and even Prince Shch. were so shaken by all this 'terror' that they were afraid even to mention some things in conversation with Yevgeny Pavlovich, though they knew that he knew very well, and did not need them to tell him, the story of Aglaya Ivanovna's latest enthusiasms. Poor Lizaveta Prokofyevna would have liked to have gone to Russia and, according to Yevgeny Pavlovich's testimony, she criticized everything abroad bitterly and with prejudice: 'They don't know how to bake bread properly anywhere, and in winter they freeze like mice in a cellar,' she said. 'At least here I've had a good Russian cry over this poor fellow,' she added, pointing in agitation at the prince, who had not recognized her at all. 'Enough of being carried away, it's time to serve reason. And all this, all this abroad, all this Europe of yours, it's all just a fantasy, and all of us, while we're abroad, are just a fantasy . . . mark my words, you'll see for yourself!' she concluded, almost angrily, as she parted from Yevgeny Pavlovich.

Notes

PART ONE

CHAPTER ONE

1. *Eidkuhnen*: Prussian railway station on the border of Prussia and Russia.

2. *no foreign bags of Napoléons d'or and Friedrichs d'or, let alone Dutch arapchiki*: Gold coins: the Napoléon d'or was worth twenty French francs. The Friedrich d'or was a Prussian coin, worth five silver thalers. The *arapchik* was one of the varieties of Russian gold coin, worth three roubles, also called the 'Dutch tchervonetz', because of its resemblance to the ducats of the old Dutch States.

3. *As for General Yepanchin, sir, we know him for the simple reason that he's well known*: According to the 'Universal Address Directory of St Petersburg, 1867–68' there were in fact four military men with the name Yepanchin in the city at this time.

4. *the hereditary distinguished burgher*: A title given to merchants and other persons of non-aristocratic rank for meritorious deeds, and passed on by heredity.

5. *the Bolshoi or the French Theatre*: The Bolshoi theatre was situated on Teatralnaya Ploshchad, and showed performances of opera, ballet and theatre by both Russian and foreign companies. The French Theatre was opened on 8 November 1833, and in the words of one contemporary observer soon became 'the rendezvous of the *grand monde*'.

6. *Voznesensky Prospect*: Dostoyevsky lived there from the spring of 1847 until April 1849, and also for a short time in 1867.

CHAPTER TWO

1.   *just off Liteinaya, towards the Church of the Transfiguration*: The church is situated on a square adjoining Panteleimonovskaya Street. It was rebuilt in 1827–9 by V. P. Stasov, after it burned down in 1825.

2.   *the farming of revenues*: *Otkup*, the sale to a private individual of the right to charge revenues on a state monopoly. Revenues on alcohol were particularly involved.

3.   *'devoted without flattery'*: A reference to the motto on the coat of arms of A. A. Arakcheyev (1769–1834), given him by Tsar Paul I. See Pushkin's poem 'Oppressor Of All Russia' (1817–20).

4.   *and the middle one was an excellent painter . . . and even then by accident*: It should perhaps be noted that Adelaida's name derives from Greek *adilos*, meaning 'indistinct, obscure'.

5.   *we don't have capital punishment*: The death penalty was abolished in Russia by Empress Elizabeth in 1753–4, but was reintroduced by Catherine the Great for certain crimes, mainly of a political nature. Dostoyevsky was himself sentenced to be shot in 1849, but reprieved at the last moment, and sent into exile in Siberia. The 1860s saw several executions in Russia. Dostoyevsky's insertion here of the words 'we don't have capital punishment' is thought to be linked to the author's desire to deflect the attention of the Russian censor from the passages in the novel concerning the death penalty.

6.   *many people have said the same thing*: Dostoyevsky is alluding above all to Victor Hugo's short story *Le Dernier Jour d'un condamné* ('The Final Day of a Condemned Man', 1829), which he knew in the French original.

7.   *'Such suffering and terror were what Christ spoke of'*: see Matthew 26:38–9, also 37, 42 and 44.

8.   *a small Napoleonic beard*: The Napoleon in question is Napoleon III (1808–73), Emperor of France from 1852.

CHAPTER THREE

1.   *'Hard work conquers all'*: The words engraved by order of Tsar Nicholas I on the medal struck in 1838 in honour of Count P. A. Kleinmikhel (1793–1869), who directed the rebuilding of the Winter Palace.

2.   *commis*: A commercial traveller.

CHAPTER FOUR

1. *Otradnoye*: The name means 'delight'.
2. *verst*: 1 verst = 1.06 kilometres.

CHAPTER FIVE

1. *the Horde*: The Golden Horde, a state formed in the thirteenth century by the grandson of Genghis Khan, consisting of most of what is now European Russia and western Siberia. After the conquest of the Russian principalities by the Mongols, Russian princes had to travel to Sarai on the Lower Volga to trade and negotiate with the Horde.
2. *'The East and South were long ago depicted'*: An inexact quotation from Lermontov's poem 'The Journalist, the Reader and the Writer' (1840).
3. I *saw a painting like that at Basle once*: Probably the painting by Hans Fries (1450–1520) depicting the severing of the head of John the Baptist (part of the 'Johannes-Triptych'), in the Basle City Art Museum.

CHAPTER SIX

1. *'Now I am going out among people . . . but a new life has begun'*: Cf. John 8:28, John 9:4.
2. *the Holbein Madonna in Dresden*: The Prince is referring to a copy of the *Darmstadt Madonna* (1526) by Hans Holbein the Younger (1497–1543) at the Dresden Art Museum. Dostoyevsky saw this in 1867.

CHAPTER EIGHT

1. *a small, dark-brown beard . . . civil service*: A decree of Nicholas I (2 April 1837) forbade civil servants to wear moustaches or beards.
2. *Avis au lecteur*: 'Warning to the reader'.
3. *the Novaya Zemlya infantry regiment*: The fantastical nature of the regiment is emphasized by the fact that its name is borrowed from a line in Griboyedov's satirical play *Woe from Wit*.
4. *Mon mari se trompe*: 'My husband is mistaken'.

CHAPTER NINE

1. *se non è vero*: The first part of an Italian saying that continues: 'è ben trovato' ('if it's not true, it's well conceived').

2. *Athos, Porthos and Aramis*: The general has in mind the heroes of Dumas's *The Three Musketeers*.
3. *Kars*: A town in north-eastern Turkey that was besieged by Russian forces during the Crimean War of 1853–6.
4. *the Indépendance*: The newspaper *Indépendance Belge*, which appeared in Brussels from 1830 to 1937, and reported on political life and cultural events in Western Europe. Dostoyevsky was a reader of the newspaper.
5. *C'est du nouveau*: 'It's something new'.

CHAPTER ELEVEN

1. *Lermontov's drama Masquerade . . . little more than a child*: The play was in fact written in 1835, when Lermontov was twenty-one. Kolya is referring to the insult delivered to Prince Zvezdich by Arbenin in Act 2, scene 4.
2. *valet de carreau*: The Russian expression, *bubnovyi valet*, is a literal translation of this term; like the French idiom, it means 'scoundrel', 'shady character'. It was found in Russian translations of Molière.
3. *Rira bien qui rira le dernier*: 'He who laughs last laughs longest'.

CHAPTER TWELVE

1. *Pirogov telegraphed Paris . . . in order to examine me*: General Ivolgin gives a fantastically distorted interpretation of a real-life event. On 1 June 1855 the great Russian surgeon N. I. Pirogov (1810–81), who was in charge of first aid to the wounded soldiers of Sebastopol, went back to St Petersburg because of his indignation at the lack of attention shown by the Russian military command to issues of medical care. He returned to Sebastopol in September. Auguste Nélaton (1807–73) was a famous French surgeon; he never visited Russia.
2. *pour passer le temps*: 'To pass the time'.
3. *Down there in Moscow . . . it was in the press*: An allusion to the trial of the murderer Danilov (a nineteen-year-old student; his victim was a moneylender), reported in the newspapers during 1866, as the first chapters of *Crime and Punishment* were being printed.

CHAPTER THIRTEEN

1. *The mighty Lion . . . yielded*: An inexact quotation of the first two lines of Krylov's fable *The Ageing Lion* (1925). Ferdyshchenko

is thinking of the last line of the fable, where a donkey is referred to.

2. *petit jeu*: A parlour game, 'forfeits'.

1. *the circumstances in which bouquets of white and pink camellias are to be used in turn*: The heroine of Alexandre Dumas's novel *La Dame aux camélias* goes walking with white camellias on some days of the month and red camellias on others. After her death, her beloved sees to it that white and red camellias are placed on her grave in corresponding order.

2. *de la vraie souche*: 'Of the true stock'.

CHAPTER FIFTEEN

1. *Marlinsky*: The pseudonym of the Decembrist author A. A. Bestuzhev (1797–1837), whose style was characterized as 'taut, lofty and impassioned' by the literary critic Belinsky, who noted the 'absence of all naturalness' in the writer's language. Dostoyevsky's ironic remark is made in the context of the popularity of Marlinsky's works among readers from a military background, from which his characters were also drawn.

2. *vershoks*: A vershok is roughly two inches.

PART TWO

1. *the Yekaterinhof pleasure gardens*: Yekaterinhof was a park with a palace, situated in the south-western part of St Petersburg, dating from 1711. In the 1820s it became one of the capital city's finest parks, containing a fashionable restaurant where musical events were held. The Pavlovsk pleasure gardens, or 'Vauxhall', were situated beside one of the first railway stations in Russia, and the word *vokzal* gradually came to acquire its modern meaning of 'railway station'.

2. *the zemstva*: Local government institutions, led by the gentry, set up as part of the land reform of 1864.

3. *Izmailovsky Regiment*: The St Petersburg Debtors' Prison (*dolgovoye otdelenie*) was located in the first 'company' of this military district, at no. 28, which was owned by the Tarasov family. In 1867 Dostoyevsky himself was threatened with incarceration there.

CHAPTER TWO

1. *the strange, hot gaze of someone's eyes*: the Russian critic R. G. Nazirov traces the theme of Rogozhin's eyes to Dickens's *Oliver Twist* (1838), where Sykes is pursued by the eyes of the murdered Nancy.

2. *Peski*: The name means 'Sands'. A part of the city inhabited by tradesmen, clerks, craftsmen, cabmen and other members of the lower middle class. The Rozhdestvensky streets got their name from the nearby eighteenth-century Church of the Nativity (Rozhdestvo).

3. *the murder of the Zhemarin family in the newspaper*: In 1868 Dostoyevsky read a story in the newspaper *The Voice* about the murder in Tambov of a family of six by an eighteen-year-old student. Dostoyevsky considered the murderer, Vitold Gorsky, a typical representative of 'nihilist' youth.

4. *the wise words of the legislator . . . courts*: A reference to Alexander II's manifesto of 19 March 1856, 'On the Cessation of War', with an inexact quotation from a passage about the future of Russia after the peace with Turkey.

5. *palki*: 'Sticks' – a card game.

6. *the Countess Du Barry*: Marie-Jeanne Du Barry (1743–93), a favourite of Louis XV of France, executed by order of the revolutionary tribunal on 8 December 1793. She begged for mercy on the scaffold, to no avail.

7. *She agreed with me . . . penny*: Cf. Revelation 6: 1–8.

8. *Pavlovsk*: From the mid-nineteenth century onwards, the suburb of Pavlovsk became the favourite summer resort of the St Petersburg middle classes.

CHAPTER THREE

1. *skopets*: A member of a religious sect, practising castration, founded in the second half of the eighteenth century by a peasant in the province of Oryol named Kondraty Selivanov. Many *skoptsy* lived in the large cities of Russia, where they occupied the status of merchants and had a reputation for amassing wealth because of their 'incapacity for all other enjoyments', according to a contemporary observer.

2. *The House of Hereditary Distinguished Burgher Rogozhin*: Rogozhin's house is thought to have been No. 33 Gorokhovaya Street.

3. *Solovyov's History*: *The History of Russia Since the Most Ancient*

Times by S. M. Solovyov (1820–79) began to appear in 1851. By 1867 seventeen volumes of it had been published.

4. *there once was a Pope who got angry with an Emperor*: A reference to Heine's poem 'Heinrich' (1822, first translated into Russian in 1843).

5. *crossing yourself with two fingers*: The reference is to the customs of the Staroobryadtsy ('Old Ritualists'), a traditionalist sect that did not accept the ecclesiastical reforms of the early sixteenth century, and was particularly active during the time of Patriarch Nikon (1652–8), who pronounced an anathema on the two-fingered sign of the cross, and introduced the three-fingered sign.

CHAPTER FOUR

1. *arshins*: An arshin was approximately equivalent to 2 feet.

2. *a certain S—*: It is thought that this may be a reference to N. A. Speshnev (1821–82), who was one of Dostoyevsky's fellow Petrashevists, and whose views had a strong materialist and atheist tendency.

CHAPTER FIVE

1. *'there should be time no longer'*: Cf. Revelation, 10:1–7.

2. *the organ*: Here, probably a barrel organ.

CHAPTER SIX

1. *Russian Millennium Day*: This was celebrated on 8 September 1862.

2. *an 'image of pure beauty'*: A reference to Pushkin's poem dedicated to A. P. Kern ('K ***', 1825).

CHAPTER SEVEN

1. *one shouldn't break the chairs*: The words derive from Gogol's comedy *The Inspector General* (1836). 'He is, of course, the hero Alexander the Great, but why break the chairs?'

2. *the senselessness of some Pushkin . . . pieces*: The references are to writings and statements of nihilist authors and publicists such as Zaitsev, Pisarev and Zaichnevsky during the 1860s.

CHAPTER EIGHT

1. *a weekly humorous paper*: Probably *Iskra* ('The Spark'), which was published in St Petersburg from 1859 until 1873.

2. *'fresh is the legend, but hard to believe'*: a quotation from Griboyedov's comedy *Woe from Wit* (Act 2, scene 2).

3. *Krylov's Cloud*: See Krylov's fable 'The Cloud' (1815).
4. *In Schneider's coat . . . fleeces students bare*: It has been established that this 'epigram' is a parody of a satirical poem about Dostoyevsky by Saltykov-Shchedrin.

CHAPTER NINE

1. *his client, who had murdered six people in one fell swoop*: Another reference to the murderer Vitold Gorsky and his victims. See above part 2, chapter 2, note 3.
2. *A girl grows up in a house . . . farewell*: An allusion to the scene in Chernyshevsky's novel *What Is to Be Done* (1863), in which Vera Pavlovna parts from her mother (chapter 2, XX). A droshky is an open horse-drawn carriage with four wheels.
3. *B—n himself*: The famous Russian physician S. P. Botkin (1832–89), who treated Dostoyevsky.

CHAPTER TEN

1. *Proudhon*: Pierre Joseph Proudhon (1809–65), the French socialist economist and sociologist, the founder of Anarchism, whose writings were widely read in the Petrashevsky Circle.
2. *the American War*: The American Civil War of 1861–65.
3. *Princess Marya Alexevna won't scold*: A reference to the concluding words of Famusov's final monologue in Griboyedov's *Woe from Wit* (Act 4, scene 15): 'Ah! Good Lord! What will she say, /Princess Marya Alexevna!'
4. *And I haven't been able to leave . . . conviction*: Here Ippolit expresses themes analogous to those of Lermontov's poem 'Thoughts' (1838).

CHAPTER ELEVEN

1. *he suddenly had a dreadful desire to leave everything here*: Cf. John 8:23.
2. *the French Archbishop Bourdaloue*: Louis Bourdaloue (1632–1704), a Jesuit and one of the most popular preachers during the reign of Louis XIV. There is a play on 'Bordeaux' (the wine) here.

PART THREE

CHAPTER ONE

1. *poods*: A pood was equivalent to 16.38 kilos.
2. *she had exceeding respect . . . advice*: Alexandra's name is derived from Greek *aleksindris*, meaning 'protection, succour'.
3. *pre-Famusov*: A reference to the hero of Griboyedov's satirical play *Woe from Wit*.

CHAPTER THREE

1. *D'Anthès*: Baron Georges D'Anthès, a Frenchman in the Russian army who spent too much time with Pushkin's wife. Pushkin challenged him to a duel, was fatally wounded and died on 29 January 1837.
2. *pay for the bottles*: A calque of the French idiom *payer bouteille*.
3. *the red cap*: I.e. a soldier's cap. Duels were illegal in Russia until 1894, when they were permitted for army officers. From 1845, the punishment for duelling included reduction to the ranks.

CHAPTER FOUR

1. *zakuski*: Snacks, light refreshments, usually consumed with vodka.
2. *'in the sky the sun resounded'*: A reference to the beginning of the 'Prologue in Heaven' in Goethe's *Faust*: 'Die Sonne tönt nach alter Weise/In Brüdersphären Wettgesang'.
3. *springs of life*: A reference to the symbolism of the last two chapters of Revelation (21:6; 22:1,17).
4. *The devil rules equally . . . known to us*: Cf. Revelation 12.
5. *Malthus*: Thomas Robert Malthus (1766–1834), English priest, economist, and originator of 'Malthusianism', the doctrine that hunger and poverty are the result of overpopulation.

CHAPTER FIVE

1. *Kislorodov*: In Russian, *kislorod* (a calque from Latin *oxygenium*) means 'oxygen'. Dostoyevsky is playing on the Greek root of the word, *oxus* ('sour'), to suggest that atheists and materialists might be thought to be people of a sour disposition.

CHAPTER SIX

1. *Shestilavochnaya Street*: The street where Golyadkin, the hero of Dostoyevsky's *The Double* (1846), lived.
2. *kurguz*: A short, tight-fitting coat.

3.   *a half-shtof*: A *shtof* was equivalent to 1.2 litres.
4.   *State Councillor*: In Russian, *deistvitel'nyi statskii sovetnik* – a
     civil service rank of the fourth class.
5.   *in the way that Napoleon turned to England*: In 1815, after the
     battle of Waterloo, Napoleon intended to flee to America, but
     because of the blockade of the port of Rochefort had to enter into
     negotiations with his enemies – the British – and was exiled to
     St Helena.
6.   *'the old general'*: F. P. Haase (1780–1853), a doctor who was in
     charge of Russia's prison hospitals.
7.   *les extrémités se touchent*: 'The extremities meet'; the words are
     those of the French philosopher Blaise Pascal (1623–62), from
     his *Pensées*.
8.   *Talitha cumi*: (Greek) 'Maiden, I say to you, arise', the words
     uttered by Christ when raising Jairus' daughter (Mark 5:41).
9.   *Lazarus, come forth*: Cf. John 11:43–4.

CHAPTER SEVEN

1.   *the renowned and classical stanza of Millevoix*: In fact, as the
     critic B. V. Tomashevsky pointed out in 1928, this stanza is not
     by Millevoix but by Gilbert, from the latter's poem 'Ode imitée
     de plusieurs psaumes' (Ode Imitated from Several Psalms, 1780);
     roughly translated, this reads: 'Oh, that your sacred beauty be
     long seen/By so many friends deaf to my farewells!/May they die
     rich in days, may their deaths be mourned!/May a friend be there
     to close their eyes!'
2.   *Lacenaires*: The criminal and murderer Pierre-François Lacenaire
     (1800–1836) was the central figure in a Parisian trial of the 1830s.
     Condemned to death, he spent the time until his execution writing
     poetry and memoirs. Afterwards, his semi-apocryphal writings
     were released to the public in print. Dostoyevsky became inter-
     ested in the Lacenaire trial while he was working on *Crime and
     Punishment*.

CHAPTER EIGHT

1.   *the learned cabinets*: the mineralogical, geological, botanical and
     other scientific collections held in German museums and universities.
2.   *Paul de Kock*: Paul de Kock (1794–1871): a French writer, the
     author of some 400 volumes of light fiction and drama, mostly
     of a rather risqué nature, and extremely popular in his lifetime.
3.   *a kind of light*: Aglaya's name is derived from the Greek word
     aglaos, 'radiant'.

CHAPTER NINE

1. *contrecarrate*: an invented word, from French. *contrecarrer*, to dispute.
2. *Fifth Street*: The fifth Rozhdestvensky street (Pyataya Rozhdestvenskaya). See above, part 2, chapter 2, note 2.
3. *with quiet steps*: A phrase Dostoyevsky heard in use among the convicts during his exile in Siberia.

CHAPTER TEN

1. *that Moscow murderer ... Zhdanov fluid*: A reference to the murderer Mazurin, who killed a jeweller with a razor, the handle of which was bound in silk to improve its grip. Zhdanov fluid was an antiseptic: Mazurin filled two bowls with it in order to hide the smell, and wrapped the body in oilcloth. A household knife, covered in blood, was also found in Mazurin's house.

PART FOUR

CHAPTER ONE

1. *Podkolyosin*: The central character of Gogol's comedy *Marriage* (1842).
2. *'Tu l'as voulu, Georges Dandin!'*: 'You wanted it, Georges Dandin!' In Molière's play *Georges Dandin* (1668), this is *'Vous l'avez voulu, Georges Dandin!'* (Act 1, scene 9).
3. *Lieutenant Pirogov*: The central character of Gogol's story 'Nevsky Prospect' (1835), whom Dostoyevsky considered Gogol's greatest creation.
4. *Nozdrev*: One of the characters in Gogol's *Dead Souls*.

CHAPTER TWO

1. *'a stick with two ends'*: The English equivalent would be 'a double-edged sword'.

CHAPTER FOUR

1. *a Chernosvitov leg*: Rafael Alexandrovich Chernosvitov was born in 1810. A Petrashevist, he was exiled to Kexholm Fortress in 1849. In 1854 he designed an artificial leg for use by war invalids, and in 1855 published a book on the subject.
2. *one of our autobiographers*: The Russian writer Alexander Herzen (1812–70), in *My Past and Thoughts* (1855–6).

3. *Voilà un garçon bien éveillé! Qui est ton père*: 'Here is a well-brought-up boy!' Who is your Father?'

4. *Le fils ... M'aimes-tu, petit*: 'The son of a boyar, and a brave man into the bargain! I like the boyars. Do you like me, little one?'

5. *Baron de Bazancourt*: (1767–1830), a French general who took part in the campaigns of Napoleon I. General Ivolgin introduces the name in order to inject some semblance of historical truth into his fantastical narrative.

6. *Charasse's book on the Waterloo campaign*: J. B. A. Charasse (1810–65), French liberal politician and military historian. Dostoyevsky read his *Histoire de la campagne de 1815. Waterloo* ('History of the 1815 Campaign, Waterloo', 1858, 1863) in Baden Baden in 1867, and possessed a copy of it in his library.

7. *Davoust ... Mameluke Rustan*: Louis Davoust (1770–1845), marshal and minister of defence under Napoleon I. Mameluke Rustan (1780–1845), his favourite and bodyguard.

8. *Constant*: Napoleon's favourite valet.

9. *Bah! Il devient superstitieux*: 'Bah! He's becoming superstitious!'

10. *'the sultry island of confinement'*: St Helena. From Pushkin's poem 'Napoleon' (1826).

11. *Ne mentez jamais! Napoléon, votre ami sincère*: 'Never tell lies! Napoleon, your sincere friend.'

12. *It's more pleasant to sit with the beans than to be without one*: The pun is more or less untranslatable – 'to sit with the beans' means to sit with one's superiors.

13. *That's from Gogol, in Dead Souls*: The words are actually 'Oh my youth, oh my freshness' (vol. 1, chapter 6).

14. *St Anne's*: The St Anne's cross, a medal for bravery.

15. *'Nurse, where is your grave?'*: A quotation from the third part of an unfinished long poem by N. P. Ogarev (1813–77), entitled 'Humour': 'Nurse, where is your grave / By the convent wall?'

CHAPTER FIVE

1. *Schlosser's* History: Friedrich Christoph Schlosser (1776–1861) was a German historian. His *Weltgeschichte für das deutsche Volk* ('World History for the German People', 1844–56) appeared in Russian translation between 1861 and 1869. Dostoyevsky had a copy of the first volume of the *History* in his library.

2. *Stepan Glebov*: Stepan Bogdanovich Glebov (c. 1672–1718), the lover of the first wife of Tsar Peter I, Yevdokia Lopukhina. He was sentenced to death for plotting against Peter, and for his

liaison with Lopukhina, who was now a nun. He was impaled after fearful tortures that lasted three days, but did not confess or show any remorse.

3. *it was a different race from that of our own era*: There is an echo here of lines from Lermontov's poem 'Borodino' (1837): 'Yes, there were men in our time,/Not like the present race.'

CHAPTER SIX

1. *Punish my heart . . . as Thomas More said*: The words spoken by the English statesman, writer and Catholic martyr Sir Thomas More (1478–1535) to his executioner on the scaffold, before he was beheaded.

CHAPTER SEVEN

1. *desyatinas*: A desyatina was equal to 2.7 acres.
2. *Non possumus*: (Latin) 'We cannot', the words traditionally used by the Pope to refuse the demands of secular authority.
3. *two million heads*: An allusion to a passage in Chapter 37 of Alexander Herzen's *My Past and Thoughts*, where Herzen reflects on the view of the ninetenth-century German republican publicist Karl Heinzen that in order to create world revolution it would be sufficient 'to kill two million people'.
4. *by their works ye shall know them*: Cf. Ezekiel 14:22–3, Matthew 7:16.
5. *flagellantism*: In Russian *khlystovstvo*. The Khlysty were an ascetic Russian sect originating in the seventeenth century and believing that each successive leader of the sect was an incarnation of Christ. Members of the sect flagellated one another with birch rods in order to reach ecstasy.
6. *the spirit tare him . . . foaming*: Cf. Mark 9:20.

CHAPTER EIGHT

1. *And perhaps . . . parting smile*: A quotation from Pushkin's poem 'Elegy' (1830).
2. *poemy*: Long poems – the term may also refer to prose works. Gogol's *Dead Souls* is a *poema*.

CHAPTER NINE

1. *lorette*: A 'woman of easy virtue'.
2. *the contemporary nihilism uncovered by Mr Turgenev*: A reference to Turgenev's novel *Fathers and Sons* (1862), which provoked a debate about young people in Russia: the term 'nihilism'

was used by several commentators to describe the mood among the radical young, characterized in Turgenev's novel by the views of its hero, Bazarov.

CHAPTER TEN

1. *the Princesse de Rohan*: The Princes of Rohan were the descendants of the ancient sovereign rulers, later Dukes of Brittany, founded by Conan, who ruled in AD 384.
2. *the St Anne's ribbon*: A decoration for civil servants.
3. *My life I'd give for just one night*: A quotation from Pushkin's *poema* about Cleopatra, which became part of the novella 'Egyptian Nights' (1835).
4. *Thou hast hid these things . . . babes*: Cf. Matthew 11:25.

CHAPTER ELEVEN

1. *Semyonovsky Regiment*: The name for the district adjoining Zagorodny Prospect (where the Semyonovsky Lifeguards had their barracks).
2. *Madame Bovary*: Dostoyevsky read Flaubert's novel (first published in 1857) in 1867, on the recommendation of Turgenev, who considered it the finest work 'in the entire literary world during the past ten years'.
3. *At the foot of the bed . . . motionless*: this image may derive from Balzac's story 'Le Chef-d'œuvre inconnu' ('The Hidden Masterpiece', 1831):

> Coming nearer, they perceived in a corner of the canvas the point of a naked foot, which came forth from the chaos of colours, tones, shadows hazy and undefined, misty and without form, – an enchanting foot, a living foot. They stood lost in admiration before this glorious fragment breaking forth from the incredible, slow, progressive destruction around it. The foot seemed to them like the torso of some Grecian Venus, brought to light amid the ruins of a burned city. 'There is a woman beneath it all!' cried Porbus, calling Poussin's attention to the layers of colour which the old painter had successively laid on, believing that he thus brought his work to perfection. (tr. Katharine Prescott Wormeley).

DOSTOYEVSKY
Crime and Punishment

'Crime? What crime? ... My killing a loathsome, harmful louse, a filthy old moneylender woman ... and you call that a crime?'

Raskolnikov, a destitute and desperate former student, wanders through the slums of St Petersburg and commits a random murder without remorse or regret. He imagines himself to be a great man, a Napoleon: acting for a higher purpose beyond conventional moral law. But as he embarks on a dangerous game of cat and mouse with a suspicious police investigator, Raskolnikov is pursued by the growing voice of his conscience and finds the noose of his own guilt tightening around his neck. Only Sonya, a downtrodden prostitute, can offer the chance of redemption.

This vivid translation by David McDuff has been acclaimed as the most accessible version of Dostoyevsky's great novel, rendering its dialogue with a unique force and naturalism. This edition also includes a new chronology of Dostoyevsky's life and work.

'McDuff's language is rich and alive' *The New York Times Book Review*

Translated with an introduction and notes by DAVID McDUFF

TOLSTOY

Anna Karenina

'Everything is finished ... I have nothing but you.
Remember that'

Anna Karenina seems to have everything, but she feels that her life is empty until the moment she encounters the impetuous officer Count Vronsky. Their subsequent affair scandalizes society and family alike, and soon brings jealousy and bitterness in its wake. Contrasting with this tale of love and self-destruction is the vividly observed story of Levin, who strives to find contentment and a meaning to his life – and also a self-portrait of Tolstoy himself.

This new translation has been acclaimed as the definitive English version. The volume contains an introduction by Richard Pevear and a preface by John Bayley.

'Pevear and Volokhonsky are at once scrupulous translators and vivid stylists of English, and their superb rendering allows us, as perhaps never before, to grasp the palpability of Tolstoy's "characters, acts, situations"' JAMES WOOD, *New Yorker*

Translated by RICHARD PEVEAR *and*
LARISSA VOLOKHONSKY
With a preface by JOHN BAYLEY

TOLSTOY

The Death of Ivan Ilyich and Other Stories

*'Every moment he felt that … he was drawing
nearer and nearer to what terrified him'*

Three of Tolstoy's most powerful and moving shorter works are
brought together in this volume. 'The Death of Ivan Ilyich' is a
masterly meditation on life and death, recounting the physical
decline and spiritual awakening of a worldly, successful man
who is faced with his own mortality. 'Happy Ever After',
inspired by one of Tolstoy's own romantic entanglements, tells
the story of a seventeen-year-old girl who marries her guardian
twice her age. And 'The Cossacks', the tale of a disenchanted
young nobleman who seeks fulfilment amid the wild beauty of
the Caucasus, was hailed by Turgenev as the 'finest and most
perfect production of Russian literature'.

Rosemary Edmonds's classic translation fully captures the
subtle nuances of Tolstoy's writing, and the volume includes
an introduction discussing the stories' influences and contemporary reactions towards them.

Translated with an introduction by ROSEMARY EDMONDS

TOLSTOY
War and Peace

'Almost in the centre of this sky ... shone the huge, brilliant comet of the year 1812 – the comet which was said to portend all manner of horrors and the end of the world'

Napoleon's invasion of Russia forms the backdrop for Tolstoy's masterpiece. At its centre are Pierre Bezuhov, searching for meaning in his life; cynical Prince Andrei, ennobled by suffering in the war; and Natasha Rostov, whose impulsiveness threatens to destroy her happiness. As Tolstoy follows the changing fortunes of these characters, scenes of domestic life are juxtaposed with magnificent battle sequences, creating an epic and intimate view of humanity. Often considered the greatest novel in any language, *War and Peace* is also a philosophical meditation on the tension between free will and fate as the forces of history move inexorably forward.

Rosemary Edmonds's distinguished translation is accompanied by an introduction and a list of the novel's principal characters.

'[A] momentous panorama of human activity' JOHN UPDIKE

'Magnificent ... *War and Peace* reaches a simplicity and gravitas unknown in Western literature outside the pages of *The Iliad*' A. N. WILSON

Translated with an introduction by ROSEMARY EDMONDS

Eugene Onegin

*'We'd both drunk passion's chalice ... there
waited for us both the malice of blind Fortuna'*

Tired of the glitter and glamour of St Petersburg society, aristo-
cratic dandy Eugene Onegin retreats to the country estate that
he has recently inherited. There he begins an unlikely friendship
with the idealistic young poet Vladimir Lensky, who welcomes
this urbane addition to their small social circle and introduces
Onegin to his fiancée Olga's family. But when her sister Tatyana
becomes infatuated with Onegin, his cold rejection of her love
brings about a tragedy that encompasses them all. Unfolded
with dream-like inevitability and dazzling energy, Pushkin's
tragic poem is one of the great works of Russian literature.

Charles Johnston's acclaimed translation has been revised for
this edition, which contains a new introduction and notes by
Michael Basker, as well as John Bayley's introduction to the
original Penguin Classics edition.

**'More than a translation, it is a re-creation. One day a young
English poet will write a sonnet to it'** *Observer*

'This Onegin is a landmark' *Washington Post*

Translated by CHARLES JOHNSTON
With an introduction and notes by MICHAEL BASKER

GEORGE ELIOT
Middlemarch

*'People are almost always better than their
neighbours think they are'*

George Eliot's most ambitious novel is a masterly evocation of
diverse lives and changing fortunes in a provincial community.
Peopling its landscape are Dorothea Brooke, a young idealist
whose search for intellectual fulfilment leads her into a disastrous marriage to the pedantic scholar Casaubon; the charming but tactless Dr Lydgate, whose pioneering medical methods,
combined with an imprudent marriage to the spendthrift beauty
Rosamond, threaten to undermine his career; and the religious
hypocrite Bulstrode, hiding scandalous crimes from his past. As
their stories entwine, George Eliot creates a richly nuanced and
moving drama, hailed by Virginia Woolf as 'one of the few
English novels written for grown-up people'.

This edition uses the text of the second edition of 1874. In her
introduction, Rosemary Ashton, biographer of George Eliot,
discusses themes of change in *Middlemarch*, and examines the
novel as an imaginative embodiment of Eliot's humanist beliefs.

'The most profound, wise and absorbing of English novels ...
and, above all, truthful and forgiving about human behaviour'
HERMIONE LEE

Edited with an introduction and notes by ROSEMARY ASHTON

GEORGE ELIOT

Silas Marner

*'God gave her to me because you turned your
back upon her, and He looks upon her as mine:
you've no right to her!'*

Wrongly accused of theft and exiled from a religious community many years before, the embittered weaver Silas Marner
lives alone in Raveloe, living only for work and his precious
hoard of money. But when his money is stolen and an orphaned
child finds her way into his house, Silas is given the chance to
transform his life. His fate, and that of the little girl he adopts,
is entwined with Godfrey Cass, son of the village Squire, who,
like Silas, is trapped by his past. *Silas Marner*, George Eliot's
favourite of her novels, combines humour, rich symbolism
and pointed social criticism to create an unsentimental but
affectionate portrait of rural life.

The text uses the Cabinet edition, revised by George Eliot in
1878. David Carroll's introduction is accompanied by the
original Penguin Classics introduction by Q. D. Leavis.

Edited with an introduction by DAVID CARROLL

HENRY JAMES

The Turn of the Screw *and* The Aspern Papers

'The apparition had reached the landing half-way up and was therefore on the spot nearest the window, where, at the sight of me, it stopped short'

Oscar Wilde called James's chilling 'The Turn of the Screw' 'a most wonderful, lurid poisonous little tale'. It tells of a young governess sent to a country house to take charge of two orphans, Miles and Flora. Unsettled by a sense of intense evil within the house, she soon becomes obsessed with the belief that malevolent forces are stalking the children in her care. Obsession of a more worldly variety lies at the heart of 'The Aspern Papers', the tale of a literary historian determined to get his hands on some letters written by a great poet – and prepared to use trickery and deception to achieve his aims. Both show James's mastery of the short story and his genius for creating haunting atmosphere and unbearable tension.

Anthony Curtis's wide-ranging introduction traces the development of the two stories from initial inspiration to finished work and examines their critical reception.

Edited with an introduction by ANTHONY CURTIS

EDGAR ALLEN POE

The Fall of the House of Usher and Other Writings

*'And much of Madness and more of Sin
And Horror the Soul of the Plot'*

This selection of Poe's critical writings, short fiction and poetry demonstrates his intense interest in aesthetic issues, and the astonishing power and imagination with which he probed the darkest corners of the human mind. 'The Fall of the House of Usher' describes the final hours of a family tormented by tragedy and the legacy of the past. In 'The Tell Tale Heart', a murderer's insane delusions threaten to betray him, while stories such as 'The Pit and the Pendulum' and 'The Cask of Amontillado' explore extreme states of decadence, fear and hate. These works display Poe's startling ability to build suspense with almost nightmarish intensity.

David Galloway's introduction re-examines the myths surrounding Poe's life and reputation. This edition includes a new chronology and further reading.

'The most original genius that America has produced'
ALFRED, LORD TENNYSON

'Poe has entered our popular consciousness as no other American writer' *The New York Times Book Review*

Edited with an introduction by DAVID GALLOWAY